THROWN

From the past comes magic, from the present, danger, gradually colliding.

Foreknowledge is a gift King Adeone needed, but never wanted. With only days to defeat his brother's latest plan, he must make the hardest decision of his life: how to face his death.

When the news reaches Amphi, the new King Arkyn must face his father's legacy. Knowing there is treachery in the shadows, he must move quickly and return to Oedran before Lord Scanlon can further his schemes.

As power shifts, more is at risk than ever before.

Copyright

Copyright © J.A.Cauldwell, 2025. All rights reserved.

Book Cover and Illustrations by J.A.Cauldwell

Pennod Press First edition, 2025

1 3 5 7 9 10 8 6 4 2

ISBN (Paperback): 978-1-917145-16-9
ISBN (ebook): 978-1-917145-15-2

Trigger Warning

This book is set in a pre-Victorian-inspired world with elements of fantasy. It includes references to difficult themes such as loss, hardship, and moral dilemmas. Some events explore the consequences of harm, societal oppression, and personal struggles, including grief and guilt.

This book is written in British English. The lack of Z might keep you awake but we like U. If you prefer a different flavour of English, I hope you find your next read soon.

THROWN

The Erinnan Legacy

Treason and Truth
Book 5 of 12

J.A.Cauldwell

<u>Dedication</u>
For Caz

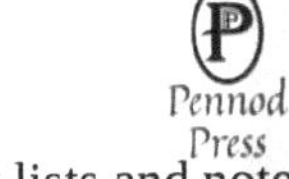

Character lists and notes on world building
are at the end of the book

The Erinnan Legacy

Treason and Truth

FROM THE PAST COMES MAGIC, FROM THE PRESENT, DANGER, GRADUALLY COLLIDING

1	TREASON	5	THROWN	
2	TERA			
3	TRAPPED			
4	TRAGEDY			

Stories From Erinna

EVERYBODY HAS A STORY AND SOMEBODY KNOWS IT

Standalone stories that may link to characters from other series.

TIES

For freebies, The Court Newsletter and to see more details and information on works in progress, please visit https://erinna.co.uk

MAPS

SNOWLANDS
RANAEGIR SEA
PALELANDS
WANDARIN OCEAN
BAYAN
ANAPARA
GARDIAN RIDGE
GARTH
Black Hills
OEDRAN
LOW PLAINS
EYLLYN
AMPHI
MACIAN ISLES
MACIA
MEITH
Shinglis
Faran's House
TRADERI
BYFA
AREAL
LUFIAN
LUFIA
ANGUIN
SERPENT ISLE
DENSHIRE
GERYMOR
CEARDEN
RY
TERA
TERASIA
JAGGED SEA
DEADLAND
POISON SEA
TAKARIN MOUNTAINS
0   50   100
MILES
THE OEDRANIAN EMPIRE

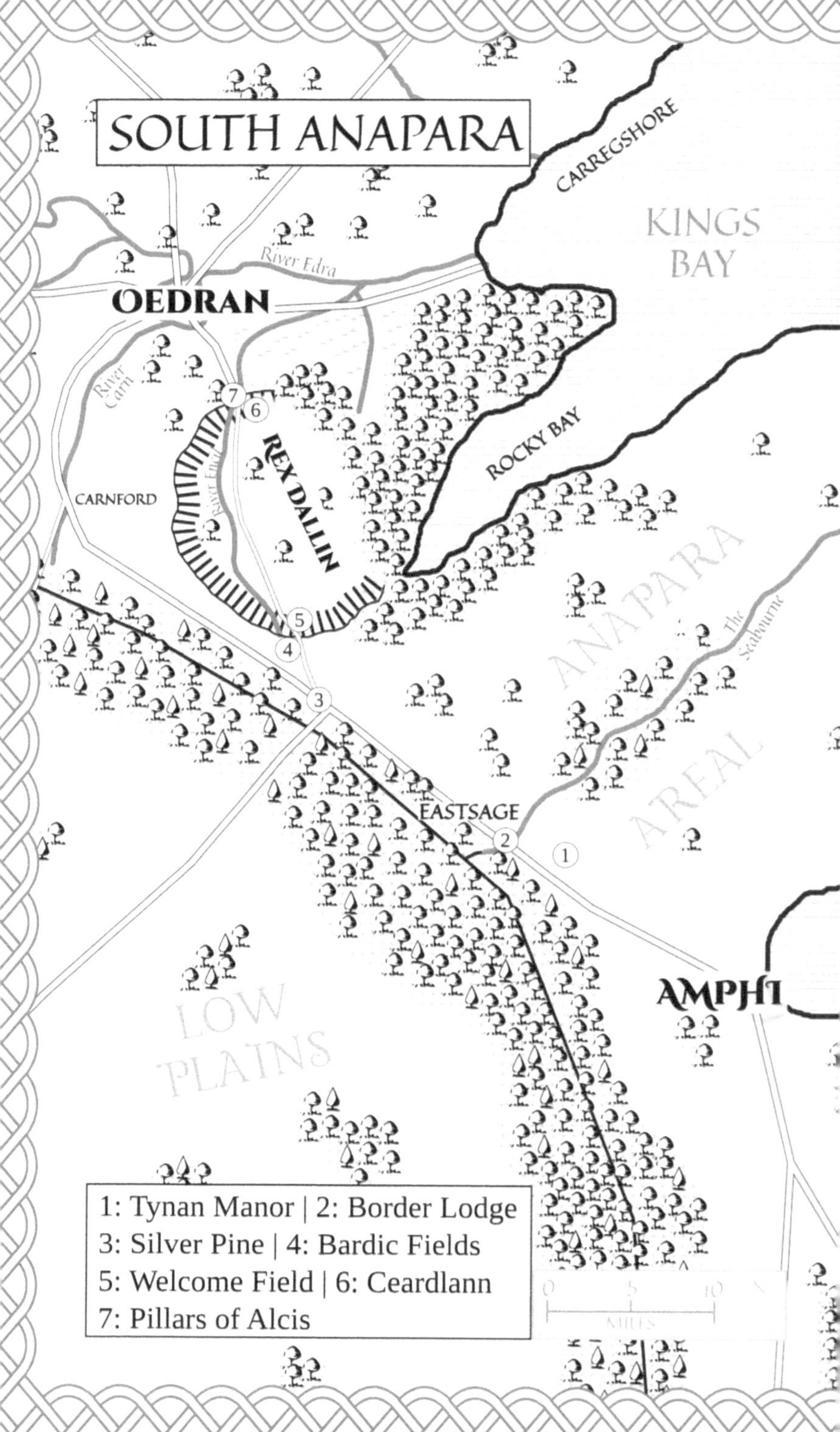

SOUTH ANAPARA
CARREGSHORE
KINGS BAY
OEDRAN
River Edra
River Carn
ROCKY BAY
CARNFORD
REX DALLIN
River Enys
ANAPARA
AREAL
The Seabourne
EASTSAGE
AMPHI
LOW PLAINS
1: Tynan Manor | 2: Border Lodge
3: Silver Pine | 4: Bardic Fields
5: Welcome Field | 6: Ceardlann
7: Pillars of Alcis
0   5   10
MILES

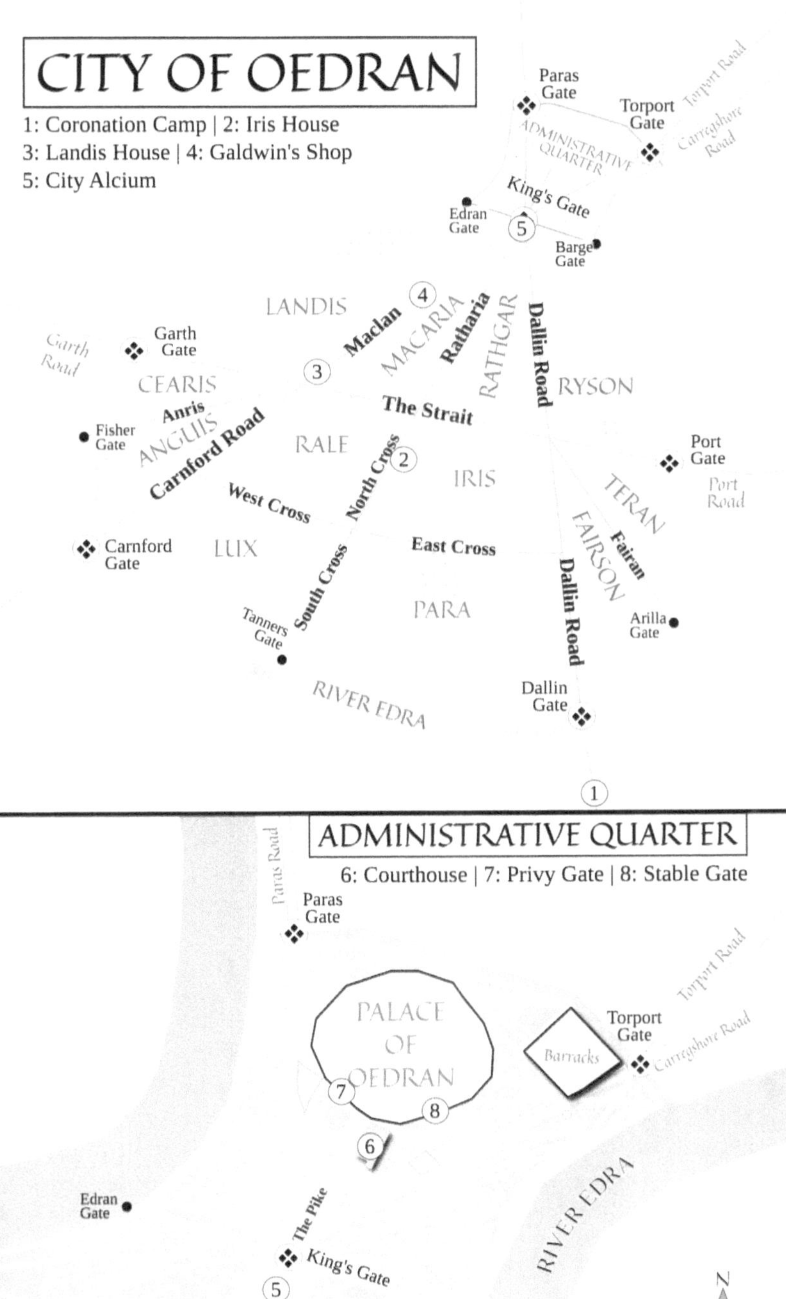

CITY OF OEDRAN

1: Coronation Camp | 2: Iris House
3: Landis House | 4: Galdwin's Shop
5: City Alcium

Paras Gate
Torport Gate
Torport Road
ADMINISTRATIVE QUARTER
Carregshore Road
King's Gate
Edran Gate
5
Barge Gate

LANDIS
Maclan
MACARIA
Ratharia
RATHGAR
Dallin Road
RYSON
Garth Gate
Garth Road
4
CEARIS
3
Anris
ANGLIIS
Fisher Gate
Carnford Road
The Strait
RALE
2
North Cross
IRIS
Port Gate
Port Road
TERAN
FAIRSON
Fairan
West Cross
South Cross
East Cross
LUX
Carnford Gate
Dallin Road
Tanners Gate
PARA
Arilla Gate
RIVER EDRA
Dallin Gate
1

ADMINISTRATIVE QUARTER

6: Courthouse | 7: Privy Gate | 8: Stable Gate

Paras Road
Paras Gate
PALACE OF OEDRAN
Barracks
Torport Gate
Torport Road
Carregshore Road
7
8
6
River Edra
Edran Gate
The Pike
King's Gate
5
Barge Gate
N

ARCHIVE

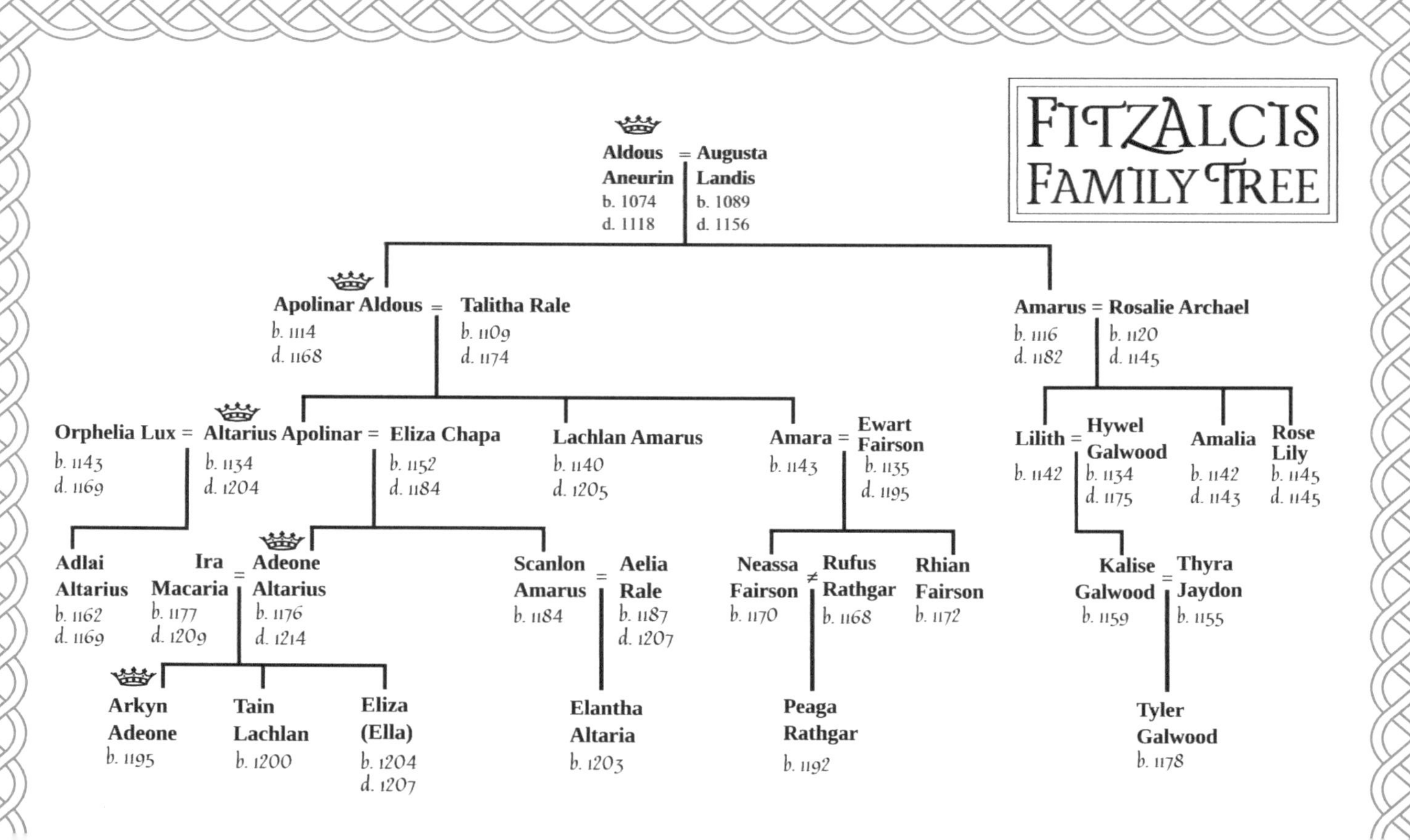

FITZALCIS FAMILY TREE

Aldous Aneurin b. 1074 d. 1118 = Augusta Landis b. 1089 d. 1156

Apolinar Aldous b. 1114 d. 1168 = Talitha Rale b. 1109 d. 1174
Amarus b. 1116 d. 1182 = Rosalie Archael b. 1120 d. 1145

Orphelia Lux b. 1143 d. 1169 = Altarius Apolinar b. 1134 d. 1204 = Eliza Chapa b. 1152 d. 1184
Lachlan Amarus b. 1140 d. 1205
Amara b. 1143 = Ewart Fairson b. 1135 d. 1195
Lilith b. 1142 = Hywel Galwood b. 1134 d. 1175
Amalia b. 1142 d. 1143
Rose Lily b. 1145 d. 1145

Adlai Altarius b. 1162 d. 1169
Ira Macaria b. 1177 d. 1209 = Adeone Altarius b. 1176 d. 1214
Scanlon Amarus b. 1184 = Aelia Rale b. 1187 d. 1207
Neassa Fairson b. 1170 ≠ Rufus Rathgar b. 1168
Rhian Fairson b. 1172
Kalise Galwood b. 1159 = Thyra Jaydon b. 1155

Arkyn Adeone b. 1195
Tain Lachlan b. 1200
Eliza (Ella) b. 1204 d. 1207
Elantha Altaria b. 1203
Peaga Rathgar b. 1192
Tyler Galwood b. 1178

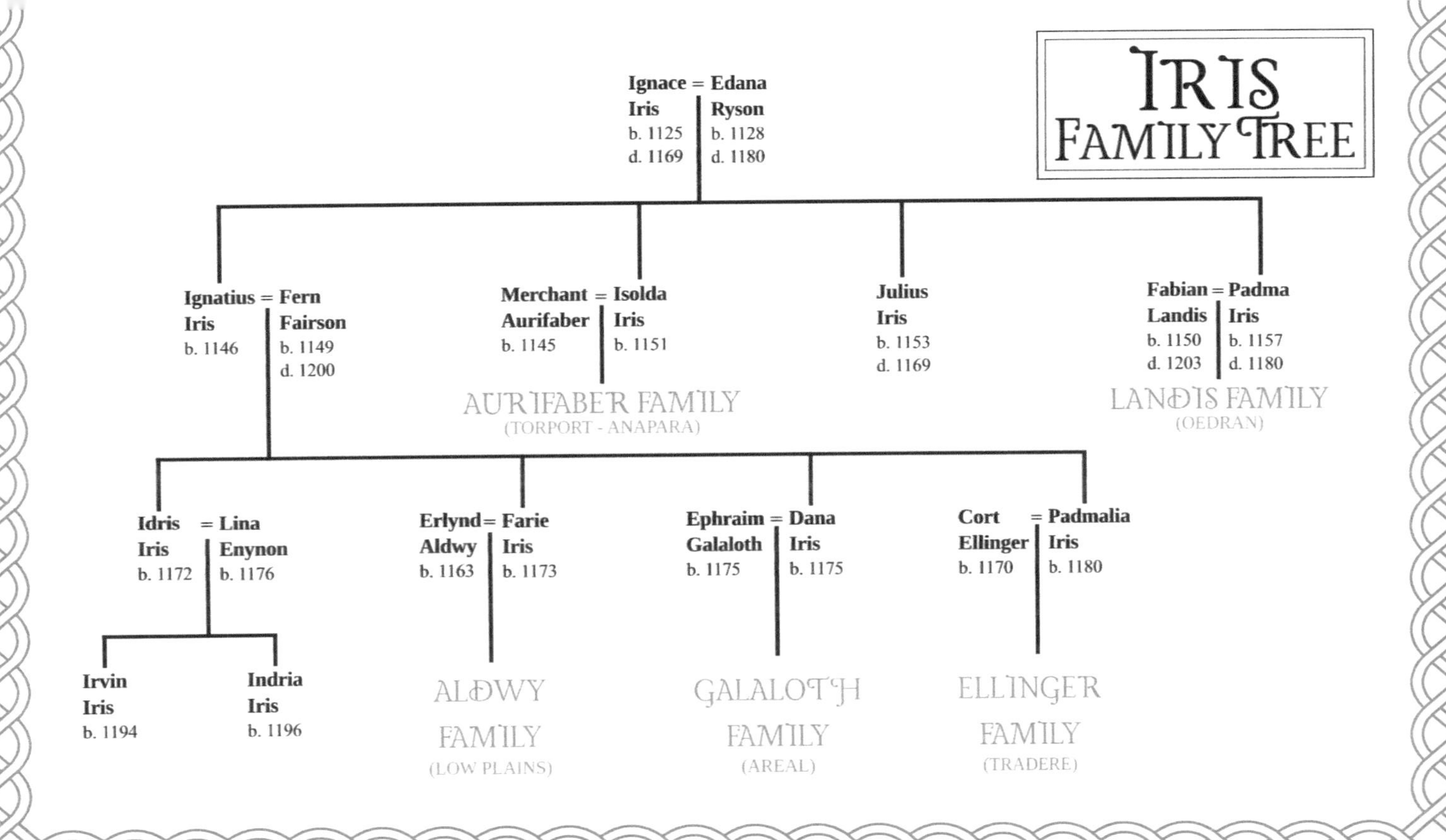

IRIS FAMILY TREE

Ignace = Edana
Iris | Ryson
b. 1125 | b. 1128
d. 1169 | d. 1180

Ignatius = Fern
Iris | Fairson
b. 1146 | b. 1149
| d. 1200

Merchant = Isolda
Aurifaber | Iris
b. 1145 | b. 1151

AURIFABER FAMILY
(TORPORT - ANAPARA)

Julius
Iris
b. 1153
d. 1169

Fabian = Padma
Landis | Iris
b. 1150 | b. 1157
d. 1203 | d. 1180

LANDIS FAMILY
(OEDRAN)

Idris = Lina
Iris | Enynon
b. 1172 | b. 1176

Erlynd = Farie
Aldwy | Iris
b. 1163 | b. 1173

Ephraim = Dana
Galaloth | Iris
b. 1175 | b. 1175

Cort = Padmalia
Ellinger | Iris
b. 1170 | b. 1180

Irvin
Iris
b. 1194

Indria
Iris
b. 1196

ALDWY FAMILY
(LOW PLAINS)

GALALOTH FAMILY
(AREAL)

ELLINGER FAMILY
(TRADERE)

CHRONICLE

1168
Accession of
King Altarius

1169
Bayan
Rebellion

1175
Altarius marries
Eliza Chapa

1176
Birth of
Adeone

1184
Birth of Scanlon
Death of Queen Eliza

1203
Scanlon marries Aelia
Rale, Birth of Elantha

1200
Birth of
Tain

1195
Birth of
Arkyn

1193
Adeone marries
Ira Macaria

1204
Scanlon drops title of Prince
Birth of Ella
Accession of King Adeone

1205
Death of
Prince
Lachlan

1207
Death of
Princess Ella
and Aelia

1209
Death of Queen
Ira. Promotion of
Wynfeld

1211
Arkyn undertakes
Terasian Review. Roth
murders Portur.

1210
Gad attacks King
Adeone at the
Guild Banquet

1209
Triniculum Plan.
Haster life-bound

1211
Anonymous notes left.
Secretaries dismissed.

1211
Landis House
burns down

1212
Tancred starts
teaching Tain

1212
Arkyn undertakes
Anaparian Review

1213
Bandit attack

1213
Tancred's history
revealed

1212
Neassa divorced

1212
Daioch life-bound
Landis history
discovered.

1213
Death of
Axton

1213
Ratharia
accident

1213
Cal shifts
for the first
time

1214
Tain's
investiture
as Justiciar

1214
Tancred
dies

1214
Adeone
assassinated

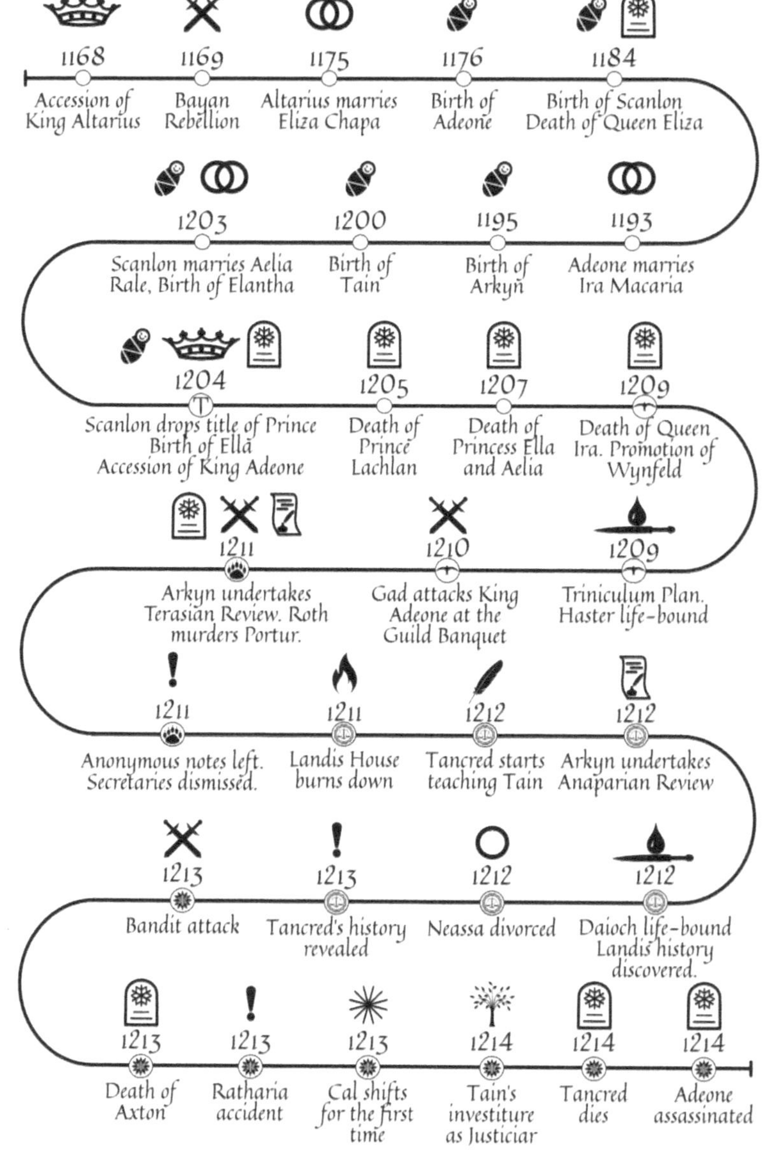

THROWN

PART 1

Chapter 1
TYSHER
Pentadai, Week 45 – 5th Lufial, 19th Geryis 1214
Palace of Oedran – King's Chambers

King Adeone's Diary: 5th Lufial 1214

Counsel was perturbing. I'm uncertain about Aldhouse – need to alert Wynfeld and mention it to Tain next year. Scanlon won't replace him but Tain may. Dinner at Landis' – an interesting talk about Cal's abilities. Festus thinks he's worth every bit of time to train him, but he doesn't know of Cal's other skills. My nearchildren were all causing havoc. The Jules were winding me up, nothing quite like a double act. Cornelia apologised, but I'd prefer them all to be relaxed.

Returned later than planned; I should take the decanter away from Festus – but he won't let me. Walked into the Inner Office without anyone warning me that the Chief was waiting, sitting nonchalantly in the semi-gloom; he'd helped himself to my whiskey – fortunately no-one had poisoned it...

"I shan't enquire how you got past my entire guard. They would have mentioned you were here."

"That's lucky, lad. I don't propose to tell you. It was better not to publicise my visit."

Adeone smiled. "Well, you old rogue, come and make yourself more comfortable with a drink. That is, unless you plan to kill me and I ought to call my guards?"

"Your life is safe with me, lad. Your sanity, however, is another matter."

"I know. I lost that years ago to your ministrations."

Laioril pulled himself up. "My lifetime endeavour, but I do have a serious message for you."

"Let's find a drink – or let me top yours up, I should say."

Laioril actually asked me to trust him! Crafty as the monkeys of Serpent Isle and many years to perfect honesty but, for some reason, not trustworthiness. I told him I'd trust him; I suppose I do with words, as long as I remember to examine statements every way possible. He's been a constant in my life, and I value his advice and support. So, yes, I said I'd trust him. He told me I'm not a medium and then, when

I objected, he actually called me 'sir': that's rare. It had the effect he wanted; I started to listen to him without joviality becoming too prominent - always possible when whiskey and his company have mixed.

"…You're something else. I didn't believe it for years. I couldn't believe it until you asked me to explain two dreams in 1209. There are myths and legends, all but forgotten now, of Erinna before Ull arrived, bringing magic with him; I've heard them from old men on my travels. These state there were forces at work even then – forces that were almost magical. A prelude, if you will, to what came with Ull. That the Majistar was sent to save a world from the effects, rather than to be the cause, of magic – the effect of the channelling of the first of our magic by the Tysher or Dreamweaver. He, the Tysher, foretold events and listened to the winds of change. He could see those passed on and could read people, the herald of a new era, breaking traditions, forcing the fractures. He made others see the hurts of the world and laid the foundations for peace, longer lasting than if he'd done nothing. The Tysher is an enigma, never fully understood. Yet they never see what they have brought into being. The Tysher may not exist in a magical world…"

Listening, Adeone was both sickened and excited. Here was a legend he'd never heard. "Why are you telling *me*, Chief?"

"You may be destined to die soon, to make way for peace and a new Cearcall. I once read this future before, but I refused to believe the legend. I saved the life of a man to prove the legend wrong. War followed; war that killed many…"

Yes, the 1169 rebellion in Bayan caused many deaths. The Chief told me to make my peace here and when death seems certain to face it. He talked of civil war if I don't. I've been trying to avoid that for years thanks to my brother's schemes…

Eyes glistening, Laioril said, "I truly wish it could be other than it is, Adeone. That's why I have fought against the knowledge and my own instincts for so long…"

"Yet how can you be so certain? After all, it is Festus who says traditions can be changed…"

"Yes, but it is you who truly believes that maxim. He merely uses it to excuse actions others would take exception to. You have changed the traditions of centuries. Young Festus Landis merely is blamed for it. Adeone, I'm truly sorry to tell you all this. All I can promise is I shall watch over everyone you hold dear as though they were of my own blood…"

"Thank you, Chief, but I can't lay that obligation on your shoulders. You're old yourself. I know your ancestors will be clamouring to claim you before long."

"I'll be here for a few years yet, lad; my ancestors are enjoying the peace and quiet."

Adeone nodded pensively. After many minutes' thought, he said, "Tell me something, Chief…"

Knowing that answer helped me sleep. I slept better than I had for years. I finally understood Laioril and why he was so certain. It didn't answer everything but it answered more than I ever expected. My dreams were vivid; I saw the days and weeks to come. They will not be easy but they will pass, as will I, into history.

18th Lufial 1214

I might be eight years Scanlon's senior, he might only be thirty, but if he doesn't kill me, I will him. Sicla! He is not going to interfere in Tain's education and inheritance. He returned yesterday. Today, he barged into my office, demanding that a mentor is appointed for Tain. I refused. James Tancred assured me Tain could carry out the duties of Justiciar without issue. Scanlon objected. He had even taken it on himself to appoint Judge Yarne. I reminded my little brother that Tain is my son and not his protégé. That he has no right to deny Tain's inheritance, just as Uncle Lachlan couldn't deny him his. He went an interesting shade.

"He comes under my jurisdiction as a young Justiciar, Sire!"

"Not in law. He is autonomous. Enough, Scanlon! I will control my son's education."

"What if you died?"

"Then Arkyn, as head of the family, would take over. As I would have supervised your education, so he would Tain's."

Scanlon sneered. "But Arkyn is not yet of age. What would happen if you died today, tomorrow or in the next three and a half weeks?"

"Are you threatening me *again*, Scanlon?"

"What would happen, Adeone?"

No, he was promising me. I saw it in his face, in his eyes, and

"His education is my responsibility. I will act as I see fit in this matter. What is more, my decision is final. Tell Yarne his services are not required."

"You may have cause to regret that!"

"I am sure you will see that it is not for long," replied Adeone. "Though, I have survived this long, have I not, *little* brother?"

"Yes, you *have*. There is one child you do not have ultimate rights over. Elantha is my daughter and she will return to my house from next year. I need to reform her education. She is too young to attend banquets. Especially as she is never demure, decorous or ladylike…"

* * *

When Lord Landis entered the Outer Office, Richardson intercepted him. "Defender, may I have a word?" Receiving a nod, the administrator drew back, close to the window, whispering, "Lord Scanlon and His Majesty have had a blazing row. It sounded like the Justiciar was trying to use emotional blackmail on the King to force someone onto His Highness' staff. I think he was using Lady Elantha. His Majesty has cancelled everything today and Tretaldai. He's also got his requests and bequests with him."

Landis frowned. "Thank you." He caught Lord Iris' eye as he entered.

Quietly, he said, "Lord Scanlon's been causing trouble."

"Does he ever do anything else?" replied Iris. He motioned to the Inner Office. "After you, nephew."

Landis grinned. "No, no, uncle, age before beauty."

Iris looked his nephew up and down. "Richardson, is he beautiful?"

A gale of laughter followed Landis into the Inner Office.

Adeone glanced over. "Are you causing trouble, Festus?"

"Why do I get all the blame? What can we do for you, Sire?"

"Witness two documents, with the time next to your signature, please."

Landis eyed his friend. "Will there be confusion, Sire?"

"Not if you remember in which order you signed them."

Landis didn't need to see the contents to recognise its purpose. He signed and affixed his seal on the first document, glancing at the King's timepiece on the desk. "We'll both go by that, Lord Iris."

Iris signed underneath Landis' signature and affixed his seal.

Adeone removed the document, waiting for the wax to dry before ringing for Richardson and saying, "My new requests and bequests, Richardson. Don't publicise the fact, please." After a drink Adeone said, "And the second. Don't forget the time, as well as the date."

"May I enquire, Your Majesty, what this document is?" asked Iris in his usual mild manner.

In a similar tone, Adeone said, "An official document, my lord. All will become clear eventually. Thank you, that's all for now. Landis, I need a word."

* * *

Three people must know my plan. Telling Landis was difficult. There are no words to describe how hard. He's been my closest friend for so long and I rarely see him as anything else, but I had to tell him as my Defender. The more I consider what Laioril said, the more I believe he's right. As the Tysher, I must avoid plunging this empire into civil war at all costs. My life doesn't matter, not in itself. I'm trying hard not to think of what my sons will go through, because my resolve will weaken, but if it's my death or thousands, I hope they will understand.

I've never seen Landis so shocked, so upset. He told me to think of my family as though I am thinking of anyone else. I explained what Scanlon had said about a protector...

"...He doesn't need long to set in motion the destruction of the empire. Not being both Protector and Justiciar and he is still Justiciar for most of the empire. Oedran alone won't save anyone."

"Oedran and your ancestors have conquered an empire, Adeone. Oedran, alone, has stood for a better world for centuries. We *can* beat him; we have before. I'll stand by you, sit by you, whatever it takes, but I'm *not* going to watch Scanlon murder you."

"Yes, you *are*, Festus; as a friend, I need your support for what I must face. He'll probably opt for the Munewid Feast; it's public and fits what he thinks I deserve for thwarting him. Arkyn and Tain will be in Amphi; they'll be safe enough. I can't do the same with Elantha, and she has been promised she can attend. I'm going to get Cal to escort her."

"No. I can't believe you'd let them witness… whatever you think he's planned."

Adeone took his friend's arm. "Festus, I'm as unhappy about it as you are. I'm going to tell Cal once Tain and Arkyn are on their way. Then I'm going to make him promise not to tell them until after I'm dead."

"Are you certain?"

Yes, I am certain, have been for longer than I've admitted. I wanted to know Festus wouldn't interfere. I asked him to promise that he wouldn't. His face clearly said I'd asked him to betray friendship. I understood but asked him not to make me order co-operation…

"Adeone, can you conceive what I'm feeling? I can't promise you this: not as your friend, not as your vassal and *certainly* not as your Defender. I'd have to face your sons…"

"Please… I know how hard it is. I've been lying that the assassins will never get me. Trust me, please. I need to face that night in the knowledge that, whatever happens, my friends are behind me, accepting my decision. I'm not even going to warn Wynfeld. I need your arm in mine as I face this, Festus. Of all men, I need *your* support."

As I pleaded with him, tears sprang in my eyes. I couldn't stop them. My heart is torn and bleeding. Landis finally gave his promise, saying he couldn't believe he was going to let a friend he had sworn to protect face death. That is the crux of the matter. He has sworn to protect me - sworn binding oaths, and I asked him to ignore them, to go against his principles, against all he holds dear. How could I? Through necessity, through nothing more than necessity. I've made my decision; I'm not calm about it, but I've made it for a good reason.

Testus tried to be formal – I couldn't bear that, not even to hide behind. I owed him honesty, and he got it – mostly.

I explained I wanted Scanlon's confederates to see the result of my requests. I warned him not to let Scanlon proclaim himself Protector. I told him I'd be informing Edward and Cal. Edward will take my requests to Amphi and the letters I've written for Tain and Arkyn. Cal, well, I didn't explain his role in full to Landis. One day, he may find out. If my dreams are premonitions, one day the empire will.

He realised I'd known I was going to die for a while. I couldn't hide that from him and he asked me how long. I explained about James Tancred...

"...He was murdered, not a doubt about that. Tain got him to defy an amendment of Scanlon's. Tancred did but knew he'd signed his death sentence. I was able to speak to him before he died. If he could face death like that then, Alcis preserve us, I will."

"Must you, Adeone? I won't ask again, I promise. It is obviously your choice – you've made that plain – but is there anything I can say to make you change your mind?"

"No, old friend, there isn't. I'll have the last laugh and I'll die with a smile in my heart knowing it. If I don't face this, there will be more than my blood shed and the empire would not survive the wound."

23rd Lufial 1214

Edward, my son's administrator (the next King's Administrator, how strange that thought is...) needed to know. Twenty-five, excellent at his job, he's never let anyone down. I asked him to swear fealty, needing the security it provides. He pointed out he's cisan but when I explained, he made no more demurral. Simkins witnessed the fealty and left us to talk – he will never understand why I've faced death.

I know I'm asking Edward to betray Arkyn; he must keep from my son my foreknowledge of death and he'll have to face Arkyn afterwards. I can only hope my son continues to be a fair man.

I told Edward I would die soon. He begged me to stop talking as I was. I carried on; I couldn't face his concern as well as my own uncertainty. I told him why I need his help and he accepted the duty without question, but I wish someone else had been there to see how much he cares. He actually thanked me for trusting him to be an administrator - that took one look into his eyes. It was far less than he's given us over the last few years. I shook his hand when he left; he knelt, of course, and wished me good luck - when he'd gone, I realised how much that simple phrase means to me.

25th Lufial 1214

I've waved my sons off to Amphi and I don't know how I did it. I want them home. I want to wrap them in hugs and hear their laughter. I need their support, but all I have is bleak silence and officialdom. I will now live or die with my decision and, as I have decided, so will I do, but my feet were leaden walking back to my office.

I sent for Cal: their best friend, their closest confidant, and I asked him to betray that friendship as I have asked Landis to betray ours, but Cal, Cal isn't yet fifteen. He'd obviously been running when he entered.

"It's nice to be reminded that you can tire, young Cal. Get your breath whilst I get you a drink. You'll need one."

Cal didn't say anything, but he did watch the King, wondering when he had become so bowed down.

Passing over a watered whiskey, Adeone said, "Sit down and listen to me carefully. Firstly, the Munewid Banquet, you'll be escorting Lady Elantha. Your father is being told it's an order. He's going to be annoyed. The reasons are difficult for me to voice and word cannot spread. You *must not* go and tell my sons. There is the empire's future resting on this and I wish it wasn't you at the centre of the web. My death is waiting for me at the banquet. I know it. Landis has promised not to interfere. I can't see him considering it a valid promise, but Scanlon has worked out a foolproof way of killing me. I can see it in his eyes. You are the only person who will be able to get out of the Palace. You know what I'm talking about. Tain and Arkyn must get the news straightaway. Delay is danger, more than you realise. Cal, I'm sorry, I feel a bastard for this. I… here, it's clean. Promise me just two things. Look after Elantha and take the news to my sons."

Wiping tears away with the handkerchief he'd been passed, Cal said, "I promise, Your Majesty. Can you not promise to try to survive for everyone who needs and loves you?"

My heart nearly broke. I told him if I could I would and then I mentioned if I didn't face this that civil war would come...

"…That is a future I would save you all from. You have become as dear to me as my own family. I hope your future is the manifestation of the good you have done us all. You deserve the best from life; do not give up in the dark moments."

Cal looked at him, unsure how to answer any of the sentiments.

Adeone continued, "I wish I had asked you sooner, but, will you not call me Adeone? Add the 'uncle' tag onto it, if you must."

Cal's emotions overwhelmed him, and I simply knelt by him and pulled him into a hug. There were no words that could be said and I doubt I could have found them if there were.

He hunted around for a change of subject. In doing so, he blew the tower apart with its own magic. He told me that Gab Linnt is an anagram of bantling! Of all people, why is it Tain's manservant... Julia came up with the information. My neardaughter is as bright as her father – Alcis help the future.

Cal told me I'd done more for him than he'd ever repaid. He doesn't know how much he's done and I'll never persuade him of it; I hope my bequests do. I told him to continue to make the world laugh. His joy in life is inspiration, and he doesn't even know it.

I contacted ReJean and got a deputy manservant sorted for Tain. It should help until they return to Oedran.

Chapter 2
BANQUET

THE KING'S HALL on Munewid Eve was dressed in all its splendour. Tapestries hung around the walls, their colours vibrant and enticing. The tables were laid ready for the feast with painted sugar sculptures of spring and summer flowers, speaking of the new year to come and the old one's passing. Entering, Adeone viewed the display with a remarkably calm frame of mind. He had made his decision and would live or die with it, as fate decreed. When his servers were tripped up entering the hall, he glanced at Landis, who simply inclined his head in response.

Cal was quieter than normal. He kept peering around the hall, eyeing the shadows, his brows knitting.

"Master Calumiel, I'm sure Lady Elantha would appreciate another dance before she retires."

Cal craned round. "Of course, Sire. My apologies, my lady…"

Elantha laughed. "I was watching you thinking, Cal, it's a rare event."

When they were dancing, Adeone allowed himself the pleasure of watching them. They were well matched and had practised much together at Ceardlann. A merchant's son escorting a Lady of the FitzAlcis might have been a break from tradition, but at least Cal cared about Elantha.

The hall doors burst open.

"Sire, there's treachery…" Ryson's words died as screams rent the air.

Landis threw himself across Adeone to protect him, but the crossbow bolt had shuddered into the King's ribcage.

Adeone mouthed, 'Thank you,' before the light died in his eyes.

Pain ripped through Landis, followed by nothing.

* * *

Pandemonium raged, with no-one certain who was in charge.

Having entered with Ryson, Hillbeck didn't wait for orders. "Guards, close the doors. No-one leaves!"

Cal caught his attention. "Sergeant, I should get Lady Elantha away – she was facing the King when—"

Hillbeck nodded. "Right, sir. You, and *only* you, take her back to the Privy Wing and stay with Her Ladyship."

"Thank you, Sergeant." He shepherded Elantha out of the hall. Only one person tried to go with him. "No, Lady Landis, you're needed here, with Lord Landis."

"Cal…"

"Trust me, my lady, please."

She was torn, her motherless blood-niece or her husband? Recognising Cal would see Elantha well-tended, she said simply, "Thank you."

Calling for silence, Iris took charge. With his habit for understatement, he said, "My lords, ladies and gentlemen, as you are aware, there has been an accident. I would ask you to remain calmly here. Sergeant Hillbeck, the guards will check everyone for weapons."

They moved Landis carefully and laid him on his front. The second crossbow bolt embedded in his left shoulder. As they turned the throne away from the hall, Iris bent to retrieve a scroll lying under it, weighing it in his hand for a second. He recognised the most likely explanation for its presence immediately.

By his shoulder, Ryson said, "They tried to make me sign it tonight."

Iris pursed his lips. Rage wouldn't bring Adeone back. "Please tell its signatories that they are not required to help, in any way." He glanced around, searching for Doctor Chapa. The King's Physician was just arriving.

"What's he gone and done this time?"

Iris lowered his voice, but the tone left Chapa in no doubt. "He's died, Chapa: assassinated."

Chapa's face drained of colour, his eyes hardening. "How?"

"Crossbow bolt."

"In a packed hall. Where was it shot from?"

"I don't know."

"You're not using your eyes, my lord. Think."

"Chapa, I realise you are distressed, but so are we all. Please remember to mind your manners," replied Iris, watching Ryson telling their peers to mind their own business.

"I said 'my lord'. Yes, I'm distressed: King Adeone was *family*. I'm also bloody furious and I'm not in the mood to be diplomatic, nor would he wish me to be. Where was the arrow shot from? Or do you want Adeone's assassin to escape, Ignatius? Because I don't and I won't face his sons having done nothing! Will you?"

Iris forced himself to be calm. In forty years, he'd never seen the doctor so determined or so upset. He glanced at the bolt, noted the angle, turned round, trying to project it in his mind's eye.

"That's impossible…"

Chapter 3
SCANLON'S REACTION
Alunadai, Week 1 – 1st Cearal, 1st Cearcis 1215
Black Hills House

"VICTORY!"

PART 2

Chapter 4
RESILIENCE

"**Y**OUR EXCELLENCY, my lords, ladies and guests, it is my sad duty to inform you of the death of King Adeone Altarius earlier this evening at the hands of an assassin."

As Prince Tain finished addressing the Amphi Court, the silence took on another depth before a rising clamour filled the hall. Tain held up a hand. Silence was speedily restored.

"I ask you to raise your goblets… Hail and farewell, King Adeone."

As the sound of the shocked refrain died away, Tain took a deep breath. "I hereby announce the accession of King Arkyn Adeone FitzAlcis. I am sure you will join me in wishing our new King long life."

As Tain made the toast, he stilled. An ethereal filigree gold circlet had appeared around Arkyn's head, glowing faintly. Tain blinked, and the illusion was gone, but the appearance stayed with him as Cal seated him with unspoken support.

Governor ReJean rose. "I am sure I speak for all of Areal when I say we are torn between shock at your father's untimely death and pleasure at your accession, Sire. If there is anything we in Amphi can do at this time, it would be our honour." Arkyn nodded in acknowledgement, and ReJean faced the hall. "I think it's best if we end the revelries."

At this, Arkyn – who'd been silent since Cal had seated him before the announcement – rose. "Your Excellency, I thank you for your support. All I ask of you and this Court is that you excuse my brother and myself if we retire."

The Governor's only reply was a low bow. Tain, who'd sat immobile and expressionless, rose and the brothers left the hall, their menservants and Cal following. Distantly, and only half aware of their surroundings, they made their way through the Palace. Memories assailed the brothers. In all of them, King Adeone was laughing, telling them the assassins would never get him.

* * *

Cal glanced ahead. His friends' pace was far slower than normal. Arkyn had grasped Tain's wrist. To support his brother or himself, Cal wasn't certain. Tain wasn't complaining though, that much was clear. The Palace wasn't dark, the candlewardens had done their jobs well, but between the pools of light lay dimmer shadows where unease dwelt. His eyes darting around, Cal noted the guards with them. Smithers, head of the Princes' Guard, was walking level with him on his right, two of his men in front. Inadvertently, Cal caught his eye. There were no words needed. There was a long night and day ahead. They walked up a flight of stairs, the heavy thud of feet and quiet breathing the only music of the moment. Behind them, the lack of chatter from the hall as people left was a noticeable void. They turned the corner of the stairs and even the quiet departure of courtiers was muffled to a susurration. Cal tried to concentrate on his stride, but memories interfered.

He didn't want to think about events in Oedran. It was too raw, but the scenes kept invading other memories. He had to face them.

Screams still rang in his ears, Elantha's heartfelt, single piercing one, as she watched the bolt take her uncle's life, most of all. When the second bolt landed, Cal had already turned her away. He'd wanted to stay, to help, but that wasn't his job. He hurried Elantha from the hall. Despair overwhelming them both. How could he inform his friends? He hadn't considered that. Elantha suggested she write. The brothers would believe her if he delivered the letter, and they had.

Arkyn's face had been deathly pale. His father was dead and cold: no laughter to help dispel the shock, no eyes softening to tell him it would be all right. As Cal watched, he saw his friend's eyes change as the weight and responsibility of kingship crashed onto him. His eyes spoke of loss but no time to grieve. Dangerous days were coming, not far in the future, not for someone else to handle, for him, here, now, tonight, today, in this hour, this minute, this moment.

Tain's reaction had been strangest. When James Tancred had died the shock and grief had hit him in an instant. Whether it had been because this news had been written, or they were in public, even that he thought his feelings could wait, Cal didn't know but his friend's composure was a surprise and inspiration.

Having expected the brothers to collapse, the reality of the dreamlike situation solidified when Tain, having just turned fifteen on the stroke of midnight, announced the tragedy.

As the news flowed unhesitatingly from Tain's lips, the silence was unnerving. The shock had reverberated around the hall and it had been absolute. Moments later the toasts drunk to the memory of Adeone, king for ten years, and the accession of Arkyn had been poignant and, for those who knew the men involved personally, heartfelt.

Yet Governor ReJean had sat stock-still his face a mask, which was strange to Cal; everyone else showed something: Tain, resolve, Arkyn, numb shock, Lady Phylicia ReJean, the Governor's daughter, distress. His own face showed control but emotion deep in his eyes gave lie to the mask. Governor ReJean though was immobile. Was it the shock or something deeper? Could he not display his feelings at the death of Adeone and the accession of a nineteen-year-old, underage, king? Arkyn was only a week and a half off being officially of age but that made everything uncertain.

Tain had finished speaking and somehow Cal found that he was seating his friend. He had begun to move away and saw a young manservant waiting to pass him two goblets of warmed wine. Cal glanced at Kadeem; the new King's manservant nodded – this wine was safe. Cal went to pass the goblets to his friends.

The young manservant whispered, "One is for you, sir; I thought you might need it."

Surprised, Cal nodded his thanks. The wine helped him steady himself. The action of drinking, of having something to do, something else to focus on helped.

Once the Governor had offered aid, and it was clear that Arkyn and Tain were leaving the hall, Kadeem had stepped forward to move the King's chair and Cal found himself moving to do the same for Tain but the young manservant beat him to it. Cal looked at him with interest. Linnt, Tain's official manservant, had kept well back. Cal was pleased; the last thing Tain ever needed was Linnt's highly incompetent and annoying presence.

As Cal considered the reactions a niggle surfaced in his mind. ReJean hadn't knelt to Arkyn, the Court hadn't knelt to him. Everyone was in shock, it was true, but Arkyn would need the gesture. ReJean had to show he supported Arkyn and acknowledge him as liege.

Cal returned to the present, blinking hard. There was too much at stake to dwell on the memories now. They were approaching a set of doors with more guards. Cal recognised Sergeant Halien. These must be the FitzAlcis Chambers. The carved double doors certainly suggested it. Cal knew enough to know they'd open onto an antechamber and, even though the corridors had mostly been devoid of people, he would be glad to get to the safety of those rooms. Cal feared his friends' true reactions hadn't yet been seen; those reactions – when they understood King Adeone had known, had expected his death that night – would be devastating.

* * *

Edward was waiting in the antechamber. He shot Cal a questioning look to receive a nod in return. The administrator knelt to Arkyn, holding out a letter, which betrayed his shaking hand.

Arkyn recognised his father's hand. "How did you know?"

"Your father's letter will make it all clear, Sire."

"I am asking you!"

Edward sensibly held Arkyn's gaze. "King Adeone knew what was coming; he bound me to secrecy. I am sorry, sir."

Arkyn took the letter, unable to work out whether he felt betrayed; at that moment, more than any other, he felt tired and numb.

Edward held out a letter to Prince Tain, who simply nodded his thanks and followed his brother into his rooms, collecting Cal with a look.

Following them, Kadeem received the order they were to leave for Oedran as soon as possible. His quick gaze assessed the situation. He wasn't needed. Bowing, he retreated as the brothers fell onto chairs, breaking the seals on their letters.

* * *

Kadeem put his head into a small room attached to the antechamber and caught the eye of the young runner on duty. "Run and wake my staff for me and ask them to come here. Then go to Governor ReJean, tell him the King and Prince Tain are leaving as soon as possible."

Kadeem turned back to the King's antechamber, ignoring the runner's confusion. Word would have spread throughout the Palace of Amphi already, the boy would understand soon enough.

Linnt hadn't moved.

Kadeem cursed; the man really was useless. "Go and pack, Linnt."

"I've only just unpacked."

Kadeem's face set. "Do it! Tonight is not the night to be obstreperous, if you have an ounce of feeling do your bloody job for once."

"I don't think you can talk to me like that, Kadeem."

"He can. He's the King's manservant and your superior," replied Edward. "I would suggest you do as he says." After Linnt had stormed out, he continued, "Did His… the King say anything?"

Kadeem eyed him. "No. Why?"

Edward shook his head slightly. "It doesn't matter. I shall go and see about packing the King's papers and desk. I do, however, wonder what to do about the papers regarding the review."

Kadeem said, "Bring them with us. The review will be rescheduled, and I doubt the King will want Governor ReJean to see them first."

"True. At least the advisors aren't here yet. It saves some work getting them organised."

Once Kadeem's subordinates reached the antechamber, Kadeem explained

34

events. With the King ensconced in his sitting room, they were to concentrate on the other rooms and liaise with the Governor, Prince's Guard and the stables. When they'd left Kadeem continued to wait in the antechamber. There hadn't been a sound from the sitting room. What was happening? He wanted to enter but reticence kept him at bay. This time was their time. They would ring if they needed anything. Master Calumiel was there as a friend, as a support and Kadeem was relieved he was.

* * *

In the sitting room Arkyn had broken the seal on his father's letter with dread. He didn't want to believe, didn't want to face the news Cal had brought, but here was the proof: a farewell letter in his father's hand. His hands shook and he let the parchment hang loosely.

Cal watched both him and Tain carefully; he, himself, was devastated, but he had not the initial horror, the closeness that Adeone's sons had – his horror had been mitigated by prior knowledge. He glanced at the grate; a small fire was laid ready. It wasn't cold but the shock of the evening meant warmth would be welcome. He reached for a candle. There was no point ringing for Kadeem. The manservant would be busy enough. Kneeling on the hearth, Cal lit the kindling, watching as it caught, then the twigs flamed and he found himself almost mesmerised. As the smaller logs caught, he put the poker to heat almost unthinkingly. Rocking back on his heels, he searched for the sideboard. Every sitting room he'd been in where the FitzAlcis were had jugs of drinks and decanters to hand. Locating it by the door, he pushed himself to his feet not even looking at his friends. He didn't want to meet their eyes yet. He had known and they had not. Pouring two goblets of wine, he took a deep breath. His angst was nothing against their grief. He glanced back to the fire. The poker was heating. A minute later, he thought he felt Arkyn's eyes on him as he crossed back to the hearth. The poker wasn't red hot but it would warm the wine enough. He plunged it quickly into the goblets, there was enough of a fizzle to reassure him.

Unobtrusively, he passed one to Tain – who had started reading the letter – before putting the other on the table by Arkyn's hand.

"It might… help is the wrong word but bring some warmth…"

Arkyn grasped his wrist. "Tell me this is a dream."

"I wish I could, sir, but it's not, truly it's not."

"Then I must read, mustn't I?"

"You must do nothing, sir," whispered Cal, "but your father wouldn't have written if he thought it wouldn't help."

Arkyn began to read.

My dear son,

I had hoped you would never read these words, that the future which I anticipate whilst writing this will never come to pass but I must have been wrong. Where can I start to explain? How can I start? You must feel so betrayed and confused by my decisions. Your tendency isn't for anger but forgiveness and I hope one day you can forgive me this decision.

A few weeks ago, I talked with someone, discovering much about myself and it settled my mind. We have always known that your Uncle Scanlon wished for my death; it would seem he has succeeded, as I always knew he would. I lied more times than I care to recall in telling you that he wouldn't. I am sorry for that, contritely sorry, but you are my son and I always hoped I would see more years of your life than I have. I am proud of the man you have become - more than I have the words to express it and, were she alive, your mother would join me in that.

I have strayed from explaining. When James Tancred was murdered, I realised Scanlon was determined to succeed. I cannot explain why that one death of the many has affected me so profoundly but it has. He, Scanlon, has tried to force a new mentor for Tain - I gave him short shrift. Trust your brother in all things legal; James taught him well. I argued with your Uncle Scanlon and saw in his eyes that my time was limited, that he was determined to succeed soon. I faced a decision so difficult I hope you are spared a similar one. To live and risk civil war or die and break yours and your brother's hearts. Civil war would have destroyed more lives than ours and it is our bounden duty to protect, not destroy. Oh, my son, I wish I could hold you as you read this but I will be far from reach. I decided to face whatever fate had in store for me. Only three people knew what I decided: Lord Landis, Edward and young Cal. Let me explain why it had to be them.

Firstly, Edward has my true requests and bequests as well as these letters and needed to know what he carried. Secondly, Lord Landis has been my closest friend for many years and I had to tell him - he has argued, spoken up for yours and your brother's feelings more than any man outside my own heart would dare to, but in the end I persuaded him to do nothing. No, I suppose persuaded is too kind a word, he respected my decisions. As my friend - I needed his support in facing my death; however, I anticipate he isn't going to adhere to his promise not to interfere, I wouldn't blame him and I would ask that you do not, that you accept whatever his actions are. He is already in torment after my request. Thirdly and lastly Cal: how can I try to excuse my impertinence of having your friend and confidant conceal from you I was going to die? I cannot, but my reason was simple: a matter of necessity. I know when I ask him to deliver the news that he will be upset, bewildered and lost, and without his friends' support. Do not blame your friend, your administrator or your nearfather; as I write this, I own their allegiance and feel awful for using it so despicably. I have warned no-one else and Wynfeld, Paturn, Hillbeck, my staff, household and guards know nothing of what is coming. I would ask that you do not use their ignorance as a matter of blame. Your uncle is devious and only has to be lucky once. It seems he was.

In time, I hope you can forgive me. In time, I hope you triumph over the adversity which besets you. There will be many dark hours and days in your fight, many days when sleep is a blessing and an overwhelming necessity, lonely days when comfort seems far astray. You will, as always, work far too hard, be far too conscientious and watch over your brother with a care I cannot... I have no doubt you will come through the trials and tribulations and see peace. You will make a world far better than I ever could. In your character is the mix mine lacks; I am at heart too mischievous; I've tamed it in recent years but you might remember before I was King. I hope you smile when you do. Your character has a gravitas that all great men need but your sense of humour is the edge that makes you great.

I do not know what my final words to you will be when we part as you leave for Amphi, but I do know my heart will be heavy watching you depart. Were you here, there is the chance you would die also and I cannot take the risk, much as I do not want you to leave. I suppose these are my final words to you now, in this letter; therefore, I shall try to make them worthwhile and honest.

You are my son and I shall try to watch over your progress

Having seen the tears flow down Arkyn's cheeks, Cal was silent, simply waiting. Tain's eyes were surprisingly dry; there was an anger in them that worried Cal, but without seeing the letter Tain was perusing he couldn't say whether it was at the letter or the facts.

Tain's anger wasn't at his father for abandoning them but at Lord Scanlon, and for more than King Adeone's death.

Both letters were long, leaving Cal plenty of time to observe his friends. He was standing; he didn't want to sit. Believing the brothers had discovered he had known for days what was coming, his silence stilled his movements. Would their friendship survive such a betrayal?

Arkyn furled his scroll first. He closed his eyes briefly for one moment before wiping them, taking a drink and pushing himself to his feet. He put the scroll on the table with careful deliberation and strode over to Cal. Tain's eyes were drawn by the movement. Cal stood stock-still anticipating the worst. Arkyn had always been more reserved than Tain but now his face was a trained blank. Cal's heart sank; he'd never expected forgiveness. He knelt as Arkyn reached him and didn't look up.

Arkyn watched his closest confidant kneel and considered what to do, he moved his hand out, palm upwards. Cal took it, turned it and kissed his signet ring. Arkyn pulled him roughly to his feet.

"Look at me."

The demand ripped through Cal as a request wouldn't. He caught Arkyn's eye and couldn't look away. Arkyn gave a sharp nod before pulling him into a warm hug. When the hug broke, Cal collapsed onto a chair, his head in his hands.

Seeing Arkyn shaking, Tain got up and pulled his brother into a tight hug, before releasing him, grasping Cal by the shoulder and leaving them together. As the door closed, Cal started to sob, the whole situation overwhelming him. When Arkyn went to comfort him, he pulled himself together. Their pain was worse than his distress.

Chapter 5
REVELATIONS
03:00

King Arkyn's Chambers – Antechamber

TAIN NEEDED to be doing something. Anything to keep his mind from dwelling on the fact his father was dead. The letter had been an ounce of comfort in the vastness of despair, but grief still strangled him.

When he entered the antechamber, Kadeem bowed but none of the anxiety left the manservant's features, his professional neutrality gone.

Somehow, Tain managed to keep his voice level as he said, "Cal is there, Kadeem. Is there anything I can be doing? I need to do something."

"What like, sir?"

"I don't know just *something*. I'll stand here giving orders and generally getting—" He broke off as Lady Phylicia entered the antechamber.

"I came to see if there was anything I could do, Your Highness."

"Thank you, my lady, but I don't know, unless…actually, there may be one thing. Is there another room my brother could sit in undisturbed? The servants will need access to all his rooms…"

"There's my sitting room, sir. It's not that far."

* * *

After they were gathered in Lady Phylicia's sitting room, she offered to stay with the brothers if Cal wanted to rest after his journey. As she said it, she looked worried; Oedran was many hours ride away. Hours that were still passing. How had Cal arrived so soon?

Arkyn noticed. "My father knew what was coming, Lady Phylicia. He had time to plan." He bit his lip so hard it almost started to bleed.

Unthinkingly, she took his hand and squeezed it.

Tain nodded his thanks and dragged Cal out of the room. A question, such an obvious question had come to him. Why had they not asked it before? Even the announcement hadn't included the information.

"*How* did father die?" As Cal told him, Tain stumbled to a chair and sat down. "Tell me it was quick."

"It was quick, sir. There's… Oh, never mind, it can all wait. Have a drink, if Lady Phylicia keeps any here."

Tain shook his head. "I'll be all right, I'll need a clear head; Arkyn isn't coping too well, is he?"

"I'd say he's coping remarkably well, Your Highness, I'm more worried that you're so calm."

"I'm *angry*, Cal. Not at my father, not at you, not at Edward or Landis. I'm furious with Uncle Scanlon, with the world, with the man who pulled the trigger, the man who… And I can't collapse. Not when we have to reach Oedran and deal with everything there."

Cal sat down. "Do you want me to check what's happening?"

Tain shook his head. "No, I expect father is being laid out and the guards are searching for the assassin, the guests dispersed and everyone going to bed. I do wonder why no lord has been in touch though."

"I expect they'll send a rider assuming the King and Your Highness will have retired for the night, sir."

Tain gave a non-committal jerk of his head. "Maybe." He got to his feet with a sigh as a determined figure entered the antechamber. "Your Excellency?"

The Governor bowed slightly. "Your Highness, forgive me. I have no wish to intrude on your grief or the King's—"

"But?"

"Shortly before you arrived here, Your Highness, I had word from your late father, asking me to appoint a deputy manservant for your stay here as Master Linnt didn't have one—"

"What of it, Your Excellency? I have no complaints about Robert."

"No, sir. I mean, I am glad. His Late Majesty informed me that there would be an explanation for Your Highness arriving in the Munewid dispatches. I had forgotten until my secretary passed me a scroll, it arrived late this evening. I was going to pass it to your administrator but considered, in the circumstances, Your Highness might want it now. The letter from His Late Majesty was perplexing and considering the events…"

Taking the letter, Tain broke the seal. What he read made him collapse onto the abandoned chair. "What? No… Linnt is actually one Advisor Bantling…"

"I *thought* he seemed familiar!" In answer to Tain's raised eyebrows, ReJean continued, "Advisor Bantling is one of Lord Scanlon's staff, sir. I met him once, maybe twice. He had disappeared though, presumed dead."

"He's looking good on it." Tain spotted a table at the right height. "Could you ask my administrator to join me please, Your Excellency? I have a report to compile. Also, Smithers, a couple of guards and Master Linnt."

"Are you going to arrest Bantling, Your Highness?" enquired ReJean.

"That's the general idea."

"Let me do so, sir," replied ReJean keeping the concern out of his voice.

"No! I shall do it." When the Governor had gone, Tain said, "Cal, where was my father shot from?"

"I don't know, Your Highness. I was dancing with Lady Elantha—"

"Sicla! Did she witness…?" When Cal nodded, Tain bit his lip and closed his eyes. Opening them again, he said, hurriedly, "Cast your mind back. *Where* was my father shot from?"

Cal hesitated. "He was seated at the dais and the bolt, the bolt was at an angle… downwards, as though it had come from a height and it was angled to his left."

Tain frowned again, placing himself behind the throne in the King's Hall at Oedran. He looked up and towards the far wall and then grasped at Cal for support.

"Unless anyone was on stilts, there's only the Viewing Gallery to match that description."

Cal collapsed onto a chair. "No!"

"This is our fault, Cal…"

"No, sir, it isn't, it *can't* be, it just can't," he ended on a whisper.

Tain and Cal shared a look that plainly said that, whatever was voiced, neither of them believed it wasn't their fault. Tain held Cal's gaze, a memory burning through him. The entrance to the ancient Viewing Gallery had been lost with the Age of Tyranny when Lord Onraet had wrested power and King Alvern had been shot from there. Tain and Cal had been puzzled about the location of the entrance. When Cal had discovered he was a shifter and could appear anywhere at will, Tain had suggested they used the skill to discover the lost location. Cal had exited from the apparently solid stone wall and had been seen moments later by one man.

"He must have told someone, Cal."

Cal nodded, his face white. "We couldn't have known, sir…"

"No but he *will* pay. Remember those plans of the Palace? When you first examined them, they were out of order and yet I hadn't handled them. He was always sneaking off… Who knows what he got up to when I wasn't in Oedran; we don't. Lord Scanlon must have planted him to find a way through the King's protection. What better way than through our households? Especially our menservants and administrators – they know everything about our lives."

Cal swallowed. "Is it enough?"

"Probably not to convict him, it's mostly circumstantial and I don't want to draw attention to your skill."

"Thank you, sir, your concern is appreciated but do you want to obtain a conviction?"

"The scroll from father helps that." He sat in silence for several minutes.

Cal respected that silence. Tain was now Justiciar of Oedran *and* the King's Justiciar, if he was present when treason was committed or discovered he had more power than Lord Scanlon did as Justiciar of the Empire, and Tain's investiture as Justiciar of Oedran had only been two weeks previously. He was to take up his duties that day. Had Scanlon made his first serious mistake? Had he overlooked the extra power Tain would have with Arkyn's accession and that he, himself, had lost with Adeone's assassination?

"Sir, hardly appropriate to mention it but happy birthday."

Tain swallowed. "Quite. Happy birthday to you also."

Cal smiled sadly. "I've had happier."

"Me too. We're fifteen, Cal."

"Aye, cisan-age. Does this mean we've got to be *sensible*?"

"In public or private?"

Cal pretended to consider. "Does it matter?"

"More for me than you, unfortunately."

* * *

At half past three, Tain pushed himself to his feet as Linnt entered the antechamber followed by Captain Smithers, two other guards and his administrator, Peter.

Tain looked at Peter. "Can you take a record of this, please?" Receiving a nod, he faced his manservant. "Linnt, whom did you tell when you saw

Cal exit from the wall in the upper servants' passageway behind the King's Hall in Oedran?" When Linnt didn't answer, Tain snapped, "Whom did you tell?" with his eyes boring into his manservant.

Still Linnt stood there mutely, no sign of defiance or elation.

From behind the manservant, Smithers said, "Answer His Highness."

It had no effect.

Tain pursed his lips. "Very well, you're dismissed from my service. Advisor Stephen Eli Bantling, otherwise known as Master Gab Linnt, I arrest you for treason. Whomever you told was instrumental in tonight's events. As you won't tell me who that was, I have no other option than to arrest you. Guards, convey him to the cells. I will prepare a report for the Chief Judge here. Be thankful I didn't discover this in Oedran."

Linnt-Bantling broke his silence. "Why?" The question was insolent and sneering.

Tain took a deep breath. "Because you would have faced me in the Justice Hall. Here you will get an unbiased trial. Take him out."

As the guards applied pressure to make Linnt-Bantling turn, a voice said mildly,

"Wait. Explain, Justiciar."

Tain swallowed, it was the first time Arkyn had talked to him formally and the seed of realisation had been sown. Trying to adjust, Tain told him.

"Is this true?" enquired Arkyn facing the advisor-manservant.

Linnt-Bantling was mute, his eyes blank. Yet Cal, watching him, had the feeling he was trying to communicate with them but soon realised he must have been wrong.

Tain walked over to the advisor-manservant. "You might not answer me, Linnt, but you *will* answer the King."

Linnt-Bantling didn't make any move.

"Take him out then," ordered Arkyn, exasperated. "If he cannot explain when explanations may save his life, he shall face the full consequences."

Angrily, Tain laid a hand on Linnt's shoulder to turn him around. Linnt threw the guards back and off him. Caught by the first, Smithers fell away from the FitzAlcis as Linnt lunged towards them. Tain sidestepped, reacting instinctively. He saw the glint of a blade and stuck his foot out. Linnt stumbled. Cal wrestled him into the wall, away from Arkyn. Tables, chairs and ornaments flew. Cal smashed the dagger out of Linnt's hand, but Linnt was strong, and they ended up falling to the floor.

"Smithers!" snapped Arkyn.

It was too late for Linnt; he was dead, having hit his head on the corner of a window sill in falling.

White and shaking, Cal got to his feet. Arkyn caught his eye whilst

Tain viewed the tableau.

"So, the report I was going to write *isn't* needed. Smithers, see this is taken care of whilst I attend on the King and sort Master Calumiel out. Oh, Peter, I will need to see Kadeem. It seems I lack a manservant," added Tain dryly.

Chapter 6

A WORRYING THOUGHT

03:42

Lady Phylicia's Chambers – Sitting Room

ONCE IN THE SITTING ROOM with the door closed on the travesty of an antechamber, Arkyn thanked Cal for his swift action.

Tain nodded. "Yes. That's saved an awful lot of questions."

Arkyn said, "What like?"

"How Cal was ever in the Viewing Gallery, without knowing where the entrance is."

"You're going to have to explain from the beginning."

Tain did so, taking into account Phylicia's unobtrusive presence.

Cal didn't pay much attention to the explanation. His heart was still racing. He'd always known there might be times he'd have to stand in the way of danger to protect his friends but he hadn't expected to be the reason a man died. He sat on his hands to stop them shaking. Closing his eyes, he concentrated on his breathing. The slightest touch drew his attention. Lady Phylicia passed him a drink with a soft smile. He nodded his thanks, almost glad someone had noticed he wasn't all right, though he didn't want to seem weak. He was sipping the wine when a knock at the door heralded Kadeem. The manservant entered and bowed with a precision Cal had always admired. It wasn't a courtier's bow, but it wasn't perfunctory either. In the moments before Arkyn and Tain finished their conversation, Kadeem's gaze had swept around the comfortable sitting room. What was he searching for? Was it instinctive?

Arkyn was saying, "I think this happened for the best, somehow." He noticed his manservant. "Kadeem?"

"I understood His Highness wished for a word. That is, if you have no objection, sir?"

Arkyn shrugged. "I don't."

"I have no manservant," explained Tain. "Master Linnt has breathed his last treacherous breath – Smithers has the story. I don't know how inconvenient it is for you but I guess it is inconvenient."

44

"Challenges appear so we stretch our capabilities, sir." Kadeem glanced at the King. "Sorry, Sire. Might I enquire how Your Highness has found Master Robert?"

Tain said, "I've not had much contact with him but I've no complaint."

"May I ask him to accompany us then, sir?"

Tain nodded. "It's the simplest solution. Check with him and with Governor ReJean that there's nothing to hold him here. If Robert agrees, he can come to Oedran."

When Kadeem had gone, Cal was finally able to ask, "Will there be any investigation into Linnt's death?"

Arkyn was silent – this wasn't his concern, it was Tain's – it was civil law not military.

Tain had been Justiciar of Oedran for mere hours but he was already faced with a conflict of interest which blinded him. He glanced at Cal's worried face and at his brother's questioning one. He heard Judge Tancred saying no-one should be exempt from the law and he'd agreed, did agree but this was his closest friend and confidant. The room at Fitz's inn where Tancred had taught him came to his mind's eye. The Judge had been right: there would be many dilemmas to face but their lessons had given him the tools to cope. He retreated into his hard-earned knowledge of the law but approached it from the fact he and Arkyn had been present and Linnt-Bantling had been a traitor.

Phylicia, sitting quietly and unobtrusively, watched the men in the room with concealed interest. The strain of Cal's question was clear on the FitzAlcis' faces but there was no doubt of the depth of thought Tain was putting into unravelling the issue. No-one was paying her any attention and she was glad she could observe without feeling inquisitive.

After several long moments examining the problem from every which way Tain said, "No, Cal, there is no case to answer. You were protecting Arkyn in a difficult situation. There was no premeditation, there were plenty of witnesses and Linnt had drawn steel in the King's presence. His death in such a manner was unfortunate but no blame can be attached to anyone. The act of drawing a blade in anger sealed his fate; he just died sooner than his execution would have been."

Cal tried to relax. "Thank you, sir, but surely someone will say it was convenient and draw aspersions about it?"

"No-one will enquire too closely as to what happened, Cal. A traitor was arrested; a traitor resisted arrest and attacked us, a traitor died. There is nothing more to be said."

Arkyn nodded. "I agree with Tain, and he knows the law far better than I do. I am interested in why Linnt reacted as he did but the reasons for it will be lost."

Tain grimaced. "Probably. What concerned me was where he got the blade from. His normal duties, especially tonight, didn't require him to carry one and I have never known him have a knife to hand before."

"Possibly fortunately if he can, could turn like that. I am horrified to imagine what would have happened if you'd been on your own with him in that mood."

Tain bit his lip. "Then don't think about it."

Cal said, "It was only when Your Highness touched him there was any reaction, and it was so disproportionate a reaction – you're well rid of him."

Tain paused. "I think you're onto something. Arkyn, can't men be conditioned not to react until there's a certain set of circumstances?"

"Conditioned is an odd choice of word," replied Arkyn, "but, yes, there are methods that could produce what you say. Hypnotism is one..."

"I don't think this was hypnotism. It was more like a fealty binding. Do you remember Lord Daioch describing how the life-bind took hold? How subtle can fealties get? How precise can the instructions be within the wording? The Judge tried to explain to me many times, and I thought I understood it but then he spoke only in terms of the fealties a king can request: life-binding, honour-binding, speech-binding and truth-binding. What if there are other ancient variations? The valley-binding exists, I talked to the Comptroller about it once and it's a subtle blend of others—"

Restlessly, Arkyn got up, running his hand over his head. "Tain, do you know how exasperating you are at times? You follow a thread so carefully and logically that I'm left with the tangled mess at the other end – the one where you've tightened all the knots!"

"Let me find my way through this puzzle then... To save you being in a tight spot."

Cal whispered, "Yes, they're always like this, Lady Phylicia."

She hastily hid a smile. "I'm not sure I understand you, Master Calumiel."

Cal raised an eyebrow. "That's a shame, my lady, because the King's face says he did and I suddenly don't feel like explaining."

"Coward," muttered Tain.

"I'm sure Kadeem would say that 'Explanations are superfluous when polite denial of understanding is present'," said Arkyn. "Thank you, Lady Phylicia, for your tact."

"It was nothing, Sire."

"I thought it was common sense myself," replied Cal.

Tain said, "Cal, leave it..."

Arkyn muttered. "Yes, it's just you've never found it, Tain – common sense that is."

"I never thought I should hunt for it." He caught Arkyn's eye with a look of startling depth.

Arkyn simply nodded in return: understanding a sentiment that had nothing to do with the words or the last few minutes. Tain's veneer was cracking for the first time that evening. Nonsensical chatter on the back of intense officialdom was a stress too far. Tain needed quiet but feared the silence, wished for peace but feared inactivity; he wanted security of place but had only the distress of upset. Arkyn watching him knew his contradictions as he knew himself and was privately worried.

Chapter 7
KADEEM AND ROBERT
03:50
Palace of Amphi

ON LEAVING THE BROTHERS, Kadeem asked Smithers to explain why the Prince was inconveniently requiring a new manservant. When he had heard the full explanation, his attitude changed and relief flowed through his veins. Making his way to the Prince's rooms, he entered the bedchamber where Robert was single-handedly packing Tain's belongings.

Kadeem stood for a moment, eyeing the ordered mayhem. "Don't you have anyone to help, Robert?" he asked, conversationally.

Robert smiled. "Seemingly not, sir. I'm not sure where Master Linnt is but I rather think *his* absence is a blessing."

"I'll lend you one of the King's footmen. Linnt is dead. He resisted arrest for treason and there was an accident, a true accident before you get any ideas."

Giving a low whistle, Robert stopped wrapping an ornament. With deliberation, he said, "Would it be wrong of me to say good riddance to bad rubbish, sir?"

Kadeem smiled involuntarily. "Only if anyone else was present. His Highness has extended an invitation for you to accompany him to Oedran, as his temporary manservant. Do you have any ties here to prevent that?"

Robert finished wrapping the ornament and placed it carefully in a straw-filled packing case before adding more straw on top from a sack. "No, sir. If His Highness requires my presence, I'll come."

Kadeem's eyes narrowed. "Is that all? No whoop of joy?"

"The situation makes it rather tactless, sir. His Highness… well he's a good kid. I'll do what I can to help. I've nothing here that keeps me here but the work, if you follow me. We've all got to live somehow, I don't mind where my job is, just that I have one."

"A good kid! I might advise him that your language leaves something to be desired."

Robert smiled. "Sorry. I'll say something else if you want."

"I dread to think what. Don't repeat anything so informal about your employer again. Alcis, it's going to be interesting with you around."

"I aim to please, sir."

"Don't take up archery," retorted Kadeem. "Your language just now aside, I was impressed in hall earlier. His Highness will need every ounce of tact and care that we can provide. I think it only fair to warn you that after Master Linnt's inauspicious employment I shall be monitoring your work carefully."

"Please inform me if I'm in any way incompetent, or wrong."

"Very well. Again, I will warn you, I have high standards."

Robert nodded. "I am aware of that, sir, and maybe I should say that so do I. Oh, Master Kadeem… Is there anything, other than the death of King Adeone, I should be aware of with His Highness? I've noticed his mood has been erratic since he arrived. Alternating high and low. High in public but very low in private. I wondered if that is normal."

Kadeem said softly, "No, it is not normal. How have you come to observe him so closely in private?"

"Master Linnt was noticeable by his absence, sir, and someone should be on call at all times."

Kadeem nodded. Robert had more about him than it appeared. "Prince Tain's depression might be due to the fact that about a fortnight ago he suffered another devastating bereavement."

Robert absorbed that. "The King did not?"

"Not to anything like the same extent. Judge James Tancred, Prince Tain's mentor, died unexpectedly. Although the King knew the Judge, he was not close to him – Prince Tain on the other hand was, as was the Prince's Administrator. You are not coming to a happy place."

"I understand, sir. Thank you for telling me. Erm, also, is there anyone other than His Highness who might know his possessions better than I do? I'm not certain what's his and what is the Palace's."

Once Kadeem had left, Robert continued but his actions were all automatic. He would be travelling to Oedran, taking over from a traitor and looking after a traumatised adolescent. He wasn't sure which of those things concerned him most.

Chapter 8
REACTION
03:60

Lady Phylicia's Sitting Room

Aᴛ ᴛʜᴇ ᴘᴏɪɴᴛ Tain's veneer began to crack a knock was once more herald to Kadeem entering. Seeing the tableau, he paused. The King and Prince were looking at each other in an odd way, one that clearly said no-one else was in the room. They were feet apart from each other yet there was no distance discernible.

Cal was saying to Lady Phylicia, "My lady, will you just show me to the King's chambers, I should check—"

Phylicia got up. "Of course."

Spotting the manservant, Cal walked over and put a hand gently on Kadeem's arm; he followed the polite warning, request and instruction and left the room with them.

Once outside Cal let out a sigh. "We're probably better letting them have some time alone."

Kadeem said, "Master Calumiel, I wonder if I may borrow your eyes?"

"Do they need to be attached to the rest of me?"

Kadeem smiled. "As it is answers to contemporary problems, and not foresight, which are needed then I believe so, sir."

"I thought your strength was philosophy not bad jokes, Kadeem."

"Desperate times, sir."

Cal gave a crooked grin. "How can I help, Kadeem?"

"I considered that you might know more of His Highness' belongings by sight than either myself or Master Robert," admitted Kadeem uneasily.

* * *

Leaving Phylicia watching to make sure Arkyn and Tain weren't disturbed, Cal silently followed Kadeem. The corridors were far busier than they had been earlier. More candles were burning, and there wasn't a shadow for a spider to hide in. A footman, runner and two guards hurried by them going in the opposite direction. Cal asked Kadeem how the preparations were going.

"We're getting there, sir. We normally take a day to prepare to leave when we've unpacked completely. So this is rather swifter but people know what they're doing and we'll be ready."

"I never doubted that, Kadeem. I... I don't know why I'm asking."

Kadeem glanced at him. "Because it's that sort of night, sir. We're all questioning everything. But questions keep our minds active."

Cal knew the last sentence was Kadeem trying for a semblance of normality. He glanced at the manservant. Was he all right? His position had changed, his responsibilities widened and he had to move the FitzAlcis to Oedran quickly. Cal wanted to ask, but the manservant might take it amiss. When they entered Tain's chambers, one of Arkyn's footmen was just leaving. Kadeem asked him to find Robert and Cal glanced around the sitting room curiously. It was smaller than he expected having seen the King's and Lady Phylicia's but its cosier atmosphere was oddly comforting.

"Are you sure I'm the best person, Kadeem?"

"The conclusion was the result of the options, sir."

"Isn't every conclusion?" enquired Cal as a manservant he didn't know entered. "You mean there was no choice. I should be flattered."

Kadeem smiled at him. "You do yourself a disservice, sir. Might I introduce Robert Burne to you, Master Calumiel? He has agreed to accompany the Prince as his manservant for the time being."

Cal swallowed. "I'm pleased to meet you, Robert, and on Prince Tain's behalf, thank you, it will take a load from him."

Quietly, Kadeem said, "It is what we are for, sir."

"If Robert follows your example the FitzAlcis shouldn't have anything to worry about."

Kadeem chuckled. "Leave flattery to the King, sir. I know how to deal with it. Before I go, I should explain your role to Robert."

"I'm the resident clown."

Kadeem inclined his head slightly. "Robert, Master Calumiel is the closest friend King Arkyn and His Highness have, but, as he says, he's also the resident clown. An extremely proficient one."

Robert said, "I understand, sir."

Cal sighed. "That's a good thing, is it? Let's get on with this, before the King realises I'm on the loose."

Kadeem squeezed his shoulder. "They'd be lost without you, sir."

"They're lost with me; it's just a different map. Come on, Robert, let's start. That way I might stay out of trouble."

Kadeem left. A short time later, Robert had made a substantial list and Cal returned to Phylicia to wait until Arkyn and Tain needed him.

* * *

In Phylicia's sitting room, Arkyn continued to watch Tain compassionately. Tain got up and crossed to the window, avoiding the gaze. After a moment, Arkyn turned away and picked up Tain's abandoned glass. He measured a splash of whiskey by eye and topped it up with water. Engrossed in pouring the drink and his own thoughts, which were certainly not stoical, he missed Tain turning back to the room.

"He…He can't be dead."

Arkyn spun round; Tain's voice had been that of a lost child, so different from the one that had been discussing fealties with such authority. His brother's fingers gripped the edge of an occasional table so tightly his knuckles were white but what struck Arkyn most was the tone: Tain was pleading for support, for confirmation of denial. Arkyn could give him the first but never the second. He crossed to his brother; confidently but caringly, he pulled him into a hug and gently prised his fingers from the table. Taking Tain's weight, he led him to the couch and then, lifting his brother's legs up so he was lying down, took Tain's shoes off. He sat on the floor, with a hand as support on Tain's shoulder. There were no tears but there was a look on Tain's face Arkyn could never describe. In those moments, he realised Tain still had a child's attachment to their father, instead of a more adult perspective and the five years age difference between them was a wealth of maturity – probably one greater with bereavement than at any other time. So, with hot eyes, he stayed; he didn't judge, he couldn't, but he did understand.

Chapter 9

ARRESTING THOUGHT

04:00

City of Amphi – Oedran Gate

THE NEWS of King Adeone's assassination sped around Amphi and its officials faster than a horse could gallop. It reached the fort and the commander of Areal, woken from his sleep, cursed more profusely than his batman had heard before. He considered that the Major of Oedran would have more than enough to do in Oedran; therefore, dealt with the practicalities of the new King's departure without reference to anyone else. He didn't need superior officers getting in the way and so liaised with the Governor directly. The new King would leave for Oedran in daylight even if everything was ready before.

Since the bandit attack in 1213, a standing order decreed a unit of the army was always to travel with the FitzAlcis. There were no forts between Amphi and Oedran. If anything were to go wrong, the commander didn't need to be found wanting. He alerted two units to be ready to ride at dawn. If that helped his promotion chances all well and good. He set another unit to clearing the road and standing guard by the Oedran Gate to prevent hold ups. He was inspecting the preparations at the gate when

51

an exhausted and dishevelled lad entered on an equally spent and bedraggled horse.

Breathless, the lad spotted the commander. "Sir, I need the Palace."

"We'll find you a new horse, first."

The lad's gaze was steady, for all his obvious distress. "No, sir, there's no time. I must see the Governor. I've news for the FitzAlcis."

"We've heard about King Adeone. Take your time and we'll get you a new horse."

"No, sir."

The commander noted the determination that tiredness was enhancing and swung into the saddle. "All right, we'll do it your way. Follow me. What's your name?"

"Caswal Hillbeck, palace courier. You can't have heard. It's not possible. I rode from Oedran within minutes... I only just got out of the Palace. The Steward closed it. I doubt anyone else will leave or get entry for hours. Was it a messenger?"

The commander had enough. "I don't think that's for you to worry about, is it, courier?"

Caswal Hillbeck swallowed. "How, Commander? I mean how?" He took stock of himself. "Never mind. Is this the Palace ahead?"

"Yes, lad, it is. Come on, you're spent, as is your poor horse. Have you changed it at all?"

"I've cooled him. He's a Swiftfoot, but I rode him harder than I should."

"In good cause. They like a gallop. Come on, the stables are this way, let's see the beast cared for."

A few minutes later, Caswal dismounted heavily and stretched. A groom hurried over to take the horse and took note of Caswal's attire.

"You've ridden from Oedran... Sicla! You've done well. We'll take care of your horse; you go and take care of yourself. There's drinks on that stand."

Caswal slaked his thirst before turning to the commander. "Where's the Governor?"

"Follow me, lad. I don't think you'll need to say much."

* * *

The commander explained the situation to ReJean, who jumped to unsubstantiated conclusions and locating guards hastened to his daughter's rooms. Where he found the target of his current suspicions talking quietly to Phylicia in the antechamber. That made things easier.

Cal was saying, "It would be good if you could, my lady. I'm not sure if I can manage both—" He broke off noting the Governor's implacable face, the presence of Caswal Hillbeck and, behind them, the commander and guards. With a sense of foreboding, Cal raised his voice slightly, "Your Excellency, the King is not to be disturbed."

Having hardly glanced at Cal in hall, ReJean pointedly looked him up and down. Velvet doublet and hose marked him out as a merchant's son. Blond hair, bright eyes and a straight posture suggested training. He bit back the order for arrest.

"Who *are* you?"

"Calumiel Galdwin, Your Excellency. My name, however, will not change the fact that you cannot, for the moment, see King Arkyn."

"Why?"

"Why it doesn't change the fact? Or why the fact?"

"The latter!"

"He is… resting," the pause was so brief that the Governor missed it.

"You're forgetting—"

Cal's patience snapped – everything that had happened, every delay of the evening and every bit of support and courage he'd witnessed in his friends was being swept aside by an official who apparently couldn't see further than the obvious.

"Your Excellency, King Arkyn and Prince Tain have had very little rest! They have a long journey ahead. It is better that they relax in uninterrupted peace."

The Governor flushed; someone Cal's age shouldn't be so forthright. As he was trying to find a response, Kadeem entered the antechamber and would have entered the sitting room.

Cal caught the manservant's eye. "Kadeem, please stay where you are. The King is not to be disturbed."

Kadeem stepped to stand beside the door to the sitting room.

Cal was glad the manservant had read the atmosphere and not disobeyed the questionable order. "Your Excellency, *why* are you here?"

The Governor snapped, "Arrest him," before crossing to the sitting room door and knocking. He entered before waiting for a reply. He was the only hereditary King's Representative in the empire; if he needed to see his monarch, no-one would stop him, least of all a belligerent adolescent.

Cal winced: it wasn't for the grip of the guards but rather for the explosion which he expected from Arkyn. He was more concerned when he heard Arkyn saying far too mildly,

"That is not a mode of entry I would have expected of you, Your Excellency. I hope there is an excellent reason for this display."

"There is, Sire. Guards, bring him in, and the courier," ordered ReJean.

Tactlessly, the Amphi guards pushed and pulled Cal into the sitting room, where he rolled his eyes at Arkyn and mouthed the single word, 'Time', to receive a nod of acknowledgement.

Entering behind Cal and the guards, Kadeem took in the drained look on the King's face and the blank one on Prince Tain's; he positioned himself carefully to be at hand if necessary. The Governor was being too confrontational for his liking. Whatever Cal was meant to have done, he knew the King wouldn't accept it. The unspoken conversation between them had said as much. ReJean was on thin ice and it was cracking. Now positioned behind the King, he saw Lady Phylicia also enter the room and cross behind the guards. They didn't need any more witnesses to whatever was about to happen. Prince Tain had noticed his friend in the grip of the guards and the stifling despondency left his gaze as it hardened. He pushed himself to his feet. Maybe the interruption would have its positive moments. Kadeem watched the door, but the commander didn't enter. He could read a situation better than the Governor. Was he trying to save his career?

ReJean said, "Sire, concerning facts have come to my attention. They raise intriguing questions as to how Calumiel Galdwin reached us tonight. This *official* courier has only just arrived. Young Galdwin reached us within two hours of your father's assassination. Two hours to ride sixty miles, and that's by the Rex Dallin – it would never work."

Barely able to hold himself up, Arkyn swayed and, with a speed that made even Cal blink, Kadeem supported him.

Still in the vice like grip of the guards, Cal caught his friend's eye. "You should be resting, sir."

Arkyn held his gaze. "Your recent endeavours are preventing it."

"I was always told practice makes perfect," remarked Cal trying to lighten the atmosphere, adding mock-soberly, "Can't think who by."

Addressing ReJean, Arkyn said, "My father knew what was coming. He had much time to plan."

"Yes, but he was there when…" protested Caswal pointing at Cal. He trailed off and dropped to his knees when Arkyn glared at him.

Arkyn smiled at Cal. "You know my father was ever foresighted but your lookalike has an awful lot to answer for. Caswal, get off your knees."

Tain broke the momentary silence. "Forgive me for interrupting, Sire. Guards, release Master Calumiel. The King and I are more than satisfied with his explanation. I'm surprised it took the Governor so long to realise there was a discrepancy. Lady Phylicia realised a few hours ago. Caswal, grab what sleep you can, or your mother will never forgive us. Kadeem will find you a spot to put your head until we leave. You will return with us. His Excellency will find you a horse. Thank you, gentlemen."

At a nod from Arkyn, the Governor bowed and left with the guards, Kadeem and Caswal in his wake. All perplexed by the audience.

Completely forgetting that Phylicia was there Tain rounded on Cal. "That was close but *two hours?* What took you so long? And whose stupid idea was it that you would shift here tonight anyway?"

"Your Highness…" Cal flicked his eyes at Phylicia who was glancing between them confused.

Tain swore, then apologised.

Arkyn put a hand on his arm. "Lady Phylicia, Cal is a Shifter; he can move between places in the blink of an eye. We would be grateful if you could promise that you won't repeat that information to anyone. All our lives, yours included, will be in danger if it becomes known."

"I understand, Sire, and you have my word to keep it secret. Will you excuse me?"

Once she'd gone, Cal said, "Just out of interest – what lookalike, Sire?"

Arkyn shrugged. "First thing that came to mind. I suppose I'll have to find one."

"No, leave the thought of it without manifestation. It's easier. I'll be my own lookalike."

Arkyn sighed. "Only you, Cal, would say that."

"You appreciate my uniqueness. Is there anything I can do?"

Arkyn sank onto a chair, fighting to keep control. "Stay out of trouble? Not annoy or show up the Governor of Areal? Sorry but I think you've already failed at both of those and—"

"Sire… I'm sorry, not you."

Neither of them noticed Tain leave to give them time together.

With a deep breath, Arkyn admitted, "The worst is the honorific."

That made Cal pause. "Not the fact Edward and I knew and expected what happened?" He sat opposite Arkyn, studying his friend, searching for something to help.

Blinking back emotion, Arkyn answered bleakly, "No. At the moment, it's the word: every time I hear it, I see father or expect him to be close by. It's not me people are addressing but it's me that must answer. Every time, it cuts the wound deeper… What do I *do*, Cal?"

"Grit your teeth and get on with it, I suppose. It won't go away, however much you wish it to. I'll try and be sparse with it, but I can't avoid it. No-one can. We're not going to insult you now, or, at least, for a while, in my case. There's not much else to be done. I suppose Kadeem would say that happy memories can cause as much pain as upsetting ones but I suppose a wittering clown like me might say that every time you imagine your father close by, he's there supporting you."

"Change my perspective, you mean?"

"I don't know what I mean, sir, I'm making this up as I go along. It's the only method I have."

Arkyn took his wrist in a vice like grip. "Cal, look at me. What did you do when father told you?"

"Other than cry?"

"Yes."

"I wept."

"Cal!"

Cal blinked. "I… I went to Tain's chambers – I knew they'd be empty; I cried and then convinced myself nothing would happen, that you'd never have to know that I'd betrayed you both."

"I take it back; you're not a clown, Cal, you're a bloody fool. You didn't betray us. Alcis, what would we have done if we'd woken to this news? You've given us valuable time. Tain was always afraid we'd wake one morning and find father had gone. We've woken from nothing but a dream of security. This is now our battle. There's no-one else to fight it and I'm glad it was you that brought the news; I wouldn't have known how to face anyone else. You've been nothing but a support tonight."

Cal swallowed. "I'm… Oh, Sicla! Did you have to say all that, sir? I'm a *clown*."

Arkyn said, "No, Cal, you're our friend, the best we could ever have. Just stop getting arrested. It's very tiring."

Chapter 10
REQUESTS AND BEQUESTS
04:36

Lady Phylicia's Sitting Room

A FEW MINUTES LATER, Tain re-entered the room, reckoning Arkyn would have had ample time to tell Cal his thoughts and Cal would have had equal time to enlighten Arkyn. He found them both talking with a drink in hand. He clapped Cal on the back.

"So whose idea *was* it, for you to shift here?"

"Your father's, sir. It's why he told me. I don't know how Cas got out the Palace; the Steward closed it. Apparently, Lord Scanlon gave orders many moons ago that if anything like this was to happen. whilst your brother was underage, then the Palace was to be closed until he arrived."

Tain nodded thinking hard. "Uncle's acting as though he'll be Protector for the next week and a half."

Arkyn paled. "Think what he could achieve if he were. Cal, can you find Edward? He'll have father's bequests..." Shaking, he stopped speaking.

Cal rose to leave, placing a steadying hand on Arkyn's shoulder in passing. He left the room with tears pricking at his own eyes. King Adeone had been like a benevolent uncle to him for years. He shook his head angrily. He couldn't break down, not now. Not with Tain and Arkyn relying on him. Behind him, the brothers were sitting hunched forward, drained and worried.

When the door closed behind Cal, Arkyn groaned. "If he's my Protector we have problems, Tain. Serious problems."

"I know that! Ten days until you're of age. What can he reasonably achieve in that time?"

"With Lords of Oedran on his side, an awful lot. Onraet took Oedran and the empire in less."

"Alvern didn't have a Defender. He also didn't have Aunt Amara."

Arkyn snorted. "True. I— Why hasn't Uncle Festus been in touch? I'd have expected him to be informing us. Of everyone, he should have been the first."

Tain paled. "Maybe he thinks we're asleep. I can't, don't want to imagine what happened but, if he was at the feast, I suspect he'll have been busy. If Hillbeck then told him he'd sent Caswal, or if he told Hillbeck to send Caswal, then he's let us know. He'll have been securing the support we need— Won't he?"

"Let's hope so," said Arkyn, pale and fidgety. "I think I followed you."

"Anyway, it's not just him, Arkyn. Aunt Amara hasn't contacted us either. They must think we're asleep. Can we be sure they'd tell us over messenger? You don't break bad news over a messenger link unless there's no choice. Isn't it more likely he'll contact ReJean once the sun's up? Is it even possible that El said she let us know?"

Arkyn's face cleared. "It's possible, yes. She doesn't have a messenger yet but she knows the principle of how to call one. That would make sense. She knows enough to bluff our reactions as well. If anyone puts things together with Cal though..."

Tain cursed. "Look, at best, El told Aunt Amara and Uncle Festus. They'll know that Caswal rode here. You've told ReJean there's a lookalike. Between all of that we can cause enough confusion. If Uncle Festus starts asking questions, decide whether to tell him or not. I doubt what happened here will be picked over for a while. Focus will be on events in Oedran. I suggest we keep it there as well."

Arkyn snorted. "I like the fact you think we'll have a choice, little brother."

Tain pulled a face. "I'm an optimist. Only answer questions when they're asked. Giving explanations without reason is not going to help. Let's worry about Oedran when we get there. I expect we'll discover that Aunt Amara has been keeping Uncle Festus, and everyone else, in line."

"Maybe I will need a Protector after all," muttered Arkyn.

* * *

When Cal found him, Edward was looking extremely sombre. "The..." Cal stalled, unable to continue; he took a deep breath and, for the first time in addressing either of his friends' staff, ignored the titles. "Arkyn was wondering if you could spare him a moment." Cal dropped his voice. "Something about you having his father's requests and bequests."

Edward nodded and retrieved a plain scroll. "How are they?"

Cal took a breath. "Not good, but also better than I thought they'd be."

"And how are you?"

"Coping, I had a bit more warning, as it seems did you."

* * *

When they reached the sitting room, Edward handed the scroll to Arkyn and stood to one side.

Arkyn ran his thumb over the red wax seal, unwilling to break the perfect impression. Breaking it would admit everything was real.

"Come on, sooner or later we have to read it," stated Tain pragmatically.

Arkyn nodded took a breath and snapped the wax. Reading the first part, a smile twitched his lips. "Uncle Scanlon won't like this." He continued reading. At one point he turned to Cal with the first true smile of the day. "You have lifetime permission for the Rex Dallin and Ceardlann."

Cal froze, stunned. To have it mentioned in the bequests of a King meant only treason could remove the right. As such, the granting of permission in the bequests tended to be restricted to members of the FitzAlcis.

Having finished reading, Arkyn passed the scroll to Tain and went to gaze out of the window. The predawn glow gave the skyline a sombre beauty. He stood for several minutes whilst Tain read the document.

"Arkyn..."

Arkyn spun round, shaking his head. Tain accepted the message that nothing else – other than what he'd told Cal – was to be made public yet. He continued reading whilst Arkyn perused the view, hugging himself. The moons were visible. Was the predawn light playing tricks? Aluna, the larger moon, appeared red, a subtle hint of unusual colour. He shook himself out of the distracting thoughts, but the feelings he'd been distracting himself from returned with painful rapidity. When he turned back to the room, traces of tears streaked his cheeks.

Tain rolled the document up and passed it to Edward. "Thank you. Keep it secure please. It might be better if you carried it on you."

"Very well, sir." At a nod from Arkyn, he bowed himself out.

58

Almost whispering, Cal said, "I'll see about some breakfast."

* * *

As Cal stood in the antechamber, a mixture of sorrow and contentment struggled for precedence. King Adeone had given him a greater gift in death than he ever expected. The Rex Dallin was the King's retreat: a valley protected by magic; it was treason to enter without permission. Cal had lived there with Tain and Arkyn but he'd known the permission he held could be revoked. Now it was as though he'd been born there, only if treason was proved would he be cast from the valley and the calm of its embrace. He hadn't realised how King Adeone had regarded him. The bequest effectively said, 'you are part of my family', ephemeral but with a weight of meaning surpassing anything else possible. He swallowed his emotion. Low energy and lack of sleep was taking its toll.

"I think breakfast might be wise, Kadeem. I'm sorry; I seem to be giving you a lot of orders tonight."

"If I didn't think they were apt, sir, I wouldn't be following them, and they're only what King Arkyn would wish. Have you taken any time for yourself yet?"

"Have you?"

"I'll get on with breakfast, shall I?"

Cal swallowed. "I think so. I'll find myself somewhere to mope."

"Sadness and sorrow are the counterbalance of life, not the face of it."

Cal rolled his eyes. "Kadeem…"

Kadeem squeezed his shoulder. "Take your own time, sir."

Cal sank onto a chair. Would the night ever truly end? Or would he be trapped in the surreal world of sorrow and sadness forever?

Chapter 11
LADY PHYLICIA
04:66
Lady Phylicia's Chambers – Antechamber

NOT LONG AFTER THAT, Cal was still sitting with his head in his hands when ReJean entered the antechamber.

"I wish to see King Arkyn."

Cal pushed himself to his feet and put his head around the door. "Sir, the Governor would like a word." He met Arkyn's blank gaze. "I'll take a message."

Tain shook his head. "Let me. You're already controversial enough."

"Such compliments, sir. How do I cope?"

Tain closed the sitting room door behind him. "What can we do for you, Your Excellency?" he enquired heavily.

ReJean glanced at Cal who shrugged at Tain before giving a slight bow and re-entering the sitting room, sitting opposite Arkyn.

"Tain doesn't trust me at all."

"If it's any consolation he doesn't trust me either," replied Arkyn.

"Does the King wish for an Arealian Ambassador, Your Highness?" enquired ReJean, unhappy to be addressing a young adolescent, whatever their rank and status, instead of his monarch.

Inwardly furious ReJean had snubbed Cal and had decided he could disturb Arkyn whenever he wished, Tain didn't hold back. "Of course he does! Sicla, how can you be so naïve as to ask? Every coronation is attended by an ambassador from each province."

"Yes, sir, but I meant to travel to Oedran with your retinue."

Tain said, "Why should the two be mutually exclusive?"

The Governor reconsidered how to talk to Prince Tain. "There is no reason apart from necessity, Your Highness."

"Governor, the night has been long and my temper is shortening with every passing moment. Get to the point."

"Lady Phylicia thinks she might be able to help. She says Master Calumiel has done so much tonight and he needs a rest, but you might need someone and she's already aware of the situation. She is my heiress; I suppose she has to start somewhere. I'm not happy but if it was a choice between her and one of the lords—"

"It would be a pleasure to accept Lady Phylicia's company. We will see she is well cared for in Oedran. I'm sure Lady Amara will be pleased to meet Her Ladyship." Tain was amused by the sudden apprehension on ReJean's face. "Your daughter will be there as your representative?"

"Yes, sir."

"Then unless the King specifically requests it, she will undertake all duties associated with that role."

"That wasn't what I—"

Tain said, "Lady Phylicia is eminently sensible, Governor. You hold the only hereditary post in the empire. I suggest, instead of making the decisions for her, you let Her Ladyship have a say in the matter."

"Sir, might she be my representative for today, the funeral and possibly the coronation? I think a more conventional ambassador would be better for the other aspects."

"You mean the meetings and devious dealings that are integral to the Ambassadors' Court."

"Yes, sir. I don't want to lose her to the snake pit," admitted ReJean.

"Very well but I think you underestimate your daughter."

"Isn't that a parent's prerogative, sir?"

"I wish I could ask mine to check," replied Tain, levelly.

The Governor cursed himself for a fool. "I'm sorry, sir."

Tain merely nodded. "Presumably, Her Ladyship will need to pack—"

"I'll send the majority of her luggage tomorrow, sir."

"Thank you, Your Excellency."

The Governor bowed and left. He found Prince Tain hard to reconcile. Instead of the naivety of youth, he heard shrewdness. Given a few years, Tain would not be a man to cross.

* * *

Shortly afterwards, Phylicia re-entered her sitting room and joined the brothers and Cal, all of whom were exhausted.

"Has your father informed you that you're accompanying us, Lady Phylicia?" enquired Tain.

"Yes, Your Highness. It was actually my suggestion."

Arkyn said, "Thank you, my lady, it was kind thought but as for your duties as—"

"Sir, father's sending a lord as well. I don't mind. I'm only fifteen; I'd rather have a few more years of freedom."

"So would I," muttered Tain to receive a sad smile from Phylicia.

"Your Highness, your duties are what you make them," observed Cal.

"Stop being a bad influence, Cal," interrupted Arkyn. "I mean to work him so hard he hasn't time to cause trouble."

"There's more than one type of trouble," retorted Tain.

Breakfast interrupted the wrangling with such good timing Arkyn momentarily considered if Kadeem had been eavesdropping.

When Arkyn had finished eating, he rose and gazed once more at the lightening sky. "How much longer? Travelling would be preferable to sitting doing nothing."

"The carts have been packed, sir," replied Kadeem. "The coach is ready. Robert has agreed to replace Linnt. I'm waiting for final confirmation from the guard."

"Then I suppose it is time we took our leave of the Governor."

Cal got up. "I'll locate him, sir."

Chapter 12

LEAVE TAKING
05:30
Palace of Amphi – Governor ReJean's Office

CAL LOCATED a runner in the corridor outside Lady Phylicia's rooms. The lad looked confused when Cal asked him for directions, as though he didn't know if he should be giving them. Cal smiled reassuringly and followed the boy.

The Governor's office was similar to the King's in that it included an outer and inner office, there was also an antechamber larger than both. Cal wondered if it served the same function as the Audience Chamber in Oedran, a more public room for the Governor to address lords. Expecting no-one other than the Governor to be awake, Cal was disconcerted to find several lords there. All talking quietly. He overheard snatches of conversation as he passed through.

"Why you, Galaloth?"

"My wed-father, perhaps?"

"Perhaps. Who's that?"

"No idea. Look, Arridge, if you or Skaner want to go…"

Cal tried to keep his face blank. He shouldn't have overheard anything at all. It wasn't for him to hear. The Governor's outer office was far calmer. The runner nodded to Cal and left as the secretary glanced over.

"Yes?"

"Could I speak with His Excellency? I've a message from the King."

The secretary's eyes said he wasn't sure whether to believe it or not but he pushed himself to his feet, knocked on the carved door to the inner office and announced Cal – or would have done if he'd remembered to ask for Cal's name. Instead, he had to say simply that someone had arrived with a message. Cal smiled to himself, at least he hadn't said a runner or courier. It was the small things that mattered.

ReJean glanced over. "What's the message?"

Cal inclined his head. "Your Excellency, the King and Prince Tain will be ready to leave within the next half hour. Other than passing on that King Arkyn wishes to take his leave, I wanted to thank you personally for allowing Lady Phylicia to travel with us. It has lifted a weight from my shoulders. The FitzAlcis are in no state for a long ride and, without Lady Phylicia's presence, I suspect they would have tried to, and I'd have had a hard time telling them not to."

"You would dare *tell* the *King* how to travel?"

Cal sighed. "Your Excellency, I have a proper respect for my place;

however, I also wish for the FitzAlcis to survive the journey. I have known the brothers for over five years and have lived at Ceardlann for most of that time. I have knelt to my friend and accepted he is our King, but his and Prince Tain's wellbeing is my priority – over and above obedience."

The Governor realised he'd heard stories about Cal for a few years but never his name. It explained the confident nature he exuded for his age.

"You are certainly an enigma, Master Calumiel."

"So I've been told, sir. We should not keep the King waiting."

* * *

Reaching the antechamber, they found Captain Smithers and Kadeem discussing logistics quietly.

Cal said, "Can I disturb them, Kadeem?"

"Certainly, Master Calumiel. Would you like to inform them we are ready to leave?"

"Thank Alcis for that. I'll be glad to be on the road. Your Excellency, please come through…" Cal entered the sitting room and passed on the message from Kadeem, who followed them in.

Relief swept across Arkyn's face. He rose and spotted ReJean. "Your Excellency, thank you for your hospitality during our stay. I obviously wish it had ended differently, but, I assure you, I will attend to everything that's been postponed as soon as possible."

ReJean knelt. "Sire, it's been an honour to have you here. I hope your next visit is far pleasanter. I cannot but apologise for the events in the early evening, and will pursue the would-be-poisoner. I will order mourning for His Late Majesty, and will send Lord Galaloth as my more traditional ambassador. May your reign be long and peaceful, Sire. If there is anything I can do, please ask."

Arkyn swallowed. He'd almost forgotten they'd nearly been poisoned that evening, and that the food taster had died. He tried to find the right words as he glanced around the room.

"Lady Phylicia, Kadeem, will you just excuse us for a minute, please."

Kadeem held the door open for Lady Phylicia as they both left.

Once the door closed, Arkyn turned back to ReJean. "How much do you know of the situation in the FitzAlcis?"

Tain opened his mouth and then shut it again.

ReJean glanced in Cal's direction.

"Let me worry about who is in the room," snapped Arkyn.

The Governor hesitated. "Your father did mention his brother was getting troublesome, sir."

Arkyn crooked an eyebrow. "Is that all?" he asked satirically. "As I am here at my accession, do you have any objection to renewing your fealty?

63

I acknowledge the privileges the Bard's line gives you, and I will not interfere in those, but this is more fundamental."

ReJean hesitated, his gaze hardening imperceptibly before his face cleared. "If it is my king's wish."

"Thank you." He stepped forward to where ReJean had knelt.

The Governor held his hands palm upward and never winced when Arkyn placed his on top. Arkyn spoke the words of a truth-fealty without really thinking about them. They'd been drummed into him from a young age. It was more a matter of rote than rule.

Words spoken, ReJean kissed Arkyn's signet ring, sealing the fealty. That was when Arkyn stumbled slightly. Cal was beside him in two strides. Ignoring the Governor's evaluating gaze, he supported Arkyn as he'd seen Kadeem do with an arm around his back, helping him lower himself into a chair.

"Thanks, Cal. This night needs to end. ReJean, thank you. Get up and sit for a moment. When father said Uncle Scanlon was getting troublesome, did he say *anything* else?"

"Not really, sir. He mentioned that there were likely to be worrying days ahead. I suppose we're in them?"

"Yes. Be watchful. Anything concerns you, I want to know about it. If treason happens here, I want to know. You tell me, not Lord Scanlon."

"I understand, sir."

"Thank you." Arkyn let out a long breath. "I should get to Oedran, but I meant my thanks for your hospitality."

* * *

The Palace had calmed down from the hectic night as they made their way to the stables. The candlewardens were looking bleary-eyed as they removed spent tapers and replaced them with new, unlit ones. The light seeping through the windows was now enough to see by. Arkyn was actually glad that the corridors weren't bright. They passed a couple of lords, who stepped swiftly aside and inclined their heads until ReJean made a small gesture, then they knelt. Arkyn hardly seemed to see them instead enquiring of ReJean what the time was.

"About half past five, Sire. It was considered better the dark couldn't hamper the journey. No-one wishes any accident to befall you on your return home."

"Thank you. I must start informing the governors…"

"Let me take that task, sir," offered ReJean. "It is not necessary for—"

"I shall be informing my officials, as far as possible, myself."

Tain said quietly, "Sir, you can't inform all at once and by the time you inform the last they'll likely have already heard from a peer."

Arkyn stopped walking and everyone else stopped around him. "Very well. ReJean, you may inform some. I shall let the Margrave, Tuchlin and Exarch know. Prince Tain, do you feel able to let the Sagamore, Visir and Dey know?"

Tain swallowed. "Of course, Sire."

Arkyn looked at him kindly. "Thank you. Your Excellency, that leaves you to inform the Pasha, Jarl and Fencible."

The Governor said, "Very good, sir, and the Satrap and Domini?"

Arkyn sighed. "I didn't mention them?"

"No, sir, not out loud."

Tain said, "I'll inform the Satrap, sir, if His Excellency will inform the Domini."

"Of course I shall, Your Highness," replied ReJean. "I can inform the Satrap also if you wish."

Tain shook his head. "No, thank you, Your Excellency. I'll be fine. Sire, should we perhaps continue?"

Pulled out of his thoughts by practicality, Arkyn said sharply, "Yes," then looked at Tain, more normally he continued, "Come on…"

Watching them carefully, Cal saw in their own ways they both wanted an argument with someone. He smiled sadly to himself – deciding to pick the right moment before igniting the match.

Once in the courtyard, the new King turned to take final leave of the Governor before entering the coach. Tain and Lady Phylicia following suit. Cal nodded to ReJean before swinging himself up beside the driver, much to the confusion of both him and the Governor. Once sure everyone was mounted and settled, Cal gave the word and the coach and carts trundled out of the yard accompanied by the clop of hooves and the jingling, clanking and clattering of the escort.

Chapter 13
GOVERNORS
06:06

Amphi to Oedran Road – King Arkyn's Coach

THE COACH had barely started to rumble when Arkyn called up Fafnir, his dragon messenger, requesting a link with Wealsman. It might be early but with two young children and a province to run Wealsman rarely slept late. They'd known each other for four years, Arkyn was nearfather to Wealsman's children, and Wealsman had also been a close friend of

Adeone's; therefore, telling him of his friend's murder was the hardest of all the messages Arkyn would bear.

"Percival…"

Wealsman scrutinised Arkyn's face. "It's bad news, and the worst you think I could hear. When and how?"

Arkyn blinked hard. "Last night. Crossbow bolt at the Munewid Eve celebrations…"

"Sicla! Are you…"

"I'm on my way to Oedran."

"That's not what I was going to ask, sir."

"It's the only question in that vein I'm going to answer for a while, Percival. I've your peers to tell."

Wealsman looked at the young man and thought, as he had before, that Arkyn's fortitude was an amazing quality. "Of course, Sire, but I doubt it's the only one anyone's going to ask you. So, are you furious or has grief taken over yet?"

"Both." He voiced the concern haunting him: "I'm not of age."

Wealsman snorted. "I can't see that being an issue. Sorry, sir, but you know, or you should, that your age has been immaterial since you ordered Roth's execution four years ago. Have some belief in yourself before you reach Oedran or everything Adeone worked for, seemingly died for, is in jeopardy."

Arkyn froze. "How dare…?"

Wealsman looked at him compassionately, "Good. Get the rest of it out whilst you're at it, Arkyn, because you've got to be calmly angry, if that isn't impossible, when you reach Oedran."

Furious, Arkyn took a deep breath. "One day, Percival, you'll say the wrong thing."

"No time like the present."

Arkyn sagged. "No and father would be ashamed of me. You only ever give me honest advice. Why am I so riled?"

"Because I'm purposefully enraging you! You're tired and overwrought, as I'm sure I soon shall be, but you need to keep fighting, not give in; no matter what your mind or body want, don't give in, Arkyn."

"I shall try not to," whispered Arkyn.

"I'm sure you shall. Can I inform anyone for you?"

"I've got to talk to Daioch and Tyler Galwood. Between Tain and ReJean, everyone else will soon be informed. Just tell your family and your officials, Percival. See the proclamations necessary are read as soon as possible."

Wealsman nodded. "I shall do my best, Sire, but I'm not in Tera."

Arkyn started. "What? Why? Where are you?"

"A few miles from the border with Areal. I'm on my way north…"

"Why? *Percival*?"

Wealsman said, "I was invited to a close friend's birthday celebrations."

Arkyn swallowed, and blinked hard. "I half wish you hadn't told me because I'd like to see you but I must order you back to Tera. You've proclamations to sign for one thing."

"As you wish—"

"I need to know Terasia's safe. I'm sorry. I feel a bastard… I—"

"Don't. You're right; I'm better being where I'm needed and my duty as your governor is currently there."

Arkyn regarded him sadly. "I'd better talk to Daioch and Tyler Galwood."

Wealsman nodded. "Look after yourself, Arkyn."

"I shall try, Percival. Make sure you do likewise."

"As it is the wish of my King, it is my command. Quick, Fafnir, close the link before he thinks of a retort."

Arkyn laughing, for the first time since receiving the news said, "Give me time, my friend, just give me time. All right, Fafnir…"

* * *

Out of the link Arkyn found Tain watching him carefully.

"Well?"

"He's upset, obviously, and trying to persuade me he's more bothered about me."

Tain said, "He probably is, from everything I've ever heard."

"True. So?"

"They will all send their obsequious and sycophantic condolences and wish to make you aware of their loyalty."

"I should be so lucky," replied Arkyn cynically "Fafnir!" (The small dragon reappeared.) "Lord Daioch, please." When the link formed, he noticed Daioch's pallor. "Did your heart burn last night, my lord?"

"Yes, Sire."

"I'm sorry for that, Your Excellency."

Daioch never hesitated. "It is your loss primarily, my King, most certainly it is, it is your loss – yours and your brother's. We in the empire mourn him, and are devastated but we have not the ties of blood."

"You were life-bound to him, Daioch, you had shared your blood in a common bond…"

"Yes, Sire, as I now am to you. These bindings follow the line. You are my King, my liege and my bounden lord—"

"Isn't that the definition of 'liege'?" enquired Arkyn trying to dredge up a semblance of normality.

"Most certainly, Sire, most certainly, but there is a slight resonance that would be missing in my words if I didn't highlight it in the vernacular."

"And it's not even seven in the morning."

Daioch smiled. "An early start sets one up for the day, my king."

"Well as I've not slept yet the early start was yesterday for me."

"Then may the days of your rule be so mirrored, Sire…"

"Alcis, I hope not. We'd never get any sleep."

"Ah, good point, sir, good point. May the years of your rule be long, seem longer through joy but *never* be devoid of sleep, my liege."

Arkyn shook his head. "I can see why father wanted you to be Tuchlin. I realise you only started in the post at midnight but there won't be any easy first days."

"I understand, Sire. It is what I am here for. Is it your pleasure that I proclaim your accession?"

"Yes, I suppose it is – born of necessity but not pleasure though."

"Of course, sir, of course. I shall attend to it directly."

"Don't let me stop you, Lord Daioch. One thing, can you send an ambassador to Oedran, please?"

"With pleasure, my king, with pleasure. May the moons bless your journey and your reign."

"Thank you, Your Excellency."

* * *

Lord Tyler Galwood, Arkyn and Tain's third cousin but some years older, looked questioningly at Arkyn as the next link formed. "It's rather early—"

"Not for me, for I haven't slept, Your Excellency."

"How can I help then, sir?"

Arkyn studied him. There was only equanimity. "What did Fafnir say?"

"Nothing. He appeared and I recognised him, so simply nodded, why?"

Arkyn swallowed. "Lord Tyler, this is hard – both Lord Wealsman and Lord Daioch guessed before I said anything." He took a deep breath. "Father was assassinated at midnight, a crossbow bolt through the heart at the Munewid Eve celebrations."

"It's certain?" When Arkyn simply nodded bleakly, Lord Tyler let out a long breath. "Sicla! Sire, I doubt you need to hear it but you have my condolences and, when I inform them, those of my family. My grandmother will be distraught…"

"Give my regards to Princess Lilith." Privately Arkyn cursed to himself. He should have informed his grandfather's cousin himself.

"Of course, but I didn't mention her for that reason."

"I never thought you did, Your Excellency."

"Good. I mean, thank you, Sire. Are you on your way to Oedran?"

68

(Arkyn nodded.) "Is the city safe? If you wish to, come to Bayan..."

Arkyn said, "Thank you but my place is in Oedran. Had I been concerned, I would not have left Amphi."

"Of course, sir. It is simple caution that made me enquire and offer."

"A caution well placed, I was nearly poisoned last night, as was Tain and Governor ReJean. I'd almost forgotten what with everything else."

Tyler Galwood, Exarch of Bayan, and well-practised courtier exclaimed, "The bastard!"

Arkyn raised an eyebrow.

"Sorry, Sire, please overlook that outburst."

"No, I think I'll agree with it."

"As you please, sir."

Feeling the wealth of meaning behind his words, Arkyn said, "Yes, as I please. I mean to succeed, cousin."

"I mean to help, Sire. Call on me, if ever you need to. I might not be Wealsman's standard but I'll do whatever I can, now more than ever. I liked Cousin Adeone and admired what he's achieved. We'll avenge him."

"Thank you. I must see if my brother has finished informing others..."

"Of course. May the moons' blessing go with you."

* * *

When the link broke, Arkyn let out a long sigh and glanced out of the coach window. From opposite him Tain enquired quietly,

"Well?"

"Oddly practical. He was somewhat tart about the whole situation. Offered us a refuge in Bayan. I won't say what he called the probable source of these troubles but it wasn't something a king should hear," replied Arkyn numbly.

"I'd get used to it if I were you."

"I never said I disagreed or was offended. Perhaps I should have curbed a continued expression of the sentiment though."

"Possibly but Lord Tyler isn't a fool, is he?"

"No. He's not. So, what *did* they say?"

Tain shrugged. "The Sagamore, very correct, long-faced and seemingly sad. The Dey, evaluating. I think that's the best expression. The Visir, smooth, even slick. The Satrap withdrew into himself. All of them though were disconcerted to find I was the bearer of the news. I'm not sure they quite knew what to do."

Arkyn frowned. "They'll get used to the fact you're an official."

Tain sighed. "I wish I wasn't, now more than ever."

"It's now I really need you to be one, Tain, I'm so sorry..."

Tain caught his eye. "Oh, you've my support, Arkyn, but I think my

69

temper might be better being under wraps elsewhere, that's all."

"We'll both be keeping the other calm then."

"We have to have our uses."

Phylicia from the other corner of the coach said, "I'm not sure anyone's noticing the lack of use, sirs."

Arkyn glanced at her. "My apologies, my lady, you shouldn't have to listen to us talking like this."

"I could put my fingers in my ears if it would help, Sire."

"I always knew Tain had that effect on people but not this quickly." She chuckled.

"I learned everything I know from my brother," grumbled Tain.

"Fortunately, that can't be true," replied Arkyn. "So, my lady, are you looking forward to seeing Oedran?"

"Change the subject then!" muttered Tain, watching the fields and scrubland pass.

"Yes, Sire," replied Lady Phylicia, "but I wish it had been under other circumstances; however, I have heard much about the city and the Palace and wish to match the stories to places – especially Prince Tain's."

Arkyn groaned. "I'm sure we can help with that. Tain what have you been telling Her Ladyship in your letters?"

Tain said nonchalantly, "Wish I could remember…"

Chapter 14
EARLY JOURNEY
08:54
King Arkyn's Coach

TIME WASN'T SOMETHING the brothers noticed as the coach rumbled along the roads of Areal and towards Anapara and home. The jolting motion lulled them out of deep emotion into a lilting trance-like state: half asleep, half awake. Caught in the drowsy world of imagination but with the constant jolting of reality cradling his body, Tain saw the situation's reality and read in it danger.

"Arkyn… We can't stop anywhere."

"Why?" The question was a sleepy, half-automatic response.

Tain shook him gently, ignoring Phylicia's presence; they had to hope she could keep confidences but, as her father's heiress, they supposed she would.

"Because Uncle Scanlon must have made a contingency for this."

"Why? He thought we'd be dead of poison."

"Did he? Can we be sure he poisoned our food?"

"It's a big coincidence if he didn't," muttered Arkyn.

"All right, I'll agree with that but he won't have wanted us to reach Oedran safely, not both of us for certain. With only me left, he'd be more certain to take power. With only you left, he has full control of the courts again. Together we're a bigger threat than father was…"

"Then why did he kill father?"

"Because the three of us would have had no trouble taking him down. Listen to me, if not as my brother as my King," urged Tain. "You can't let us stop en route to Oedran."

"The horses will need a rest," murmured Arkyn.

"Then tell them to find a good site. Where were we planning to break the journey?"

Arkyn pulled himself out of slumber. He shrugged. "I left everything to Kadeem…"

"Botheration!"

"Border Lodge was to be the first stop, sir," said Phylicia quietly. "I overheard a conversation. People forget I'm here."

Tain caught her eye. "Never, my lady, I just thought I could trust you."

She smiled. "You can, sir, but maybe I can be more use than as a mute decoration."

"Your Ladyship is probably far more observant than we are at the moment," said Arkyn. "What are your thoughts on Prince Tain's fears?"

She considered. "Are you sure, absolutely sure, that Lord Scanlon was involved in King Adeone's murder?"

As one Arkyn and Tain said, "Yes!"

"I can't explain the intricacies of our family situation to Your Ladyship but it is probable the attack was at my uncle's order," elaborated Arkyn.

Phylicia considered again and her face was oddly compassionate. "Then I would say His Highness is likely to be right. I wouldn't stop where predictably you would. Border Lodge is certainly out. My maternal uncle has a manor not far from the lodge but on a different road—"

"We can't take this cavalcade on anything but main highways, my lady. The roads are less forgiving."

She considered again. "Maybe this coach and some of your guards could detour, sir. If the rest carry on past Border Lodge and stop to rest on the Anaparian side of the border, we could then rejoin them. It would be a delay of an hour, two at the most and Uncle Tynan would welcome you without being too stuffy."

Arkyn looked at Tain, who was biting his lip. "What do you think?"

"It's worth taking a chance, Sire. What's the worst that can happen?"

Gazing out at the passing farmland and scattered buildings, Arkyn replied, "Kensal asked me that once," referring to a confidant who had died in a bandit attack.

"Sorry, but I think we might be less likely to find trouble if we go via Lord Tynan's."

Arkyn considered for a couple of minutes. "Very well. We'll prevail on Lord Tynan but take only four guards with us."

"Why, sir?" enquired Phylicia.

"There are several important items on the carts that mustn't get into the wrong hands."

Tain said conversationally, "Haven't you noticed we've two units of the army with us, Sire?"

"Obviously I haven't," replied Arkyn tartly. "We need to stop."

Tain reached up for a cord and pulled. The coach began to slow and two moments later Smithers and Kadeem were talking to the FitzAlcis.

Cal availed himself of the spare corner of the coach and listened to the plan. "Whose idea was it, my lady?"

"Mine actually."

He looked momentarily surprised. "I think Your Ladyship is going to be a pleasant companion…"

She smiled. "You mean I might join the madness?"

He chuckled. "I think Your Ladyship already has. How much *did* Prince Tain tell you in his letters?"

"Enough, Master Calumiel, for me to want to visit Oedran when His Highness is there; I just wish it was under other circumstances."

"Don't we all?" He was silent for a moment before saying, "Won't your uncle mind?"

"Not a bit. We ought to warn him if it's decided."

Cal glanced at the group of men. Smithers shook his head slightly, so Cal said, "I wouldn't. Fine deception it would be if someone took advantage."

"Are you saying you doubt my uncle?"

"No but what about everyone on his manor?"

"He wouldn't employ them if they weren't trusted," pointed out Phylicia without ire.

"Linnt was trusted, Jacobs and Stuart were trusted – they were former secretaries in Oedran – trust is not a mark of a man's loyalty only his employer's possible gullibility."

Tain groaned. "Kadeem, can you stop talking to Cal? He's picking too much up."

Cal said, "So you do listen to me, Your Highness?"

"Only when pushed."

"As I recall, you tend to do the pushing – into the pools if I'm not mistaken."

"Don't let me cramp your style."

Arkyn interrupted softly, "Children, behave. Lady Phylicia will be wondering if you can be sensible when you're together."

"Don't we all wonder that?" said Smithers before hastily apologising.

Arkyn frowned. "How long have you been guarding Prince Tain, Captain?"

"Three years today, Sire."

"I'm impressed you've survived this long – most people would be gibbering wrecks by now."

Tain sighed. "Shall we continue on our revised route, Sire?"

Chapter 15
LORD TYNAN
10:12
Areal – Lord Tynan's Manor

LORD TYNAN'S MANOR was a pleasant stone built, two-storey structure which seemed to meld into the surrounding landscape as though it had been there from the first breath on Erinna. Its sandy stone façade wasn't grand and Tynan – a portly man – fitted the relaxed building like a glove. On hearing a coach with guards was approaching, he bustled out of his front door to await its arrival. There were no sweeping steps up to the door here, just an ancient homely wooden porch with untamed creepers growing up it.

Phylicia eased herself from the coach first, insisting she did so to give her uncle a moment of relief. He smiled when he saw her.

"Phyl, you're looking more beautiful and more like your mother each time I see you. Wyndham, wouldn't you say she's looking like my sister?"

"Avo, milord, I would. Milady. Horses to see to."

Phylicia smiled at her uncle's steward. "Thank you, Wyndham. Now, I ought to do this right." She turned towards Arkyn. "Sire, might I present my uncle, Lord Walter Tynan of Areal, to you?"

Tynan's face registered incomprehension before he said, "My dear boy, if this is true then your father must be... I'm sad to hear it, so very sad." He knelt. "My liege, my loyalty and hospitality are yours."

Arkyn swallowed, trying to keep emotion in check. "Thank you, Lord Tynan. Please get up..." He introduced Tain and Cal. "We're rather trespassing on your hospitality, my lord, but when Lady Phylicia said you lived so close…" He trailed off, before continuing, "Her Ladyship insisted it wouldn't inconvenience you."

Tynan smiled at his niece. "It's open house here, Sire, always has been always will be. We'll see your horses well-tended whilst you come and take your ease for half an hour. I'm guessing you're for Oedran and quickly. Come in, come in. If there's anything you need…"

Whispering, Tain asked Cal, "Will you or I use the 'dear boy' line first?"

"To our King?" replied Cal seriously.

Tain raised an eyebrow and Cal pursed his lips trying not to laugh.

Arkyn caught the look. "What are you two planning?"

"Us? We never plan anything, sir. It just sort of happens," admitted Tain with injured innocence.

Tynan meanwhile said, "Nip and find your aunt, Phyl. She's about here somewhere– t'would only be fair to warn her."

Phylicia smiled. "If the King will excuse me."

Arkyn caught her eye and nodded. She left and Lord Tynan led the way into a sitting room. He waved affably to well-padded chairs upholstered in dark reds and browns. Arkyn sank onto a chair, its webbing welcoming his form in an easy embrace.

"Is there anything I can do, Sire?"

Arkyn managed to smile. "You're already doing it, my lord. It is a while since I have felt so welcome. Please sit down, it is your home, and it seems ceremony is ill placed here."

Tynan sat opposite Arkyn. "I hope you don't mind but I've never been a friend of ceremony, even with my wed-brother being Governor. I've never got on with the palaver, sir. Amphi I see occasionally but I'm happiest when Phyl visits me here. Far less trouble all round."

"I can imagine there is."

"Aye. Home is for relaxation and private lives for home. I'm lucky though; I can say that and carry it out – must be hard for my niece to be 'on show' all the time."

"Yes, it must."

There was a knock at the door before Arkyn could reveal any more of his feelings and Kadeem entered bearing a laden tray.

"My, you were quick, lad," stated Tynan.

"Speed is measured merely by comprehension of relativity, my lord," replied Kadeem with a straight face.

Arkyn said, "My manservant has a unique outlook on life, my lord – fortunately." He caught the manservant's eye.

Blank faced, Kadeem asked, "Tea or something stronger, Sire?"

"Tea is fine, thank you, Kadeem."

"Sir. Your Highness?"

"Tea, please. Is my new manservant not around?" enquired Tain.

Kadeem said, "He is attending to other matters, Your Highness. He is using his initiative."

Arkyn groaned. "Oh dear. A manservant with initiative looking after His Highness…"

"Surely that is a good thing, sir," remarked Tynan, accepting a cup of tea, trying to gauge the atmosphere.

Kadeem saw a spark in the King's eye and simply handed cake round whilst the new monarch said,

"As Kadeem might say, perspective is relative to experience, my lord."

Tain sighed. "Between all of you I might just admit to a bad name."

"Bad names don't cross my threshold, Your Highness; they're kept in their place," observed Tynan. "Mischief isn't the same thing. I've heard Your Highness has much skill in making people laugh."

"That's one way of putting it, my lord," replied Arkyn. "Might I ask how you heard?"

"Oh, we talk of this and that when my niece visits me, Sire. She's a good memory but never gives us specifics, just the gist."

"Tain, what *have* you been telling Lady Phylicia?"

His brother shrugged. "Mostly the truth – well, no… *the truth* but not all of it; be thankful for that, Sire."

"Hmm…"

For all his appearance of geniality, Tynan was turning over the revelations of Arkyn's visit busily in his mind. The youngsters looked washed out, tired, drained and fighting to keep in control. He chatted aimlessly, trying to draw their minds away from their journey and the reasons for it. He was beginning to wonder where his wife and niece were when the door opened and they entered, dropping into curtsies as Arkyn rose to greet them.

Introductions slickly accomplished, Lady Tynan said, "I've prepared a room, Sire, if you wish to refresh yourselves before your onward journey. Or even, if you simply wish for some solitude."

Arkyn said, "Thank you, my lady. That was thoughtful. I'm sure my brother will be pleased."

Tain muttered, "There's that bad name again," before saying, "Sire, I shall scream if there's an assassin." He pointedly bowed and left as though in emphasis of something unsaid.

* * *

Outside he found Kadeem and Robert waiting patiently.

Robert said simply, "This way, Your Highness."

75

"Thank you, Robert, and thank you for agreeing to accompany me back to Oedran."

"It is a pleasure, sir." Robert replied to Tain eloquently raised eyebrow, "I enjoy travelling, Your Highness, truly I do."

They entered a pleasant upstairs room. Washing water, razors and clean clothes were laid out. He freshened up, only slightly self-consciously with a strange manservant present and far less self-conscious than had it been Linnt. Returning downstairs he rejoined his brother. Arkyn glanced at him but continued listening to his hosts, then as Tain took up the conversation Arkyn excused himself and also freshened up. The thought that they might wish to had been kind and he wondered whose idea it had initially been. Kadeem was quiet and Arkyn recognised that for the moment the puzzle was better left to mystery; his manservant was being official and Arkyn wasn't in the mood to challenge it. As he went to rejoin Tain, he said simply,

"How long until we can continue, Kadeem?"

"About twelve minutes, Sire."

Arkyn simply nodded, not wanting to acknowledge again that the honorific was abhorrent to him.

* * *

As he re-entered the room where his hosts and brother were ensconced everyone rose. Tain studied him carefully and received a mutual look in return. Tynan pretended not to notice. Arkyn explained they would soon be ready to leave.

"That is truly a shame, sir," replied Tynan. "Never mind – soon isn't now. Do you have provision for your onward journey or is there anything we can help with?"

Arkyn eased himself into a chair. "My lord, you and Her Ladyship have already done more than you realise. Tain, where's Cal?"

"Causing trouble somewhere probably. I think he went to check how long we'd be here."

Tynan said, "How long do you expect it to take you to reach Oedran? Is there anyone we can inform of your journey?"

Arkyn shook his head. "No, thank you, my lord, it is more important that you talk of our visit here to no-one. It will become known in time but I would rather that, for now, our journey was private. I do feel the need to stretch my legs before being in the coach though. Would you mind if we took a walk?"

Tynan rose. "Not at all, it's a beautiful day. We've some interesting gardens here…"

A more polished courtier than her husband Lady Tynan nevertheless

76

said, "Yes, an awful lot of dedication has gone into leaving them seemingly untouched by human hand because—"

"I like the wildness of it," protested her husband.

"—They have been untouched by human hand for a couple of years."

"They sound intriguing," said Arkyn.

"Aye, they're not bad," replied Tynan. "I just have to find a good gardener. Our last one left for a job at Amphi Palace courtesy of my niece."

"I only recommended him, uncle, it was father who offered the job," observed Phylicia.

"I'm sure it has worked out best for everyone if Your Lordship likes untamed gardens," observed Arkyn.

Tynan laughed. "Aye, maybe so."

The gardens had a pleasant aspect and, although they were wilder than most gardens of lords, they were not unpleasant for being untended. Phylicia showed Arkyn many highlights and soon Kadeem appeared to say that they were ready to leave at the King's convenience.

Before they got back in the coach, Arkyn said, "Truly, thank you, Lord Tynan. I have been made more than welcome and you have my unreserved thanks for it. I was apprehensive about arriving unannounced for your sake, but maybe I should make more stops like this."

Tynan bowed slightly, "Sire, you *were* welcome. I hope you drop by another time, and leave it spontaneous, anticipation is a dreadful emotion."

Tain echoed his brother and Phyl gave her uncle a hug before taking her place in the coach.

As it rattled off Tynan said to his wife, "They're doing well for saying."

"Yes. I'm surprised Leander let Phyl go with them."

"They'll be glad of the support today."

"Mm. I wonder if it isn't an extra strain," remarked Lady Tynan.

"I don't think so. When's that lass been a strain to anyone? Come on, we'd better stop the gossip," added Tynan with a sigh.

"Let 'em have their gossip, what harm can it do?"

"Enough – especially today. There was a lot not being said. I might not like politics but I do understand the sub plots." He spied his daughter. "Where were you, Sophia?"

"On a ride, father. Guards didn't let me come back. Is Phyl here?"

"No, you've missed her. She was on her way to Oedran."

Sophia looked puzzled. "But the FitzAlcis are in Amphi—"

Lady Tynan raised an eyebrow. "Go and freshen up."

When she'd gone, Lord Tynan said, "She'll find out."

"But *we* won't have gossiped about it. I listen, you know."

Chapter 16

CAVALCADE

THE COACH with its escort of guards and servants approached the small hamlet of Eastsage with its longhouses and curious inhabitants. Smithers' quick gaze noted the soldiers arraigned as lookouts, the huddles of villagers and the captain riding to meet them. He stiffened, his left hand gathering the reins of his horse, whilst his right reached for his sword, his eyes searching to right and left. The captain reached him.

"We *were* attacked. Two of my men are wounded. Arrow wounds both, not intended to kill, just as a message to stop but we didn't. The carts are all safe but we had a bit of a set to with the felons. One got away. Don't think he'll be back, now he knows our strength."

"Where was this, Nolan?"

"South side of Border Lodge. We were slowing, the horses tiring, it's been a fair pace for cart horses. We were out of sight of the lodge and watchtower but close enough for someone to have considered the horses would be tired."

Smithers absorbed that. "Right. Tell them to be ready to move. The wounded will have to come with us for the meantime. We'll continue straight through but slowly enough for you to catch us." He dropped back until he was level with the coach. In response to a raised eyebrow from Arkyn, he said, "We're continuing straight through, sir. The carts were attacked. It sounds half-hearted but one bandit got away."

"He can happily report that we weren't there and hopefully it means that we should be unexpected in Oedran."

"Wouldn't it be better to be expected, Sire?"

"And leave time for incriminating evidence to be stashed?"

* * *

A few minutes later, Arkyn said, "Tain, I think we should get off the main highway and go via the Rex Dallin. We know it's safe."

Tain looked at him. "Not everyone has permission."

"If I take them through, they do."

Tain bit his lip. "I'd actually forgotten for a moment. We should warn the resident guards."

Arkyn nodded. "I'm not talking to the Comptroller over messenger. Not today. Where's Caswal? He can warn the southern sergeant. There's Welcome Field. We can stop there next. The horses will be tired by then.

They can roam for a while and we can… well, get frustrated."

"And imagine we're the Bard back in safety after braving the Age of Tyranny's worst years. Welcome Field was named in his time, I believe."

"Yes. He used to rest there before heading for Ceardlann. Any men he took into the Rex Dallin were welcomed there, hence the name I suppose. Let's restore its use."

Tain nodded. "Seems sensible. Smithers!" When the captain appeared a few moments later, he continued, "Is Caswal Hillbeck still with us?"

"He's snoring nicely, sir," replied Smithers with a grin. "He even slept through the attack, apparently."

Arkyn said, "Wake him, with my apologies, and tell him to ride to Guard Lodge, and inform the sergeant on duty we'll all be arriving soon. Tell him we'll need the full complement of men to accompany everyone to the Pillars of Alcis and they're to meet us at the gate. Then tell Kadeem we're going via the Rex Dallin. He knows the way, or he should."

"Is that wise, sir?"

Tain said quietly, "You've your orders, Smithers."

"What made you say that?" enquired Arkyn once Smithers had left.

Tain sighed. "He shouldn't be questioning you, sir."

"He's head of my guard."

Tain bit his lip. "Is he? I thought he was head of mine now."

Arkyn frowned. "I'm sure that consideration is relevant when we're in Oedran and there's an option."

Tain swallowed. "Sorry, but he *shouldn't* be questioning you."

Sensing a sibling argument on the horizon, Phylicia said, "It's odd: the Bard was my ancestor but I know next to nothing about his life. Did he really take men into the Rex Dallin during the Age of Tyranny? Wasn't that impossible? I thought the valley was impenetrable from the moment King Alvern was murdered until King Arlis chose to leave or died."

Arkyn said, "He was a brave man, Lady Phylicia, and found a way around the precautions. Your family's star stone was used to temporarily break the barrier, I believe. Tain probably understands it better than I do."

"I doubt it. You've had more years reading about it," chimed in Tain.

Arkyn looked at him, clearly asking him to take up the conversation. "Maybe Phyl would like to hear the whole story. We've a few hours to fill. Sorry, Lady Phylicia, I hope you don't mind me calling you Phyl, I think Lord Tynan was responsible."

She smiled. "I don't mind at all, Sire. It makes for smoother conversation."

Arkyn nodded before gazing unseeingly out of the coach window.

* * *

Tain watched his brother for a moment before turning back to Lady

79

Phylicia. She was curious rather than judgemental; a small part of Tain began to appreciate how strange the whole situation must be for her. He wondered if like him, she was away from home for the first time.

"What do you know about the Bard, my lady?"

"Honestly, that he was my ancestor and helped restore King Arlis to the throne in Oedran. Nothing more. It's rather reprehensible but father's always so busy and it seemed wrong to ask other people to explain my family history. I don't really have free access to our library either. Father always said when I was older I could choose what I wanted to read but until then it was up to my governess."

Tain nodded. It wasn't unusual for children to have reading chosen for them. He wondered where to start.

"Well, let's go back a generation. King Alvern Abadin conquered Terasia in 720. The day that Tera fell, a girl was born to one of the overlords. King Alvern took baby Orla and promised to marry her when she was fifteen. He had her raised in Oedran and was good to his word. Although King Alvern had two sons, Arlis and Everis, she had three. When he'd discovered she was carrying an illegitimate child, Alvern had banished Queen Orla to the Rex Dallin with his sons, who were growing up away from the plagues and famines of the city. As soon as her third son, Maldwyn, was born, he was taken from her and out of the valley. The following day King Alvern was murdered."

Tain paused swallowing. He glanced out of the coach window. The details of Alvern's murder were so similar to his father's that it sliced through him again. Scanlon had used history, used the example set, to murder his own brother. He balled his fists. Two kings murdered by crossbow from the Viewing Gallery. He couldn't dwell on it.

"He was murdered on the orders of his Chancellor, one Lord Onraet of Southern Areal. At the moment of his death, the Rex Dallin magically sealed itself, protecting King Arlis and his family. As Onraet's rule took hold the Age of Tyranny was born and Maldwyn grew tall. He had been taken to a manor where boys were taught to be bards. Skilled in music and storytelling, knowledgeable and hot headed, he travelled the roads of Anapara. He must have said the wrong thing to someone because he fled Oedran with Onraet's men chasing him. He broke through the magical barrier to the Rex Dallin; he had been born there, he had right of entry. The men chasing him couldn't even see the entrance at that point, the magic still being strong. Arrested and taken before Arlis, the truth of his parentage emerged. Between them the sons of Queen Orla began to plan to restore Arlis to Oedran. Seventeen years had passed. They knew they needed the support of the empire, of its lords if they were to fight Onraet."

Tain idly wondered if Onraet had felt those first tremors. Had there been prophecies to give him sleepless nights? Oddly, he hoped there had been. Even knowing the end of the story, he hoped that somehow Onraet had spent years watching his back, watching the shadows.

"In the end, Maldwyn left the safety of the valley, travelling many hundreds of miles building support. He never gave his name. So, he became known as *the Bard*. His name was used only in the valley or with his closest companions. As time passed, he knew he had to build an army for Arlis, but an army needs somewhere to hide, and that wasn't going to be easy. On a visit to Ceardlann, he and his half-brothers decided they had to use the valley. They started laying down stocks of grains, building warrens and recruiting smiths. To hide their endeavours, the Bard spread word of a great gathering on the plateau, by the ancient Silver Pine Road. No-one thought anything of it. The great fair annually drew people from Anapara, Areal and the Low Plains, and, as years passed, further afield, but not all who arrived left on the road. They would quietly descend into the valley with the Bard, to be welcomed and escorted to where they were needed. After Onraet's defeat, stories of how it had come about were told and the area of the plateau that the Bard had used became known as *The Bardic Fields*."

Tain glanced at Arkyn. His brother was restlessly dozing. He reached for a blanket and tucked it around Arkyn. His brother was going to need every ounce of support he could give him. Just like Arlis had needed Maldwyn's.

* * *

At just gone two in the afternoon, Arkyn awoke properly due to one particularly harsh jolt. Tain and Phyl had been watching the countryside pass talking about their intertwined family histories. They heard the shouts of the men, the clatter of the hooves and the rumble of the coach wheels. They rocked with the motion of the vehicle but from all they felt disassociated, remote. A shouted comment broke through their ambivalence and, almost at once, the horses slowed and the coach pulled up. Arkyn and Tain glanced at each other. What was wrong now?

Cal was on the step. "The coachman thinks that the horses need half an hour's rest."

Arkyn nodded. "Then they'd better have it. Can you clear the area around the coach, Cal? Tain and I need to talk."

As Cal left, Phyl said she could do with stretching her legs, if they'd excuse her. Appreciating her tact, Arkyn did so. When he was sure that they wouldn't be overheard he looked at Tain.

"We've got to decide how we'll handle arriving in Oedran."

"That might handle itself. You'll have to go to father's office. I'm guessing there'll be a fracas somewhere. Father seemed to know... Seems to have planned something. I'd like to find out what."

"You and me both but I don't know if I'm ready to face it all. Can I even do the job?"

Tain pursed his lips. "I don't hear anyone doubting your capabilities. They've been singing your praises since Terasia. More seriously, if you don't face it this evening, you'll be even less ready to face it tomorrow, and face it we must."

Arkyn groaned. "True. There's something else. Smithers will be looking after you from the moment I enter the Inner Office. Hillbeck will be head of my guard." He saw Tain's frown. "I can't take action against people when father knew what was coming and didn't tell them—"

"They'll try to resign—"

"Let them. I'm not going to be accepting anything."

"If you don't, won't it appear a weakness?" enquired Tain. "You have to do something."

"But what can I do? I can't dismiss Paturn or Wynfeld, I shall not accept anyone other than Uncle Festus as Defender, and, right now, I need one; moreover, the King's Guard is nothing without Hillbeck. I could at a push dismiss Pixney but who would I put in his place? He's more than equalled Haster—"

A quiet voice from outside remarked, "Sir, it wasn't Hillbeck on duty."

Arkyn and Tain exchanged a resigned glance.

With a trace of exasperation, Arkyn remarked, "I thought I said make sure we're not overheard, Cal."

"I am doing. I'm standing guard so no-one else comes near. Simple really when you think about it."

Arkyn growled, "Then stand on the step and make yourself even more useful and then learn the meaning of 'clearing an area'."

Cal was on the step leaning on the door. "Sorry, sir, but I thought it was more sensible if I stuck around. Anyway, before you throttle me, or before His Highness does, it wasn't Hillbeck on duty. Your father changed at the last moment. He said Hillbeck had spent enough celebrations on duty he could have that night off. It was Kilbride."

Arkyn and Tain shared a glance, the King saying, "I wonder why he did that."

Tain shrugged. "Probably because he knew you'd need Hillbeck. We can't let the murder of father go by without acknowledgement that someone failed in their duties. The empire will expect something. I agree you need Paturn, and Wynfeld from what I've heard you say of him. Hillbeck, I'm sure, will try to resign, but letting him go would be a disaster—"

"I expect Lord Scanlon simply wants you to dismiss everyone in a rage so that you leave yourself vulnerable. He's engineered this event so you take action against those most loyal to you," observed Cal. "If I were you, sir, I wouldn't give him the pleasure. There's more ways of making your authority known and respected than by dismissing the men who keep you safe."

Arkyn caught Tain's eye. "I didn't know Cal could be sensible."

"He gets these fits on him, best leave him to them. They pass soon enough," replied Tain levelly.

"Yet not with the rapidity of my friend's…" muttered Cal.

"He's admitting he's slow as well. I've been waiting ages for that."

A polite but hesitant cough distracted Cal. Far enough off not to overhear anything stood Kadeem with a tray of drinks and food. Cal turned back to the FitzAlcis.

"Much as I hate to deprive you both of pleasure, Kadeem obviously thinks you'll be hungry. Shall I let him come and be solicitous?"

"Is there a blanket we can put on the ground?" asked Arkyn.

Cal nodded. "Yes, Lady Phylicia is currently utilising it."

"Then we three shall join her and let Kadeem avoid a balancing act."

Chapter 17
REX DALLIN
16:12

Anapara

ALMOST TWO HOURS LATER, Kadeem pointed out the silver pine waymarker to the advance guard, telling them to follow the track that led from it. Captain Nolan nodded, and they moved seamlessly from highway to track without confusion or jolting. The clopping and trundling hooves and wheels became muffled and Kadeem momentarily wondered if that would disturb the FitzAlcis or bring them reassurance. He scanned their surroundings; they were well onto the plateau now. The scrubland stretched either side of them for miles, specifically kept unfarmed as a defence for the Rex Dallin. Without farms there should be no-one in the vicinity. Nolan also glanced around; he didn't know this place and was intrigued. Did Kadeem really know the way? The road was unassuming, unmetalled, a country track. A short time later he realised there were no potholes and, in that moment, understood its unassuming appearance was part of its defence. For all its simplicity, it *was* still maintained. Idly he wondered how many other roads and tracks were so deceptive, leading to places passing travellers would never consider.

Turning in his saddle, Kadeem nodded significantly at Cal who saw the unimposing southern gate of the Rex Dallin was fast approaching. Cal whistled loudly and everyone slowed up. Swinging himself down he stood on the coach step.

"The valley is in sight, sir. It's a steep descent; it might be better if we go first."

Arkyn nodded. "That seems sensible. Everyone else can take their time and join us at Welcome Field. Is the sergeant here?"

Cal glanced around. "He's just making his presence known, sir."

"Good. Let him know my orders, Cal, would you? I'll speak to him when we're all settled."

"He's handling the responsibility well, isn't he?" remarked Tain once Cal left.

"Yes. I wish none of us had to though, but he's slipped into the role very well."

"What role is that? Dogsbody?"

"Seemingly so. Maybe it should be FitzAlcis' Dogsbody?" murmured Arkyn despondently.

"I'll tell him of his new title. Will you add it to the list of ceremonial positions? Make it—"

"Tain…"

"Yes?"

"Shut up," said Arkyn tolerantly.

A couple of minutes later, Cal tiredly pulled himself onto the step again. "Sergeant Baris wonders if you'll be taking the militia with us, sir?"

Arkyn started. "I can't see any reason for them to come, can you, Tain?"

"Other than for your safety from the Pillars of Alcis to Oedran, no."

"I doubt there'll be any trouble for us there. Uncle will expect us at Carnford tonight. He won't expect I'll take people through the Rex Dallin because he never would. No, I think the army can return to Amphi, Cal."

When he was told, Nolan said predictable things.

"Those are your King's orders," remarked Cal ending the discussion. Smithers hid a grin.

"You're sure you're ample protection for your King?" remarked Nolan.

Cal caught Smithers eye. "Do not disparage the Prince's Guard, Captain Nolan. It is unwise. As for myself, I have had some weapons training."

Smithers hastily swallowed his laughter at the understatement. "Captain, the King and His Highness have been my concern for some years. Please accept that I will protect them with all my skill and any tool to hand."

Cal raised an amused eyebrow. "This isn't getting the King to Oedran."

Smithers nodded. "Good point, Master Calumiel. Will you accompany the coach still?"

"Of course, Captain. Sergeant Baris, your men on the Rex Dallin side of the gate. Smithers, the Prince's Guard and the army on this side, and you're to be the last one to enter, make sure no-one unauthorised does so because the last thing needed now are treason charges."

* * *

Arkyn and Tain alighted from the coach and walked into Welcome Field, suddenly aware why it had been dubbed that. Its thick hedges around three sides gave a feeling of protection, of the valley's embrace. The old stone in the centre of the field once more had a fire on it and a couple of guards were brewing tea. Arkyn found himself smiling without being aware of it. The guards saluted and Arkyn said simply,

"Just carry on, Silversley. It's a welcome sight."

The guard nodded. "There's a couple of chairs over yonder, sir, if you need to sit down. We thought we'd anticipate Master Kadeem."

"Congratulations on succeeding."

With a beaker of tea in hand. Arkyn studied the craggy cliff face that made up the fourth side of the field. A rivulet of water ran down its face and into a pebble lined stream that crossed the field. Everyone else, even Phyl, had stayed on the other side of it, as though it was an invisible barrier. There was only him and Tain in this third of the field, and he was glad. They didn't need to keep careful control of their emotions. The valley welcomed them with calm.

"Landis still hasn't been in touch."

Tain glanced at Arkyn. "Nor has Aunt Amara. What are you thinking?"

"Nothing. I don't know. It's beginning to worry me, but unless we stay in the valley, we have to face Oedran."

"I don't think staying here is a good idea, even though we want to. Why don't you send Cal to see what's happening?"

Arkyn considered that. "Because I don't think the lookalike story would stand up to Aunt Amara's scrutiny. I don't want to be in the position of lying to her either. It wouldn't be fair."

"Or safe," said Tain. A moment later he added, "Who do you trust in Oedran? Are we walking into a trap?"

Arkyn swallowed. "I don't know, on either front. No. I do. I trust Aunt Amara, our nearfamily – or I did, until Uncle Festus was noticeable by his absence. Elantha, I trust her to my marrow. The Iris family—"

"How about the King's Guard?"

"Father didn't tell there was to be an attack. He's asked me not to blame them."

Tain hesitated. "Doesn't mean they didn't betray him."

Arkyn closed his eyes. "I trust the men we have with us. I trust Hillbeck. He's of this valley. I cannot let paranoia take such a hold, Tain. I can't. I have to hold on to the thought that men are loyal, that they mean their oaths." He opened his eyes. "At least until I catch them breaking them and then there'll be no mercy."

"For a moment there, I was worried."

Arkyn snorted. "I'll face Oedran, Tain. I'll face what is waiting for us, and I swear on all our ancestors that I'll protect their legacy."

"We face it together."

Arkyn looked sideways at his brother. "I could leave you in the valley, just in case."

Tain's eyes narrowed. "No."

Arkyn winked. "I wouldn't dare. I need Ceardlann to survive."

After twelve minutes of peace, Tain broke it saying, "ReJean thought about refusing fealty."

Arkyn looked at him sideways. "Yes."

"What would you have done?"

Arkyn shrugged. "I had to hope he wasn't going to be that stupid. If I hadn't asked for it... well... He had used words but not actions to acknowledge the change of circumstances. Those actions matter. Father, grandfather were always clear about that."

"Yes, but *ReJean*. Sicla. Even if treason were proved against him, nothing could be done without your word. When was the last time a ReJean swore fealty, actually knelt and swore fealty in person?"

"A few hours ago," said Arkyn flippantly. He put his beaker of tea down, rubbing his hands. "I don't know. The scrolls would have to be examined but we're not living in normal times. I was *there*, on the day I... on the day... I don't know, Tain. Do you think I was wrong?"

Tain shrugged. "No. The ReJeans have a lot of protection thanks to Ancestor Arlis, but there's responsibility with those. You didn't ask for speech, honour or a life-binding, so it's been no more than you'd ask any lord in the empire." He watched his brother's face. "Anyway, nothing says that he can't still betray you if he's so minded."

Arkyn snorted. "You never cease to amaze me, little brother. Honestly, you could have said a hundred things that would have been better than that, and not for the first time today. Next time I need reassurance, I'll ask someone else."

"It's true though."

"Yes." Arkyn caught Tain's eye. "I know it. The only vassal I can be absolutely sure of is Lord Daioch."

Tain returned his look. "There might be a couple more but he's the one who can't change his allegiance."

Picking up his beaker, Arkyn didn't reply. He knew it was true. Whatever he wanted, whatever his heart told him, any time he felt safe, he wasn't. He blinked hard and returned to watching the rivulet of water.

* * *

An hour and a half later, they continued on their journey north, all suitably refreshed, the horses cooled and fed and the guards relaxed. Those who had ridden from Amphi were curious, looking around the valley but they felt the cloaking safety and let the stress flow from them; none of them would ever forget the journey simply for the fact they were in the Rex Dallin but what would stay with them primarily was that feeling of safety. The Rex Dallin guards though, used to the enveloping atmosphere, were watchful; they watched everyone and most were considering their own sorrow at the reason for the ride. Some, those who knew Arkyn and Tain well, also considered the future as well as the past: what was to come, as well as what had been lost.

* * *

The coach slowed once more, Arkyn glanced out of the window – they were three-quarters of the way through the Rex Dallin. He looked at the guard riding alongside the coach window.

"Why have we stopped, Halien?"

"There seems to be an elderly gentleman blocking the route, Sire."

"What all of it?" asked Arkyn dryly. "Find out who it is please."

Halien moved off. What he heard as he approached the small group was Kadeem saying,

"It's really *not* a good time, Chief."

"Let me decide that, lad," replied Laioril. "He's not asleep, is he?"

"Probably not now. I take it you'd like to see him?"

"Aye. Dunna fret. I've guessed what brings you north. I might be able to help."

Kadeem nodded. "Many stranger things have been known, Chief. Come on then."

"Thanks, lad, but I can see my way plain enough."

Smithers said, "I'll escort you, sir."

Kadeem muttered, "Oh dear," before saying, "No need, Captain Smithers.

87

As Chief Laioril says, he can see his way."

Smithers looked at Kadeem and then at a bright-eyed, amused Laioril. "Ah. After you, Chief."

"They've got you well trained then, lad. Don't worry, I don't need a herald." He reached the coach door. "Evening, lads."

Arkyn sighed. "I might have guessed you'd be the hold up, Chief. You'd better join us before all my Oedranian staff and household have heart-attacks at your absurd manner."

Once in the coach Laioril said, "Aye, well, I thought you might appreciate a spot of normality, *Sire*."

Arkyn swallowed. "Stick with 'lad', Chief."

"I thought you might say that." He looked round. "Tain and..."

Phyl smiled. "Lady Phylicia ReJean. I answer to Phyl though."

Laioril scrutinised her before saying, "Greetings, lass. You've all your future ahead."

"Haven't all the living got that, Chief?" murmured Arkyn as they moved off.

"Aye, but some have lived longer than their remaining time. I'm sorry about your father. I'll miss him."

Tain bit his lip and turned away from the Chief's bright eyes.

Laioril took his hand. "Tain, loss is hard, you know that, lad, better than many your age but don't let it wreck your spirit; no-one would want that. Face the world head on, focus on what they gave you and what you think is right. Watch the stars in darkness for they shine all the brighter."

Involuntarily Tain caught Laioril's eye his own distress clear in his. He wanted to talk so much in that moment but only in private with the Chief. His need for reassurance, for strength, clear in his gaze.

Arkyn said quietly, "You've not asked anything, Chief."

Laioril held Tain's gaze but answered Arkyn. "Lad, details don't change the main fact. There are times for details and times for facts. There are also times to forget both and I'm good at forgetting things."

Arkyn nodded. "I've noticed. I just wondered if you had any reason for joining us."

Laioril glanced at him. "Other than to see if you were all right?"

"Oh. We're lousy but then you guessed that. When did you arrive?"

"A couple of days ago, give or take. We're at Encampment Field. I hope you don't mind."

"Not at all. Stay as long as you wish."

"Thank you, lad. Does the Comptroller know?" enquired Laioril.

"I expect he's guessed but I don't know if anyone's informed him. We couldn't face it..."

"That's understandable. Where's young Caswal? I thought I spotted him lurking. Susan also ought to be told…"

Arkyn motioned to a guard and once Caswal had ridden for Ceardlann, said, "Chief, will you come to Oedran? For the funeral, at least. I know the Wanda don't attend coronations and don't offer allegiance, or are obliged to, but I think father would have wanted you to say goodbye."

Laioril murmured, "Aye, lad, if you wish it, I'll come – of course, I'll come. I'd be honoured."

"Thank you. I'd like you there – we'll need all the support we can get and father held you in high esteem."

"Before or after frustration, lad?"

"Integral to it, I think."

Listening to the conversation, Phylicia realised she'd never considered the FitzAlcis could accept intense informality and she began to see them properly as people whose emotions could overwhelm them. She began to admire their fortitude and respect their composure in equal measure.

The Chief was chuckling, and the sound was like a breeze blowing away cobwebs of misery. His eyes were bright, a reminder of life in the midst of thoughts of death but there was no flippancy in his soul for all there appeared to be in his quips. He was talking to Arkyn but his eyes constantly strayed to Tain.

"Lass, just move onto this seat for me…" Once Phyl moved the Chief continued, "Tain, lad, lie down. No. No arguments. I'm not listening to them, and it'll take too much energy to continue for no reason…" He slipped a hand behind Tain's head and whispered, "You're overtired and overwrought, let me help…"

Tain replied, equally as quietly, "There's no time to sleep…"

"Nonsense, lad. There's an hour at least…"

"Not yet, Chief."

"All right but keep lying down – rest, if not sleep, will help."

"Tell him that."

Laioril smiled. "Oh, I shall." He moved his hand and squeezed Tain's shoulder. "Take strength from your memories, lad, not heartache." He turned to Arkyn. "I ought to get down before we reach the Pillars."

A few moments later, Arkyn gave the order to stop. When the coach pulled up Laioril opened the coach door and nimbly jumped down. He and everyone else was surprised when Arkyn followed suit. They walked a short way from the coach and when they couldn't be overheard Arkyn said,

"I'm worried about Tain. He's hardly acknowledged what's happened."

"He will, lad, but, when he does fully, he'll collapse. He's focusing on making sure he's got the wherewithal to face what might await you in

Oedran. Has he been rising and falling as a wave does with calm and rage?"

Arkyn considered. "Yes. I hadn't seen it but yes. He has had moments of serious despondency but also amazing clarity and if not calm, a level-headedness that is surprising."

Laioril nodded to himself. "He knows you need him. Even if you don't want him to, he's giving you strength. He's keeping enough in reserve but he's fighting for you as well. Shielding you, as you do him."

Arkyn closed his eyes. "I can't let him—"

"Lad, he's doing what he needs to, to get through the day. Your lethargy is a blessing at the moment for you've learnt to cope with exhaustion and it masks some emotions. He's young, lost his mentor as well as his father in less than a fortnight and he hasn't found his way of coping with official life yet. You'll need each other over the next few months, whatever you both might think in the heat of an argument, and you'll get frustrated with each other because, whatever you want, things have changed, and he knows it; you won't be able to gloss over it, Arkyn, however much you wish to. He won't let you and he's right not to. Oh, look, I'm annoying you already."

Arkyn made himself relax. "Sorry, Chief, I know you only ever give advice that is honest."

"Do I? Live and learn. Now, whatever he wants he should soon be in a light sleep. It'll refresh him. Do you want me to help you to one?"

Arkyn eyed him. "No thank you. I didn't realise it was a skill of yours."

"There's a lot no-one realises about me. It's something I've picked up on my travels. If you, or he, need to talk, lad, you know where I am. We'll be here for some weeks…"

Arkyn nodded. "Thank you, Chief."

"Don't thank me; I'm raiding your kitchens and forest."

Arkyn smiled sadly. "You're welcome to. What you give and will give is worth more than that. I better return…"

Arkyn pulled himself into the coach and smiled at Phyl who motioned towards Tain; his eyes were closed, and he was breathing more deeply than he had.

"Never trust the Chief to give in. Are you comfortable, Phyl?"

"Yes, thank you. Chief Laioril is an interesting gentleman…"

Arkyn said softly, "Yes, he is, and he cares deeply. Though I do wonder how he knew…"

"Did you not ask him?"

"No. We have a mutual understanding. The FitzAlcis don't ask him awkward questions and he doesn't tell us as many lies." He saw the look on her face and chuckled. "His way of putting it. Is there a blanket for Tain within your reach? It must be getting near eight."

Phyl passing over a blanket looked at a small silver and enamelled timepiece that hung at her waist. "It's a quarter and six past seven, sir. We've made good time for a cavalcade."

"We have, but I wish it had been better still. That's a pretty timepiece."

"It was my birthday present from my father, sir."

Arkyn nodded and looked sadly at Tain; he wondered what their father had done about their birthdays. They had formally celebrated them in Oedran a couple of weeks previously but the exchange of presents hadn't been made. Watching his brother, he thought about Laioril's words. Tain was fighting for him, shielding him, strengthening him. He wished it wasn't the case, but he'd recognised the truth in Laioril's words. Tain had done all three with their discussions, with their strategising and even when dealing with ReJean. It should have been the other way around. He should have been the one protecting Tain. He blinked. Cal too. He'd let Cal organise them, relay orders, be his voice. Cal hadn't said anything about it, had simply taken on the task. Arkyn rubbed at his face. Necessity was the cruellest determiner of fate.

* * *

Laioril returned to camp considering events. He called up his messenger; so rare an event that his messenger was perplexed, but the dark-skinned man with whom the link formed was astonished.

"I didn't realise phoenixes existed, Laioril."

"Chief Darshan, you should know King Adeone was murdered last night at the Munewid Eve festivities."

Head of all the nomadic Wanda, Darshan said, "A sad day. The stars have made room for him and I must think. There have been many rumours and signs brought to my attention of latter years. Yes, I must think and we must meet. The age has changed. Certainly it has. I am a day from Amphi, having hoped to introduce myself to the young man who is now King of Oedran."

Laioril said, "I am sure that can still be arranged."

Darshan's dark eyes bored into Laioril's blue. "I believe you but do not make rash assumptions. I must consider how to present myself to Arkyn of Anapara… He will need much support."

"Not for the conclusion of his duties he won't," remarked Laioril.

"Support has many forms."

"And many disguises. Maybe we could meet on the Bardic Fields? I'm a day away."

"A suitable place. Two days' time?"

Laioril nodded. "Two days, lad. I'll be there."

Chapter 18
OEDRAN

20:48

Oedran – Dallin Gate

As THE DALLIN GATE OF OEDRAN rattled by Arkyn caught a glimpse of surprised guards. He drew the coach's curtains almost closed, not wanting the obvious interest. The slower pace through the city caused him to ponder what was waiting. He half-heartedly woke Tain.

"We've just crossed The Strait."

Tain rubbed his eyes. "I'll kill the Chief. Who was at the gate to welcome you?"

"No-one but then we didn't expect anyone."

Tain bit his lip. "I expected Wynfeld, from what you've told me."

"Something will have prevented him."

"What prevented him is the worrying thing."

Arkyn met his gaze. Nothing else needed to be said.

* * *

Minutes later, Arkyn and Tain caught each other's eye again as they heard Smithers discussing their entry with the Palace guards. When they alighted from the coach, Tain raised a questioning eyebrow.

"The Palace *had* been closed, sir," replied the captain.

"Who's here?" enquired Arkyn stretching slightly.

Tain glanced around the stables, touched Arkyn's arm and nodded to a couple of stalls.

"Ah." Arkyn motioned to the chief groom. "When did Lord Scanlon arrive, ReShard?"

"Around two by the stable clock, Sire, with his manservant and guards. All the Lords of Oedran are also here. I believe there's a Lords' Council occurring."

"Thank you, that's all."

Once ReShard was out of hearing, Arkyn looked at Tain who raised an eyebrow eloquently before motioning to Smithers to lead the way.

Without any sort of discussion on their destination, they walked through the Palace to the King's Chambers in the Privy Wing. It didn't matter where the Lords' Council was being held, they would be summoned to the Inner Office. Arkyn fixed his gaze straight ahead, ignoring the salutes and glances from unnerved guards. Tain beside him had none of his normal bounce and energy. They had been stealing themselves all day to face this walk, where once they had run. They didn't even realise they had fallen into hierarchical step with Arkyn just ahead of Tain just ahead of Phyl. Cal, following, was more aware of their surroundings and the guards. Less than a day before the Palace had been busy humming with expectation for the feast, now silence pervaded its halls and corridors.

As they approached the Audience Chamber, Sergeant Hillbeck saluted smartly and poignantly.

The new King took a deep breath. "Your nephew's safely at Ceardlann with his mother. Thank you." Before Hillbeck could reply, Arkyn had passed into the Audience Chamber and stopped astonished as his nearmother swept into a deep curtsy. He walked over to her, raising her. "Aunt Cornelia, what are you doing here? Is Uncle Festus here?"

Lady Landis glanced at an uncomfortable Cal. "He was wounded last night. I thought you'd know."

Cal took a step back as Arkyn turned towards him. "I couldn't find the right time and then, unfortunately, I forgot what with everything else. I'm truly sorry, Sire, my lady..."

Incredulous, Arkyn snapped, "The right time!"

Tain, who'd whitened, touched his arm. "Aunt Cornelia, how badly hurt is Uncle Festus?"

"He took a crossbow bolt below his left shoulder blade. It knocked him unconscious for hours. He's lucky to be alive but he insisted on being at the Lords' Council, nothing I or the doc said could do any good. Lord Iris and Lord Rale tried as well, but he wasn't having any of it, sir. It was a close thing. I've still not given you my condolences..."

Arkyn shook his head, his heart plummeting once more. "They didn't need to be stated explicitly; you're obviously worried about Uncle Festus. Are your chambers made up here?"

"Yes, sir, but, with permission, I'll take him home tonight. He shouldn't be moved too much, you see, not that he's listening... I'm sorry, I'm..."

Arkyn wrapped her in a hug, swallowing back his own emotion. "Take him home and make him behave, Aunt Cornelia. Everything else will wait." He paused listening. "The Lords' Council is here then, and it sounds like pain is adding an edge to my nearfather's volubility. It almost seems a shame to disturb them." He would though, and now he had to face it without his nearfather's strength. He swallowed. Without his Defender's strength. It explained why Landis hadn't been in touch, but there was no reassurance in the explanation, only dread.

Chapter 19

LORDS' COUNCIL

IN THE INNER OFFICE, Scanlon was making his views known. "Stop obstructing matters, Landis, or I'll have you arrested."

"By what right and on what charge, Scanlon?"

"Don't address me with such familiarity! I'm the Justiciar! That's all the right I need to charge you with treason and order your execution before dawn." His eyes flashed with loathing and triumph.

Landis' face set. "Strange indeed, you are not a prince, you dropped the title of your own volition. We have been wed-brothers, kith if you will, though I am never so reluctant to admit it. You are not Justiciar of Oedran, your post does not include this city from midnight last night; therefore, you have no jurisdiction here by right. You cannot arbitrarily order the arrest and execution of anyone under the title lord—"

"Enough!"

"Lord Landis is perfectly correct in all of that, Lord Scanlon," observed Lord Ryson.

"Keep your nose out of this, lawyer."

"I don't think I will, Lord Scanlon. I am the only other here present with an in-depth knowledge of the King's Law and I don't appreciate seeing it twisted to fit unfolding events. You have no authority to order Lord Landis' arrest; therefore, please do not put yourself in a position that might be damaging."

Landis said, "Thank you, Elidir. Lord Scanlon, all I have been trying to say is that there is another requests and bequests: one which was witnessed after the one here. Until that is found no-one can assume a protectorship, no-one can assume any power that wasn't already granted to them by King Adeone."

"So what power are you daring to address me by in this?"

Landis took as deep a breath as he could, "Because I am still the King's Defender! As such I *do* have the power to order arrest for treason where I think there is a motive at work that is treasonous."

"I am simply trying to make sure that the King has nothing to worry about on his return. If Your Lordship wasn't so obstreperous this matter would have been resolved hours ago," raged Scanlon.

"Resolved in whose favour, Lord Scanlon? We are here to protect the interests of the King. I cannot see that a protectorship that might not be what King Adeone had in mind is protection of King Arkyn's interests;

it is simply a way of seizing power. Can we be sure that King Adeone included a clause for a protectorship…?"

"Arkyn is not of age, Landis!"

"Please be less familiar when speaking of the King. We are all aware King Arkyn is a week and half off being of age but he has been named King's Representative five times—"

"And abused the power."

"I'm sorry, my *lord*? Abused the power? How? Are you daring to question the erudition of your King?" enquired Landis dangerously.

"He had the temerity to replace three of four governors—"

"Let me see, Portur: replaced because he was dead. The Domini: replaced because Lord Iris and His Late Majesty had well-founded concerns. The Sagamore: not replaced. The Fencible: replaced due to the fact that he was being manipulated into unwise decisions. Obviously, none of them needed replacing!"

Iris said quietly, "Festus is right, Lord Scanlon, there is nothing sinister in King Arkyn's previous decisions. I did advise King Adeone to replace the Domini and my opinion was garnered for the Fencible. Can we please get this discussion away from the slanging match it is becoming? We are meant to be holding a Lords' Council, not crucifying our King."

Landis collapsed into his chair. "You're right, Lord Iris. My apologies."

Lord Scanlon sneered at him, "Almost sounds as though you're in the wrong, Festus."

Landis eyed him. "Then appearances can truly be deceptive…"

* * *

Arkyn listened to the raised voices for a moment before entering the Outer Office. His father's administrator rose and then knelt poignantly. Arkyn took a deep breath.

"Thank you, Richardson, please get up and tell me what's happening."

A voice from the other side of the room said, "The Lords of Oedran and Lord Scanlon are playing the power game, Sire. I would say it keeps them out of trouble but should I get my hands on them they'll find the opposite to be true. Have you slept yet?"

Arkyn crossed to the kneeling doctor and helped him back to his feet. They looked at each other and simply nodded in understanding.

"Take a guess, doc."

"That's a no then. Can I advise you go to bed?"

"You can advise it, but I'm not going."

"That was predictable. Do you want my report now?"

Arkyn said, "How long is it?"

"Very brief. A crossbow bolt, just above the heart. Death, almost instantaneous. Lord Landis took the second bolt but Lady Landis has explained that one. I'm bloody furious."

"We're all angry and I know you were close to father. If you want to have some time off, I'll understand."

The doctor glanced between his charges. "Not likely, sir. I've got to make sure you're both sensible; he'd want that, so would Eliza if she could have known you. I'm family; I'll have time off when you do. I'll see Kadeem and Linnt and make sure you've something to help you sleep well. Now, if I might ask a favour, can you please tell Lord Landis to come and be a good boy? He's being far too volatile for my liking and there's a chance he may listen to you."

"I shall do my best, but not quite yet."

Chapa said, "Thank you, Sire," knelt once more and kissed Arkyn's signet ring but in taking the King's hand, he gripped it tightly in mute support.

Arkyn squeezed back before catching Richardson's concerned eye. "*All* the lords are present?" he asked the former King's Administrator.

"Yes, sir, the lords and your uncle, Your… Sire. I thought it was better that I stayed. I truly am sorry; you have my condolences."

"Thank you, Richardson. You have ours. You worked alongside of him for so long you were a friend to him. Could you send for Lady Amara please? Cal, will you announce us and then stay in the Inner Office?"

* * *

"King Arkyn Adeone FitzAlcis of Oedran and the Empire, His Highness Prince Tain Lachlan FitzAlcis, Justiciar of Oedran, and Lady Phylicia ReJean of Areal, my lords."

Everyone rose, turning to face the entrants. Five knelt immediately, six hesitated before kneeling, one exceptionally white. From the corner of his eye, Arkyn was surprised to see Tain kneel. Phyl entering behind him, and Cal shutting the door, also knelt. Lord Scanlon was the last to do so. The door closed on the Outer Office and Arkyn made his way over to what was now his desk. He sat down in the chair, his face blank.

"Thank you, you may rise." His gaze noted his nearfather's bandages. "Sit down, Landis, you've obviously been injured."

Landis said quietly, "Thank you, sir," collapsing gradually into the chair accepting a glass of whiskey from Lord Rale.

Tain had moved to stand beside Arkyn, meaning Scanlon had been pushed further away, next to the Lords of Oedran who were known to support him.

Keeping his temper in check, Arkyn enquired mildly, "What is this gathering for? There is no doubt as to the succession, I would have thought.

Obviously if the poisoner in Areal had done a better job, there might have been. Iris, as King's Counsellor, maybe you would care to explain."

"Lord Scanlon called a Lords' Council, Sire, to look at the issues arising out of your father's assassination," replied Iris without emphasis.

"Interesting. Lord Scanlon, on what authority did you call it?"

"I am the highest official here, sir." Even Scanlon faced with Arkyn in that moment couldn't be completely disrespectful. Arkyn's mild manner had the room enthralled.

"Hmm. Why did you call it in the Inner Office? Only the King or his Advocates, in the absence of the King, can call meetings in this office—"

"I am FitzAlcis."

"I am hardly forgetting that; I am just trying to ascertain why you'd make such a potentially devastating mistake. You are only a lord; therefore, you cannot call a meeting in the Inner Office. If you rely on the argument that you are my uncle then you cannot call a Lords' Council because you are of the FitzAlcis; however, that aside, was there any issue in particular that has gripped your discussions?"

Teran said, "The matter of a protectorship."

Arkyn eyed him, waiting.

After a moment Teran added, "Sire."

"Of course. My administrator has my father's requests and bequests but before we examine that maybe someone would care to tell me whether the assassin has been detained."

"No, Sire," admitted Landis carefully. "Everything possible was done. I was unconscious but Uncle Iris took charge. Ryson was also instrumental in securing exits from the hall."

Arkyn's eyes lingered on him for a moment before moving to Iris then slipping to Ryson. "If you were unconscious, Landis, maybe Lord Iris or Lord Ryson would like to explain what was done."

Iris said, "The hall doors were closed as soon as it became apparent that there was an attack, Sire. The guards mentioned that no-one had passed them for some minutes prior to the closure. Doctor Chapa made a few comments about observation and we were left with the horrifying and unbelievable truth that the assassin had been in the Viewing Gallery. Forays were made throughout the Palace but no-one was apprehended and the guards hadn't seen anyone carrying a crossbow... Every manner of person in the Palace has been searched. Not one crossbow has been found, beyond those carried by the guards. Those take different bolts to the ones used last night."

Lord Ryson added, "The Steward has closed the Palace, Sire, and it has stayed under closed orders all day. There should still be a chance—"

"There's no chance whatsoever," interjected Arkyn hollowly. "Let us not deceive ourselves, gentlemen. A courier managed to bring news to Amphi. This place is not secure. No, my father's murderer is long gone."

Lord Iris hesitated. "My king, there is little news I would dread to be the bearer of more than this but King Adeone was, it appears, legally assassinated. When we moved His Late Majesty, we discovered a scroll – it is in front of you, Sire – signed by six Lords of Oedran."

Arkyn blanched, grabbed the scroll, unfurled and read it. He thrust it at Tain, who read it before saying,

"Legally this document has basis in law. Morally it is an outrage." He faced the Lords of Oedran whose seals were affixed to the document. "If you have one iota of self-preservation, I suggest you kneel and keep your gaze lowered in the presence of the King! You are all forsworn! How dare you ever to have presumed to rise in the first place? Be glad I do not call the guards to arrest you!"

"Prince Tain—"

"No, Sire. This document might have a basis in law but it is not complete! There is at least one seal missing for it to be indisputably official and they know it. There is not a majority here."

Arkyn looked at the lords who *had* all knelt. "We are waiting for one more person, before I read out my father's wishes regarding the protectorship you have been debating for so long. No, Lord Scanlon, be *silent*! When that has been read, you will all of you return home under house arrest conditions until I have time to examine the consequences of this document. I hope that is clear."

Landis made to stand. "Sir, I shall go and organise it."

"You're not going anywhere. Cal, ask Edward to alert the barracks' duty captain, please." (Cal bowed and left.) "Lord Rale, would you mind pouring me a drink please? Thank you. Water will be fine. Is there anything else anyone wishes to tell me immediately about the events in the hall?"

There was a general shaking of heads but Ryson did say, "Not that can't wait, Sire."

Arkyn nodded. "Thank you…" He took the water from Finian and sipped it. He got as far as saying, "Now, this council…" before Cal announced Lady Amara and remained in the room.

Chapter 20
PROTECTOR?

21:12

King's Chambers – Inner Office

As HIS GREAT-AUNT ENTERED, Arkyn got to his feet in greeting, and Landis also pushed himself up.

Tired though she was, Lady Amara snapped, "Young Festus, what do you think you're doing? You're wounded! Sit down this instant or I'll whip your feet out from under you." She gave a brief curtsey and her tone became compassionate. "I'm glad to see *you*, Sire."

Arkyn smiled sadly. "I you. Please have a seat."

Amara glanced around the Inner Office, noting the kneeling lords. "Were those idiots responsible for last night's atrocity? Huh. Never did have the sense they were born with. Their ancestors will denounce them for this. I know. I met some of them. Young Scanlon, I'm not interested in your comments; I'm busy being acidic. Who else? Ignatius, how nice to see you here. Keeping everyone in line still? Good, it's what they need. Elidir, you're growing more like your father. Young Rale, hmm, you're just growing. Gerens, still being good? Yes, Sire? Of course, you needed me here for some reason other than to keep the Lords of Oedran in line."

A smile played about Arkyn's lips. "I need you to hear part of father's requests and bequests."

"I'm sure I can do that."

"Thank you. Cal, can you ask Edward for the document, please?" Moments later he said, "Lord Iris, Lord Landis, can you assure us that these signatures and seals are yours, please?"

Tain handed the document to Lord Iris and then Lord Landis. When they'd affirmed their signatures, he passed it to the other Lords of Oedran to show there was no conspiracy and then to Scanlon.

Scanlon's eyes narrowed. "The date's the same as the copy we found."

"The time is later," remarked Lord Iris. "King Adeone was most insistent that we recall in which order we signed them."

Retrieving the document, Arkyn said, "Thank you, my lord. The portion of the document I will read out is specific to your earlier discussion… 'My principal bequest is the Oedranian Empire, which I leave by hereditary right, to my eldest child Prince Arkyn Adeone FitzAlcis, be he of age. If I die before he is of age then I name Lady Amara Talitha FitzAlcis, daughter of King Apolinar Aldous as his Protector, if she sees fit, up to his twentieth birthday'—"

Arkyn paused. Scanlon's furious intake of breath hadn't been subtle.

99

Amara glared at him. "Well, young Scanlon?"

"Nothing, Aunt Amara."

"No, I didn't think it *would* be anything. Sire, carry on."

Arkyn had the niggling suspicion she was enjoying herself. He took up the document again, "It continues, 'If my elder son predeceases me then the inheritance will pass to my next born, Prince Tain Lachlan FitzAlcis, with the same protectorship. If Lady Amara predeceases me then I name my Defender Lord Festus Landis as Protector. I would have it noted as my request that on no account is Lord Scanlon Amarus FitzAlcis ever to be Protector of my sons or be involved in the running of the empire in a way that such a post would demand.'" Arkyn looked at his shaking uncle. "It is part of King Adeone's final decree that you have no hand in the monarchical government of the Oedranian Empire. What is more, he knew an assassination attempt would be made during the Munewid celebrations. It seems, after all the battles of will over the last few years, he had the last laugh. Leave these chambers immediately."

When Scanlon had gone, and his angry footsteps had retreated, the new King faced the six kneeling Lords of Oedran. "Get out!" he snapped, not caring how blunt he was or the shortness of the phrase, it all encompassed his feelings.

Chapter 21

FAMILY, NEARFAMILY AND FRIENDS

21:16

King's Chambers – Inner Office

ONCE ALONE with the loyal lords, his companions and aunt, Arkyn said, "Lady Amara, what is your decision?"

"Oh, you know I've never been bothered with all the politics," lied Amara. "You can cope admirably. There are times when this convention for a Protector is ridiculous and wrong. There's no law requiring it. Though, if you want any advice, you know where I am. Now, if you'll excuse me, young Arkyn, I'll say goodnight. I need my beauty sleep as much as ever."

Arkyn rose as Amara did. He walked out from behind the desk and gave her a hug. "Thank you. I'm sorry to have dragged you out."

"Don't be. I wouldn't have missed that for the world. Anyway… I'm truly sorry Arkyn, Tain. He shouldn't have died like that."

Arkyn bit his lip, trying to stop the tears flowing. Tain walked over and gave Amara a hug. She nodded to them both and then turning to the door spotted Phylicia.

"Who are you?" she enquired.

Arkyn pulled himself together. "Sorry. Might I introduce Lady Phylicia ReJean. She was kind enough to travel with us."

Phylicia dropped a short curtsy as she met Amara's eyes.

Amara smiled at her warmly, "Thank you, Lady Phylicia. You'll have to come and see me. It is years since I went to Amphi; I'd like to hear how the city is doing."

"I'll certainly be pleased to talk to you about it, my lady."

After Amara had left, Arkyn turned to the assembled lords not knowing what he was going to say or even how he was going to say it. Instinct took over. "Thank you, my lords, for remaining true to your oaths." He took note of the ones who were still present and acknowledged Ryson was there with delayed surprise. "I hope you will not find it a discourtesy if I request privacy – the day, I am sure, has been draining for us all. Cal, can you see the Steward about Lady Phylicia's rooms, please? My lady, feel free to stay here in the meantime. Lord Landis, I would also have a quick word with you."

The four lords not invited to stay, rose and bowed. Cal held the door open for them before leaving on his errand.

"Uncle Festus, where is father?" enquired Arkyn.

Landis whispered. "Next door. Do you want me to come with you?"

Arkyn shook his head. "No, I think Tain and I must do this ourselves. Thank you though. Could you stay here?"

Arkyn and Tain entered their father's bedchamber. There, looking relaxed, as though he merely slept, was King Adeone. With tears streaming from his eyes, Arkyn walked over glancing down at him. Dry-eyed, hands shaking, Tain fought for control. They each bent down and placed a kiss on their father's brow, trying to come to terms again with how much their lives had changed. Arkyn had a few years in which Scanlon couldn't legally assassinate him using the same trick as he had done to kill his father. It would take all their combined ingenuity to evade the illegal attempts. Eyes shadowed with emotion and exhaustion they exchanged a glance, stark reality on their faces. They swore, then and there, they would always protect each other. They left the bedchamber, Arkyn still wiping tears away. Landis tried to hide his concern by carefully handing around drinks before raising his own in a toast.

"To King Adeone Altarius, good friend, excellent father and protector of the empire. May you rest in peace, Adeone."

Phyl was touched she'd been included in the toast as four glasses were raised and drunk from.

Arkyn sighed as he put his glass down with studied exactitude. "Uncle Festus, father left you permanent entry to the Rex Dallin."

Landis paled further and blinked back tears. He raised his glass again in a silent toast. "I hope I never do anything to warrant it invalid, Sire."

"So do I. I can't bear to think of you as a traitor. When did he tell you he knew he was going to die?"

"The 17th of Lufial, Sire. He had a massive argument with Scanlon about Prince Tain's education now Judge Tancred has died…"

"Murdered more like…" muttered Tain. "Don't look shocked, Uncle Festus. I know he was murdered. The Judge had years left in him. It was my fault as well. I made him deny an amendment of Scanlon's. I suppose I am responsible for father's death if that is what sparked the row."

Lord Landis held out his good hand and when Tain took it gripped it as hard as he could. "No, you are not. Your father and uncle had been at boiling point for years. Any row could have sparked it and the very fact that your father was legally assassinated meant that Scanlon must have been planning this for a time, for far longer than the origin of that disagreement. To get six lords to agree on anything normally takes a year in itself. Your Highness, you are not responsible. I am. I knew your father expected an attempt and I… I took an oath to protect his life and I stood by and watched him face death. I am to blame."

Arkyn spoke up, "No, Uncle Festus, you're not. The only people to blame are the six lords who affixed their seals to that document. You're right that father and Uncle Scanlon have been outwitting each other for years. In the end father may have died but he certainly had the last laugh. Scanlon was so certain he'd be Protector."

Landis nodded but was conscious he was gripping Tain tightly. He looked at him in apology and saw complete dejection in his features. Instead of letting go he pulled his nearson down until Tain was kneeling and as carefully as he could pulled him into a one-armed hug and held him. It seemed like half an hour later when Tain pulled away, embarrassed for needing the support. There was a knock at the door and Cal entered.

"Sir, Lady Phylicia's rooms are ready and Kadeem says yours are too."

Arkyn nodded. "Then, Lady Phylicia, might I just thank you again for all you've done and wish you a peaceful night's sleep."

"Thank you but it was nothing, Sire. I will say goodnight though."

Once they were alone, Arkyn, Tain and Cal exchanged solemn glances.

"How did you get word?" asked Landis. "We tried but—"

Arkyn replied numbly, "Cal brought it. For once, Uncle Festus, I'm going to say that's all the explanation you'll get. I'm sorry."

Cal interrupted, "Sire, if it isn't too much, could I say goodbye to your father?"

Arkyn nodded. "Certainly. He's next door."

Landis watched him leave. "There's no need to be sorry, sir. Have you eaten at all today? You all three look like you've had little sleep."

"We've had some food but now you mention it I am hungry."

"If you will excuse me, I'll see that your menservants know you're retiring. Though I think Kadeem will have—"

"Uncle Festus, you need to go home," stated Arkyn quietly. "I shouldn't have kept you so long; the doc will have my guts. Please be sensible. We can't lose you as well."

Wincing, Landis got to his feet, as did Arkyn. The Lord of Oedran took his nearson's hand, and, ignoring Arkyn's protestations, knelt before kissing the King's signet ring saying,

"My liege."

Arkyn pulled his hand free and crossed to the windows behind the desk. Staying where he was, Landis watched him carefully.

"Uncle Festus, I thought I was the fool around here," whispered Tain.

As Cal re-entered a few moments later, Arkyn, obviously emotional, said, "Thank you, Lord Landis. Get yourself home and well."

Tain and Cal helped Landis get up. Cal continuing to support him to the Audience Chamber and the waiting carrying chair.

As Landis settled himself, Chapa took Cal aside. "How are they?"

"Lousy, doc. They've hardly eaten or slept since they got the news. They were frustrated by inactivity in Amphi, then by the journey and Lord Landis just put his foot in it. I ought to go and pick up the pieces."

"Take care of yourself as well."

"I won't. You should know that."

Chapa muttered. "Aye, I know. We none of us do."

Landis his good hand in his wife's said, "Cal... tell him I'm sorry."

"Only if you promise to get better for him."

Landis glanced between Chapa and his wife. "I'm under orders."

Cal grinned. "You certainly are, my lord, and mine don't rank as noticeable." He sobered. "Lord Landis... I'm sorry for your loss."

Landis blinked hard. "Thank you, Cal. Look after yourself as well as your friends."

Quarter of an hour later, as they left the Inner Office, Arkyn said, "I'll never forget today, Cal. Thank you."

"It's what friends are for," replied Cal. "Shall I say goodnight?"

Arkyn nodded and, seeing he was spent, Cal bowed slightly and walked quickly away to control his own emotions.

Chapter 22
SLEEP BECKONS
21:54
Palace – Privy Wing

BARELY ABLE to hold himself up, Arkyn walked to his chambers with Tain beside him, an infallible and silent support. Neither of them was in ignorance of the fact that any conversation would be grist to the gossip mill. Debates were for far more private locations. At the door of Arkyn's chambers, Tain looked at his brother to receive a shake of the head. Arkyn didn't want company; he wanted time to absorb what had happened and to remember his father as he had been: a figure of authority but someone who still knew how to laugh. Arkyn was terrified he wouldn't be able to live up to him.

* * *

Tain entered his own chambers to find a fresh bright-eyed Robert, who served him dinner with slick ease and a quip or two. He tried to raise a smile but couldn't manage it. It was refreshing though to have someone willing to crack a joke. When he'd finished eating, unable to say what he'd tasted, Tain rose and walked over to the window. He sat in the window seat and gazed blankly at his reflection.

"Sir, there's a hot bath and, forgive me, you should try and sleep."

Tain looked round blinking. Kadeem occasionally told his brother he needed to rest but Linnt had never said it to him. He found it was nice, in a way, to know someone was looking out for him.

"Thank you, Robert. Can you wake me at half seven please? Let Peter know I want to see him then as well."

"Certainly, Your Highness. Have a restful night."

Tain left for his bathroom. He nearly fell asleep in the bath. Dragging himself out of it with difficulty, he dried himself off, put on his night tunic and walked into his bedroom to find the covers turned back and all but one candle extinguished. He rolled into bed and blew that candle out. Fatigued as he was, he lay thinking for a long while before finally drifting off.

* * *

Arkyn had entered his antechamber to find his manservant waiting. Kadeem knelt. He looked shattered and Arkyn realised that where he'd been able to catch some sleep on the journey, Kadeem hadn't.

Arkyn slipped a hand under his manservant's elbow to help him to his feet. "Go to bed, Kadeem. Someone else can sort me out."

Kadeem caught Arkyn's eye; there was more emotion present than

Arkyn had witnessed before.

"Not tonight, sir, please."

"If you insist."

"I do, sir."

"Thank Alcis," replied Arkyn with genuine relief. "Send everyone else off for the night. I'd rather be alone."

Kadeem nodded, stifling a yawn. "Very good, sir."

A few minutes later Kadeem served Arkyn's dinner and seeing the King's mood was currently controlled by exhaustion said,

"Sir, today is over. Tomorrow is a new day but first you need to sleep."

"I know, Kadeem, but I can't seem to rid my mind of everything."

"If you wish to talk, sir, I am willing to listen."

"Thank you, but I think I have talked too much today. I want to run and hide, I suppose, but I won't. I have six treacherous lords to speak to in the morning. Why..." Arkyn trailed off and eating his dinner contemplated the changes his life had undergone. He had never actually asked his father how he'd coped with the change and, although he'd known the change would happen, he realised he'd never truly prepared for it.

There was the sound of soft footsteps and a polite cough. Arkyn pulled himself from his preoccupations.

"Kadeem?"

"Your bath is ready, sir."

"Thank you. I..."

"There really is no need to say anything, sir, unless you wish to. Tonight is for memory, contemplation and exhaustion."

Arkyn clapped Kadeem on the shoulder in passing. A minute later, relaxing in the warm bath water, Arkyn found tears running down his face and was glad that these tears were falling where no-one could see, for these he couldn't stop even had he wanted to. He closed his eyes to absorb the feeling.

Apologetically, Kadeem woke him. "Sir, surely bed would be better for sleeping?"

Arkyn murmured, "You're probably right. Help me up."

Kadeem offered his arm before wrapping a warm towel around Arkyn who dried himself off and donned the nightshirt Kadeem passed him. Entering his bedchamber, Arkyn collapsed into bed and slept, comforted by the familiar surroundings.

Kadeem cleared the bathroom, set everything ready for the morning and rolled into his own bed without undressing. A young member of the household found him early the next morning and carefully removed his shoes, undid the top buttons of his tunic and draped a blanket over him before lighting a small fire in the grate. An hour later Kadeem's deputy woke him and the manservant idly wondered who'd tucked him up.

* * *

Meanwhile, Cal walked through a silent city and quietly entered his house. His father was still up. Cal nodded at him before wearily making his way to the stairs. His father's voice stopped him in his tracks.

"Where have you been all day?"

"Supporting my friends after the legal assassination of their father. Strangely enough to the rest of the empire it still looks like murder. That's what it was. Please excuse me, Pa, I'm exceptionally tired it has been a long day for saying it started yesterday morning."

"You've not slept since then?" His father sounded shocked.

"I had to go to Amphi to break the news," replied Cal continuing his ascent without waiting for a reply. As he got ready for bed, there was a soft knock on his bedroom door. He opened it tentatively; his father handed over a decanter and glass.

"Have one. Might help. Then again might not."

After his father left, Cal poured a measure of whiskey and drank it with tears streaming down his face. He poured himself another and another. By the time he was on his fifth, he was drunk and the tears still flowed. Sobbing, he slipped into sleep.

* * *

Throughout the night, the clerks of the King's Office were copying out proclamations by dictation. They were sent to every major building in Oedran and every town in the empire, from those they were copied again and read in every village. It was a long, slow job but they had been working in shifts all day. As darkness enveloped the Palace, the first riders were sent out. The official buildings in Oedran could wait a couple of hours. Those riders needed to be on the road. The nearest towns would wake to the news being cried in the streets. The reign of King Arkyn Adeone had truly begun.

PART 3

Chapter 23

NEWS REACHES THE BARRACKS
Alunadai, Week 1 – 1st Cearal, 1st Cearcis 1215
Oedran – Administrative Quarter – Barracks

ARKYN AND TAIN had barely left Amphi when Wynfeld was glancing through the Munewid Eve reports, checking the day's duties, noting the parades required and checking the orders for summer recruitment. His batman tutted as he requested breakfast at his desk again. There was too much to do with the Petitionals a day away and the city population swelling as people arrived for them. Nothing was particularly unusual in any of the reports. He finished his breakfast, as the Intelligence Captain, in charge of spying, arrived with the morning report.

"Beaver, why the concerned look?"

"Erm, two things, sir…" Beaver explained the first.

Wynfeld cursed. "All of them?"

"Yes, sir. It doesn't get any better. The Palace is closed. The courier was turned away. Nothing in or out. The guards said the order came from high up. So who knows, but I thought in light of the reports from the empire we should be worried…"

"Damned right. Come with me."

* * *

Two minutes later, Wynfeld was saying, "General, the Palace has never been closed before. We should be worried."

"Fiddlesticks," observed Paturn. "It used to be closed regularly and if that report is correct the King will be making checks and having the Palace searched before tomorrow's Petitionals."

"We were meant to be helping with that, sir. It's on today's orders."

"His Majesty has many men who can do those checks. You're worrying unnecessarily. The King might even be testing you to see what you'll do. Don't overreact. Just attend to your other duties."

"Sir, should we at least talk to Prince Arkyn?"

Wiping his mouth, the General, dismissed Beaver with an easily read look. "Wynfeld, I thought you cared for the Prince."

Wynfeld said, "I do, sir, but if anything happens—"

"You're under my orders first! And I have given you ample of those this morning. Return to your duties, Major. I'm not going to be paranoid and hauled before His Majesty to explain an overreaction. Is that understood?"

"Yes, sir," replied Wynfeld with grave misgivings.

* * *

Once outside, he and Beaver made their silent way to the Major's office where Wynfeld said,

"It's nothing to worry about, apparently. We're not to do anything about it… Those are our orders. I don't want to hear that you've gone anywhere near the Palace today. Is that understood?"

"Yes, sir." Beaver saluted and left, contemplating the order. As he reached his office, a small smile played over his lips and he called up his messenger, a three-headed dog named Canois.

"Any chance of a link with the Herald?"

The dog looked around the office, licked its paws and, at the same time, said, "No. He's unreachable."

Beaver tried to catch one of the six eyes. "How about the Steward?"

"The same. No-one in the Palace can be reached before you ask any more tiresome questions."

"Aren't you in a helpful mood?"

"Depends which head I've got on. You'll have to get inventive, won't you?" With that Canois disappeared.

Beaver swore. There were legends of magical globes at the Palace but could they stop messenger communication? Rather more perplexed than worried he returned to the Major's office and relayed his discovery.

Wynfeld said, "Interesting. I wonder what other things those globes can do. I wish Butterworth was here—"

"Can't you recall him, sir?"

"His Majesty wishes his talents elsewhere. What about our friendly scryer?"

Woodroyd pulled back from his obsidian mirror. "Odd, sir, nothing. I can see the outline of the Palace from above but, when I try to get close, it's just blackness of a void. It's like the area doesn't exist. I've heard of something like this happening if you try to scry into the Low Plains – something to do with a mass of magic or Ull's curse or something. I'm not quite sure what. It's an interesting phenomenon though. Personally, I've never come across it before. I guess it's the result of the Cearcall a few hundred years ago. They had a hand in the Palace, I've heard."

"You and most of the empire, Woodroyd. Can you try the Low Plains and see if the result is the same?"

The scryer was incredulous. "Not from here, sir. Only a seer could do such a thing. The furthest I can get is Dellwood. I'm not the best scryer but even the best would only get to Carnford from here. No, you need a seer, or I need to travel to the borders of the Low Plains. It's just over a day's travelling…"

"Better luck next time. All right, dismissed, and not a word to anyone else about this little problem." When Woodroyd had gone Wynfeld said, "Any more ideas?"

Beaver shrugged. "Wait, sir. Unless you want me to try and get one of our contacts in?"

"Do you want to be court-martialled? If anyone is to defy the General, it will be me. I won't ask anyone else to. Get on with your day as normal and I'll let you know if I need anything."

Once Beaver had gone, Wynfeld considered the problem from every angle before going to inspect some rather hungover troops and giving them a tongue-in-cheek pep talk, with anecdotes, about the damage drink can do to reputations. By the end of it, the men were laughing and some of the worry had left Wynfeld. Maybe the General was right; maybe there wasn't anything to be concerned about.

The General however wasn't convinced. He might have told Wynfeld it was nothing to worry about but that didn't mean it was true. He tried to contact people in the Palace himself to receive the same reaction Beaver had. He thought about contacting one of the governors but if there was no messenger communication possible from or to the Palace that wouldn't help. He smiled to himself and trusted in the Intelligence Regiment ignoring stupid orders.

* * *

As night fell in the barracks, a clerk lodged himself where he could see the gates. The safest time to leave was around four in the morning; the gate guards would be tiring towards the end of their shift, the next shift not yet awake. The hidden clerk had hoped it would be a relief regiment on duty but it wasn't. That was unfortunate, an unforeseen error in his plan. After the Munewid, he'd been sure that the General or Major would have given this regiment the night off, but maybe it wasn't too much of a problem; they knew him, true, but they wouldn't, therefore, question what he was doing as rigorously. He'd taken to leaving and entering the barracks at weird times for months, to allay suspicion if he ever did have to run. He'd taken his belongings, again in bits, to an inn and he'd pick them up first thing the following day. There was nothing left in the barracks. He'd have vanished completely.

As soon as he'd heard the Palace was closed, he'd realised the attack had happened. His contact had been clear the day before that the clerk was needed to deflect the Major should messages arrive during the day. The message about the Lords of Oedran had proved the attack had succeeded. When he didn't pass it on, he realised that he'd committed provable treason.

111

He'd expected release, euphoria even. He'd have avenged, in some measure, the wrongs he had suffered, but bile rose in his throat as his stomach roiled. If he didn't leave, he was a dead man. Wynfeld wouldn't stop hunting him, and, once found, he'd be tortured if he didn't talk, but it would be certain death if he did. They wouldn't have to hunt far for the proof. Too late, he realised he'd been careless.

With the Palace open once more, he'd managed to messenger his contact, his panic clear to read. His contact had said simply to follow the plan, to leave in the early hours. More notice was taken of men entering the barracks, not leaving them.

From his hidey-hole, he stiffened as he spotted a palace courier at the gates, he glanced at his timepiece, one of the last things of value he owned, and noted that it was about three. Damn, it was too soon. He should run now, just leave but he couldn't move, trepidation leadened his feet and his muscles froze. Even from where he was hiding, he heard the curse.

"Wake the Major and give him this."

"He won't be happy, sarge."

"You're telling me. Go."

* * *

Major Wynfeld woke to his batman shaking him.

"What's happened?"

"Palace courier, sir."

"Finally. Time?"

"Three, sir."

The Major groaned and rolled out of bed, "Where's the courier?"

"Allen has the message, sir, it's rather erm…"

"It's what?"

"Not good news, sir. Not good at all. You'll need to wake the General."

Wynfeld sighed. "Just what I didn't need after yesterday. Allen!"

"Here, sir."

"What's the message?"

The soldier handed over the proclamation and beat a hasty retreat before the Major could finish reading the top line.

Wynfeld went white, swearing. "Sicla! Wake Beaver. I want him in my office as soon as maybe. I'm to the General." Deep within him lay not only apprehension and shock but also a terrible sadness for he had, in spite of all, truly liked and admired Adeone from their first talk, the terrible day Queen Ira had died.

* * *

The General's batman was protective, but Wynfeld's more-direct-than-normal approach worked; he ignored him, and walked into the General's quarters. Woke him with something related to tact, but distantly and unacknowledged, and saluted.

"You'll want to know this, sir."

"I better, else you're looking at retirement, Wynfeld."

"We might be anyway, sir. King Adeone's been assassinated—"

"Sicla, death and damnation! When?" demanded the pale General.

"Munewid Eve. King Arkyn's already back—"

"What did we know beforehand? Any bloody inkling, Wynfeld?"

"No, sir. No whispers of an attempt, and nothing's been in or out of the Palace today. I mean yesterday. I informed you I was worried."

"You did, and I didn't listen, but, before we're summoned, you'd better discover something. This falls directly in your remit, Wynfeld. I expected you'd ignore the orders I had to give. How sure of the new King's regard are you? Will he forgive you this?"

"How can he, sir, how bloody can he?"

"That is for you to ponder. Get on with it. I've a proclamation to read to the men on duty."

"Sir."

* * *

As Wynfeld entered his office Beaver saluted. "Is it true, Major?"

"King Adeone was assassinated on Munewid Eve. King Arkyn's home. I have the proclamation in my hand, what I don't have is any bloody information. What do you know?"

"What you've told me, Major."

"Not good enough, Beaver. I can't face King Arkyn with effectively, 'We know nothing'!"

"You might have to, sir."

"Do your bloody job or else you might not have one. The General expected we'd have found this out already."

"How? He gave us orders to do nothing…"

"You don't question the General!"

"Sir."

Wynfeld, thinking privately he'd have liked the question answered, took a steadying breath, "Do we at least know where Lord Scanlon is?"

Beaver looked surprised, "Here, sir, he arrived shortly after noon. It was in the evening report."

"Not the copy I read it wasn't. I'd have put that fact together with the whole bloody Prince's Guard and entourage turning up, don't you think? Who copied the report?"

"Jacobs, sir."

"Arrest him – keep him in solitary and keep an eye on Stuart as well. I want a report at dawn. I want to know every particular of what happened, Beaver, and I want to know we have the assassin before I report to our new King."

"Sir."

Beaver left and Wynfeld collapsed into a chair. He took two minutes to collect his thoughts before turning his mind to the gathering of information. Glancing at a timepiece he swore roundly; it was half past three, far too early for most of his contacts to be awake. He picked up the evening report, scan read it to make sure, read it in more detail to be certain and then walked quickly to Beaver's office.

* * *

Beaver giving a briefing. He hesitated as Wynfeld entered and several bleary-eyed sergeants turned and saluted.

Curtly Wynfeld said, "Carry on."

Beaver hesitated slightly before doing so. Wynfeld listened with half an ear, watching the sergeants. There was an array of emotions crossing their faces: surprise, determination, concern and uncertainty. As Beaver ended the briefing, Wynfeld's stance changed marginally but enough for the captain to notice. Beaver made his final comments watching Wynfeld carefully, but the Major didn't wish to add anything that his presence hadn't already done. He did, however, detain one of the sergeants with a vice like grip when he went to leave. The other sergeants glanced at each other meaningfully and left rather more quickly than intended, glad it wasn't they who had been stopped.

Beaver watched the Major carefully. Wynfeld was known to be conscientious, sharp and determined. He'd been head of intelligence gathering for over five years and didn't miss much. Beaver was privately wondering what he'd spotted but was sensible enough to keep silent.

Wynfeld pushed the confused and hapless sergeant onto a chair and enquired, far too mildly, "Why are you concerned?"

That foxed the sergeant, he'd expected some sort of accusation. "Erm, I'm not sure how my unit can help, Major. We've no palace contacts, all ours are in the southern half of the Lower City."

Wynfeld smiled. "Good. You're just the people I need."

The sergeant, feeling no happier, glanced at his captain. Beaver, however, said nothing.

Wynfeld said, "I need the last aluna-months' worth of reports checking. The copies I have as opposed to those here – at least the last month. Any anomalies I want highlighting, date, time, compiler and copier, by seven."

"Major—"

114

"You've got your orders, Sergeant." It was Beaver and not Wynfeld who had spoken.

Wynfeld said, "I wouldn't ask if I didn't need to know, Sergeant. But I'll just add this, if I discover you or your men have covered anyone's back you'll be court-martialled. Is that clear?"

The sergeant swallowed. "Yes, sir."

"Good. I want you and your men reporting to me in twelve minutes."

The hapless sergeant left and Wynfeld turned to Beaver. "As information reaches you it's sent to me and the General. Is that understood?"

"Yes, sir."

* * *

When Wynfeld reached his office, the Commander of Oedran Barracks was waiting for him. Wynfeld raised an eyebrow in invitation and the commander said simply,

"What can I do, Major?"

"When we've more information, I'll let you know. I've sent for the duty captain. If you have any contacts that can help, get information from them. Don't forget, I know who your uncle is, and that you meet with him."

The commander said simply, "I'll have a think, sir, and report back to you if I discover anything. My uncle is notorious for his reticence."

"As soon as possible, Aurifaber. Oh, and discreetly send out another patrol around the Palace. I don't want a large military presence, but I also want to know we're not going to receive any more surprises."

"Sir."

* * *

The duty captain was sitting in the guardroom of the main gates with his head in his hands, bleakly considering what the future held, and had been doing for most of his shift. His men had more recently told him what the proclamation said and left him alone. He'd been on duty at the barracks the night before instead of being at Court, instead of witnessing what had happened. He cursed. This wasn't a good day however he looked at it.

One of his men entered the guardroom tentatively, "Captain Rathgar, the Major wants to see you."

The captain sighed. "I had a feeling he would. Thank you."

He walked through the barracks acknowledging the salutes of the men, and in passing the commander saluted automatically.

The commander said softly, "I'm sorry for the news, Rathgar."

The captain nodded and carried on. He walked into the Major's office and saluted, realising events were fast becoming his worst nightmare.

Major Wynfeld watched him enter with a shrewd, evaluating gaze. Captain Peaga Rathgar, Lord Peaga Rathgar, the King's second cousin and Lady Amara's grandson, had the air of a tortured soul. Wynfeld had never had the impression that King Adeone and Lord Peaga had been close but many men would have conflicting emotions as the news broke.

"My lord, I'm sorry for your loss, but we have a job to do. Has anything come from the Palace tonight?"

The captain seemed confused as he replied dejectedly, "Only that the six lords, including my cousin, are under house arrest conditions, Major, there's been nothing else."

Wynfeld stilled. "What?"

"Lords Rathgar, Cearis, Teran, Anguis, Lux and Para are under house arrest conditions, Major. I thought…"

"That's quite enough, don't you think, for me to be informed?" asked Wynfeld curtly.

Peaga was genuinely confused. "I did, sir. I sent one of your intelligence clerks with a message as soon as I got the orders from Administrator Edward at about half past nine. I was surprised not to receive a response. I thought you had had an early night…"

Wynfeld said shortly, "Two points, Captain: one, I *never* have such an early night and two, if I don't reply to that sort of message, you make bloody sure I've received it. I don't want your excuses; I don't want your apologies. I'll consult with the General and decide what charge you're on. When on duty you're a captain first, not a lord. Which clerk did you tell?"

"Erm, I can't remember his name, sir – one that used to work in the King's Outer Office. I thought he was the right one."

Wynfeld swore. "Jacobs?"

"Yes, sir. Goes around glowering a lot."

"Thank you for that startling observation." There was a recognisable knock on the door. "You'd better get back to your duties. Yes, Beaver?"

Beaver entered and held the door for the departing captain. "Erm, Major, I hate to make your night worse but Jacobs has run."

* * *

Eventually when the whole barracks was awake and milling around, Jacobs found the strength to move. He hurried away from the gates, skirted the administrative area where he was known and walked quickly to the service area. He'd found his bolt hole here months ago, and he eased himself into it. It was amazing how many small spaces lay hidden in buildings and he'd found one behind the kitchens. Warm and with a promise of food if he was careful, he could hide here for days if need be. He tried to think. Would anyone be able to point to him? Or more precisely, would anyone have noticed his wanderings around the barracks? Stuart had been schooled not to ask questions and had been keeping his distance for a long time anyway, uncaring about Jacobs, but Jacobs hadn't forgotten him and the fact that it was Stuart's mistakes that had made matters worse when they were dismissed from the FitzAlcis' staff. Without that blundering, Jacobs could have talked King Adeone around but Stuart had admitted to the threatening notes by his very face if not his words. No. Stuart wouldn't be an issue and he didn't think anyone else cared enough to notice his movements. He'd be safe for a time. Once the initial few days were over, he could find a way to leave.

With that cheery thought, he decided to talk with his contact again. By the time the conversation was over, Beaver had discovered his disappearance and the hunt for him was on.

Chapter 24
MORNING
Cisadai, Week 1 – 2nd Cearal, 2nd Cearcis 1215
Prince Tain's Chambers – Bedchamber

A VOICE CALLED Tain out of sleep. Not the normal voice. This one had different harmonics. Pleasanter harmonics. He pushed himself up rubbing the sleep from his eyes. A deft hand quickly rearranged his pillows so he could sit up comfortably. Tain nodded in thanks as, yawning, he lent back into them once more. He looked at the manservant momentarily puzzled, then the events of the last two days washed back over him in sickening realisation. He wasn't given time to dwell on them as the manservant – Robert, that was his name – asked blithely,

"I've got your breakfast here, sir, if you'd like it now."

Rather surprised, Tain said, "I wonder what my father will…" He took a steadying breath, "…*would* have said if he knew you were giving me breakfast in bed, Robert."

"I'm afraid, I can't help Your Highness with that puzzle. A more mundane one though I might be able to."

Tain sighed. "What more mundane puzzle?"

"Would Your Highness like a bath this morning?"

"Please."

"Very good, sir. Your administrator is waiting in your sitting room, when Your Highness is ready."

"Let him come in."

"If you'll forgive me, Your Highness, it's not, well…"

"Get on with it, Robert."

"Forgive me, sir, but I was always taught that the household and staff of a lord or prince remained firmly in their allotted places and rooms."

Tain raised an eyebrow.

Robert hesitated. He had started the conversation, but it might see him sent back to Amphi if he'd overstepped. "I understood it to mean that your manservant never enters your office, unless asked to provide refreshments, or if you want to see them, and your secretary never enters your privy chambers, Your Highness."

Tain listened with interest whilst eating his breakfast. "That's what I was taught but Linnt said it wasn't really observed anymore. How come my breakfast is actually hot?"

Robert smiled. "There is a small kitchen in these rooms, sir. I'm bringing it back into working order."

"I'll say it's a nice change. I never knew about the kitchen… I'd better see Peter before I take a bath."

"If you'll permit me to move the tray, sir, it might make it easier."

Two moments later, Tain's feet fell straight into his slippers. "You'd better lay out a formal tunic for me in my dressing room. Not full formal, just enough to make people pause for thought."

"Of course, Your Highness. Your tailor has delivered a couple more since you've been away that might be appropriate."

"Bring them in here then and I'll choose."

Robert held the door to the sitting room open. Once it closed behind Tain, he reckoned he had about six minutes to clear the evidence of breakfast away, run the bath and find the tunic. He started to run the bath first – he'd lit the fire under the copper long before he'd woken the Prince so the water was hot – then he moved the breakfast remains. After that, he rootled around in the dressing room, quickly hooking the new tunics off the rail and a couple of others, collected the belt rack and laid them out in the bedchamber. He'd just turned the bath taps off when Tain re-entered the bedchamber.

* * *

Tain greeted Peter pleasantly. "Morning, Peter. I need briefing on what Lord Scanlon was trying to achieve by a protectorship. Ask Major Wynfeld. He might have some idea. I have my suspicions but that's all they are. Next, I want to know if I can order the arrest of the six traitorous lords. I need to know what the law is in that respect. Did they need to have half or a majority? I have always thought it should be a majority but they might have found a loophole. I'll see you at the Courthouse in an hour or so."

The administrator didn't miss the Prince's dull eyes, at odds with the tone of his greeting. "Very good, Your Highness. If you'll permit me to say though, the lords will have had more time to find the loopholes if

118

there are any."

"Yes, but anything will buy our new King time. Tell me, Peter… Was Robert rude when you arrived?"

"No, Your Highness. He was polite and correct."

"Oh. Right."

Hearing the strain replaced by slight despondency, Peter asked, "Is there anything wrong, Your Highness?"

"Other than the fact my father was murdered two weeks after my mentor?"

"Yes, sir. I can see those strains written clear in your manner."

Tain straightened his shoulders. "I'm truly realising what it all means, Peter. That's all."

Taking heed of the dismissal that had crept into Tain's voice, Peter left.

Tain gazed out of the window for a couple of minutes. The last early morning mists were lying in the gardens below. A couple of gardeners were chatting as they took a break. Half of him appreciated the fact that for some life continued as normal. There might be more interesting gossip for some days but life still had to be lived. Taking a breath, he re-entered his bedchamber. Somehow his perception of the world had changed again.

* * *

Robert bowed as Tain entered and Tain nodded in acknowledgement. Then he glanced at the bed, and around the room, favourably impressed by the obvious change from when he'd left. He glanced at the tunics.

"The tailor has begun to understand what I like. Tell me, Robert, as you're so free with your opinions which do you think would be appropriate in the circumstances?"

Not knowing whether that was a rebuff or not, Robert took the Prince at his words. "Not the full green, Your Highness."

"Why's that?"

"Well, sir, I am thinking that at some point during the day you will be seen in the company of King Arkyn. The tailor won't have had chance to prepare our new King's formal wear yet, so he will be in his formal dress as the heir to the throne, not as the King. Also, your mourning wear hasn't yet been made, though it should be here later today…"

"Yes, I mustn't clash or be seen to be more formal than my brother today. Nicely reasoned, Robert. So, of the two left, my preference is for the one with the green vertical middle piece and the interlocking curvilinear pattern on the lower portion of the sleeves."

"The one on your left, Your Highness?"

Tain caught a twinkle in his manservant's eye, "That would be the one. I was taught to describe everything in detail. Linnt seemed to take pleasure in misinterpreting me."

Robert said, "Well, sir, I hope I shall never be found wanting in that respect. Which belt would you like to go with it?"

Tain looked between the belts and tunics. "The one... I'll try it your way, third in from the left, I think."

"That would be the one that matches the interlocking curvilinear pattern but is chased in gold, Your Highness."

"That would be the one, Robert. Lay them out in the dressing room, please. I'll even let you choose the dagger to adorn the belt and the shoes to clad my feet whilst I go for my bath, if it's ready."

"Ready and steaming nicely, sir."

"You're very efficient, Robert."

"I aim to please, Your Highness."

Robert smiled as the Prince went to take his bath. He wasn't doing anything out of the ordinary. The couple of days he'd spent working with Linnt had, with the events of the morning, made him realise the Prince wasn't used to an ordinary manservant let alone one of the standard he should have. That was something he could try to remedy in however long he worked for the Prince directly. For Robert didn't fool himself it would be longer than it took for the King to find someone from Oedran, more used to the Palace, and appoint him. He, himself, would be returning to Amphi within the next couple of months. Not that this interlude wouldn't have done him some good in Amphi. Being even a temporary manservant to the Prince had to have advantages.

* * *

When dressed, Tain was at a loss. He'd asked to speak to Peter so early to give his administrator time to gather the information he needed but it left him with little to do for the next hour. He didn't want to go for a walk in the morning mists, and yet he didn't want to do nothing either. He'd got so used to doing something or having others around to talk to. Cal was at home and, if he had any sense, wouldn't be up yet. Arkyn also wouldn't be getting up for another hour at least. Kadeem would refuse to wake him after the previous day's exertion and rightly so.

Tain stood by the windows watching the gardeners weeding and trimming around the edges of the paths. There was something methodical and calming in their routine. He was pulled out of his reverie by Robert entering and enquiring if he needed anything else.

Tain realised there was something he could do: get to know his staff. Tancred and his father had always insisted it was important; so, in answer to Robert's question, the Prince said, "No thank you, Robert; however, before you disappear tell me something... How many times did you cover for Linnt in Amphi?"

"Sir?"

"Don't play coy, Robert. I know there were times when he wasn't where he should have been, or hadn't done what he should have. Kadeem was irate on one occasion at least."

"As you say, Your Highness, there were a couple. I put them down to the fact that Master Linnt was in a strange place. He had never been in Amphi before, unlike Master Kadeem."

"I suppose that is true enough. How long have you worked there?"

"Since I was ten, Your Highness. So, eight years. I started as an upper, before moving to the footmen."

Tain had never heard of uppers so asked what it was.

"Someone who goes around and wakes people up so they are ready for their day's work, sir. I was woken by one this morning. They might be called something different here, I suppose."

Tain nodded. "I don't get to know who does what. It is the Steward's responsibility."

"You have other things on your mind though, Your Highness."

"You can say that again."

"You have other—"

"Not literally, Robert," muttered Tain glancing back out the window, not looking at anything in particular.

"Sorry, sir."

Tain looked at the manservant and spotted a spark of amusement. "Stop being hypocritical."

"Certainly, Your Highness. What gave me away?"

"Your eyes. I've seen mischievous eyes once too often." *'Every morning in the mirror,'* Tain continued in his head.

"I shall try to curb them, sir."

"Why?" asked Tain.

"I thought you disapproved…"

"No, I'm just weary. To tell you the truth, it is a pleasant change. There is too much solemnity at the moment."

"With good cause, Your Highness."

"I know. Yet it is our pain, no-one else's."

"Sir, the empire has lost one of the greatest kings in its history. We all have something to mourn."

"Not all, Robert. Not those lords who signed away his life. As for being one of the greatest kings, he had no battles to fight, no victories to his name."

Robert went grave. The Prince's tone had been strained. He tried not to see his shaking hands. Was the Prince even aware they were shaking?

He was balling them occasionally, trying hard to keep his focus.

"Maybe those things don't make a great king. For there are more battles and victories than are simply measured in military might. King Adeone fought many battles for the people of the empire. He'll not be forgotten, Your Highness."

Tain biting his lip nodded. He took a steadying breath, "That is far truer than I think you can realise. Far more, I suspect, than I do."

"Maybe, that is how it should be, Your Highness."

"Even if it isn't, we'd never know enough to find out. Now, do I have to tell you what you see and hear in these rooms stays extremely private?"

"Well, sir, although you have no need to, it might be better you do. That way if I ever do tell anything you can take appropriate action knowing that you did tell me and I have no escape."

"Well, Robert, I must tell you that whatever you see and hear in these rooms stays private and, in fact, stays in these rooms, is that understood?"

Robert gave an appreciative and respectful smile, "Perfectly, Your Highness. Just here?"

"No, as you well know. Anywhere I am and anywhere you are, when working for me. Actually, anywhere you are whilst you are in the employ of the FitzAlcis on or off duty. Now, stop making me say everything you know already."

"Thank you for the clarification, Your Highness, and my apologies."

Tain nodded mutely. He turned away from Robert again biting at his lip. Emotion welling up in his throat for no good reason. The gardeners had moved on and the mists were clearing, being burnt off by the sun of what was, to Tain, a new world. He could still feel Robert's presence behind him but couldn't turn and show the man his emotion. The presence lifted, a moment later the door closed with a muffled thump.

Tain took a deep breath. Walking back to his dressing room, to collect his signet ring, he found Robert there. Both of them hesitated, but Tain, realising there was an awkward pause, said,

"Thank you."

Robert inclined his head slightly. "It's what I'm here for, sir. Now, I'm afraid to admit I forgot to attach your belt pouch this morning…"

"Oh. Very remiss of you, Robert. How will you live with yourself?"

"By remembering we're all fallible, Your Highness. It's the only thing that keeps me going some days."

Tain snorted gently as he undid the aforesaid belt and passed it over. "What about the other days?"

"I look in the mirror and tell myself one day I might be handsome but, until then, I'll have to live with the mistakes of my parents marrying."

Tain asked simply, "What would they say to that, I wonder, Robert?"

"Last time I mentioned it they said I could never regret it as much as they did because I only see my reflection, I'm not blighted by having to look at it all the time." He knelt so he could strap Tain's belt properly.

Tain hardly noticed his presence. Linnt had always made him feel uncomfortable. "It sounds like you have a good relationship with them, Robert. You won't want to stay in Oedran."

"It may sound like that, sir, but there are many reasons I started working when I was ten." He pushed himself up and caught Tain's eye. He was surprised to see the Prince nod in understanding.

Tain simply said, "Where's my signet ring, Robert."

"One second, sir. I'll locate it."

"It feels like a game."

"That's all life is, Your Highness."

"Now you sound like Kadeem."

"I suppose I have picked things up from him, sir. A short acquaintance can do that I understand."

"Apparently. I suppose I'm as ready for the day as I'll ever be."

Robert nodded and smiled. "I hope the world is ready for Your Highness. Good luck, sir."

Tain swallowed. "The world must go on and it needs leaders. Thank you, Robert. That's all for now. Let my guards know I'm going to the Courthouse, please."

Robert left. Did the world know how much responsibility it put on shoulders so young? He was impressed though. Even with the last hour Tain had shown the guts he had. He would meet challenges head on.

Chapter 25

WYNFELD AND PETER

08:06

Barracks – Major Wynfeld's Office

THE DOOR TO Major Wynfeld's utilitarian office had hardly been shut since the moment he'd got to his office after seeing the General. News flowed in with haltering steps and none of it good. At around eight in the morning, his corporal entered. Wynfeld raised an eyebrow in invitation.

"The Prince's Administrator is wondering if you could spare him some time, Major."

Wynfeld was puzzled. "You'd better show him in… Administrator, welcome once more to the barracks. How can I help?"

Peter closed the door. "Good morning, Major. Prince Tain wishes to know if you have any suspicions about what *exactly* Lord Scanlon was planning when he pushed for the protectorship."

"Administrator, I report to the General or our King – no-one else without their permission."

Peter eyed him. "Are you sure you want me to go back to the Prince and tell His Highness that was your reply? I am not at liberty to disclose all his reasons, but I can tell you that one is so that he can brief the King when he rises. Shall we say it would save you some difficulties if you were to explain?"

Wynfeld smiled. "You've settled in well, haven't you?"

"I did train as a lawyer."

"So I recall. Take a seat. What I'm going to tell you King Arkyn will discover anyway and I doubt I'll survive its revelation. We got word of the assassination at three, by our clock, this morning when the proclamation was delivered. Every man I have is currently trying to discover as much as we can. You probably know more than I do."

Peter swore softly. "Let's share our knowledge."

By the end of their conversation, Wynfeld felt better. "The six lords must have been certain that Lord Scanlon would be triumphant, or they were plain bloody stupid. Do you know if Lord Ryson was approached?"

Peter shrugged. "No. I've no idea. All I do know is he wasn't dismissed with the other lords and, from what you've said, something happened to make him aware of the attempt but too late."

"Yes. I know that Lord Scanlon tried for reconciliation a year or so ago and, from what I can determine, was rebuffed, but one doesn't rebuff Lord Scanlon without consequences. I'd tell His Highness to be careful of Lord Ryson still."

"I don't think I'll need to tell him, Major. It's a shame we don't know more of the specifics. Where did they all sign this document and when?"

Wynfeld said, "I believe the 'why' is equally important."

"They have to declare that to the King in their audiences this morning. Will they be escorted to the Palace? The mood in the city is likely to be black at this news."

"Yes. I'm expecting something resembling a riot. The yeomen and City Guard are on alert for one and, much as I am loath to do so, so are the men on duty here. I don't however think the Palace will be the focus of the rioters' attention, if it gets that far."

"You are thinking that the six lords will be?" Seeing the truth of his question, Peter paused for a long moment. "Prince Tain doesn't need the stress of a glut of arrests, Major."

"I understand."

"Good. I've spoken to Edward. From what has been said, if you don't have a summons by eleven, it will be late this afternoon or evening, or maybe even tomorrow. I'd see there's a brief report of what you know for the King to read and be open about the lack of knowledge. Don't try to hide it, for heaven's sake."

"I hadn't planned to hide it."

"Understood. I've got to get to the Courthouse. His Highness is due there."

Wynfeld rose as Peter did. "Administrator… Watch your back."

"From what you've told me, you watch yours, Major. Good morning."

Chapter 26
JUSTICIAR OF OEDRAN
08:30
Oedran – Administrative Quarter – Courthouse

TAIN WALKED to the Courthouse feeling distinctly strange; he'd been in the building many times but never yet as the Justiciar. In the circumstances it was best to enter quietly and, therefore, he entered the building by the unimposing rear entrance, the closest to his office.

As it was early not many people were around and Tain was glad; the couple of people he met simply moved aside for him but he could feel their eyes following him along the short section of corridor. The Justiciar's office was three rooms: an administrator's office, the Justiciar's private office and then a dressing room or servants' area.

Entering his administrator's functional office, Tain was still queasy. Two desks – his administrator's on his left, and a smaller clerk's desk to the right of the door straight ahead – were offset by scroll shelves and cabinets. The faint aroma of all offices lingered: old parchment and paper, sealing wax and beeswax candles. The back of a fireplace in the corridor kept the room comfortable in winter.

As he entered, his gaze took in a man lounging at the clerk's desk. As soon as he noticed Tain, the man rose and bowed with little of the relaxed air he'd held before. There was something vaguely familiar about him, but Tain didn't get chance to ponder the puzzle as Peter opened the door to the Justiciar's Office and followed him in, closing the door behind them.

Tain took in the room that was now his office. It felt so much more impersonal than it had when he'd visited it with Tancred at his side. Even though the sun streamed through the windows on his right, a chill suffused his skin. Would it always have been like this, or were other events making it so onerous? His administrator's patient silence didn't help, nor the careful, evaluating gaze.

For want of something to say, Tain asked, "Who was that in the office?" as he sat down in the well-upholstered, wingback leather and velvet chair behind his desk.

"Jenkins, sir: he's your Chief Lawyer. Judge Tancred recommended him to your father for your staff. He was basically reporting for duty."

"Right. I suppose I'd better talk to all my lawyers, hadn't I?"

Peter nodded slightly, "I don't think any of them will mind if it isn't for a couple of days, sir. They realise that you're busy."

Tain made a small noise of incredulity. "What a wonderful euphemism. Although it is also true. You know the worst thing, Peter? Although I know father wouldn't wish me to be sombre, I can't find even a smile within me."

"Hardly surprising, Your Highness. They'll return though. When my father died, I couldn't smile or be idle for a long time."

Tain looked at his administrator and nodded in thanks. He didn't often confide in anyone other than Cal and Arkyn but he'd needed to say something. To acknowledge what had happened.

After a pause, he said, "I presume you and Edward are co-ordinating my official life."

"Yes, Your Highness."

"Oh, good. If there are any meetings at the Palace, I'll probably need you there to take notes. So, get another person to sit in the office to field messages and the Keeper when he decides I need a break. I can imagine what agreements there were between him and Judge Tancred."

Peter nodded; he'd overheard a couple of them. "Very good, sir." Deciding that normality would probably help, he continued, "There's some information on the Assassination Law on your desk, and I've put lists of both your staff and the people currently working at the Courthouse to hand for you to examine if you wish."

Tain nodded. "Surely the last is the business of the Keeper."

"Technically, yes, sir, but I thought you might be interested."

"What you mean, Peter, is that you thought it might take my mind off other things."

"Something like that, sir, yes," admitted Peter, self-consciously. "I also thought you *might* be interested. For one thing, if you'll forgive me, it is unusual for the Justiciar to take an interest in the situation. It might make people feel valued if they get to hear that you know they exist, sir."

Tain gazed at Peter levelly. Should he upbraid his administrator for presuming to decide what would interest him? No. That would be Scanlon's way and Peter had only tried to be helpful. He needed that honesty. "I'll take a look. Anything else you thought I should be interested in?"

Relieved not to be receiving anything other than a seriously phrased enquiry, Peter said, "Only the list of today's trials, sir."

"They're still going ahead?" asked Tain incredulously.

Peter swallowed. "Yes, sir. Lord Scanlon's orders."

Tain's chin set. "Please see if the Keeper has a moment."

The Keeper's office was opposite Tain's, and so he received the summons almost immediately. He arranged his official robe quickly, but carefully, and walked the short distance to Prince Tain's office. He entered without fuss and bowed precisely. He had been appointed in Prince Lachlan's tenure as Justiciar and his post was a lifetime one so Lord Scanlon had never been able to replace him. He was a kindly man who nonetheless held respected authority and had kept the justice system in Oedran running with an absent Justiciar.

Looking carefully at Prince Tain, he said, "My condolences on the loss of your father, Your Highness. He will be sorely missed."

"Thank you, Keeper. I see my uncle decided the Courthouse will continue as normal."

The Keeper said, somewhat sadly, "Yes, sir. Technically it doesn't have to stop for the days of official mourning following the proclamation."

Tain nodded. "I know, I just didn't think he'd not acknowledge the assassination of his brother. Can I give an order for a later date?"

"Of course, sir."

"Then, for the day of the coronation and the day either side of it the Courthouse will close. The yeomen for one will be too busy. Officially, it will be to celebrate the accession of King Arkyn."

"Right, Your Highness. Three days should go down well."

Tain grimaced. "I thought it might. Just let it be known. By the time uncle finds out it should be too late for him to attempt to stop it without appearing to be what he is, a complete heartless git. It might even force him to do the same in the empire."

The Keeper fought down a smile. It would be interesting working for the Prince. He'd obviously grasped the situation and had formulated some ways of dealing with it. The Keeper sensed Tancred's hand in the young man's outlook and methods. There was something subtly devious that could, quite easily, deny all knowledge of other methods, and be believed. Prince Tain was now running the judiciary and justice system in Oedran. Technically if he was ever unsure, he should ask his uncle.

That was unlikely to happen. Judge Tancred's death had left a void, but the Prince would need to find someone to fill that gap on his own, otherwise there'd be less trust there. If he asked, the Keeper would help wherever he could. If it was anyone else, the Keeper would have to get them checked.

Personally, he was relieved he would be answering to the Prince. He had disliked working for Scanlon who would easily have fitted into Onraet's regime during the Age of Tyranny.

Prince Tain waved to a seat. "Out of interest, how much 'urgent' business is currently stored in your office for me?"

The Keeper said levelly, "Enough, sir. Your uncle has been absent, especially over recent months."

"Yes. What's the first thing that can't wait?"

"I think it could all wait another fortnight, sir."

"By which, you mean it's already waited so long people have found a way of coping."

"Yes, sir. Everyone will be surprised if anything changes until after the coronation."

Tain hesitated. "Maybe that would be a good thing, Keeper. Have you heard the rumours that I don't know what I'm doing?"

Who had told the Prince about them? The Keeper tried to be diplomatic. "Yes, sir, but I'm certain no-one believes them."

"Of course they believe them! I think I might as well start as I mean to go on. I'd like to prove them wrong. Arrange a time tomorrow for us to go through your list of the most urgent things to do. I'd also like a list of all the current Oedranian judges. Unofficially, I'd like a list of the Anaparian ones as well. I'd like to know how many judges the city requires so we can try to make sure we should never need an Anaparian judge during my uncle's remaining tenure as the country's Justiciar. I'd rather not give him an opening for planting more spies in this Courthouse. I'm sure you can appreciate why."

"Yes, sir."

Tain nodded. "Are any checks made on the people working here?"

"Checks, sir?"

"Into their background and whom they meet with."

The Keeper shook his head. "Not exhaustively, sir. Occasionally, if I have concerns about anyone then yes, Your Highness."

"I think for all our sakes we ought to make sure that, in the top echelons especially, we know who is talking to whom. I'd also like to know who I can put a measure of trust in and who to tell things to that I want to get back to my uncle. He'll have filled this place full of his spies before he left; I have no doubt about that."

"I think he's been doing it for a couple of years, but I can't prove it. He's too wily for that. I'll get on to the checks straight away."

"Thank you, Keeper. When it comes to my staff, they have already undergone a check, although they don't know it. Also, apart from talking to the Intelligence Regiment about them, don't mention them to anyone."

"Of course not, sir."

"Right, thank you, Keeper. That's all for now. I have to read some information and lists that Peter kindly left for me."

"I'm sure you appreciate the thought, sir." The Keeper saw no brightness in the depths of Tain's eyes. "We'll all get through this somehow, sir."

Chapter 27
GALDWINS
07:12
Oedran – Galdwins' House

AT THE GALDWINS' HOUSE, the morning found the master of it in a thoughtful, annoyed, mood. He sat at the scrubbed wooden table, a bowl of porridge slowly diminishing in front of him. He added a dollop of stewed apple from the bowl his wife had put out. There was a hint of honey running through it. He wouldn't be catching a cold soon then. His brain processed the thought without him actually considering it. Life experiences had a lot to answer for.

Watching him, his wife wondered if it was a wise idea to interrupt his musings. On balance, she thought perhaps it was.

"Did Cal come home last night?"

"Yes," growled Master Galdwin. "He's in a state. The King's dead. Well, King Adeone's dead. Something about legal assassination but Cal said it was still murder. He looked atrocious."

"No! The poor Princes… King and Prince I should say. I wonder if we can do anything? They've done so much for Cal over the years."

He glanced at her. "I'm not certain about that, and, quite frankly, they've more than enough people running around after 'em. The FitzAlcis aren't my favourite people at the moment."

"Why not?" asked his wife, confused. "They've just lost—"

"Aye, maybe, but why did it have to be Cal who went to Amphi to break the news? He was exhausted last night. I hadn't even got the heart to tell him off for not letting us know where he was."

Madam Galdwin smiled to herself. "See, I keep telling people you've a heart in you somewhere. I'm sure Cal would have been happier breaking the news than letting anyone else do so. They're his friends."

"Yes, and we're never let to forget it," muttered Master Galdwin. "Where are the children? They should be up by now."

"They're moving about. I hope they don't wake Cal. What time did he return? I never heard a thing."

"Late. I hope he slept…"

"I'm sure if he'd been up for so long, he will have done," said his wife.

"That or the whiskey should have seen him asleep."

"See, there's that heart of yours again."

"Fat lot of good it ever did me. Too many children running rings round me because of it," grouched Master Galdwin.

She smiled at him, "Go on with you. You're muttering out of habit. Morning, Hal."

"Morning, Ma. So where *is* the golden boy?" asked their second eldest.

Master Galdwin clipped him round the head. "A bit of understanding wouldn't go amiss. I want you in the shop in twelve minutes."

When his pa had gone, Hal rubbed his head. "What's happened?"

"King Adeone's been murdered. Cal's been to Amphi and back, breaking it to the Princes… There I goes again, the King and Prince."

Hal grimaced. "Oh, right. Ma, don't you ever wonder what Cal knows being around 'em so much? I mean, he must overhear things."

"Stop being nosey. You'll never find out, and I doubt anyone else will either. Their business is their own, especially now. Anyway, eat up; your pa wants you in the shop."

"Why me? Why can't Cal…?"

"Because he wants you there, and Cal didn't get back till late. Go on."

Hal eventually mooched out of the room. One by one, the rest of the Galdwin children found out what had happened. Louisa looked the most distressed, the others inquisitive.

Crispin had removed the glass from Cal's hand without waking him and replaced the decanter in its normal spot. His father glanced at the level. It was less than he'd have thought Cal would manage after having been around the FitzAlcis.

* * *

It was nearly ten when Cal finally rose. His father looked at him carefully. For saying he'd had such a long couple of days he looked remarkably bright.

"Well, lad?"

"Thank you, pa. If you don't mind, I should go and see if there is anything I can do at the Palace."

"Well, today you can but don't forget you've work here as well."

Cal nodded. "I won't. I really wish I could be in two places at once."

His father walked over to him and took him by the shoulders. "Cal, you're my son. I'm sorry King Adeone's dead, my condolences are truly with your friends, but I'm not going to stand by and see you in danger or hurt. Do you understand?"

Cal swallowed; it was more than his father had ever admitted to him before. "Yes, pa, and I appreciate it but my friends' hearts have been broken and I suppose it's at times like this that they need every friend they have for they have precious little family left and even less they can trust."

Master Galdwin absorbed that. "Be careful. Go on."

Chapter 28
BREAKFAST MEETING
09:18
Oedran Palace – Arkyn's Chambers

ARKYN WOKE SLOWLY, light dragging him from the depths of emotional and physical exhaustion: even rage had no place there, even dreams were debarred but it wasn't a restorative sleep. He'd been tossing and turning for most of the night, and true depth of sleep hadn't taken hold until the early hours. He disentangled himself and rolled onto his back. What time was it? He didn't particularly care past the thought it was day. He stared at the ceiling, at the curtains and the furniture – anything to stop him thinking on other matters. The sun was bright and seeing its light around the curtains, he sighed. It had no right to be shining, no right to mock with light his shadowed heart.

The servants' door opened and Kadeem entered on soft feet. He obviously hadn't expected Arkyn to be awake because he was carrying the water carafe and glass that normally sat on Arkyn's bedside table. Maybe he had stirred Arkyn's sleep when he collected them but Arkyn knew better than to suggest it.

The new King looked at his manservant and merely smiled a constrained and wan smile. Kadeem gave a short bow and passed him a drink.

Taking it, Arkyn hoisted himself into a sitting position, eyeing his manservant, unsure what to say.

Kadeem removed the necessity. "I'll open the curtains, sir. Your bath is prepared and I'll order breakfast. I've laid your tunic out but if you wish for a different one just ring for me."

Arkyn swung his legs out of bed, and nodded, appreciating not only Kadeem's tact at not highlighting the change of circumstances but in also ensuring that there were no questions to answer and so in the negative his manservant had become a positive miracle.

Twenty-four minutes later Kadeem bowed slightly deeper as Arkyn entered the sitting room looking every inch a prince and surpassing it to look the King. He met Kadeem's gaze levelly, and the manservant wondered for the first time in years where Arkyn got his fortitude from.

"Will I do, Kadeem?"

Matching the King's quiet tone, Kadeem said, "Never more so, sir."

Arkyn managed the smallest of smiles as he sat down. "Alcis, I'm tired."

Kadeem gave a small nod of understanding. He poured a glass of milk and when he passed Arkyn on his way out of the room, quite without thinking, he squeezed the King's shoulder.

Arkyn felt Kadeem's uncertainty from using such a recognisably intimate gesture and nodded slightly not saying a word. That hint of understanding was worth the whole empire to him, for at that moment it meant far more.

* * *

Thirty minutes later, Kadeem quietly announced Prince Tain.

Arkyn toying with his breakfast omelette and bacon, getting less appealing the colder it got, glanced up. "Thank you, Kadeem. He'll probably need a glass." He pushed his plate aside and reached for some toast and jam.

Kadeem left on soft feet.

Tain crossed to the table and sat down next to Arkyn. "Have you slept?"

"Yes. Why do I look awful?"

"No more than normal. Do you want any more toast?"

Arkyn sighed. "Feel free. Have you breakfasted?"

"Yes, but a while ago now. Any jam?"

"Of course. How I forget my hosting skills."

"Sorry but I'm peckish."

Kadeem returning with a glass and fresh pitcher of juice asked, "Can I fetch Your Highness anything?"

Arkyn said, "Offer him food and he'll never leave us alone, Kadeem."

Kadeem inclined his head but waited until Tain replied.

"No, thank you, Kadeem. I'll just finish my brother's breakfast."

As Kadeem left, Arkyn passed over the butter. There was a pause whilst they looked at each other knowing the other was making light of the situation.

Arkyn finally said, "It's happened."

Tain swallowed. "Yes."

That was all they could find to say to acknowledge their new positions and relationship to each other.

A few minutes later Arkyn asked dryly, "Why were you so hungry?"

"Apparently it's because I'm still growing – into what I don't enquire too closely."

"Probably wise. What time is it?"

"Must be quarter past ten."

"What?" asked Arkyn shocked. "Do you realise how much I've got to do today?"

"Yes."

"Then—"

"No-one argues with the doc's recommendations, you know that, and Edward's been busy, as have Richardson and Peter."

"They don't know what I want done," stated Arkyn, visibly stressed.

"There are, however, things that need to be done, however you wish them done. The six lords have been summoned and then there's—"

"Tain, how can I face being in the Inner Office? I can only see father or grandfather there."

"Me as well, but you've got to," admitted Tain. "Shirk this, for whatever reason – good or bad – and you'll have trouble with everything else and lose face. Feelings are for private moments."

"*You* say that? You once told me off for having no feelings."

"I was overwrought and young. Now anger is producing lucidity. You *must* face this," stated Tain holding his brother's gaze.

"I will – in my heart, I know I will – I just doubt my resolve."

"You shouldn't ever doubt that – you've far more than I ever have."

"I don't believe that. Tain…" Arkyn trailed off.

"Yes?"

"Will you be there?"

What had it cost Arkyn to ask him that? Tain's gaze softened slightly. No longer persuading, merely supporting. "Yes. I didn't simply invite myself to breakfast because I was hungry."

"No, that was convenience, wasn't it?"

"Certainly. It's given you or me, come to that, food for thought."

Arkyn got up, frustrated. "There are times and places, Tain."

"Yes, but if we can't find laughter somewhere, somehow we're lost, Arkyn, we're just lost."

"You've not smiled, let alone laughed, yet."

"I didn't say it was a flawless argument. Mine rarely are," said Tain.

"That's given me a wealth of confidence in your abilities."

"At least it was honest."

"True. Come on, let's face this before we end up arguing over nothing," replied Arkyn, his stomach glad he hadn't eaten a large breakfast.

Chapter 29

KING'S SENTENCE

10:36

King's Chambers

Arkyn and tain entered the King's Chambers in companionable silence. Three of the six lords were in the Audience Chamber and it was clear the guards were not letting them talk to each other. The King ignored them as he crossed to the Outer Office, then nodded Edward through into the Inner Office.

"What's first, Edward?"

Edward looked at the King, glanced at the Prince who made a non-committal jerk of his head.

"A briefing from the Justiciar on the ramifications of the assassination, sir," replied Edward assessing the King's mood.

"Thank you. I wondered why he was following me around."

Edward bowed out, recognising an attempt of normality.

After a couple of moments examining the view, Arkyn turned to his brother. "You'd better get on with it."

Tain watched Arkyn's face. "They needed a majority, which they didn't have but, due to the complication of a vacant lordship, we'll be arguing for years if we arrest them for treason. There is, however, a small, nearly forgotten, piece of legislation in the treason laws, Sire, which might be of use in this case. Can I explain?"

Arkyn said, "I rather think you'd better, Justiciar." How odd it was to be guided by his younger brother, whom until now he'd been guiding.

"I don't care for the title but thank you. Have you ever heard of a King's Sentence?" When Arkyn shook his head, Tain continued, "I'm not surprised, former Justiciars have been rather careful of the power gifted to them with the oath but I think it's important. Justiciars have dominion over all breaches of the law, or rather in the justice meted out in response to them or, more specifically, seeing justice is meted out. The law in this case, though, hasn't been breached provably in a court of law. Their actions exist in the grey area where law is powerless but action must be taken. It is in this that the King's Sentence becomes relevant. It is a piece of legislation that allows you to legitimately take action for injuries that do not fall under the law. The lords haven't committed treason as such, nor are they planning it – as the action has already happened – there is no evidence that they are treacherous towards you—"

"The position of King is continuous, only the incumbent changes."

"True, Sire, but, in law, the position is the incumbent from the moment of accession. To continue though, the lords know that they cannot be arrested, tried and executed on the evidence we hold. We would need to know that they now, today, were traitors, not their actions of a week past."

"That's ridiculous. Are you telling me that someone could attempt to kill me and if I didn't catch them, I couldn't prosecute them when I did?"

"Is that a trick question? If you haven't caught them, how can you prosecute them? Anyway, no I'm not. The lords used a piece of law to assassinate father, it is that law under which we now view their actions. That law overrides the regular treason laws. All that is different is the sentencing. If they had had five lords or seven, there would be no doubt: in the first they have committed treason, in the second they have not. The situation is that in having exactly half the number of lordships as signatories and with one lordship in our protection the argument that they had a majority is ambiguous and the sort that lawyers will argue not for hours or days but years and centuries; I cannot see the benefit of allowing lawyers that privilege whilst the lords who signed the document are in Oedran and can plot more, can you, Sire?"

"What's the answer you want? You lost me at the beginning of that and I've not caught you up yet."

Tain sighed. "Just say no."

"No."

"Thank you. Then the option on our law books open to you is a King's Sentence. You hold the fealty of the lords, and you'd better get them to renew it before you take the route of the King's Sentence. Under that fealty they have specific obligations, as you know."

"Yes, not to harm me; it didn't do father much good."

Tain swallowed. "I know but listen to me, please. The fealty means they *must* obey your instructions as though they were law. That's important. Like a lot of courtly speech, the phrase 'your wish is my command' is not idle but born out of fealty obligations."

Arkyn grasped the back of the chair behind the desk. "I know that; what I don't know is what your point is."

"Proclaim a King's Sentence, bound on their fealty, for injuries done to you by the assassination. The sentence is simple, exile. You can't order execution; I can't order arrest, trial and execution but we can get them out of Oedran."

"Is that any safer?" enquired Arkyn sceptically.

"Splitting them up over hundreds of miles? Yes, I think so. Recall one every year, test their fealty and send them out again if you want to."

Arkyn considered for a couple of moments. "I could exile them anyway without going through the palaver you suggest."

"Of course you could, Sire, but you'd have every one of their lawyers filing petitions, disputes and shouting that the exile was illegal; thereby playing straight into Uncle Scanlon's hands. Proclaim it as a King's Sentence and they can't do a thing, not a thing. The only small issue…"

"There's always one."

"There has to be a limit to the sentence. At least it's wise to impose one. That way it can mitigate any challenges they could make. I'd suggest six years." His brother crooked an eyebrow. "I'll be Justiciar of the Empire by the time the sentence is spent, it covers the time they can't use the same method to assassinate you, and it doesn't feel excessive."

"If they had only attempted to kill father, they'd have died. How is six years of exile sufficient?" enquired Arkyn stonily.

"It isn't. On any level." Tain hesitated. "We risk stirring unrest if we exile them for life. We can't risk father's sacrifice."

Arkyn swallowed so hard he thought he wouldn't get his voice back. "I want to avenge him."

"And we will, Arkyn. You have my word, but today is not the day."

Unmoving, they held each other's gaze, the promise and wish burning through both of them. The journey might be long but they were starting it there, in the Inner Office, where their ancestors had ruled for centuries.

Eventually, Arkyn said, "King's Sentence… What's the history?"

"Came into being during the Age of the Cearcall, Sire. Last used in around 777; your knowledge of the law will in fact enhance your standing."

"Will it? The parallel is concerning. Wasn't that the end of the Age of Tyranny when King Arlis wiped out the Chancellor's family? All that he hadn't killed in battle, that is," concluded Arkyn dryly.

"Yes, sir, but it shows you mean to end tyranny as our ancestor did, that you won't tolerate the empire being put in jeopardy."

"I'll take your word for it. Do you think we're living through an age comparable to the Age of Tyranny?"

"I think if we fail in stopping uncle those left will certainly do so," said Tain gravely.

"Then we mustn't fail."

"We must not."

Two moments later, Arkyn asked, "What terms do I impose on the exile? They're still going to plot."

"If they are going to plot to kill us, they will plot. You might be able to persuade them that pausing for thought is a good idea."

"How? Come on, Tain, you always have been better at devious dealing than I have. What threat can we hang over them to make them think twice?"

Tain thought for a moment. "Tell them to leave their families in Oedran. If anything is found against them, their heir will stand trial. If they're a widower or bachelor, say that marriage won't be permitted, and any children born outside marriage won't be recognised."

"That is nasty!" Arkyn's face, however, was in the first stages of a grin. "But it may work. How do we make sure that the lords actually go?"

"You do have an army. I've heard it is useful in such situations."

Arkyn nodded. He couldn't stop the lords communicating over messengers, but he could have them watched. He called for Edward.

"Yes, Sire?"

"Do we have the files on the six lords under arrest?"

Edward said, "Yes, sir. The Major's sent over a copy of his as well. He's also sent a brief report of his findings so far, Sire."

"So far?"

Tain interrupted, "Could you bring the files in, Edward? I'll explain."

Arkyn turned to him as Edward left. "What's going on?"

Tain sighed. "The barracks discovered what had happened at three this morning when they received the proclamation, Sire."

"How do you know that?"

"I asked Peter to talk to Wynfeld to see what they knew. I needed the information to formulate a response. I'm sorry, sir, I know I should have had permission to talk to the Major, but you were snoring."

"Snoring?"

"All right, asleep. Are you mad?"

Arkyn took a deep breath. "At any other time, I might have been." He turned to his administrator who had returned with the requested files. "Thank you, Edward. I'll need to see the Steward after all this." When Edward had gone Arkyn said, "He's worried."

"We all are," admitted Tain.

"Yes. I've got to disband father's household."

"Add it to the list. They'll know things have changed and your household is small enough to amalgamate easily. Simkins and Richardson were left decent pensions."

Arkyn nodded and flicked open Wynfeld's report. Tain took Lord Teran's file and for half an hour they were immersed in reading and discussing options. Arkyn formulated instructions for Wynfeld to follow regarding each exile and had Edward send them. He didn't want to see the Major yet. When his administrator had confirmed he'd sent the instructions, the King said simply,

"It's time."

Chapter 30
LORD TERAN
11:00
Inner Office

LORD TERAN SWAGGERED into the Inner Office, oblivious of the precarious position he was in. His permanent sneer only enhanced the impression he believed he was untouchable, that Arkyn couldn't claim revenge for the assassination.

"Teran, it is traditional that you kneel. I would suggest it is a tradition best upheld," said Tain authoritatively.

Looking at Teran, Arkyn raised an eyebrow.

Teran shrugged. "I've sworn fealty before and don't have bad news. Your father only required we knelt for those. He changed that *tradition*."

Arkyn's eyes narrowed. "How fortunate you mentioned fealty. That's exactly what you're going to renew. So, when you kneel, you'll hold up your hands as well."

"And if you don't, that is provable treason, Lord Teran," added Tain.

Teran eyed them both. "Lord Scanlon wouldn't try me."

"You are not in his jurisdiction," replied Tain. "King Arkyn wouldn't need to put you on trial if you refuse to swear fealty here. Your treason would be perpetrated in his presence. You would die before dawn."

Teran knelt, glaring.

Arkyn crossed to him. "Your hands, Teran. You will renew your broken oath or I will have to take other measures."

"You cannot arrest me, Sire. Not for something I had a right to sign."

Tain interrupted, "There are other options, Lord Teran. That document didn't have a majority of the lords' signatures on it. The Lordship Macaria still exists; it needs to be taken into account. If you do not want to see the inside of a cell, might I suggest you acquiesce to your King's request. If you do not, it will not only be yourself who suffers. You're jeopardising your rather large family. It is brave but misguided to do so."

Teran's eyes narrowed during Tain's speech. He held up his hands for the King to take. Arkyn renewed his oath kept Teran kneeling as he returned to his desk – where, for the look of the thing, Tain seated him before standing back a pace.

Arkyn was quiet but determined as he said, "Teran, you must declare your reasons for your actions to me."

Teran sneered more openly, "He cared nothing for tradition, nothing. He sent you, a mere boy, to meddle in Terasia as a result a former minor lord is now in charge of the province and his deputy is a complete nobody. Where is the respect lords and overlords deserve? Where is the polish this empire had when those of hereditary power were given the dues of their blood? The empire has sunk into mediocrity over recent years. It's nothing. Apolinar was the last great King of this empire. Altarius only kept people happy; his power wasn't truly respected or feared. As for Adeone, he was nothing but a limp rag by comparison. Those are my reasons; I wanted a chance at changing things for the better."

Arkyn didn't look at Tain; he sat instead regarding the lord in front of him silently for several moments before saying mildly,

"There is one post in the empire – bar those of the FitzAlcis – that has hereditary power by law: that is the Governorship of Areal for as long as the Bard's line lasts. Your *titles* are hereditary, not your *power*. Your power is the gift of kings, not a right of birth. I am proclaiming a King's Sentence on the wrong done to me under your seal. For six years you will not leave Terasia. You will be escorted to Tera, a house will be found for you within the city bounds and that will be your residence. You will not be involved in the governance of that province, you will not interfere with the Margrave's tenure or with the Deputy Governor's, or any of their officials, you will not plot against them, me or my heirs and family. You will arrive in Tera within a cisluna-month of today and should you not, measures will be taken. Your family is to remain in Oedran; if you dabble in treason or leave Terasia your son will stand trial for treason. I am aware your daughter is married to Lord Penrod Silvano; it will be their decision if they have anything to do with you in Tera. Before you dare argue, remonstrate, or even to tell me I can't do this, you should know that this is provided for under the treason laws and it has been brought about by your own actions. All the terms of your exile are bound on your newly renewed fealty. You may go."

Lord Teran's face reddened with rage. "What about the Etanes? What will you do there? Are they to be disbanded? Is your reign tyrannical?"

Arkyn said, "It would make my power respected and feared. The Etanes are my concern, not yours. Go. The guards know of the terms of this exile and will escort you from the city before sundown."

"I'll not leave Oedran – not today, not tomorrow, not ever."

Tain moved to the side of the desk. His hand idly on his sword hilt. The air crackled with emotion. His brother's next actions would say more about him than what had gone before. Teran's defiance risked everything.

Arkyn sat back. "You are refusing your liege's instruction?"

"I expect *His Highness* will tell me that's treason."

Tain didn't say a word. He didn't need to. They all knew Teran couldn't be executed. There were no witnesses to his defiance. He'd called their bluff, but that didn't mean he'd won.

Arkyn rang the bell and when Edward entered said, "We require Lord Teran's guards." When the men were there, Arkyn continued, "Escort, Lord Teran to Oedran Prison. He is to be held there until a prison cart can take him to Tera. It is perfectly acceptable to me that he is put with the common prisoners."

The guards saluted, hauled Teran to his feet and marched him out.

Teran struggled to remove their grip but the guards tightened their hold. He was marched through the Audience Chamber to exclamations and questions.

Tain and Arkyn heard the guards state that Teran was under arrest. The clamour increased but the footsteps receded.

* * *

Tain let out the breath he'd been holding. "What did you just do?"

Arkyn snorted. "Not have him executed, and hopefully made sure the others are more circumspect."

"They're never going to simply accept it. *Did* we consider the Etanes?"

"I thought you'd have a plan for that."

"Looks like we'll have to formulate one then."

Arkyn nodded before saying, "This still feels wrong."

"You're coping well. I've never truly seen you in action before today."

"Likewise. Even a chill went down my spine when you told Lord Teran that you'd put him in a cell."

"Whereas you actually did. Was I responsible for that?"

Arkyn hesitated. "It's always worth following through on a threat."

"I suppose." Tain sank onto a chair. "They can't honestly have thought we'd miss the fact there wasn't a majority."

"Ah, but, if Scanlon was Protector, I wouldn't have had a say. By the time my birthday came round, it would have been too late. They certainly miscalculated. Let's talk with Lux next. He's leads and they often follow."

Chapter 31
CONFINED ORDERS
11:18

Barracks – Major Wynfeld's Office

WYNFELD RECEIVED the instructions, raised an appreciative eyebrow at the way his King was dealing with the assassination instigators. Was Prince Tain behind the idea of the King's Sentence? He called for his corporal, asking to see the day's duty rotas. When he had allocated units to escorting the lords to their exile, he took note of the other names on the list and sent for two young captains, both of whom were a little too close to events for his peace of mind. He told his corporal he would see each separately.

Lord Chander Teran arrived first and saluted smartly. He might be heir to a lordship but in the barracks, when faced with superior officers, he was a captain and no king worth the title would interfere with that.

Wynfeld said, "At ease, Captain Teran. What do you know of events?"

"Nothing, Major."

"Are you sure?"

"Yes, sir. I've been here. I was on duty on Munewid Eve and yesterday. I come off duty tonight. I only know what the proclamation said."

"Have you had any contact with your family since yesterday?"

Chander Teran swallowed. "Mother did get in contact last night, sir."

"What did Her Ladyship tell you?"

"That father was under house arrest. Is it true?"

Major Wynfeld considered him solemnly for several long moments, "It was. There will be a further proclamation soon. Your father and the other lords who signed the Assassination Document have been exiled from Oedran under a King's Sentence. Shut up, Captain. You're confined to barracks today; it is wiser and safer for you. I don't trust the mood in the city. I hope that's clear enough."

"Major, I think I should be supporting my family."

"Do you indeed! Your family have helped rip the heart out of this empire and have potentially caused civil war. You swore to serve your King, that oath hasn't changed even though our monarch has. Your duties are here today and you will not be relieved of them under any circumstances. If I find you have disobeyed me then, heir to a lordship or not, I will court martial you. Is that clear enough?"

"Certainly, Major Wynfeld. Can I ask where my father is being sent?"

"Tera."

Chander Teran let out a long breath. "I'll inform my sister. Thank you, Major." He saluted and left, shakily. In the corporal's office he saw Peaga Rathgar. "Worse than I thought."

Peaga watched him go and squared his shoulders. The corporal nodded him into the Major's office.

"Close the door, Captain."

Peaga did so before saluting.

Wynfeld considered him for a moment. "Your cousin has been exiled to Garth, for six years. I suggest you don't leave the barracks today."

"Sir, I would like leave to go to the Palace…"

"To see whom?"

"My grandmother or King Arkyn."

"What for?" asked the Major shortly.

"A feeling that I should. I might be able to help."

Wynfeld said, "I think you'll help more by not getting in the way, Captain. Do you think our King will even have time to see you after the events your cousin helped to instigate? Anyway, technically you're on duty until this evening, you might be asleep but you're not on leave."

"Then tonight, sir…"

Wynfeld looked at the young man. "Have you woken up to the situation, Captain Rathgar?"

"If I have, sir, what difference does that make?"

"Depending on which side you're on quite a damned lot!"

"Must I choose a side, Major?"

Wynfeld's face hardened. "In this, every man will. Your cousin ordered the assassination of the head of your family. Is that stark enough reality for you? Whose world would you rather live through? You're officially our King's family, Captain. Sooner or later, you must decide. Will you follow Lord Rathgar or your King?"

"Maybe the future isn't so easy to predict, Major. I could propose a middle road…"

Six minutes later, Wynfeld said simply, "You're still to remain in barracks today. As I told Captain Teran, I don't trust the mood in the city. I do not want to have to explain to King Arkyn should you be harmed."

Peaga hesitated. "Erm, about last night, sir… What charge am I on?"

The Major considered him. "Next round of duty is to be evening and all night. Anything else?"

Peaga silently cursed; he couldn't attend Court for a month. He'd have to face his grandmother because of it and so facing anyone else was going to be the least of his troubles.

* * *

Once dismissed, Peaga headed straight to find Chander. He found him in his quarters, ashen and shaking.

"It can't be true, Peaga."

"It is. I'm confined to barracks; I guess you are as well."

Chander took a breath, trying to control his shakes. "Yes. I'm not even going to see father and I don't know how long the exile will last."

"Six years."

"*What?* No, it can't be… *Six*? Sicla's Cavern, Arkyn must be mad."

"If he is, I don't think anyone is going to dare voice it. He'll relent…"

"He won't," said Chander. "Especially not if Landis gets to him."

"Then we'll have to face it. We might not like it but—"

"Face it? Peaga, six years of exile is a death knell to them and us. You should have heard how the Major spoke to me. Munewid Eve, before the assassination, he'd never had been so blunt. Was he as bad with you?"

"He certainly wasn't pleasant but then I messed up last night and he didn't get some vital information."

"Did you mess up on purpose?"

Peaga eyed him, "Why do you think that?"

"I just wondered…"

There was a knock at the door and one of Chander's sergeants when bidden said,

"Sir, we're losing three units for escort duty. Orders have just come. We need a prison cart for Lord Teran. Apparently, he defied the King. He's at the prison and needs collecting."

Captain Teran jumped up. "That's the last straw…"

Peaga put a hand on his shoulder. "Captain Teran will be with you momentarily, Sergeant." When the sergeant had left, Peaga continued, "Calm down. You don't want the men to see how much this has affected you. It will undermine your authority. Cool, calm and collected. There's nothing we can do about the exile but we can make sure the escorts remember that your father and my cousin are still Lords of Oedran. Your men answer to you first. Maybe we can help without the Major being aware. We won't win a war with such a strategy but we may undermine him and win a battle."

Chander looked at him. "So we may. You're shattered."

"I'm for my bed. I was on night duty. I'll see you in the mess later."

"We're already in one!"

Chapter 32
LUX, RATHGAR, PARA AND ANGUIS

11:18

King's Chambers

THE FURORE of the Audience Chamber had been mitigated by the fact the guards prevented the lords from talking to each other. Looks passed, curses followed but, throughout all, Lux had watched the door to the King's Corridor where the tramp of feet, the noise of a struggle and the rapid cessation of both, with an exclamation of pain, suggested the guards might have assaulted Teran. If that were the case, the guards weren't bothered about reprisals. If they weren't bothered about those, then what had happened in the Inner Office? What was facing them all? He stood stock-still, his arms behind his back. Teran and he had known what they signed. The others? He could take an educated guess. Even knowing what they signed hadn't been treason, there were allowances for it in the law, but how would it be twisted? He wasn't a fool. They needed seven lords. Revenge would come in many forms. If he was to be executed, maybe he could bargain with the knowledge he had. Would a boy, two boys dare execute six Lords of Oedran? He thought back to the night before. There was no knowing what those boys would do. Grief and anger raged within them. Scanlon should have been Protector. Where was he now? Lady Amara had cut his plans to shreds. They needed time to regroup. As Edward motioned to his guards, he squared his broad shoulders. He had valid reasons. Petty though they might seem, lords' authority shouldn't be belittled in counsel.

The guards didn't accompany him into the Inner Office. That was something. There were no witnesses to their discussion. Lux eyed the King. Grief was hidden from sight, but determination was wrought on the young man's face. Well, determination could work both ways.

"What fate awaits Lord Teran?"

"The fate that awaits you all if you defy me," said the King without emphasis. "Before we proceed, you will renew your broken fealty."

"I broke no fealty. The law is clear."

"Please explain to me where the law states that fealty is not broken when you conspire to, and succeed in, assassinating your liege," requested Prince Tain.

Lux eyed him: the Prince was fifteen, yet he looked both older and younger at the same time. His dark eyes spoke of age but his face of youth.

"King Arlis' decree is clear. It is legal to sign an Assassination Document!"

"Legal, yes, if you have a majority of Lords of Oedran; however, nowhere does that decree state that fealty is not broken. King Arlis, Prince Everis would have considered your actions a betrayal, as does King Arkyn, as do I. You are forsworn, Lord Lux. Doubly so as you did not have a majority."

"We had a clear majority of lords who were of age!" raged Lux.

"If only law was simple. I would blush for your ignorance if it wasn't beneath me," said Tain. "Lord Lux, Teran defied the King. Will you follow his fate?"

"I have not been told what that fate is!"

"You do not wish to know," stated the King. "Tell me, Lux, have you followed the last few years' reviews?"

"With incredulity," sneered Lux.

Arkyn nodded. "So have many, but I haven't heard anyone state I was indecisive, easily manipulated or that I don't follow through when I promise something. So, I promise you now that if you don't renew your fealty, I shall consider you forsworn today, now, outside of the provisions of the Assassination Document and Decree. The full implications of that I expect you to understand. If not, please ask my Justiciar for clarification. He is more than able to provide it."

Lux straightened his back. "The Justiciar will not object. Where is your Protector?"

Prince Tain audibly sighed. "Sire, it seems the Lords of Oedran are as ignorant as they are defiant today."

The King snorted. "I have been noticing the same thing, Your Highness. Lux, you stand in the presence of my Justiciar. Lord Scanlon lost his position as the King's Justiciar on my father's death. He may still be Justiciar for the provinces but he is *not* the King's Justiciar with rights over treason. That is now Prince Tain." The King pushed himself to his feet. "Will you still defy me?"

"And your Protector?" demanded Lux, churning over the revelation. Had Scanlon lost so much power with King Adeone's death? Would they have been better murdering the two boys in front of him first? His fingers itched for his dagger or sword, but he hadn't been permitted to wear either by his guards. He would remember their manhandling to prevent him.

The King's eyes narrowed. "Would you like to face her whilst defying me, Lux? Lady Amara has qualities made for such moments."

Lux considered saying yes. It would delay what was coming, but it would also make it worse. Lady Amara had knowledge the two men in front of him didn't. He paused. When had he stopped thinking of them as boys? They were that: young, inexperienced. He shivered.

"No, I thought not," stated the King.

Sharp eyes, a sharp mind and a reputation for following through. Lux knelt. He needed to get out of the room without the order being given for his execution. After that, he could regroup and plan.

He swore fealty with a dollop of rage. It physically burnt through his veins as he spoke the words. He'd sworn fealty at King Adeone's coronation. All Lords of Oedran and lords in Oedran and surrounding lands did so. All lords within the empire swore fealty to the King through his Representatives or would swear fealty to the King through those who had sworn fealty to the Representatives. Like a web over the empire, the bonds of fealty tied men to the King, to the empire, and few questioned it. They would lose their lands, their position and likely their life if they raised a murmur of protest. The fealties didn't just bind the lord swearing them but all their family as well. Lux thought back to Adeone's crowning, to the Fealty Swear then. No. His blood hadn't burned within him like this. He was certain, if he could see them, the veins in his hands would be fiery. The King held his gaze with every request. Every response stuck in his throat for a moment but he renewed his fealty to the King. Would it override the other? Well, he'd been forsworn once, again wouldn't be a problem. The end of the process reached, he went to push himself to his feet.

"I don't think so," said the King. "Stay where you are and explain your reasons for signing the Assassination Document, Lux."

Lux reddened. "You cannot keep me kneeling!"

The King crooked an eyebrow. "I have heard politer responses. Do not forget to whom you speak, or measures will be taken."

Lux reddened. "You dare—?" He checked himself. He had to get out of the room with his life and no greater fealty demanded. The King had only requested a truth-fealty, he didn't want to push it higher, and he definitely didn't need a fealty reading. "Fine. Your father cared nothing for traditional dues of the lords. Absolutely nothing. He would happily see us undermined and do nothing about it. During counsel he would belittle us. He did it to me, to others. He demanded loyalty but gave us none of our dues in return. He ignored us at Court, refused to give us positions and discounted our advice. He was more than content to dine with the cisan but wouldn't join our tables. When he showed me up in counsel, I decided not to take the insults any longer."

Why did it sound so much less than it felt? Lux saw the King's eyes harden. There would never be understanding and sympathy from him. He was too much of his father's mould. They had destroyed one soft monarch and gained another. Well, he'd done everything requested of him. They couldn't take any reprisal. He had acted within the law.

"Lux, your reasons are not only short-sighted but lack substance. You were belittled in counsel? If that is so, it would have been your own actions that merited such a response. Did you wake up this morning and believe you had forged a better world? Did you congratulate yourself on the distress you have caused? Did you believe that I could do nothing? I see you did. I must disillusion you; there is a small piece of law you seem to have missed in your self-congratulation. Under the treason laws, I am exiling you from Oedran for six years as a King's Sentence. I will not permit any marriage and any illegitimate children will not be recognised. You will travel to Lufia alone, apart from one servant and the guards I am sending to ensure you get there. You are not to leave Lufian for those six years. Before you leave, you are to speak to no-one. Go."

Lux's blood boiled. He tried to find any words to express how much that wasn't going to happen. He wouldn't be bullied like this. He wouldn't be forced to leave Oedran.

"Or you could follow Lord Teran's fate," suggested the King.

Lux pushed himself to his feet, flung the door open and strode through the Audience Chamber. He was not going to accept this… this… sentence, or whatever it was. He stormed along the King's Corridor and down the Golden Stairs before heading for Lord Scanlon's chambers. He needed to know what the King was doing.

* * *

Scanlon listened. That was one thing you could say for him. Reaching the end of his recitation, Lux took note of the look in Scanlon's eye. It wasn't what he'd expected. He'd expected outrage, but there was quiet acceptance, or what seemed like it.

"Lufian is not a wilderness, Lux. I suggest you leave before King Arkyn decides to arrest you as he did Teran. I don't believe defying the King in this is at all productive."

"You can't sit there and let this happen, my lord! Not when—"

Scanlon's eyes flicked to the doors. "Are you asking me to defy the King for you, Dyfrig? I won't be doing that."

"It's not just me! He's going to exile every one of us. You—"

"I am FitzAlcis, Lux. Remember that. I suggest you let the listening guards escort you to your new home."

Lux stormed out the room. His guards were indeed standing either side of the door waiting.

"As you've no family, the escort and your manservant are waiting at the stables, sir," said the sergeant in charge. "We have orders to detain you if you do not follow the King's instructions."

Lux strode through the Palace without uttering another word. He'd make sure he reached Lufia on his terms. Whatever Lord Scanlon had meant about it not being friendless, he would be the highest ranking lord there apart from the Sagamore. There were compensations in that.

Scanlon watched him leave with narrowed eyes. So Arkyn was playing that game, was he? Divide and conquer might be an ancient tactic but it wouldn't work out quite the way the boy wanted. Still, he'd wait until they'd all had their audiences. It wouldn't be too much longer.

* * *

In the Inner Office, Tain said, "I rather suspect you're going to get the same story from the others."

"I know I am. Let's get it over with."

147

Having seen one of his fellow lords marched out of the King's Chambers, and the other storm through them enraged, Rathgar argued less in the hopes of more leniency. It was clear to him that their plan hadn't worked. It had been clear the night before. Would the fact that one of the King's family had grown up at Rathgar House mitigate the reaction? If his Uncle Rufus had been more circumspect when it came to the failure of his marriage, he could have used Aunt Neassa and Peaga as leverage. Instead, they were beyond his reach because of the divorce. He cursed his uncle; more, he cursed Lady Neassa for having agreed to, asked for, the divorce.

He reaffirmed his fealty without arguing and gave his rehearsed reasons without blinking. He had lost legally acquired land in 1211 because Adeone had taken a merchant's side, undermining his position as a Lord of Oedran. The divorce between his uncle and wed-aunt had been rushed and their side hadn't been heard. It sounded less justified when spoken within the Inner Office than it had elsewhere. He hunted around for something else. He blustered for a good half minute but both the FitzAlcis in front of him showed their understanding that it was bluster.

He heard out the King without speaking. So, he was to go to Garth in Bayan, to be in exile for six years without his family. Well, that wasn't as bad as execution. A lot could happen in six years, even if he was to be under the watchful eye of Lord Tyler Galwood, third cousin to the man exiling him. He pushed himself to his feet and left without another word, but he walked calmly through the Audience Chamber. He would be back, and, when he was, much might have changed.

* * *

Lord Anguis acted much as Rathgar had. He complained that Adeone had ignored the Lords of Oedran, especially since Queen Ira's death. That Adeone's refusal to consider remarriage had belittled the lords and their families. He added that his authority had been made worthless by Edward whilst the administrator was training in the Outer Office. Denied entry to see the King by a foundling-orphan of no family – and, therefore, no standing – such a thing was a disgrace but instead of dismissing the then clerk, Adeone had had the temerity to give Anguis a dressing down instead, and Edward had been made Arkyn's administrator. Where was the respect due to the Lords of Oedran if that could happen?

When he'd gone, Arkyn said, "Don't let Edward know that one."

"I wasn't going to, don't worry. They seem a little upset by the outcome."

"Yes. Para next?"

* * *

Para thought that his term as Ealdorman had been undermined by Lord Iris, on Adeone's instruction, that the banning of weapons in Oedran had been tyrannical and unnecessary that it was undermining Oedran's status as a great city. He also thought Adeone's dismissal of Judge Tancred's past spoke of weakness and insulted the ancient order. Arkyn exiled him to Paras in the north of Anapara and banned him leaving a twenty-mile radius of the city.

Drained from the altercations, Arkyn watched him leave. They were all parroting each other but with different incidents. The threads were there, a lack of respect for tradition, a dismissal of importance, but where had been their loyalty, where had been their proof they had raised their disappointments with his father? The Petitionals existed for a reason. The lords all had a right for the King to listen to their concerns. They hadn't voiced them to anyone but each other.

There were footsteps resounding in the Audience Chamber again. Someone needed something from him or his office, but he needed to see Cearis. The last of the six.

Chapter 33
SCANLON
11:66
Inner Office

THE DOOR to the Inner Office flew open and Scanlon entered. "This is illegal and you know it."

"Do come in, my lord," stated Arkyn.

"Where's your Protector? She should be here to stop such stupid and outlandish decisions."

With deceptive mildness, Arkyn said, "Aunt Amara believes in me far more than you do, Lord Scanlon; she has told me to get on with things, that I don't need her holding my hand and how true that is if this is your reaction. It seems I am able to undermine you of my own accord."

"Whatever else the relationship—"

"I am now your King, Lord Scanlon; you will remember that for as long as I am on the throne, crowned or not! Your plans might have gone wrong, I might not be able to *prove* you were behind this but it does not mean we both don't know it. Your confederates are exiled, as I presume you have heard, I would suggest that if you wish to object so publicly to my decisions you accompany them, but chose which carefully, won't you."

"Unfortunately, I must remain in Oedran for the funeral."

"I don't believe you're invited. Get out," spat Arkyn.

"It is unwise to antagonise me, as your father discovered."

"Is that an admission of guilt, Lord Scanlon?"

"I have no guilt to admit. If I leave, I take Elantha with me."

Arkyn swore. "Do not use her as a pawn in this."

"She is my daughter and will be obedient to my wishes. She is not to return to Ceardlann, she can come to Black Hills."

Arkyn ignored Tain's curse. "As King, I am requiring my cousin's presence in Oedran. If you remove her from the city *now*, you will be expressly going against me, Lord Scanlon, and that *is* treason."

Scanlon sneered. "Very well, I require a house in the Administrative Quarter for my daughter. The Palace is too impersonal."

Arkyn said, "I will see to arrangements but you are not required at the funeral. I suggest you find some pressing matter requiring your attention elsewhere."

"Then I shall return for the coronation as Justiciar."

"Lord Scanlon, I am Justiciar of Oedran," stated Tain. "It is my job to be at the coronation and to crown the King."

"You are not of alunan-age; you have not your full power yet. Do not presume to instruct me in this!"

"It seems I do have the right amount of power for this. Lord Rathgar as Ealdorman passed the crown to the Moonshi at father's coronation as you were travelling back from Terasia. Now the Justiciar of Oedran is here, is the King's Justiciar, and as such I will be taking my full role. I will acknowledge my brother as my King and forgo any right to the crown whilst he lives. Why *did* you take so long to return from Terasia in 1204? Did you not want to publicly do the same for father? You didn't even proclaim his accession in Tera in 1204. You did nothing to acknowledge his accession formally! I will—"

"How dare you—"

"Quite easily, Uncle Scanlon. And stop interfering in the Courthouse! It was not up to you to decide what would happen there today, or have you also forgotten that?"

Scanlon took a breath to argue the point but Arkyn said mildly,

"Lord Scanlon, I've already asked you to leave. Please do so now."

With overstated emphasis and a pointed sneer, Lord Scanlon gave a florid bow and stormed from the room. He wasn't going to be dismissed from Oedran like that. Certainly not when his friends were being exiled. Leaving at the same time would make it appear as though the King had exiled him. That wasn't going to happen.

* * *

Tain let out a long breath. "Sorry, Sire."

Arkyn got to his feet and took his brother by his shoulders and held

150

his gaze. "Thank you – that must have cost you a lot."

Tain swallowed. "No more than I wished to pay. Are you all right?"

"Yes, I knew that row was going to happen. I just feel dreadful for El."

Tain nodded. "Me too. We've not seen her yet."

"No, and now I've got to tell her... Edward!"

The administrator entered the Inner Office. "Sire?"

"Where's Lady Elantha?"

"Talking to Lady Amara, Lady Phylicia and Master Calumiel."

Arkyn relaxed. "Thank heavens. Can you ask her to come here?"

"Yes, sir, but there's still Lord Cearis waiting for his audience and becoming whiter by the minute and then there's the Steward..."

Chapter 34
CEARIS
12:00
Inner Office

CEARIS ENTERED the Inner Office and, without anything being said, he knelt. Arkyn saw no defiance, but he did recognise something deeper: it wasn't fear, it was complete acknowledgement that he was in the King's hands and he didn't expect to live.

Arkyn renewed his oath before saying, "Explain."

Cearis looked up and then away before looking back. "It was a game, sir. Nothing more. It was just a game..."

Arkyn was incredulous as well as furious. "Are you telling me you didn't think that anything would come of signing an Assassination Document? Are you expecting me to believe that?"

Cearis swallowed. "I didn't know what it was, I was asked to witness something, I didn't... Oh, Sicla."

"Who asked you to sign it?" enquired Arkyn sharply.

"I can't. I willingly gave an oath, a binding oath. I can't speak of it..."

"An oath?" said Tain. "To someone other than the King?"

"Yes, sir," whispered Cearis.

"You realise you've admitted to treason, don't you, Cearis?" enquired Arkyn inwardly cursing. Had others done the same? Should he have checked to see if they had?

"Yes, Sire, but not against you. I didn't agree with your father's *policies* but I never disliked *him*. I thought I was helping reverse some of those policies not destroy him. There's no reason for anyone to believe me, I know that, there's no reason at all but I swear to you, Sire, I never

151

meant you or His Highness harm. I swear…”

More calmly than Tain expected Arkyn asked, “Where do you think this will end, Cearis?”

“I don’t expect to see the dawn, Sire,” whispered Cearis.

Tain turned his back on the Lord of Oedran, leaned forward slightly and murmured in Arkyn’s ear,

“Useful double-agent, if you need one. He’s a bachelor, there’ll be serious problems to sort out if he’s executed.”

Arkyn glanced at him and then at Cearis and shook his head slightly. “Cearis, your technicality that the treason wasn’t against me might just be the sort a lawyer will argue for years. You, I take it, have no wish to be in a cell for those years?”

“Not particularly, Sire.”

“How fortunate…”

When Lord Cearis left, he was exiled to Cearden in Denshire for six years under the eye of the Visir.

Tain snapped, “You could have used him to our advantage!”

“Who says I haven’t? He’s been speech-bound. That was clear.”

“Then you’ll never find anything out from him.”

“We shall see,” replied Arkyn. “Maybe a nervous Lord of Oedran will reveal more than words. Now for the Steward…”

Chapter 35
STEWARD
12:12
Inner Office

WATCHING THE STEWARD enter the Inner Office, Arkyn’s gaze narrowed. The man was acting as though there was nothing wrong. His walk had the confidence of a man sure of his position and power. His whole demeanour made Arkyn uneasy and annoyed. The control he’d found in Tera, though, flowed again in his veins as he enquired calmly whose orders the man should follow.

“Yours, Sire,” replied the Steward.

“And before mine?”

“Your father’s, sir.”

“So, explain to me why, without mine or King Adeone’s express command, you closed the Palace after the assassination,” ordered Arkyn.

“I had received instructions to do so from the oldest member of your family in your absence.”

Arkyn stilled. "Lady Amara might be ageing but her memory is still razor sharp. She has no recollection of those orders."

"Forgive me, Sire. I meant to say the oldest *male* member of your family, in line with tradition."

"An interesting choice, given you are aware of the history of that member of the family. Did you attempt to contact myself or Prince Tain to inform us we were orphaned?"

"Sir, I—"

"NO, YOU DID NOT!"

Tain broke in, "Steward, I would suggest this is the point where you kneel and ask the King's forgiveness for what is effectively a form of treachery and could be construed as treason. You did, knowingly, follow orders of someone not authorised by either King to give them."

The Steward blanched and knelt. "Sire, I acted in good faith, your age meant I had to look to your uncle for orders."

"My age? Maybe you conveniently forgot that my age was immaterial to my father when he named me his Representative once again a week ago. When were you planning on sending word to Amphi?"

"When your uncle arrived, sir, but I was told word had been sent."

"Who by?" demanded Arkyn.

"Sergeant Hillbeck said it was in hand, sir. I had a hall full of courtiers to deal with, feed and find places for them to sleep, Sire. I had the Palace to keep running under—"

"Did you warn my uncle of my return?" interrupted Arkyn.

Still kneeling, the Steward said, "No, sir. I presumed Sergeant Hillbeck would do so or he'd have informed Lord Landis who would. I was dealing with matters in the Palace at large."

Arkyn would check he was telling the truth but it might have saved the Steward. He would need to take some action but the Steward hadn't made things any worse. They couldn't trust him, but they needed more to arrest him. Far more. Arkyn's age *had* complicated matters.

The Steward took advantage of a pause to say, "Sire, I—"

Tain frowned. "Steward, you will speak only when spoken to."

Arkyn said, "Thank you, Prince Tain. Steward, I would remind you that no-one is indispensable and that you do not have the authority to close the Palace without my order. You will, as Prince Tain implied, remember your place. *All* orders received by you from my uncle are to be forgotten. Is that clearly understood?"

"Yes, Sire."

"Good. Now, leave before I get my Justiciar to arrest you."

The Steward rose and bowed out backwards. Arkyn turned to the window, every muscle in his body taut.

"Are you all right?" asked Tain.

"No. I'm bloody not and you know it! The Steward is a damned traitor and I can't prove it."

"Yes, but now he knows that you know and will modify his behaviour. He's been mouthing off in private for a long time that you were too young to be a King's Representative. Now he's seen that you're old enough to be King and he's scared. He'll be more careful. Are you calming down?"

"Not really." Arkyn let out a long breath. "I think we need to see El and we should have done so earlier."

Chapter 36
ELANTHA
12:18
Inner Office

WHEN EDWARD HELD the door open for Elantha, she entered the Inner Office hesitantly, before dropping into a curtsy so precise it seared Arkyn's heart. Crossing to her, he wordlessly pulled her up, wrapping her in a hug.

Feeling tears pricking at his eyes, Tain poured some drinks. When he turned back, Arkyn had tears streaming down his face and their cousin was sobbing. He sat down. They didn't need him, and it was his fault. He and Elantha had always had an uneasy relationship. His brother had been kinder to her, but seeing her so upset all he wanted to do was protect her. She shouldn't have been alone.

She gradually calmed down and Arkyn guided her over to where Tain was sitting brooding.

Elantha glanced at him. "Tain."

Getting up, he pulled her into a hug, surprised by the strength of the one she returned. He wiped her eyes dry. "I'm sorry you had to see it, El."

"But maybe, for me, it was better than imagining it."

Arkyn asked softly, "Do you want to talk?"

"Aunt Amara's been listening, and she actually has a soft side. So's Cal. He didn't know what to do when it happened but he was so kind. He didn't want to leave but you had to be told. I only took the sedative so he'd go to you."

"Thank you, little flower," whispered Arkyn, oddly aware that she hadn't sat with him, but had stayed with Tain.

Blinking back tears, she took a deep breath. "Father's told me you're organising a house for me in the Administrative Quarter. Must you?"

154

Arkyn said, "It was that or Black Hills, El. I'm sorry."

"But I still won't see you…"

"You will," stated Tain. "We'll make complete and utter nuisances of ourselves; you will welcome the peace and quiet."

"Will I go to the funeral? Father said, as he wasn't to go, I wouldn't but I didn't believe that."

Arkyn actually swore. "Yes! What did Aunt Amara say?"

"She told him to leave before he got a dose of her mind. Can she come and live with me?"

Arkyn chuckled. "Tempting but I think she's going to be making sure Tain and I are behaving ourselves."

"That's probably needed more. When will I move? Will Maria come with me?"

Arkyn glanced at Tain. "Let's see how long we can drag it out for, shall we? I reckon it should be a couple of aluna-months at least."

Elantha swapped seats, snuggled into his shoulder and started sucking her thumb. "Good."

He slipped his arm around her. She was bonier than she had been. A growth spurt he'd not noticed before. He caught Tain's eye. There was something in his brother's gaze that spoke of pain and regret but also understanding and concern.

After a couple of moments, to the surprise of the brothers, Elantha said, "Arkyn, can you speech-bind me?" as though it was a normal part of the conversation.

Arkyn sat her up and took her shoulders. "Why on Erinna would I want to do that, El? You're my cousin not an official or lord."

She shrugged. "Because I know about Cal being able to shift, and I'm scared of father. He'll make me reveal things and I don't want to."

Tain said, "That's a good point."

"I'm not doing it!" exclaimed Arkyn, numb with shock.

Elantha took his hand. "Please, Arkyn. I know what I'm asking. Truly I do. I found all Tain's notes one day. You know it's right—"

"You *read* my notes?" interrupted Tain.

"Yes. Well, those not in shorthand, and some of your textbooks. My governess said I had to broaden my mind."

"More than I ever did."

Absentmindedly, Arkyn muttered, "Children, behave." He studied Elantha's pleading face, then glanced at Tain. "Honestly, what do you think?"

Tain pulled a face. "You'll regret it if you don't. El's willing, she knows the risks with it but more importantly she knows what will happen if she's *not* speech-bound. I'd say it's a very adult decision to take but one she obviously wants to. Isn't that about right, El?"

Elantha nodded, knelt by Arkyn and took his hands. "Please, Arkyn."

Arkyn couldn't take his eyes off her. Eleven years old, blonde hair tied up neatly, soft blue eyes inherited from her mother, fragile, showing signs of growing into a beautiful young lady, who shouldn't even know about speech-bindings let alone be asking for one and accepting the consequences. She was making a decision men three times her age would never contemplate, but maybe that was the point. In her innocence she had surety and certainty of purpose. More importantly no-one would contemplate that she was bound. Tain didn't think it was a bad idea. He'd never have suggested it. Neither of them would have done, but Elantha had. She'd thought far enough ahead to see a danger they'd been blind to, and was brave enough to recognise its costs.

Closing his eyes momentarily, he stood. Taking her hands, he spoke the words of the speech-binding fealty automatically, but he thought about Tain's idea on how specific the bindings could be and decided that Elantha's would be different. He amended it so that only the clause of not repeating anything that he wouldn't want repeating was included. He didn't mind if she annoyed him with what she said, and it wasn't fair to the girl to stop her doing so.

At the end Elantha said, "I wouldn't have minded, Arkyn."

He wrapped her in a hug. "But I would, little flower. I would. Will you come and dine with us this evening? Me and Tain."

"Of course. I should let you get on. You're both busy annoying people. That is, annoying other people—"

Tain threw an arm around her shoulders. "Let me guess, that's how Cal described it?"

"Well, actually, it was Aunt Amara, but he seemed to agree."

"I bet he did," said Arkyn. "Has he told you of his arrest yet?"

She became intrigued. "No. I'll ask him."

"Good idea. Sire, do you need me for the moment?" enquired Tain.

Arkyn eyed him. "You want to rub it in, don't you?"

Tain shook his head. "Actually, I was thinking I might need to go to the Courthouse and you might need to organise a few things without me."

Arkyn swallowed. "All right. I'll see you later."

After Arkyn had given Elantha another hug, Tain said quietly, "It's just an office, Arkyn, and Edward is still your administrator."

Arkyn clapped him on the back. "Thank you. Go and cause trouble elsewhere."

* * *

Once they'd gone, Arkyn sank into a chair and put his head in his hands.

Edward didn't enter and, for those brief moments, Arkyn was relieved. He needed this moment of readjustment alone, needed to come to terms with the horrifying fact fate had caught up with him and the future had arrived in one blinding, stupefying blow. This was the first moment he'd had to consider what came next, as well as everything that had happened over the last two days. He'd been in Amphi to undertake a provincial review, that would have to be rearranged. Then there was the poisoning he, Tain and ReJean had narrowly avoided. Taken with the assassination it sent a chill through him. The journey and events of the previous evening hardly figured in his thoughts. For the moment, they were dealt with. He needed to see Paturn and Wynfeld, start looking at the wider situation but for the moment, he needed to see if his instinct was right. He rang for Edward, who entered with pure professionalism but an edge of concern which couldn't be hidden.

Arkyn never hesitated. "Before the mayhem continues, I want to know how many people had their lives attacked on Munewid Eve. Mine and Prince Tain's were, Lord Landis was, father… I expect there were others. Initially keep your enquiries discreet and concentrate on those people close to my family."

Edward nodded. "I understand, sir. What about the Governors?"

"ReJean was attacked at the same time as myself and Tain. Check with Wealsman and Galwood first – they're the closest. Check with Wynfeld and Paturn, not for intelligence but to see if they were targeted. Also, send in Hillbeck please."

Chapter 37
HILLBECK AND KILBRIDE
12:42
Inner Office

SERGEANT HILLBECK'S record was not unimpressive. Having saved King Adeone's life in 1209, he'd served in the King's Guard since and been the senior officer of it since 1212. He'd developed an efficient relationship with King Adeone, formed from mutual respect. He didn't fool himself though as he waited for a summons from King Arkyn. He and his men had failed. Their job was to protect the King. He wasn't expecting King Arkyn to be forgiving. He'd sent his nephew to Amphi to inform the new King of events knowing that, without Lord Landis, no-one would consider it for some time. He received the summons, took a deep breath and entered the Inner Office, saluting smartly.

Arkyn nodded in acknowledgement, seeing the uncertainty in the sergeant's eyes. "Hillbeck, I'm not replacing you as head of my guards. I am however going to have to dismiss Kilbride and I know that will cause you problems."

Hillbeck visibly relaxed. "We'll cope, sir. It's not unexpected."

Arkyn raised an eyebrow. "Are my actions so predictable?"

"No, Sire. Most thought I'd be gone as well and several of the guards who were on duty expected to be under arrest – at best dismissed, at worst they expect to lose their lives."

"In a different time, and situation, they might well have done so."

Hillbeck frowned. "Sire, what could be worse than the assassination of King Adeone whilst they were on duty, charged with protecting him?"

Arkyn took a breath. "My father not expecting it. If that had been the case, you'd all be facing disciplinaries. I am not such that I can blame you when my father didn't inform you he knew there was to be an attack. As it transpires, you couldn't have done anything as the assassin was in the Viewing Gallery."

Hillbeck paled. "His Majesty *knew*… Sorry, Sire, I meant—"

"I know what you meant. Just don't make such a mistake publicly or after the coronation. I'd rather not be accused of knowing my father was to die." He ignored Hillbeck's attempt to apologise, instead saying, "As you're valley-born, I'd like you to accompany me whenever I return there." If that didn't let the sergeant know he was still trusted, nothing would.

Hillbeck smiled sadly. "Of course, sir. You're missed when you're away from home."

Arkyn merely nodded in thanks. "When Kilbride comes on duty, warn him privately if you wish, but don't let anyone else know."

"Right, Sire. Thank you." He saluted and was gone before Arkyn could draw another breath.

Chapter 38
DETAILS
12:48

Inner Office

ARKYN CALLED for Edward once more and moved to one of the other tables in the room. He could only stand so much of fate. He nodded for his administrator to take a seat.

"I suppose there are a hundred odd arrangements to make, none of which I even wish to contemplate but that I have to. Firstly, my father's…"

he took a deep breath, "…funeral. That will have to be soon. I suggest Imperadai. Tell the Steward and set up a meeting to arrange details today. Secondly, my coronation. That will have to be next Imperadai. It can't be left any longer. I come of age then and coronations are normally Imperadai. Things will need to be set in motion for that. City officials and military officers. Who's Ealdorman?"

"Lord Landis, Sire."

Arkyn swore. "That makes it interesting. Do we know how he is?"

"Doctor Chapa mentioned that he shouldn't be attending any meetings, sir. I think he said something along the lines of 'if he knows what's good for him', in a resigned sort of voice."

That was believable. Arkyn considered. "I can't ask him here, I'm not brave enough to stand Chapa's remonstrations or Lady Landis' concern. I can't even use the next or the last Ealdorman for this, or any of the other six lords involved with my father's assassination. Who's left?"

Edward realising the King's mind was befuddled said, "Lords Fairson, Iris, Ryson and Rale – although he's still underage."

Arkyn took a breath. "It had better be either Lord Iris or Lord Fairson. Of the two I'd say Iris would be better but I can understand if he wishes to be excused."

Edward said, "Forgive me, sir, but he's not likely to consider that he could be excused."

Arkyn made a non-committal jerk of his head. "I'll speak to him today, and soon, please. I'll also contact Landis by messenger. I'm not having him strain himself unnecessarily. I'll tell whichever lord takes over until Landis is well to liaise with him but he's not to get up."

Edward smiled. "Good luck, Sire."

Arkyn tried to return the smile. "Are you trying to say that he won't listen to his liege's request?"

"Yes, Sire. I am."

Arkyn caught his eye. "You might have a valid point. All right, Edward, draw up a preliminary timing for today, please, and start collecting people together."

* * *

Left alone, and in temporary limbo, Arkyn got up. There were no documents on the desk, everything had been cleared. That meant there was no distraction in the room. He walked over to the bedchamber door and hesitated, a hand on the handle. Taking a breath, he entered. His father looked like he merely slept but there was no hue of life, no animation. Crossing to the bed, Arkyn knelt by it, emotions battling within him. In the depths of his mind feelings of betrayal niggled. His father shouldn't have left them, shouldn't have considered that it was right to face his death. Then, almost as though it had been whispered in his ear, he heard a voice saying,

'Maybe you don't know the whole story.'

Arkyn turned, but he was alone in the room.

He sighed and pushed himself to his feet. He watched his father's face for a couple of seconds before bowing slightly, as though he was still alive, and leaving. As he pulled the door to, he turned to find Lord Iris waiting patiently. As soon as he saw Arkyn had noticed him, he knelt and stayed with bowed head. Iris was one lord Arkyn knew he could trust to keep a confidence. Friend of his grandfather's, trusted by his father, he had been at the right hand of kings for almost half a century. His father had granted Iris the title of King's Counsellor, a post that had been empty for around a century. Arkyn asked him to rise in a level voice.

Iris rose but the look he gave Arkyn was concerned. "Sire."

Arkyn smiled sadly. "I am finding it difficult to adjust, my lord."

"That is hardly surprising. Most men find it difficult when their parents pass on; to lose your father to such violence doesn't make the transition easier, Sire, quite the opposite."

"I should be more focused though."

"Sir, you and your father were close; I know that as do many others. If you didn't feel everything I assume you're feeling, it would be extraordinary. Take your time and come to terms with it as you can."

Arkyn moved behind his desk. "Thank you, my lord." It was all he could think of to say.

"You may call on my support whenever you need it, sir."

Arkyn's lips twitched. "How fortunate. Lord Iris, you obviously realise that Landis is incapacitated. He's under orders to rest for a few days – and they are Chapa's orders, so I daren't even try to disobey them."

Iris chuckled. "Understandable, Sire."

"Thank you. The problem is my coronation. It will have to be next Imperadai; as Ealdorman, Landis obviously has a myriad of duties to perform. If you wish to do so, will you undertake some of those duties? Liaising with His Lordship, obviously."

Iris said carefully, "Sire, I am more than willing to help but it would be wrong for me to take over from my nephew."

"I completely agree. I hope my nearfather will be well enough on my coronation day to play his part but until then he *must* rest. A crossbow bolt shuddered into his shoulder; it's surprising he's not maimed more. You saw how white he was last night. He physically can't do anything. Mentally – well there's been questions about that for years."

Iris smiled. "I understand, sir. I hope he does."

Arkyn nodded. "He will. Keep him fully informed of what's happening. Bring a secretary with you, if you want to, to transcribe the whole of the meetings so he can read a full account if he wishes. I just need a Lord of Oedran I can trust in his place and I can think of none better than you. I trust Lord Fairson but he hasn't the experience you've got, and Lord Rale is far too young."

"What of Ryson, sir?"

Arkyn said, "He's a lawyer. I'll leave his help for Prince Tain. Will you do this, Iris, or shall I ask Lord Fairson?"

Iris nodded. "I'll do it, sir. I shall go and inform Lord Landis."

"I'll also contact him and Lady Landis. I'd go in person but—"

"Your place is here, sir. The Landis family will understand that."

Arkyn relaxed. "Thank you. Edward will let you know what meetings are planned."

Iris bowed and left without another word. He said to Edward, "I've accepted the King's proposition, Administrator. If you could forward details of the meetings I'm required at to my secretary I'd be grateful." More quietly he continued, "Keep checking on the King."

* * *

Arkyn called up Fafnir, asking for a link with Landis. When the link formed Landis was still pale.

"Uncle Festus, how are you?"

"I'm fine, Sire," replied Landis, unconvincingly. "What can I do for my King?"

Tears sprang in Arkyn's eyes. "I…" He took a breath and pulled himself together. "You're under Chapa's orders to take things easily, aren't you?"

Landis drew a breath. "Never have listened to him, sir."

"You have to now – if only for a few days."

"Sire, the next couple of weeks I should be doing more than the last couple of years—"

"Landis, stop. Concentrate on getting yourself better."

"Does that mean I don't need Chapa, sir?"

"Unfortunately, for you, you do need him."

"What of my responsibilities, Sire?"

"Iris will be in the meetings for you but he'll be reporting everything to you for you to agree or not."

"It could make things long-winded, sir," pointed out Landis dully.

Arkyn said, "You're not being cut out of the planning, Landis. Get used to the idea."

"Right."

Strains were appearing on his nearfather's face. Arkyn softened his tone, "Father's funeral is set for Imperadai."

"Will I be allowed to attend, Sire?"

"Of course you will be! I don't care if you have to be carried there on a stretcher. We're *not* saying goodbye to father without you there. I'd rather postpone than that. I'm just glad it's not your funeral as well!"

Landis half-whispered, "Right, sir. Thank you."

Arkyn studied him. "Get some sleep, Uncle Festus. You need it."

Before his nearfather could reply he'd nodded to Fafnir to close the link. Once faced with his office he recalled Fafnir and got a link with Lady Landis.

"How is he, Aunt Cornelia?"

"Bad. He keeps trying to get up."

"Don't let him, he looks atrocious. Is Chapa still with you?"

"Yes, sir. I've given him a room, if that's not inconvenient for you."

"Of course it's not. It saves me from his remonstrations. I know it's a losing battle, Aunt Cornelia, but try to stop Uncle Festus from fretting. I've asked Iris to liaise with him about the preparations for the funeral and coronation."

"He feels responsible, Arkyn."

"He's not! Uncle Scanlon is. He has to recover. I can't lose him as well, not now."

Lady Landis said, "I'll do my best, sir. I can't promise he'll be sensible but I'll do my best."

Arkyn nodded. "Thank you. Father's funeral is set for Imperadai; my coronation is to be on my birthday. I would like him at both."

"Then he better be good. Now, Sire…"

Arkyn smiled wanly. "Don't worry, Aunt Cornelia, Kadeem and Edward are taking care of me."

"I never truly doubted it, sir, but you need to take care of yourself as well. Would you like Julius around for any duties?"

"I hadn't considered it. I'll let him know if I need him. Thank you, Aunt Cornelia. Really, thank you."

Chapter 39

ATTACKS

EXITING FROM the link with Lady Landis, Arkyn found he was looking straight at Edward and Kadeem.

"You decide who goes first."

Edward deferred to Kadeem.

"Lunch is laid out in the triniculum, sir."

Arkyn sighed. "Bring me a plate of something out here. I'll eat whilst Edward gives his report."

"Is it wise to set such a precedent, sir?" asked Kadeem.

"It's hardly a precedent, I've done it before. Just do your job!"

When Kadeem bowed and left, Arkyn eyed an unnerved Edward. "What did you need to see me about?"

Edward hesitated, almost as though he was going to say it could wait. Registering the King's mood though, he said, "I have the reports about attacks, sir. General Paturn wasn't aware of any direct attack but he did change his plans for the evening at short notice. Major Wynfeld was attacked by an assailant whom he disarmed, and who is now enjoying the army's hospitality. The Margrave mentioned his guard caught a man who'd taken a shot at him, and again the man is enjoying the army's hospitality. The Exarch had a fire in the Citadel and, if he hadn't left his rooms early, he would have certainly been there changing for their banquet."

"None of them thought to mention it to anyone in my office? Or even me – come to that – when I spoke to some of them."

"They have all mentioned that by comparison the matters were trifling and not worthy of notice."

"They were their exact words, were they?" asked Arkyn shrewdly.

"That was the gist, sir, of every reason."

"See they all get my thanks and tell them I'll talk to them when I get the chance." He paused as his manservant put down a plate of bread, cheese, ham and apple slices in front of him along with a goblet of water. "Thank you, Kadeem, and my apologies. Edward, what's the first meeting?"

Kadeem bowed and left as Edward said,

"One with the Moonshi about funeral arrangements, sir. After that's concluded, he'll take over aspects of the organisation, if you delegate any to him, and it can be proclaimed ..." Edward carried on for several moments before concluding, "By which time, Sire, the evening will have arrived. Will you be dining with Prince Tain?"

"Yes, and Lady Elantha."

"Very good, sir. I'll let Master Robert and Maria know. The other thing I'll need to know for this evening is whether you plan to be at Court. If you do the Steward will obviously need to make preparations."

Arkyn took the goblet in his hand. Kadeem hadn't given him a glass, which could break; that said everything about his understanding of Arkyn's mood. "I don't think I can face that as well, Edward."

"Very good, sir. I'll not be arranging any evening meetings, Sire."

"Time is short."

"If you insist, I can utilise the time, sir, but I thought the last two days have been stressful and an evening of peace might be more beneficial."

"You mean I need to have an early night?"

Edward smiled. "I'm less practised than Kadeem is, sir."

"Maybe. What time is the meeting with the Moonshi?"

"As soon as you are ready. His Benevolence had arrived in the Palace before I could ask him to attend, Sire."

Arkyn nodded. "Give me twelve minutes, Edward. I'll finish my lunch and then see him."

Edward bowed and left.

Arkyn finished his lunch, moved the plate and goblet to the sideboard then rang for Kadeem.

When the manservant entered, he knelt.

"Get up! I'll be far angrier than I was earlier if you don't."

Kadeem rose. "I'm sorry, Sire, I overstepped the bounds."

"Concern can manifest itself in many ways. I'm sorry for my reaction."

"There's no need to apologise, sir."

Arkyn raised an eyebrow. "Let Edward know I'll see the Moonshi."

Chapter 40
IRIS, CHAPA AND LANDIS
13:30
Oedran – Landis Lordship – Landis House

LORD IRIS LEFT the Palace in a sombre frame of mind. His new King had shown resilience but, having worked with him during trying times before, Iris had never doubted he would. He made his way to Landis House and confidently walked through the doors without announcing his presence. He had been welcome here without question since his sister had married Landis' father. He wasn't, however, unnoticed, and a footman walked over to take his cloak.

"I'm here to see my nephew, Backery."

The footman smiled – the manner of greeting saying far more than anything else. "Doctor Chapa is currently with His Lordship, my lord."

"Then I'll not get in his way. Maybe you could let Lady Landis know I'm here."

Before the footman could reply, a gentle voice said,

"Good morning, uncle."

Iris turned. "Morning, Cornelia."

"Come through. I'm glad you're here. It might stop him fretting."

Iris nodded. "How is he?"

As they entered the drawing room, Cornelia said simply, "He watched his closest friend murdered and nearly died himself: not too good."

"Stupid question, I agree."

"Not really. I just feel useless."

"You're never that. He'd be lost without you."

She looked surprised. "Uncle Iris?"

"I don't normally say such things, but that doesn't mean I don't observe them. I'm your nearfather. I know you better than you might think."

She sagged. "Of course. What else have you observed?"

He eyed her. "You need to stop worrying about everyone, if only for a few hours, lass. Doctor Chapa's seeing to Festus. King Arkyn and Prince Tain are keeping busy, and King Adeone, may the moons bless him, has been laid out. Take a couple of hours for yourself."

"What of Lady Elantha?"

"I admit I do not know, but I expect she is well-tended."

Cornelia said, "She shouldn't be alone. I'll see about having her here for a few nights."

"If you wish, I'll mention it to the King but I think with Festus injured it might be better to be without the disruption."

"I should see if—"

Entering the drawing room, Chapa placed his bag on the table. "He's sleeping, Lady Landis – probably not for long but he's quiet at least – it makes a change. Morning, Lord Iris. I'm afraid you can't see His Lordship yet – well, you could *see* him but getting coherent sense out of him might be harder than usual."

"I do need to talk to him on the King's business, Alair," replied Iris.

"I'm sure they know how to make my life harder. Very well. When he wakens, you may have six minutes with him. No more."

"Thank you."

Lady Landis said, "I'll send for some refreshments…"

Doctor Chapa's gaze missed nothing. "For two, my lady."

"Please join us, doc."

He smiled. "I was planning on staying, to make sure that Lord Iris behaves himself. I was going to suggest you go for a lie down."

To his surprise she snapped, "Not you as well! I have a house to run, a sick husband, six children to care for, two nearchildren to worry about, a niece to be concerned over and a nephew who is noticeable by his silence, not to mention my husband's nephew who's due back from the Low Plains imminently with their ambassador. I'll rest when I can!"

Iris looked at Chapa and metaphorically ducked. The doctor was in a determined mood to match Lady Landis'.

"My lady, you have a steward and a housekeeper, your children will respect your need for solitude and are comfort enough for each other. Let me worry about the FitzAlcis, I've plenty of practice. Lord Rale, I'm sure, can ask his peers for advice, and Lord Emrys isn't here yet and won't be until tomorrow at the earliest. You will please go and lie down for a couple of hours – doctor's orders. Go on, shoo."

"Doctor Chapa, imagine what my husband and nearsons would say if they heard you ordering me about like that."

Chapa snorted. "Forgive me, my lady, but I think they might say I was right – then give me a roasting for my expressive statements." He walked over and took her hands. "You care deeply, Cornelia, more than most know. You must grieve also before you do yourself harm. Festus is asleep, he'll never know. Please…"

She looked into his kindly piercing eyes. "Have you?"

"Grieved? Not yet. Festus is keeping me busy."

"He's usually to blame. Have you a—"

He whispered, "I'll come and see you settled. Lord Iris, I shan't be long."

* * *

When Chapa returned, Iris said, "How do you get away with your audacity, Alair? I've never worked it out."

The doctor smiled ruefully, "I don't give people chance to think, I suppose. 'Twas ever so."

"I remember. How *are* you?" He received a piercing look.

"Furious, if truth is to be known, and very, very sad."

"King Adeone meant much to you," said Lord Iris simply stating fact.

"Yes. My cousins all do. We Chapas are made that way."

Iris nodded. "As I have observed many times. King Arkyn acknowledges the kinship?"

"Yes, I am fortunate in that, but he is not so close. Adeone was Eliza's eldest and caught my heart from the moment he was born. I will never

166

forgive Lord Scanlon his schemes."

"The proof is lacking."

"*Proof!* Proof is for lawyers and the courts. I have only my heart and head – which, as King Altarius was wont to point out, gets me into trouble."

Iris chuckled. "Aye, I suppose it does. I wonder what his reaction to this would be."

"You would have more idea than I do. You were his friend; I was merely his doctor."

"No, Alair, you were closer than that."

Doctor Chapa murmured, "Maybe at the end but not when younger."

"Youth is often a barrier, or at least a difference in age is."

"Yes. Talking of barriers are you free now?"

Lord Iris eyed him. "Of what?"

"In his final days King Altarius told me some things he normally never talked about. I think he needed to ease his mind. The revelations were nothing about his family affairs, he never told me those, but amongst the recollections of his youth he mentioned a mistake he'd made. He'd speech-bound a close and valued friend in his rage at that friend daring to question Lord Dunius' execution—"

"Did he name his 'friend'?" asked Iris.

"No, but it wasn't difficult to deduce for it certainly wasn't Lord Ewart; Lady Amara's reaction would have been known. King Altarius had few he named as friends, Ignatius, especially ones close enough to question his decisions in 1169 and still live."

"Whom did you tell?"

"No-one. King Altarius' confidences were just that. I simply hope that you're now free."

Lord Iris said, "I've been as free as I can wish since 1211. King Arkyn inadvertently broke some of the binding. He told me he wanted to hear my opinions whether good or bad, and King Adeone had instructed me to follow his wishes as though they were the King's."

"Ah. I thought it had to be a king who broke a binding made by one."

"I said I was as free as I could wish. I am still speech-bound. It is safer for everyone, especially now."

"Maybe."

"It is. I was a Chief Advisor, a Deputy Chief Advisor and now I am King's Counsellor. In the binding is security. I cannot, even if I wished it, reveal anything confidential."

"I see your point, my lord." Doctor Chapa poured himself another drink. "Do you ever find life lonely with the friends of our youth gone?"

"Not lonely but maybe there is a level of understanding missing. King

Altarius knew me as a young man, King Adeone as a middle-aged one and King Arkyn as an old or elderly man. They all see my advice differently. King Arkyn would never speech-bind me for a mistake, not because his principles are so different but because I pose no threat as an old man. Young are threatened by youth not age."

"Very true."

"Yes. I see young friendships and youthful bonds and know that, a couple of generations on, the future young will not understand those bonds as we are in turn misunderstood by the current young generation."

Doctor Chapa said simply, "Every manner of thing has its cycle."

"And in its turn its revolution."

"That is one thing we must avoid."

Iris nodded. "Most certainly. The six lords, who signed the Assassination Document, have been exiled, Alair. It's all that could be done, but it doesn't mean it's over..." There was a knock at the door, and Lord Iris answered it mildly. "Yes, William?"

"Lord Landis is asking for the doc, my lord."

Chapa got to his feet, picked up his bag. "I'd hardly taken a drink. Can't you make him behave, William?"

Iris said, "I'm coming as well, and don't blame William, you're the one who's meant to be making Festus sensible."

"My lord, I don't think—"

"So a lot of people have noticed, Alair," quipped Iris.

* * *

Carefully wedged so that no weight was primarily on his wound, Landis looked up as Doctor Chapa entered and then saw Lord Iris.

"Uncle?"

"I can wait, Festus."

Landis rolled his eyes. "That's a shame. Doc, where's Cornelia? William was being evasive."

"Resting. My orders. Is that all you dragged me out of my comfortable seat for?"

"Good and no. This dressing is feeling odd."

"Sit forward, my lord. Could you steady him, please, Lord Iris?" Dressing seen to, the doctor said, "Six minutes, Lord Iris," and left.

"He's very acidic at the moment," observed Iris once they were alone.

"He's very upset," said Landis numbly.

"We all are. Now, I've got to tell you..."

A few minutes later Landis said, "What about the funeral?"

"They're drawing up the order now. Someone's going to have to write the homage for the FitzAlcis.”

“No!” Landis was vehement. “No. They cannot be put through that. Let others do the homage.”

“Who?”

“I’ll think. I would, but I know Chapa won’t let me. King Arkyn and Prince Tain *mustn’t* feel that they have to do it. They have faced so much.”

“Tradition—”

“Can be changed! Their father was murdered. Who would be in a rational frame of mind?”

“Not all the traditions of the world can be changed, Festus.”

“No, but King Arkyn and Prince Tain mustn’t be distressed further.”

“Is it right to question their ability to cope?”

“No, but look behind their eyes. It would not do for them to break down at the funeral. Be watchful of Prince Tain. He will convince you that he is coping, but he has lost James Tancred also—”

“Were they that close? I had heard rumours.”

Landis nodded. “Yes. James was… well, yes, they were that close. Prince Tain inherited Tancred’s library, and it’s an inheritance which hasn’t been boxed up until he’s twenty. It’s in the tower at Ceardlann.”

“I understand. I shall be watchful of his care. Festus, tell me truthfully, will you recover from this wound?”

“If no infection sets in, yes. My left arm will be weakened for life but at least I live. I must face the King soon. I failed to defend Adeone—”

Iris said, “You did all you could.”

“It wasn’t enough! There are things I must explain to the King, when he has time. I must also tender my resignation as Defender and Chief Advisor. Rayburn should do well enough in the latter post now.”

Iris sighed. “Don’t be daft. It’s at times like this I glimpse your mother in you. King Arkyn is unlikely to accept either. Get well and when you’re in a more rational frame of mind give it due consideration. I shall advise the King as best I can in your absence but I cannot advise that traditions can be changed.”

Landis smiled wanly. “That is my line anyway. I’m not sure how long I’ll be incapacitated for. Do you mind the extra duties?”

“Not at all. Is Chapa looking after you or bullying you?”

“Both more than I deserve. Someone ought to keep an eye on him.”

“I’m sure they will. He’s partial to a drink and a spot of reminiscing.”

Landis nodded. “I’d noticed.”

“It will do you both good.” Iris talked for a time about everything but recent events as Landis simply listened numbly. Eventually, Iris said, “I’ve got to get back to the Palace. Is there any message?”

Landis closed his eyes. "My love, loyalty and care to my nearsons." He opened his eyes. "Make sure that they're alone when you deliver it."

Iris smiled. "I shall." He pointedly closed the curtains and left.

Outside the room, Doctor Chapa said, "That was only eighteen minutes, Lord Iris. Congratulations."

"I'll go back and have another go if I surprised you, Alair."

Chapter 41
MOONSHI
Mid-morning
Oedran – City Alcium

THE MOONSHI HADN'T been at the Munewid feast; he'd heard the news when his deputy handed him the proclamation. They had exchanged no words for a full minute before the Moonshi had said in a voice deadened by sorrow,

"Start preparing for the funeral. I will attend on the King."

He glanced at the timepiece on his desk. Was the King even in Oedran? He had been in Amphi at the Munewid. He ran down a mental checklist of people to ask. Called up his messenger and contacted Richardson. The administrator looked strained but informed him the King was in Oedran and would have matters to deal with until the early part of the afternoon.

Once the link broke, the Moonshi pushed himself to his feet. They had much to do to prepare the City Alcium for the funeral. They'd need to know when the King wanted to hold it, and send out of Oedran for the wood they had in storage for the pyre. That could be brought to Oedran in small amounts over days. There was no reason to highlight its arrival. They would have to move the King's Lull into position in the centre of the alcium. Its marble simplicity would hold the King's bier during the funeral ceremony before Adeone started his last journey to join his ancestors.

He opened a drawer and took out a key, weighing it in his hand. The candles would need to be lit. Trying to keep calm, he drew out a long heavy package. The wax candles inside would burn for a day. They would need replacing daily until the funeral.

He made his way to the main alcium and told two of the alcia talking quietly in huddles to get the Great Stand. They hurried away. When they returned, he motioned to the centre of the circle. It could be moved later, but for now, one candle would burn there, day and night. A focal point for the empire's grief. At every alcium a candle would burn for King Adeone's memory.

Once the candle had been lit, he left the alcium and its whispers. Making his way to the King's Alcium he unlocked the door. He found the King's Stand and placed the candle on its spike atop the intricate gilded pole. Here were motifs of empire, of conquest and of nature. He moved its heavy weight to the centre of the room and lit the candle from another, then snuffed out the smaller. He sat crossed legged at the side of the room, emptying his mind of all but the light, then allowed it to fill with memories of Adeone. The boy he'd seen, the adolescent, his marriage, the blessings of his children, the funerals for King Altarius and Prince Lachlan, the tearing grief at the passing of Princess Ella and Queen Ira, all the memories crowded into his mind, and he sent them to the heavens with the light of the candle, tears starting in his eyes.

He got to his feet and bowed in the direction of the flame. He left the room as though someone slept there, locking the door behind him. King Arkyn had the only other key. There would be peace for the candle to burn and no draughts to disturb its flame.

After lunch, he changed his robes. The full-length garment of white edged with silver was too informal for this moment. It might do within the confines of the City Alcium, but it wasn't just the King he was attending on. It was the new Guardian of the Heavens as well. He asked one of the alcia to sort out his coach. It wasn't the day to walk through the streets.

He shrugged the loose-fitting silvery robes on over a linen tunic. They shimmered even in the dim room. He reached for a belt and changed his mind twice on which to pick. Carefully he unlocked a drawer and took out the formal sash for his robes. Goldwork weaved a tendril like pattern between stars on a silver cloth that kept its shape. The gold buckle set with diamonds, moonstones and white opals complimented and contrasted the belt and robes. Opulence was in every thread. He examined the folds and flow of the robes in the mirror. Satisfied there was no bunching, he reached for his cloak. His hand went for his official one, silver with silver embroidery and gold highlights. He pulled his hand back, looking at the collection and took out his black cloak. Dark as night with only a badge of office stitched into its silk. The twelve-pointed star on a night sky stood out clearly but not so much as to offend anyone. He reached for a leather scrip with pencils and paper inside. There was no knowing if he'd need it. He expected the King would send for him, but there were many reasons why a young man so suddenly bereaved might need to talk.

* * *

He reached the Palace questioning his choice of outfit. He didn't know King Arkyn well, but he had heard rumours that the new King was particular about appropriate dress. Should he have chosen black robes? He cursed

171

himself. He probably should. The King was in mourning, the Palace was in mourning, the empire was. He had chosen the wrong thing. He couldn't get this meeting wrong. His continuation as Moonshi was solely at the King's wishes. He had the coach return to the City Alcium. There were times for the opulence of position but today wasn't one of them.

He changed more quickly than he'd dressed. The black and silver shot silk robes appeared a dull silvery grey. Far more appropriate for mourning. He changed his sash for the black silk one chased with silver, and the buckle for one of silver with jet and black opals. It was much more appropriate. It was his formal mourning wear, after all.

* * *

The second time he entered the stables, he alighted as though it was the first. His gaze swept around the yard. It felt no different to normal, as though nothing had changed. He supposed for the men there, it hadn't. They still had the same horses to tend, the same routines to follow. Walking at a measured pace, he made his way to the Outer Office. He'd inform Richardson... no, Edward, that he was in the building and then find somewhere to wait. If the Court was open, he'd go there. If not, there was Upper Hall. He didn't fancy standing for hours in the Audience Chamber. After a short conversation with Edward, he decided that waiting in the Audience Chamber was best. The administrator was right. He shouldn't attend Court before knowing the King's wishes and he was too late to lunch in Upper Hall, so it would be very strange for him to be there. What he heard about expected plans made him worried. There was too much to do. He called his griffin messenger and told his deputy to be ready to meet him on his return.

He watched Lord Iris enter and leave. The elderly Lord of Oedran seemed bowed down by the weight of events. Too late the Moonshi realised he didn't know enough detail about King Adeone's passing. He re-entered the Outer Office and asked Richardson. What he heard made his blood boil and his throat close. Richardson passed him a glass of water, which showed an understanding beyond words.

* * *

It was around half past one when Edward informed him the King would see him. He entered the Inner Office and knelt, his robes draping elegantly around him. With the King's word, he rose.

"The condolences of all the ancestors' guardians are with you, Sire, in this most trying of times."

The King managed a wan smile. "Thank you, it is much appreciated, Your Benevolence. Now, we have several formalities to conclude in this meeting. Firstly, do you wish to continue as Moonshi?"

172

"If my King wishes me to." How was the young man so calm after everything he'd faced over the last two days?

"I do. Please take a seat. My father's funeral—"

"Administrator Edward mentioned Imperadai is under consideration."

"Yes. Does that pose any problems for you?"

"Not for the City Alcium, Sire, but two days is a relatively short time to organise it," replied the Moonshi arranging his flowing robes. He shouldn't have interrupted, the King's face said as much.

"It seemed appropriate. I'd also be surprised if certain matters, such as the guest list, haven't already been prepared."

"I think someone has been slack if it hasn't been, sir. Will there be ambassadors here from the most distant provinces by then?" enquired the Moonshi. Was he trying to get more time? He didn't know himself.

"I doubt it. Waiting for them could put it back to Alunadai and that would mean my father's body has been left for over a week... I would rather he was at peace before that." The King put the pen he was in danger of breaking back in its rest.

"I tend to agree, sir. Would nightfall on Imperadai be acceptable?" There wasn't much else the Moonshi could say. The King's feelings were plain, his distress although contained was revealing itself. If they had to work more quickly than expected, then they would work more quickly.

"Yes. Obviously, the funeral will be held at the City Alcium. Can you get the items you need for it in time?"

"Yes, sir. Some are already in storage and have been for some time." He saw the King's face. "It's standard practice, Sire, no morbid premonition."

"Obviously, I'd like to send my father to our ancestors with due regard to ceremony. I would have liked Lord Landis to help bear his body, but that is not possible. For now, we'll say that the bearers will be those Lords of Oedran who are still here. I will be asking Lord Julius if he will take his father's place. There should be one Landis as part of that procession."

"It would be wrong if there wasn't, sir," said the Moonshi. "Not only because Lord Landis was His Late Majesty's most steadfast friend through all the years, but because King Adeone was nearfather to the Landis children."

"Quite. That makes five bearers, I'll have to find someone else."

"Is there not another close friend of His Late Majesty?" enquired the Moonshi. "Or maybe a relative from Queen Eliza's family?"

"I shall have a think." The King's eyes narrowed. "I do not want anything to go wrong, Moonshi, I hope that's clear. Major Wynfeld will be in touch regarding security."

"Not the King's Guard, sir?"

"They will have plenty of other things on their mind. Now, my father's ashes won't be residing in the City Alcium…"

"Sire?" What was that about? The Moonshi tried to keep a neutral face. The ashes of the FitzAlcis had rested at the City Alcium for centuries.

"In my father's requests was a line to the effect that he wants his ashes taken to Ceardlann. I will be honouring that request as diligently as I will be honouring all the others. I'll inform you of when we'll be taking the ashes to the Rex Dallin in due course."

Troubled, the Moonshi said, "Of course, Sire. May we at least raise a plaque in memory of King Adeone?"

"I'll be extremely displeased if you don't, Your Benevolence. It is his ashes we are transporting not the memory of him. Can you liaise with my office and draw up proceedings?"

The Moonshi rose. "Of course, Sire. Might I add that the King's Alcium is there should you feel need for solitude and contemplation over the coming weeks and months."

"Thank you, but I should hope it's always there, Your Benevolence."

The Moonshi bowed and left, his mind a whirl. Two days to arrange the funeral. He caught Edward's eye.

"Who am I liaising with in the Ealdorman's absence, Administrator?"

"Lord Iris, Your Benevolence. His Lordship will be expecting you to call on him this evening. His secretary will have the details. It would be best to anticipate some changes at late notice. The King requires your personal oversight on all matters. Allow your deputy to take other business for the next fortnight. The coronation will be next Imperadai."

The Moonshi let out a long breath. "Very well, Administrator." He left the Outer Office feeling as though he'd run a mile.

Chapter 42
LORD FARAN
13:66
Inner Office

ONCE THE MOONSHI had gone, taking with him the scent of beeswax, cedar and sandalwood, Arkyn sat back, wrung out and drained of every internal support. He pushed himself to his feet and walked round the office, trying to get his head straight. The exercise failed, so he called up Fafnir and, moments later, was in a link with Lord Faran – another of his father's close friends.

Faran studied the young King's face. "Sire, my condolences. Your father will be sorely missed."

"So I keep hearing but I doubt that many appreciate how much. Faran, was your life attacked the same day or night my father died?"

Faran paused. "How—?"

"Was it?" asked Arkyn more sharply than he intended. Too much rested on the reply, on the tangential evidence.

"Yes, Sire. An arrow was a little too close for comfort when I was out riding. My companions couldn't find anyone in the woods though."

"How close is 'a little too close for comfort', my lord?"

"It tore my tunic sleeve and scratched my arm, Sire."

Arkyn said, "You didn't think anyone here needed to know?"

"Under the circumstances, sir, I thought it was negligible."

"Not coincidental?"

Faran took a breath. "Yes, sir, but I rather hoped I'd overestimated the significance."

Arkyn eyed him. "I don't think so. There were around ten other attacks that night: myself and Prince Tain amongst them. Do you still think the attack on you was negligible?"

Lord Faran whistled. "Maybe not. I'll get my men scouring the woods and alert the army that there are probably bandits in the area again."

"I doubt that the person who shot at you was a bandit but it should keep the fort on their toes. Tell me or my office if anything else occurs, Lord Faran, or if you hear of any other close shaves that night. Do I have your word that you'll do that?"

"Of course, Sire. Might I make enquiries to that end?"

Arkyn momentarily closed his eyes. "Don't let anyone know what information you're after, my lord. I'd rather no false reports were made in mistaken belief of coincidence."

Faran nodded. "I'll be discreet, sir."

"Thank you." Arkyn hesitated before asking, "Who is the Sagamore sending as ambassador?"

Faran gave the name of another Lord of Lufian.

The King again paused. "I thought the Sagamore would have more sense than to send Toral. I won't interfere with his choice but how quickly can you get to Oedran?"

"A couple of days solid travelling on the mail routes with changes."

Arkyn bit his lip. "You might miss the funeral but… Can you come?"

Faran relaxed. "I'll set off as soon as I can, sir."

"Thank you. I'll let you go and pack."

* * *

Arkyn exited from the link more drained than he'd been at the start of it.

A supportive hand guided him to a chair.

"I've spoken to the Margrave, sir…"

Shaking slightly, Arkyn motioned for his administrator to continue.

"He was concerned about you, Sire, as you've no doubt predicted, but he suggested I called up Lord Faran and Lord Camlyn—"

"Faran was attacked," stated Arkyn.

"I'm not surprised, sir. Unfortunately, Lord Camlyn was killed."

Arkyn's hand shook. "How?" It had been too much to hope that everyone would have survived Scanlon's attempt to wipe out Adeone's closest friends and family.

"Poisoned whiskey, sir. Captain Ballard from the fort at Perivale is investigating. He was involved in exonerating Lord Camlyn a couple of years ago. He's aware of the delicate nature of the investigation."

"Good. Tell him I want the murderer caught and not someone hanged for something they didn't do."

Edward nodded. "Of course, sir. There's one thing I should mention…"

Arkyn took a deep breath. "Only one?" When had he stopped shaking?

"Lord Camlyn's requests apparently included a codicil. I'm sorry to say that you're Lady Mellonia's guardian, sir."

Arkyn rubbed at his nose. "Of course. Father mentioned that Lord Camlyn had done that a while ago. Her nearparents…"

"Are named as local guardians in Bayan, sir."

"Tell them I'll be in contact as soon as possible but will respect Camlyn's requests; however, all estate matters will be overseen by me every year."

"That's a lot of work, Sire."

Arkyn sighed. "I meant I'd be sending someone to go over the books. After Lady Daia's experience in Terasia I'm not letting any steward think he has free rein. Who am I seeing next?"

Edward said carefully, "Advisor Rayburn is outside, sir, but I can ask him to come back."

Arkyn shook his head. "No, I'd better see him. I want and need to."

Chapter 43

ADVISOR RAYBURN
14:00
Inner Office

RAYBURN WOKE that morning turning over events of the previous day. Whilst the King and Prince returned from Amphi, he'd had to face the immediate issues within the Palace. He'd woken the morning after the assassination to the news of it, having not attended the feast. Hillbeck had briefed him on what had occurred. Landis was incapacitated and everyone who had been at the feast was getting what rest they could. The King had been informed, or it was assumed he had been informed as messenger communication wasn't working. Rayburn had cursed openly at that. How could they not know if King Arkyn knew he was King? He informed the King's Advisors of events before striding to the Herald's office, where the Herald's Help informed him it had been at the Steward's order. Thanking the secretary, he strode to the Steward's office where Secretary Welard informed him there were standing orders detailing the Palace had to be closed until the Justiciar arrived, but that the Steward was asleep and wouldn't be available for hours. Cursing he wandered to the Outer Office. There was too much that needed to be done. There would be the funeral and coronation. True, King Arkyn was underage but not by much. He wanted, needed to familiarise himself with the protocols for an underage accession. The best person to ask would have been Lady Amara, but there was no way he would disturb her grief. The discussion with Richardson had been tense. Richardson was no longer the King's Administrator and grief was written into his eyes, but not for his post. Rayburn had been surprised to see him. He didn't live in the Palace. Apparently, King Adeone had said there'd be an early start to the day, so he'd slept at the Palace.

They had decided they should put in place a contingency for cancelling the Petitionals, whilst organising the funeral and coronation. They had reckoned on King Arkyn's return being the following day at the earliest. Rayburn had tried to work, tried to concentrate but hadn't succeeded. He'd returned to the Outer Office in the early afternoon to go over more detailed plans. He and Richardson were still talking when Lord Scanlon strutted into the Outer Office as though it was his own, demanded King Adeone's requests and bequests and proceeded to read it, scoffing at some and openly grinning at others. He'd never even enquired where King Adeone was laid out, what had happened or whether King Arkyn had been told. He'd simply ordered that a Lords' Council would take place in an hour and left for his own chambers far too full of glee.

The memory still made Rayburn furious. Act, even if you didn't feel it, *act* for decency's sake. His brother had been murdered. It wasn't something to celebrate. Certainly not so openly. Oh, he'd not said anything about it being something to celebrate, he wasn't that stupid, but his whole manner had said it instead.

They'd managed to delay the Lords' Council with Landis' help, though Rayburn hadn't hung around for it. He'd been summoned by Lady Amara at quarter to nine. Minutes later, Kadeem had informed her that the King was home. She'd told Rayburn to wait. When she later told him what had occurred, he was relieved and slept better than expected. His morning had been a juggle of consulting with Edward and waiting for a summons.

* * *

Rayburn knelt on entering the Inner Office. He glanced unobtrusively at his new King. They'd worked together in different times and so he recognised the King was feeling the strain of the day. He didn't however move.

"Get up, Rayburn. Thank you."

He still didn't move.

"Advisor?"

"Sire, if ever I find out who orphaned you, who pulled the trigger, I shall kill them," replied Rayburn with absolute sincerity. As the King moved towards him, he wondered if he should have kept that opinion to himself.

"Thank you for the sentiment but Prince Tain would arrest you."

The King had bent slightly to help him back to his feet. Rayburn took Arkyn's hand.

"I swear I shall serve my King in whatever capacity I can. May the ancestors bear witness to this my oath." He kissed Arkyn's signet ring. "I am your servant."

"Thank you. Now, if you don't get up, you'll find I'm more than a little annoyed and I've already been tested beyond normal endurance."

Rayburn got to his feet. "What can I do to alleviate that burden, Sire?"

Arkyn looked at him and sighed. "I will presume you know Landis is incapacitated. You're in charge of my advisors until he is fit again."

"You don't wish me to stand aside for Advisor Caple—?"

"If I wished that he'd be here!"

Rayburn inclined his head slightly. "My apologies, sir." He waited for the King to say or do something but nothing happened. "Sir?"

Arkyn started. "Sorry, Rayburn, I was miles away."

"Sometimes it is the best place to be. Can I get you a drink, Sire?"

"Please, and pour yourself one whilst you're at it."

"Thank you, sir. Anything in particular?"

"You decide."

Rayburn noted the forming lethargy and poured two drinks: a whiskey for himself, and a plain glass of water for Arkyn. When he was emotional or tired the King never chose anything alcoholic.

Taking the glass, the King said, "Your memory is good, Rayburn."

"Not particularly, sir. What can I do?"

"We need to look at my advisors: those who made up my staff as a prince and the King's need to be amalgamated, as far as possible. I would like you to remain in post and Lord Landis will still be Chief Advisor."

Rayburn nodded. "Might I make a suggestion, Sire?"

"It's your job."

"True. Don't worry about your advisors until after your coronation… No, sir. I can understand you wish to resolve the situation but there's little time in which to do it justice. Simply let Edward inform Caple and your previous staff that decisions will be made soon. I can talk to Caple and relay that you truly haven't forgotten and that because of Lord Landis' incapacitation I'll be heading the King's Advisors for the meantime."

"He might argue."

"I don't think he will, Sire – not by the time I've finished."

The King smiled wearily. "Don't make enemies over this. Caple will feel pushed out."

"I doubt that, sir. No, truly I do. We've not had much chance to absorb anything that's happened, but no-one will expect Lord Landis to be asked to resign. For myself, I'll serve however you wish. It is only because Lord Iris became King's Counsellor that I was ever recalled to the King's Advisors. If not, I'd probably still have been heading your previous advisors – therefore, is it strange that you've asked me to continue, Sire?"

"Confidence of purpose is sometimes dangerous," remarked the King eyeing him thoughtfully.

"Yes, sir, it is but for the moment, I suspect, you need someone who has worked both for you as a prince and for the King's Office…"

"You know, I begin to worry that I'm easy to read, Advisor."

"No, Sire. I'm a presumptuous fool."

"Maybe. There's also another matter you might advise me on. The barracks didn't find out about the assassination until they received the proclamation."

"Sicla!" He shouldn't have just gone to sleep after the King returned. He should have gone to see Paturn and Wynfeld. He cursed himself in his mind. Why hadn't he thought to do so?

"Anything more helpful to suggest?" asked the King dryly.

"Yes, sir, sleep on it." That might give him time to see Wynfeld.

"I did say 'more helpful'."

"My apologies, Sire, but it's my advice. You had an exceptionally long day yesterday and today, from what I've heard, has been emotionally straining. This needs clarity of thought and it will give the General and Major more time to discover what they can."

"Are you helping to cover their backs, Rayburn?"

"No. I'm trying to make sure everyone is in a calm frame of mind."

The King sat back, strain etched into his features. "You're probably right. I suppose you'd better let my advisors know, and tell Edward to let you know of any meetings…"

Rayburn got up. "Of course, Sire. Might I make a suggestion?"

"Yes."

"Take a break, sir, even if it's only six minutes."

King Arkyn simply nodded and watched as Rayburn left. The advisor knelt on the threshold before rising and closing the door softly.

* * *

Edward glanced over. "Advisor?"

"I'm confirmed in post, Edward—"

"I never doubted that would happen."

"Thank you. I've persuaded King Arkyn to worry about his advisors after his coronation. Could you let me know of any meetings I'm likely to be needed for? I'll let the rest of the King's Advisors know the situation and also those from when he was a prince. I've also just advised the King to have a short break. I'm not sure if he will."

Edward glanced at the Inner Office door. "Thank you." He lowered his voice, "I must admit Chapa's on standby for this evening; the King's exhausted."

"Wouldn't you be? How much more has he got to do today?"

"Got to? Nothing much. Will try to do…"

Rayburn chuckled. "Far too much. Good luck."

"Thank you, Advisor."

"You'll need it. I spy the Steward approaching in a foul mood." Rayburn wondered if he should wait and see why the Steward was in a bad mood. Would Landis have done so? Possibly, but then he'd have had an absolute right to. Edward would contact him if he was needed; he had no doubt about that.

Chapter 44

JENKINS

Early Afternoon
Oedran

TAIN MEANWHILE had hugged Elantha, gone with her to the nursery, been hugged by his old nurse, fussed over more than he wanted and escaped only just maintaining a mask of maturity.

He headed for the Courthouse; the building was the focus of his duties as Justiciar of Oedran and contained eight courts including the ancient Justice Hall. After everything that had happened over the previous couple of weeks, part of him wanted to meld into the mouldings but he had to stamp his authority into people's minds; therefore, he took the conscious decision of entering by the majestic front of the building. The atrium was a bustle of people: lawyers, witnesses and students mingled in an ever-changing crowd. The light green lawyers' robes were easily spotted. The uncertainty of witnesses gave emphasis to their presence. The students were simply gossiping. Tain could take an educated guess at the subject matter they were discussing. Within the mass of people was a glimpse of a teal robe.

Tain turned to his guards. "Lyndon, ask the Keeper to join me please."

"Keeper, sir?"

"The gentleman in the teal robes."

Some of the crowd had noticed the presence of the guards and then, by association, Tain. They glanced at each other before bowing and moving aside. The lawyers were now the uncertain ones, the witnesses curious, and the students had stopped gossiping, if only momentarily. The Keeper received the message from Lyndon, turned abruptly on the spot and made his way over to Tain where he bowed with practised ease.

"Justiciar, I hope your endeavours this morning have been fulfilling."

Tain considered that. "I would say they met with the King's approval. I can't say as much for the six Lords of Oedran who signed away King Adeone's life. The results will be proclaimed tomorrow morning. We will go to my office, Keeper."

The Keeper smiled. "Of course, Your Highness. Please..." He waved his hand and Tain crossed to the doors of the ancient Justice Hall. Two lawyers hurriedly held them open. Tain nodded his thanks. Was it really just over a fortnight since he'd been here, taking his oath to Truth and Justice in front of his father and Judge Tancred?

* * *

As he crossed the threshold, the sound of magical trumpets proclaimed his presence but there were no trumpeters here, the sound washed over him and then into his bones. He could not hide in this place. He could not forgo what he had sworn. The doors thudded closed behind him. He stopped in his tracks.

The Keeper looked at him compassionately, "Maybe the long way round would have been better?"

"No. I had to face it."

He entered the main body of the Justice Hall and paused once more. The fanfare had stopped and the absence of sound was eerie. The centuries closed in around him. He glanced at the Justiciar's Seat, his seat, his court, his responsibility. The power of place and position washed over him in a crescendo of realisation. He froze once more, wishing Judge Tancred was there with his reassuring presence. The Keeper beside him – like previous keepers beside previous Justiciars – was an infallible support. As though lead was in his feet, Tain walked up to the bar and ran his hand along the polished walnut desk. He didn't want to speak, and the Keeper kept silent. This was a moment that had to happen in private: Tain accepting what was facing him as a new Justiciar.

The Prince moved around the bar and up to the Justiciar's Seat. He grasped the tall back, realising how throne-like it was and resented the feeling. He was an official but not a King of Justice. His numb mind glanced at the carvings, the symbols of justice in harsh relief on the sides but not the back panel. He knew he had to face it and so slowly sat down, looking at the Justice Hall in front of him. He took a deep breath and thought rather than voiced his greeting.

He could have sworn that, on the edge of his mind's hearing, he heard the faintest whisper of a reply, as though spoken by someone on the brink of death. He tried to relax and closed his eyes, again feeling the presence of history all around him. He pushed himself to his feet and once more business-like nodded to the Keeper.

* * *

The Keeper simply held open Judge's Door and then the one into Peter's office. Tain nodded to Peter before entering his own office. He collapsed into a chair and pointed to the one opposite.

The Keeper sat down. "What's happened, sir?"

Tain explained in more detail than he'd planned to.

The Keeper listened intently and at the end said, "Has anyone warned your lawyers that they're superfluous yet, sir?"

"Don't be daft, Keeper, of course they're not. I need to meet Jenkins and I don't need facetious comments getting in the way."

"Ah, then that might be a conflict of interest. Jenkins has many qualities, but he has his faults also."

"What faults?" asked Tain suspiciously.

"He has a unique way of expressing himself."

"Get to the point, Keeper."

"He is noted for being sarcastic, dry and cynical but he is the best lawyer in Oedran – unfortunately for his career under Lord Scanlon he won't twist the law."

Tain forced himself to relax. "He sounds the sort of man I need."

"Yes, under more pleasant times I'd agree, but I'll make sure he realises now isn't normal."

Tain nodded. "It might be wise. Sicla, no. I'm not starting with telling my staff to change, not today. I'll be terse instead. Ask Peter to send for him, please."

"Very good, Your Highness. Shall I also send you the list of trials for tomorrow to verify?"

"If it's ready. Oh, you should know I asked Lord Scanlon to keep his nose out of matters here. You have my authority to emphasise that if, or rather when, needed."

The Keeper hid his surprise. "Thank you, sir."

"Or refer him back to me. I'm not... The oath granted me the right to control Oedran judiciary as I wish, didn't it? In every way? It's only tradition that means he might be able to... It's not law, is it? I couldn't find any that said it was."

"You are Justiciar of Oedran, sir. As you say, it is tradition that means people may try to appeal to him." He added in the privacy of his head that it became rather an interesting problem if anything happened to the Prince, for there had to be a Justiciar of Oedran.

"Good. Judge Tancred did explain but it's all a muddle. No-one seems certain and there's never been a conflict of interest before – not like mine and Lord Scanlon's anyway."

"Actually, sir, Prince Lachlan wasn't enamoured of Lord Scanlon's methods, in much the same way that Your Highness isn't, it was just that Prince Lachlan was at the end of his tenure not the beginning."

Tain swallowed. "Ah. Let's hope my tenure lasts long enough for me to be full Justiciar for the Empire then. Please ask Jenkins to join me."

The Keeper bowed and left. He passed on the summons to Peter, who sent a runner to Jenkins before saying to the Keeper,

"Life is suddenly complicated."

"Think how he feels, Peter."

"I am doing. It's not that long since I lost my pa."

The Keeper nodded. "How are things for you and your family?"

"All right. It's fortunate I'm in this job, it's helped. I still thank the old Judge every day in my mind."

"Aye, he saw you right, but he also saw the Prince right at the same time."

Peter watched him leave and contemplated that carefully.

* * *

A few minutes later Jenkins breezed into the office. "It's nice to know he acknowledges my existence, Peter, but should I be worried?"

Peter smiled. "He's in a delicate mood, Jenkins, be careful."

"I shall endeavour to shelve my personality."

"I'll believe that when I see it."

Jenkins grinned. "I must have been appointed for a reason."

"I wish I could ask the Judge if it was anything I did that meant I was lumbered with you on His Highnesses staff."

"Such compliments. Do I get announced, Administrator?"

Peter rolled his eyes. "Certainly." The administrator opened Prince Tain's office door, walked through and held it open. "The incorrigible one, Your Highness, who answers to the name of Lawyer Jenkins."

Tain nodded. "Thank you, Peter, that's all. Jenkins, come in please. I've been reading your file."

Jenkins entered and bowed. "Oh dear. Should I apologise now, sir?"

"It depends how much you think you'll annoy me. Take a seat, there are several matters I need to explain to you. Then I want to discuss my staff."

Jenkins sat down. "Very good, Your Highness. Might I just ask if you warned Peter that we had already met a couple of years ago?"

Tain shook his head. "No, I had forgotten myself. I thought I recognised you though."

"It was just after the Judge had agreed to teach you, sir."

"An adjournment of a case! Two weeks."

"Well remembered, sir."

Tain said simply, "Thank you. Right. I've been told you have your faults. What are they?"

Jenkins met Tain's shrewd gaze. "I expect it might refer to the fact I say what I think and don't tend to hold back sir. I have a sarcastic and cynical edge that many find highly annoying. I'll happily apologise in advance for all my faults."

"At least you recognise them."

"Someone's got to, sir. Though various judges have kindly made sure I know them, in detail. Their endeavours are heart-warming."

"Better than someone trying to stab you in the back with them. As you

184

have admitted to them, I'll try to lay out some rules. I don't mind straight talking, I don't mind people holding their own opinions but try to moderate the sarcasm and cynicism if anyone else is around."

"I'll try, Your Highness. I must admit I was slightly surprised when the Judge approached me. I'd have thought more deferential people would have been appointed for your staff."

"Maybe everyone else will make up for it and you're the balance."

"Maybe, Your Highness."

"Or maybe the Judge realised that I'd need every good lawyer in Oedran."

"Sir?"

"Do you think that my father's assassination was engineered by the six lords alone?"

Jenkins' shock was clear in his voice. "Who else would do it, sir?"

"Lord Scanlon…" said Tain and explained a bit more concluding with, "He wants me to mess up, so no-one will put any faith in me. It will be partly your job to make sure that I don't."

"I'll do my best, sir."

"Good. On that note, you should be aware that the Judge and my father both recommended I never simply rely on one person's word when it comes to the law. So, from today, if I ask for any information there will always be two people working on it simultaneously and separately."

"Make it three, Your Highness. With two, you might get to the point where you have a disagreement with no majority. Three, you should always get a majority."

"Won't that seem excessive?"

"For a time, sir. Your staff will have to learn to cope. I have eight lawyers currently under my eye. Scrap the hierarchy that was suggested and employ an extra lawyer, then split the lawyers into three teams of three and utilise that structure to implement the triple checking of facts. Put one man in charge of two others and then rotate the subordinates on a seasonal basis. That should eliminate, at least initially, any chance of fixing things. Lord Scanlon will find it hard to turn anyone against you if they are constantly being observed by different people. Also tell your staff that they are likely to be approached by traitors. It will make them watchful. I doubt any of them wish you harm already. I know for a fact many of them dislike Lord Scanlon's methods and are hoping that you will bring some tolerance back into the Courthouse."

"Right. You might be right when it comes to the hierarchy so find another lawyer, please. Will people question my motives if I see to it in the next couple of days?"

"Not as much as if you do it later in your tenure."

"Good. How are your offices arranged here?"

"I can show Your Highness more easily than I can describe them, sir."

"Then I shall find time to look around them later today, probably before I return to the Palace, but if I'm called away, I'll come back as soon as I can. If, for any reason I can't make it, I'll let you know."

"Right, sir. Would you like any of the other lawyers there as well?"

"I'll leave that to your discretion though probably not the whole lot. I'm not feeling up to large crowds at the moment."

"Of course, sir. I should have thought."

"Maybe but, when it isn't your family, you see things differently."

Jenkins was surprised; he wouldn't have thought a fifteen-year-old would have recognised that. "Possibly, Your Highness. We were all shocked by the events and you're probably sick of hearing condolences but all your staff wished me to express theirs. We never thought we'd live to see such an event and we cannot ever believe that your father was anything but the King he appeared to all true subjects of the empire. The empire was flourishing under his rule—"

Tain who'd risen and walked to look out of the windows, to hide his face, said, without turning round, "Stop, Jenkins. Thank you for all your kind words but please just stop."

"Sorry, sir."

Tain composed his face and turned to the lawyer. "Is there anything you need from me at the moment?"

"A miracle, Your Highness…"

Tain frowned. "What like?"

"Could you age five years overnight, do you think, sir? We could get rid of Lord Scanlon then."

Tain said, "Ah, that would be what you meant when you said you were cynical."

"Not me, sir, never."

"And there's the sarcasm!"

Jenkins chuckled. "I was always told to start as I mean to go on."

"When you get to the cliff edge you're meant to stop! I thought the Judge would have told you that before."

Jenkins nodded. "Oh, he did, sir, many times. I worked directly for him when I was newly qualified."

"Really?"

"Yes, sir. Fifteen years ago now."

Tain stilled. "That would have been in the year I was born then?"

"Yes, sir."

"When Prince Lachlan was Justiciar of most of the empire?"

"Yes, sir."

"So when you say you worked for the Judge, did you actually mean you worked for my great-uncle?"

Jenkins took a breath. "Indirectly, sir. I was never part of His Highness' staff officially."

Tain sitting down nodded. "Call *me* cynical, Jenkins, but you were therefore one of his unofficial staff who checked his official staff?"

"How do you work these things out, sir?"

"When you can't see for the fact you've just been blinded by the obvious, it might well be staring you in the face."

"Would you know if it were staring you in the face if you have just been blinded, sir?"

"Jenkins..." said Tain tiredly.

"Your Highness?"

"What would you call your answer just then?"

"Impudence, sir? Or a lawyer's trick."

Tain looked at him. "When I use metaphors don't try 'a lawyer's trick' on them."

"I'll try to remember, Your Highness."

They eyed each other for several moments. Tain's mind was whirring with possibilities. If Jenkins had worked for his uncle, even indirectly, he might have more idea than most about Lord Scanlon.

"Why do you want me to age five years? And my memory isn't that bad, so don't just repeat what you said before, explain your reasoning."

Jenkins considered. "You're Justiciar of Oedran, sir, and the King's Justiciar. That's helpful. It breaks some of Lord Scanlon's stranglehold on justice but Oedran, when alone, relies on its name, not its might. The empire is vast, opinions vary, whispers become storms. You can't stop a storm. You might stop a whisper, if you're in the right place, but that place might not be Oedran. Until you're Justiciar of the Empire, those whispers can gather and spread and Lord Scanlon won't do anything to stop them. He will add more. He did it to Prince Lachlan as the power shifted. By the time Prince Lachlan retired, some were saying Lord Scanlon was what the empire needed. That's what he wanted at the time. When Prince Lachlan died, when it was clear that Lord Scanlon was secure for years, then the whispers changed again and they worked against your father, then against your brother, and now against you. Whilst the power shifts from Lord Scanlon he'll do everything to discredit Your Highness, but you know that. In five years' time, his power will break. What happens then? Well, I doubt King Adeone was being so forgiving of his brother because he wanted to be. The laws surrounding the power division between King and Justiciar are strong. The lords are notoriously jumpy about divisions of power. I expect King Adeone was waiting for Your Highness to be of age, so that the power then resides with you and Lord Scanlon has nowhere to hide. You will truly then be his equal in law and he could take the consequences of his scheming."

Tain pursed his lips. "I'm sure you'll see the whispers don't spread."

"I'll add it to my list, sir."

* * *

Twelve minutes later, Jenkins left to reorganise Tain's staff and Peter entered with some documents.

Tain caught his concern and simply said, "I'm all right, Peter."

"Yes, sir. I never doubted it for a second." When Tain eyed him, he amended his statement. "I should have said, I only doubted it for a second, sir. How was Jenkins?"

"He was… different."

"Yes. He is. Notorious is another word for him, sir."

"I hope to match his skill in that respect. What are all those papers?"

"Tomorrow's trials and information from the Steward – a guest list for the funeral – I think it might need amending, sir – with the King's consent obviously – a preliminary order of events for the funeral and a list of meetings that Edward has sent over. The King hasn't seen any of it yet to my knowledge."

Tain nodded. "Right, let's have a look." Two minutes later he said, "Get me the Steward, Peter, and, yes, I expect him to come here."

<h1 style="text-align:center">Chapter 45</h1>
<h2 style="text-align:center">GUEST LIST</h2>
13:54
Courthouse – Prince Tain's Office

TAIN WAS ON EDGE waiting for the Steward. He had to speak to him before Arkyn read the guest list but he also needed to keep his temper, and the Steward was not his favourite person.

The gentleman entered with pursed lips and a frown that should have been lost at the door of the Courthouse, if not Tain's office.

Tain didn't invite the Steward to sit by word or gesture. The man needed to realise he'd acted foolishly. They wouldn't forget though they might appear to forgive.

"Steward, the guest list for the funeral needs amending. Why are Lady

188

Rhian and Lady Neassa not included?"

"Lady Rhian had planned to be at Ceardlann for a few days, I believe."

Tain stared. "Steward, I was planning to talk to the Amphi judges today. I presume you were planning something other than discussing a king's funeral. Plans change! My father's cousins are to be added to the guest list immediately. Had they been in Tradere, they would have been informed of the date so they could have attended if at all possible."

"Your Highness cannot invite every family member, sir; it is for the King to change the list."

"I have no intention of inviting *every* family member, some certainly won't be attending, but Lady Rhian *will* be invited, as will Lady Neassa. You've also missed off Calumiel Galdwin."

The Steward almost sneered. "He isn't family, Your Highness, nor is he an official, or of a high enough social standing."

Tain's features set. "He will be there if he wishes it."

"As I have said, *sir*, the King must be the one to amend the list."

"I would amend it before my brother sees it."

The Steward said, "Your Highness, I think you are forgetting that you're only fifteen and I am aware of protocols."

"I am well aware of my age, it has hardly been missed. Or were you asleep during the celebrations and my investiture? No? As for your grasp of protocol it seems to be somewhat lacking, or am I meant to have forgotten why you were summoned to the King this morning? You have made errors of judgement that make me question your motives. You might remember you recommended Linnt to be my manservant: a traitor. Another unfortunate error of judgement, was it?"

"No-one could have foreseen that, sir."

"You weren't worried when he asked you to further his career, when he requested you put him forward, and when he used subtle manipulations to make you? You see, Steward, I know a lot more about that appointment than you have reckoned on."

The Steward barely turned a hair. "I recognised a healthy level of ambition. That was all, Your Highness."

Tain let the comment pass; it was unlikely to be true. "There is also the complete mess you made of the *protocols* surrounding the death of King Adeone. Do not expect me to have forgotten so soon. What's more, do not try to defend your actions again. I am certainly not in the mood to listen to a load of—"

"Your Highness must—"

Something snapped inside Tain. "*My Highness must…?* I think you'll find, Steward, my Highness *must* do nothing. You will remember that."

The Steward reddened. "I have an appointment with the King, sir."

Tain wondered whether to contact Arkyn to check; however he decided to leave the Steward to dig himself into an even larger hole.

* * *

Arkyn had barely drawn breath from his conversation with Rayburn when Edward announced the grim Steward. It seemed the man hadn't even had the decency to catch his breath. With a glance at Edward, who shook his head minutely, Arkyn enquired what was wrong as his administrator left.

The Steward replayed the meeting with Tain. Arkyn's features set halfway through and the set was perfectly timed to make the Steward think he was doing the right thing continuing. When he reached the end, he was therefore perplexed by Arkyn's response, delivered in a cold, hard tone.

"You will never speak to Prince Tain in that manner again. If anyone was in the wrong, Steward, it was you. Would you have presumed to tell Prince Lachlan whom he could invite to King Apolinar's funeral? Or is it simply because my brother is young that you talk to him thus? You're to apologise to Prince Tain and you're *never* to walk out on him again. You wait for him to say you can leave. On that note, get out of this office before I make a decision that proves damaging to you."

The Steward left, barely remembering himself enough to bow. Arkyn waited two minutes before calling Fafnir and requesting a link with Tain.

* * *

Tain said, "I'm sorry, sir. Knowledge of what the Steward is got the better of me."

Through gritted teeth, Arkyn growled, "I'm not annoyed at you, Tain. I'm bloody furious with him. How he dared to come and tell me like that. As though I'd ever say you were in the wrong to him..."

Tain shook his head. "He's a fool. Though I think I know his game..."

"Chess?"

"Not quite but not far off. He's trying to set us against each other. Trying to create discord that Uncle Scanlon can use to his advantage."

"Yes, but does he know it, I wonder."

"Possibly or he might not realise the full enormity of his methods."

Arkyn sighed. "Are you all right?"

"I'm better now."

"Good." Arkyn paused. "I suppose I ought to... I dread to think what Edward's got lined up for me."

Tain rubbed at his face when the link broke before putting his head on his arms and trying to block out the world for a couple of minutes. The scents of leather, wood polish and parchment charmed his senses but a small thud, in an office that should have been silent, disturbed him. He

190

sat up searching for the source of the noise. Robert apologetically bowed. He'd tried to be unobtrusive putting Tain's late lunch on one of the tables. Tain nodded for the man to leave – he'd completely forgotten about lunch. Crossing to the table, he was intrigued to find that all the food had a freshly prepared look, as though Robert had made it himself. He toyed with it for a couple of minutes and then heard Maria saying,

'Are you going to eat that, sir, or simply mess it around? It was made to be eaten you see, and it's what it does best.'

He tucked into the food and felt better for it. He made his way back to the desk and rang for Robert to clear. The manservant entered and Tain for want of something to say managed,

"That was delicious, thank you, Robert."

"My pleasure, sir. There is a small kitchen area here, similar to that in Your Highness' chambers."

"I never knew that. I expect it is a legacy of Prince Lachlan. I can't imagine my uncle would have had it added."

"It is a likely explanation, sir. Is there anything else I can get you, Your Highness?"

"No, thank you."

The manservant inclined his head and left with the tray.

Once on his own, Tain considered Robert. He was certainly different from Linnt. It was late for lunch and Tain had completely forgotten about eating. Linnt would simply have ignored the situation.

Chapter 46
LORDS' DUTIES
14:36
Inner Office

ARKYN CALLED EDWARD into the Inner Office. "Get the rest of the Lords of Oedran here in two hours…"

Once Arkyn had finished explaining, he read some of the information that had been flowing into his office all day: reports assuring him everything was in hand for the funeral, that all was well in the empire, the first reports on the lords' demeanour during their house arrest. It was all things he needed to know, but nothing that he could concentrate on. Was it grief? Probably. It was certainly exhaustion from the day travelling, even in the coach. He returned to the reports. Lord Teran had fought all the way to the prison. He allowed himself a small smile. The Custodian of Oedran Prison had put him in a solitary cell. That was unfortunate and

191

not what he'd ordered. Then he cursed to himself. He'd only said it was acceptable to him if Teran was put with the common prisoners, not that he was to be. Still, maybe the threat had been enough. He'd leave the city by nightfall. He wasn't certain the other exiled lords knew what Teran's *fate* had been. Ambiguity had many uses.

He poured himself a drink. It already seemed like a long day and it wasn't over yet.

* * *

In line with Arkyn's wishes, Lord Rale was informed the meeting was happening but he was not required to attend as he was underage; however, shortly before the meeting was due to start, he requested an audience.

"Rale?"

Finian swallowed. Arkyn's tone had been more official than he'd expected. "I'm hoping you won't mind if I'm at the meeting, Sire."

Arkyn eyed him. "Why do you need to attend, my lord?"

Finian hesitated. "Because Aunt Cornelia is asleep, Uncle Festus hasn't been informed because he's meant to stay in bed and you can bet quite a lot of money that, if he knew it was happening, he'd be here. I suppose I'd like to observe, sir, so that, when he finds out, I can tell him what happened. Lord Iris will have more than enough on without running back and forth unnecessarily to Landis House. If I can observe it solves a lot of problems and, I suppose, I'm also curious, Sire."

"All right, but you are *observing*. As it is, Landis didn't need to be here. You'd better just wait outside until everyone's here. Oh, Finian, you should have a mentor for such meetings…"

Finian smiled. "I'm sure I can ask one of my peers to help, Sire. Leave it to me."

Arkyn watched him leave. Why was he uneasy at that proposition? Could it be Finian's grin had been eerily like Lord Julius' when he had a mischievous scheme on?

* * *

A few minutes later, Edward announced Rale, Ryson, Fairson and Iris before taking his place at the clerk's desk.

Arkyn waved everyone to a table and wasn't surprised that it was Lord Iris who seated him.

"My lords, forgive the sudden nature of this meeting but events have been sudden. All Lords of Oedran bar yourselves and Landis have been exiled from Oedran, and all but Para from Anapara as well. Lord Para is confined to the north of the country. It will be proclaimed in the morning. By then all the signatories of the Assassination Document will have left Oedran. Their duties here must be undertaken by others. I will not entrust them to members of their respective families; therefore, we need to come to a workable and agreed arrangement. Landis already looks after three provinces and undertakes their respective duties; so, I am not proposing to put more on his shoulders." Privately he wondered who would be the first to suggest provinces to take. There was power in representing them. If it was Iris, his motives wouldn't be because of the prestige. Rale couldn't take any. Fairson and Ryson were listening intently. Were they interested in what he had to say or the opportunities?

Iris watching the young King's face got up, bowing slightly. He crossed to the sideboard and poured the King a drink. Placing it by the King's hand he half-whispered, "We'll do what we can, Sire."

"I have no doubt *you* will, Lord Iris – probably more than you should."

Fairson said, "Lord Iris speaks for us all, Sire. We're appalled by events. We'd realised that there'd be issues—"

"I'm happy to take on Terasia and Serpent Isle, sir," interrupted Ryson.

"Why those in particular?" enquired Arkyn. So it had been Scanlon's erstwhile friend to pick first, interesting.

Ryson said, "Practicality, Sire. Terasia is the sister province to mine of Gerymor, with Lord Wealsman as Margrave it should be less problematic. Serpent Isle because I've heard the sea air is meant to be good for one."

Arkyn regarded him for a moment. The reasons made sense for Terasia. Serpent Isle was geographically close to the other provinces. As the spice isle it had riches but Gerymor did as well being a source of gemstones. Either Ryson was interested in those riches, or he was practical in his choices. After a moment, Arkyn said, "I'll tell the Margrave to make your life difficult for anticipating ease, shall I?"

Ryson smiled. "As my liege wishes but, seriously, Sire, they do seem the most practical for me."

"I agree, my lord. At the end of this meeting, you'll sign an agreement to that end. Lord Fairson, do you have any preference?"

"Denshire and Lufian seem sensible, sir. I'll take Bayan as well—"

Iris said, "Gerens, I'm not in my dotage or senile. I will take my fair share. Stick with Denshire and Lufian. I'll take on Bayan and Anapara."

Arkyn considered both him and Fairson. The younger lord didn't seem fazed or annoyed by the interruption. He simply motioned that if Iris was happy so was he with a flick of his hand.

"They are large provinces, Lord Iris, and you'll have duties as King's Counsellor," Arkyn reminded him.

Iris smiled. "To echo Ryson: the Exarch should make life easy, sir."

"Do you insist, my lord?"

Iris held his gaze. "I do, my liege."

"Then so be it." Arkyn turned slightly. "Edward, do you have the agreements for Their Lordships?"

Edward rose – the ink still drying on the last. He walked over and placed them in front of the relevant lords, before fetching the sealing wax and a lighted candle.

Arkyn said, "Take your time to read these agreements, they will be binding until further notice. If you still agree, please sign and affix your seal to them. Then pass them round so that you can act as witnesses to your peers' decisions. Lord Ryson will, I'm sure, explain any legalese should it be required. Lord Rale, you are not required to act as a witness."

Finian said, "If the law and you permit it, Sire, I would like to."

Arkyn eyed him. "Ryson?"

Ryson, reading the document, answered distractedly, "Lord Rale's over cisan-age and is a Lord of Oedran, sir. There is no impediment as long as there are other witnesses."

Arkyn recognising an official note in Ryson's voice said, "Thank you. Then, Rale, you may. Out of interest, my lords, whom did Finian ask to act as his mentor in here?"

Ryson looked up. "Me, Sire."

Arkyn nodded. "Thank you. Finian, your reasons?"

"I thought lawyers should stick together, Sire."

Arkyn smiled. "Heaven help us. It'll be interesting when you've graduated!"

The room was silent for several minutes but soon all the documents were signed and witnessed.

Arkyn said, "Thank you, my lords, that has made the situation far easier. You'll be receiving paperwork in copious amounts soon. Including a Calendar of Court Presidings. That's all for now… Ah, actually, Lord Iris, I could do with a word. Lord Ryson, I'd be grateful if you'd wait outside for a few minutes."

Everyone but Iris bowed and left.

Arkyn looked at the oldest of the Lords of Oedran. "I do know why you were made King's Counsellor, Lord Iris, in full."

"I did not realise that, Sire."

"No, I thought not," said Arkyn dryly. "You've taken on an awful lot today; do not do too much, please. Accept Fairson's help if your conscience will allow – at least for the next couple of weeks. After that, time will tell, but the exiled lords will be gone from Oedran for long enough for Finian to be of age. When he is, one of your provinces will fall to him. I am thinking Bayan."

Lord Iris said, "Sir, Anapara may be better. There are fewer contentious issues and also less travelling."

Arkyn smiled. "Let the young travel and let my office have your experience and wisdom, my lord. I'd rather your expertise was here in our home province."

Iris inclined his head. "Very well, my liege."

Arkyn eyed the elderly Lord of Oedran. "You've not sworn fealty yet."

"My loyalties haven't changed because of what happened, sir. I swore loyalty and fealty to your father and his heirs – you are that heir and therefore circumstances dictate you're my liege. I will however confirm it in the traditional way next Imperadai."

Arkyn swallowed. "Thank you." He hesitated. "Lord Iris, I feel as uncertain as I did in Terasia."

"Then, Sire, your reign should be great," replied Iris with a smile.

"Very amusing. I think you know what I meant."

"I think perhaps I do, sir. Take it a day at a time."

Arkyn nodded. "Oh, I almost forgot, your True Dallin—"

"I'll bring it in the morning, Sire."

"You mistake me. Please keep it."

"Sire, I've not returned to the Rex Dallin in years."

"That is immaterial to me." Arkyn continued more softly, "Keep it please. There might be need of it and I'm happier knowing you have it."

"Very good, Sire. My thanks," replied Iris watching the young man.

Arkyn avoided the look. "Could you ask Ryson to join me, please, I need to know what happened on Munewid Eve."

"Would you like me to stay as King's Counsellor, sir?"

"No, thank you."

Chapter 47
RYSON'S TALE
17:00
Inner Office

LORD RYSON RE-ENTERED the Inner Office and knelt. That simple action said more than words could have done to Arkyn. Ryson was expecting Arkyn's mood to darken, which meant he'd likely guessed why Arkyn had asked him to wait.

"Please get up, my lord, and have a seat. I'd like to know what happened at the banquet and why I have read and heard reports that you burst into the King's Hall with Sergeant Hillbeck yelling treachery at the moment my father was killed."

"Might I request Prince Tain is also present, Sire?" replied Ryson. "Given everything that has happened I think he should hear this as well."

Arkyn regarded him for several moments during which Ryson looked back, completely at ease.

Finally, the King said, "Then, until he arrives, please wait outside."

* * *

Tain arrived quarter of an hour later and walked unheralded into the Inner Office. "I suppose you thought I needed a break, sir?"

"No. Lord Ryson asked for you to be here. I'm about to get an explanation about his part in all this."

Tain bit his lip. "Oh."

Two moments later, Ryson sat down looking remarkably relaxed. Arkyn regarded him silently.

Tain said, "Lord Ryson, what happened on Munewid Eve?"

"It's hard to explain, sir," replied Ryson. "Some time ago, Lord Scanlon visited Oedran; you are aware we used to be friends, and that is how the situation will stay, but he tried once again to twist my perception. I wouldn't oblige and he left in a temper. Major Wynfeld is aware of this, Sire, I report to him whenever Lord Scanlon's visited me. I had the uncomfortable feeling that Lord Scanlon was after more than reconciliation but I wouldn't let him explain what. I didn't want him in my house and I continue in that. Shortly afterwards, I met a man I became intimate with. On Munewid Eve, I became concerned about his motives; he made comments designed to alter my perception of King Adeone. I threw him out of my life and will pass his details, given the following events, to Major Wynfeld."

"Pass them to His Highness also, if you're that concerned, Ryson."

"As you wish, Sire. I left my house that night looking forward to the banquet, oblivious to anything else. Whilst I made my way from the stables to the Court, Lux stopped me, asking for a word in private. I didn't think anything of it. We went into a room and the other exiled Lords of Oedran were there – all but Cearis, that is. Teran and Rathgar blocked my exit, seemingly accidentally. They unrolled the Assassination Document, dipped a pen for me and made it quite clear I was expected to sign. It was also made clear to me that if I didn't my work as a lawyer and as Provost of the Law School would become untenable. I know you only have my word for this but on any oath you wish, in any place you name, I would swear to this: I told them I was not going to oblige, and that they were fools to think they would ever get away with it. In fact, I said some rather blunter things and the next thing I know I'm waking up with a blinding headache. The blow didn't break the skin, but it left me unconscious for some time,

196

and I don't know who struck, for at that time the lords were all in front or to the side of me. I might suspect it was Cearis but frankly he hasn't the strength either physical or of purpose. I was surprised to see his seal on the document. Anyway, Sire, I came to and was flooded with apprehension. I tried the door, but it was locked. I thought for a moment and then banged on the door. After quite a while, one of the nearby guards must have heard, for the door was unlocked. I pushed my way out. I ran, as fast as I could towards the King's Hall. I literally bumped into Hillbeck. I've never been so glad to see anyone. I told him what had happened and he joined me in the race to the King's Hall. We entered too late, Sire, and I will understand if you take action for that."

Arkyn glanced at Tain who said, "Reading."

Arkyn nodded, pushing himself to his feet. "Lord Ryson, please kneel."

Ryson moved to a clear area of the room and did so. He was completely relaxed. Tain wondered about speech-bindings and whether truth-fealties were strong enough to overcome them but it was too late to mention it, and, as it turned out, he needn't have worried anyway.

Arkyn took Lord Ryson's hands. "In truth, have you ever sworn any oath of allegiance to any but a king?"

"In truth, my liege, I have not."

"In truth, Lord Ryson, have you wished harm on any of my family?"

"In truth, my liege, only Lord Scanlon."

Tain inwardly raised an eyebrow.

"In truth, Lord Ryson, how much of the tale you related was the truth?"

"In truth, my liege, every word."

"Forget all but my last question."

Ryson kissed Arkyn's signet ring when the King released his hands.

Arkyn sat back down. "Get up, please, Lord Ryson. It seems you did everything you could to prevent the attempt and you have our thanks for that. I'm sure Prince Tain will see your career as a lawyer and Provost is unhampered by your actions."

Tain nodded. "I shall do my best, Sire."

"Thank you. Ryson, if it helps to ease your mind, I am certain that nothing you could have done would have prevented my father's death; circumstances were set against you."

"I shall always wonder, sir," replied Ryson sadly.

"That is natural but I do not blame you in any measure. That's all."

Ryson bowed and left, leaving the two brothers eyeing each other with a look that spoke volumes.

Eventually Tain said, "That was revealing."

"Yes. I wish I'd known it this morning."

"Mm. This way the lords think they've got away with it. I shall file the information safely away. Now, Sire, you need a break and I have to inspect my staff's offices."

"I feel like I'm drowning in a never-ending sea."

That had come out of the blue. Tain looked at his brother. "Me too. The expression sink or swim has startling meaning at the moment."

"You can say that again!"

"The expression—"

Arkyn simply sighed. "One day you'll not take me literally. How do I put up with you?"

"I have no idea, sir."

"Tain, stop the 'sir', we're in private."

"Sorry. I thought I'd get into the habit."

"I'll ask the Moonshi if he's got a spare one then."

Tain's eyes narrowed. "About taking you literally, Arkyn – ever thought I might have picked it up from somewhere?"

"Uncle Festus, it's all his fault. I don't suppose you could stay and talk for a bit?"

Tain was torn; he really wanted to say yes but he ought to say no.

Arkyn saw the struggle. "Never mind. You've got your duties as well now. I keep forgetting."

"Why don't you come with me instead?" offered Tain. It was one way to make sure his brother didn't get mired for a short time.

Intrigued but pleased that Tain would want him there, Arkyn said, "Why not? Sure you want the King to come along?"

"I suppose I have to put up with it if the King wants to, wouldn't I?" muttered Tain.

"Yes; however, do you want *me* to come?"

"Would I have offered if I didn't?"

"I don't know how to read people at the moment."

"Arkyn, you're still my annoying older brother for all you might be King. I can remind you of the fact at regular intervals if you want."

Arkyn shook his head slightly. "Annoying must run in the family."

With a flourish, Tain opened the door for the King. Arkyn gave him a friendly buffet as he passed. The secretaries all rose and bowed.

"I'm going to annoy Prince Tain for a time, Edward. To prove to Kadeem it isn't work, you'll stay here."

"Very good, Sire," replied Edward watching the brothers leave, privately relieved there was something to make the King take a meaningful break.

Chapter 48

FRUSTRATION
17:36
Courthouse

AT THE COURTHOUSE, Tain made his way to his office confidently. People turned as they realised that Arkyn was with him. Some hesitated, unsure what to do, a couple knelt as they passed, others stepped aside inclining their heads in an obeisance to both brothers.

Arkyn's skin crawled. He rarely entered this building and hadn't expected to for a long time. He couldn't recall his father ever entering the Courthouse apart from for Tain's investiture. He wanted to mention it, wanted to talk about it with Tain, to find a line they could agree on, but the corridors weren't the right place.

There were two people in the administrator's office attached to Tain's. Peter held open the door to the Justiciar's office and would have left but Tain said mildly,

"If Jenkins has got over the shock of the King being here, ask him to join us please."

Two moments later, the lawyer entered and knelt to Arkyn, highly confused by his presence. Arkyn nodded at him to rise.

"The King thought he'd join us," explained Tain.

Arkyn shot him a tricky look but Tain ignored it.

Jenkins said, "We could wish for nothing more, sir."

"That almost sounds like you doubt His Highness' skills," remarked Arkyn, watching the lawyer.

Jenkins shook his head. "Never that, Sire, especially not after this morning. His Highness needed no help with the concept of a King's Sentence. I, on the other hand, did."

Arkyn glanced at Tain and raised an amused eyebrow. "Your relationship should be interesting then."

Jenkins said, "That's one way of putting it, sir."

Tain closed his eyes for a second before saying, "Jenkins!"

"Jenkins, be careful what you say," advised Arkyn. "Until His Highness is twenty, I also have an oversight of his staff and my temper is rather short at the moment."

Tain re-evaluated if he was pleased by Arkyn's presence. "Jenkins, let my lawyers know the King is here. When you return, we'll be ready to come and inspect your offices."

Jenkins bowed, *very* precisely. "Your Highness. Sire."

When he'd gone, Tain said, "Are you *trying* to undermine me?"

"I was trying to do the opposite," stated Arkyn.

"Except now Jenkins thinks I need you to hold my hand, *sir*."

"I doubt it. Your lawyers and staff will need to realise who they're talking to and acknowledge it."

"Yes but—"

"No, Tain. Your authority is low at the moment. We've got to raise it. Become more tolerant later by all means but for the immediate future people must recognise you as a figure of authority not just a young prince – Jenkins especially and his tone was anything but respectful – oh it tried to be, which makes me concerned about how he normally talks to you."

Tain silently fumed.

Arkyn sighed. "All right, I'll let you do it your way, for the moment, but, if I'm here, your staff will remember who you are. You heard what the lords said—"

"They were grasping at anything they could, Arkyn! They were acting on Scanlon's instructions but couldn't say it. Can't you realise that?"

"I do but they also believed some of it. We know father and tradition weren't firm friends—"

"That was never a bad thing before today," said Tain accusingly.

Arkyn took him by the shoulders. "And it isn't now, but—"

"If you change, you'll have let them win, you do realise that?"

Arkyn didn't know whether to shake him or walk away; it had been the truth and it sliced through him, wounding his heart.

Tain took in Arkyn's dejected face. "Sorry."

"No, Tain, I am. I shouldn't have interfered. I'll apologise to Jenkins."

"No, you won't, that would undermine your authority."

Arkyn swore. "Are you hunting for ways to be awkward today?"

"What's so special about today? I'm always awkward."

Arkyn turned away, running his hand through his hair. "*Nothing* is special about today," he whispered. "It's just horrific."

Tain regarded his back for a moment before turning him around and giving him a brief but poignant hug. "We'll get through this."

Arkyn swallowed. "I suppose we'd better view your offices."

Tain nodded. "I suppose so. Are we going to behave ourselves?"

"Probably not. Did I ever tell you about the first inspection I did of the barracks?"

"Yes. I'll try to match it."

Arkyn didn't move. "Tain, I am sorry. I was out of order over Jenkins. He's your staff."

Intrigued by the apology, Tain nodded in thanks. "You were also right. Don't worry; you're just adjusting to all the authority you've got."

Arkyn shook his head. "More like the responsibility that goes with it is crashing down on my shoulders in one crushing weight. I *will* apologise to Jenkins as well."

Tain shook his head. "No, you *won't*, Sire. It would be even worse. Jenkins knows what his faults are, to apologise will look as though you condone them, which you don't. I'll make sure he's all right."

Arkyn's eyes raked over his brother's face. Where had Tain's confidence come from? Three days ago, he'd been guiding his brother, not the other way around. These were Tain's first days as an official. When he'd faced those same days— Realisation dawned. Tain was at that point now. The point of knowing what should be done, wondering if he was doing it right and then dealing with things hoping someone would tell him if he wasn't. Arkyn cursed himself, feeling foolish. In Terasia, he'd had to face Portur's murder and Roth's treason alone and he'd done it. Why had he doubted Tain could face his first days as Justiciar? His brother could handle his staff and adapt to his changing position.

Watching his brother, Tain wondered what was going through his mind. Arkyn's silences often spoke volumes but this one wasn't revealing. He was about to enquire what had caught his brother's thoughts when Peter entered.

The administrator gauged the atmosphere, frustration lingered in the air. What had that been about? Did he need to warn Edward or Kadeem? Neither brother gave anything away as they turned towards him.

"Jenkins has returned, sir."

Tain nodded. "Ask him to come in then."

Watching Jenkins as he entered and bowed, Arkyn noticed something in his bearing he'd missed before. The lawyer's eyes never left Tain. He wasn't looking for instruction, he was anticipating needs. Arkyn considered that. Maybe some of the lawyer's manner had been bluster covering concern. It wasn't a normal day for anyone.

Tain glanced at Arkyn's thoughtful stance. "Is there anything we should know before I view the offices, Jenkins?" he asked before Arkyn could speak.

"No, Your Highness."

"Then let's go. Sire, will you join us?"

"I will. I've hardly ever been in the Courthouse and I'm curious," answered Arkyn truthfully.

Jenkins said, smiling, "Then come again for a full tour of the building, Sire. It has some intriguing areas, if you know where to look, and as for its history, that in itself is fascinating, even aside from the architecture."

"I might do that, Jenkins. if it wouldn't cause too much concern."

Tain almost flinched.

"Concerned is a lawyer's base state of being, sir. No-one would notice a little extra," stated Jenkins, lips twitching.

Hurriedly, Tain said, "Just lead the way, Jenkins."

Arkyn caught his brother's eye and winked. Of all the responses, Tain hadn't expected that; he shook his head and allowed Arkyn precedence. Arkyn put a hand on the small of Tain's back and propelled him through the door ahead of him.

Peter attached himself to them as they left the office. They made their way to a wider corridor by the library. Opposite this was a set of rooms and Peter held the door open for them. As they entered three men rose and bowed.

Tain was shown round the offices with a deference Arkyn was pleased to see. The offices consisted of a set of interlinking rooms with filing areas, which already held masses of documents.

"What are all these?" asked Tain.

Jenkins said, "We're not sure, Your Highness. They were left by Lord Scanlon's lawyers when they moved to the Justice Office in the Palace. These rooms are used by the lawyers of the Justiciar of Oedran as opposed to the Justiciar of the Empire, sir."

"It might be as well if you found out what is there this week."

"Very good, sir. I'll get a couple of the junior lawyers and scribes onto it first thing, if Peter can spare the scribes?"

Tain raised a querying eyebrow at Peter who nodded.

"That shouldn't be a problem, sir. Jenkins, tell them His Highness has authorised it or tell me how many you need."

Arkyn smiled slightly. Peter was politely showing Tain that what he wanted he got. Tain never doubted it, but he liked to give the illusion it might not be the case. Judge Tancred had always said using people's wish to have a choice in something was important.

Tain talked to all the lawyers who were there individually with as much verve as he could manage. Arkyn began to see the strains of a full day's work on his brother's face. Two minutes later, Tain began to feel what his brother could see and left for his office. They reached it to find Robert laying out refreshments for them with a timing that showed expert anticipation.

Chapter 49
DECISION TIME
18:24
Courthouse

WHEN TAIN AND ARKYN left the Courthouse, it seemed someone had decided a coach was needed for the short journey to the Palace. Tain raised an eyebrow at Peter.

"Master Robert, Your Highness."

Robert who was holding the door of the coach open resolutely didn't catch the Prince's eye.

"Robert?"

The manservant said, "It is the end of a long day, Your Highness."

Arkyn put a hand on Tain's shoulder. "Thank you, Robert." Once in the coach, the King continued, "He had a point."

Tain sighed. "What made you think I wouldn't acknowledge it?"

"Nothing. It depends on the way you were going to."

Tain sagged. "Have *some* faith in me, please, Arkyn."

"I've more than some, Tain, but you're tired and I'm worried."

"That feeling is mutual then. What else have you got to do today?"

"Dismiss Kilbride."

"Ah." Tain hesitated. "Can I be there?"

"All right."

A couple of moments later, Tain said, "Isn't there a ceremony for dismissing one of your guards under this sort of cloud?"

"Yes, but I was going to spare him that."

Tain frowned. "I don't think you can without undermining the decision."

"In what way?"

"Too weak to show your displeasure publicly. Kilbride will be labelled the scapegoat… It would be like me sentencing someone to imprisonment but then letting them have the freedom of Oedran at the same time."

"Unfortunately, he is the scapegoat, Tain. He's being dismissed because I have to dismiss someone," admitted Arkyn.

"Then make it good, make it worthwhile. Maybe you were right and it *is* time to play by the rule book, sir, at least for a while."

"I couldn't face anyone today, not to do something so drastic."

"Then face it tomorrow," replied Tain. "Warn him, if you must, but leave the formal dismissal for tomorrow."

Arkyn nodded. "I'll need to familiarise myself with the procedure."

"Let someone else tell you it. Make them earn their pay."

"I'll tell them that was your idea. Shouldn't we be there by now?"

Tain glanced out the window of the coach. "We're being delivered to the Privy Gate by the looks of things."

Arkyn rolled his eyes. "Do you think Robert and Kadeem are related?"

Tain let out a long breath. "I hope not. Can you imagine two philosophical menservants looking after us?"

Arkyn shook his head. "I really don't want to. Tain, if I'm only warning Kilbride, you go and relax. You'll be there at the audience, I promise."

Tain sighed. "All right."

* * *

Arkyn entered the Outer Office in a frustrated mood. Richardson, Edward and the secretaries all rose. Arkyn motioned Edward to precede him into the Inner Office.

Once the door had closed Edward said, "Sir?"

"I'm going to have to go through the whole palaver of dismissing Kilbride properly, aren't I?"

"Unfortunately, it might be better, sir."

"You'd better warn Rayburn that I'll need talking through what I've got to do. Unfortunately, I know the first bit. Get Kilbride and Hillbeck in here please."

Edward bowed and left, worried by the King's mood. It had been depressed all day but now tiredness was being bolstered by fledgling anger and frustration, and Edward wondered who'd be caught in the effects of it.

* * *

Hillbeck and Kilbride entered sombrely. Kilbride, obviously apprehensive, knelt as Hillbeck saluted.

Wanting to keep the interview short, Arkyn said, "Kilbride, I have no option but to dismiss you from the King's Guard and I'm going to have to do it publicly. This is simply by way of a warning."

Hillbeck's eyes shot to the King's face; there had been no hint of anything so formal earlier in the day.

Kilbride said, "Sire—"

"I'm sorry, but you don't get to speak to me. I'm obviously not happy with the situation, but you were in charge of King Adeone's safety on Munewid Eve and you failed."

"Sire, Kilbride knows and understands the situation," said Hillbeck. "He has written a formal report of his actions that day and everything else he was aware was occurring but I think mostly he just wanted to say sorry."

Arkyn looked at Kilbride, who lowered his gaze, and then to Hillbeck, who didn't. "I don't think that 'sorry' is enough in this situation. Kilbride, tonight you will reside in a cell before tomorrow's dismissal. That's all.

204

Wait outside. Hillbeck, a word."

Hillbeck watched the King's face as Kilbride left the office. He saw more than Arkyn realised; he saw what Edward had, drained emotion giving way to something more worrying: feelings of frustration eating on themselves, concerns and fears consuming each other like an ouroboros, a constant cycle, mentally more draining than the emotion of loss. It was disquieting for anyone facing him in stressful situations.

Arkyn's manner betrayed nothing of self-doubt, of unease or agitation as he asked Hillbeck for a verbal report of what had been done by the King's Guard and whether the sergeant required anything from him.

Hillbeck explained the part the King's Guard had played, more on what he'd heard and concluded with, "We're currently hunting for the entrance to the Viewing Gallery—"

"Stop, immediately."

"Sir?"

"It's simple, Hillbeck, stop hunting for the entrance. That mystery is better left as it has been for centuries. I will not sanction its rediscovery."

"Sire, I am worried that there is an assassin who knows the entrance and your guards do not."

Arkyn eyed him. "Tell Pixney to increase the men on the second and third floors on this side of the King's Hall; tell him I want the servants escorted through the passages, if you must, but you have my orders. If you're that concerned, concentrate on catching the bloody assassin."

"Very good, sir. I'll make sure the orders are carried out."

Arkyn jerked his head in dismissal. His orders were nonsensical, and they both knew it, but he couldn't face the discovery, face having to acknowledge the place his father's assassin had stood. He didn't want Tain or Cal put in the position of acknowledging it either for they were blaming themselves for the entrance being discovered. It wasn't fair. None of it was. They shouldn't have ever had their fun used for such ends. He shouldn't be here, in the Inner Office, dismissing loyal men, refusing to listen. He shouldn't be having to face down the Lords of Oedran, exile them, wonder about their motives, mourn his father, support his brother, protect his cousin, fail at protecting her. He shouldn't be having to outwit his uncle, face him down, have Tain face him. His father shouldn't have died, shouldn't have faced death, shouldn't have made his friends betray him, shouldn't have confused his administrator's loyalty, shouldn't have forced his nearfather's hand. It wasn't fair, none of it. He thumped the desk. The world shouldn't have changed. Exhaustion was emphasising his anger and he didn't have the strength left to fight it.

Chapter 50
COLLAPSE
18:48
Inner Office

EDWARD ENTERED, carrying documents. He let the door close, walked over to the King's desk, putting them down. "Sir, go to your chambers for a bit. This will all wait."

His head on his arms, Arkyn said, "No it won't, Edward! The world doesn't stop because my father was murdered."

Edward murmured, "Then it should! Sorry, Sire… I…" He cursed and walked quietly away.

"Edward…"

The tone surprised the administrator, it was soft, questioning but not accusatory, yet there was still a concerning harmonic there. He turned back to the King.

"Why did he tell you and not me?"

Edward swallowed. "I wish he hadn't, sir, but I think he hoped, truly hoped, that there would never be a need for you to find out…"

"There nearly wasn't; I nearly died of poison…"

"No, Sire. I think His Late Majesty hoped that all the signs were wrong that he'd actually survive the attack."

"Yet deep down he knew he wouldn't. I can feel my anger building against everything and before I lose all reason, I need you to know I understand that it wasn't your fault."

"Thank you, sir."

"I just can't accept that he didn't… that he…"

Brokenly at first Arkyn started talking and then finding a flow of words he continued, his voice gradually getting louder. In the Outer Office, Richardson dismissed the other secretaries and walked through with them to the Audience Chamber. He told the guards on the dais to go for a break and mentioned to Hillbeck on the doors exactly why he was closing them. He returned to the Outer Office and simply waited, listening as Arkyn poured forth his anger at the whole situation and thanked the moons that no-one else could hear him. He'd watched his new King grow up. Half of what he said he'd never have said without grief being present. It wasn't his heart but a twisted reflection of it. Gradually quiet fell once again but it was some time before Edward left the office.

"Edward?"

"Leave him be, sir…"

"He didn't mean it."

206

Edward sat in a chair. "Maybe not, but he said it. Where's everyone?"

"Gone for a break. I have my uses…"

"I wish I had mine."

They heard the bell ring and Edward got up.

"No, Edward, I'll answer this."

* * *

Arkyn was slumped by the windows, shaking, cradling himself. Tears had coursed down his cheeks unchecked. His fists were balled, white knuckles hinted how tightly.

Richardson crossed to him, slipped an arm around his back and helped him into the chair behind the desk. He prised the King's fists open. He hadn't done any damage. He knelt by Arkyn's chair. Not out of deference but out of care.

"You're going back to your chambers, sir."

"No, I'm bloody not!"

"Yes, you are. You've had your rant at the injustice of the world, at your father's decisions, at Edward's seeming perfidy, you've shed more tears than I think you have over the last two days and now you need to sleep. No, sir. I've known you since before you took a breath in this world and I swore to Adeone that I'd help look out for you when he put you in my arms before you were a day old. So, am I to be forsworn when he'd most want me to help?" As Arkyn started shaking again, Richardson said, "Come on, lad, there should be no-one but Hillbeck and Edward about. I saw to that."

Arkyn got shakily to his feet. "I…"

"Hush, sir. Lean on me, metaphorically or literally. I'm retiring; I haven't anything to lose in telling you the truth…"

Arkyn accepted the support. "Don't be so… Richardson, I'm tired…"

"I'm not surprised. Come on, your bed awaits and I'm sure Kadeem's there to tuck you in."

Arkyn sagged. He didn't have to make a decision if Richardson took the lead and he needed not to make a decision.

Richardson opened the door. "Nip and make sure that there's no-one in the corridors, Edward – that includes the guards."

Edward nodded and was back moments later to say the coast was clear.

The only guard remaining was Hillbeck, and he took one look at Arkyn and walked ahead of him.

Once in the antechamber Hillbeck saluted and left. He shook his head, but that was as much as he ever said on the whole thing.

Kadeem wordlessly took the King's weight from Richardson. With Edward opening the doors, he guided Arkyn to his bedchamber. Once in a comfortably warm bed, Arkyn looked round. His mind clearing.

"Where's Edward?"

"He's gone to sort something out."

"Get him for me, Kadeem."

"Is that wise, sir?"

"Just do it."

Edward entered the bedchamber and knelt.

Arkyn swallowed, closing his eyes. "I'm sorry."

Edward got up and crossed over to the bed, taking the glass of sedative from Kadeem. The manservant left them alone.

"Don't be, sir."

Arkyn looked him in the eye. "I am sorry…"

"It could have been anyone there. I'm glad it was me. I deserved it."

"No, you didn't. You were sworn to secrecy because of necessity, not because you wanted to betray me and I should never have suggested otherwise. It wasn't fair."

Edward carefully placed the glass of sedative down, knelt and kissed the King's hand. "I am always your man."

Arkyn sighed deeply. "I never truly doubted that. Please get up; I'm sick of seeing people kneel and of hearing declarations of loyalty – for all I appreciate them. I'm not sure I'll be back at my desk tonight."

"I should hope not, sir! That is, you need your rest."

"I think I do."

That was a step in the right direction then.

"Kadeem's disappeared, Sire. So, I suppose it's my job to say that there is a sleeping draught from the doctor. It may be an idea to take it."

"With coaxing like that you can take Kadeem's job…"

Edward smiled. "My expertise is in other areas, sir. Will you take it?"

Arkyn nodded, took the sedative and then lay back on his pillows. "Thank you, Edward."

The administrator bowed and left.

A few minutes later Kadeem entered the King's bedchamber. "Can I get you anything, sir?"

There was no reply. The manservant padded over and, trying not to disturb Arkyn, removed a couple of pillows before putting a log on the fire and blowing out the candles. The King needed the sleep of oblivion.

* * *

Richardson looked up as Edward re-entered the Outer Office. "Well?"

"He's apologised. I just don't know if I'll ever forget what he said."

"Neither of you will but he didn't mean it, not deep within himself."

"I know that but it was still said."

"And don't you think he'll curse himself with it for years to come as much as you'll curse that you did what was asked of you?"

"I can't curse that. King Adeone had the right to ask me and by following his wishes I did less damage, I think, than if there had been no-one there who could deliver those letters."

"You're probably right. I wish he could have trusted me..."

"He hoped he was wrong," pointed out Edward. "What would you have done if he'd said to you that he would be dead by the end of the banquet?"

"Had every precaution put in place," replied Richardson without a pause.

"Would that have been successful?"

"We'll never know."

Edward shook his head. "Unless you knew of the entrance to the Viewing Gallery, it wouldn't have been. If any other method had been chosen there was always a hope that you might have prevented it but there was no way of preventing what happened. Even Lord Landis was unable to do anything."

"For him there were other obligations," admitted Richardson.

"Yes." Edward glanced at the Inner Office door. "I'll never presume to know their minds but by not telling anyone, King Adeone knew no-one could be blamed. Do you think it's possible that why he did what he did? That it was to protect men King Arkyn will need?"

Richardson considered. "Giving Hillbeck the evening off certainly suggests that. I wouldn't put much past King Adeone when it came to protecting his sons' interest. Now, I'm for home. Leave everything and lock the doors."

"Will you eat here, sir?" asked Edward.

"You can't face everyone on your own can you?"

"Not really."

"Then I'll tell them that you want something in your room. No, no-one will be surprised. You've been working hard. It's one of the perks of being the King's Administrator..."

Edward smiled half-heartedly. "If I am still that."

Richardson snorted. "Then you don't recognise the lies of anger. Come on, you need food and I need peace."

"Please stay, sir, I could do with some company."

Richardson nodded. "I think I could as well and, Edward, I'm no longer the King's Administrator, there's no need to call me 'sir'."

Securing the doors, Edward stilled. "No, I am. How did I end up here?"

"By hard work. Come on you need dinner."

"Damn," cursed Edward. "The King had planned to dine with Prince Tain and Lady Elantha…"

"Whilst you were with the King, I cancelled that arrangement."

"You didn't know…"

"He wasn't in any fit state for anything but bed, Edward; sometimes it's easier to tell them than to pick up the pieces afterwards."

Edward sighed. "I'll try to remember that."

They entered Secretaries' Corridor and Richardson put his head round the door to the runners' room.

"Who's causing trouble in here then?"

The three lads jumped up.

"One of you nip and tell Upper Hall that Administrator Edward would like dinner for two in his room and when Denny starts moaning tell him I sent the message."

When Richardson rejoined Edward all they heard was the swift departure of one of the boys and absolute silence from the others.

Once in Edward's room, Richardson sank onto a chair. "Definitely one of the better rooms this."

"Is it?"

"Mm. It used to be mine at one point. Then I got married and a house, and when Adeone became King, well, I was asked if I wanted a room here and I said I'd only need somewhere to lay my head. The Steward took me at my word."

Edward smiled. "I wondered why you had the room you've got."

"Because the Steward and I have a long-standing agreement to annoy each other. I'd have thought you'd have worked that one out by now. He's from an illegitimate line of the Ryson family."

"I'm not bothered about his past, just how to stop him infuriating the King, especially after today."

"Get interested in people's history, Edward; you'll need every lever you can get. It's not an easy job being the King's Administrator."

Edward said, "It's not an easy job being an administrator."

"No but it gets more complicated. I made it to the position of King's Clerk the year Adeone was born. By the time Lord Scanlon was born I was working in the Outer Office and I'd thought it was hard work to get there. It was nothing to when Adeone became King."

Edward swallowed. "Today *has* been rather busy."

"Yes, and tomorrow will be worse. Imperadai with the funeral will the worst day until the day before the coronation. I'm going to make you an offer, and I don't mean to tread on your toes. Do you want me to stay and help until after the funeral? Traditionally, I should leave tonight."

Edward looked at him, "Yes, I'd appreciate it, and not for me. I'd never have persuaded King Arkyn to go and rest."

"As I said, it's easier to tell them sometimes."

"He'll also be annoyed if he doesn't get a chance to talk to you properly."

"He doesn't need to."

"This is King Arkyn we're talking about; he doesn't need to do a lot but he still does," pointed out Edward.

Richardson laughed. "True. Adeone does live on in his sons."

"Mm and you're going to escape the mayhem. You'll miss King Adeone, won't you?"

"Yes."

"Do you wish to reminisce? I don't mind listening."

"Thank you. There are some stories I certainly can't tell my wife but are worth the hearing, and I know he wouldn't have minded."

Edward poured two drinks. "I'm intrigued."

Chapter 51
SAMARA
Afternoon
Lufian

IN LUFIAN, Lord Faran had packed bare essentials and his wife, who was helping, said,

"Is this wise?"

He shook his head. "Probably not but he asked me to go, Kyla. I think he needs someone with him who is removed from the situation. Wealsman would have been the better man, but he's running Terasia."

"But why you? It's not as though you got off to the best start, is it?"

"Maybe that helped," mused Faran. "The bandit attack was unfortunate, but it was dealt with fairly and the result was he knows he can trust me, as Adeone knew he could. There can't be many men like that and the others are all governors."

She said, "Yes. Why aren't you more involved with running Lufian?"

"Are you rejoicing or complaining?"

"Rejoicing but I have wondered why Adeone didn't give you some post or other."

Faran looked at her. "I told him I didn't want anything, that I was happy as I was, with just the occasional stint of teaching at the Lufia Advisors' School, that's as much involvement as I actually want. Adeone needed one friend who wasn't influential."

"I suppose so. Wealsman wasn't though, not until recently."

"Wealsman, darling, was Adeone's spy in Terasia but he was always going to be influential."

"Were you his spy here?" she asked with narrowed eyes.

He kissed her. "I had my uses. Now, do you think they'll have hitched the coach yet?"

"I should be thankful you're taking a coach, I suppose. I half expected you to be riding."

In the interests of marital harmony, Faran forbore from mentioning that once on the road that was exactly what he planned to do.

In the entrance hall, his eldest daughters were waiting. Lucille looked worried and Faran simply kissed the top of her head.

"I'm for Oedran."

She watched him. "Can you pass on our condolences, father?"

He nodded. "Of course. I'm sure the King will appreciate them. Where's Samara?"

"She's sound asleep, father… and still teething…"

"Ah, then I won't wake her and have her screaming the place down. Give her a hug for me. Now, you four, be good for your mother."

Lady Faran said, "They always are. It's only you they play up with."

* * *

The empire's roads were littered with lodges where the King's mail riders could change horses or get a coach. Lord Faran had enough standing to be able to use them at will, and, with the news spreading through the empire like wildfire, the lodge keepers were not stupid enough to argue when he mentioned the King had requested his presence in Oedran.

The first lodge they stopped at was close by the borders of Lufia, Bayan and Tradere, at a place called Shinglis. It was an important road junction and as such the lodge was large and well equipped, the lodge keeper was also known to and knew Lord Faran. As soon as the lord's coach drew up, he swore.

Faran alighted swiftly and the lodge keeper left his office to greet him.

"Lord Faran, I presume you're heading for Oedran?"

"I am, Withers. I just need a horse…"

"It's what we do best, my lord, but what of your coach."

"I'll leave it here and collect it on my return journey. I need to make Oedran and quickly."

"My lord, night is not far away, surely it would be better to continue in the coach and leave it at your next stop."

"It's rather cumbersome. I promised the King I'd be with him as soon as possible."

"It wouldn't be much time difference, my lord…"

"Withers… You are aware of the events in Oedran?"

The lodge keeper sighed. "Yes, my lord, word reached us earlier today. All lodges have been informed by magical messenger, a rare event."

"So was the assassination. My point is that King Arkyn's temper is going to be frayed; would you like me to explain what caused my delay?"

A polite cough behind them made them both turn.

Faran eyed his coachman. "Yes, Juan?"

"Master Withers isn't the delay, milord, Mistress Samara is."

Faran stared uncomprehendingly at him. "What?"

"Mistress Samara, sir, snug under the seat, asleep to the world…"

Faran strode over to the coach and looked down at his youngest daughter, then at the bemused coachman.

"Have you tried to wake her?"

"Yes, sir, but without luck."

Faran nodded, he looked again at his daughter. "She didn't climb in and drug herself, I assume."

"Erm, no, milord, that would be rather odd."

Faran brushed his daughter's hair from her face. "Can you drive strange horses, Juan?"

"Should be able to, sir."

"Good. I'll contact Her Ladyship, put her mind at rest. You contact Henri to come and collect our horses. Get them to hitch the new horses to our coach and we'll have to continue to Oedran in this."

"The horses may be uncertain with a strange coach and driver."

"I'd have thought mail-horses were used to it, Juan, but one of the lodge lads can come and help if you want. Please arrange it."

* * *

Two moments later Faran said, "She's here, Kyla. Juan found her."

"Thank Alcis. I was so worried, but I didn't want you to feel you had to turn back. I'll send someone to…"

"No. Look, she can come to Oedran. There's still a nursery set up for the FitzAlcis – well, for Lady Elantha."

"We can't impose, it's ridiculous."

"Listen carefully, someone put Samara in the under-seat storage on a nice little bed but drugged her so well she's still asleep. They did it for a reason. I doubt it was a pleasant one. I was going to have left the coach here to pick up on my return, berate me later. It would have been in one of the lodge's outhouses and the lid would have been too heavy for her to lift. This was attempted murder, Kyla. Whom can we trust?"

His wife looked physically sick. "I'll investigate."

"Wait for my return. Samara may well tell us in her own way then. Laugh it off as adventurous spirit because there's someone in our household destroying our lives and this time I mean to find them."

Lady Faran nodded slowly. "I'll play dumb. Just bring her back safely."

"I will. She'll be well-tended as King Arkyn's neardaughter. I rather suspect he'll be pleased to see her again."

"She might be a distraction for him, I suppose. Be careful, love."

"You too. Keep an eye on all the girls."

Chapter 52
MELLONIA
02-01-1215

Bayan – Lord Camlyn's House

MELLONIA CAMLYN of Bayan couldn't believe her tidily ordered life had been turned upside down so quickly. She'd gone to bed on Munewid Eve trying to persuade her father to let her stay up for the change of year. She hadn't argued but she hadn't been happy at his refusal.

"Another year, young one," was all he'd said.

The argument that Lady Elantha in Oedran was allowed to attend the banquet there, and she was younger, had gone unheeded. The fact she turned fifteen on the stroke of midnight had been pause for thought but not a reversal of the decision.

Now she didn't know if she was glad she hadn't seen her father die.

She had been woken by her nearmother. It had been strangely formal. She'd been told to get up and go to the study, where her nearfather said,

"Lady Mellonia, I regret I must tell you your father has died."

It was after midnight her numb mind had proclaimed, it must be, she was being addressed as 'Lady' but she hadn't comprehended anything else for many moments. Tears wouldn't come, not there, not where there had been laughter. Her eyes searched the room, hunting for the lie.

"Died?"

"Yes."

"But he was well when I went to bed. He was well, uncle, he was well." That was the key point; he hadn't been ill: elderly, yes, but not ill.

The glances had flown between her nearparents. Communication the like of which she could only begin to understand.

Her nearfather had said, "I'm afraid your father was poisoned."

She'd grasped that, "Food poisoning you mean? But surely the doctor…"

"No, Mellonia, poison administered for precisely the purpose of his death. In his whiskey."

"But you're still here…"

"I drink brandy, girl!"

"Of course you do, uncle," whispered Mellonia. "Can I go back to bed, please?"

"I suppose so. Do you wish to see him?"

It had taken all her resolve to say, "Tomorrow."

She had sat on the edge of her bed for hours. Sleep was elusive, she grew cold but uncaring of the cold. How? Why? So many questions and so few answers. Her nearfather wasn't someone who would ever explain. The questions would probably be answerless forever.

There was one that wouldn't: what would happen to her?

* * *

She had been drawn and quiet all through the following day, not wanting to think about anything. The servants were all kind, but she'd needed solitude, or un-expecting company. Her father had been laid out, and she had looked down at the peaceful face and wondered why, for all she felt desperately sad, the tears would not come.

* * *

She was sitting numbly in the library on the second day of the year when snatches of conversation from the study filtered through to her.

"News from Oedran is grave. King Adeone is dead also: assassinated."

"Surely then…"

"King Arkyn has returned to Oedran, but it was clear that the time isn't right to burden his office. We'll have to take the child with us."

"Will he permit that?"

Her nearfather said, "He won't know for days and we can't move here – dearly as I'd like to."

"Be careful, love, walls have ears."

"Perhaps not, it's the nosy servants hiding behind the doors that do."

"We should still be careful. Who knows what tittle-tattle those servants will make of innocent comments?"

There was a pause for a few moments before her nearfather said, "I suppose this was Camlyn's requests."

215

"No-one seems to have found another. I've had every room searched."

"So, yes, it is. Good. It names us, my dear, as her local guardians so we can act in her interests here."

Her nearmother said, "Good. We wouldn't want to lose her to Oedran."

"No, nor the handling of the estate. At fifteen she's ripe for marriage. I've a few in mind. Camlyn wouldn't hear of it."

"He was a sentimentalist, love, that's all."

"Then we are the pragmatists. We'll leave as planned, whatever that interfering captain says."

"I'm sure he'll be mindful of his place."

Half an hour later, Mellonia was still sitting in the library, running her hand over the leather covering of a book her father had once given her on birds, beautifully illustrated it brought back happier times.

Her nearmother entered. "Mellonia, we're leaving in the morning."

"It's all right, aunt. I shall be perfectly content here."

"Your nearfather thinks it is better that you come with us. There will be too many memories here."

"They are not bad, aunt," anything was worth a try.

"Nevertheless, we are your guardians and it is our responsibility to see you are cared for."

"Not forgetting the Camlyn lands of course and my guardian is the King, aunt. Father told me his arrangements," she watched the effect of the statement on her nearmother's face. There was a flicker. Lady Dennison hadn't expected her to know.

"I'll not be spoken to like that, young lady – neardaughter or no. Come and pack your things."

"But I was right, the King is my guardian."

"The King is dead," snapped Lady Dennison coldly.

"King Arkyn then."

"He is a little preoccupied by weightier matters."

"Maybe empathy will draw his mind in this direction."

"Maybe so, but we can speak to him as easily from Meaden Hall as from here."

Mellonia said, "Yes, but this is my home."

"You're not leaving it for good, young lady. Come and pack."

"Must I?"

"Yes."

* * *

As they walked into the hallway, Mellonia spotted the house steward and the steward spotted her. He inclined his head smartly.

"My lady, do you have a moment?"

"Of course," replied Lady Dennison.

With a poise that Mellonia was going to remember for years, the steward said, "I beg your pardon, madam, but I was actually speaking to Lady Mellonia as my mistress."

"I'm coming," said Mellonia. "Aunt, will you ask Mary to find a suitable trunk or two? It would help if I knew how long I was to be absent for."

"Initially a couple of aluna-months."

"Thank you." She followed the steward into his office. "Give me some news I want to hear, please."

"I'm sorry, my lady, I don't think I have any. I just thought you could do with a rescuer."

"Thank you. Apparently, I'm to go with my nearparents in the morning."

"Aye, my lady. I knew your father's arrangements but with King Adeone's assassination some things are more urgent in Oedran. All we've been told is that the King is aware of the situation – that you have been orphaned, that is – and that he has agreed to your nearparents being local guardians but estate matters will be overseen by an Oedranian official every year."

Mellonia sank onto a chair. "I bet they weren't happy. Promise me something: don't leave here. They're going to try to marry me off. They inherit the greater part of the lands if I die and if I don't marry someone who is beholden to them..."

"They don't have the control they think they do, my lady. Your mind is a match for theirs. Listen, they scheme and plot but it is the King who has the ultimate say. If they try anything not of your liking, inform him."

"That won't do anything, probably make it worse. A King's ward, I sometimes think, is in a double prison, but I couldn't tell father that."

Her steward sat by her. "Maybe it's time you know your family history; well, your immediate family history. It's not all glorious. Your father saved the Camlyn lands but at the expense of his father's life."

Mellonia swallowed. "Grandfather is never mentioned."

"No. He helped lead the 1169 rebellion."

"*What*?" Her eyes scoured his face, hunting for a lie that wasn't there.

"Yes. Your father disagreed with his father's principles, walked into the Oedranian camp, got himself honour-bound to the FitzAlcis, procured entry to the Citadel in Garth, without the rebels knowing about his sojourn into the Oedranian camp. No-one's certain what he said or did but, by the end of the day, the gates were open to the Oedranians and several men were dead, including your grandfather. Your father never spoke about that day. When Lord Galwood's father retired as governor, your father was asked to step in. He refused. His actions had many repercussions.

I'm not even sure if King Adeone was aware he was honour-bound, I very much doubt King Arkyn is, but it does mean that when something was requested of him by the FitzAlcis, he had less chance to refuse than many another lord. I don't know on what terms your guardianship was mooted but it might explain why he agreed so quickly."

"What else don't I know?"

"Probably quite a lot, my lady. There'll be a lot now no-one knows."

She swallowed and tears started falling. The steward looked at her and, as though she was still six and had simply fallen over and grazed her knee, he picked her up and sat cradling her.

After some time, he said softly, "Can I advise you, my lady?"

"You're the steward…"

He passed her a handkerchief. "Get yourself a messenger. I know it's not considered proper for ladies but, quite frankly, stuff propriety. Don't tell your nearparents but have that safety net."

She nodded. "I'll think about it. Hume, do you know why they are my nearparents?"

"Because before you were born your father had settled his bequests on them as he didn't expect to have a child so he thought that it would mitigate the fact you're here."

"Oh. That explains a lot."

"Doesn't it?"

She got up, rearranging her skirts. "Thank you. Watch over everything and keep the house running as it should. Meaden Hall isn't so far as to be inaccessible if I need a break from propriety."

"If you don't want to leave, say the word, lass, and we won't let you."

Mellonia sighed. "I wish I could but there would be repercussions I couldn't save you from. I'll bear my soul in patience."

"As always. Take courage from the small things and hope from the spaces between the bad. Your father's funeral will be Hexadai. You'll have to be back for then."

* * *

The following morning, her nearfather snapped, "Really, Mellonia, the animals are not coming, nor the birds! We are not turning our house into a menagerie. They belong here."

Mellonia sighed rather than said, "So do I," before adding in a normal voice, "Uncle, my animals are my friends."

"Then we shall introduce you to people. The creatures will be well-tended here."

Mellonia faced him. "You can force me to leave home to suit your whims but I will not leave all my friends."

Aware of the hall full of servants, Lord Dennison said, "You may bring the dog and the little bird. The dog we can train for the hunt."

Mellonia thought, *'Maybe not,'* before saying, "Thank you, uncle."

Hume watched them leave with misgivings. He said under his breath, "A brave lady of her father's mould. I hope she isn't too unhappy."

The housekeeper beside him replied, "Be optimistic, she speaks her mind well. There'll be liveliness at Meaden Hall."

Hume smiled. "Aye. Do you, like me, wish you could see it?"

"Of course. Her father would be proud."

"Her father was."

PART 4

Chapter 53
MORNING AND ORGANISATION
Tretaldai, Week 1 – 3rd Cearal, 3rd Cearcis 1215
Inner Office

KING ARKYN entered the Inner Office the following morning wanting a few minutes privacy. He closed the door on the Outer Office and crossed over to the bedchamber where his father was still laid out. His hand rested on the handle for some moments before he took a deep breath and opened the door. He stopped on the threshold. Candles burnt in all the sconces, as Simkins silently kept vigil. When Arkyn entered, the manservant crossed to him and, inclining his head, would have left – apparently and unusually for the Inner Office and not his own quarters – but Arkyn gripped his wrist.

"Thank you."

"I felt someone should be here…"

"It should have been me," murmured Arkyn.

"No, sir, you've far too much else on. I have a lot of free time."

Arkyn tightened his grip. "I'm sorry, Simkins."

"That, sir, is my line. I failed your father and, therefore, I failed you. I should have known everything wasn't right. I should have seen he was putting things in order. Whatever was in his bequests for me, and I've heard a couple of rumours, I don't deserve."

"Cocswallop."

Simkins glanced at Adeone's lifeless form. "No, sir, it's my conscience, and I've been sitting here since yesterday reconciling my mind and coming to this decision."

"Wait for me in the Inner Office, please."

Simkins left.

Arkyn knelt by the bed, trying to clear his thoughts. He had a busy day to face and hadn't expected to face Simkins resolve as well. His eyes travelled to his father's left hand. He frowned, looked at the right hand and the frown deepened. He glanced around the room but couldn't see what he was searching for. Entering the dressing room, feeling like he was violating something, he pulled open one drawer and then another and another.

* * *

Eventually he re-entered the Inner Office, shouted for Edward, asked for his father's requests and bequests and Richardson, and when he had the former in his hand, and the latter was in the office, he said,

"I should have spoken to you yesterday. I'm sorry I didn't manage to."

Richardson glanced at Simkins, wondering what had happened. "We did speak, Sire."

"Actually, you ordered me to go to bed. No, I don't want your apologies, Richardson; you were right. What I'd like is for you to knock some sense into Simkins. He's refusing the bequest my father left him because he doesn't think he *deserves it*."

"Will you excuse us, sir?" enquired Richardson.

Arkyn nodded and watched as Richardson pushed a reluctant Simkins into the triniculum. What would the administrator say to his long-term colleague? Whilst he waited, he asked Edward to send for Rayburn.

* * *

After some time, Richardson and Simkins re-entered the Inner Office. Arkyn raised a questioning eyebrow.

"Simkins wishes to say something, sir."

Arkyn motioned for him to do so.

"My decisions are my own, sir."

Richardson turned to Simkins swearing under his breath. His hands half reached out as though to take the manservant by the shoulders and shake him. Pursed lips didn't do his frown justice.

Oddly more amused than annoyed, Arkyn said, "They are, Simkins, and as none of us are in a calm frame of mind all I shall say is that the pension will be paid to you in line with my father's wishes. You did so much for him, whatever you believe at the moment. I respect your decisions but I have to uphold my father's last wishes and those definitely included yours and Richardson's future wellbeing. My own grief is of a different mould to yours; mine is making me sombre and yet angry, yours is making you intractable and stubborn; as for yours, Richardson, we won't mention last night but direct and caring probably covers it... What I will say though is, now is not the time to make important decisions. You both have families to support as well as yourselves and father knew that. You both have pensions to the same amount that your yearly wage was, that was his wish, and your houses in Oedran are yours for your lifetime rent free."

Simkins said, with feeling, "If he wasn't already dead..."

Arkyn got up and walked over to him, Simkins eyed him nervously, but all Arkyn did was take him gently by the shoulders. "But he is, Simkins, and he knew you'd find out when it was too late. I thought you appreciated his sense of humour."

"Not being on the receiving end of it, I don't, sir. I'm sorry; I shouldn't be speaking like this. Why are you tolerating it?"

Arkyn glanced at Richardson who diplomatically left.

"Because after last night I have no right to comment on what anyone says in their grief. Please accept it, Simkins."

Simkins swallowed, obviously trying to maintain a professional mask. His eyes met Arkyn's. He nodded, too choked to speak.

Arkyn relaxed. "Thank you. Now, I don't think keeping vigil is helping you, for all I appreciate it. What's happening about my father's chambers?"

"I'll… I'll start clearing them, sir. I couldn't…"

"If it's any consolation, neither can I. Let's face this head on, Simkins. Ask for Kadeem's help. There's something I'd like you to locate. Father used to wear my mother's ring, the Queen's Ring, it's not on his hand but his other rings are, you've not removed it?"

Simkins looked worried. "No, sir."

Arkyn said, "I'd like it found. First though, if you've been up for as long as I suspect, you are to go to bed and get some rest."

"Thank you, sir."

"I've got to face another day. Ask Richardson to join me, please."

Simkins finally did what tradition dictated he should have done as soon as he'd seen Arkyn and knelt.

"Stop improving my mood, Simkins. It doesn't suit you."

Hearing the irony, Simkins smiled and rose. "Of course, Sire."

* * *

Richardson re-entered the Inner Office a moment later, with his professional demeanour restored.

"Will you accept the bequest?" enquired Arkyn.

"Yes, Sire, for your father's memory not because I actually agree with the amount."

Arkyn said softly, "Father was liberal when his generosity had been earned. Simkins has accepted. What did you say to him?"

"Nothing that apparently had any immediate effect, sir. He told me that he would be accepting it but that, it seems, was to shut me up. How did you convince him?"

"It's called persistence. I believe you are well-practised in the art. That aside, could you stay and help Edward for a couple of days? My accession was so… sudden that nothing had been previously prepared."

"Edward and I came to an understanding to that end last night, sir. It is under his control."

"It seems I am anticipated at every turn," said Arkyn.

"Kadeem might advise you to take a different road, Sire."

Arkyn eyed him. "Ask Edward and Advisor Rayburn to join me please, Richardson, before you put my manservant out of a job."

Richardson with a small smile bowed and left.

* * *

When Edward announced Rayburn, the advisor knelt.

Sitting down at his desk, Arkyn said, "Rayburn, I don't expect you to kneel when you enter and leave. Please get up. Edward, we'll need my diary for today. Rayburn, have a seat."

Edward returned two moments later carrying three pieces of paper. He handed one to the King and one to Rayburn, keeping one in his own hand.

Arkyn looked at it. "I wish efficiency was something I could complain about at times. Thank you for anticipating the meeting."

Rayburn scanned the day's meetings. "Sire, you also need to see the General and Major Wynfeld."

Arkyn nodded. "Yes, and soon, but I want to talk to you about it, first. I also need to talk to you about the procedure for dismissing Kilbride. I've been advised to go for the full effect."

"I think that's wise, Sire. Edward, the King will need about half an hour for the audience. The protocol requires the entire King's Guard to be present. The Palace Guard or Prince's Guard can take over door duty for the duration of the audience. If a Defender has been appointed, they should be present and carry out the dismissal. Because of Lord Landis' incapacitation that isn't possible today. I suggest, therefore, that either the General or Major are present as the highest officers under your command, sir. I would also recommend that Prince Tain is present, given the reason for the dismissal."

"I have already told him he will be. I've not yet seen him this morning but I must soon."

Awkwardly making a note, Edward said, "His Highness is currently at the Courthouse, Sire."

"Thank you, Edward, and for heaven's sake sit down and use the desk. Looking at this list, it seems weighted to the funeral arrangements. What is happening about the proclamations?"

Edward said, "The proclamation of your accession has been delivered to all towns within a day's moderate mail-ride of the cities. By the end of today, every town in the empire should have received it and it should have been proclaimed in each. Your father's funeral has been proclaimed for tomorrow evening in Oedran. The proclamation for the coronation date, due to the fact it could be stated with certainty was included with that of your accession. It is standard practice when an underage king accedes. The proclamation for His Highness' appointment as Justiciar of Oedran had been dealt with by King Adeone."

Rayburn said, "I believe your administrator is too efficient, Sire."

"Yes. Edward, you're ruining illusions," added Arkyn dryly.

"My apologies, Sire. I have had Richardson's help."

"True. As well as the funeral arrangements, I'll need a meeting about the provincial ambassadors. I take it none have yet arrived?"

"No, sir. We're expecting the Low Plains' Ambassador by tonight, along with Lord Galaloth of Areal to aid Her Ladyship, and probably the Traderian Ambassador also. Bayan, and whoever the Domini sends, should be here tomorrow. Lufian, Denshire and Terasia on Pentadai. Gerymor, all being well, on Hexadai. For the Isles and Pale Lands, it depends on the winds, the Equinano was at Meith, she's picked up their ambassador. The Fencible has said they won't wait for the Equinano and their ambassador set sail yesterday on the navy ship the *Queen Sonila*. So far, they've reported favourable winds to Torport. The Serpent Isle Ambassador I'm expecting an update from shortly but he did say that, if it looks unfavourable, he'll put into port off the coast of Areal and travel via the mail routes. They should all be here by Septadai. The timings have been estimated from the mail routes, sir, so there might be some variation. Those are the best scenarios for travelling with luggage."

Arkyn nodded. "I'll need to see the list of who has been sent but later is fine. Lord Faran is also due. I've invited him to stay. He can have his regular rooms in the Privy Wing. Everyone else will be in the Court rooms; I'll need to see the Chamberlain. I'll see the ambassadors as soon as they arrive. Oh, Sicla... Edward, I must see Lady Rhian."

Edward nodded. "She's not in the Palace, sir."

"I still need to see her wherever she is. Do we know how Landis is?"

"I've not heard anything negative, sir, so I presume he's healing."

"We need to check," said Arkyn. "Where Lord Landis is concerned I've found it better to not presume anything. Now, I'm acutely aware the fact the official calendar has been blown to the winds by magic. What has happened about the Petitionals?"

Edward said, "An announcement was made that they were postponed. You will need to decide what happens this year, Sire."

"There's no real precedent," added Rayburn. "When Lord Onraet killed King Alvern, and instigated the Age of Tyranny, it was at the end of the Grievances, sir, and he simply did away with the practice altogether. It was reinstated and renamed to the Petitionals on King Arlis' accession."

"Edward, could the official calendar start on the Alunadai following my coronation?"

Edward hesitated. "I'll investigate, sir. The only clash I can envisage is the Ambassadors' Court will be in full swing."

"Then they can enhance the proceedings."

Rayburn listening to the King's swift manner smiled to himself, he enjoyed working for Arkyn, if only because officials became flummoxed and he was anticipating some fun once the solemnity of the next few weeks was past.

Chapter 54
SUMMONS
10:24
Oedran Palace

THE GENERAL AND MAJOR received the summons with tinges of apprehension. Wynfeld had retreated into one-word answers, knowing the King was going to be furious that they hadn't stopped the attack. The General was also taciturn. He'd served three kings; would the fourth require his immediate resignation? He would understand if that were the case, and Wynfeld could take over, but his future also lay in the balance.

Salutes greeted and followed them through the Palace but so did wary eyes, expectation and anticipation. Hillbeck on the doors to the Audience Chamber said conversationally,

"I hope, sirs, you're not going to do anything stupid."

Wynfeld glanced at him sharply as Paturn replied.

"That would depend on one's definition of 'stupid' and I don't want to hear yours, Hillbeck."

"In that case, General, don't let me prevent your immediate audience."

Edward greeted them in the Outer Office. The fact it *was* Edward and not Richardson made the situation far more real than it had been before.

"General, Major, the King is still talking with Advisor Rayburn but I shall inform him of your arrival, if you could wait here."

* * *

By the time they were announced, Wynfeld was more apprehensive than he could ever explain. He entered the Inner Office, saluted his King and stood feet four-square watching the young man's drawn features. He looked tired, unsurprisingly tired and almost a defeated air hung about him. Advisor Rayburn's face, though, gave nothing away.

Paturn had saluted and knelt. Wynfeld followed suit. If the General considered they should kneel then they would.

The King's reaction to the two subservient and nervous officers was succinct. "Get up!" Once they were on their feet, Arkyn glanced at the General, then at Wynfeld. "Explain."

Paturn said, "I really wish I could, Sire."

It was so lacking in substance, so obviously bleak that, for the first time, Wynfeld saw the General as fallible.

"There was no hint, Sire. I've men examining old reports but other than noting the six lords were on speaking terms, and individually hosted dinners at which Lord Scanlon was present, there has been no hint of what was planned," explained Wynfeld, his eyes never leaving Arkyn's.

"Is that the whole truth?"

Wynfeld said, "Yes, Sire, but we've uncovered other issues. Well, one issue: Jacobs was filtering information when he was copying reports. We've enough rope not only to hang him but to truss him up as well. He was sly, and only by comparing reports, which should be the same, have we discovered it. There's no doubt he'll be executed."

Arkyn got to his feet. "I thought the agreement was that he did mundane work, Wynfeld! Who let him near anything else?"

"I don't know, sir. I wasn't aware of it until I was told that Lord Scanlon's arrival was in the evening report but it wasn't in my copy."

"So, you can't say for certain that you had no hint," retorted Arkyn.

"Yes, sir, I can. The men would remember it and after the events no-one is daring to hide anything."

"Jacobs had better be detained and in solitary," fumed the King.

"He's run, sir," Wynfeld admitted, still holding Arkyn's gaze. "He prevented me getting told that the six lords were under arrest, and, when I sent men to apprehend him, he wasn't to be found."

Seeing Arkyn was speechless with fury, Rayburn said, "Is there *anything* else, Major Wynfeld?"

Wynfeld didn't look at the advisor. "There's a report with Edward for our King. It details all we've managed to discover so far."

Arkyn found his voice. "Anything to add, General?"

General Paturn said, "Yes. Sire, we both feel that we failed King Adeone and wish not only to offer our condolences but also our apologies, and, if necessary, our resignations."

Wynfeld inwardly winced. They hadn't discussed it, even though it was a likely outcome. His King's face darkened.

With rage emphasising his voice, Arkyn snapped, "What *good* would your resignation do? Would it help the situation? You would deprive me of the highest officers of my army. No! Major, I'm surprised you would even consider it as a viable course of action."

The General's face became a fixed picture.

"I failed your father, sir, and in that I failed you," replied Wynfeld, his gaze steady. "Ultimately, I'm in charge of collecting intelligence. I don't believe anyone can dispute that we missed this, most devastating, plot."

Arkyn watched Wynfeld's face, thinking of all the times they'd worked together. He said tiredly, "No, no-one can dispute that fact, *no-one*. Now, listen to me carefully; my father had prior warning of his death. He knew what faced him. I shall not be taking action against his closest advisors and officials because he chose to keep the knowledge private. I *will* be taking action against incompetency and treason. Kilbride will be dismissed, but that is currently all until I have better facts to hand. You two, however, don't need to worry."

The General said, "Sire, your decision is beneficial to those whom you release from obligation but are you certain it isn't detrimental to your authority?"

Arkyn's temper flared once more. He whipped round to face the elderly General. All he saw was concern. "Paturn, my decision is final! I am not making the pronouncement from a youthful blindness to consequence; I am trying to upset my uncle's plans. He will expect me to take vengeful action against all who should have protected my father. That would not advantage myself, it would not be valuable to the empire, I hesitate to add that there would only be one person who could possibly gain from such hasty action and, I think, not one of us here wish for him to feel victorious in any small measure. Major, you will give the intelligence regiment a reminder of their duties. I need to know that there is nothing amiss there. *You* will talk to every man in the regiment and see if anyone had any concerns. *You* will ascertain if they reported it to anyone. If they did, and no action was taken, *you* will follow it up until you have satisfied yourself that there is no traitor within that regiment. I want Jacobs caught. I want to know who decided he could be involved with confidential matters, and I want Stuart under lock and key until the whole matter is resolved."

Wynfeld said, "Very good, Sire. Would you like an observer with me when I conduct the interviews?"

Arkyn raised an eyebrow slightly, "If you think it is a good idea, I shall send someone along."

"I would be happier, in this circumstance, Sire."

"Good. Now, you both look like you've not slept. Go to bed. I shall see you for the Military Audience. Every officer in Oedran, whether officially on leave or not, will be expected to be there. Details will be with you shortly."

* * *

When they reached the barracks, Wynfeld and Paturn made their way silently to the latter's office and sank into chairs.

Paturn said, "You'd better catch Jacobs. The audience we had was, I believe, so short on Rayburn's recommendation. King Arkyn's temper will not stand a long wait."

"I know our King's temperament, General."

"No, you did. They change when they become King."

* * *

In the Inner Office, Rayburn had said, "May I ask how His Late Majesty came to know of his imminent death, sir? Because it obviously wasn't through his official intelligence gatherers."

"I don't believe it was one man's word look or deed. It must have been a series of circumstances and an aptitude for reading people. I don't want to think about it. He made his decision; I live with the consequences of it. I'm not happy that Wynfeld's men knew nothing, and took so long to find out what had happened, but I shall consider more leisurely what to do about it. I know Paturn's and Wynfeld's work, and know this wasn't their fault. I shall consider what the consequences will be when I've all the facts to hand. Father asked me not to lay blame for their ignorance, and I shan't but I shall take action if it is proved that there was negligence leading to ignorance. I shall also take action over Jacobs. They knew why he was employed there. They knew he and Stuart were posted there from the FitzAlcis staff for threatening behaviour, for want of a better term. How could they be so blind, so stupid?"

"By the sounds of things, Wynfeld and Paturn didn't know anything about it, Sire."

"No but there are two Captains of Intelligence and they did!" There was a knock at the door and Edward entered tentatively,

"Sir, Lady Rhian is here."

Arkyn nodded. "That's all, Rayburn."

Rayburn knelt as he left. Arkyn was considering what he could say in response to that when his father's cousin entered the office.

Chapter 55

RHIAN

10:36

Inner Office

LADY RHIAN DROPPED into a curtsy that showed many years' practice as Arkyn crossed to greet her, waiting until they were in private before speaking.

"Cousin…"

She looked up at him. "Sire."

He shook his head slightly. "I… please don't. I've enough of other

231

people treating me like fragile glass. I'm sorry…"

She got up. "How are you?"

"Do you really want me to answer?"

"If it will help."

"Sad and angry. My temper's erratic…"

"That's not surprising, sir."

He passed her a drink. "Were you in hall when it happened?"

"Yes."

"How are you coping?" he asked, not that he needed to, her face spoke for her more clearly than words could.

"You didn't get me here to check I was all right, sir."

"Actually, I did. I saw more than you might think when you visited Ceardlann last year, and here, and, well, I can put two and two together and get five."

She swallowed. "Yes, I loved Adeone, and no I'm not coping. Can we please leave it there, sir, I am my mother's daughter and I have no intention of breaking down here."

Arkyn crooked an eyebrow, a smile twitching at his lips. "Does quoting Aunt Amara in awkward situations work?"

"Mostly," admitted Rhian wryly.

"I'll try it. Have you had your invitation to the funeral?"

"Yes, this morning," she admitted, closing her eyes momentarily.

"I hope it said you'd be close by me."

"I don't think the Steward is particularly observant."

"No, neither do I. He'd missed you off the list, and Cousin Neassa."

Tears welled as she fought for control.

That had cut deeper than Arkyn realised it would. "Tain put him right before I saw the list. The fool – that is the Steward not Tain for once – had also missed off Cal."

"He always was a little man trying to make a point," she spat. "If nothing else I was Adeone's cousin!"

"Yes but the Steward is a traitor. I'm sure of it," confided Arkyn. "I just have no proof and, whatever I say, I've no-one to replace him with yet. Be careful, cousin."

"Does mother know any of this?" asked Rhian.

"I haven't told her and I rather suspect Tain won't."

"I think it might be better if she doesn't know," advised Rhian. "You might, however, get the evidence you seek if she does."

"I'm keeping Lady Amara as a sort of secret weapon."

"She said she was made your Protector."

"Yes, but I was unsure if that was a capital P or not," remarked Arkyn.

"You would have appreciated how she demolished Lord Scanlon."

"Oh, I can imagine. You know, whatever she said, she's watching out for you now."

"That's a good thing, is it?"

"Speaking as her daughter, yes – but as a concerned member of your family, possibly."

Arkyn nodded. "If we're being honest, I'm not sure what we'd do without her. I wish I'd met your father. He must have been special."

Rhian shrugged. "They were chalk and cheese, sir, but it worked. From what I've heard, I wouldn't say she bullied him into marrying her but he didn't argue when she suggested it."

Arkyn chuckled, a true laugh, it felt like the first he'd had since receiving the news. "I can imagine not."

There was a knock and an apologetic Edward entered.

Arkyn rolled his eyes at Rhian. Had his administrator been waiting for some sound other than soft conversation? "Yes, Edward?"

"Lord Faran has been in touch, Sire. He's asked if you could contact him, when you get time. Apparently, there's been a slight problem. I'm not sure what. I thought it best you knew."

"Faran?" enquired Rhian.

"I invited him here, my lady," explained Arkyn.

"Good, sir. I'm pleased you did that. I shouldn't stop you talking to him."

Arkyn glanced in dismissal at Edward. "You can, cousin."

"You have far too much on for me to disturb you any longer, sir."

Seeing she meant it, Arkyn said, "I suppose I should say thank you. Cousin Rhian, father is next door, if you want to say your private goodbyes before the funeral."

She blinked hard. "Thank you, Sire, I think I will. I'll leave by the servant's corridor—"

"No, you won't! Come through here. I don't mind what is happening, if I'm in a meeting or not. You're not leaving these chambers any other way."

In reply, she simply curtsied and left.

* * *

Arkyn called Fafnir and obtained a link. "What *slight problem*, Lord Faran? That phrase normally means bad news for me."

Faran said simply, "Your young neardaughter decided to come along for the experience, Sire. My conscience advised me to warn you."

"Thank it for me. Is there more to this than you're telling me?"

"There were circumstances which were concerning, yes, sir, but, at the moment, she's simply adventurous. It's the safest explanation."

"Will this slow your arrival at all, my lord?" enquired Arkyn.

"Hopefully not, sir. Samara and I have come to an understanding."

"I look forward to seeing you both. Where are you currently?"

"We'll be in Oedran this evening, Sire," admitted Faran.

"I beg your pardon?"

"Coming to Oedran at the current time means we get the best horses, and we travelled through the night."

Arkyn said, "There was no need."

"Yes, there was, Sire. I can delay if you wish."

"No, no don't do that. I'm just surprised. I'm glad you'll be here for the funeral. I hope you'll help bear father's body to the Alcium."

Faran swallowed. "It would be an honour unlooked for, sir."

Once out of the link Arkyn passed Edward the information that Faran was due imminently and settled down to read yet more reports and deal with funeral arrangements and Kilbride's dismissal. Neither of which helped his mood, or his feeling of being overwhelmed.

Chapter 56
KILBRIDE DISMISSED
12:24
Inner Office

JUST BEFORE LUNCHTIME, Tain entered the Inner Office saying, "There are a lot of guards hanging around doing nothing, Sire."

"I thought there might be," muttered Arkyn. "Has Rayburn seen you? It should have been Landis doing this, or the General or Major, but the first isn't able to and I sent the others to get some sleep…"

Tain nodded. "Yes, sir. I'll do it but people might mutter I'm being given a lot of authority for my age."

"I didn't think Hillbeck was a good idea," replied Arkyn. "He's worked closely with Kilbride. It wasn't fair on either of them."

"I'm sure he would have coped."

"So am I but I thought it might be… It might help."

"You mean I can take my anger out on someone?" replied Tain.

"Or feel like you have." He paused and answered a knock at the door with a simple, "Come."

Iris entered and bowed. "Sire."

Tain glanced at Arkyn and then at Iris. Why was the Lord of Oedran present? His duties wouldn't include the dismissal of a guard.

Arkyn said, "Lord Iris, thank you for coming. I thought that you would be able to tell Landis we did everything correctly."

Iris smiled. "No-one ever doubts that, sir." He glanced at Prince Tain. "Your Highness."

"Lord Iris."

The elderly Lord of Oedran sensed the Prince's unease. "As an observer, it's not my place to interfere, Sire, but, if you wish me to, I am more than willing to undertake the dismissal."

Arkyn saw Tain's set face. "Thank you, my lord, but Prince Tain is more than content with his role. Let's get it over with."

Iris opened the door before following Arkyn and Tain through the Outer Office to the Audience Chamber. Rayburn announced the King to the assembled guards and took up his position at the King's left hand, once Arkyn was standing in front of the throne with Iris at the King's right, where Landis would have been standing had he been present.

Standing on the second of the five central dais steps, Tain took a deep breath. "You have all taken an oath to serve and protect the King of Oedran, to lay down your lives in the protection of his. On Munewid Eve, that oath was broken and King Adeone Altarius FitzAlcis died at the hands of an assassin. Those men who were on duty that night now make yourselves known to King Arkyn."

Nine of the men present stepped forward and knelt.

"Will those men currently on duty please step forward and remove their weapons?"

The men who were kneeling whitened, but surrendered every sword.

Tain took a deep breath. "In such times there is one ancient method of recompense, execution. Feel the point of the blade on your spine and consider your oaths."

The nine who had disarmed their fellows, looked at each other uncertainly. Had they been ordered to make the first move towards execution?

Hillbeck glanced at Arkyn's resolute face. "Men, you have your orders."

Tain tried not to see the semi-circle of kneeling men, each with the tip of their own sword resting on their spine, whilst a colleague held the hilt with a bowed head, as though waiting for the kill order, which all the guards believed they were.

Tain continued, "Yet there is one of your number missing. Where is the man you answered to that night? Bring in Kilbride; he can witness the plight of the men under his orders."

Kilbride entered the Audience Chamber barefoot, escorted by two of the Prince's Guard. He momentarily closed his eyes, before looking at the FitzAlcis' implacable faces. He walked forward slowly. Had things changed since he was arrested the night before?

As the sergeant stood a few paces from the bottom of the dais steps.

Prince Tain said, "Sire, this is the man who failed King Adeone. Sergeant Duncan Kilbride."

"Sergeant no more," replied Arkyn.

"Is it your wish he remains still to guard you?"

"No. He shall not bear arms again in the name of the Kings of Oedran."

Tain nodded to his own guards, who tightened their grip on Kilbride. The Prince descended to the disgraced guard and took off his weapon belt, laying it on the dais.

"He no longer bears arms, Sire."

Arkyn said, "He is protected, where was the protection for King Adeone?"

Tain used his dagger to cut the leather thongs securing the former guard's breastplate and greaves, continuing until Kilbride was left with his tunic and hose only – at which point he was made to kneel.

"Sire, as Kilbride left King Adeone undefended, so now is he."

"Then he is to be exiled from Oedran at sundown."

Tain said, "Let it be known, Kilbride is an outcast from Oedran. Take him out."

All the guards watched as Kilbride was escorted out of the Audience Chamber by one of the Prince's Guard, whilst Tain's sergeant stood in the centre of the doorway to emphasise the audience wasn't over.

Taking a deep breath, Tain continued, "Sire, there are still nine men awaiting your judgement. Is there any action you wish to take?"

"No."

Confused relief passed over the guards' faces.

"King Arkyn acknowledges that circumstances were weighted against you," said Tain. "So there will be no executions, *but* be true to your oaths, here to be renewed, lest his mercy fail you."

The nine men holding the swords at their colleagues' necks relaxed and let the points drop.

"Sire, your guards," stated Tain.

To the silence of relief, Arkyn said, "Not quite, Prince Tain. There is a vacancy for a sergeant. I would ask of you Lyndon's service."

"May he serve his King as loyally as he has served the Prince's Guard."

Standing in the centre of the Audience Chamber doorway, Lyndon paled. This explained why he'd been told to escort Kilbride without being able to refuse.

"Sergeant Jost Lyndon, will you join the King's Guard?" asked Arkyn.

"I will serve however you wish, Sire," replied Lyndon.

Arkyn nodded. "Then you will be first to take the oath."

Whilst the men were taking their oaths of allegiance to Arkyn, Tain murmured, "Hillbeck, the King doesn't wish Kilbride to be publicly evicted from the Palace for fear of the reaction of the people of Oedran. He thinks they might harm Kilbride if it becomes known what's happened here. Let him leave quietly. I suggest Terasia as his destination."

"Is that an order, sir?" asked Hillbeck sagely.

"I think it probably was, yes. Let the Margrave keep an eye on him. The King's not felt good about doing this but he had to."

"I know, sir. I'll see it's set straight."

"Thank you."

Arkyn took the oath of the last guard. "Sergeant Hillbeck."

Hillbeck walked forward and knelt in front of Arkyn, his was probably the most important oath of everyone's.

"Sergeant Dean Hillbeck, do you hereby swear to protect and serve the King of Oedran, to command his guards, and to act always for his safety?"

"I do so swear, Sire."

"To forgo personal safety, to face death and to lay down your life for the King of Oedran?"

"I do so swear, Sire."

"Do you acknowledge your only allegiance is to the King of Oedran from this day forth and swear to take orders from none other than the King?"

Hillbeck held the King's gaze. "May the valley be my protection and my balm, for my master shall ever be the true lord of it."

The room froze, all but Tain who nodded to himself. The rest of the assembled guards and Rayburn thought Hillbeck had just refused the last request, thereby committing treachery if not treason. Lord Iris was assessing what he knew of the Rex Dallin. Was the assumption of treason correct? Only he and Tain weren't surprised when the King said,

"So be it. The Lord of Ceardlann, and not the King of Oedran, holds and requires your absolute allegiance; follow no other man's order without his permission. Be your silence at such requests proof of your bond."

Hillbeck kissed Arkyn's signet ring and rose. He bowed slightly. "Sire, may your guards resume their duties?"

"They may."

"Men, salute your King and liege!"

Arkyn swallowed as every guard present saluted. He smiled as Hillbeck said,

"Men, dismiss – we've already held King Arkyn up enough."

When the men had left the Audience Chamber, Arkyn said to Hillbeck, "You didn't need to declare your origins quite so publicly."

"It was time, sir. You are the first true Lord of Ceardlann for many generations as you were born there. Our loyalty has ever been to the

Kings of Anapara but you are truly our lord as well. May the valley ease your burdens and bring you strength and peace.”

“Thank you,” whispered Arkyn, holding his gaze.

Hillbeck stepped back, saluted, inclined his head and left.

Once outside, one of the men said, “What was all that about, sarge?”

Hillbeck smiled to himself. “The King understood, Coppard. What makes you think you have to?”

* * *

Iris and Rayburn followed the King and Prince to the Inner Office.

When the door closed Rayburn said, “Forgive me for asking, Sire, but I’m your Military Advisor and have discovered an oath I know nothing about. It’s rather worrying.”

Arkyn chuckled. “Prince Tain will explain. He will do it more justice – no pun intended.”

“How much do you know about the Rex Dallin, Rayburn?” asked Tain.

“Not much, just that I’ll be executed for treason if I step foot there.”

“How succinct. Well, Hillbeck was born there, and, as such, has certain privileges, one might say, when it comes to serving the head of the valley, currently the King of Oedran. He simply exercised that privilege and claimed the Lord of Ceardlann as his liege not the King of Oedran.”

“That’s treason.”

“No because they are currently the same person.”

“But, what’s the difference then?”

“Ah, for that you’d have to visit.”

“Prince Tain, stop teasing,” said Arkyn tolerantly. “The difference, Rayburn, is simple: the magic which protects the valley and binds the inhabitants to its head is profound and not completely understood, they are born into fealty and it’s a stronger fealty than any I can request, bar a life-bind. View it as though Hillbeck has life-bound himself to me without drawing blood. The fact I was born in the valley is meant to mean far more for such oaths. Do you now understand?”

“I may in time, sir.”

“So may we all. Hillbeck seemed to know what he was doing; I wasn’t going to argue. Will you stay for lunch, Rayburn?”

Rayburn inclined his head slightly. “I’m afraid I can’t, sir, I have a meeting with the Moonshi.”

Arkyn nodded. “Well, don’t let me keep you from it but do remember to eat.” Rayburn left, and the King turned to Iris. “Lunch, my lord?”

Iris hesitated. “That would be an honour, Sire.”

Arkyn eyed him. “Do you truly have time, Iris? And do me the honour of telling me the truth.”

Iris sighed. "I was meant to be seeing Landis, Sire, but he would more than understand."

Arkyn nodded. "He would but, instead, I hope that he approves of today's events when you update him."

Iris said, "There is nothing he can disapprove of, Sire. Your Highness, may I say how impressed I was. That audience cannot have been easy."

"Thank you, Lord Iris; your good opinion is worth much," replied Tain.

Arkyn said simply, "Thank you, my lord."

Once Iris had gone, Arkyn and Tain looked at each other – only one thing on their minds.

Tain said, "If only Hillbeck's gesture was that simple, Arkyn."

"I didn't think Rayburn needed the complicated explanation."

"He thinks he got it though."

"That's just a fortunate coincidence."

Chapter 57
ARRIVALS
Afternoon
Inner Office

WHEN LORD GALALOTH of Areal arrived, he alighted from his coach with well-hidden curiosity. He'd never visited Oedran, not even for his wedding. He helped his wife alight as the chief groom hurried over. The man's seniority marked by the way everyone else stepped aside, as well as a brimless hat with a horse emblazoned on it.

"My lord…?"

"Galaloth of Areal."

"We weren't expecting a coach, sir."

Lady Galaloth said, "That we know. Do you have a lad who can show our coachman to Iris House? My father is happy to take care of it for us until we leave."

"Your…" ReShard hesitated. "Of course, my lady. I'll see it done. The King's requested you attend on him immediately, Lord Galaloth. I'll find a runner."

"No need," said Lady Galaloth. "I know the way."

They left and, once well clear of the stables Lord Galaloth chuckled. "You enjoyed that."

She smiled a quiet smile. "I've heard Idris' stories of that man's ambition. It might make him think twice next time."

"Who? The chief groom or your brother? And can you really remember your way to the Inner Office?"

"Yes. As long as we don't enter Court and take the right turning for the Golden Stairs, it's not too bad. And *you* can't enter Court anyway until you've seen the King."

Galaloth grimaced, though his beard and moustache hid much of the reaction. "You can, I suppose?"

"Yes. I was presented to King Altarius when I was fifteen. Not that he didn't know who I was anyway, but it's the presentation that matters. I knew King Adeone—" she stopped abruptly. "I can't believe he's gone. He was so full of life. Father, well… We were of an age."

"Your father schemed for you to marry King Adeone?"

"Scheme is too strong a word," said his wife. "He wouldn't have been upset if his gaze had travelled to me. Everyone was taking bets on Nia, Lady Daioch now, but he chose Ira. I was on my first visit to Areal when that happened. Of course I returned for their wedding. I can't believe she's gone as well. King Arkyn was born the year we married and I've not been back since."

Galaloth slipped his arm around her waist, supportive and loving. "We must make time to see your family whilst we're here."

She leant into his broad chest. "That would be nice but if Idris gets on his war horse about things, I might show a side you've not seen before."

He chuckled a deep-throated laugh. "You're a mother. I expect I've seen or heard it before."

At the doors to the Audience Chamber, the sergeant on duty asked their names. Giving them, Lady Galaloth wondered what else had changed. She'd never been asked for her name by the guards before. Was it a consequence of the assassination, or something King Arkyn wanted that his predecessors hadn't? Conceivably it could be both.

The Outer Office had different occupants but the layout and furniture was reassuringly familiar. The King's Administrator rose to greet them. A younger man than she expected.

This time her husband gave their names. He had the surety she'd always loved in him.

The administrator's gaze never wavered as he said, "Thank you, my lord. Could you wait in the Audience Chamber, please, whilst I ask Lady Phylicia to join you?"

They retreated there without a word. The spacious room had always fascinated Lady Galaloth with its painted murals. The handful of times she'd been in it, she'd been passing through. It had been rare but occasionally

King Altarius had invited their whole family to dine with him. Had he been assessing her? It was possible. She'd never considered it before, but the meals had all been after she was fifteen, and a couple of them Adeone was present. She swallowed. He'd been good company, amusing, quick-witted, bright in a way her husband wasn't. Energy had flowed from Adeone. She wanted to talk about her memories, but the silence quietened her tongue.

A couple of minutes later, Lady Phylicia entered. She greeted them with smiles and a shy confidence.

"Lady Galaloth, I wasn't expecting you'd come as well."

"I hope you don't mind, Lady Phylicia. I thought father might be glad of some support."

"Of course. Lord Galaloth it's nice to see you. I should tell Edward I'm here."

* * *

As Lord Galaloth and the ladies entered, Arkyn registered the way they entered as much their physical presence. Lady Phylicia was leading, and he had the sickening realisation that he'd not seen her or spoken to her since the evening of their arrival. She must think him unfoundedly rude. Why was there never enough time in the day for everything he had to do?

Once clear of the closing door, Galaloth knelt swiftly, his cloak falling in artistic drapes around him. Arkyn was at once aware that this man felt secure and sure of himself. He didn't miss the quick evaluation the lord did to get his bearings, nor the fact that Lady Galaloth didn't have the same reaction. Her obeisance was so precise it showed her roots were not Arealian. She had been in the office before.

"May I just present Lord Galaloth as an Ambassador of Areal, Sire?" said Phylicia softly, "and his wife, Lady Dana Galaloth, daughter of Lord Iris of Oedran?"

Arkyn managed to smile. "Of course you may, my lady. Lord and Lady Galaloth, please rise. Welcome to Oedran. I hope your journey wasn't irksome. Lady Galaloth, it is a pleasure to have you here once more. I expect your father will be pleased. He has been an invaluable support."

As she pushed herself to her feet, Lady Galaloth replied. "My father has ever been honoured by the trust of the FitzAlcis, Sire. It is more than life itself to him."

Arkyn watched her for a moment. "We have been fortunate to have his regard. Lord Galaloth, I hope your duties won't be too onerous. Lady Phylicia will let you know where the divisions will lie. It is unusual for there to be two coronation ambassadors from one province, but I have no doubt that everything will settle down."

Lord Galaloth blinked, obviously assessing the fact a fifteen-year-old girl was considered his superior. If it had been a different situation, Arkyn might have let his amusement show. Phylicia was a ReJean, only one step below the FitzAlcis in the politics of the empire. Galaloth would have to cope. Arkyn had little doubt Phylicia had discussed the subject with Lady Amara. If the hours the ladies had spent together had been all about embroidery, he'd be exceptionally surprised. Embroidery and his aunt weren't often in the same room. Well, not with her needling the fabric.

He continued, "Your rooms should be ready for you; my administrator will provide the information. I hope to see you at Court soon and at my father's funeral tomorrow."

Galaloth inclined his head. "Of course, my king. May the moons bless your reign."

"Thank you, my lord. Lady Galaloth, I'm sure there will be many at Court glad to welcome you back."

She smiled. "I shall be pleased to see them, Sire." Her eyes softened. "Though I wish it had been in other circumstances. My sisters and I have often spoken of returning for a visit, but we never imagined this. Farie decided to come with Aldwy but…" she trailed off. "My apologies, Sire. Thank you for the welcome."

Arkyn tilted his head slightly. "Your elder sister is visiting as well?"

"To help support her husband and our father, sir. Yes. I didn't wish to give the impression we were using events as a family reunion. I'm sorry."

Arkyn swallowed. "No. No apology. Use it for that. I think it would have pleased father somehow. That something pleasant, however small, however large, has come from his sacrifice. We *all* need that."

She held his gaze. "My heartfelt condolences are with you, sir. Your father… always made me smile and laugh."

Arkyn couldn't do anything but nod. Her simple statement had hit him too hard. His father had made a lot of people smile.

Seeing it, Lady Phylicia said, "Lord Galaloth, Lady Galaloth, with his permission, we should let the King continue."

Arkyn pulled himself together. "Thank you. Lady Phylicia, could you stay a moment please?"

When alone with her, he let out a long breath. "How are you?"

"I'm well, sir. I have been enjoying Lady Elantha's and Lady Amara's company. It has been an interesting time."

Arkyn's lips twitched. "You've not been too shocked, have you?"

Phylicia laughed. "I had heard rumours about Lady Amara, sir, but she has been kind. She has said she'll look after me at Court as well."

Tongue-in-cheek, Arkyn muttered, "Oh dear," then more seriously added, "I'm glad. I'm sorry I can't currently be more involved in your visit."

"I understand and don't mind, Sire."

"Thank you. I've got to decide when I am going to be at Court."

"Isn't it one of those things which is decided for you, sir?"

"Apparently not, my lady."

She frowned, thinking. "Maybe when all the ambassadors are here, sir? That should make it nice and simple."

"Yes, that might work. Thank you. You obviously have a career as an advisor ahead of you."

"Can you persuade father of that, please? He simply sees one of marriage and children."

Arkyn chuckled. "I shall see what I can do. I think the time you've spent with Lady Amara has been beneficial."

Phyl grimaced. "Sorry, Sire. Maybe it's made me state my views."

"As I recall, you stated them perfectly well before you met her."

"Maybe I did, sir. I should let you continue."

"Thank you, my lady."

* * *

Once in the corridors of the Palace, Lady Galaloth let out a long breath. Looking at King Arkyn she'd been taken back years. It was almost disconcerting how similar the kings she'd known were in appearance.

The runner showing them to their rooms was quiet. He wore a black armband as all the palace staff were doing and would do for some time.

In the privacy of their rooms. She sank onto a chair, her head in her hands. She had overstepped so many lines in the Inner Office. Her father would have a lot to say when he found out. Her husband squeezed her shoulder in mute support.

"I let you down," she whispered.

He shook his head. "No. You didn't. He appreciated your words."

"Why did he want Lady Phylicia to stay then?"

He sank into the chair opposite. "I don't know. I doubt it was because of anything you said. She might tell me."

"I don't think she's that naïve, love. The King's wanting her to take the lead for Areal."

Galaloth shrugged. "She may be more visible, but I've enough to do. ReJean was precise about how much she should be mired. He wants me to get Tradere's side of the trade issues. He doesn't think the Satrap is being honest with us. Lady Phylicia can't deal with that."

Lady Galaloth raised an eyebrow. "Oh, men always think they have the monopoly on such matters. Without us, you'd be lost."

He chuckled, leaned over and kissed her. "I know it because you never let me forget it. Lady Phylicia may one day be at the centre of such discussions but for now I have to represent her father in such things."

His wife's lips twitched. "Keep telling yourself that. I suppose I ought to present myself to Lady Amara. I'll change and freshen up first. Would you like to meet her?"

Galaloth considered. "I've seen her before but you'll tell me the correct answer is 'yes'. Is she as formidable as everyone says?"

"She has a certain presence. I've never heard of anyone arguing with her, not even the Kings."

"And you think it's a good idea for me to meet her?"

"I think it's a better idea for your career than ignoring her."

"Should Lady Phylicia…" He trailed off, waving his hand to finish the thought.

"Not needed. I've been presented to Her Ladyship before. I also survived the experience so don't look so worried."

* * *

They waited in Amara's antechamber until a maid collected them. Lady Amara was seated writing at a desk. Her younger daughter pushed herself to her feet as they entered.

"Dana! I'm so glad you've come."

The ladies fell into a hug.

Lady Galaloth smiled. "I wasn't expecting to see you, my lady. At least, not for a time. I was going to see where you were and give you warning."

"Oh, no warning needed. It's good to see you. Cornelia will be pleased as well. Oh, sorry, Lord Galaloth. I didn't mean to stop the introductions."

Lady Amara's eyes narrowed but she didn't turn round. "Yes, you did. You thought you'd give him breathing room."

Rhian's lips twitched. "Maybe. Lady Amara, Lord Galaloth of Areal. Lady Galaloth you will remember."

Amara turned to face them. "Yes. Dana, you've not changed at all. I appreciate you'd have given my daughter warning but not me. Lord Galaloth, welcome to Oedran. I hope you're aware of what's required from an Ambassador of Areal. Lady Phylicia certainly is."

Dana's lips twitched. There it was. The straightforwardness that kept even kings in their place. Her husband floundered for a moment before replying.

"Lady Amara, it is a pleasure to meet you."

Amara crooked an eyebrow. "Is that all I get?" She caught Dana's eye. "You've trained him well. Your father will be proud. Sit yourselves down and tell me the news from the Amphi Court. I expect your Munewid Eve banquet was ended almost as abruptly as ours."

Dana sat at the corner of the silk upholstered couch. "Yes, my lady. It was. So many of us were shattered by the news. Prince Tain… He won a lot of respect in those minutes, as did King Arkyn. To receive news like that, to then sit in full view of the Court… They are certainly inheritors of the finest FitzAlcis strength.”

Lady Amara’s eyes narrowed. “As opposed to the worst?”

“I’m not sure there are any such traits, my lady.”

Amara’s lips twitched. “Your father has a lot to answer for. Does he know you’ve arrived?”

“He should by now. We sent our coach to Iris House. Your chief groom seemed rather perplexed we’d arrived in one. Are all ambassador’s meant to ride here?”

“It’s generally considered quicker, but not essential. I’ll see what can be done to accommodate your coach here. You don’t want to have to wait to visit people.”

“I thought Your Ladyship might consider it rude if I did not present myself immediately.”

As they jousted in words, Lord Galaloth found himself enjoying the experience. He didn’t often witness his wife dissecting consequences and events with like-minded ladies, or with such aplomb. When they talked of the signatories of the Assassination Document, he also discovered his wife had a wealth of expletives. He began to wonder who the ambassador was. By the time they left, he didn’t think it was him.

Chapter 58
BARDIC FIELDS
Late Afternoon
Anapara – Plateau – Bardic Fields

CHIEF LAIORIL of the Wanda would tell stories from history to any who would listen, but there was one he hardly mentioned unless asked for it: the murder of King Alvern and the birth of the Age of Tyranny. As soon as he heard how King Adeone had been killed, he cursed that history wouldn’t let Alvern’s story die.

Laioril had taken his tribe south through the Rex Dallin, much to the consternation of some of the inhabitants, who knew the Kings tolerated him, but feared for their livestock with the Wanda’s notoriously loose concepts on ownership of meat that moved around. Laioril though wasn’t quite as bad as his reputation suggested: he never poached from the poor.

Chief Darshan had had a rather longer journey from south of Amphi but it wasn’t the distance that mattered, and he pitched his tents hours ahead of Laioril's leisurely arrival. The evening found them sitting by the fire, with drinks of summer wine eyeing each other with interest. It was the first time that they'd met face to face.

"Should I mention your messenger, Laioril?"

"Not if you don't want me to mention your father's indiscretions to your family, Darshan."

"Is that a threat?"

"Depends how well you know me. So, these portents of doom—"

"I never said the rumours and signs that had been brought to my attention were portents of doom. I have been considering them though. I'd be interested to know your thoughts on the new King of Oedran. I have heard rumours of him but you know him better than any rumour."

"And you trust me to give you an unbiased opinion?" enquired Laioril.

Darshan eyed him. "I trust you to give an opinion, let your conscience be the judge of anything else."

"You asked for it."

By the end of Laioril's thoughts on Arkyn and a bit more on the situation all Chief Darshan said was, "The next few years will be interesting. Thank you, Laioril, I should contemplate what you have told me and watch the stars; the moons have already revealed their thoughts on the events."

"So, you believe in such signs absolutely."

Chief Darshan pushed himself to his feet and actually gave Laioril a slight bow. "For now, I shall think on what you have said, Laioril."

When his counterpart had left, Laioril muttered, "An enigma wrapped in a riddle, hidden in a mystery and placed in a puzzle box."

A female voice said in amusement, "Met your match at last, Chief?"

"Your ears are too sharp, Miranda. Do you have another bottle of wine with you?"

She sat beside him, took his beaker and poured him a good glug before pouring her own drink. She held up her beaker.

"To King Adeone."

Laioril nodded. "Aye, to Adeone, lass." He took a drink. "Elderberry, his favourite."

She smiled. "What else? Will we be near Oedran soon, Chief?"

"Why?"

"I've a bottle for Lord Landis and from what I've heard he'll need it."

The Chief said, "We'll make a special journey, lass; he'll need more than the wine."

Chapter 59
IDRIS
Early Evening
Court Wing – Galaloths' Rooms

LORD GALALOTH and his wife re-entered their rooms talking quietly of their plans for the evening. Now the King had greeted them, they were free to attend Court. As an ambassador, Galaloth had freedoms at Court that other visiting lords didn't. He didn't have to wait to be presented *at Court*, he could attend as though it had already happened. Entering their sitting room, they were greeted with,

"I knew you'd arrived when your coach did."

Dana smiled. "That's how one normally knows people have arrived."

"Yes, but normally the guests are in the coach," replied her brother. "Does father know you're using our stables as a coach house?"

"Yes. So will Farie. He didn't raise a murmur of protest."

"Did you give him the chance? Galaloth."

"Idris. Did you come here for any reason other than to greet your sister?" asked Lord Galaloth, privately riled by the peremptory tone.

"Just to see whether you wanted me to make any introductions and to catch up on your family news."

Dana shrugged. "I'm sure I can manage with the introductions. I've just introduced my husband to Lady Amara."

Idris sat back down. "Ouch. If you've survived that, Galaloth, you'll survive Court without a problem. Have you seen the King?"

"Yes. Immediately we arrived."

"How is he?" asked Idris.

"Looking well," replied Dana before her husband could. "I can't imagine how difficult the last few days have been. He and Prince Tain handled themselves with remarkable dignity in Amphi when the news arrived… I can't believe King Adeone's gone."

Her husband squeezed her hand. A gesture of understanding that made her eyes well. She blinked back the tears. Oedran was full of memories of her youth, of her hopes and her dreams, of friends and family.

"How's father?"

"Busy. Taking over for Festus where he can." Idris saw her face. "He was injured by a second bolt. He'll live but he's under Chapa's orders to take things easy. I sometimes think that doctor has more power than the King."

Dana chuckled. "He certainly doesn't have that, but he does have a way with the FitzAlcis and lords. I'll have to see Cornelia. I hear they've quite the brood these days. She shares family news in her letters. I should

247

let her know I'm here before rumour does." Pushing herself to her feet, Dana crossed to a small desk and drew out a sheet of paper. Ignoring her brother and husband, she started writing.

Idris looked at Galaloth. "You've not broken that habit then, Galaloth?"

"I don't see a habit to comment on, Idris. Are any other ambassadors here yet? I forgot to ask the King's Administrator."

Idris shook his head. "None. You are the closest. Though I expected ReJean to send Skaner or Arridge."

"I think my wed-family might be why he asked me," replied Galaloth. "I'm not saying with Arridge being His Excellency's wed-brother that I didn't expect him to be sent, but I think Skaner is too set in his ways to find favour with a young King."

"There's a statement with a story behind it," remarked Idris. "So what took you so long to arrive? I mean the King made it here in a day, not three. It will have been noticed."

Galaloth smiled. "Family affairs and, with Lady Phylicia here as an ambassador, my swift arrival wasn't as imperative as it might have been."

Idris frowned. "Lady Phylicia is Ambassador for Areal? Then what are you?" he asked perplexed.

"Ambassador for Areal also. King Arkyn accepted the arrangement. I am due to meet with Her Ladyship in the morning to learn where the division is. I expect ceremonial aspects will be Her Ladyship's, and I will attend to other matters. I'm interested to know who my fellow ambassadors are to be. I obviously know Lord Aldwy will be one, but as a former Tuchlin that isn't surprising. Have you heard of any others?"

Listening to her husband and brother talking, Dana pulled out a second piece of paper and penned a short line to Rhian.

They've already started the gleanings. Are we meant to enjoy playing the game this much?

She could imagine the smile it would raise, that she hoped it would raise. Rhian had been paler than she'd expected. The events had taken their toll. She listened with half an ear to the conversation until she heard Idris start talking about the events of the Munewid. He'd been present. Of course he had. Had it only been Septadai? Three nights ago. She sat next to her husband, who put his arm around her without hesitation. He glanced at the notes.

"Three, love?"

"Yes, Cornelia, then Lady Neassa, and a quick thank you to Lady Rhian for earlier. Oh, I ought to let Lady Fairson know I'm here as well. I won't be writing to any other Lady of Oedran."

Idris raised an eyebrow. "It's believed no-one but the signatories knew what was planned, Dana."

"Oh, and what difference does that make?" she demanded. "Disgrace follows the family. Or don't you remember how hard we had to work because of Aunt Isolda?"

"Not particularly hard. Father was King Altarius' confidant. The disgrace our aunt brought on our family was expunged by the Bayan Rebellion and the loss of grandfather and Uncle Julian."

"For the men, yes. Not the women." She saw her husband's confusion. "Our aunt married without the King's permission. She had to leave Oedran, so did her husband. They live in Torport now. She has the longevity of the Iris family, that's for sure."

"Do you write to her?" asked Galaloth.

"Occasionally," admitted Dana. "She made contact when I married you. Tried to reassure me that life could be enjoyed beyond Oedran. I found it a kindness I wanted to return."

"Father would be livid to know that," said Idris.

"Doubt it," replied Dana. "It's far in the past." She didn't add that her father wrote to her aunt as well. The only person in the Iris family who didn't was her brother. He had always been conscious about his position. Probably as their father was still living, unlike every other Lord of Oedran of his generation.

"Well, Aunt Isolda hasn't set foot in Oedran since her marriage."

Dana eyed him. "Actually, she has. She sought permission to visit, when her husband came on business, from Queen Ira. She received permission by return of courier. She obviously didn't attend Court, but she has been back to Oedran. That was Ira all over though."

Galaloth decided to break up the sibling argument. "So will you write to the Ladies of Oedran?"

She shook her head. "No. It's a different situation. They aren't blood relatives, their husbands are regicides, and I had far too much respect for King Adeone to undermine King Arkyn. I know Cornelia, and Malti Fairson, Rale and Ryson are unmarried, as is father. The others have never bothered to write to me. Nor do I wish to renew what little acquaintance I had with them."

"I understand," said Galaloth. The fire of retribution was in his wife's eyes. He'd never seen it blaze so brightly. Idris crooked a discreet eyebrow. He knew his sister's temper.

Chapter 60
NURSERY TALES
Evening
Inner Office

DURING THE AFTERNOON, Arkyn's temper found a level. The Inner Office was a peaceful place to work, but he still couldn't reconcile himself with being there.

"Sir, Lord Faran's coach has been spotted at the King's Gate."

Glancing at his timepiece, Arkyn put the document he was reading aside. It was about eight o'clock. Certainly time to finish for the day. He got to his feet.

"Thank you, Edward. I'll go and greet him. Can you sort my desk out, please? You'll see what I've signed. Let Prince Tain know dinner's been delayed. I'd have thought we'll be ready in about an hour. Lord Faran may join us."

* * *

Arkyn made his way to the stables swiftly. If the coach had been spotted at the King's Gate, Faran would soon be at the stables. As he entered the stableyard, Faran's coachman was negotiating the yard, and the grooms were suddenly uncertain. Arkyn motioned for them to continue. He watched as one indicated to Juan where to go. The chief groom tried to make his way over but was prevented by the manoeuvres. Arkyn shook his head at ReShard. There was no need for the chief groom to greet him.

Once the coach had drawn to a halt, Arkyn crossed to it. He couldn't have sat waiting in the Inner Office but he wasn't sure why he'd wanted to greet Faran publicly either. Was it to finally put to rest rumours of the lord being out of favour following his own inauspicious visit?

Faran alighted carrying his daughter and concentrating on his balance. When he straightened up, Arkyn held his gaze for a brief moment. Surprise was in the Lord of Lufian's gaze. The briefest of moments later, Faran knelt and inclined his head. Arkyn was oddly glad the grooms and stableboys kept the yard clean. He offered Faran his hand to help him to his feet.

Untangling his own, Faran took the King's hand and kissed the signet ring. "Your vassal, Sire."

Arkyn wanted to say something dry about the predictability of Faran's response but all he actually said was, "Thank you, Lord Faran, please get up." Seeing Faran struggling, Arkyn bent down and lifted Samara gently from him. "Let me take Samara, my lord. No, it's no trouble." He stood looking down at his drowsy neardaughter. "Come, let's go in. There are rooms prepared.”

Halfway to the nursery Samara awoke and stirred.

Lord Faran said, “Sire, your neardaughter is strong.”

“I’m sure, as you put it, we’ll come to an understanding.”

* * *

Maria smiled at the sight of Arkyn with his neardaughter. “Shall I take her, sir?”

“No, Maria, not yet.”

He disentangled Samara from the cocoon and carefully put her down. She started toddling around, exploring her surroundings before crying.

“Samara, what’s the noise for?” asked Faran kindly.

“Ty.”

“Ty is at home, Samara.”

“Who or what is Ty?” asked Arkyn.

“A toy squirrel she cuddles, sir. It’s soft, and she’s rather attached to it.”

“Ah. Maria, the old toy box of my sister’s, could you bring it please?”

Both Maria and Lord Faran said, surprised, “Sire?”

“Maria, please. All of Ella’s most precious toys mother put elsewhere at Ceardlann but there may be something soft that Samara can have. It seems a shame they’re locked away if they can help. If there’s nothing there, we can find something else, I’m sure.”

Knowing that memories of all Arkyn’s deceased relatives would be painful in his mind, Faran murmured, “Sir, it isn’t necessary. The memories must be—”

“They are but let me deal with them, Faran.”

Two minutes later, Maria set the softest toys out.

Arkyn said quietly, “Shall we find a different Ty for you here, because Ty is poorly at home.”

He didn’t see Maria and Lord Faran smile at each other and didn’t hear them leave.

Samara reached out and touched all the toys before taking a rabbit.

Crouching down next to her, Arkyn asked, “What will you call him?” She burbled and Arkyn smiled. “Tell me tomorrow. Did you enjoy your journey here?”

She watched him with clear brown eyes, before trying to say something that Arkyn was sure was ‘Nasty, here?’

“No. Who is nasty, Samara?”

Gazing at him, she put her thumb in her mouth. Toddling over, she leaned against him, clutching the toy rabbit to her.

Having realised that they were alone, he said, “Samara, I’m just your nearfather, ignore anyone who tries to tell you anything else, especially if they say I'm important, I'm just your nearfather. We'll have to find you some more toys for a start. Are you tired?"

She nodded, and he carefully got to his feet. "Sleep in here. I need to talk with your father tonight. Will you be good for us?"

She looked at him through sleepy eyes. He continued to hold her until she was asleep before finding her cot and carefully laying her down. He stole from the room and out into the corridor. He saw Maria and Faran talking softly.

"She's asleep in her cot, Maria. Keep an eye on her and send for Lord Faran or me if she gets fractious."

Maria said simply, "If there's real need of course, sir."

"Where's El?"

"With Lady Amara, sir. I think they're comfort for each other."

"I hope so," murmured Arkyn, his eyes wandering.

"Are you—"

"I'm fine, Maria. Lord Faran, before you retire, I'd like a word."

* * *

Once in his chambers, Arkyn said, "She's lovely."

"I rather think so too and when I find who tried to kill her, I'll be rather more successful with them."

"She asked if 'Nasty' was here – or at least I think she did. Any ideas?"

"No but the girls might have. I'll ask Kyla to talk to them, or—"

Arkyn passed him a drink. "Let Samara do the talking. She's bright enough to convey her meaning."

Accepting the drink, Faran smiled. "Yes, I was impressed, Sire, with how comfortable you were with her."

"Impressed? Such a compliment. I'm the second oldest of my generation in my family and nearfamily. I've spent much time with younger children." He sighed. "Thank you for coming, father would have appreciated it."

Faran studied the young man in front of him and resolved one day to see him without a catastrophe having happened. For the moment, however, he said, "It was nothing, sir, just what my conscience prescribed. Can I help in any way? Anything, no matter how small or seemingly trivial."

"I'm sure having travelled from Lufia with virtually no stops and little sleep you'll need to rest, but, after that, if you insist, I'm sure there'll be something someone can find."

"There's always something, Sire. I apologise for the complication of Samara's presence."

"Don't, truly, don't. I'm pleased to see her. What exactly happened?"

Faran told the story from the moment he'd agreed to travel to Oedran, through the discovery of Samara to the arrival at the Palace.

When he'd finished Arkyn said, "It *is* rather worrying, isn't it? Not that you need telling. Do you want me to send a captain along to investigate?"

"No, Sire. Thank you. I think that might lead to danger for the rest of my family. Samara *will* tell us in her own way. It's just... after Princess Ella died whilst King Adeone was visiting and then Damso died in suspicious circumstances, then there was the bandit attack on you, sir, and odd little things happening, I—"

"Ella died at Ceardlann," Arkyn reminded him. "There's no blame can be attached to you for that, nor for the bandit attack. I thought you knew of Apposer Nallvir's findings."

"I do but you must still have doubts, and I feel someone is manipulating my life because your father and I were close."

"They probably are, and you're not the only one being affected. I'm sorry for it... I don't know if I should be telling you this, but I was in father's office when Nallvir relayed his findings."

Faran stilled. "Sir?"

"I don't think I'd ever seen father more relieved than in those moments, or better pleased."

"He cared deeply, sir, about many things but—"

"Faran," the tone was both a warning and a gentle admonishment.

Faran sighed. "Thank you for telling me, it does help, but I'm not going to be happy until I've caught whoever it is in my household."

"I can understand that. If you need my help for anything, ask. I was pleased when you were exonerated, for what it's worth."

Lord Faran looked at him seriously. "It's worth a lot, sir, thank you. I've not been fortunate when the FitzAlcis have visited me."

"Then I'll have to come again and see if we can make it third time lucky. I'm sure the idea won't concern any of the Lufian officials."

"Don't worry about them, Sire. Come for yourself. You're welcome whenever you wish. I mean that, it's no courtly statement."

"Thank you. I don't get many invitations to visit places; I think lords are too afraid of the upheaval."

Faran laughed. "Ah well, my conscience is a fickle companion, but it says that friends are always welcome and I have no intention of arguing because I get good company. The fuss, I'll employ others to deal with."

Arkyn chuckled. "That, my lord, sounds like a perfect solution."

Chapter 61
DINNER?

TWO MINUTES LATER, Kadeem entered and announced Tain. Lord Faran got to his feet and looked at the young Prince. They'd met many years before but Tain had grown and changed so much that he was virtually unrecognisable to the Lord of Lufian. Faran realised that Tain was one man whose features would constantly change. In a few years not many who were simply acquainted with him in passing would recognise the adult from the child.

Arkyn said, "Tain, do you remember Lord Faran?"

Tain nodded. "Of course I do. He ran all around the lawns at Ceardlann with me on his back."

Faran smiled at the recollection. "I'd almost forgotten that, Your Highness. How are you, sir?"

"I think that question is better not answered, my lord. My apologies."

"Why, Tain?" enquired Arkyn.

"I'm bloody furious. I daren't even be in court because I'll take it out on some defendant who doesn't deserve it."

"How long have you been at the Courthouse today?"

Tain avoided his brother's searching gaze. "Longer than I should have been, obviously. If I've not been with you, I've been there, but that's where my duties lie, isn't it, either with you or there."

Arkyn got up and walked over to him, he took him roughly by the shoulders. "No. You've also got to look after yourself."

Faran watched the brothers. He crossed to the decanters and poured Tain a drink. It wasn't his place to comment on such fundamental issues. He was there as a support for Arkyn, not to antagonise any situation or take sides. He passed the watered whiskey to the Prince who took it with a nod of thanks.

Arkyn said, "Come and sit down and relax. Please, Tain, be sensible. I can't be worrying about you as well – more than I already am, that is."

"Obviously I'm an added burden."

Arkyn swore. "I meant nothing of the sort… For heaven's sake, haven't we got enough trouble in the family already, or are you looking for a way of causing more?"

Faran got up to wait elsewhere.

Tain glanced at Arkyn. "Sorry."

Arkyn said, "So am I. Faran, sit back down. Tain, after tomorrow you're to take time for yourself. See Cal for a bit. Get out of the Courthouse and Palace, go for a ride or something. Have you seen Cal since we returned?"

Head hung, Tain bit his lip, shaking his head.

"That explains a lot. Make time to see each other. You're close; you don't want to lose it because of this mess."

"Will you come for the ride?"

"If I can."

Faran sensing the end of the argument said, "Might I ask who Cal is?"

"He's our friend," replied Arkyn. "He's lived with us at Ceardlann for a few years; he's the same age as Tain and has a similar mischievous streak."

"Which is obviously nothing like Arkyn's," muttered Tain.

Faran smiled. "Is he the gentleman with the disapproving father?"

Arkyn paused. "Yes, but we get around that – or father did for us."

Tain glanced at him. "We'll have to tell Master Galdwin that we're not letting Cal out of our lives, won't we?"

"It'll become clear, Your Highness," stated Faran.

Kadeem entered and half bowed. "Dinner is ready to be served, sir."

Arkyn pushed himself to his feet. "Good. Thank you, Kadeem."

Faran waited until the manservant had left before saying, "You hadn't yet dined? It's late—"

"Would Your Lordship's conscience let you dine before your guests have arrived?"

Chapter 62

FRUSTRATION AND FUTURE

Late Evening

Oedran – Para House

LORD KENELM PARA had barely seen his father the day before, for the militia hadn't let them talk whilst Para packed bare essentials and started on his journey to Paras. With the proclamation that morning, all the heirs and families of the exiled lords discovered King Arkyn's reaction to the assassination. Documents had been delivered by palace couriers outlining in full the terms of the exile and, if there was speculation rife in the city, there was cold-blooded rage in the houses of the six lords.

Kenelm invited his two closest friends for dinner and they arrived together. Both had been off duty, and both wanted to talk away from the barracks and the many ears Wynfeld had there. They registered Kenelm's black mood as soon as they entered the house. The evening would be interesting. As soon as they shed their cloaks, drinks were passed to them

255

and the servants disappeared.

Kenelm flopped into a chair. "Did you get to talk to them?"

Lord Chander Teran shook his head. "No. I was on duty and it was made plain to me that I wasn't to leave the barracks."

Lord Peaga Rathgar nodded. "Same for me. Mind you, I doubt Cousin Rathgar would have wanted to see me."

Kenelm said, "No, maybe not. Did you try to intervene?"

Peaga sighed. "I know a lost battle when I see one…"

"Basically not then. I never took you for a self-serving coward, Peaga."

"He's not," interrupted Chander. "Arkyn was always going to take action, no-one, not even Peaga's grandmother, could have stopped that."

"Lady Amara was made Protector," grumbled Kenelm. "She could have done something…"

Peaga said, "I very much doubt it, Kenelm. If I'd thought there was any hope, I'd have tried to see her but there wasn't."

Kenelm glanced at his companions. "So our fathers are exiled, Chander and I are hostages for their good behaviour and you can do nothing, is that what you're telling us, Peaga?"

"Yes," agreed Peaga.

"Lady Amara must know more about what the King intends than we do. Can't you enquire?"

"If you think it's that easy, you obviously don't know her."

"Scared of her?"

"What makes you think I'm any different to the rest of the empire in that regard? You don't want to cross her, Kenelm, and I certainly don't."

Chander attempted to mediate. "That's understandable from everything I've heard but she *was* named Protector and Kenelm has a point. We're your friends; we need to know where we stand. It's not nice thinking we're used to force our fathers' behaviour."

"My cousin is exiled as well!" snapped Peaga.

"Yes, but you're not officially part of his family, are you?" sneered Kenelm. "I mean you're not in the same place we are."

"What do you mean? I grew up under his roof and call it home!"

"Yes but, as was pointed out in your parents' divorce, the head of *your* family is the King because you're the close descendant of one."

Peaga snorted, "Yes, and since when did they pay attention to me? I'm the last generation of that line it applies to. I'm not even to be part of the family group at the funeral. They don't have to acknowledge any child I might have as being of FitzAlcis descent, and it was only because father lost his temper publicly that mother was remembered. That and the fact Aunt Rhian was visiting… and possibly, or probably, that Lord Landis was present…"

"Well, *he* got what he deserved," said Kenelm doing a crude impression of Landis attempting to save Adeone's life. He continued bitterly, "I bet he thought up the exile as well."

"He's not been in the Palace since the Lord's Council."

"There're messengers! And, for that matter, he apparently didn't leave for a while afterwards. Who knows what he was advising then. If it wasn't him, I take two other bets…"

Chander said tiredly, "Who?"

"That upstart merchant's son who's suddenly appeared, who was in the room when our family were arrested. A trader's spawn witnessed our family's fall. I won't be forgetting that. Nor that Arkyn allowed it…"

As he lapsed into silence, Peaga said, "You said two bets."

"Oh, yes. Well, if it isn't the trader's spawn, then it's probably that lily-livered lawyer," the sneer in his voice was evident.

Chander, genuinely confused, asked, "Who?"

"Ryson. You know, he turned his back on Lord Scanlon because his sister told him to and then, after the damage was done, she disappeared and he had the audacity to claim the events happened the other way around. No, I've three people I want to destroy. The rules have changed. Play all before you lose anyway."

"Be sensible for once in your life and let it go," growled Chander.

"Wake up, Chander! It's not about anything but what future we want for ourselves. Our fathers are exiled, we're hostages – they have to play to the King's rules or we will be executed! I don't think it will be long before they wake up and realise they've created a worse monster, because Arkyn will have more revenge on his mind. I'm not going to tamely fall without having contributed to the fight. Father has to behave but I don't!"

"Kenelm, be careful, you're drunk and from what I can tell have been for some time. Who knows who's listening—" pointed out Peaga.

"Oh, this place is full of spies, we know it. My sister may even be one; she's so close to Julia Landis. You could easily be one, Peaga, or you Chander. Can't trust anyone, even those I thought I could…"

Peaga sighed. "You need bed, Kenelm."

"No, I don't. I need a woman. Ever had a woman, Peaga? I bet you haven't. Course Chander has. Takes after his father. Two bastards already and we all know about Chandra and why she was really married off—"

Chander's fist flew out and Kenelm finally fell silent: unconscious.

"He never does know when to shut up," grouched Chander.

Peaga snorted. "Nice right hook. Let's get him to bed. How's Chandra?"

"Happy. She wanted marriage. I'd have known if she hadn't…"

"No-one, other than drunken fools, think anything else. Do you think he meant what he said?" asked Peaga, taking Kenelm's legs.

"No. He's drunk. He'll have a hangover and a re-think in the morning. When are you next on duty?" Chander slipped his arms under Kenelm's lifting him. They started manoeuvring him out of the drawing room.

"Midnight. You?"

"It was meant to be tomorrow night but we have to be at the funeral. I'm surprised the King even permitted a representative of each exiled lord. The General understood. Commander wasn't too happy; I've lost my leave days for a month…" Chander paused, catching his fleeing breath.

"But you're effectively obeying a summons, aren't you?"

"That wasn't why. I called the commander a pratt – no, not a pratt, an ignorant fool and an upstart trader. Didn't take it too well. A week ago, I'd only have received a dressing down, father's exile means they can turn the knife – if the Major's tone wasn't proof enough, that was."

"What will you do?" enquired Peaga as they navigated the stairs.

"Accept it. The General won't rescind it. The King won't accept any petition, even supposing I was stupid enough to try, as I'm under the commander's orders and it's a military matter first. I just amuse myself with the look on the commander's face. You'd have liked it. You could see all the veins standing out. I might do it more often."

Peaga grinned. "Make sure I can see it."

"All right. We should make a pact and get Kenelm to lose weight!" said Chander rolling their friend onto his bed and leaving him there.

They didn't let Kenelm's drunken state interfere in their evening. They still sat talking in the drawing room, ate a far better dinner than the barracks would provide, before leaving Para House laughing at the thought of Kenelm having missed it.

Chapter 63
MARIA AND MEMORIES
Late Evening
Arkyn's Sitting Room

ONCE ON HIS OWN, Arkyn didn't even look at the timepiece. It had been a long day but he wasn't ready for sleep. He told Kadeem he was going to the nursery. When Kadeem mentioned it was late Arkyn shrugged. He wasn't going to wake anyone up. Kadeem inclined his head and stood back. Arkyn eyed him.

"You're not coming to keep me out of trouble?"

"I rather thought you wished for privacy, Sire."

"Thank you." Arkyn left his chambers feeling the same sense of illicit freedom he had when he'd sneaked out of the nursery years before to see his grandfather. He walked down the Golden Stairs, ignoring the guards' confusion. The Privy Wing was his home. He would wander about if he wanted to. He entered the nursery without alerting anyone to his presence. Maria put her book aside and pushed herself to her feet as he entered the sitting room.

Arkyn smiled wryly. "Kadeem told you I was on my way."

"It gives him a purpose, sir."

Arkyn snorted. "Yes." He listened for a moment. "Is Samara having trouble settling?"

"A bit. She'll be fine. Faith's with her."

Arkyn hesitated. "Can you find something else for Faith to do?"

Maria eyed him. "I could, yes, but—"

"Please."

A few moments later, Maria re-entered the sitting room. "She's gone, sir. Do you want me to stay?"

Arkyn nodded. "Very much so." He crept into the night nursery and smiled at his wailing neardaughter. "Ssh… Come here, Samara." He picked her up confidently and held her carefully.

"She keeps coming to the edge of the cot," whispered Elantha.

"Why aren't you asleep?" replied Arkyn in a like tone.

"You need to ask?"

"Maybe not. Sorry." Without thinking he was rocking back and forth gently and his neardaughter was calming down.

"I think she wants company," said El quietly. "She's used to having sisters around."

"True but they're a bit far away," whispered Arkyn.

"Would it help if she slept with me?"

"I don't know but you don't have to—"

"I know but she keeps holding out her arms like she wants me to pick her up. She just seems to want someone else with her."

"She might roll out of your bed," whispered Arkyn as Samara stopped crying.

"True." El hesitated. "But we'd probably both sleep better."

Maria whispered. "I could find the training guard, sir. It should still be here. We've not used it since you were all little but it would stop Mistress Samara rolling out if Her Ladyship doesn't mind."

El smiled. "I'm offering, Maria."

A couple of minutes later, Maria placed the guard into the slots and El made room for Samara. Arkyn put his neardaughter down, careful not to wake her. She stirred, but settled when El brushed her hair gently.

Arkyn smiled. "Will you sleep now too?"

El shook her head. "I can't. Will you read a story?"

He hesitated. "Probably best not to light a candle but I could tell you one of Laioril's badly."

El chuckled. "Sounds good."

Neither noticed Maria leave them alone.

When Arkyn was sure El was asleep, he tip-toed out of the night nursery. He sat in his favourite place from years gone by. The window seat looked over the gardens, but for the moment he gazed at the stars.

A few minutes later, Maria re-entered the room to retrieve her book. "Sorry, sir. I thought you'd gone."

"No. They're asleep though." He looked at Maria. "I've been cowardly."

She sat down. "I very much doubt it."

He smiled wryly. "Uncle Scanlon's insisting El moves into a house he controls. I can't fight him. I'm not strong enough at the moment. I want to, he wants me to so he can label me tyrannical. I'd almost do it for El, but we'd lose, as things are we'd lose, and I don't know whom I can trust. Not really. Uncle Festus is too badly injured to lend me his strength. I've all on maintaining a semblance of a Court with so few Lords of Oedran. It's worse than that though because it means I'll have to disband this nursery."

Maria said, "It was going to happen soon anyway, sir. Don't feel bad on our accounts."

He watched her for a moment before turning back to the stars. "What will you do?"

She shrugged. "What I've done before. Go and see family, stay for a time. I'll find another post when I return. There will be one somewhere."

He pushed himself to his feet. Crossing to the chairs he sank onto one. "What do you *want* to do?"

She considered. "Go with Lady Elantha. Look after her."

Arkyn blinked hard. "I can't let you. Not because of you or her. I wish you could be with her but Uncle Scanlon... I can't let you work for him. He's cruel. His household rules... No. I can't."

Maria caught his eye. "That's your parents in you."

"Not just them." He broke the eye contact. "Tell me something, do you want to start afresh?"

"Truthfully? No. I will need to though."

Arkyn considered. "Where do you consider home, Maria? Humour me."

She chuckled. "All right. I guess Macarian House. I don't dislike it here, or at Ceardlann, though I feel out of place there, but Macarian House holds a good part of my heart."

"There are memories there," whispered Arkyn.

"Aye. Many of them. I was fifteen when I first worked there. Your grandmother was a kind lady. Took me on, no questions asked. When your mother was born, I was already caring for my nephew but she didn't care. Said she trusted me. Your grandfather left the decisions to me when Lady Macaria passed. Said he'd seen he could trust me. So, I brought up your mother. Of course, when she went to Garth for that year, I couldn't go with her, so I visited my family, but there was no doubt I'd be there when she got home. When your father courted her and they married, she asked your grandfather to keep me on. Of course, she fell with you quickly but by that point your grandfather had had a bout of apoplexy and I was nursing him. She wanted me to head up her nursery. I'm not sure what King Altarius said, but nursing Lord Macaria and running a nursery in different residences was going to be tricky. So she asked why her father couldn't be nursed in the Palace. She told me Adeone gaped at her until she pointed out that he was wed-family. King Altarius took a bit of persuading but we brought Lord Macaria here. I continued to nurse him and when you arrived care for you as well. All Ira wanted was her family together and cared for. Your father and grandfather must have trusted her because I don't remember any other discussions on the matter. When Lord Macaria passed to the ancestors, you were fractious for weeks. You'd taken to sleeping by him. Of course, Macarian House was mostly shut up then. The staff dispersed but she found jobs for everyone. There's still a small staff there, but you know that." Maria fell silent seeing Arkyn's grief-stricken eyes.

"I didn't know that about Grandfather Macaria. I felt like I should have known him but I couldn't grasp a memory."

She smiled sadly. "He'd have liked you. You do them all proud."

He knelt by her, taking her hands. "Not just them, Maria. You too. You've brought up all of us. My mother, me, my brother, sister, Elantha, let's not forget Wynfeld and Cal as well, plus whoever else has been foisted on you by circumstance whether for a day or a year. You've helped mould who we are. So, this is my promise to you. You can live at Macarian House for as long as you want, or here, or Ceardlann. Wherever we are, wherever we hold sway, you have a home with us. A home and a pension. No, I don't want anything by way of reply. You are part of our family. You will always have that place in my heart."

She lightly touched his chin, and he met her moist eyes. "Your heart is worth more than your crown."

He chuckled. "Don't tell the empire that. I'm quite attached to my heart."

"I wish they could see you now," she whispered. "You have the best of them all.”

Before he could reply, the door opened and Lord Faran entered.

“My apologies, Sire. I’ll—”

Arkyn pushed himself to his feet. “Samara’s next door asleep on Lady Elantha, my lord.” He nodded to Maria and left without looking at Faran.

In the nursery, Faran hesitated. “Did I blunder badly?”

She shrugged. “Yes. We were talking of Lady Ira and King Adeone.”

Faran sank onto a chair, his head in his hands. “Damn. I didn’t mean to, Maria.”

“He knows that. Mistress Samara’s a sweetie. She’s got your smile.”

Faran sighed. “I should go and apologise to the King.”

“No. Let me explain. You see your daughter if you want to.”

* * *

Maria entered Arkyn’s chambers with a jolt of the familiar. She found Kadeem and asked if she could disturb Arkyn.

He crooked an eyebrow. “What happened? He came back rather quiet.”

“Lord Faran interrupted our reminiscing. It’ll only take a minute.”

Kadeem nodded. “Pretend you slipped by me.”

She entered Arkyn’s bedchamber to find her former charge curled up, hugging himself. She sat on the edge of his bed saying,

“Lord Faran sends his apologies. He wanted to apologise in person.”

Arkyn didn’t say anything.

“He’s like that. Always has been. He was here, studying, when your parents married. I think he might have asked for your mother’s hand if Adeone hadn’t shown an interest. Though Macaria might not have granted it with Faran being a first-born son. She enjoyed his company. Danced with him frequently before your father proposed. He stood up for her as well when your father’s attentions made things awkward for her. I suppose what I’m trying to say is he’s a good man.”

Arkyn rolled onto his back. “I know that, Maria. At least I know he’s a good man. I just… Thank you for what you said earlier. The precipice feels further away than it did.”

She squeezed his shoulder. “Have faith in yourself, Arkyn.”

“Will you accept my offer?”

“Which part?” She asked with a smile.

“Any or all of it. Living wherever you choose, accepting you’re like family to us. Letting me take care of you as you have of us. Phrase it how you want. An easy retirement. A rest well earned after all of Tain’s tricks.”

She chuckled. “Ah, that brother of yours has turned some hairs grey. I am honoured by the offer…”

262

"Then please accept it," said Arkyn.

"I shall. Thank you."

He sat up and gave her a hug. "Good. Anything else you need?"

"Hair dye," she said with a laugh. "Come on, sir. You get the sleep you undoubtedly need. That brother of yours must be easy work compared to running the empire."

Arkyn grinned. "Don't tell him that."

Chuckling she pulled the covers straight over him and left with a wink.

Chapter 64
LANDIS AND FARAN
Imperadai, Week 1 – 4th Cearal, 4th Cearcis 1215
Oedran Palace

THE MORNING DAWNED without a cloud in the sky. It promised to be a clear day and night ahead and, whilst getting dressed, Faran was glad. The funeral needed calm dry weather.

He entered the Outer Office half expecting it to have changed, but it hadn't. He hadn't been sent for but Richardson took his appearance without any concern. When Faran asked if the King needed anything, the former King's Administrator deferred to Edward who was with the King. Faran passed a couple of minutes of small talk with Richardson before the Edward left the Inner Office and asked him to join the King.

Arkyn looked over at his entry and enquired pleasantly, "Did you have a restful night, my lord?"

"I did, sir."

"Good. After everything last night, I was thinking. Will you do the homage at father's funeral? Tain and I have been advised against doing it…"

"Who by, sir? It's not anyone's business but your own."

Arkyn said softly, "Lord Iris passed on the message from Lord Landis. If it had been anyone else then I'd have agreed with you."

"Ah. Then of course I will, sir. Doesn't Lord Landis wish to?"

"He is severely wounded. A crossbow bolt landed in his shoulder."

"I shall go and visit him, Sire, if I may?"

"Please do and, whilst you're there, get Doctor Chapa to check the injury you received on Munewid Eve. I've not forgotten, even if you're trying to hide it."

"Thank you, sir, but another doctor would be—" began Faran.

"Are you worried about Chapa's comments?" asked Arkyn.

"Possibly, sir, but I also thought he might have his hands full with your nearfather."

"The sparring does them both good."

* * *

At Landis House, Faran was greeted by Lord Julius, Landis' elder son.

Once the initial introduction and greeting were over Julius said, "Are you here to see father, Lord Faran?"

"I am, or at least that was my intention. Is he in a fit state to be seen?"

"Probably. I'll check. Do you know the way to the drawing room?"

Lord Faran said, "I've not been here since the rebuild but I see some rooms are still the same. I'll find my way."

Julius hared off and Faran was reminded of Festus as a young man. He smiled and walked toward the older drawing room.

"Good morning, Lady Landis."

She turned, startled. "Faran! When did you arrive?"

"About four minutes ago."

"I meant in Oedran. I didn't know you were expected."

"Oh. Last night. It was a rather swift journey."

She smiled. "It must have been. Sit down and tell me about it."

Soon afterwards, Doctor Chapa entered the drawing room. "How is my patient meant to rest with all these interruptions, Lord Faran?"

"He'd be bored without them, doc, and you'd have an even worse time," remarked Faran. "How are you?"

"Feeling terse."

"What's new? Seriously, Chapa?"

"Ask me after tonight. I've had a message from the King. Roll up your sleeve and I'll see to your scratch."

Faran said, "Surely another room would be better, doc."

Lady Landis smiled. "Don't mind me. My husband is a map of scars. I'll see about refreshment for you and Festus whilst you're talking."

Once she'd gone, Faran said, "Why are you trying to hide what you're feeling, doc?"

Chapa cut off the old bandage. "Because I daren't show it. I'll be no good to help anyone. I should be glad I've got so much work on because, if I hadn't, I'd get maudlin."

"Don't you think Adeone's memory might deserve it?"

"Yes, I do! When I can I will."

Faran nodded. "I've invited Richardson to my rooms to reminisce in a couple of days. Join us."

Chapa swallowed, looked at Faran and then away. "If I can, my lord.

264

This 'scratch' of yours… You should amend the description, I suggest 'wound'. Has your daughter suffered at all after her adventure?"

Faran accepted the change of subject. "Not to my knowledge."

"I'll come and check her over, if you've no objection, just to make sure."

"Of course. Thank you."

* * *

"Apparently we should compare scars," muttered Landis when Faran entered his bedchamber twelve minutes later.

Faran poured himself a cup of tea. "You'd win. How are you feeling, or at least healing?"

"The doc says everything is knitting together, which is probably why I feel like needles are pricking all over me, I don't think it's solely down to his unguents. What brought you here?"

"I heard you'd got into trouble, and the King's asked me to do the homage at the funeral. I wondered if there was anything you wanted to say."

"Thank Alcis he's been sensible," said Landis. "Come and sit down. William, where are you?"

His manservant appeared as if by magic. "My lord?"

"Can you pour us both a drink please? Something worth drinking, His Lordship is particular."

"Festus, are you trying to give me a bad name or simply looking for an excuse?" demanded Faran. "I'm perfectly happy with tea."

"The excuse seems good to me. Now, this speech…"

Chapter 65

UNEXPECTED ARRIVAL

Afternoon

Oedran – Carnford Gate

AT THE CARNFORD GATE of Oedran, an exhausted, unshaven, bedraggled rider reined in, motioned to a guard and enquired the way to the Palace.

"I could tell you, aye. Who are you?"

The man considered. "Call me an unexpected ambassador."

"In that case, no I can't. No ambassador is currently unexpected."

"Thank you for your help," replied the rider, with a hint of irony. How could anyone expect an unexpected ambassador and, therefore, how could they deny the existence of one? He rode forward, taking in the city in front of him; so this was Oedran. It made his home city look like a small town. He rode slowly up the street. Had he been right to come? He could return without the King ever discovering he'd arrived, but no; there was

265

more than one reason for his journey.

A more major road, crossed his path. Another man in uniform stood at the junction. He hailed him.

"Which way is the Palace?"

The man crossed to him. "Ambassador?"

"Of a sort. What gave me away?"

"The fatigue on your face, my lord. Straight over here, then any major road that carries on the way you're riding. You'll come to Alcium Plaza, straight over that, by going around the Alcium, be careful of the preparations for the funeral, through the gates into the Administrative Quarter and then straight ahead, you'll not miss the Palace. Bear right around the wall if you want the stables."

The mounted rider nodded. "Thank you. You've been most helpful."

"Might I know who's asking?"

The man smiled. "I'd rather the King discovered my presence when I see him, but, truly, thank you for your help."

The guide grabbed the bridle. "Here, you ain't planning to harm him, are you?"

"No, quite the reverse. I promise you, on whatever you wish, that I am not planning the King harm."

The guide eyed him. "Still need your name."

"What right do you have to request it from me?"

"I'm one of the yeomen. It's our job to keep these streets safe and we're not having an easy time of it since the news broke. There's three murders we can't be bothered to solve because the men said that King Adeone deserved to die. I'm not going to help anyone who'll cause the young King distress."

The rider considered. "I'm not going to cause a riot but if you insist," he leaned down and whispered his name into the man's ear.

The man swallowed. "Ah."

"As to the murders, remember every man has a family who deserve an explanation of their loved one's death whether they are FitzAlcis or cisan born. Investigate the murders; if you find nothing that is a different matter from ignoring them altogether. Now, might I ask your name?"

The man gave it. "I ain't going to tell a soul, sir. I promise."

The rider nodded. "I wouldn't tell a person either, Rushton."

* * *

At the Palace Stables there was less interrogation, tired arrivals who were ambassadors were becoming common.

The groom who took the bridle of the horse asked, "Where's your luggage, my lord?" Ambassadors were always lords with luggage and normally an attendant. He frowned slightly. Something wasn't right, but it wasn't his place to question a lord. Guards could do that.

Dismounting heavily, holding himself up against his horse, the rider said, "When you find it, let me know. Which way is the Inner Office?" If he didn't think about the aches it might be easier.

The groom whistled a piercing whistle, and a runner appeared. "Here, show His Lordship to the Outer Office, lad. Lend him your shoulder too."

* * *

Aching with every step, the rider entered the Palace, its corridors stretching before him seemingly without end. Gritting his teeth he followed the runner. He needed a bath to ease these aches. Somehow, now he'd stopped riding, it was worse, but it always was. He wanted to notice the corridors, the frescos, the gilding and paint, but he concentrated on putting one foot in front of the other. What was coming would require far more strength. He rested a couple of times on the Golden Stairs. The runner hesitated, asking if he needed help. He didn't, but catching his breath was welcome. He asked how much further it was. Hearing they were almost there, he straightened up. It wouldn't do to appear as though the ride had cost him so much.

They reached the Audience Chamber doors and the first problem.

"Good afternoon, Sergeant Hillbeck. I'm not here. I'm an illusion."

When he'd gone, Hillbeck's co-guard said, "Who was that, sarge?"

Hillbeck said simply, "That was an illusion."

In the Audience Chamber the runner hesitated. "Outer Office is through those doors, sir."

"Thanks, lad. Here…" The rider tossed him a silver talence.

"Cor, thanks, sir."

Once in the Outer Office, the unexpected arrival said, "What kind of mood is King Arkyn in, Edward?"

The room stopped; there was no other word for it. Four men, three of them dumbfounded, turned to the entrant. The fourth taken aback by the undertones of informality in the question.

The visitor crooked an eyebrow. "Lost for words? If only you each had a mirror… I'll announce myself." He took off his cloak and put it on a chair with his riding crop before turning to the two administrators. "I'm pleased to see you both again, but it must be bad if you're *still* lost for words. What's the arrangement of the Inner Office?"

Edward managed to say, "The King's desk is straight ahead of you. Let me announce—" It was too late.

Richardson and Edward held the other's gaze.

267

Richardson said, "Kenton, Marcle, I suggest you go for a short break. Give it half an hour."

Kenton glanced at the Inner Office, nodded and pulled Marcle out the room, none too subtly, but he knew the visitor and Marcle did not.

* * *

Arkyn glanced over as the door opened; he froze looking at the kneeling man in front of him – speechless for many moments and long minutes.

When the new King found his voice, he snapped, "I gave you an order, Wealsman!"

"I returned to Tera, Sire, and *then* I came north."

Arkyn hardly heard him. "How dare you leave Terasia without permission? I needed you there; I need you there more than ever now I've exiled Teran."

Still on his knees, Wealsman said, "Frankly, Sire, I don't know how I dared; all I know is that I had one murdered friend and one I wanted to support and Ernst is capable. I've signed the proclamations and I've been in contact with him at every stop and change of horse, other than at night. I bet I know more about what's happening in Terasia now than I do when I'm there. I'm here, Sire. Do you want me to leave?"

His temper at boiling point, Arkyn snapped, "Would it matter if I did? I've half a mind to strip you of your post and call my guards. Your care for your province has diminished."

Wealsman looked at him compassionately, "Then do it, sir. Call your guards. My care for Terasia hasn't changed but my closest friend was murdered and the nearfather of my children is in need of support. My loyalties have never been so torn. Maybe I was a fool to come. Maybe I should have sat fretting in Terasia but I *couldn't*..."

"Sicla's Cavern, you're bloody *Margrave*, Percival! You can't follow personal wishes – just as I can't. I don't want to be in Oedran but I have to be. I can't abandon my duties and I thought you wouldn't." Arkyn's voice began to break.

"I have conflicting definitions of abandon and duties – maybe I took the wrong side. When I asked the way to the Palace, two men refused to tell me because I wouldn't tell them who I was and why I was asking. They thought I meant you harm but I never have and I never will. Any harm I've done has been unintentional. From what I can gather Adeone's funeral is tonight. I'll be gone tomorrow. You can say I was never here. I'll leave at the end of the funeral and take a mail coach. I'll be back in Terasia before the week is out. I never wished to distress you."

Arkyn said, "And that's a good enough apology, is it?"

"No. There isn't one, is there, Arkyn? I've betrayed your trust," replied

Wealsman sadly, his heart aching as much as his limbs.

After a few moments, Arkyn took a deep breath. "You don't need to apologise and you haven't." He finally crossed to his friend and offered a hand to help him to his feet.

Wealsman kissed the King's signet ring. "I'm sorry, Arkyn. By the time I came to my senses, I was in Oedran. I just had to come, had to be here."

"No, I'm sorry. For myself I'm glad to see you." He pulled Wealsman to his feet.

"The King isn't?"

"He's a fool who's annoyed you didn't go back to Tera."

Wealsman studied Arkyn intently. "I did, sir. Ask me on any oath you want. Take a fealty reading. I went to Tera, spent the afternoon running my staff ragged and then took a mail-horse and rode for Areal. I changed horses as often as I could, at night I used a mail coach." He groaned. "You might say I'm aching a bit."

Arkyn saw drained emotion in his face.

"I also forgot my luggage," continued Wealsman. "It was quicker. Kristina's berated me. I now understand; I shouldn't have appeared like this, not in this state. I must be some apparition."

Arkyn remained silent and Wealsman waited.

Eventually, the King said, "You definitely need a new tunic and a shave. You can't have ridden all that distance. Sicla. It must be close to a thousand miles. You must have been galloping all the way."

"I'd have ridden twice that and more, Arkyn. I wanted to be here. Not my best decision but it came from my heart."

"It's not your worst; truly, it's not your worst." He looked at Percival. "Father's next door, they're about to shroud him. Go on through before you're too late."

* * *

Percival entered the bedchamber. Recognising one man with his back to him, he said, "Simkins, can you give me a few minutes?"

Shocked, Simkins turned. "What…? My lord! Your Excellency, what on Erinna are you doing here? Does the King know?"

"You mean you didn't hear his reaction to my arrival?"

"I wasn't concentrating on that. I've found it better not to hear anything."

"How fortunate. Do you mind if I…?"

Simkins shook his head and waved everyone out. "Take what time you need, sir. Ring when you leave."

Wealsman said, "I'll ring and help with the shrouding."

* * *

Once Percival left the room, Arkyn sank onto his chair, trying to relax.

269

He considered what Wealsman had said and contacted the Deputy Governor of Terasia. Ernst was a direct gentleman who confirmed Wealsman's story in such a way as to leave no doubt as to its veracity. The Deputy Governor of Terasia also confirmed that a house had been found for Lord Teran, and that it was a distance from any acquaintance he might claim in Tera, adding the Lord of Oedran should reach the city in just over a week.

Arkyn sighed. "The difference between mail routes and cavalcade pace is never more pronounced. Thank you, Ernst; I shouldn't keep you any longer. Lord Wealsman should be with you by Alunadai."

"Sire, if you want Lord Wealsman in Oedran, tell him to stay and I'll cope here."

"Between us, Ernst, I'm not sure I have any effect on him."

"If that were true, he'd still be in Tera, Sire."

Arkyn pondered that as the link broke.

* * *

Once faced with his office, Arkyn tried not to consider what his reaction had been. It had been sickeningly official and officious. Percival never disregarded his duties. He should never have doubted that. He now had to mitigate it somehow. He got a drink and sat down before calling for Edward and arranging rooms and provisions for Percival's stay. He discovered that his administrator had already anticipated everything needed with an efficiency he was notorious for.

Arkyn finished by saying, "I'm not sure how long he's going to be here: certainly tonight. I'm not having him ride straight back to Terasia."

Edward smiled. "Good, sir. I mean… Oh, Sicla…"

"Thank you for the underlying concern. I'm sure he'll appreciate it. As for dinner tonight, much as I'd like Percival there if I invite him, I'd have to invite others and it would get complicated; therefore, it will still be private as arranged. I'll breakfast with Lord Wealsman tomorrow, which hopefully should stop him running off. Let Kadeem know." After the briefest pause, he added, "Ask Kadeem to attend on His Excellency whilst he settles in. That should keep Wealsman out of trouble."

Edward's lips twitched as he nodded and left.

* * *

When Wealsman re-entered the Inner Office, the King knew he had been right to travel north. He walked over, clasped Wealsman's shoulder.

"Thank you."

Wealsman said, "I'm not going to ask how you're coping."

"The worst is that he knew, Percival, he knew and he still walked into the King's Hall. Oh, he didn't know the means but he knew he wouldn't

270

walk out of that banquet.”

“Sicla! I didn’t know that. How are you keeping it together, Arkyn?”

“Because I must; it’s as simple as that, I *have* to. Landis took a crossbow bolt to the shoulder as well. It was a co-ordinated attack. So far everyone close or important to us was attacked that night, other than General Paturn but he changed his plans at the last minute. You, Tyler Galwood, Wynfeld, Landis, not to mention the fact that the Amphi food taster died of poison – meaning myself, Tain and ReJean were targets, also probably Lady Phylicia ReJean as well. Can you imagine if all those attacks had succeeded?”

Wealsman paled. “With your permission, I’d rather not until I’ve slept.”

“Probably wise.” Arkyn sagged. “I feel it will never end; I’ll be forever chasing peace as father was.”

“Every game concludes; it might be slow but the end will come.”

“Will we win though?”

“That is for the future, Arkyn, just play the game as well as you can.”

“How? I feel like the board has been ripped from under me and the pieces toppled.”

“Then find a new board and pick up the pieces… Listen to me, I could be Kadeem – sorry for that.”

“I’ll forgive you.”

Wealsman smiled. “Thank you. Is there anything I can do? However small, however insignificant, personal or professionally – *anything*?”

“I don’t know at the moment, I really don’t… Percival, I know how close you and father were, I never truly begrudged the fact neither of you told me in 1211, but I wish I’d made that clear to him. He never quite believed me.”

“He was like that. He still felt guilty even after reassurance; he just hid it well. Don’t regret any part of your relationship with your father, even the rough times had their place and you were never angry with each other for long.”

“Did you get caught in the middle?” asked Arkyn tiredly.

“No. You were both too principled. Can I give you some advice?”

“Of course.”

“These next few weeks are going to be bloody tough. Face them head on and then take some time off. Get through the funeral and your coronation. Get through the Ambassadors’ Court and the first month of the year. Then go to Ceardlann. The world will look changed on your return.”

“It already does, Percival, but I think I know what you mean. Thank you. I might follow your advice.”

“Surprise me and do so.”

Arkyn said wanly, “I do listen to and follow advice, Percival.”

"I know that, as do all around you…" Wealsman studied Arkyn's face. "I was ever a fool when it came to friendship, but through my folly and forwardness I hope you know I truly do care, I'm not trying to get rid of you so everyone gets some peace from the mayhem."

"Then we're fools together. Edward's sorted you out some rooms, you look ready to drop."

Percival smiled wryly. "I suppose everything is reversed with my visit here. You're telling *me* to rest."

"I'm sure given time you'll manage to reassert yourself in that regard, Percival. I'll just try not to give you chance."

"I appreciate a challenge, Arkyn."

"Oh, good," replied the King dryly.

Chapter 66
MUTUAL FRIENDS

Late Afternoon
Oedran Palace – Privy Wing

WEALSMAN REALISED the efficiency of the Palace as soon as he stepped foot in his rooms. He'd been unexpected and had arrived with no luggage, but there was everything he could need there from a clean tunic to shaving gear to writing materials, and Kadeem waiting patiently.

In a genuine voice that spoke a thousand sentiments more, the manservant said, "I'm pleased to see you, Your Excellency."

"I you, Kadeem, but I wish it was in happier circumstances."

"Aye, sir. We all do. I have a bath prepared if you'd like it."

"I forgot you're a mind reader. Show me the way. I honestly can't wait."

Deep, steaming and fragrant, the water enveloped him. He groaned. Over nine hundred miles from Tera to Oedran. He had managed to rest a bit in the coaches overnight, but whatever he'd tell Arkyn, he'd ridden more than was sensible, or had ever attempted before. Endurance riding was a hobby, but maybe, as he aged, he shouldn't be doing such long rides. He let the water soak the aches for several long minutes. It would work its magic. Reaching for a cloth, he scrubbed at his legs. The water turned murky around him. Arkyn hadn't mentioned his state, beyond the tunic and shave but, as the water darkened, he realised he'd been fortunate. Travel stained didn't quite do that state justice. He yawned. Lavender wasn't always the best option, though it did help aches. He made sure the rest of him was presentable before pulling himself out of the bath. The blisters on his hands probably needed seeing to, but they could wait. For now, he needed to dress and visit a couple of people.

He entered the bedchamber with a towel wrapped around him. Kadeem was waiting with another gentleman. In answer to Wealsman's raised eyebrow, the manservant said the King had ordered a massage for him. Wealsman wasn't going to complain about that.

The King's masseur worked methodically and in silence, whilst Wealsman struggled to stay awake. Master Glew was good but not up to Terasian standards. Still, anything to help his muscles.

Once dressed, he asked Kadeem whether the King had organised anything else.

"I've been told you'll be dining with Lord Faran, Your Excellency."

Wealsman crooked an eyebrow. "Faran of Lufian? He's here?"

"He and his youngest daughter arrived yesterday, sir. His rooms are next door. If you wish to sleep before dinner, I can wake you later."

Wealsman shook his head. "I would rather see Lord Faran before dinner, and then I've a call to make in Oedran. Do you think anyone would object to that?"

"Your Excellency, you're His… a King's Representative. No-one will dare say anything." Kadeem caught his eye. "I *am* glad you're here, sir."

Wealsman sighed. "I had to be. Is he… well."

Kadeem hesitated. "It has been a stressful few days for everyone, Your Excellency. The King has been drawing on his resilience."

Wealsman sank onto a chair. "I was afraid of that."

"We're keeping an eye on him, sir."

"I never doubted it. I should see Faran. Then, would it be possible to borrow a coach to take me to Landis House?" asked Wealsman.

"I'll see one is sent to the Privy Gate, Your Excellency. Would you like me to accompany you?"

Wealsman met the manservant's eye. "Not if the King is drawing on his resilience. He'll need you. Tonight especially."

* * *

A footman showed him into Faran's sitting room. The Lord of Lufian was writing busily with notes strewn across a table. When Wealsman was announced he got up.

"Your Excellency, I'm pleased to meet you at last. Come on in. You've had an interesting journey, and one that may well go down in history. Fawcett, a drink for the Margrave – he looks like he needs one."

Wealsman smiled. "I'm pleased to meet you also, Faran. What are you working on? A whiskey would be good, please, Fawcett. Thank you."

Faran waved to a chair. "The homage. I was about to contact you when

I was informed you'd arrived. Have you any memory of Adeone you'd like included?"

Wealsman smiled. "Plenty but I don't think some of them are appropriate. Let me have a think…"

A few minutes later Faran said, "Do you want to read the homage or help bear Adeone's body? I won't mind; you were one of his closest confidants. I think there was only Landis who might have been closer."

Wealsman shook his head. "You do yourself a disservice, Faran. My arrival will not upset any plans, I hope. I'm here to say goodbye to one friend and to support another. That is all. I am not here as an official."

"Which of us is?" pointed out Faran. "I don't think the homage is right for an official to say."

"No, maybe not. Would you mind if I had a read of it?"

"Not at all. Come and see what you think."

Wealsman smiled. "Then I need to call on Lord Landis. I hear he's been wounded."

"Yes, quite badly. You'll meet him later. We're invited to dine at Landis House."

"Are we? I thought I was dining with Your Lordship."

"You still are."

"True. I should perhaps see Lord Landis beforehand though."

"Of course. Now, this homage…"

* * *

Wealsman left Faran's rooms three-quarters of an hour later. Faran didn't need the disruption in his day. A courier, acting as his guide, was rather confused by Wealsman's manner. He was Margrave of Terasia, an overlord in Terasia – which gave him near equivalent status to a Lord of Oedran – and a King's Representative – which surpassed it – not to say a close friend of the King; therefore, it was unusual in the extreme for such a high official to not only ask him his name but also something about himself. Craig decided that things must be different in Terasia – or Wealsman was somehow making fun of him.

As they left the Palace by the Privy Gate, Wealsman stood for a moment surveying the bustling scene. He saw not a crowd but individuals congregating: there were merchants, servants, craftsmen, housewives, lawyers, vagabonds, street sellers and soldiers and every shade between. The soldiers caught Wealsman's attention.

"Craig, may I go to the barracks?"

"Certainly, Your Excellency, but you'll need a password to enter."

Wealsman considered, contacted Edward and two moments later had the day's password without question. He pulled himself into the waiting coach. The bath and massage had definitely helped. Hopefully a good night's sleep would set him right for the ride home. Optimism and determination, there was nothing quite like it.

The guards on the barracks asked for Wealsman's name as well as the password. Wealsman pointed out the password was all that was required and if they were asking at the Major's orders then he was going to see him, if they would supply a guide.

With an unerring knack for self-preservation, the sergeant called for one of his men and let Wealsman enter. Craig waited outside with the coach half wishing he could enter to see who objected next.

The barracks hummed with activity and anxiety. Wealsman's gaze missed nothing as he walked to Wynfeld's office. His guide delivered him to a corporal and left.

Wealsman gave his name before saying, "Is Major Wynfeld available for a quick word, corporal?"

The corporal's scepticism could have been framed.

Wealsman chuckled and handed over his seal. Eyeing it uncertainly, the corporal took an impression, hesitated and handed it back.

"The Major is busy, Your Excellency. Maybe I could arrange a time."

"I'm only here for the funeral," said Wealsman, deciding, in the interests of the corporal keeping his job, never to reveal the greeting to Wynfeld.

The corporal grimaced and glanced at the door to Wynfeld's office. "The General's there, sir."

Understanding flooded into Wealsman's mind. "Is he? Then I'll interrupt them. I don't expect you to, corporal. The Major will understand."

"It really isn't necessary, sir. Have you ever met the General or Major?"

"I am about to meet the General but the Major and I are known to one another." Wealsman knocked on the office door and heard Wynfeld say,

"It had better be important."

Entering the office without replying Wealsman smiled at the look on Wynfeld's face and, in reply to the General's rather blunt…

"Who in Sicla's Cavern are you?"

…he said, "Percival Wealsman, General Paturn. It's a pleasure to meet you. Good afternoon, Major Wynfeld."

Wynfeld saluted. "Welcome to Oedran, Your Excellency. What brought you north?"

The look Wealsman gave him was level and his gaze unflinching.

Wynfeld sank onto his chair. "My apologies, Your Excellency."

"Accepted, Major," said Percival still watching him. When had such a confident and competent officer become so bowed down?

"How long are you in Oedran for, Your Excellency?" asked Paturn.

"Until the morning, General."

"Surely you've not ridden all this way just for the funeral, sir."

Wealsman looked him in the eye. "Not *just* the funeral, no, General, but my friend's murder was the motivating factor."

Paturn held his gaze. "Aye, it would be. My apologies, Your Excellency. I should leave you to talk. Wynfeld, I will need that information as soon as possible after Lord Wealsman has left."

"You'll have it, sir," said Wynfeld as the General left. He waved Wealsman to a chair. "We both put our foot in it, didn't we, Your Excellency?"

Wealsman said, "To be honest, yes, you did."

"My apologies, once again. How are you?"

"Tired and aching, both physically and mentally."

"I presume the King knows you're here."

Wealsman explained about his ride and his arrival.

At the end, Wynfeld said, "You've not told me everything, have you?"

"No, Major, nor will I."

Wynfeld frowned. "I had realised my credibility had diminished, but I have just realised how much."

"It has done no such thing but there are words spoken between friends that remain between them."

"Of course, but what I said was true, and there's no surprise in that. I've made enough mistakes before; King Arkyn won't forgive me this."

"In your own words, what happened?"

"Are you asking for our King?" enquired Wynfeld.

"No, for shared time in Terasia, for what happened there and the respect that was garnered."

Wynfeld explained, in tones which betrayed many conflicting emotions.

"What are you doing about it all?" asked Wealsman when he finished.

"I can only pick up the pieces and I'm not doing that too well. The assassin disappeared and no-one admits to knowing anything. We've been speaking to every guard, palace employee and guest possible. I'm hunting through past reports to see if there is any hint. I'm hunting hard for Jacobs but there's no sign of him – someone's harbouring him but I don't know who, and it can't be the exiled lords – we've gone through their houses on one pretext or another – and we don't know what he's planning or what he's been ordered to do…"

"Could Jacobs be your assassin?"

"No. He's never held a crossbow to our knowledge and we've dug deep into his past. The bolt gave nothing away but the weapon might if we had it, which we don't."

Wealsman said, "What can I do, Major?"

"Your Excellency, surely you want to rest."

"We do share some traits: overwork is one of them. I'm a King's Representative, make use of me."

Wynfeld hesitated. "There's nothing I can think that you can do, my lord. I've any warrant I need—"

"Let me talk to Stuart," requested Wealsman.

"He knows nothing."

"Faced with me he might remember something."

Wynfeld smiled. "Your Excellency, I'm not sure that is quite fair."

Wealsman made a non-committal face. "Maybe not, but surprise does much to aid recollection, and I really can't be any worse than you."

Still smiling, Wynfeld realised he was pleased to see Wealsman, and he'd been reassured by his presence.

* * *

Brought to the interrogation room from his damp cell, Stuart wasn't feeling cooperative, but nor was he feeling loyal to Jacobs either. He sat down and faced his interrogators. He swallowed. Predictably Major Wynfeld was there looking tired and, for a brief moment, Stuart was glad before he noticed Lord Wealsman.

"Ah."

He remembered being questioned by Wealsman subtly when in Terasia about the anonymous notes. That man had a memory he didn't want to run up against twice. The Terasian officials had been clear, Wealsman was fair, but it was useless trying to deceive him. Running up against Wynfeld was nothing by comparison to Lord Wealsman's memory.

Wealsman smiled. "Good afternoon, Stuart."

"Is it?"

"That may depend on your answers."

"I've told him all I know," said Stuart nodding at Wynfeld.

Wealsman smiled. "I'm sure you think you have. Now, you can either elaborate or face life in a cell. You and Jacobs are morally inseparable."

"Not since he got me dismissed, we're not. I should never have believed him. I couldn't get away from him even when I wanted to, and now I'll suffer for his bloody idiotic actions."

"Yes, rather unfortunate that," observed Wynfeld. "Depending on your co-operation we could alter that or make it worse."

Wealsman said, "Major, there are laws that might contradict that stance."

"We're in a military camp, Your Excellency, and Stuart is still bound by his oath to the FitzAlcis. They transferred him here. He could be said to be bound by military law."

Wealsman smiled mirthlessly. "So he could. Stuart, what do you know

277

about Jacobs' sudden promotion?"

Stuart glanced between his interrogators and considered that he'd never been asked that before in that way and so answering honestly was easy.

* * *

An hour later, Wealsman rang the bell at Landis House. A polished footman opened the door and stood to one side; it was clear Wealsman was a lord.

"I'm Percival Wealsman. I'm here to see Lord Landis, if possible."

"Of course, Your Excellency," replied Backery. "This way please."

They were crossing the hallway when a mild voice said, sardonically, "Let me guess, you're about to disturb my patient?"

Wealsman turned to face a grey-haired, blue-eyed man with a piercing gaze. "Is His Lordship well enough to be disturbed?"

"That's the question, isn't it? Who are you?"

"Percival Wealsman."

Chapa looked at him carefully. "Are you really? Hmm. Let me guess, you're here at the King's instruction."

Wealsman said, "Actually I'm not. Might I ask your name?"

"Doctor Chapa."

"Ah."

They eyed each other for a long moment. Two men who'd heard a lot about each other meeting for the first time. Their curiosity wasn't hidden, nor did they try to hide it.

"Come on then," said Chapa. "His Lordship's been better but he'll want to meet you."

Wealsman nodded in thanks at the footman. "Doctor Chapa… I'm sorry for your loss; I know you were close to Adeone and he to you."

"Thank you," replied Chapa neutrally. They continued in silence until they reached an upstairs door. "Wait here, Your Excellency." He entered a room. "Are you behaving yourself, Lord Landis?"

"Who's been telling you otherwise?"

"No-one. They're all too loyal to you. I've tried bribery. It didn't work. I've a visitor for you."

Lord Landis said, "Who?"

Percival heard the smile in the doctor's voice as he replied.

Landis said, "Sicla's Cavern! I'm getting up. No, doc, I'm not listening, give me your arm."

"It's rather attached to me."

"I can remedy that if you don't help."

Two moments later, Chapa left the room. "He's as ready for you as he'll ever be, Lord Wealsman. I suppose it's useless to tell you not to wear him out."

* * *

Wealsman entered the room, looked for the first time at Lord Landis and found he was being evaluated at the same time. They were silent for long minutes before Landis said,

"Does Arkyn know…?"

"Yes."

Landis considered the significance of the shortness of the response. "Sit down. We should perhaps go elsewhere."

Wealsman said, "Here is fine, my lord."

"My name's Festus. If we can be informal about our mutual friends then we can call each other by name, can't we?"

"Of course. How are you? The doc's gone."

Landis sank onto his bed. "Not good. I'll survive but Adeone didn't. There are decisions I have to make because of that."

"Do you want to talk about them?"

"No. It would put you in an awkward position. Adeone would have appreciated your presence, but you know that. Does Arkyn?"

Wealsman explained what had happened and what he'd done.

Landis laughed. "Good for you, Percival. Arkyn will appreciate it more when he's past the funeral…"

They talked for a few minutes before Landis rang the bell and told his manservant he was getting up properly before asking William to show Wealsman to the study.

The manservant said, "Of course, my lord. I'll ask the doctor to—"

"No, you won't. He'll send me back to bed."

* * *

Once alone, Wealsman looked around Landis' study with interest: a room that was comfortable, rich but not ostentatious. The wood gleamed with polish and the sun streamed in the windows. Curiosity getting the better of him, Wealsman opened a door to find a well-stocked library. He entered and read the titles of the volumes. He smiled and nodded to himself. There were a few novels, volumes on history, reference works about several provinces. Wealsman found himself holding a scroll on deception. He sank onto a comfortable chair, unrolling it. He read the first line and smiled.

Deception is a skill to be acquired and a liar will rarely deceive successfully.

Wealsman considered that; it was true people who lied at every turn were usually discovered, or distrusted through small signs.

He continued reading for several minutes struggling against fatigue. He blinked hard but, the next thing he knew, someone carefully removed the scroll from his hands. Blurrily he opened his eyes.

279

"I always knew that text was a soporific but I didn't think it had such an immediate effect, Percival," said Landis smiling.

"I was intrigued. My apologies for exploring."

Landis eased himself into the chair opposite. "Don't apologise. You're welcome to explore all you wish. I hear you're dining here this evening."

"Apparently. I assumed you'd know when Faran informed me."

Landis smiled. "I believe he asked my wife. He knew I wasn't to be disturbed, or, at least, that the doc thinks it better that I'm not..." He paused, looking caringly at Lord Wealsman and then at a timepiece. He rang the bell, and when William answered said, "Can you see a guest room is prepared for Lord Wealsman, please?"

When the manservant had gone, Wealsman said, "Lord Landis?"

"You're obviously exhausted. There are a couple of hours before we must leave for the Palace. Please rest. Don't worry, I'll see you're there but you've ridden hard. Take some rest whilst you can."

Wealsman yawned. "I did not, and do not, wish to inconvenience yourself, Lady Landis or your household."

"They're used to it. Adeone was a regular guest."

They both chuckled.

"Yes, he did turn up at unexpected moments." Wealsman rose. "I'm sorry to miss dinner; Adeone said your cook was worth the friendship."

"He said yours was worth the puddings."

Wealsman yawned once more. "He was right. Excuse me; I can't seem to stop yawning. It's not quite the image I wished to portray."

"At least it's honest. Do you regret coming north?" enquired Landis.

Wealsman sighed. "No." Then with feeling he added, "I regret causing Arkyn distress."

"Don't we all," murmured Landis. "How is he? I've not seen him outside of a messenger link since the night he returned."

"I suppose he's coping as you might expect until foolish friends blunder in," Wealsman admitted. "I honestly couldn't tell you, Festus. I don't think my arrival showed him at his best."

"Had Adeone been shrouded when you arrived?"

"No. I helped Simkins and the Moonshi do that after Arkyn dismissed me. Why?"

"If you were that close to the event, Arkyn would have just looked on Adeone for the last time. His emotions wouldn't have been under his control," explained Landis both glad to be able to add reassurance and oddly frustrated that Wealsman had been able to help, when he couldn't.

Wealsman crossed to the window and examined the view. "I couldn't have timed it worse, could I?"

Landis walked over to him and put his hand on Wealsman's arm. "No but maybe it was better that a friend was there. Arkyn will be emotional at the moment, however good he is at hiding it."

Wealsman nodded. "I know, Festus. Thank you. I wish I could stay for longer but my duties call me to Tera and if I stayed for even a day, I would not return for months. I wish to support Arkyn as much as I can—"

"The support you give Arkyn, and gave Adeone, is not, and was not, confined to being here in person. If it were you'd have sadly failed over recent years."

Wealsman said, "I think I may have done."

"No. You are tired and have had a hard journey so I shall be kind and simply tell you that you're a fool. You've never let either of them down. You need rest before you say anything else you might regret." He rang the bell again. When William answered, he asked, "Which room?"

William smiled. "If you'd like to follow me, Your Excellency. Doctor Chapa wonders if you have a moment, Lord Landis?"

"Not if he's going to berate me," replied Landis to general chuckles.

* * *

Faran arrived shortly afterwards and found Chapa and Landis talking, each with a drink in hand and emotion on their faces.

"Is Lord Wealsman here yet?" he asked, accepting a drink from William.

Landis said, "He's happily sleeping in one of my guest rooms."

"Good. He looked like he needed it but he insisted on meeting you before dinner."

"What time did he leave you?" After Faran answered, Landis continued puzzled, "I wonder who else he visited then. He didn't arrive here until about three-quarters of an hour ago."

"Does he know anyone else well in Oedran, or that he would have heard about enough to wish to meet them?"

"Not that I can think of. Oh, wait, of course, there's Wynfeld. He was stationed in Tera during the last review."

Faran smiled. "If he went to the barracks, it would explain it."

"Yes. I wonder what he and Wynfeld discussed."

Chapa said, "I expect they discussed the apprehension of the assassin, my lords. I should leave you to dine."

"You're joining us, Chapa," stated Landis.

"Am I?"

"Yes, of course you are. It will give you more chance to rebuke me and you know you wish to."

"I want you well, Festus, for Adeone's sake," whispered Chapa.

Faran glanced at him, it was the most heartfelt comment he'd heard

281

the doctor utter yet.

Landis said, "There are some wounds you can't heal, doc."

"I know," said Chapa dejectedly.

Chapter 67
FUNERAL
Dusk

Oedran – City Alcium

AS DUSK FELL, a solemn procession wound from the Audience Chamber at the Palace to the City Alcium. King Adeone's bier was born on the shoulders of Lords Iris, Fairson, Ryson, Rale, Faran and Julius. Immediately behind them walked Arkyn, Tain, Elantha, Lady Amara, Lady Rhian and her sister Lady Neassa. Lord Landis was with them, although he was in a carrying chair at the doctor's insistence and his private relief. Behind them were the doctor and former chief merchant, Henry Chapa, representing the Chapa side of Adeone's family. Arkyn had insisted on their presence and insisted on them being part of the family group. Behind them came Landis' children as Adeone's nearchildren but walking with them was Cal, again at Arkyn's insistence. Then there were the ambassadors, including Wealsman, the officials of Oedran and other invitees. Guards flanked them all: King's Guards, Prince's Guards, Palace Guards and the militia all took a part in the procession – from escorting the body of the late King, to lining the route along The Pike to the King's Gate, then to the City Alcium. Once there, the sombre-clad Moonshi greeted them, flanked by black-clad alcia who took the weight of the bier from the lords and reverently carried it inside the City Alcium. In the centre of the main circular space the King's Lull sat ready to receive the bier holding Adeone's body. It was placed there for all to see with candles lit around it.

Shrouded in a white silk cloth shot with gold threads, Adeone lay on a bier covered in scarlet velvet. Arkyn and Tain knelt next to him: Arkyn at his right hand, Tain at his left. Each inclined his head and waited, never moving a muscle, never portraying anything but steely resolve.

A couple of feet from the bottom of the bier stood Lady Amara, Lady Elantha and Lady Rhian, the young girl between the older ladies, to the right of Rhian stood Neassa clasping her sister's hand. Elantha already had tears running down her face and Arkyn was desperately trying to resist looking at her, for he knew her grief would ignite his. Gradually the officials filed in until, around the FitzAlcis, there was a complete ring of people.

The Moonshi nodded to the alcias and, around the edge of the chamber, every candle was extinguished. The only remaining light was from the candles around the King's Lull, illuminating the richness of Adeone's shroud and the circlets on Arkyn's and Tain's heads.

Lord Faran walked forward until he was standing at Adeone's head; glad now he'd accepted the burden of reading the homage, for seeing the brothers kneeling he didn't know how they'd have coped.

As people listened to the story of King Adeone's life they found themselves smiling as reminiscences from his friends and family were dropped into the dialogue with tact and appreciation. Doctor Chapa had recalled a troublesome birth, and added it was probably an apt herald. Henry Chapa, the banquets at which Adeone had let his prankster-imagination run wild. Lord Landis had asked for Adeone's life with Ira to be remembered, and Lady Landis had asked that Faran mention that whatever else Adeone had been he had been a father and nearfather first. Then at the end came Percival's contribution.

"Friendship through trouble is Lord Wealsman's recollection of King Adeone, friendship and an aptitude to listen and through listening to ease burdens, to banish the nightmares of the mind. There is, in that, a lasting tribute not many men earn, for King Adeone always put others before himself, whether that was personal friendships or his duties as King. He was a laughing prince, an erudite king, a kind father, nearfather and friend. He was everything great about Oedran and its empire. I would ask that you remember the man, not the glamour of the king, but the man who supported his friends and family, who loved and lost, who saw the morning and the evening as moments of beauteous change. Tonight is our farewell to him. Let us make it honest, let us send him to our ancestors from our hearts, loved and respected and written inextricably into our history."

Silence fell, silence absolute and unflinching, no-one moved a muscle, no-one even seemed to breathe. Then, from the balcony surrounding the central domed area, solo flute music wafted: gentle, a susurration of feeling. In these tunes were memories and meaning, alive for all to hear. Tain and Arkyn closed their eyes and listened as their father's soul was played to the stars. People found themselves smiling, and then weeping as the music and atmosphere tugged at something within them.

When the music became a simple melody, Tain and Arkyn rose, moving to stand with their family, to allow the alcia to carry the bier out to the pyre. Amara put a steadying hand on Arkyn's shoulder, and Rhian nodded with understanding at Tain. Together they followed the bier out.

Carefully, and without obvious jostling, the guests reorganised themselves. Arkyn and Tain stood with an arm around Elantha, flanked by Lady Amara and Lady Rhian.

The Moonshi stepped forward. Once all the guests were assembled, he said in a voice trained to carry, "Adeone Altarius FitzAlcis, once King, may the ancestors greet you and make you welcome. Let the stars be brighter with your presence, let your memory here never wane lest we forget your sacrifices. Be at peace, beyond the cares of this world."

He lit the pyre.

As Arkyn watched the pyre flame into life, sorrow burnt within him and it hurt; there was no ease for this, no balm. Aware he had to stay standing, every muscle was under control but the control was breaking him. Suddenly he was aware that Lady Amara had moved and standing next to him was the one man whose presence he hadn't realised he'd missed.

Laioril whispered, "Lad, watch the stars greet your father, not the flames: the flames will burn within you, the stars bring you peace. They are the balm of the night."

Arkyn did as suggested.

"Now listen, lad, listen to the sound of the city."

Arkyn tried. "I can't hear anything, Chief."

"No, lad. I know. The city watches the stars as well."

Watching the flames, anger raged inside Tain. He wanted to find who'd done this to them, find them and deliver justice. Everyone had been focused on the Assassination Document, but no-one seemed to remember a man had pulled the crossbow trigger: a man unknown and unapprehended. It would be a long search; the only men to know the identity were exiled. He hoped that the assassin would be discovered, captured and face the consequences. He glanced at Elantha and simply hugged her to him. Laioril was by Arkyn; he hadn't seen or heard the Chief arrive. How long had he been close by? Had he been in the shadows of the dusk, simply waiting until he was needed? Or was it until he wished to be present?

After a time, Arkyn and Tain were both aware people had gone: they were being left alone with their closest to mourn their father in private.

Arkyn looked at his brother and simply held out an arm. Still supporting Elantha, Tain moved over to him and accepted the support. From nearby, Lord Landis watched them for a moment feeling utterly hopeless. He'd let them down. He had known there would be an attack, and he hadn't prevented it. Adeone's wishes had left him shackled but now he knew he should have done more, his nearsons had needed him to prevent this and he hadn't, he'd failed.

From beside him Laioril said, "Blaming yourself, lad, won't help."

"Shut up, Chief."

"No. You did what Adeone wanted."

"But not what was right, not what a Defender should, not what a nearfather should. There's no convincing me otherwise so save your breath."

Laioril looked at him kindly, so kindly that Landis almost broke.

"Lad, this time is for Adeone's memory not self-recriminations. Think of the good times lest guilt wrecks your memories. He was the laughing prince, wasn't that *your* line? Remember the laughter, lad, and remember that when he met you, he hadn't laughed properly since his mother died. You made him that laughing prince of your memory."

Landis swallowed and, looking away, nodded, but it hadn't been his line.

Wealsman had stood with the ambassadors – he hadn't wanted a higher place, although Arkyn had offered him one and willed him to accept – but he didn't leave with them. He waited and watched. He saw Arkyn struggling for control, watched as a man he didn't know spoke to the King and noticed Arkyn's posture change. His eyes tracked the gentleman and saw the exchange with Landis. Then the man walked towards him.

"Percival Wealsman? I'm Laioril."

Wealsman grasped Laioril's wizened hand. "I've wanted to meet you."

"Aye, lad, I you. Do you happen to have any whiskey with you? It was a nice drop…"

"No. I'll send some north."

"Thank you, lad. Are you watching the flames or the stars?"

Wealsman said, softly, "I was actually watching Arkyn."

Laioril nodded. "Aye, lad, we all are but watch the stars greet our friend and remember all the good times with him, all the whiskey, his unexpected visit and remember what brought you north."

"I can't forget, Chief, even if I wanted to."

"No, lad, I know. Just send the memories with him to the stars. They will sustain his light."

When Wealsman turned to reply the Chief had gone.

From close by, Cal watched everything with tears pricking at his eyes. He hadn't known the laughing prince, he hadn't really known the erudite king, what he had experienced was the kind man who took trouble over everyone. They were his memories: memories of Ceardlann, of evenings laughing, of hours spent watching a family closer than any other he knew.

As he looked at the flames, he murmured, "Goodbye, Uncle Adeone."

PART 5

Chapter 68

MORNING IN OEDRAN

Pentadai, Week 1 – 5th Cearal, 5th Cearcis 1215
Oedran Palace – Tain's Bedchamber

PENTADAI DAWNED as clear and beautiful a day as the previous one and Tain woke early. He lay gazing vacantly around his bedchamber; his father was gone and the future had to be faced. He rang for Robert.

The manservant entered. "Good morning, Your Highness. Did you sleep well?"

Tain said, "I feel refreshed, so I suppose I did. What time is it?"

"Half past six, sir. Are you wishing to get up?"

"That's the general idea as I'm awake."

"I shall see to your bath, sir. Is there anything else I can do straight away?"

"Reverse time?" suggested Tain.

"Ah, I believe that's a bit beyond my skills, sir, but, if it were not, I would certainly oblige."

"Your first failing, Robert."

"Yes, sir."

"How will you cope?"

"By reminding myself that I cannot do everything, Your Highness, and, although I wish I had a Ullian Spirit, I'll continue to attempt to do the best job I can with the skills I have. Alternatively, I'll search for a timer and ask them to help."

"Timers are rare, your duties I'm sure are time consuming enough."

Robert said, "Any pun intended, Your Highness?"

Tain sighed. "No, that one was purely unintentional. Thank you, Robert."

* * *

Wealsman rose to discover his tunic had been laundered and a small saddlebag of provisions was ready with a shaving set and a note to the effect he should pack the spare tunic he had acquired. He did so before making his way to the King's rooms.

He entered the antechamber and rang the bell. A footman he didn't recognise entered, and he reminded himself that Arkyn's household had changed since his trip to Terasia.

He said simply, "I'm Percival Wealsman. I was asked to breakfast with the King."

"Of course, Your Excellency. Please follow me." Once in the sitting room the footman said, "King Arkyn hasn't yet risen. Can I get you anything for the meantime?"

"No, thank you. Do you know when he will rise?"

"No, sir. I shall ask Master Kadeem to join you."

A few moments later, Kadeem entered with his customary soft tread. "How can I help, Your Excellency?"

"When is the King likely to rise?" asked Wealsman turning from the window and its view of the gardens.

"I was leaving him to rest, sir."

Wealsman nodded. "Then maybe I would simply be better returning to Tera…"

"Without saying goodbye, I would advise against it, sir. The King would be most upset and I would ask you do not make me deliver the news of your departure."

Wealsman sighed. "He's not happy I'm here."

"Actually, sir, he *is*. He relaxed enough to ask for a drink last night."

Wealsman paused. "I'd have thought he'd have been too emotional."

"Obviously something or someone has helped, sir."

"Kadeem, I've blundered in. I should blunder out again."

Kadeem eyed him. "Your presence is expected at breakfast, I believe."

"Apparently so."

Kadeem swallowed. How far would good service go when putting a King's Representative and friend in his place? "Then, whatever else your relationship is, Your Excellency, he is the King."

"So he is. What's the time?"

Kadeem relaxed. "Quarter to nine, sir."

Wealsman considered that. "Then I should stay here; it can't be long before he wakes. I wonder, is there a book I could borrow to keep me out of trouble?"

Kadeem smiled. "Follow me, sir." He led the way to a small library in Arkyn's chambers. "I shall advise Your Excellency when the King wakes. Until then I hope there is diversion here."

"Thank you, Kadeem."

* * *

Arkyn finally awoke and rang for Kadeem.

"What time is it?"

"A quarter and six to ten, Sire."

Arkyn sighed. "You thought I needed to rest?"

"Yes, sir. I thought it was better than getting the doctor involved. Rest is an effective healer."

Arkyn said, "Apparently so. I'd better get up. Can you check what time Tain and Cal are going for a ride please? If it's before lunch, I'll join them. Let Edward know I'm taking the morning off."

"I've informed Edward already, sir, and His Highness said that they'll be leaving at around eleven."

"Is there anything else you've anticipated?" enquired Arkyn.

"Not that springs to mind, sir. Your robe, Sire."

"Stop changing the subject."

Kadeem lips twitched. "My apologies, Sire. Shall I order breakfast?"

"As it's so late is it worth it? It will soon be lunchtime."

"I believe breakfast is an important meal, sir, and Lord Wealsman is waiting for you."

Arkyn grumbled, good-humouredly, "All right, I'll have breakfast; if you don't tell me off, he will."

* * *

The footman who had greeted Wealsman informed him that Arkyn had woken and escorted him to the sitting room. Wealsman simply perused the view contemplating his ride north and the ride south to come. He was so lost in thought he didn't hear Arkyn enter.

The King crossed to him. "Thank you for not simply leaving."

Wealsman turned to him. "I foolishly nearly did."

"Yes. I thought you might. I was the fool yesterday."

"Nonsense, Your… Sire."

"It was the shock. I'm glad you're here. Thank you for what you said about father."

Wealsman looked at him. "It didn't just apply to Adeone… I'm sorry I've not had a chance to meet Prince Tain."

Arkyn noted a spark of latent mischief in his friend's eyes. "Oh, no, I'm not putting you two together. Father was always against it."

"I never could work out why, sir."

"Yes, you could. I'm going for a ride with Tain at eleven; I might let you have a few minutes together," conceded Arkyn.

"Thank you, sir," replied Wealsman laughing. "But I was hoping to have left by then."

Arkyn nodded. "Why are you fretting to leave?"

"The King wishes me to be in Tera."

"I'll have a word and let him know he's being stupid."

"Arkyn, it's where I should be. We both know it," replied Wealsman holding his gaze.

"I wish you could stay for longer."

"My duties *are* in Tera and you need a Representative there on your coronation day. I've done what I wanted to, I've said goodbye to Adeone and I've seen you. Let me leave."

Arkyn swallowed. "All right but you'll breakfast first and I'll help

291

your ride as only I can."

Wealsman looked worried. Adeone's mischievous character ran in both his sons. Tain's was apparently obvious, but Arkyn had crafted his so it hid below the surface – hidden and yet visible to any who knew him well. When it had an airing, quiet humour emanated from him but the dry mischief was normally used to help not hinder, therefore it was with anticipation, if not apprehension, that Percival waited for Arkyn to explain.

A few minutes later Arkyn handed over a True Dallin. "Take a mail-horse and ride via the Rex Dallin. It'll cut hours off. I'll have a sergeant meet you and ride with you through the valley to show you the way. Once you're through the southern gate follow the track until you reach the main road. Turn left and you'll be right for Areal. Then you *must* break your journey at Border Lodge. The lodge keeper will look after you; ask him what the weather's like in Terasia. I'm sure you'll recognise his reply."

Knowing Arkyn so well, that didn't reassure Wealsman. "Sir…"

"No, Percival, I don't want your objections."

Wealsman gave in. "I'll give the Dallin back to the sergeant."

Arkyn shook his head, "No, you won't. Take it with you. One day you might need it. Just don't lose it. Then there's this…" He handed over a tiny gold scroll, no longer than a thumbs length. "I don't think Edward would ever prevent you seeing me but…"

Wealsman took the King's Token that granted entry to see the King no matter what was happening. "Sire, I'm going to be in Terasia."

"You've proved you can be here quickly and without me ever getting warning as well – and, for that matter, without permission."

Wealsman smiled. "I won't be doing it again."

Arkyn searched his face. With a genuine smile, he said, "That's a shame. Take it, Percival, it's the first I've given out and I'm glad it's to you."

"Thank you, Arkyn."

They moved to the triniculum as Kadeem announced breakfast was ready to be served. The table was laden with chaffing dishes containing bacon and potato cakes, and scrambled eggs, then there were platters of toast and pots of butter, and preserves.

"Someone thinks we'll need energy today then," said Arkyn looking at the spread.

Wealsman glanced at an innocent looking Kadeem. "Ruling the empire is hungry work, Sire."

Arkyn snorted. "How's Kristina? You said she's berated you…"

As they exchanged family news, Wealsman was considering his situation far more seriously than his light-hearted talk would suggest. As they finished the meal, he laid down his knife with such careful precision Arkyn groaned.

"Do I want to know, Percival?"

"Whilst I'm here, sir, I'd like you to renew my fealty. Adeone didn't, wouldn't, when he made me an overlord. If I am to take the fealty of the overlords, of any lords in Terasia, I would prefer it for mine to have been renewed by my king."

Arkyn watched Wealsman's calm face. It spoke of an inner certainty and confidence. "You realise the implications as I'm not crowned?"

Wealsman shrugged. "Yes. I also realise that it will still be stronger than that which I swore through Lord Portur at your father's coronation. What's more, I'd like you to make it honour-binding."

About to object, Arkyn paused, seeing determination in his friend's eye. There was only one question in his mind. "Why?"

"Because it should have been taken when I was made an overlord. I appreciated Adeone's gesture, more than he or you would ever believe, but for my own peace of mind, for his memory and your safety, I would like you to take that fealty before I return south."

Arkyn pushed himself up from the table. "Wait here." He left the room, wanting privacy. Entering his bedchamber, he sat on the bed, head in his hands. Percival had been a stalwart support since 1211. The fact he'd ridden north said everything about their relationship. He didn't need to enforce it. A quiet doubt seeped into his mind. Why did Wealsman want this? Why had he really come north? Cursing, he called up Fafnir. He needed advice but a specific sort of advice and only one man would have to keep it secret.

* * *

"My apologies for disturbing your morning, Lord Daioch…" Arkyn outlined Wealsman's request and the reasons the fealty hadn't been taken in Tera in 1211. He appreciated the way Daioch listened without interrupting. The normally talkative lord was grave when Arkyn finished.

"Might I enquire, Sire, just enquire, why you're talking to me about this?"

Arkyn grimaced. "Your life-bind."

"Ah. Yes. Well, sir, if I may be completely honest—"

"You're Tuchlin for a reason, and I asked for advice."

Daioch chuckled. "True, sir, very true. I would say let the King decide this rather than the friend. The divisions can be difficult to navigate for everyone, but you haven't requested it. Lord Wealsman has. You aren't showing distrust, Sire, most certainly you are not. You would be respecting his wishes to accept. Though I understand, more than understand, why you are hesitant."

Arkyn absorbed that. "I'd need witnesses and Lord Landis is injured."

293

"Those witnesses don't have to be lords, sir. Though, I hear Faran is prowling the corridors of the Palace once more. He is far more discreet than his manner lets on."

"I wouldn't say he portrays himself as indiscreet." Arkyn paused. "Ah. What are you trying to tell me, Daioch?"

"If he wasn't so… quietly determined, he'd be Sagamore, but he argued that he was more use not being a governor, and your father let him get away with it." Seeing Arkyn was still wary, Daioch said, "You can trust him, sir. I would stake my life on it."

Arkyn snorted. "You just have. When Faran was proved innocent, father's relief was palpable."

Daioch tilted his head slightly. "Faran was a confidant of your father, far more than I ever was. A step below Landis, maybe, but a confidant."

"Thank you. I guess I don't need to tell you this was exceptionally private, do I?"

Daioch chuckled. "Not at all, sir, not at all. I can feel your wishes."

"I was afraid of that. I'll let you continue."

* * *

Once the link broke, Arkyn continued thinking. Daioch was right. The King should decide this, as he'd decided about ReJean's and Elantha's fealties. He recalled Fafnir and asked Faran to join him. Kadeem would be the other witness.

He rejoined Wealsman and Kadeem, who were now in his sitting room. His manservant caught his eye and would have left if Arkyn hadn't shaken his head. Wealsman had pushed himself to his feet, caution on his features. Arkyn leaving the room had obviously concerned him.

"Against my wishes as a friend, I will take your fealty as your King," said Arkyn, a lump in his throat.

Wealsman relaxed. "Thank you. I'm sorry it's so difficult for you."

Arkyn shrugged. "There have been and will be more difficult fealties and days. We're waiting for Faran to join us as my second witness. I can take fealties privately, but I prefer to follow convention whenever possible."

"I am glad there will be witnesses, sir. I wish I could stay for the formal Fealty Swear."

If Faran hadn't entered at that moment, Arkyn might have found himself asking Wealsman to do that but the complications wouldn't be worth it.

Wealsman knelt and swore to serve Arkyn as his vassal, to never dishonour his own name, the FitzAlcis name or empire and to defend the King and the empire. When he kissed Arkyn's signet ring at the end, he relaxed. As though he'd once more found his place.

Arkyn knew there was more to it than that. The higher the fealty, the more power was in the words, the stronger it bound them together. He'd felt it with all the fealties he'd taken and knew he would feel it again. Strength flowing to him, reassurance flowing from him to his vassals. Even with El he'd felt something.

He turned to Faran. "Thank you, my lord. On your fealty, please keep this between us."

"I am yours to command, my king," said Faran, bowing before leaving.

Arkyn cursed quietly to himself.

Wealsman chuckled. "I can say the same if it helps."

Arkyn struggled against his instinct to curse louder. "I'll cope if you don't, Percival. Let's sit comfortably for a moment. Kadeem, do you have the package that Simkins found?" When he had it in his hands, Arkyn said, "This was with father's things. It's obviously for you."

Wealsman took a package and letter. The latter he put in his belt pouch, before opening the former. He laughed but there was raw emotion in his eyes.

Arkyn glanced over. "Dare I ask?"

"A chess set, sir. His own, I believe."

Arkyn leaned over, checking. "Yes, it was. I'm pleased, Percival."

"I can't take this with me on a horse, sir."

"I'll send it on. He left Kristina a couple of jewels and Daia one. Do you want to know what his official bequest to you was?" asked Arkyn.

"I didn't think… He gave me so much in life."

Arkyn smiled. "It's a small ship that will be built; his line was that he hoped it would avoid you getting a sinking feeling when thinking of him."

"That's Adeone. What on Erinna will I do with a ship?"

"Sail somewhere?" suggested Arkyn.

"When, sir? I'm a little occupied as your Margrave."

"Then maybe use it for trade."

"I'm debarred from trade as an overlord," pointed out Wealsman.

"Not for importing for your own use you're not. Or I'm sure you know a couple of handy merchants who'd rent it from you."

"I'm convinced – your middle name is definitely 'devious'."

Arkyn smiled. "Actually, it's Adeone."

"I always said they meant the same thing."

* * *

Arkyn and Wealsman made their way to Tain's chambers just before eleven and were greeted by Robert, who informed them that Tain had gone to the Courthouse but would be at the stables for eleven.

"Why do I bother trying to help him?"

Robert unsure whether it was a rhetorical question replied, "Because you care about him, sir."

295

Arkyn pursed his lips. "Thank you, Robert."

"My apologies, Sire."

"There is no need to apologise but I would be grateful if you refrain from commenting for the time being."

Wealsman touched his shoulder. "Sire, shall we go to the stables?"

Robert cursed himself for a fool when they'd gone. Had there been no need for an apology because he'd gone too far? Was it the mistake that would cost him a job he was beginning to enjoy? He'd soon find out.

* * *

When they reached the stables, Wealsman said simply, "I should get going, Sire. Will you apologise to His Highness for me?"

"I will but I should be apologising for Tain. Are you sure I can't convince you to stay one more day?" asked Arkyn.

"I am, sir."

Arkyn motioned to a groom holding a mail-horse. "Thank you for coming, Percival. Truly, thank you."

Wealsman knelt. "Your servant, Sire."

Arkyn pulled him to his feet. "I thought servants did what they're told. You're my friend, Percival, which seems to mean the opposite."

Wealsman took the reins and swung into the saddle. "In that case, Sire, might I offer some advice?"

Arkyn sighed. "I've already taken the morning off."

Wealsman's eyes twinkled. "Make it the day. Look after yourself, sir."

Arkyn smiled. "Ride safely."

The Margrave bowed in the saddle and moved off trying to control his memories. 'Ride safely' were the last words he'd said to Adeone when face to face; he hoped they weren't the last words Arkyn and he would exchange in person.

Chapter 69
POIGNANT RIDE
Late Morning
Oedran Palace – Stables

GLANCING AROUND THE STABLES, Arkyn found Ponder saddled and waiting, his reins held by his groom. Walking over, Arkyn took them.

"Thank you, Simon. He looks well."

The young groom inclined his head. "He's been enjoying the freedom of the paddock, Sire."

"He's looking good on it. Aren't you, old boy?" As Simon bowed, and moved back a few paces, Arkyn said quietly to Ponder, "Come on, we're going for a ride, well we are when Tain and Cal appear. Do you fancy a gallop? Or has all the rich grass of the paddock slowed you down?" Ponder nudged him and Arkyn laughed. "Yes, definitely the grass. You'll get fat, you know. What will I do then? Hey, old boy?"

Arkyn became aware the chief groom was bearing down on him. He cursed to himself; couldn't the fool see he didn't want to be disturbed? ReShard bowed, and Arkyn merely raised an eyebrow.

"Sire, I was wondering what you wished done with Pursuit."

Arkyn was considering how to control his temper to best effect when from behind him Tain said, without controlling his,

"The King will inform you in due course! Remember that our horses are part of us! Get back to your other duties."

Arkyn turned. Tain looked like thunder beside him, dark eyes flashing.

Once ReShard had gone the King said, "Thank you, but…"

"No 'but', Arkyn, please. He's a bloody fool."

"Why are you jumping in such a lot?"

Tain swallowed. "I'm your brother, Sire, it's my job to remind people who they're talking to. Sound familiar?"

Arkyn sighed. "Yes. Wealsman's left. I wanted to introduce you."

"I didn't realise he was going so soon. Sorry." He glanced around. "Is Cal not here?"

"Not yet it seems."

Tain called Pesky, his aptly-named, rainbow-coloured dragon messenger, and obtained a link with his friend. "Where are you?"

Cal blushed. "Erm, still in the shop, sir. I'm running a little late."

"We'll come to you then. We'll bring Darky."

"Well, actually, sir, I'm not sure I can—"

Tain looked at him. "Is your father being awkward?"

"Not exactly awkward, sir, but—"

"Have you told him, Cal?"

"No."

"Then we'll have to. Come, please. I think we all need it."

Cal simply nodded.

On hearing the reason his friend wasn't there, Arkyn mounted, catching his groom's eye. "Can you bring Darky along please, Simon?"

"Of course, Sire."

The groom swung into the saddle with a graceful ease and Arkyn smiled to himself, he realised he'd never really noticed his groom in the saddle before but it seemed he was an admirable horseman.

Once through the stable gates Tain said, "Where are we going after collecting Cal?"

"I had thought to go to Wynwood, if that was all right, but we're heading in completely the wrong direction."

"Then how about a ride around Oedran?"

Arkyn nodded. "Sounds fine to me. Being out of the Palace is pleasant; it's oppressive at the moment. How's the Courthouse?"

"Busy. I don't know if I'm enjoying it or not. I think I'm missing the Judge more than I'll admit."

"I think you probably are as well. You know I have every faith in you, don't you?"

Tain hesitated. "Yes, but you know little of the law, Tancred knew it well and it's the faith of a peer I need, I suppose. Uncle Scanlon's never going to give it me, is he?"

Arkyn snorted. "I'd be more worried if he did. Tain, believe me, you'll be fine. Jenkins said that he was impressed, didn't he?"

"Yes, in a roundabout way."

"How are you getting on with him?"

"Fine. We've settled into an understanding."

"What's that? If I dare ask," muttered Arkyn.

"He said he's done everything he can to lose his sarcasm – including taking it for a long walk on a dark night but it had found its way home – so, as long as he's careful with others around, I'd rather have honesty than sycophancy."

"Be careful he doesn't use that as an excuse for being rude."

Tain nodded. "I will be."

* * *

Some minutes later, they dismounted outside the Galdwin's shop and entered companionably. The customer who was there didn't just look uncertain but terrified.

Tain said, "Please excuse us for interrupting. Master Galdwin, is Cal available?"

"He's fetching stock, sir. Why?"

"We're going for a ride and would appreciate his company."

"He'll be a few minutes but I could do with his help today."

"We won't be long, Master Galdwin; you have my word on that," said Arkyn calmly.

Master Galdwin's eyes narrowed, but he saw them without the trappings of office, for once. "Be as long as you need. If you don't mind, I'll carry on?"

Arkyn nodded and, a moment later, the customer left.

Master Galdwin, straight-backed and without hesitation, said, "Sire, my apologies and my condolences. Your father and I may have had our moments of disagreement but I'd come to respect him."

"Thank you, Master Galdwin, it means more than I think you realise," admitted Arkyn. "I'm going to need to talk to you officially soon about a couple of bequests for Cal but it's nothing to worry about. I'd be grateful if you didn't mention it to him."

Intrigued, Master Galdwin nodded. "Right you are, sir. This sounds like Cal. He's certainly damaging enough for it to be. Cal! Be careful!"

Cal entered with two bolts of silk under his arms: one scarlet and one emerald. He put them on the counter before bowing to Arkyn.

"That just holds us up even more, Cal," said Arkyn, mock jestingly.

His friend grinned, "Makes a change it's me, sir, and not Prince Tain."

Tain said, "Can you leave that bad name elsewhere? It was happily asleep."

Arkyn clapped him on the back. "We'll wake it up, it probably needs the exercise." He turned to Master Galdwin. "Are you *sure* you don't mind?"

"Take him away, sir, he's nothing but trouble to me." He hesitated. "Sire, Your Highness, as a family we wanted to do something but we didn't know what…"

"Master Galdwin, Cal's company means more than you can imagine."

"Aye, sir, well that aside, it's your birthdays about now and we hope that you can accept these bolts of silk from us as a gift."

Arkyn and Tain glanced at each other with evident surprise.

Tain said, "But Master Galdwin—"

"No but, Your Highness, a simple yes or no is all I need. It was Cal's idea. He said, quite rightly, we're cloth merchants and good cloth is hard to come by."

Arkyn and Tain glanced at their friend, who shuffled his feet.

"Thank you, Master Galdwin. We will accept with pleasure and thanks."

"Yes. Thank you, Master Galdwin," added Tain.

"Shall we go, Sire?" enquired Cal, uncomfortably.

* * *

Once they were all in the saddle the King said, "Cal?"

Cal swallowed. "His Highness is growing so much he needs new clothes every few months."

"Cal!"

"Sorry. I… I don't know. I mentioned it in passing but father grasped the idea. He'll blame me but if he hadn't wanted to…"

Arkyn nodded. "Will you tell him we really do appreciate it? I'll see the tailor and ask if my coronation wear can be made with it."

"Now *that* I hadn't expected."

"It's a good idea though," added Tain mischievously.

299

Their ride around Oedran was interesting. Tain remembered walking through the city shortly after his mother had died; it had seemed like streets full of people had disappeared at the approach of him and his father. Now a path was cleared and people made their obeisance to Arkyn. Silence went before and followed them. It was eerie and disquieting but within Arkyn there was a nugget of appreciation.

A street flower seller cautiously approached them and held out three small posies. Arkyn, Tain and Cal took them with a word of thanks and noticed that the seller simply walked away. Arkyn looked at the posy in his hand and considered it was all the lady had had to give to show her feelings. He swallowed and picked up the pace very slightly. Tain and Cal glanced at each other and flanked him without a word.

Tain said quietly, "Palace?"

Arkyn caught his eye, glad of the understanding. "I think so. Cal?"

"It's fine by me, sir," replied Cal. "Will lunch be an option?"

"He's hungry, isn't he?" said Arkyn amused

"He's not the only one," admitted Tain blithely.

They were entering the Administrative Quarter when a scuffle in his peripheral vision caught Cal's attention. He turned, hand automatically reaching for a dagger, but his belt was bare. He took in the scene: a man being restrained, a knife hitting the pavement. He caught the eye of the man being detained there was a look of reckoning in it that sent a shiver down his spine.

He looked for Hillbeck, the sergeant flicked his hand and the guards closed in. Arkyn and Tain didn't appear to notice.

Cal dropped back and murmured, "What was that about, Hillbeck?"

Hillbeck shrugged. "Probably an everyday chancer who happened to get noticed because of people getting held back to allow us through. It happens. I doubt it was anything else."

Cal's frowned, but he didn't question the sergeant further. It wasn't his place to, but he doubted anything that close to Arkyn happened by chance.

* * *

To save a flight of stairs, they went to Tain's chambers. Tain rang for his manservant. "Lunch is in order, please, Robert, and could you find some water for these flowers and send the King's to his chambers?"

Arkyn said, "Actually, Robert, mine can go to my office please."

"Very good, Sire. What about yours, Master Calumiel?"

"I'll be taking them home with me, Robert. Thank you."

When he'd gone, Tain crooked an eyebrow at his brother. "Your office?"

Arkyn shrugged. "To remind me. It was an interesting ride."

"Yes, it was. Did the same happen when you were riding to my house?" asked Cal. His friends were being far more pragmatic than he expected.

Tain paused. "I can't recall, it was quiet but I don't think people were kneeling. We were a bit busy wrangling."

"Well, sir, you don't want to get out of practice I suppose."

"Arkyn, that was cheeky, aren't you going to stop it?"

"What makes you think I'd succeed?" asked Arkyn blithely.

"A certain tag on your name."

"Oh, *that*. It doesn't count for anything in your private chambers, which means, little brother, he's *your* problem."

Cal simply sat there smirking.

"I've never had any influence on him," muttered Tain.

Arkyn replied, "I am very grateful for that – most of the time he's bad enough without your influence."

Cal said flummoxed, "How did you manage to turn that on me, sir?"

"With practice," pointed out Tain.

After a couple of moments, Arkyn said, "What was that at the King's Gate, Cal?"

"Hillbeck reckons the man was just a chancer carrying a dagger who got caught because you were passing, sir."

Arkyn considered. "What do you think?"

Cal hesitated. "I hope it was that simple."

"You don't think it was, do you?" asked Tain rhetorically. "Why?"

"Does instinct count as a valid reply?" asked Cal. "I don't know. I might be seeing shadows everywhere. I just happen to think the safest place in the empire isn't near you two."

Arkyn snorted. "Well, that's definitely not something I'd hear at Court."

Cal blushed. "Sorry, sir. What I meant—"

"We know what you meant," said Tain without emphasis, "and you're right. Arkyn can't deny that. What do you think we should do?"

"Discreet enquiries as to what happened would probably be an idea." He couldn't tell them what he'd felt, what he'd seen in the man's eyes. That would make them warier than they needed to be.

Arkyn called up Fafnir and asked Edward to check with the Chief Yeoman. Word came back half an hour later that there had been nothing suspicious in the man's story, so they'd confiscated the dagger and let him go on his way with a warning. Cal's blood ran cold.

Chapter 70

A JOURNEY OF DISCOVERY
Late Morning
Anapara – Road between Oedran and the Rex Dallin

WEALSMAN RODE SWIFTLY through Oedran with a guide, who would show him the way to the Rex Dallin. As Wealsman was wont to do he got talking to the guide who explained the city they were riding through. Once over the Dallin Bridge and onto the Rex Dallin road, they spotted the signs of a camp being laid out and Wealsman reined in, looking at it.

The guide said, "I believe this will be the coronation camp, sir."

"It certainly looks like it." He turned in the saddle and looked back at the walls of Oedran. "Right, on, I think."

"This is Dellwood, Your Excellency."

Again, Wealsman reigned in. "Dellwood? Where's the inn?"

Less than a minute later, they dismounted swiftly and Wealsman entered the inn by the closest door. It led directly into a utilitarian kitchen and he was faced with a man frying bacon.

He smiled. "I never thought that was one of your skills, Fitz."

The former captain turned around, frying pan in hand. "I'm dreaming. It can't be you, Lord Wealsman, because you're in Tera, I know it."

"Sorry, Fitz, it is me. How are you?"

"Hungry. Bacon cob, Your Excellency?" asked Fitz with a pause.

"Sounds good. I can't be long. I'm on my way back to Terasia."

"Back? I thought you were just arriving."

"No, that was yesterday afternoon. Thank you."

Fitz said, musingly, "How come I didn't spot you at the funeral? I'm getting slack."

"I didn't want to be spotted, Fitz."

The former captain sat down. "Did King Arkyn know…"

"Yes. I didn't spot you either." Wealsman joined him, his back against the table, legs stretched out to give him some relief. Riding was painful.

"I kept back. Kept an eye on those slovenly guards."

"They're not that bad."

"They are. Think this would ever have happened if I were still in charge? Not likely," muttered Fitz. "I'll tell you something else, my lord, I'm not going to sit here and wait for something else to happen."

"You've retired, Fitz, and Hillbeck is fully capable."

"Aye, well…"

"Did you hear about Kilbride?" asked Wealsman.

"Not enough was done. If King Altarius had been in that position…"

"Are you doubting Arkyn, Fitz?"

Fitz frowned, shocked. "No, I'm not. That lad's got more about him than we know."

"You'll never convince me otherwise. My point was that when Kilbride was dismissed Arkyn renewed all the oaths. Do you know what Sergeant Hillbeck did?"

"No," admitted Fitz.

Wealsman explained.

"Did he now? That's interesting. That is strength of a different kind. I can't match that one. Maybe I'm better here after all."

Wealsman smiled. "You make a good bacon cob. I'll take it with me as I should be on my way. Raise a glass to Adeone for me."

Fitz said, "Hold it right there and we'll raise one now."

* * *

A mile down the road, the guide said, "This is as far as I can go, Your Excellency. Those are the Pillars of Alcis, marking the boundary of the Rex Dallin. Good luck on your ride south."

"Thanks, lad. Here, have a drink on me and maybe raise the glass for the memory of King Adeone and the health of King Arkyn." He passed a darl over.

"Aye, sir, I'll do that and I'll raise one for your good fortune."

* * *

Wealsman rode across the ford swirling around the Pillars of Alcis and found a smile on his lips. He took in the sight of the valley ahead. Pastures and meadows stretched away in front of him, marred only by the presence of a seemingly underdressed sergeant.

"Lord Wealsman? Can I see your Dallin, please?"

Wealsman passed it over.

"Thank you, Your Excellency. It's this way."

Percival hesitated. "How far is it to Ceardlann?"

"A mile, sir, but the King never mentioned anything about—"

Wealsman weighed the Dallin in his hand. "No, because I never did. This token grants me entry to anywhere in the valley, yes?"

"Yes, sir."

"Then I wish to detour by Ceardlann. It won't take long, I promise."

Percival studied the approaching house as soon as he saw it. The double-fronted, half-timbered façade with a tower to the left looked welcoming and homely. Adeone had considered it home, considered it was where his soul was. Wealsman could almost feel him here, far more than he had in

Oedran. He swung out of the saddle and hesitated.

The sergeant said, "Walk straight in, sir."

Wealsman did so. The wooden panelling was a contrast to the Palace and there was an atmosphere here of peace. He looked around, turning on the spot, his mind constantly taking in details. At one revolution it took in a footman watching him with amusement. He stopped turning. Dizzily he stumbled. The footman caught him.

"Might I ask who you are, sir? We weren't expecting anyone."

Wealsman steadied himself. "I'm… Where's the Comptroller?"

"In his office."

"Could you show me the way? I'm Percival Wealsman."

The footman smiled. "I'm Joe, sir. This way. Welcome to Ceardlann. Will you be staying for long?"

"No, about half an hour. Why?"

"I would have prepared a room, sir."

"Without instruction from the King?"

Joe smiled. "There are some names that open doors, Your Excellency, and yours I have heard many times. Anyway, that aside, you hold a Dallin. Those are issued by the King so you are welcome here whenever you wish to stay."

Wealsman said, "It's a bit far from Terasia, but thank you."

Joe knocked on and stuck his head around a door. "Comptroller, Lord Wealsman wonders if you have a moment."

"Of course I do, Joe. Come in, my lord. Would you like a drink?"

Wealsman entered and looked around the cluttered office. "Water, if possible, please, Comptroller. I'm pleased to meet you."

The Comptroller, an ageing man with mild manners said, "I you, my lord. What brings you here?"

Wealsman settled back in a chair. "I'm on my way home. The King kindly let me come through the Rex Dallin. I thought I could do something in return."

"What is that, sir?" enquired the Comptroller.

"See how you are. I understand you didn't attend the funeral."

"No. My place is here. I have no wish for the ceremonies of Oedran. I sat and remembered under the stars. I will see and speak to King Arkyn when he is ready."

Wealsman said, "I think he wants to be here."

"This is his home, my lord, of course he does. Oh, he might reside in and rule Oedran but this is home. It was for his father and more so for King Arkyn; he and Prince Tain were born here," replied the Comptroller.

"So I understand. We've strayed from the point of how you are."

"I'm an elderly man; grief has been my companion many times."

"I'm a youngish one and it's not unfamiliar to me but it still hurts, still cuts deep. This was no normal death, Comptroller, and I know you were close to Adeone."

"Aye, my lord, as were you. Maybe your understanding, your visit is all that needs to be said."

Wealsman took a sip of water. "Maybe. Would you… Could you show me around Ceardlann? I've heard much of this house but never thought to see it."

The Comptroller got to his feet. "Why did you *really* come, sir?"

Percival rose, wincing. "To see how you are. Adeone would have wanted me to and so, I believe, did Arkyn. He gave me that Dallin for a reason."

The Comptroller said, "It acts as a shortcut on your journey."

"Yes, but that wasn't the only reason. I know Arkyn well, as you do, Comptroller. He cares deeply but has little time at the moment."

The Comptroller led the way from his office. "How is he? I keep worrying about him and Tain."

* * *

The ride through the Rex Dallin brought one more surprise. The guide led him through the King's Meadow, over the trout stream and circled Encampment Field before joining a lane that would take them south. Wealsman glanced into Encampment Field.

"Is that the Wanda?"

"Yes, sir. Laioril's tribe camps here every year." He took a good look. "Hang on, I don't recognise half of those people. We should stop."

"Of course. I met Laioril briefly last night."

Laioril glanced between Wealsman and the sergeant, grinning. "Yes, there's more than my tribe here, lads. Chief Darshan and I had business. Don't worry, we'll all be gone soon and I'll make sure no-one gets left behind."

The sergeant said, "Look, Chief, your permission——"

"Is a mystery to all, I know. I'll swear that it covers this eventuality."

"Oh, aye? On what, you old rogue?"

"On my life, because that's the price I'll pay if I'm wrong. Sergeant, there's good reasons why Chief Darshan is here, and it will become clear presently. Now, you just show the lad to the gate."

"Chief, will you swear on Adeone's memory that you're not lying?" asked Wealsman, his gaze never leaving the old man's face.

"Aye, on Adeone's memory and dreams."

Their eyes met with shared grief for several long moments.

Wealsman said, "Sergeant, that's good enough for me. I think it would be good enough for the King. Shall we resume our journey?”

The sergeant eyed Laioril distrustingly. “Of course, Your Excellency.”

When they were a way from the camp, the sergeant said, “That was all very well, sir, but I don’t trust Laioril: kings might, I don’t.”

“I would in this. Do you know the reputation of Chief Darshan?”

“No. Should I?” asked the sergeant.

“Probably not. He is said to be the Wanda King.”

“But… What does that make Laioril?”

“Even more trouble. Let them be, Sergeant, I would expect they’ll have left in just under a week.”

<h1 style="text-align:center">Chapter 71</h1>
<h2 style="text-align:center">LUNCH</h2>

Early Afternoon
Tain’s Sitting Room

ARKYN, TAIN AND CAL were halfway through lunch when Robert announced Lord Faran and Samara. Arkyn smiled as they entered.

“My apologies, Sire,” said Faran. “Had I known you were lunching, I’d not have disturbed you.”

“Join us, Faran. I’m sure Prince Tain won’t mind,” replied Arkyn.

Tain shrugged. “Not at all. Robert, a place for His Lordship and maybe Samara could have her own.”

“Nonsense. Samara, come and sit on my knee,” said Arkyn.

Faran walked with his daughter over to Arkyn and lifted her up on to his knee saying, “Don’t wriggle.”

Samara laughed.

“Were you addressing me or your daughter, Lord Faran?”

Faran taking his place said, “My daughter, Sire, my conscience is just convincing me of that fact.”

Tain said, “So I should hope, my lord. Might I introduce Calumiel Galdwin to you? He keeps us in line.”

Cal laughed. “Your Highness, nothing could be further from the truth.”

“You’re right, since you came into our lives no-one’s managed to keep us in line.”

Arkyn said mildly, “Samara, shall I tell them to behave?” (Samara looked up at him.) “Children, behave.”

Faran chuckled. “Master Calumiel, whatever your role, I’m pleased to meet you.”

306

"I you, my lord," replied Cal. "I hear your journey was interesting."

"I would advise that, if at all possible, Master Calumiel, you don't traverse three provinces in two days. A more leisurely pace is preferable. If you won't take my word for it, I advise you talk with Lord Wealsman."

Arkyn said, "I shall try to make amends for such a journey when I find the right means, my lord. Until then, I get the feeling I've been sabotaged from returning to my desk and I thought, with Percival gone, I was safe."

"Samara wished to see you, sir," replied Faran innocently.

Arkyn nodded. "I'm sure I believe you, Faran. So, Samara, what shall we do for an hour?"

Tain and Faran sat talking whilst Arkyn and Cal entertained Samara. Watching his brother relax, Tain caught Faran's eye.

"Thank you."

Faran said, "I can't imagine what Your Highness means."

Tain eyed him. "Imagination and knowledge are two different things, my lord. How are your rooms?"

Faran accepted the change of subject gratefully. "They are fine, Your Highness. I stayed in them for years when studying here, and several times since. They even feel a bit like home."

Tain nodded. "Always a nice feeling. Father made these my chambers and I've felt comfortable here since the first day. I love the views…"

Faran crossed to the dual aspect windows; he sat in the window seat, examining the view. "I can see why, Your Highness."

Tain joined him. One window looked towards the Palace grounds the other out and over the walls to the Administrative Quarter of the city. The uneven skyline added interest and beauty to the view.

Arkyn glanced over and saw Tain and Faran were comfortable with each other. He was glad. Faran was undemanding company; he didn't hunt for conversation or push for anything. Arkyn suddenly understood how important that was. All the men he was close to were the same, they took a step back and as far as possible treated him as a person with feelings. He was brought out of his reverie by Samara tugging on his tunic.

Lord Faran stole a glance at them and smiled, but he wished Adeone had been able to see how easy Arkyn was with Samara. How long would it be before Arkyn married and had a family? There'd be pressure on him to do it soon now he was King.

After three-quarters of an hour Samara was showing signs of tiredness. Arkyn picked her up.

"I think you need a nap. Let's find your bed."

Faran got to his feet. "I'll take her, sir."

Arkyn shook his head. "It's on the way, or near as makes no odds. I have to face my desk sooner or later today."

Once they'd gone Cal said, "I should also get going, sir, father will be wondering where I am."

"No, he won't. He knows where you are. He might not like you being here but he knows where you are."

Cal eyed him. "Your Highness, who taught you pedantry?"

Tain's eyes hunted out the corners of the room. "Father and Uncle Festus with a touch of the Judge to help the lesson. Stay for a bit. I've got to go back to the Courthouse but not quite yet and—"

"All right, I'll stay. What do you want to do?"

Tain pulled him to his feet. "If you weren't better than me, I'd suggest some swordplay, but, as you are, let's get out in to the fresh air, I'm stuck inside a lot at the moment."

Chapter 72
GUARDIAN AND WARD
Afternoon
Inner Office

WHEN ARKYN REACHED the Inner Office, he contacted Mellonia Camlyn. Given the circumstances, he should have done so before but time had always run out. He'd never spoken to her or her father before and so, rather self-consciously, he asked Fafnir to form the link.

Mellonia looked pale, but she greeted Arkyn with a small smile.

The King said, "How are you?"

"Erm, I'm... How are you, Sire?"

Arkyn accepted that. "Quite. I was sorry to hear about your father. Is the captain making a nuisance of himself?"

Mellonia said, "I don't know. I'm not at home, sir. I was sorry to hear about King Adeone."

Arkyn nodded. "Thank you. Did you ever speak to him?"

"No, sir."

"No, I never spoke to your father either. Circumstances have thrown us together, my lady, like leaves in a storm."

"It has been stormy," she admitted without thinking.

"In what way, Lady Mellonia?"

"It doesn't matter, sir."

He said, gently, "Yes, it does. Where are you, if you're not at home?"

She hesitated. "I'm at Meaden Hall; my nearparents house. They insisted I came here but only because they couldn't move into home... They wanted to."

Arkyn considered that. "How old are you, my lady?"

"I'm fifteen, sir, and please, call me Mellonia. If you're my guardian, it's daft to be formal."

Arkyn smiled. "If you'll call me Arkyn."

She swallowed. "I hadn't considered that, sir."

"Will you? Just in links like this, if it's easier to reconcile."

She looked at him and then nodded. "Yes, all right. Thank you... Arkyn."

"Not at all, Mellonia. Now, if we're going to be informal, tell me exactly what's been happening?"

So Mellonia did.

At the end of the explanation, Arkyn said, "Right. That's going to stop. Do you want to be at home?"

"Yes. I do. It's my home. I've only good memories there. Hume, the steward – my steward, I should say – has been there for years and he's a good steward, he's always been good to me. I'd be looked after..."

Arkyn smiled. "By the sounds of things, I've a gentleman very similar looking after Ceardlann. When is your father's funeral?"

"Tomorrow, Sire."

"Then you'll return home from tomorrow."

"Thank you, so much. Won't my nearparents object?" she asked.

Arkyn said, "I'll let them, then I'll point out that it's the same as other situations in the empire. Lady Daia Sansky has been living at home, on her own with her staff, since her father died. She has a Terasian guardian, for want of a better expression, but she manages her lands herself and lives where she wishes to. Your situations are very similar. I'll ask her to contact you. She knows me relatively well so she can tell you how to deal with me..."

Mellonia smiled. "Thank you."

"It might help to know you're not alone. As for your nearparents' schemes, I'll keep an eye on them. Your lands are yours, my lady. No-one else's. I'll be sending someone to make sure that they're not being mishandled by your steward, but that is a precaution only and due to the fact it was discovered that Lady Daia's steward was doing so with hers. It's nothing for you, or him, to worry about," finished Arkyn.

"So, what exactly are my nearparents my local guardians for?"

Arkyn smiled. "Standard practice for wards in the empire. It means you've someone close on hand to look out for you but it doesn't always work. From what you've said, I think you and I are better talking directly, don't you?"

She nodded. "Yes, sir… Arkyn. Probably. Won't you be busy though?"

"As you said, probably but I'm responsible for your happiness and care, Mellonia, so, if you need me, I'll be there for you. It's really that simple."

"I can't see that I'll be that important though."

"I can't see that I am either, but, if enough people try to convince me, I might believe it. Mellonia, don't worry about me, I've plenty of people organising my life."

She considered him, her round face framed by ringlets of her brown hair. "If you're going to worry about me, Arkyn, it's only fair I return the compliment, isn't it? I mean, I don't want to lose you as my guardian."

"Don't you?" he asked with a crooked eyebrow.

"Not considering the options, no."

He laughed. "I think that was a compliment."

"Maybe I should rephrase that?"

"I wouldn't. The spontaneity was just right. I should speak to your nearfather. Wish me luck."

She smiled and he realised that, even in their brief discussion, she'd regained some colour and her eyes were brighter.

"Of course. Good luck, Arkyn."

* * *

When faced with his office again, Arkyn pondered for a moment on how to approach the issue with Lord Dennison. He decided to see what happened. Fafnir opened the link and Arkyn found he was looking at a long face, brown eyes, straight nose and a handlebar moustache.

"Sire, my condolences on the loss of your father."

"Thank you. I've spoken to Lady Mellonia—"

"As her guardian here, sir, I would be grateful if you'd let me know before you speak with her."

Arkyn stilled. Was Dennison truly trying to establish dominance already? He was more foolish than expected. "I'm sure you would, my lord, but such a consideration works the other way as I'm her guardian. You should not have removed her from her home without my express permission or that of my office. She will return there from tomorrow and she will reside there until she wishes otherwise."

"Sire, she is young. I don't know what she's said to you, but it surely isn't right that—"

"Dennison, she is of cisan-age and is sensible. She wishes to be at home; therefore, that is where she will be. There are plenty of other wards in the same situation."

"Sir, I have watched her grow up and I think—"

"Are you doubting my judgement, Dennison?"

The lord never even turned a hair. "Not at all, Sire, I'm just—"

"It sounded remarkably like you were. You may have seen Her Ladyship growing, but I have had some years of assessing people very quickly."

"Sir, she may not be in a rational frame of mind at the moment."

Arkyn's tone turned cold. "I think I know how grief affects people, my lord. How far is your home from Lady Mellonia's?"

"Not more than a couple of hours ride, sir."

"Oh, for heaven's sake, what *are* you worried about? It's not like it's the other side of Bayan, is it? Stop your manipulative games, my lord. Lady Mellonia is going home and you're staying in Meaden Hall. If you think changes in her circumstances are needed, you do not force them on her, you talk to me. Is that understood?"

Dennison looked at the King's implacable face. "Yes, Sire. I shall discuss it with yourself or your Protector," privately thinking that King he might be but he obviously knew nothing about life.

Arkyn's frown deepened. "My Protector... I am sure Lady Amara would be enthralled to hear your reasoning. When I said stop your games, Dennison, I meant it! You'll get your dues as Lady Mellonia's nearparents, but not if I think you are using her to further your own ends, I hope that's clear as well. And make no mistake, I will take action if you defy me."

Dennison's mask slipped as his eyes narrowed. "What would you like doing about Camlyn's requests and bequests, Sire?"

Arkyn considered. "Pass the document to Mellonia. She is her father's heiress. I'll let her know that you're doing so. Now, my lord, should you need to contact me, please don't hesitate to do so."

"Thank you, Sire," replied Dennison thinking that was the last thing he was going to do, but it vied for position with contacting Lady Amara.

* * *

Arkyn broke the link and straightaway asked for one with Mellonia. She smiled as the link formed.

"Sir?"

Arkyn looked at her levelly.

"Arkyn?"

"I've just spoken with your nearfather. He'll be passing your father's requests and bequests to you to keep. Do you want me to ask the Exarch to give you a hand with them?"

She shook her head. "No, sir. If my nearfather knows I've read them then he'll have to abide by them, won't he?"

"Yes."

"And to think I was worried that my guardian would be the King."

"You still can be, I won't be offended."

She grinned. "I don't think I could be now if I tried. I can see why father did what he did in 1169."

Arkyn frowned, perplexed. "What did he do in 1169?"

"Don't you know?"

"Haven't got a clue. Are you going to be coy about it?"

She tilted her head and Arkyn saw a spark of mischief in her eyes and he was glad for it. Glad he'd got her smiling.

She explained in very few words and Arkyn looked at her surprised, "He told you that?"

She shook her head. "Hume did, just after father died. He was trying to explain why father made my guardianship over to the FitzAlcis."

"It's certainly interesting, but your father made your guardianship over to us for other reasons," admitted Arkyn. "There was a bit of trouble brewing for him and it secured your future whatever the outcome."

"Oh. What was the trouble?"

"I have no idea, Mellonia," said Arkyn, for once lying. She didn't need the knowledge that Lord Scanlon had been trying to wrest her lands from her. It was bad enough that her nearfather was trying to do the same.

"Does anyone else know?"

"I doubt it now. Shall we live with the fact I'm responsible for you?"

She nodded. "I suppose so. Thank you for telling me."

"That's all right. Now, I'd better go and depress a few officials."

She laughed as the link broke. Arkyn sat for a time contemplating what she'd revealed. If her father had done that for the FitzAlcis, he'd make doubly sure Mellonia was protected. He contacted her steward, told him what had been arranged and noted the relief in the man's eyes. He was glad his lady was to be home. It reassured Arkyn, but he wouldn't tell Hume everything yet. Dennison had been flexing his muscles when faced with a younger man in authority. Hopefully that contretemps would be their last.

Arkyn rang for Edward and when his administrator entered the Inner Office said, "Ask Prince Tain to join me and add Lady Mellonia on to the list of people I need to write to on a regular basis. I doubt I'll forget but, if she's on the list, you'll give me time to do it."

Chapter 73

UNCERTAINTY

WHEN EDWARD INFORMED Tain that Arkyn was asking to see him, Cal went home and Tain made his way back into the Privy Wing and up to the Inner Office instead of going to the Courthouse. He nodded to Edward and went to enter the Inner Office.

"Sir, please let me announce you."

"I've taken lessons off Lord Landis, Edward."

The administrator inwardly cursed. "Of course, sir."

Tain winked and entered the Inner Office without another word.

Arkyn looked over. "Did I miss the knock or wasn't there one?"

"I can't remember," admitted Tain. "I was too busy telling Edward not to announce me. What can I do for you?"

Arkyn explained his meeting with Dennison, concluding with, "He's a fool, but Mellonia will be safe enough at home. It got me thinking about father bequests. We've not discussed them, especially the ones for Cal."

Tain eased himself leisurely into a chair. "Ah. I thought his were apt. What's troubling you? It can't be the entry to the Rex Dallin—"

"Actually, it's the sword. Master Galdwin's not going to be happy when he finds out Cal can wield one, let alone that father left him that one."

Tain shrugged. "Maybe not, but there's nothing he can do about it. There's not much more anyone can teach Cal about wielding a sword. He disarmed Uncle Festus."

"True. I just think the friction would aggravate the situation again."

"I don't think Master Galdwin needs a reason to, Sire. He's admitted he respected father but he still doesn't like Cal's involvement with us. Tell Cal about it. I'm sure he'll appreciate it."

Arkyn nodded. "What of the third bequest?"

Tain bit his lip, knowing why Arkyn wasn't being explicit. No matter how trusted people were, there were some things better kept private and mentioning it out loud tempted fate, tempted someone to walk through the door without knocking – though of the two people most likely to do that one was incapacitated and one was Tain who said,

"I would wait for that one, at least for a couple of years. He'll have to know soon but maybe when everything else has died down."

"I'll have to tell Master Galdwin about it, it's not insubstantial and as Cal's not of alunan-age yet his father has to be told. I can't see him being happy, can you?"

Tain shook his head. "No, but I think, if you explain carefully, it won't be too bad. Can I also suggest that you wait until after your coronation? You don't need the stress of dealing with Master Galdwin as well as that."

"I suppose that makes sense. There's something else, Tain, something that I've not mentioned because I didn't want to worry you but I've had Simkins and Kadeem hunt high and low and they've not found it…"

Tain frowned. "What?"

"Mother's ring. The Queen's Ring, which grants entry to the Rex Dallin, is gone. I'm sure father was wearing it."

Tain frowned. "He certainly used to. Is it at Ceardlann? Mother kept some jewellery there and father would have considered it safe."

"I'll have to check."

"Have you spoken to the Comptroller yet?"

Arkyn shook his head. "I don't know what to say. I sent an invitation for the funeral but he politely declined. He doesn't like to leave the valley. In fact, I'm not sure he ever has."

"Have you told him about father's requests and bequests?"

"No, again I don't know what to say."

Tain looked at Arkyn. "The truth won't hurt. Father asked we scatter his ashes in the King's Meadow so he wouldn't be imprisoned in death as he had been in life. I think you'll find the Comptroller will understand."

Arkyn swallowed. "Imprisoned in life. I never thought father saw it like that until I read it in his writing, but I can understand what he meant, there's so much expectation and so many things that have to be done that one can't be oneself."

Tain bit his lip, before saying, "Are you feeling trapped?"

"Yes. Are you as Justiciar?"

Tain simply nodded, biting his lip.

"Is there any way I can help?"

Tain gaze shot to him, surprised. "That would give you even more to do and no there isn't really. Is there anything I can help with for you?"

"You've got enough on."

"Yes, but I'm sure Oedranian justice can manage without me for one day. As long as I sign off tomorrow's trials it'll be fine – even if I'm only here as support."

Arkyn swallowed. "I've got a meeting I can't see the point of with the astrologer in about quarter of an hour."

Tain looked puzzled. "What on Erinna for?"

"Apparently, it's traditional. Do you want to stay for it?"

Tain said, "If you think I can help, then yes."

"No, I think with you here I'll curb my frustration better."

"I thought *I* frustrated you."

Arkyn grinned at him. "Mostly you do but when the choice is between you and astrologers, I think the astrologers might win."

Chapter 74
ASTROLOGER
14:54
Inner Office

ARKYN WAS RIGHT, he became frustrated. The meeting included Advisor Rayburn, the Moonshi and the astrologer as well as himself and Tain. His own mind constantly wandered to everything else that needed to be done, the small details and the large, and the parchment at his hand was scrawled with more notes about that than about the meeting he was in. The stars were telling him they had gained a soul when Erinna had lost one. He didn't need the astrologer to tell him how it affected the world.

Tain watching Arkyn was worried. He'd seen his brother in many emotions over the previous few days, but read the frustration. Arkyn would soon snap and it wasn't going to be pleasant.

Advisor Rayburn sensed the tension though he couldn't explain why it was prominent. Why was Prince Tain present? It wasn't a matter that required the Justiciar. Glancing up from his notes he caught the Prince's eye and followed its flick. Sicla. Had he time to stop the King's explosion?

The Moonshi had had virtually no contact with the King or Prince, even through the previous bereavements they'd suffered. King Adeone had always kept such family matters private and so he didn't read into the situation the warning signals Tain and Rayburn had sensed.

The astrologer, used to a lone existence, was happily oblivious to it all. He was saying, "Aluna was red this Munewid, Sire. She flamed with the injustice of the event but there is more to it than that. It is said that a red moon heralds a new Pennod, or era, or age of the world. There have been six Pennods so far that we recognise and if we are entering a new one it is indeed significant. There are accounts, trustworthy accounts that say a red moon was seen the night of the battle where Ull appeared, then—"

Arkyn rose. "Is there anything in this recitation that pertains to the murder of my father or matters more pressing this week?"

The astrologer looked up at Arkyn's face and pushed himself nervously to his feet. "It is traditional that we apprise our King of our current thoughts before the coronation."

"Would you like me to apprise you of mine?"

Before the astrologer could answer, Tain murmured, "Sire…"

Arkyn glanced at him then strode from the Inner Office.

Tain looked at the meeting's attendees. "Please wait here."

Worried, the astrologer said, "I didn't mean to cause our King any distress, Your Highness."

Tain hesitated. "I think the distress was truly the work of others, this has simply been a catalyst of reaction. Excuse me a moment. Advisor, might I suggest everyone has a drink?"

* * *

Tain found his brother hiding in the King's sitting room with his head in his hands. "What was that about?"

"Leave me alone, Tain."

"No. You wanted me here for a reason so, King or not, I'm not going anywhere. What was that about?"

Arkyn glared at him. "Were you listening to the same drivel I was?"

Tain rolled his eyes. "Yes. The astrologer can't read a man as well as he can the stars…"

"Father's dead, gone, cold. No damned words are going to ease that or bring him back! Nothing in the movement of the heavens can help."

Stung, Tain said, "Do you think I don't know that, Arkyn? Do you?"

Arkyn glanced at him and then away. "No, of course I don't. I'm sorry."

"Maybe someone else needs to hear that apology. You might not like it, Arkyn, but you're Guardian of the Heavens as well as King. You have to have meetings with them and unfortunately this isn't going to be the only one that is boring, frustrating or seeming nonsense but occasionally they may be useful. I think there's a lot of good that could come from listening to the astrologer. So what if you don't believe it, don't want to recognise it, but he thinks we're starting a new age of the world. Use that fact, use it for all it's worth, use it as the good. Make people believe that by supporting us they are supporting a better world, a fairer world, a more just one, a glorious pageant of an empire. It's worth a try, isn't it? Isn't it worth listening to the madness to reach the sanity beyond?"

"Have you been talking to Kadeem?"

"No, unfortunately I can blame no-one for that phrasing but myself. Arkyn, come on, you're King. We all hate aspects of our jobs. I hate the thought of sending men and women to prison or execution but I'll have to do it. One hour of drivel might pay off for years of contentment. Please come back to the meeting, or claim fatigue. I'm sure they'll believe it…"

"You're trying to tell me I look terrible, aren't you?"

Tain said, "No need, I'll find a mirror instead. Have you got a headache?"

"Yes. It's a fifteen-year-old brother with delusions of knowledge."

"That can't be me, I'm not deluded. Seriously, Arkyn, are you unwell?"

Arkyn sighed. "Yes, I've a headache. How did you guess?"

"Because it's the only time you get snappy." Tain rang the bell and, when his brother's manservant entered, said, "Kadeem, when we're in the Inner Office give it a couple of minutes and then bring a headache remedy for the King."

Kadeem glanced at Arkyn who simply nodded saying, "Prince Tain has some grand plan; I think, as always, it's safer not to enquire."

"If you weren't King, I'd say you were a coward," muttered Tain.

"There are some compensations then." Arkyn pushed himself to his feet once Kadeem had left. "Do I have to go back?"

"Of course you don't, *Sire*, but it might be prudent to."

Arkyn sighed. "Right. Promise to intervene before I get that bad again?"

"Only if you'll catch my eye."

"Attached to the rest of you or not? Don't answer that. Come on, let's face the astrologer."

Tain hesitated, then as Arkyn went to pass him, touched his shoulder. Catching his brother's eye, he pulled him into a hug. They hadn't acknowledged the others' pain for too long, both mired by everything else. His brother returned the hug with a strength that gave away how much he needed it.

Tain blinked as they broke apart. He held open the door. "After you."

Arkyn said softly, "Tain… Thank you."

"Thank me *after* the meeting."

* * *

In the Inner Office, Rayburn had poured the Moonshi and astrologer a drink and then seated himself.

In his deep mellow voice, the Moonshi asked, "Should we perhaps rearrange the meeting for another time?"

Rayburn glanced at him. "That has not been requested. If it is King Arkyn's wish we will be informed."

"You have worked for him before?"

"Yes, for a few months. He is not prone to these outbursts, but the events of the last few days have been harrowing for the FitzAlcis brothers. They would be harrowing for any family but it must be doubly hard when the focus of the empire is aimed at you. Can we say that we would cope any better? Yes, we knew King Adeone but we had not that deep-seated attachment to him, and the FitzAlcis brothers were close to their father."

"King Adeone will be sorely missed," said the astrologer.

Rayburn nodded. "Yes, but King Arkyn will be a great ruler for us; I have no doubt. Moonshi, we'll need to discuss the preparations for the coronation now the funeral is past."

The Moonshi said, "Of course, Advisor…"

* * *

Not long afterwards, Arkyn and Tain re-entered the office. Tain seated his brother and passed him a drink. Only when Tain was also seated did Arkyn request everyone else resume their places.

Speaking gravely and as though he meant every word Arkyn said, "My apologies for that interlude, gentlemen, especially to you, astrologer. You were explaining about Pennods, I believe."

The astrologer swallowed. "Yes, Sire, thank you. There are currently six recognised Pennods, or ages, or chapters or eras of the world. The Age of Anarchy or Emergent Kingdoms is the time before Ull's arrival here. Then there is the Age of Ull or the Coming of Magic, those years when Ull was alive on Erinna, interestingly this proves that not all Ages of Erinna are long. Then came the Age of the Cearcall, before the Early Empire or the Age of Battles," he hesitated momentarily and Arkyn said,

"And following the murder of King Alvern the Age of Tyranny…"

"Erm, yes, Sire. It is also known in some texts as the Age of the Bard though for purists this isn't quite right. Anyway, the next age is the one that many astrologers are sure has just ended. As yet there is no specific name for it; hindsight is often the motivating factor in naming an age of the world…"

"Yes, I doubt Lord Onraet was wont to call his rule the Age of Tyranny," observed Tain innocently.

Arkyn's lips twitched. "I'm sure he didn't… Come. Ah, Kadeem, thank you. Excuse me a moment, gentlemen." He took the headache remedy. "Now, ignoring His Highness' startling observations you were saying, astrologer?"

Tain muttered, "Startling?"

Arkyn caught his eye and winked.

The astrologer pretended not to notice. "Thank you, Sire. The new ages seem to be heralded by a red moon, more specifically a red greater moon: when Aluna blushes the world changes. Some call this moon the blood moon, that reference was especially used during and after the Age of Tyranny. The red moon was seen again this Munewid and it heralds change on Erinna. We cannot say that this change is either good or bad, that it will bring battles or prolonged peace and for this I am sorry, Sire. I realise that it is not the way that one should flatter kings and say that everything will be blessed and good but the murder of King Adeone was not a blessed thing. Your accession is welcomed, indeed anticipated, but it is marred by sadness at the events that wrought it. The stars weep for

318

your father as much as man, their light has been dimmed over recent days and shooting stars have been seen throughout the empire—"

The Moonshi said, "I think what the astrologer is trying to say, Sire, is that your father will be sorely missed but your reign will be great."

Arkyn glanced at the Moonshi. "Really, I'd say that he was saying that he hadn't got a clue what was going to happen whilst trying to dig himself out of a large hole. Let's not mince words, my father was murdered and the current future is uncertain. My coronation will happen but there are six exiled lords and a hand manipulating them. Shall we really deceive ourselves?"

Tain rubbed at his forehead. "Sire…"

"Yes, Your Highness?"

"Maybe we should live the future instead of anticipating it."

Arkyn nodded. "A wise course of action."

The astrologer said, sadly, "That's me out of a job then."

Arkyn laughed, much to the surprise of everyone else present, he said, "Not necessarily. Show us all the magic of the stars whilst Prince Tain tries to keep our feet bound by terrestrial cares."

The astrologer smiled. "I can certainly try, Sire."

Tain glanced at Arkyn. "So can I."

"Oh, good," said Arkyn dryly.

Half an hour later the astrologer and Moonshi left, in no doubt that they wouldn't be discussing the meeting with anyone else. It had been such a mixture and contrast that, until the next meeting was over, they could not tell whether King Arkyn was partial to astrology or not.

Within the Inner Office, Arkyn enquired, "How often do those meetings occur, Rayburn?"

"King Adeone managed to talk them down to once every couple of months, Sire."

"Oh good. Do not mistake me, I'm sure they're valuable but I don't think my head is in the right place for them at present."

"Hardly surprising, Sire," replied Rayburn. "Might I enquire if that remedy is working or would you like me to inform your administrator that you're taking some time off?"

"I'm sure it will work better given a little longer. Maybe you should check what the next meeting is."

Once the advisor had gone Tain said, "Really?"

"It'll go."

"Don't run yourself ragged, Arkyn."

"There's only so much time. We've a tight deadline to work to."

"I know…" He hesitated. "I'm worried about you."

Arkyn crossed to him. "Don't be. Let me worry about you instead. That's the traditional way…"

"Traditions can be changed."

"Oh… leave Uncle Festus' expressions to him. What are you up to now?"

"I've got to return to the Courthouse, if you don't need me. There are a couple of cases I ought to be briefed about and the trials that have occurred over the last couple of days to look over… Everything that I said could wait actually."

Arkyn sighed. "You'd better go. Is it… *Are* you all right with it all?"

Tain glanced at him and then away. "I'm… coping, yes. I wish the Judge was here to help but I can only try to be the Justiciar he taught me to be."

"Is there no-one else you can turn to for that side of things?"

"I don't know whom to trust. The Keeper is no judge, nor ever was. I'm fortunate that James was thorough in his teaching."

"You've really not had a good time recently, have you?" whispered Arkyn. How had he managed to forget that Tain had been grieving even before Munewid Eve?

"Neither of us have, Arkyn, but no. I've lost my mentor and father in the space of a fortnight and I'm now Justiciar of Oedran and my brother is King. Not only have two supports of my life been torn away from me but a sickening officialdom has come in the middle of a third."

"Forget the officialdom is there, for both our sakes," said Arkyn, still whispering.

Tain dropped his voice, "It wouldn't help, Arkyn. You know that. If I don't remember and remind people no-one else will take us seriously. As you reminded Jenkins so I remind others."

Arkyn grasped him by the shoulder. "Don't be alone because of it."

"Nor you. Come for dinner later."

Arkyn smiled. "Why not? Cal and Elantha?"

Tain hesitated. "I'll see they're there, if they want to be."

Arkyn noted the hesitation. "We need the madness."

"I thought, according to you, I was mad enough without anyone's help."

Arkyn merely raised an eyebrow.

"Very non-committal. Will you excuse me, sir?"

Arkyn glared.

"I'll take that as a yes then. I'll see you later."

Arkyn clapped him on the back. "More than likely. Let Edward know on your way out."

Tain left with an ironic bow but once in the Outer Office became more sober. "Edward, the King will be dining with me tonight. If she wishes to, Lady Elantha can join us and could you send an invitation to Cal? I'm going to be showered with work as soon as I set foot in the Courthouse."

Edward smiled. "I shall attend to it directly, Your Highness."

Chapter 75

PRACTICE MAKES PERFECT

Late Afternoon
Courthouse

WHEN TAIN ENTERED his outer office in the Courthouse, Peter rose. "Edward's informed Robert about the dinner this evening, Your Highness. The invitation has been sent to Master Calumiel and Lady Elantha has said she'll be there."

"Oh, thank you, Peter. That's efficient of you both, as always. You know I forgot to ask Edward to let Robert know."

Peter smiled as they entered Tain's private office. "Standard procedure, Your Highness." He took the Prince's cloak. "Shall I inform Jenkins of your arrival, sir?"

"Do you have to?"

"I believe sooner or later your Chief Lawyer will need to speak to Your Highness, but I can make it later than currently planned."

"Very amusing. I suppose I'd better see him. Is Robert here?"

"Not currently, sir. I can send for him."

Tain shook his head. "No, it's all right, I'm sure I can find where the decanters are hiding."

"What would Your Highness like to drink?"

"Water for now, please."

Two minutes later, Peter had hung Tain's cloak in the dressing room and returned with a sparkling Denshirian glass jug full of water and an iridescent drinking glass. He poured a drink for the Prince.

"I'm not sure I'm up to Robert's standard, Your Highness, but is there anything else I can get you?"

Tain said softly, "You're doing all right. For now, that's all. Thank you."

* * *

Six minutes later, Jenkins entered the office and bowed an official and exact bow. Tain looking over said conversationally,

"Who is the show for, Jenkins?"

"Practice makes perfect, Your Highness."

"Which didn't answer the question asked. Congratulations on proving

321

you're a lawyer once again."

"Practice makes perfect, Your Highness."

"I suppose you find that amusing?"

Jenkins smiled. "Practice…"

"Jenkins!"

"My apologies, sir."

Tain looked him in the eye. "Do you mean them?"

Jenkins said, "Practice… Sorry, sir. Yes I mean I apologise for getting Your Highness frustrated but not if I make Your Highness smile."

Tain rolled his eyes, "I appreciate the thought. Sit down and depress me with a long list of trials. I'm sure you'll be getting enough practice at that to become perfect very quickly."

Jenkins smiled. "I'm impressed, sir – not one note of irony."

"That could be because I wasn't being ironic – or sarcastic, for that matter. I may, however, have been being facetious. Get on with it. I've not got long."

Jenkins nodded, sobered and gave concise information. He handed over two reports outlining the cases in hand with notes on the laws that pertained to them and the precedents list for every outcome. Tain examined them whilst Jenkins was talking, making notes at the same time. By the end of the briefing Tain had filled a couple of sides of parchment with shorthand and glancing at a timepiece said,

"That's all for now, Jenkins, thank you."

After the lawyer left, Tain took several deep breaths, trying to still his pounding heart. He read the documents he'd been given more fully in conjunction with the notes he'd made whilst Jenkins was there before setting them aside. He picked up other documents Peter had left. They were obviously bundled together with a summary of what was included on the top. Tain read it only slightly puzzled before glancing at the signature of the person who'd sent it. He rang once more for Peter.

"If Advisor Rayburn isn't with the King, ask him to join me, please."

Peter said, "Of course, sir. Might I tell him why he's required?"

"I've read the summary document."

* * *

Half an hour later, Rayburn entered Tain's office and bowed precisely. "How may I help, Your Highness?"

"Come in and have a seat, Advisor. Are you sure I'm not dragging you away from something important?"

"Your Highness comes second only to the King, sir," replied Rayburn. "There are plenty of advisors for me to delegate less urgent things to."

Tain tilted his head slightly. "Can I call on the King's Advisors?"

"When, in less than a week, you're going to crown him, yes, sir, I think you can," observed Rayburn.

Tain swallowed. "Actually, that's what I wanted to make sure about. Am I going to crown him?"

"Why do you doubt it, Your Highness? You're his brother; you crown him and forgo your rights at the same time."

"My age. Being alunan I come of age at twenty. It's only tradition that makes us mark our fifteenth birthdays as we enter our adolescence. Legally, I am Justiciar of Oedran but does that mean anything? If he could have done, Lord Scanlon would have stopped it."

Rayburn nodded. "Yes, sir, he would have done, and he tried to from my understanding, but that conflict is, for the moment, past. If I might advise you, do not dwell on it. Let Lord Scanlon's peculiarities lie undisturbed."

Tain bit his lip. "Rayburn, I know you're aware of the situation, but please be careful what you say. Lord Scanlon is still of the FitzAlcis, whatever else he might be and whatever the FitzAlcis think of him."

Rayburn inclined his head. He might have underestimated Tain. "My apologies, Your Highness, I shall follow your wishes."

"Thank you. I also expect they are the King's. Now, to the question of the coronation."

"Do you have a lawyer who is an expert in the differences between the cisan and alunan sections of society, sir?"

Tain frowned. "I honestly have no idea." He rang for Peter and posed the question to him.

Peter replied, "Not amongst your lawyers, sir."

"That, Peter, was a lawyer's answer. Is there anyone who can help?"

Peter said, "Well, actually, s...sir, it was the subject of my thesis."

Tain raised an eyebrow eloquently, "I knew you'd come in useful. Take a seat…"

"If you'll excuse me for a moment, I'll get a scribe to sit in my office."

When Peter had gone, Tain said, "Peter still surprises me, Rayburn."

"I suppose that's the advantage of having a lawyer as your administrator, Your Highness."

"You did say advantage? We're talking about lawyers."

Rayburn laughed. "So we are, sir. I shall try and find an apt expression that isn't derogatory."

Peter re-entered a couple of moments later and sat down. "How can I help, Your Highness?"

"Rayburn will explain."

So Rayburn did.

With a lawyer's pause, Peter said, "Your Highness, it's only traditional that you consider yourself alunan. It's not written into any law that the FitzAlcis are in any section of society. Before the Age of Tyranny, it was accepted that they were neither alunan nor cisan – definitely not cisan – and that's because the FitzAlcis are crowned, are royal and are of the heavens. It was part of the problem that led to the Age of Tyranny and so King Arlis, when he reclaimed the throne, simply accepted that by considering his family alunan he had disposed of one threat to them. There are still, however, odd hints that things are different in the FitzAlcis. For example, if you don't mind me using Her Ladyship as an example, Lady Elantha carries a title but is under fifteen."

"She carries the title because she was born a princess but when Lord Scanlon dropped the title of prince, King Altarius insisted that she still held a title."

"Quite so, sir, but no-one made any move to say that it couldn't happen. In fact, all the FitzAlcis carry titles before they're of age. In law titles are carried only when fifteen or over, the manner of address before that is simply 'mistress' or 'master'."

"So, is the conclusion that I'm not alunan?" enquired Tain.

"Yes, sir, or at least in law Your Highness is not, in traditional conception you are. I suppose another example would be that Your Highness assumes part of your inheritance every year between the ages of fifteen and twenty, in strict law that would be prohibited as you are not of age for a member of the alunan. The progression of your official life is further complicated because it is proclaimed by decrees and, therefore, technically a form of law, but that confusion aside—"

Tain sighed. "I think I get the point, but it was far easier when I thought I was alunan. Peter, as I am now, can I legally crown my brother?"

Peter said, "Yes, sir. Your Highness has an official post – one gifted by King Adeone, which is important – you are the only brother to the new King and you are his heir."

Tain swallowed. He'd not even thought about that. The academic theory of forgoing his rights was very different to the reality of being his brother's heir. His hand shook. "Thank you, Peter. that's all for now." He glanced at Rayburn. "I'd better read these proceedings then."

"Yes, sir. Your Highness will be in many of the meetings concerning the coronation and some decisions will reside with Your Highness. Should you need any advice, please don't hesitate to ask for me."

Tain nodded. "Thank you, Advisor Rayburn."

* * *

Sometime later the door to the dressing room opened, and Robert appeared.

"Can I get Your Highness anything?"

Tain glanced at him. "You tell me; you organise my life so well."

Robert said, "Maybe a drink, sir, before Your Highness heads back to the Palace?"

"Admirable. Something stronger than water though."

"Not a good day, sir?"

"It's a day, Robert. I'll be ready to leave in twelve minutes."

"Very good, sir. Your coach will be waiting."

"I can walk."

"I never doubted that, sir, but it will drop Your Highness at the Privy Gate and I hesitate to mention it has already picked Master Calumiel up. He's waiting next door."

Tain sighed. "Thank you. You'd better get him a drink as well." He rang a bell and when Peter answered said, "Send Cal in, please, Peter."

Cal waited for Robert and Peter to leave before saying, "You're looking depressingly official, Your Highness."

"That statement was designed to make me feel normal, was it?"

"I can't say it was designed at all; it just got said. Having a good day?"

"Stop being facetious and I might tell you. You might as well sit down. I'm going to be a few minutes."

"Oh good, that means half an hour or more."

Tain picked up the list of the next day's trials. "Shut up moaning, some of us have a position to maintain."

"I always said you needed to practise more."

"Don't you start," muttered Tain, much to Cal's confusion.

Half an hour later they walked out to Tain's coach and settled themselves for the short ride to the Palace.

Cal said quietly once it moved off, "Getting lazy now you're Justiciar?"

Tain shrugged. "It was Robert's idea. I think he's probably saying I'm looking tired without saying it."

"He could be right, Your Highness. Will it be a late dinner?"

"Depends how much talking you do," said Tain acidly.

"It takes two to converse, sir."

"Only one for a monologue."

"Damn!"

"That's not like you, Cal."

"I have to let you have the last word, Your Highness." Cal grinned. "According to palace protocol but as we're not there yet…"

"Practice makes perfect I suppose," said Tain dryly.

Chapter 76

BORDER LODGE

Early Evening
Border Lodge

LORD WEALSMAN HAD LEFT the Rex Dallin sergeant at the southern gate, where another guard waited with a fresh horse. The well-maintained track intrigued him. He wouldn't go astray. The bleakness of the plateau seeped into his mind, reassuring him that the valley's calm was safe.

There was a slight breeze blowing from the south, from the Low Plains, warm and inviting, ideal for any ride.

He took a long drink of water from the flask the guard had attached to the saddle. He tried to remember noticing the turning for this track on his gallop to Oedran and couldn't.

He patted his horse's neck, reins held tight. The horse wanted to gallop. Wealsman scanned the track ahead. No potholes, no tree roots. He let the reins hang looser and urged the horse on. The power ran through him as the gallop began. He ached still but there was nothing like this, nothing like the breeze becoming a tempest through his hair, nothing like the rhythm of the horse below him, the pounding of its hooves on the beaten earth. He leaned forward. They could go faster than this. The horse sped up. Wealsman wanted to yell his joy at the speed, at the freedom. Until the last few days, he'd not ridden like this for years. His bones were singing. He'd pay for it later, when the blood stopped racing through his veins, when he rested, but right now, he wanted the speed, the exhilaration. They were private on this track in a way the main highway wasn't. He saw it come into view. Too soon!

He reined in the horse, watching the road for a time. All looked well. There were a few carts towards Oedran and a few mail riders, one galloping along the raised King's Highway spoke of the times. Couriers sent hither and thither bearing the news, bearing the responsibility of delivering it safely. These mail riders had endurance born in their souls, and, having ridden more miles north than even they would contemplate in one go, Wealsman appreciated them far more.

Wealsman joined the King's Highway and urged his horse on. The firm footings of the road, with its earthen surface, was maintained for mounted riders and the horse revelled in the sustained gallop. They found their pace; every horse and rider had a different one. They needed to maintain this for a few miles. He should change the horse at the next lodge but it wasn't tiring. They sped past. A boy was holding another horse ready. How did they know he was due? Silly question, his ride south wasn't private.

So many orders to get him a horse, get him to the Pillars. Nothing was private in Oedran. He leaned down, into the horse's neck, whispering encouragement. The horse's stride lengthened slightly. It was pacing itself, slowing every so often, speeding up again. If he could have done, he'd have bought this horse without a second thought. They were matched in ways he hadn't felt with others.

He thought he'd misread the mile marker at Eastsage, they sped past it but it turned out he hadn't. Border Lodge appeared more quickly than he'd anticipated and he truly realised the shortcut that Arkyn had provided and blessed him for it.

As he entered the lodge, he dismounted swiftly. The horse was breathing heavily but it nickered as though laughing. Percival patted it, whispering his thanks.

A stable lad, no more than fourteen, hurried forward. "New horse, sir?"

"Please, lad. I'm naming this one Wingfoot, but he won't carry me much further. My name's Percival Wealsman. Is the lodge keeper about?"

The lad grinned. "Aye, sir. Inside. I'll see to Wingfoot. The King's been in contact, I believe."

* * *

Wealsman entered the lodge and knocked on the door marked *Lodge Keeper*. A hesitant voice with strange harmonics bade him enter.

"Good afternoon, I'm Percival Wealsman. I believe the King may have been in contact?"

"Yes, Your Excellency."

"Good. Do you know what the weather's like in Terasia?"

"I believe it's set to be fair, sir."

The man's eyes flicked and some sixth sense made Wealsman duck. The knife whipped over his head and his elbow met the assailant's stomach.

"Be careful," was the lodge keeper's helpful comment.

Wealsman said conversationally, as he twisted the man's wrist, "Such a consideration would never have occurred to me, keeper. My thanks."

Once the dagger dropped, Wealsman twisted the man's arm up his back. "My apologies, sir. I have you at a disadvantage. Lodge keeper, would you mind checking him for weapons?"

The lodge keeper swallowed. "Well, now you mention it, sir, yes I would rather."

Wealsman eyed him. "I would remind you of my name, keeper. That is all, just my name."

The lodge keeper moved forward and patted the man down. "That's all there was, sir, just the dagger Your Excellency removed."

"Check his boots."

"Oh."

"And now take his belt off. I'll hold his arms, you secure them." All the time the man was muttering and struggling. Wealsman said kindly, "Shut up. It won't do you any good. Did you think that because I have guards, I don't know how to defend myself? You have a lot to learn in the short time left to you."

"What do you mean?" The question was rough.

"I might be a simple man at heart, but I am also a King's Representative and as was amply proved during King Arkyn's visit to Terasia in 1211 it is treason to attack one. Now, will you be quiet or do we have to go to the tedious effort of silencing you?"

The lodge keeper was watching with something close to admiration as Wealsman's politeness left the assailant speechless.

Wealsman turned to the lodge keeper. "Now, sir, what *is* the weather in Terasia like?"

The lodge keeper balled his fists. "Atrocious, sir. The King was apparently most insistent on that fact."

Wealsman laughed. "I thought he might be. Thank you for realising it could be used as a warning. Is there somewhere we can detain this man?"

* * *

A few minutes later, the lodge keeper sat down shaking. "He had my son, sir. I'm sorry."

"No, thank you for the warning. I might suggest that in your job you need to be a bit more forceful when the fight goes your way, but that is all. Where is your son now?"

"I'll find him, he can't be far."

"Let your staff do that. How old is he?"

"Ten, sir."

"Not old enough to defend himself then?"

The lodge keeper sighed. "Try telling his sisters that."

Wealsman snorted. "I know the feeling. Now, tell me what happened."

The lodge keeper told how the man had simply walked into the lodge that morning when he and his son were together, overpowered the lodge keeper, beating him where it wouldn't show and then tying him up. Taking his son somewhere and coming back, explaining exactly what would happen when Wealsman arrived.

Wealsman listened. "Right. Well, the felon will have to come with me. I'll stop by at Amphi Palace and hand him over to Governor ReJean. Will you witness to his attack on me?"

"Yes, Your Excellency."

"Can you please write a statement then, and include what you've told me. I'll get a couple of your lads to witness it and then I'll tie the traitor to a horse and gallop him all the way to Amphi."

The lodge keeper smiled. "About your onward travel arrangements, Your Excellency, King Arkyn was apparently most insistent and therefore your transport has changed."

With amused resignation, Wealsman said, "Do tell me how."

Two minutes later, he was looking at the how and unbeknownst to him a smile crept onto his face. He saw a lightweight envoy coach. Large enough for one man to travel in, or at a squash two men. It included a seat, a wider berth for sleeping, a cupboard for victuals and paperwork, a small table and a hanging lamp. A trunk could be tied to the back and, if necessary, there was a spare place beside the driver for any attendant. One was kept at all primary mail lodges. Some would have been inveigled into service by the ambassadors as they were known to be quick when pulled by a pair or four; maybe not as quick as galloping, but with changes ready at every lodge, there wouldn't be much difference. His limbs would thank Arkyn for weeks to come.

The lodge keeper smiled. "Does this suffice, sir? We have supplied a pair given the call on our horses at the moment. That necessity should ease south of Amphi."

Wealsman nodded. "Yes, thank you, keeper. Where will I swap it?"

"In Tera, Your Excellency. I did mention the King was insistent."

Wealsman laughed. "I shall endeavour to thank him. But it does rather leave the question of what to do with the man I've arrested."

"We'll tie him securely to the luggage rack, sir. He won't slip off that, you may be assured."

"I must find out who he is as well."

The lodge keeper said simply, "From what I've heard of the King's journey to Oedran, he'll be the bandit that escaped when the cavalcade was attacked not far from here. Seems someone worked out you'd be coming south, sir."

Wealsman nodded. "A likely explanation. Thank you, lodge keeper. Please see I get your statement shortly. I wonder, is there any chance of a meal whilst you write it? Bread and soup will do."

* * *

A few hours later, Wealsman's coach rattled into the Palace of Amphi's stableyard. Grooms hurried forward and promises were made that the coach would be ready to leave again in a few minutes.

Wealsman said simply, "I need to see the Governor but do hurry if it would make you feel better. I also need a few guards."

329

The head groom waved over a couple of uniformed men.

Wealsman addressed them simply, "I'm Percival Wealsman. Attached to the coach is a man who attacked me with intent to kill. Please put him in your cells whilst I inform His Excellency of events."

* * *

ReJean started as Wealsman was announced. "I wasn't expecting to talk with you, Percival. You're looking well."

"I feel drained but, then, today *has* been taxing."

"Not to mention the last few but why today in particular."

Wealsman explained about the traitor. "I'd stay to deal with it myself, if I wouldn't be treading on your toes, but I do need to reach Terasia."

"Leave it to me. He won't see the dawn."

Wealsman relaxed. "I'd rather King Arkyn didn't find out what's happened for a few days, weeks preferably – he doesn't need the stress – but get out of the assailant who he is and let Major Wynfeld know."

"Before he left for Oedran, the King insisted I informed him of all cases of treason in the province. Border Lodge is officially Anapara but you've brought the felon here. Are you asking me to break my word?"

"How exactly did he phrase the request, Leander?"

"That I was to tell him and not Lord Scanlon, which will cause enough repercussions as His Lordship is still our Justiciar."

"And ours in Terasia." Wealsman considered. "I don't think you'll be breaking your word if you wait to tell the King, Leander. No, I don't, as long as you don't tell Lord Scanlon. If His Lordship asks you, feign amnesia and contact the King immediately, then let me know. I doubt Lord Scanlon will ask. When I'm reported as having been here, he'll know the attack failed. Oh, don't look like that. He nearly killed you on Munewid Eve."

"I've yet to see evidence he was behind the attack, Percival. I know the FitzAlcis have strife within their ranks but I cannot believe Lord Scanlon would order the murder of his own brother and nephews, let alone others that may have been targeted. Fires happen, accidents out riding happen. Camlyn was elderly. No. I need more proof than I've been offered before I can point fingers."

Wealsman lips pursed. "ReJean, be careful. You are doubting your liege's word." He held the Governor's gaze. "Lord Scanlon's advisor was planted as Prince Tain's manservant, was instrumental in the assassination and turned murderous when confronted. If you wish for evidence, consider those actions. Then try to locate someone who was previously in Lord Scanlon's employment. It might be circumstantial, but it still happened."

ReJean swore. "I'd forgotten that. It was rather busy that night."

330

"I can only imagine. How was he?"

"Who? Oh, King Arkyn? Stoical and sad. I wasn't allowed near unless I insisted. That young merchant's son overstepped a few times."

Wealsman eyed ReJean. "Cal Galdwin?" Seeing the truth, he chuckled. "Oh dear. You do need to be careful of that prejudice, Leander. He's a close confidant of the King and Prince. They don't seem bothered by who his father is. Times have changed from King Altarius' day."

"Yes." ReJean caught Wealsman's eye. "Not always for the bad. Did you see my daughter?"

"I believe so. There wasn't much time for introductions. She was near me in the funeral procession, but it wasn't the night for talking."

"Of course. How was the funeral?"

"It went well…" After a couple of minutes Wealsman said, "I should go. Thank you for your help."

"I hope the rest of your journey is uneventful."

"So, Leander, do I. Is there anything you need of me at the moment?"

ReJean smiled. "If there is, it can more than wait. All business it seems must. I'll come with you to the coach."

* * *

Once in the stableyard ReJean said, "My best to Lady Wealsman, and be sensible on your journey home, Percival, you're irreplaceable to the King and your province."

Wealsman said softly, "Thank you. I appreciate your confidence in me but all our provinces would be lost without us and the FitzAlcis have always held the ReJeans in high regard."

Governor ReJean chuckled. "Read the Bard's story when you can; you might be surprised. Safe trip."

Chapter 77

DEMOTION AND REVELATIONS

Hexadai, Week 1 – 6th Cearal, 6th Cearcis 1215

Inner Office

IT WAS HEXADAI, but Arkyn was at his desk, still reading reports that he hadn't had chance to with the mass of meetings about the funeral. He glanced over the standard military reports; flicked through palace ones but missed nothing. He reached for the next: a report from Wynfeld on the barracks' situation. It explained much Arkyn wished he'd known before.

He sent for Rayburn, Wynfeld and Lord Faran but told Edward he'd see Rayburn before the other two. He needed advice and Rayburn was an expert in military matters. The advisor entered the Inner Office and knelt swiftly.

Frustrated, Arkyn snapped, "Get up. I've told you before I don't like kneeling officials as my father didn't."

Rayburn said, "Sire, I feel it is right, given the circumstances of your accession that the fact you are King of Oedran is reinforced."

"That does not have to include you kneeling at every opportunity!"

"Sir, my conscience is my own."

"Not in my office it's not. Get up!"

Rayburn got to his feet. "My apologies, Sire."

There was something in the way the advisor apologised, calmly but sincerely that cut through Arkyn's frustration, making him reconsider. "No, Rayburn, please accept mine. I should not have snapped. Of course your conscience is your own, I certainly don't wish for the handling of it. I have enough trouble with mine." He motioned to a chair, using the moments until his advisor sat down to arrange his thoughts. After the exiles, the funeral had been the most pressing concern. He had a brief respite before the coronation and considerations over oaths and fealties would consume his time.

Wynfeld's private report detailed the whispers that were growing. Whispers he'd hoped would be silenced with Kilbride's dismissal and the lords' exiles. There was little point starting with pleasantries.

"People – the Court, the empire – are wondering if I've finished taking action over the assassination. I've taken all I can for the lords, and Kilbride's dismissal addressed the apparent shortcomings in the King's Guards; however, I must question why the intelligence regiment never discovered something was happening. In his last letter, father asked me not to blame others when he didn't tell them there would be an attack. I will not blame them for the events; yet, I cannot believe that the activities of the six exiled lords were never under suspicion. Especially as Jacobs manipulated the regiment. Given everything, I am thinking of demoting Beaver."

Startled, Rayburn said, "Sir, resignation if you are determined to take action would surely be better and there would be a large gap to fill."

"I am asking Fysher as co-captain of the intelligence regiment to retire; he was instrumental in giving Jacobs confidential work. There's no evidence on which I can court martial him for treason though. Back to Beaver, I feel that he will be better under the army's mantle. I'm considering exiling him for a couple of years as well."

"Sire, I do not mean to question your decisions, but is that wise?"

"I am sending him to Lufia," revealed Arkyn without emphasis.

"Lufia? Might I ask why?" enquired Rayburn, perplexed.

"The second city of the empire… Were you ever apprised of the conclusions following the bandit attack on me and my entourage a couple of years ago?"

Rayburn said, "Only that His Lordship was innocent, Sire."

Arkyn considered for a few moments. "Then you might not recognise in full why I am sending Beaver to Lufia. Apposer Nallvir got the feeling that there is treason high in the government of Lufian. Where else, then, would you recommend I send one of the best spies this empire has? One who is apparently disgraced?" Arkyn watched a small smile creep over the advisor's face.

Eventually Rayburn said, "Sire, I believe you are more cunning than many will credit."

"I'll take that as a compliment."

"Please do." The advisor sobered. "If there is treason high in Lufian government it is worrying."

"Not just there. Nallvir suspected the same in Bayan. The Exarch has already dismissed three officials who were being loose tongued."

Rayburn said, "Curious. Might I ask who is in your mind for Captain of Intelligence?"

"If Wynfeld has no suggestion, I thought Lyndon. He's from the army but he's also apprised of the situation. I know I've only just taken him into the King's Guard, but, had I known about this before, I'd have arranged something else."

Rayburn sat for a few moments before saying, "I think you should speak to the Major before you take any action, Sire."

"You disagree with the notion?"

"I neither agree nor disagree, sir, but the Captain of Intelligence must be right for the job; there is no room to make a mistake in that particular appointment, or even an appointment that might not be the best man even if it isn't a mistake, as such—"

"Carry on digging, Rayburn. You're doing an excellent job."

Rayburn swallowed. "That's me, sir. Whatever I do, I excel at."

"Apparently." He rang for Edward. "Are Lord Faran and the Major here?"

"Lord Faran is, sir. Unusually, the Major hasn't arrived yet."

Arkyn nodded. "Thank you, Edward. Come on in, Lord Faran. Do you know Advisor Rayburn?"

Faran smiled. "I do, Sire. We studied together at the Advisor's School."

"Ah. Then further explanations and introductions are superfluous."

Rayburn smiled. "I am sure we'd still discover facets of each other's characters, Sire."

Faran glanced at Arkyn. "Those are probably better left hidden, Rayburn.

What can I do for you, Sire?"

Glad of the change of subject, Arkyn waved to a chair. "I need to know how far you were apprised of Apposer Nallvir's findings following the events which greeted my arrival in Lufian, Lord Faran. Did my father ever confide the unofficial findings that didn't make the report?"

Taking a seat, Faran said carefully, "I was told he had found me innocent, Sire, and nothing more."

Frowning, Arkyn answered a knock at the door. Edward announced Wynfeld, who entered sluggishly, slightly slumped and dull-eyed. Concern ripped through Arkyn; he pushed himself to his feet, before recalling he shouldn't physically support anyone.

Turning, Rayburn pushed himself to his feet. "Major, have you slept?" He remembered where he was. "My apologies, Sire."

"Don't apologise. You took the words out of my mouth. Wynfeld?"

Wynfeld relaxing from his salute said, "There's been little time, Sire."

"We'll see. Sit down, before you fall," ordered Arkyn.

Rayburn stood aside so Wynfeld could take his chair and found another. Arkyn didn't take his eyes from the Major but Wynfeld hardly met his gaze. Faran was looking between them, concerned. Arkyn steadfastly ignored him. When Rayburn was seated again, Arkyn said,

"Lord Faran, Major Wynfeld, I'm going to ask Captain Fysher to resign. Captain Beaver I am thinking of demoting and sending to Lufia. Wynfeld, I'd like your thoughts please."

"It is less than I expected, sir."

Rayburn glanced at the King. "What did you expect, Major?"

"At least one court martial and an execution. We failed dismally."

"Father didn't inform you of his suspicions," pointed out Arkyn.

"We shouldn't have needed suspicions, Sire! We shouldn't have needed those. Six lords who we've been watching engineered this and not a bloody word, not one hint, and, even if there was, I'm not sure those layabouts would have recognised it. I'll damn them all to eternity—"

"Major Wynfeld, remember yourself!" snapped Faran.

"I don't think he's forgotten who he is, Lord Faran," interjected Arkyn. "Wynfeld, do I have your support for this?"

"Yes, sir, of course you do. Would you like me to inform them?"

"No, thank you. I was considering promoting Lyndon to captain, to replace Beaver. If there is no-one you would prefer?"

"In this, I would not now presume, my king."

Arkyn said frustrated, "Then I won't keep you any longer, Major, but I will give you one order and I will check you have obeyed it..."

Wynfeld finally looked at him properly. "Sire?"

"Go and sleep. I shall see you for the Military Audience and I hope you will be your normal self." When Wynfeld had left, Arkyn rang for Edward asking him to request the General made sure the military doctor saw Wynfeld.

Less familiar than Rayburn was with the situation, Faran was making internal notes. The Major wasn't just an officer of the army. King Altarius would have upbraided him for appearing in such a state. Adeone would have been concerned, probably would have ordered the Major to rest, but ordering the doctor to attend on him? Probably, possibly, not. Faran hadn't missed Arkyn's impulse to help Wynfeld physically. The Major was trusted, that had been clear for years, but the level of concern Arkyn had shown went beyond that for a trusted official. Maybe the susurration of a whisper was right: Wynfeld and the King had a relationship that went as deep as confidants. Faran tried to recall what Adeone had told him. Wynfeld had worked for Lord Macaria, had known Queen Ira well, had been carrying her when she died. What else had happened that day, or the days following? Something had. Something which had drawn Arkyn and Wynfeld together. Mutual grief? Possibly. He tried to recall anyone who had met Ira and not loved her. Maybe he should call by the nursery and talk with Maria. He didn't want to say the wrong thing. Adeone had trusted Wynfeld to be and remain Chief of Intelligence. Arkyn didn't seem minded to alter the situation, even after a spectacular failure of intelligence. Yes. He needed to fathom the situation out. Maria, maybe Fitz, even Richardson should be able to help him understand where Arkyn's loyalties lay and why.

For the moment there were more immediate concerns. "Sire, might I clarify why I'm here?" enquired Faran once the door closed on Edward.

"Because Nallvir believed there is treason high in Lufian government. I need you to know why I'm sending Beaver into your country and I need you to help him and never reveal what I've confided."

"The last is always a given, Sire. Were Apposer Nallvir's findings any more specific?"

"No. He suspected the same in Bayan; the Exarch is aware."

"Is the Sagamore, sir?"

"No. Tyler Galwood is family; there are greater ties at work. I had assumed father would have confided in you given the findings…"

Rayburn said, "Your Majesty, would you be happier discussing this without my presence?"

"Why do you wish to leave?" asked Arkyn.

"I don't wish to, sir, but I simply thought that you might find it easier to discuss Nallvir's findings without my presence. I could interview Lyndon and report back, if that would also help?"

"Then you'd better do so. I thought you weren't aware of the findings," observed Arkyn, his eyes narrowing.

"Even I, lowly advisor though I am, Sire, can tell there's more."

Arkyn snorted. "I knew you were employed for a reason. That's all, Rayburn, and don't kneel…" When the advisor had left, Arkyn muttered, "I really don't know why I bother telling him not to."

Lord Faran chuckled. "He's always been a law unto himself, Sire. As a student he actually studied."

"Is that what students are meant to do?"

"Meant to doesn't guarantee compliance, sir. You should talk to your nearfather about it. If he made one lecture in three, I'm surprised. I made slightly more, but Rayburn, I believe, attended them all." He noted Arkyn's mood. "What were Nallvir's full unofficial findings, sir?"

Arkyn's gaze softened. "He believed your son was murdered, but couldn't pinpoint the culprit without a freer remit than he had. He wasn't sent to distress you, Faran, and was exceptionally conscious of that fact."

Faran whitened. "He should have shelved his finer feelings!" He got up and walked to the far end of the room, obviously trying to contain his emotion. He couldn't leave the room before Arkyn dismissed him but he couldn't stay looking at the compassion in his eyes. He'd believed Damso had been murdered since he'd seen his body but there had been no proof, nothing to grasp or to follow. He stared at the gardens wanting his family, the living breathing heart of him, at his side.

* * *

Arkyn left the Inner Office, without alerting Faran that he was doing so. He hastened to the nursery. Entering, he winked at Elantha.

"I'm after Samara…"

"She's next door. Have you got six minutes?"

"Not immediately, little flower. I'll be back. Lord Faran is in need of support, and I can't give it him."

"What's happened?" asked Elantha, troubled.

"I've told him that we believe his son was murdered."

"I understand."

"Thank you… Ah, Samara, come and see your father." He picked his neardaughter up and simply carried her contentedly through the Privy Wing to the Inner Office. Faran was still staring out of the window. Arkyn crossed over to him.

"I might not be good at giving people a hug but I believe I know a girl who is, don't you, Samara?"

Faran turned to him and Arkyn saw the bright emotion in his eyes. He simply passed Samara over. "I'll be in the nursery when you want to face the world again.”

Lord Faran simply nodded and sat in a chair, hugging Samara to him.

* * *

Returning to the nursery, Arkyn entered it quietly and sat in the chair opposite Elantha. “How are you?”

She swallowed. “How are you?”

“Quite. Come here, little flower. We’ve abandoned you, haven’t we?”

“You’re both busy. Cal’s dropped by…”

“Always knew we kept him about for something,” quipped Arkyn.

“Don’t be mean to him.”

“See my last comment.”

Elantha sat on his knee and he wrapped his arm securely around the young girl. She started crying and he shushed her kindly.

Two minutes later Maria entered, unaware that Arkyn was there. She took in the scene and walked out again. There was nothing she could do for them in this, and she hadn’t missed the fact that Arkyn also had tears in his eyes.

In the end Lord Faran disturbed them when returning Samara to the nursery. The young girl looked at Arkyn and Elantha and toddled over to them. She tried to clamber onto Arkyn’s knee as well.

“Come away, Samara,” said Faran, noting the emotion.

“No. ‘Ncle… Eltha…”

Arkyn murmured, “She’s all right, Faran. Come on, Samara, I’m sure Elantha doesn’t mind being clambered on.”

Lord Faran walked over and lifted Samara up onto the chair arm. Arkyn put his spare arm around her so she didn’t fall but Samara clambered over Elantha and buried her head in Arkyn’s chest. After a moment she gave Elantha a hug as well.

Lord Faran watched the scene for a moment before quietly leaving.

Samara looked for him. “Pa?”

Arkyn glanced around. “He’s busy, Samara.”

Elantha wiped her eyes. “As are you. I was being daft. Come on Samara. Let’s find the rabbit your Uncle Arkyn gave you…”

Arkyn almost sighed in relief when he got feeling back in his legs. “El, I don’t care how busy I am if you want me here…”

“You’d never get anything done,” she replied. “I’ll be all right. Maria’s taking good care of me.”

“I’d hope so too. I wish I’d more time, El…”

“You’ve got your duties. I wish we were at Ceardlann.”

Arkyn said, “So do I. Do you want to go there for a time?”

"Not without you and Tain, not at the moment. Maybe later. After everything quietens down."

He gave a strong hug. "Be brave for both of us, El."

* * *

Leaving the nursery, Arkyn found Faran waiting in the corridor. There was something reassuring about his tact, and disconcerting in his quiet adherence to protocol. Arkyn hadn't dismissed him; therefore, he would remain available. He'd have to be careful about that. Keeping Lords of Provinces waiting around might enhance his authority, but it wouldn't enhance his safety. He motioned they'd walk.

They entered the Outer Office without having spoken a word. Another revelation. Faran wouldn't force conversation. That also revealed he'd been in close to them for years. Most people would have at least tried to find out if they could help with anything.

Edward's face was a mixed picture of relief and concern as he held open the Inner Office door. There wasn't anyone waiting, but that didn't mean everything was well. After the door closed, he sighed.

"Edward's looking worried. I've obviously delayed something."

"It's my fault, Sire."

"Nonsense."

"Sir."

Arkyn said, "Oh, stop pretending to agree."

"My conscience told me to, sir. Thank you, for everything today. For telling me the truth and for getting Samara. She helped more than I can ever explain."

"Maybe you don't need to explain, Faran," replied Arkyn quietly. "I thought you needed your family."

"You are very caring, Sire. The empire is fortunate in its King, but your friends and family are blessed in you."

"Smooth, my lord. I should see what Edward was fretting about."

* * *

After the subsequent meeting, Arkyn said, "Please stay for a moment, Paturn." When the other attendees had all left, he continued, "If I see Wynfeld looking like he did earlier again I shall be exceptionally annoyed. He was almost sleepwalking! He can't work like that and I want you to make sure he doesn't. Is that understood? Good. Now, I'm going to ask Fysher to resign and I'm going to demote Beaver and send him to Lufia."

"When, sir?"

"As soon as I've heard about their replacement." He rang for Edward, "Is Rayburn here?"

"Yes, sir."

338

The advisor entered and knelt.

The King said, "I'll soon throw something at you, Rayburn."

"Thank you for the warning, Sire. I shall duck."

Arkyn's eyes narrowed. "Have you interviewed Lyndon?"

"Yes, sir. He seems a good candidate. His record is clean."

"Lyndon, Sire?" enquired the General.

"I'm going to promote him to Captain of Intelligence. I want to leave Smithers with Prince Tain and Hillbeck I need. Lyndon was the next in line for a promotion to captain. If I'd still been a prince he'd have been promoted by now. He's bloody good at his job and after what's happened I'm not going to promote anyone from within the regiment."

"Very good, sir. Has the Major been consulted?"

"Yes. He made no demurral but then he wasn't exactly at his best but I think if he'd objected, he'd still have said something."

"Then it seems we have a new Captain of Intelligence."

"Let's get them all here and we will have."

* * *

Arkyn eyed the two Captains of Intelligence. Neither of them were facing him with equanimity. Beaver in particular seemed morose.

"I'm not going to be diplomatic about this," stated Arkyn. "Your combined incompetence has resulted in the assassination of a King of Oedran. I have read your reports on the matter and they amount to the fact that you knew nothing and have discovered nothing substantial in the last few days. Fysher, you put a disgraced secretary in charge of copying reports, one who was a margin away from having been arrested for treason. What's more, he's still not been apprehended; therefore, I advise you to resign before leaving this office."

Captain Fysher took his commission out of his breastplate and handed it over. "I expected worse, Sire."

"Thank you, you may go."

The now former captain knelt and left.

Arkyn turned to Beaver. "Fysher wasn't directly in charge of intelligence gathering, Beaver, you were. I cannot explain my feelings at the moment but I think you could say they aren't good; however, your skills are valuable, your knowledge important. Before you relax, I am demoting you to sergeant and posting you to Lufia. The Sagamore is in need of a sergeant to help his protection captain. You will fill that post."

Beaver said, "Demotion, sir?"

"Yes, to sergeant. Don't make me spell this out to you."

Beaver stood for a moment, all emotions flitting across his face, anger, relief, despondency and a flicker of comprehension. "Lufia, Sire?"

339

"Lufia. I shall expect you to be leaving the barracks in the next two days. Lyndon will be taking your place there, please hand over to him as soon as possible. You may go."

Two moments later, Beaver had left and Lyndon was saluting.

"Lyndon, I'm promoting you to Captain of Intelligence, reporting directly to Major Wynfeld as Chief of Intelligence. You're taking over from Fysher and Beaver with immediate effect. Here's your commission. Fysher should have left the barracks before nightfall and Beaver is to hand over to you and then march to Lufia as a sergeant. The General will explain anything else you need to know. Thank you for your service in the Prince's and King's Guard."

Confused, Lyndon said, "Sire? What on Erinna do I know about spying?"

"Ask yourself what Wynfeld knew when he started and you might have your answer. That's all."

Recognising the tone, Lyndon saluted and left.

The General said, "If you'll excuse me, sir, I'll see Lyndon is accepted back at the barracks."

"Do so. Thank you, General." Once he'd gone Arkyn relaxed. "Do you think Beaver understood, Rayburn?"

"Yes, sir, I do. I'm just worried that he might be an obvious spy."

"I hope so – as long as he doesn't get killed for it. That's all, Rayburn."

"Thank you, Sire," said the advisor, kneeling as he left.

* * *

Arkyn sent for Hillbeck and informed him what had happened.

"I'd just got him up to scratch, sir," commented the sergeant.

Arkyn glanced at him. "I'm sorry, Hillbeck, but there weren't many men to choose from."

"I understand, Sire. Do you have anyone in mind for the promotion?"

Arkyn shook his head. "No, you choose. It can be one of the men in my Guard but not one who was on duty on Munewid Eve, if there's no-one suitable yet we can both keep our eyes open."

Hillbeck nodded. "I'm sure I'll find someone, Sire. Do you have a couple of minutes?"

Chapter 78

BEGIN AT THE BEGINNING
Late Morning
Oedran Palace – Advisor Rayburn's Office

THE FIRST MEETING Prince Tain found himself part of for the coronation proceedings made him face up to the fact that he was an official outside the Courthouse as well as within its bounds. The meeting was held in the Palace, within the area set aside for the King's Advisors. Peter showed him the way, and Tain walked into the relevant office confidently.

A couple of moments later, Rayburn had apologised for not thinking to hold it at the Courthouse, been reassured and admitted the attendee list had changed because of the King ordering the Major to get some sleep.

Tain nodded. "Who's going to chair the meeting?"

Rayburn said, "Your Highness, sir, unless you delegate."

"No, it's all right, I'll do it."

A few minutes later Rayburn's secretary announced the other attendees and settled himself down to take notes. Peter waited until everyone else was seated before joining the table.

Tain said, "Gentlemen, in five days the King is to be crowned, more precisely I will be crowning King Arkyn in the City Alcium. I've read the information that Advisor Rayburn has sent to me about the proceedings and the procession, but we all have different parts to play. I think it would be best if we start at the beginning and then work our way through it. So, let's take King Arkyn's ride out of Oedran on Tretaldai. I'm not looking for specifics, just the general idea of what's going to happen. Rayburn, your notes said it was traditional for a king to leave in the early evening."

"Yes, Your Highness. I'd suggest, with the King's consent, that about four by the Court Clock would be right."

Tain nodded. "That seems sensible. We entered by the Dallin Gate when we returned from Amphi, and so it's beyond there we'll camp that night. General, I presume you or the Major has everything in hand."

General Paturn said, "Yes, sir. The camp is being erected about half a mile outside the Dallin Gate, we're fortunate that it's not one of the main roads into the city. Your father's coronation camp was on the port road as he'd returned from a review via that route earlier in the year. It caused, if I may say so, absolute havoc."

"I can imagine. As you say though, the road to the Rex Dallin is not a major one by normal reckoning. In fact, a camp there must be rare."

Advisor Rayburn said, conversationally, "The last we could find a record of was King Arlis', Your Highness."

Tain stilled. "That can't be right."

"I'm afraid it is, sir."

"Sicla! The parallels are concerning."

"No, sir, simply coincidental. Both kings are returning to the city after the assassination of their predecessor. We are centuries apart and there has been no battle to reclaim Oedran."

Tain swallowed. "Very true. Isn't the coronation ceremony merely a ceremonised version of King Arlis' entry into the city after the battle?"

"It is, sir," admitted Rayburn.

Tain said, "Right. I advise that none of you mention this *coincidence* to the King. He does not need the weight of fate adding to." He took a deep breath. "General, I hope the King's tent will be appropriate and not a standard military one."

"The tent and trappings being erected are those used by King Altarius during the Bayan Rebellion, sir. His Late Majesty liked his comforts," replied Paturn.

"Good, thank you. You'll need to make provision for some of the Court as well and myself, I'm afraid."

"It's in hand, Your Highness."

"Whose hands?" enquired Tain.

"Mine and the Major's, sir, and, with Your Highness' permission, I'll deal with the meetings and let him get on with the practicalities."

"Of course. You'll need at least one regiment outside Oedran and probably more. We'll have a meeting to discuss what's needed later. At the gates of Oedran, we need to work out who will bar the King's entry."

Advisor Rayburn said, "It's normally the Ealdorman, Your Highness."

Tain considered. "It can't be Lord Landis; he'll have other duties that morning as King Arkyn's Defender. Who is Ealdorman next year?"

"Hang on, sir, I'll find out. Erm, it should have been Lord Rathgar, Your Highness, but as he's in exile Lord Iris has taken his duties so I presume he will be," finished Rayburn, furling the scroll.

"Then it looks like Lord Iris will be the man."

The General said, "Sir, should a King's Counsellor stop a King?"

Tain eyed him. "I think the fact of who Lord Iris is and what he represents is greater than that objection, General. Unless you're offering to do it?"

"I am the King's to command not to impede, Your Highness."

"Yes, quite. If Lord Iris objects, we shall think again but as the eldest Lord of Oedran, I think he is appropriate. Does anyone else not?"

Rayburn and the Moonshi glanced at each other; both said, in unison,

"No, sir."

Rayburn added, "I'd like to see His Lordship's reaction to the idea that anyone else takes precedence."

Tain nodded. "Yes. Moonshi, once the gates are opened, are you happy with your role?"

"Yes, Your Highness."

"At the City Alcium, King Arkyn will wait outside for a few minutes whilst the guests arrange themselves, do you have enough alcias to mean that is quickly accomplished?"

"Yes, Your Highness. I'd say the delay should be minimal, a couple of minutes only. Ideally there'd be none but I can't work miracles."

Tain said wryly, "That's unfortunate, Moonshi. The crown will be at the Alcium from the night before. Do you have sufficient security to guard it?"

The Moonshi nodded. "Yes, sir. It will reside in the King's Alcium and there's only one door to the room and crypt below. I'm informed two of the King's Guard and two of the militia will be standing guard all night."

"General, none of the men who were on duty the night my father died are to be part of that guard," ordered Tain.

"The King has made it plain that the matter is closed, Your Highness," pointed out Paturn, troubled.

"I'm not reopening it; I'm stating that it would be better if that night they had other duties. I don't want to wake up on Imperadai to the news that anything has happened to the crown. Is that clear?"

"Yes, sir."

"Good. Where are the tokens that are attached to the crown?"

The Moonshi said, "They're currently in the care of the King's Jeweller. The morning of the coronation, each ambassador will be given the relevant token. They push into the crown via small holes and will all be checked beforehand. The coronation ring, I will have in my possession."

"Do not lose it, Your Benevolence. Who will be carrying the crown for the ceremony?"

"My deputy, Your Highness."

Tain was so obviously considering the idea that everyone else was silent for a long time.

Eventually Tain said, "Your Benevolence, will you listen to an idea? Rayburn, I'd like your thoughts as well, please. First, however, please answer a question: were any new alcias inaugurated at the Munewid?"

A slow smile spread over Rayburn's face and all he did was nod at Tain; nothing to his mind needed adding on the matter but the Moonshi was puzzled.

"Yes, Your Highness, but I can't quite see the relevance."

"How many swore to guard the ancestor's memory?" enquired Tain.

"In the City Alcium just one, Your Highness."

"And in the city as a whole?" probed Tain.

"I could discover the information, sir, but I do not have it to hand."

"Right. I'd like the young man who was inaugurated at the City Alcium to carry the crown at the coronation."

The Moonshi hesitated. "It is the traditional due of my deputy, sir."

"As I realise but it is also traditional for a king to accede at the *natural* death of his father. I shall not dwell on my feelings of recent days, nor shall I discuss the King's, but I think a younger man would be better. You could also say that they started their new duties at the same time. As did I, for that matter. I suppose what I'm trying to put into words and failing to do so is the wonderful but simple air that this could add to proceedings, an air that wouldn't be intimidating to any: just two young men, facing their futures." On the edge of hearing, Tain heard Rayburn mutter,

"Make that three."

The Moonshi said, "I think I know what Your Highness is trying to say and shall give the matter my attention."

"Thank you."

The Moonshi inclined his head slightly before turning to Rayburn. "Advisor, what are your thoughts? His Highness wished for them."

The advisor shrugged. "I think it's a brilliant idea. If it were up to me, knowing the King as I do, I'd say yes straightaway."

Tain asked, more for everyone else's benefit than his, "Why are you so convinced, Rayburn?"

"Other than one must never disagree with a prince, Your Highness, I was involved in the setting up of King Arkyn's previous advisors. He insisted that a new graduate was appointed to his staff."

Tain said, "Thank you. Moonshi, maybe you could let me know your answer by tomorrow. Now, when we leave the Alcium, the King will set off slowly for the Palace, to allow for the entourage which accompanies him time to mount. We will need an official outside the Alcium, co-ordinating the horses and getting them in the right order. Has that been anticipated?"

"Yes, sir. Lord Fairson has said he'll find someone," replied Rayburn.

Tain nodded. "Good. He can have the responsibility for the horses from the time the King leaves Oedran to his return to the Palace. Obviously, he needs to be in the entourage but he can have the oversight."

"I'll inform him, Your Highness."

"Thank you. When we return to the Palace, Steward, you will greet King Arkyn with the heads of the different sections. We'll be entering at the main gates and not the stables. The Palace Doors will be closed until the King dismounts. You walk out to greet the King and ceremoniously pass him the keys to the Palace. If you get anything wrong, you can be assured action will be taken on Pentadai. The King will enter the King's Hall by the Great Doors, walk forward and be acknowledged by the Court. Once that's completed, I will escort him to the King's Chambers where the King will lunch. Steward, you'll have to liaise with Kadeem to ensure that the King's Chambers are ready to move into that day. I say *liaise* but Kadeem is in charge of that, so, give him any help requested. All those who are to swear fealty must be gathered in the Audience Chamber by three. Rayburn, the order in which the lords swear fealty will have to be drawn up and a proclamation to the effect that any who wishes to can petition the King—"

"That went out yesterday, Your Highness."

"Good, thank you. Steward, the Audience Chamber will have to be prepared. I vaguely recall it is set with mirrors and scarlet and gold drapes?"

The Steward nodded. "Yes, Your Highness. The panelling actually revolves to reveal the mirrors. Each one is being checked overnight when the King is elsewhere and cleaned. Hopefully the night before the coronation they will all turn and we will hang the drapes."

"There is no *hopefully* in this, Steward," stated Tain. "It will be done. Once the Fealty Swear is over, the King will retire and ready himself for the banquet. The banquet will start early and finish late. Are the kitchens preparing for it?"

The Steward said, "Of course they are, sir. I am adept at my job."

Tain looked at him. "Of course you are. When the King retires from the banquet the day is over and, at the latest half an hour later, the Court should leave. Pentadai is a holiday, Hexadai the start of the Ambassadors' Court. Did I miss anything, Rayburn?"

"No, Your Highness."

"Good. Now, let's get down to finer details, or at least work out what you need me for."

* * *

When everybody had gone Rayburn said, "Your Highness, might I ask you something? Is it wise to antagonise the Steward?"

Tain said simply, "Probably not but I can't forget what a fool he was. Can you get my speeches to me as soon as possible, so I can start learning them, please?"

"Of course, sir. You should have them by this evening."

"Thank you. Was that meeting all right?"

Rayburn smiled. "Yes, Your Highness, it was perfectly fine." As the

Prince left, Rayburn relaxed. It had been fine, but he could tell the King and Prince were brothers. Time to have taken a breath would have been nice. He wondered if they went through things so quickly to disconcert attendees or because they preferred it.

Chapter 79
SCANLON
Early Afternoon
Inner Office

LORD SCANLON ENTERED the Outer Office, ignored the secretaries and Edward, entered the Inner Office, where he gave the most perfunctory bow he could.

Arkyn said, "Lord Scanlon, it is *traditional* to let my administrator announce you. If nothing else, I expect you to knock."

"And I expect Festus will ignore it and not be reprimanded."

"He holds a King's Token, you do not. What can I do for you?"

"Elantha shouldn't have been at the funeral. As her father—"

"What was the expression father used to use? Oh yes, paternal by right but not by endeavour. Tell me, Lord Scanlon, when was the last time you took any interest in her as a person and not a pawn to be pushed about? When did you last listen to her, to what she wants in life, to understand her feelings?"

"I'm concerned she doesn't disgrace me; her feelings are irrelevant."

Arkyn riled. "She has never disgraced anyone!"

"Apparently, she showed her emotion all through the funeral—"

"Emotion that her uncle had been murdered! That is never a bad thing. Get out!" ordered Arkyn.

Scanlon ignored him. "Sir, I expect a house to be available for her within two weeks."

"Expect what you want. The house will be ready when I have time to attend to it. Until then, your daughter is well cared for. Now—"

"Then there's the fact of her association with that merchant's son. Whatever your father *mistakenly* believed was right for princes I do not agree is right for my daughter. She will cease the association."

"I don't think you should be dictating Elantha's life to such a degree. If she wishes to see Cal, then I will hold no objection. He is a friend..."

"A merchant's son is not a suitable friend for the FitzAlcis."

"Then how do you cope with life? You are the grandson of a merchant, Lord Scanlon! You seem merely to be trying to twist perception to bring misery for your daughter. I will not stand by and see that happen. Now, didn't you have some pressing business at Black Hills? If not, I suggest you find some. I've requested you leave before, now I am telling you to. Otherwise, I will get my guards to remove you."

"You wouldn't dare."

"Edward!"

Edward opened the door. Scanlon pushed past him in a rage.

"Yes, Sire?"

"I was going to say that Lord Scanlon is leaving, but it seems I have no need. Warn Maria that he's likely to be upsetting Lady Elantha; if, when he's gone, Her Ladyship wants to see me, I'm free."

* * *

Half an hour later Elantha was announced. Arkyn got up and wrapped her in a hug.

"Is it true I can't see Cal?" she asked.

"No. Your father doesn't wish you to but he won't be here for a while."

"He was so horrible about it."

Arkyn hesitated. "I'm sorry. I probably didn't help. I told him I wasn't going to support his wishes and that he had to leave. I've also told him to leave Oedran."

"Before your coronation? Won't people say he should be there? They said it at the funeral."

"Who did, little flower?"

"I'm not sure. I just heard a couple of the lords saying it. They said that it wasn't right he wasn't there, that Uncle Adeone was his brother."

Arkyn nodded. "The mutterings are better than his presence would be. In time people will understand. Once they do, they'll realise why I don't want him at my coronation, and why father wouldn't have wanted him at the funeral."

"If father's not to be there, am I going to be at the coronation?"

"Yes, you'll be there. Look, shall we forget who your father is between us? You're my family, from which branch doesn't matter. Your father is just an unfortunate complication in empire matters not in our relationship."

She looked up at him. "Are you sure? He said that fathers are always the... the determiner of their daughters' position, or something like that."

"That shows how little he knows us. Will you try to believe me that I don't hold him against you?"

She swallowed. "I can try."

"Good."

"Are you really busy, Arkyn? Phyl and I were going to take a walk around the grounds. Do you want to join us?"

"I'd love to, but how harassed was Edward looking?"

She grinned. "Pretty bad. One day you will come, won't you?"

"Yes. I'll make sure of it."

* * *

Two hours later Edward entered with a small smile on his face. "Lord Scanlon has left for Black Hills, sir. He said, as he obviously wasn't required by the King, he wouldn't dignify Oedran with his presence."

"Those were his exact words?"

"Other than the fact I formalised his reference to you, Sire, yes."

Arkyn let out a long breath. "Thank Alcis for that. I don't suppose he committed treason when referencing me, did he?"

"Unfortunately not, Sire."

"A shame but, until my brother is twenty, we'd still have a problem trying him, I suppose," mused Arkyn. "Did he give any indication of when he'd be back?"

"No, sir. I could contact His Lordship's Administrator and ask."

"No, it's all right; I'll cope with the uncertainty."

Chapter 80
GUARDING DUTIES
Late Afternoon
Inner Office

IN A MEETING WITH the King, Chief Yeoman, General Paturn, the captain of the Palace Guard and the captain of the City Guard, Tain felt like he was drowning in a sea of information. How did people absorb so much? Four people throwing ideas at each other across a table was disorientating. It wasn't easy to determine where the meeting was going and where it had reached.

He caught Arkyn's eye. The King was sitting back listening. A slightly ironic note entered his brother's eye. Everyone had forgotten their presence and Arkyn was waiting to see who would remember it first. As Tain realised, the recriminations started.

Arkyn's face tautened. "Gentlemen, return to the matter in hand. None of us have all day. Paturn, have you picked the regiment for the proceedings before the Dallin Gate?"

General Paturn turned to Arkyn. "Yes, Sire. The elite regiment is returning from Bayan border. They should be here in two days."

"Have you sent their replacement? I'd rather the bandits didn't gain that foothold again."

348

"I have, Sire: a regiment that was here. Your father suggested it at the end of last year."

"Good." Arkyn shifted his attention to the Chief Yeoman. "I want a report on your plans by five tomorrow. I understand there'll be a presence on every road from the Dallin Gate to the Alcium and back to the Palace, but I also want the buildings on the route cleared of people the evening before the coronation and kept like that until the event is over."

Paturn said, "People will not like that, Sire. Tradition dictates—"

"General, I know what tradition dictates. I know that they can watch but it may have escaped your notice that there is still an assassin on the loose, as is Jacobs."

"No, it hadn't, sir, and I doubt it ever would."

Arkyn looked at Paturn's implacable face. "My apologies, General. Prince Tain, you're remarkably quiet; what are your thoughts?"

Tain knew what Arkyn wanted him to say, but he agreed with the General. "There is no precedent for the action that I can recall, Sire."

"You don't agree with it?"

"I wish I could, but I don't see how it can be achieved completely."

The General spoke up, "If someone wants to get into a house there is always a way, Sire. His Highness is right, I'm afraid, the logistics are almost impossible."

Arkyn turned to the others. "Aldhouse, as Chief Yeoman, what are your thoughts?"

"My view is the same, sir."

Arkyn saw there was no point asking the two captains they were both nodding as the Chief Yeoman gave his reply. He was brought out of the preoccupation by Tain saying,

"If anything happens, sir, I, for one, will not rest until we've got to the source of it."

Arkyn caught his eye. There was apprehension ill hidden on his face. Tain met his gaze and Arkyn saw his unease was shared. Arkyn broke the look.

"You'd better all make sure you have enough men on the streets then." He turned to the captain of the City Guard. "Which area are you taking?"

"We're going to be on all the gates and street corners, sir."

"Right. Do you have enough men?"

"For that, sir, yes, but we've no spare."

"Very well. Prince Tain what's happening with the Prince's Guard?"

Peter, there to take notes for Tain, passed the Prince a piece of paper. Tain glanced at it briefly and then put it to one side saying, "You'll be guarded by them from the beginning of the process, to the Alcium. When you leave, the King's Guard will take over."

"Who's guarding you?"

"The same men. There are enough of them, Sire."

Arkyn nodded. "Gentlemen, I'd like to emphasise that, although this is my coronation, if anything happens to His Highness you'll all be looking at retirement a lot earlier than expected."

The General knew the threat was serious, but he raised an ironic eyebrow anyway. He'd been due to retire for a few years. Arkyn simply smiled wryly in acknowledgment of the fact. The smile was wiped from his face as Tain said,

"I, gentlemen, would like to emphasise that it is the King's *coronation* and if anything happens to him, I'll throw every law I can at you. At the moment, I have an academic outlook on the law. I follow it to the letter."

Arkyn chuckled at the look on everyone's faces. Peter was grinning discreetly. Tain had spoken with the passion his administrator recognised as truth but also as nerves. No-one replied, but they understood the message.

* * *

At the end of the meeting, after having gone over the route and details for the procession, Arkyn asked the General to stay and a look kept Tain there as well.

Once the door had closed on everyone else, Arkyn eyed the General. "I'm not happy concerning the situation regarding the buildings lining the route."

"I know, sir but there is no time in which to work it out."

Tain who'd been trying to think of the solution for most of the meeting said, "Sire, you need a canopy. It would stop anything getting at you from above. Also dissuades people from being in the buildings if they can't see you ride past."

"We'd need a reason—" started the General.

"Do we happen to have an aeromancer around?" asked Tain.

"Why?" enquired Arkyn, suspiciously.

"What's the weather likely to be for your coronation?"

"It's summer; so, either sun or rain."

"Right, you're either being protected from getting sunstroke or from being drenched to the skin. Paint it with the heavens and you can claim that it represents our ancestors' protection."

Arkyn's lips twitched. "Who'd carry it?"

"We'll work something out, Sire. Does it meet with your approval?"

Arkyn nodded. "Yes. Maybe the years you spent trying to outmanoeuvre our attendants have been well spent."

"I have my moments. I'll speak to the palace carpenter."

Arkyn said, "Good. Now that's sorted, General, I ought not to keep you from your duties any longer."

"Sire." The General saluted and left.

* * *

Tain's eyes tracked Paturn's retreat. Once the door closed, he said, "Are you all right? You seem on edge."

"I feel like a fraud," admitted Arkyn.

"You are. After all, you're no better than anyone else… Arkyn, you're doing fine."

"Will anyone tell me if I'm not? Would you? Now?"

Tain looked at his brother. "Whatever made you think I'd stop simply because you've become King? Family tradition is hardly on the side of being deferential in these circumstances. Anyway, I did say you were wrong over clearing the route."

"Yes. It was the tact you used that worried me."

"I can be diplomatic you know," muttered Tain.

"First time for everything."

"It must run in the family."

Arkyn sighed. "You always have an answer, don't you?"

"Can't imagine what you mean!"

"I'm sure you can't. What are you doing now?"

"Standing in here talking to you."

"Tain!"

Chapter 81

PREPARATIONS

Early Evening
Outer Office

TAIN LEFT THE INNER OFFICE and stopped for a word with Edward. The administrator's desk showed how busy he was, but, on registering that Tain wanted a word, his face did not.

"How many of the ambassadors have arrived, Edward?"

"All but Serpent Isle, sir. He's due to dock tonight, and should be in Oedran tomorrow morning."

Tain nodded. "Then the King will be at Court tomorrow night. I'll see to arrangements."

Edward hesitated. "Has the King agreed to this, sir?"

"I'm not burdening him even more, Edward. Though, sadly, I'm adding to your load. Issue a full summons for Court, include all the King's Advisors and city officials, even if they've not attended in the last year.

"Very good, sir. Does that include Lord Landis?"

"I'll talk to Doctor Chapa."

* * *

Tain made his way to the Steward's office, where the secretary was rather perturbed by his presence.

"Is the Steward available?"

"He's just talking to the Chamberlain."

Tain said, "Is he?"

Two moments later, after the Chamberlain left, Tain entered the office and sat down. The Steward made to do the same, but Tain raised an admonishing eyebrow.

Pursing his lips, the Steward stood straighter. "Sir, I don't mean to be disrespectful—"

"You'll still manage it. The King will be at Court tomorrow night."

"I've been trying to find out when he'd be there for a few days now. We need a couple of days for preparations…"

"You've had ample warning that our new King would be entering his Court. I could understand your manner if on Cisadai the King had decided to attend Court, but we've been back in Oedran for almost a week." Tain stopped talking and swallowed. "For almost a week. You have had plenty of opportunity to anticipate what is required. If everything isn't right for the King's entry, I'll see he knows where to lay the blame. It will be a test of your stewardship."

"Your Highness, please recall you're not yet of age and therefore—"

"Steward, you're not high enough in favour to get to remind me of anything. I am FitzAlcis, I am the King's Justiciar and I will be making sure King Arkyn is shown the respect due to him. This is not a new concept. Tomorrow night our new King will enter his Court. He's to be greeted by the presiding lord, a banquet is to be held and everyone is to be in sober clothes, the pages and ushers also – their list of wear includes mourning wear before you start to tell me that they might not have it. All ambassadors and lords and ladies in Oedran will be present as well as the King's Advisors and city officials. Liaise with Edward about the summons."

"Who will be the presiding lord, Your Highness?" enquired the Steward. "It should be Lord Landis."

"That you will be told soon." With that Tain left for his own chambers. Once there, he asked Pesky for a link with Doctor Chapa, who studied him carefully.

"Your Highness?"

"I'm fine, doc. How's Uncle Festus?"

352

"Healing well, sir. Are you sure you're fine?"

Tain ignored the question. "Is he able to be up and about yet? Arkyn is going to Court tomorrow; Landis should be the presiding lord."

"No, sir. He's not going to be there for that."

"I thought you said he was healing well."

"He is but not fast enough. He did some damage at the funeral. He'll try to do too much at Court, especially if he's there to greet Arkyn. No, I won't hear of it."

"He'll find out. I've given instruction that every lord and lady over cisan-age is to be there."

Chapa said, "He can find out, sir. My concern is his health and that he's well enough to attend the coronation in line with the King's wishes."

"He'll want to be there tomorrow night, Chapa."

"Yes, he will, but not as presiding lord and not for the whole night."

"You'd let him be there if those conditions were met?" asked Tain.

"I suppose, *unintentionally*, I did say that," replied Chapa dryly.

"Leave it with me. How long can he attend for?"

"A couple of hours, sir."

"Would the banquet be acceptable?" asked Tain.

"Physically, yes, sir, but be aware that mentally he might have some barriers to overcome."

"He won't be the only one."

"I shall be on hand."

Tain swallowed. "Thank you, doc."

* * *

Over dinner, Arkyn said, "Should I be worried by your arrangements?"

"Probably, but you could have faith in me instead," muttered Tain.

"Contrary to what I'm about to say, I have that. I'd like people in full formal wear, including you. Unfortunately, that means your circlet as well for the time being. I'll have to wear mine too."

Tain frowned. "Any chance of a reprieve? I hate the ostentation."

"No. It's there for a reason." Arkyn smiled. "I also want the Greeting Room brought back into use. Not only for tomorrow night. Given events, I need to use every tool to keep the Court in line."

Tain crooked an eyebrow. "Not because you hate entering Court alone?"

Arkyn shrugged. "That as well." He changed the subject. "Rumour is you gave the Steward another dressing down."

"Who told you?" Tain sighed. "Fine. Yes, I did, but I didn't say much."

"Just enough from what I heard. Is Uncle Festus being let out?"

"For the feast only. Lord Iris is presiding."

Arkyn swallowed. "I'll be sitting where father was when…"

353

"Yes," whispered Tain.

"There's no way around it, I'll just have to prepare my mind for it."

"Me as well. I've seen Pixney. Guards will be in every corridor on the side where we know the Viewing Gallery exits. They'll escort the servants through the passages as well. That had already started."

Arkyn said quietly, "It was at my order. Is Cal going to be at Court?"

"Do you want him there?"

"Yes."

* * *

Tain dressed quietly the following evening. Court shouldn't be a chore. He should be looking forward to seeing people, to the semblance of normality. Though it wasn't normal and never could be. He hadn't attended as an official before. He hadn't even attended as a right, only by invitation on specific evenings or feasts. He didn't know everyone but they would know him. Even before setting foot through the gilded doors the clamour, favour seeking and stares were an anathema to his soul. He couldn't avoid it forever though and nor could Arkyn. Whenever they appeared for the first time after recent events it would be the same: nudges, looks and whispers would follow their every move. He had to face it, face the speculation and the hours ahead with grace. There were modes of behaviour expected not just of courtiers. Arkyn's evening would be one of showing favour to those who had remained loyal, to ambassadors, all without causing offence to others. Tain watched his reflection for a moment; without Landis present it would fall to him to control the flow of people around his brother. It should fall to him anyway, but Landis was far more practised at the art.

Robert was waiting patiently with his filigree circlet: the gold and emeralds glinting. Tain closed his eyes. He didn't want its ostentation. It wasn't that he didn't care about his position, it just felt wrong in his bones. The ancestors were richer with souls, he shouldn't be shining. He strapped on his belt. Black leather to match his black tunic and hose. Emerald green banding edged the tunics but against so much black its colour was faded, muted. Maybe the silk had been dyed darker. He didn't want to examine it to find out. He wanted the evening to be over. Catching Robert's eye, he realised his manservant was waiting for a comment.

"It's nothing good getting me through the situations at the moment, Robert, it's simply a form of rage."

"Rage is underrated, sir, but you've more composure than you realise."

Tain sighed. "I'm not convinced."

"Then don't question what it is, sir, simply accept it and try not to lose your heart to a locked box."

354

Tain shook his head. "The operation would be tricky." He settled his belt more securely. The dagger and sword weighed him down, but they were as necessary as the circlet for showing rank. He glanced down.

"Get me a different buckle, Robert. I don't want the gold."

Robert hesitated. "Master Kadeem—"

"I asked for a different buckle, not an explanation," snapped Tain feeling sick. Robert was doing his job.

The manservant gave a slight bow, his face a blank. Had Arkyn passed on a message to Robert through Kadeem? It wasn't improbable, but they'd discussed dress the previous evening. Maybe Kadeem had just been helping Robert find the right outfit. His new manservant wouldn't know all the protocols and expectations yet.

His manservant had left the circlet on a table. Tain eyed it. Why did it rile him so much? It was a circle of gold, striking against his black hair it was true, but just a piece of metal.

Robert was hovering. "There are no dark buckles, sir."

Tain cursed. "Fine, leave it, but get one made please." How was it he didn't have one dull buckle? He glanced back at the circlet. That was how, that was why. His ancestors had a lot to answer for.

"May I...?" Robert waved at the circlet.

There was no escaping it. Once he wore that circlet, he would be his ancestors, what they had wanted their descendants to be. He collapsed onto a chair. His head in his hands.

Robert's eyes were on him. The manservant's concern crawled over his skin. The dressing room door opened and shut. Robert had left.

Tain rubbed at his face. He didn't have the time for this sort of angst. Taking a deep breath he stood, faced himself in the mirror and reached for the circlet. It was time to become the official, the King's right hand, the Prince of Oedran, the Justiciar, not the boy from Ceardlann acting a part.

The circlet settled on his head with an oddly reassuring weight. It didn't crush him as he thought it might. The expectations on him might though.

He left the dressing room to find Robert waiting patiently with his mantle. He let the manservant arrange the split rectangle of fabric over his shoulders and drape it formally from his right shoulder to his left, pinning it in place with a badge of office, a golden tree in a circle. More gold. More opulence. More reminders.

"Thank you, Robert. I'll expect you in hall."

"Of course, sir. Good luck, Your Highness."

* * *

Tain entered Arkyn's chambers without waiting for a footman to announce him. He didn't need announcing to his brother. There would be days,

355

weeks, years ahead when they couldn't avoid it but he didn't want to lose every bit of their relationship to their positions. He still needed to observe formalities with others present but, as they weren't, he'd remain himself.

Entering the sitting room, his plan was shattered. Kadeem was entering from the servant's door. Had Robert alerted him? Either way it forced formality. Tain caught Arkyn's eye and bowed, then caught the cushion that came flying towards him. He clutched its softness to him.

Arkyn crossed to him and pulled him into an enveloping hug. One they both needed. Fragile and friable. The evening had to happen but neither of them wanted it.

Arkyn said, "I'm meant to be the one with nerves."

"I didn't know there was a monopoly on nerves."

"Do you think it would help?"

"No. Kadeem's holding your mantle."

"Practicality doesn't suit you."

Tain watched as Kadeem walked forward with his brother's mantle. His own felt odd. Like the circlet and sword though, it gave them standing. Kadeem moved round to check how the black and scarlet shot silk hung at Arkyn's back. Tain caught his eye. Quietly the manservant held out a black buckle. Swallowing, Tain took it with a nod and sad smile. Whilst Kadeem continued to fuss, Tain swapped the buckles over. It was a small thing in the wealth of other details but he felt easier in his mind. If Arkyn noticed, he didn't say anything. Tain left the gold buckle on an occasional table. Kadeem would sort it with his normal practicality.

When his manservant stepped back with a quick nod, to show he'd finished, Arkyn turned to Tain. "Shall we get this over?"

Tain bit his lip. "It feels too soon."

Arkyn squeezed his shoulder. "Even if I don't do a formal speech, I must be seen to welcome the ambassadors. Do you want to make your entrance another day?"

Tain wanted to say yes. His mind screamed out the answer but his lips wouldn't voice it. He noticed Kadeem's stance. Slightly turned towards Arkyn wasn't strange but the worry was.

Tain studied his brother's face, instinct giving way to reason. If Arkyn could face it, he would.

"Why would I ever want to forgo this experience? We'll face the horde together, sir."

"Let's hope they're ready for the experience," muttered Arkyn, pulling Tain to his feet.

Chapter 82

COURT

THEY ENTERED the Greeting Room of Court without having spoken during the walk there. They both knew what faced them. Arkyn's gaze swept around the room. The tiled floor was no different to most of Court. The walls, adorned with pictures of his ancestors and vistas of the empire, made a statement that couldn't be misinterpreted. Power was in this room, in who was invited to be there. Arkyn's gaze swept over the two dozen or so individuals congregated: his family, nearfamily, Cal, Lords Iris, Fairson, Rale, Ryson and Faran, Idris and Irvin Iris, and thirteen impeccably dressed ambassadors. Iris as presiding lord knelt as Arkyn entered. Everyone else present except for Tain, Lady Rhian and Lady Neassa followed his example.

Arkyn took a deep breath. "You may rise, my lords and ladies."

He glanced around the room again. Cal was still kneeling. Arkyn crooked an eyebrow. Lips twitching, Cal gave him a look that said that he didn't class as a lord and certainly not as a lady. Arkyn returned one which said Cal had better get back to his feet. Cal did so but the look he gave Arkyn wasn't amused, it was supportive.

Arkyn turned his attention back to Lord Iris who pretended he hadn't seen the exchange.

"Thank you, Iris. Is everything ready?"

"Yes, sir. Shall I…?" He motioned to the door into Court.

"Please. I shall be in the FitzAlcis Chamber shortly."

Iris bowed and left. Arkyn crossed to the ambassadors, passing a few words of conversation with each. Had they settled in? He hoped that Court wouldn't be too onerous. Did they all know each other? Had they recovered from their journeys? Had they spoken with his governors to let them know of their safe arrival in Oedran?

He tried not to concentrate too much on who the men were. Certain of his Representatives hadn't thought particularly hard about the appointments. If they had, they'd have realised that just because he'd met a lord before didn't mean he wanted to see them again. They all had their roles to fill though and as long as they followed his expectations, they would be welcome at Court. He wasn't yet secure enough to ask for changes in ambassadors, however tempted he might be. Lady Phylicia didn't seem at all perturbed by her place amongst them.

He spoke quietly to the Lords of Oedran, thanking them for attending, and had crossed for a word with his nearcousins and friends when the door opened and his great-aunt entered. He glanced over and, in that glance, spotted knowing looks between the ambassadors. They expected him to show displeasure that she hadn't been present to greet him. Arkyn's inner thoughts were the exact opposite.

He smiled warmly as he moved to join her. "Perfect timing, aunt." He held out his arm.

She caught his eye, amused, and linked her arm through his. "Glad to oblige, Sire. I thought it would be crowded if I came too soon. Rhian and Neassa are about here somewhere."

Her daughters walked forward from the corner they'd been occupying. Rhian's pallor made the white marble surfaces colourful.

Arkyn held out his hand to her, forgetting the assembled dignitaries behind him. "Can I help, cousin?"

She shook her head.

Amara watched them with knowing eyes. "You could let her face the hall another day, sir."

Rhian swallowed, closing her eyes. The truth of the statement clear.

Arkyn grasped her hand. "Cousin?"

She took a deep breath. Her eyes flew open. "I will face it tonight, Sire, with the rest of my family."

He searched her face. The FitzAlcis strength ran in Rhian. It might have been tempered by Fairson calm but it was there.

"Then we'll enter as a family."

Tain said, in a voice to carry, "Make way for King Arkyn."

Arkyn entered the wider Court with his aunt beside him and Tain a slight step behind. His cousins a step behind that and then the Lords of Oedran, ambassadors and everyone else rearranging themselves in a semblance of precedence. He knew without looking that Cal would have waited until last.

* * *

The Anapara Room wasn't busy, but Arkyn spotted a welcome face. "Merchant Chapa, join me."

The former Chief Merchant of Oedran, cousin of Doctor Chapa and Arkyn's late grandmother, bowed before crossing to join the procession. His quick gaze evaluated the order, he caught Arkyn's eye.

"Where would my king like me?"

"I'm sure you know your place in my heart."

Amara's lips twitched. "Henry Chapa, behave yourself."

Arkyn winked and moved forward. Merchant Chapa chuckled to himself but much as Tain tried to motion him to join the family group, he waited until the lords had passed. He fell into step with Cal.

358

"You must be the Galdwin I'm hearing so much about."

Cal hesitated. "I can't answer that without knowing what you've heard, Merchant Chapa. There are a few of us."

"True. How are you?" asked Merchant Chapa watching Arkyn and Tain.

Cal hesitated. The merchant wasn't asking how he was, he was asking how his friends were. "Better than expected in the circumstances."

They exchanged a knowing glance as Arkyn, Amara and Tain entered the FitzAlcis Chamber to a fanfare of trumpets.

Arkyn crossed to the centre of the room, under the stained-glass dome, with his companions fanning out behind him. Lord Iris was waiting. As Arkyn reached the centre of the room, he knelt, head bowed. As one, all the lords, ladies, merchants and officials in the room followed suit, leaving Arkyn standing with Lady Amara and Tain at his side, Rhian and Nessa remained standing. The Court was the King's, but family weren't presented.

Arkyn held out his hand to Iris. The elderly Lord of Oedran took it and kissed the signet ring.

"Your servant, Sire. Your Court awaits your pleasure."

"It is my pleasure to welcome you to it. Please rise."

Lord Iris did so. When he was back on his feet, everyone else rose.

Arkyn said in a voice loud enough to carry, "My brother Prince Tain is hereby recognised to be my heir, let this Court show him due respect."

Tain knelt. "I am nothing but my King's servant here."

Arkyn held out his hand and when Tain kissed the signet ring said, "You are far more than that, Prince Tain." He applied a slight pressure and Tain got back to his feet. The King turned to Lord Iris. "For my Court, do you recognise Prince Tain as my heir?"

"I do, Sire." The Lord of Oedran faced Tain and, with precision, bowed. "Your Highness, may the King never want for your support."

Tain said, "The King should never be in want of anyone's support."

Arkyn gave a slight nod. "Lord Iris, we shall continue."

As Arkyn started his walk around Court, Tain went to follow. From behind him, he heard their great-aunt say,

"Lady Phylicia, you've met my daughters…"

He smiled to himself. If Phyl could survive an evening at Court in Lady Amara's company, then she'd handle the snake pit with ease. The other ambassadors and lords were splitting into groups. Tain's gaze swept around the room. Lord Idris Iris was talking with two ladies he didn't recognise, Irvin and Indria Iris were nearby talking with the Landis siblings. He ignored the heirs of the exiled lords. They weren't there for anything other than convention. Maybe they should have banned the families from attending Court at the same time as exiling the lords. Shame he hadn't thought about it at the time.

* * *

Cal watched his friends leave and everyone rearrange themselves. Merchant Chapa didn't seem keen to rejoin the other merchants, so Cal stayed talking with him. He'd heard enough about the merchant to feel like he knew him, and it seemed that was reciprocated. They shared stories of mutual acquaintances, walking slowly around the rooms of Court.

Merchant Chapa let Cal lead, and where they went intrigued him. "Are you shadowing them for a reason?"

Cal pulled a wry face. "Maybe it's habit, but the King wished me to be present this evening. So, I thought staying within sight was wiser."

"Stranger things have been known." Merchant Chapa followed Cal's eyeline. It was fixed on Arkyn and Tain but not in the same way others would look at them. He was checking if they were coping, not looking for an opening or trying to get their attention. "Ever thought about just walking up to them and asking?"

Cal blushed. "Sorry, Merchant Chapa. I'm not practised at this."

"You will be. It does take time. Then you have to remember how to be in private."

"I might survive that experience better. I'll miss Ceardlann."

Merchant Chapa squeezed his shoulder. "I doubt it'll— Seems you're wanted. Go on, I'll find someone else to annoy."

Cal smiled slightly. "I've enjoyed our talk, Merchant Chapa." He crossed to Tain's side. "Sir?"

"Is Merchant Chapa looking after you?"

"He was, Your Highness."

"What did your father say?"

"Not much, sir: officially, I'm currently in bed."

Tain turned his snort into a cough. When Arkyn looked round, Cal bowed and returned the King's smile. When Arkyn resumed his discussion with Lords Galaloth and Aldwy, everyone else in the room was watching Cal and Tain.

Cal said, "Oops, it looks like I'm still the unknown and therefore interesting one here tonight. How will I live with the notoriety, sir?"

"I'm sure if not living with it is your ambition it could be arranged."

"Your Highness' concern for my welfare overwhelms me."

"Courtier!"

"I try, sir. I wouldn't want all of Spellen's tutelage wasted. Would you advise me to mingle?" enquired Cal, knowing Tain's attention should be elsewhere.

Tain turned to an usher. "Ask Lord Julius Landis to join us please."

Julius appeared and took in Cal's presence. "Is he already causing trouble, Your Highness?"

Tain took note of everyone else around them. "Lord Julius, would you mind introducing Cal to a few people? I'm a bit busy this evening."

"Certainly, Your Highness. Come on, Cal, we should be able to increase your notoriety."

Tain groaned but went to join Arkyn who, in a brief lull, said, "Is Cal all right?"

"Yes – Julius should be looking after him, Sire."

"That's a good thing?"

* * *

Julius steered Cal away from the FitzAlcis. Cal hesitated but didn't make any demurral. Once they were relatively private, Julius clapped him on the back.

"You'll cope, Cal. Come on, you know most of the people I'm talking to. If they've not wandered off."

"Why would they ever avoid Your Lordship?"

Julius snorted. "I should never have doubted your ability to find the apt observation. Given two of them are my sisters, I can think of several reasons."

Cal chuckled. "Maybe Lord Irvin will— My apologies, my lord. I didn't see you." He'd collided with a young lord wearing the double narrow stripe of the heir to a Lord of Oedran, the same as Julius wore. The narrow strip of lesser lords gave them the slang-name of narrs on the streets of Oedran. The Lords of Oedran were *wides* due to the wider stripe of their formal wear. For some reason the slang came into Cal's mind as the young man looked him up and down with a sneer, before walking off with an expression that suggested he'd smelt something foul.

Julius snorted. "That's Kenelm Para. Don't feel like you have to apologise to him. No-one would care if you tripped him up."

"He would, I suspect," said Cal. "Anyway, he purposefully walked into me. I expect it was to see how I'd handle it."

Julius snorted. "He's a worm."

They were passing two ambassadors deep in conversation. Cal couldn't help but hear their discussion.

"It needs fixing. If the Satrap won't take action—"

"His Excellency is gathering the facts. It's on the town to sort it out—"

"If they were doing so, that would be a different matter—"

Arkyn or Tain would doubtless have asked what it was about, but he couldn't. Their badges of office denoted Denshire and Tradere, but that didn't tell him what they were discussing. Julius didn't seem to have heard them at all. Was that normal? He supposed it must be. Court was known to be a boiling pot of gossip and intrigue. Maybe if everyone heard everything it would send them mad. To him it sounded important but maybe it was normal, just another passing comment, dissection of a situation that didn't mean much in the vastness of the empire.

Julius was crossing to where the Landis and Iris siblings were talking with Lord Rale. Cal inclined his head to the young Lord of Oedran.

Finian grinned. "Evening, Cal. Couldn't you escape Julius' clutches?"

"His Highness thought to keep us both out of mischief together, my lord," replied Cal. "I believe he wanted Lord Julius to introduce me to a few people. I'm sure he'll get around to it eventually."

Everyone laughed.

Julius was the picture of injured innocence. "If I might have a chance, I will with pleasure. You obviously know Lord Rale, my sisters, you probably remember Lord Irvin, so might I introduce Calumiel Galdwin to you, Lady Indria?"

Irvin's sister smiled. "It's a pleasure to meet you, Master Calumiel. I've heard much about you from our companions."

Cal wished he could say the same. "It's a pleasure to meet you, my lady. I hope you're having a pleasant evening."

"It's always nice to meet new people," said Indria shyly.

Julia chuckled. "Cal's night will be brilliant by that measure. Where are my nearcousins, Cal?"

"In the Tradere Room last I knew, my lady. How's Lord Landis?"

As talk turned Cal tried to concentrate on his companions but his eyes were roaming around the room. He saw individuals congregating but his mind registered something else, an undercurrent of tension. Everyone was waiting. When he'd attended on Munewid Eve he'd been with Elantha, a slight step removed. He and El had joined Court only for the feast. When he'd attended for the banquet to mark Tain's investiture, he'd mostly kept to himself and talked with Elantha and Tain. He hadn't truly been in the midst of courtiers before. He was both fascinated and terrified.

* * *

Around half past eight by the Court Clock, an usher nervously approached Prince Tain. Tain looked at him questioningly and the man said,

"Lord Landis and Doctor Chapa have arrived, Your Highness."

"Thank you. Ask them to wait in the FitzAlcis Chamber." Tain crossed to Arkyn. "Sire, Lord Landis and the doc are here."

Arkyn glanced at him. "Thank you."

Two minutes later, they entered the central chamber. Landis moved to meet them, timing his steps so they met almost under the central dome. He knelt, as Iris had, took Arkyn's hand and kissed the King's signet ring. Supporting Landis more than it appeared, Arkyn helped him back to his feet, saying to the room at large,

"A chair for Lord Landis."

"No, Sire, I shall stand whilst my King does," stated Landis.

"And a chair for the King," requested Tain. He glanced at his brother and nearfather. "Simple solutions are often the most effective."

"I wasn't aware a solution was needed, Your Highness. Lord Landis was going to sit down at my instruction."

"Sire, I never would sit whilst my liege stands: tradition dictates." As soon as he said it, Landis sighed with resignation and mouthed as Tain replied,

"Traditions can be changed."

Arkyn laughed. "Well, whatever the outcome it seems we both get the chance to take the weight off our feet. Lord Landis, are you comfortable?"

Landis wincing said, "In my liege's presence I am always comfortable."

Arkyn looked at him and raised an eyebrow slightly.

"Yes, Sire, thank you."

Half an hour later, the Steward announced that the banquet was ready and Arkyn got up. Lord Landis, aware of how carefully Arkyn had been skirting the issue of Adeone's death during their talk whitened slightly and stayed where he was.

The King said, "Landis?"

"Might I be excused the hall, Sire?"

Arkyn glanced at Tain and then at Doctor Chapa who simply shook his head slightly. "We all have to face it, my lord, I would appreciate your support."

"Then lead the way, sir." When Arkyn turned away, Landis closed his eyes and pushed himself to his feet. An arm supported him. He opened his eyes. "Your Highness?"

"There is more than one type of support, my lord," stated Tain.

"Maybe so, sir, but given events it is not right for Your Highness to support me."

"Uncle Festus, don't talk nonsense. It's either me or Doctor Chapa."

Lord Landis winced. "I'm caught between magic and the explosion."

Tain said softly, "We are at Court, Lord Landis."

Landis glanced at him. "My apologies, Your Highness."

"They are accepted. Come on, you're on the King's left."

Landis swallowed. "No, it's not right. Iris has taken my duties tonight."

"Lord Iris insisted. The King wasn't of the mind to object."

* * *

Tain delivered Lord Landis to the dais before taking his own place on Arkyn's right. Arkyn took a deep breath before sitting down, steadfastly trying to ignore the memories, conjectures and imagination taking over. He concentrated on everyone entering the hall and taking their places. Once they were all settled, instead of immediately opening the banquet, Arkyn got back to his feet, motioning for everyone else to stay seated.

He said, "A week ago tonight events in this hall were such that they'll never be forgotten. I sit now where King Adeone did; many of you were present as he died at the hands of an assassin. That assassin is yet to be caught, and I would ask if any have knowledge of who he was, they inform my office. If accusations are made without foundation and with malicious intent, there will be repercussions. Munewid Eve saw many attacks on men and women of importance throughout this empire and the perpetrators are all being sought and will face justice when discovered. I have heard murmurings that it is wrong that Lord Scanlon was not at my father's funeral and has left Oedran; I would ask that he is left alone with his feelings at his brother's murder." Arkyn took a breath and continued, "There is one man whose contribution to events I have not been able to mark." He turned to his nearfather. "Lord Landis, I have heard reports of how you sought to protect King Adeone with your own body, how you were injured in that pursuit and I have seen the effect of your wound. You have my thanks for your action and I would ask that this Court give you due honour for it. My lords, ladies and gentlemen here present, please raise your glasses in a toast to Lord Landis for his selfless action."

As the refrain of the toast died away Lord Landis said simply, "Sire, my thanks but I didn't do enough. I would like to tender my resignation as your Defender."

Arkyn's erratic temper boiled within him but he controlled it with a skill that impressed Tain.

"Lord Landis, I do not accept. You are my Defender. Let it be known throughout the empire."

"I am ever my liege's to command," stated Landis without emotion.

Arkyn sat down and, with a flick of his hand, opened the feast. His face was such a careful blank that Tain was worried.

"Are you all right, Sire?"

Arkyn glanced sideways at him and then turned to their nearfather. "Why on Erinna did you do that, Landis?"

"I failed to save him, Sire; it is not the action of a true Defender."

Aware the whole Court were watching, barely above a whisper, Arkyn said, "I'm going to say this once, Uncle Festus: I know father told you, I know what he bound you to do and not do, and you still tried to save his life so *don't* tell me you're not a true Defender. Do you understand?"

"Your wish is my command, sir."

Arkyn said, "And now answer my question, please."

"I understand your words but cannot reconcile them with my feelings. In time I may, Sire."

"Then we shall none of us mention it again. You're my Defender, Uncle Festus, get used to the idea."

Landis inclined his head, wincing.

"How much pain are you actually in?" enquired Arkyn kindly.

"A not inconsiderable amount, Sire, but it will pass. I'm sure whiskey or wine will help."

"It may, but I'd rather see if the doc has anything better for it. Kadeem!"

Two minutes later Lord Landis took the painkiller Chapa passed him.

"Did you notice Lord Kenelm?" murmured Tain to Arkyn.

Arkyn looked at his brother before glancing around the King's Hall for Lord Para's heir. "No, why?"

"He didn't observe the toast."

"Sicla. What do you think I should do?"

"You've only my word for it," pointed out Tain.

Arkyn said, "Not quite." He turned to the servers. "Kadeem, please ask Lord Irvin to join me."

Irvin Iris received the message, glanced at the dais, caught the King's eye and got to his feet. He made a slight bow before walking up the dais steps and along the back of the dais until he was beside Arkyn's chair, once there he knelt.

Arkyn sighed. "Get up, my lord; your grandfather is a bad influence."

Iris watched his grandson and the King carefully. Unless asked to he wasn't going to comment on the observation. He'd learned where those lines were many years ago when he'd crossed one.

"Did Lord Kenelm partake in the toast?" enquired Arkyn.

Irvin resisted the impulse to look at Kenelm. "No, Sire."

"He didn't miss the moment?" After Irvin shook his head, Arkyn asked, "How are you so certain, my lord?"

"He actually said 'not likely', Sire," admitted Irvin.

"Thank you, my lord, that's all. Kadeem…"

As Irvin left, Kadeem stepped forward. "Yes, sir?"

"Ask the Steward to join me please."

Conscious of his diminished credibility, the Steward knelt when he reached Arkyn – thereby, unintentionally, making the Court aware of it.

"Lord Kenelm Para has a ban on attending Court until Imperadai. Please see he leaves immediately," said Arkyn decidedly.

"Very good, Sire. I will need to record the reason."

"Insulting behaviour and failing to follow my requests."

Arkyn watched out of the corner of his eye as Lord Kenelm was told of his ban. The young man made a predictable fuss in leaving.

Landis said, "I'm truly not worth the trouble, Sire."

"I'll decide that, Landis. Don't forget, he had insulted me as well."

"Then three days is surely not enough, Sire."

Arkyn sighed. "Are you looking for ways to be awkward tonight?"

"No, sir, they just seem to be finding me."

Arkyn chuckled. "Then I hope you can lose them as easily."

Tain listening with half an ear heard his brother's amusement. Part of him was glad, glad that even for a moment his brother had forgotten where he was sitting. He couldn't though. Couldn't forget. His eyes flicked to the Viewing Gallery. Had his father seen the bolt that took his life? Had he watched a shadowy figure take aim? He closed his eyes. He didn't want to see the hall, or imagine that night.

From beside him a soothing voice said, "Deep breaths, young Tailan."

He steadied his breathing, before whispering his thanks to his great-aunt. Had his distress been obvious? Would he be judged for it? Did he care if he was? Not particularly. The mood throughout the hall was subdued, and not all who had been at Court were there for the banquet. They had slipped quietly away. Maybe they were also fighting memories.

Chapter 83

TERA

Evening

Terasia – Tera – Margrave's Residence

THAT EVENING Wealsman's coach rattled into the courtyard of the Margrave's Residence and discharged its load. Having directed the driver to the stables and to find a meal and bed, Wealsman entered the Residence and smiled as his wife came towards him.

She said, "You're looking better than I expected."

"Arkyn thought I needed taking care of. I've had an envoy coach."

"Yes, on that note he's contacted me and Ernst. I'm—"

"No, don't tell me. I really need to find a way of bribing Fafnir."

Kristina ignored him. "I'm to see you have a good night's sleep, and Ernst is to make sure you manage a relaxed day tomorrow."

Wealsman muttered more to himself than Kristina, "Definitely devious."

She continued with, "You can see Adeona and Vian tomorrow, I'm not having you wake them now. I hope you weren't commenting on Arkyn…"

On reaching their private rooms, Kristina said, "How was your trip?"

Wealsman told her. When he reached the events at Border Lodge, her blood ran cold.

"You see that's why Adeone insisted you had guards—"

"I can take care of myself."

"So could he and it didn't—" she bit back the rest of her thoughts.

Percival said softly, "I'm sorry. You were right, you always are." He hunted for a change of subject. "I passed Lord Teran on my way back. We happened to be at the same lodge for a few minutes. He's not happy."

"Good. I hope when he arrives, he'll be even worse."

Percival sighed. "I can only act within the terms of his exile, love."

"Is that all Adeone deserves?"

"No, and you know it, but I have to let others make the point overtly. Arkyn's done what he can. If I did what I wanted, Teran would never breathe past our first proper meeting, but I can't do that. I'll not have him enter this Residence after the first meeting, and, having watched his ego, I'll keep him and Silvano apart."

"That'll be hard, they're kinakin."

"Just because their children are married doesn't mean they have to see each other. Penrod is Arkyn's ward as he was Adeone's. Chandra was so relieved to leave her father's house I can't see that she'll want cosy nights with him. No. I'll make my feelings plain, but I can't expel him from Tera."

Kristina sat down next to her husband. "I'm sorry, I'm so sorry, Percival."

Wealsman hugged her to him as he understood the reason for her words. "He left me his chess set."

She squeezed his hand. "Then you'll have to teach us to play."

He kissed the top of her head. "Bless you for that. You know, he stopped my nightmares, years ago, when he first came here; he talked them out of me when I was drained by them one day, wouldn't let it go, knew he could help. I've never suffered since. I never quite thanked him for that."

She pulled him to his feet. "Yes, you did. Some thanks are portrayed by more than words. You're maudlin tired: come on, bed."

"I don't want to sleep."

"No, but you can talk as easily there."

He did. By the time he'd relaxed, and the memories were flowing, so were silent tears for his lost friend. Kristina held him until they dropped to sleep, privately glad the grief was manifesting itself.

Chapter 84
FEALTIES

WHEN TAIN ENTERED the Outer Office the following morning, Rayburn was already waiting. The advisor was talking quietly with Edward, going over Arkyn's diary. It struck Tain in that moment how much had changed. Not Richardson, Edward. Not Landis, Rayburn. He hadn't even consciously acknowledged that. The obvious change – his brother, not his father – yes, he'd acknowledged that, but so much else had altered and he'd been too immured by grief and anger to notice, to acknowledge, to accept.

The moment the secretaries got to their feet, Edward and Rayburn broke off their conversation. The weight of the previous night descended onto his shoulders again. He had to be the official, especially when it came to a meeting discussing fealties, the procedures and protocols. He was now recognised formally as his brother's heir.

Tain said, "Are you delegating *anything*, Rayburn?"

Rayburn replied smoothly, "Of course, Your Highness, but the King expects my presence as his advisor."

Tain let that pass with a nod. "Edward, is anyone else due?"

"Lord Iris, Your Highness, to represent Lord Landis."

"Then we'll wait for him. Rayburn, correct me if I'm wrong, but I presume you'll be here to brief the King about the coronation banquet?"

"Of course, Your Highness, with the Steward."

"What time are you retiring at night?"

Rayburn smiled. "When my day's work is done, sir, as for everyone at the moment."

* * *

Two minutes later, Arkyn looked up as they were announced. "Morning, Prince Tain, Lord Iris, Advisor Rayburn. We'll use one of the tables. Thank you, Edward." Once seated, the King said, "Fealty Swear, I believe."

Lord Iris said, "Yes, sir. It's not as daunting as it may seem, Sire."

"Not for you, maybe, my lord, but you're not the focus of attention and have attended how many?"

"Just your father's, sir. My father was alive for the coronation of King Altarius, although he died during the rebellion the year after."

Arkyn hesitated. "I didn't realise that, my lord. I'm sorry."

"Thank you, Sire, but it was many years ago. I obviously swore fealty when I became head of my family and then with your father's coronation."

"Of course. Rayburn, maybe you could explain the event to us."

Rayburn said, "Certainly, Sire. The Fealty Swear will be held after lunch on the day of your coronation. Whilst you lunch, sir, all the lords currently in Oedran and the immediate lands will be gathering in the Audience Chamber. The order drawn up will be those Lords of Oedran who are of age, the ambassadors, Lords of Provinces, any more minor lords and then anyone who has requested to swear fealty. Unless, you wish otherwise, Sire, Lady Amara has pointed out that by then you'll be crowned and she doesn't necessarily see her presence as required—"

"How exactly did Her Ladyship phrase that, Rayburn?" asked Arkyn, his lips twitching.

Rayburn swallowed. "Must I, sir?"

Arkyn's eyes gleamed. "I think I would like my Protector's actual words." If nothing else he needed a laugh.

"Erm, Her Ladyship said she'd witnessed enough fools swear fealty and being on her feet for long periods isn't good for her at her age."

Arkyn snorted. "I shall accept her decision. Though I will add I do not think all my vassals are fools. So, that's the order of precedence then."

"Yes, sir. As heads of their families, it is then accepted that others in their families have also sworn fealty. For example, Lord Iris, if I may, Your Lordship swears fealty for all your family, Lord Idris and Lord Irvin are not required to individually swear fealty, though they may ask to. The fealty you swear at a coronation binds your family."

Arkyn asked, "Is that recognised in law?"

Prince Tain, feeling strange but slowly getting more used to his official life, said simply, "It is, Sire."

"Completely?"

"Yes, sir. When the head of the family dies and his heir takes up the mantle of *the* lordship, as Lord Iris has said, fealty is renewed but until then the younger lords of a family are bound by the fealty of the oldest."

Arkyn said, "Very well but exactly how? I mean, if someone swears fealty at my coronation it is truth-binding, so are you saying every male member of their family is also bound in truth to the King?"

"Yes, Sire."

"What if they have more children after that?"

Tain said, "The same applies, sir."

"What if I request a greater fealty, say honour-binding?"

Tain said, "My understanding is that is bound to the person only, sir. Honour, speech and life-binds are very powerful and therefore different rules apply."

Arkyn mulled that over. "If I were to ask someone for one of those, would the rest of their family still be bound in fealty?"

Tain said, "Through convention, yes, Sire."

"But not law?"

Tain hesitated. "That could have lawyers arguing for a long time."

Lord Iris said, "Sire, is there any particular person in mind?"

"No, it's merely the logical progression of thought. We might as well continue before I take a simple meeting into depths never before plumbed out of curiosity."

Rayburn said smoothly, "Sire, you need to feel comfortable with the concepts involved; it is no problem to explain them."

"You have explained, I am just taking things too far."

"Sir. The Lords of Oedran, as I have said, swear fealty on your coronation day, along with lords from the immediate hinterland of Oedran. Men of standing can petition to, but there has only been one to do so, the Chief Merchant – will you accept his petition?"

Arkyn considered for a moment before saying, "I will."

"Thank you, Sire. Now this year the procedure is slightly more problematic because of the exile of the Lords of Oedran who signed the Assassination Document. You have already taken their renewed oath but there must still be confirmation of fealty on your coronation day, before that they were swearing fealty to an uncrowned king."

"What difference does that make?"

Tain said simply, "It means that if anything happens before your coronation their fealties are not bound to your heirs, Sire."

"The fealty wording is the same."

"When you are crowned the significance changes, you are King Absolute; you have sworn your own oaths to the empire and therefore the fealty is two-way. Until then it is an understanding that you will make your vows that exists, and it is to that understanding fealty is sworn. Once you are King Absolute then the significance changes. Before the empire existed, the new king was crowned directly his father died, at the latest a day later. That amount of time left no space for ambiguity. With the empire, especially in the early years, the heir to the crown could be many miles away and there was normally a longer gap. He was acknowledged as king by proclamation but his actual crowning was later. The fealties as we know them are older than the empire; they were in existence during the Age of the Cearcall and as such are designed with the fact that there is a King Absolute on the throne and no space between death and coronation. The laws that govern fealty have never been properly updated to reflect the fact that there is a gap."

"Prince Tain, I publicly acknowledged you as my heir last night. Are you saying that what I did wasn't legal?"

Tain shook his head, "No, Sire, I'm not, it was. I'm saying that no man currently owes me direct allegiance as your heir, only as father's heir presumptive. If I wasn't father's heir presumptive then your pronouncement would be legal but not binding on your vassals... In three days, all this becomes academic, sir. Do you really want me to go into the legalities?"

"No. Just over a week ago it was academic and yet you seem to know a lot about it."

Rayburn said, "His Highness knows more than I do, Sire."

Tain said, "I found the laws intriguing, and had the best authority on ancient law as my mentor."

Without irony, Arkyn said, "He'd have been very proud. If the exiled Lords of Oedran need to renew their oath to a crowned king, surely I have to recall them."

Rayburn looked at Lord Iris, then the King. "I think I'll just defer to His Highness, Sire, I may learn something myself."

Arkyn chuckled. "Prince Tain?"

"You don't need to recall them, Sire. It is quite simple; you add the phrase 'For all your family' to the fealty swear. It was common when lords were in the army subduing newly conquered provinces, or aiding their integration I should say."

Arkyn said, "Right. Have you anything else to add?"

Tain said, "A couple of points, sir."

"Should I ask what?" enquired his brother with a sense of foreboding.

Tain looked at him. "Advisor Rayburn said only one person, who isn't a lord, had asked permission to swear fealty. I have a request from one other and I also have a request for myself."

"What request?"

Tain pursed his lips. His brother wouldn't take the requests calmly. "Cal and I wish to swear fealty."

"Your Highness is not required to," stated Rayburn hastily.

"I rather think he knows that," commented Arkyn dryly. He looked at Tain; he'd never considered the idea before. "Lord Iris, Advisor Rayburn, leave us for a moment please."

Without a word they left, Rayburn once more kneeling as he did so.

Once the door closed, Arkyn looked at Tain. "Is there any law to stop Rayburn kneeling?"

"No, sorry, Sire. There may be one for quite the opposite though. Why did you ask them to leave?"

"You don't have to swear fealty, Tain. You'll be doing enough and more by crowning me..."

"As you said, I'm aware of that. Arkyn, you're King, you're my brother and I want people to see I recognise both sides of that relationship. I'm not going to plot and scheme, I'm not going to accept anyone else as King whilst you're alive and I won't try to usurp you. So, before anyone gets any ideas, I'd like to make my decision public, but it's more than that; I'm asking because I believe in what I'll swear. I'll mean every word."

"I can't even use the argument that you don't know what you're doing, can I? You're only fifteen—"

"I am crowning you, Sire, and, if you want to argue the responsibilities appertaining to a person born alunan, might I send for Peter to explain that actually we're not? And if you want to use my age, I'll just point out you took El's fealty and she's younger."

"Tain, have you found an answer to every objection I could make?"

"Carry on objecting and we'll see. Please, don't block me on this. I know what I'm doing and there are more sides to this than I've explained."

"Such as?" asked Arkyn, eyes narrowed. Tain was devious, but this wasn't mischief, there was no light to his voice, no spark of anticipation in his eye. His certainty was dumbfounding.

"If I swear fealty – as your brother, Justiciar and heir – no-one else can refuse to for the duration of your reign, no-one, Arkyn."

Defeated, Arkyn absorbed that. "So be it. Thank you. As for Cal..."

"He's as determined as I am, Arkyn."

"Damn. I didn't want that obligation in the friendship."

"Come on, do you think that it will make any difference? It's not as though he's ever truly dropped the formality, is it? He's acted like he's bound for years."

Arkyn sighed. "All right but tell him… Just tell him… thank you."

Tain nodded. "I will. Shall we get Iris and Rayburn back in?"

"Not yet." Arkyn watched his brother's face for so long that Tain blushed. Arkyn ignored the heat, but held his brother's gaze, searching for something, though he wasn't sure what. "I should make you one of my advisors."

Tain hesitated. "As your Justiciar I am not technically doing anything outside my remit. Officially, I am a sort of advisor."

Arkyn shook his head. "You know more about fealties than Rayburn."

"As I said, I found it interesting. There's a whole chapter about it in the book that the Judge gave me for my birthday last year."

Arkyn closed his eyes for a moment. Images playing through his mind, of sunlight and carefree laughter. Warmth flowed through him with sadness in its wake. "I've not forgotten it was your birthday..."

"I never thought you had," half-whispered Tain. "It's not been the time to celebrate, has it?"

"No. Nor will my birthday be. I've your presents put by…"

"Give it a couple of days – after your coronation."

"Alcis, no!" exclaimed Arkyn. "I'll be snowed under by coronation gifts. Tonight? We can dine together and forget all this."

Tain swallowed. "No, not tonight. Tomorrow? Shall we invite Cal also? I've got to give him his."

"You didn't give it to him before we went to Amphi?"

"Well, no, because I thought I could ask him to Amphi for a couple of hours and give it to him then; did you give him yours before we left?"

Arkyn shook his head, "No and for the same reason. There's one I'll send to him this evening. Father left a present for him and a letter with it."

Tain nodded in understanding, "He'll not want us watching when he reads that."

"No. Let's get this meeting over with."

Chapter 85
FIGHT
Morning
Oedran – Galdwins' House

THAT MORNING Cal's brother, Crispin, entered the kitchen. Excitedly he said, "Cal, there's a wide in the shop asking for you?"

"Which?" asked Cal curiously. He hadn't expected any of them to seek him out. It wouldn't be Landis for Crispin knew him. The only good thing was it couldn't be any of the exiles.

"Don't know. Looks vaguely familiar. Youngish."

Cal entered the shop and smiled as he inclined his head. "Lord Rale, how are you?"

"Just about fine, thank you. How did you find Court last night?"

"Interesting, my lord, but could you keep your voice down: I was early to bed last night."

Finian grinned. "Fair enough. Cal, I was wondering if you knew how the King and Prince actually are. I don't want to disturb them, not with the coronation to arrange but I wondered if you knew…"

"Surely Lord Landis has…"

Finian shook his head. "Uncle Festus isn't saying much, Cal. Too tied up in his own grief and getting better. I think he's using all his strength to keep himself together. It was surprising how well he seemed last night. None of us want to burden him with anything else… We all feel like we're waiting for something else to happen…"

Cal nodded. "When it comes down to it, we are, aren't we, Lord Rale? We're all wondering where he'll strike next. Not that we should be discussing this at all."

"No. I know, but there's no-one else outside of my family I can talk to. We've all talked till we're dropping with exhaustion."

"I can imagine, my lord." The shop bell rang. Cal looked over Finian's shoulder; quick as lighting he pulled the young lord round behind him.

Two cloaked men had entered the shop, inconveniently leaving their knives in their hands.

"Can I help you, gentlemen?" asked Cal, all too aware his sword was elsewhere. He needed to keep one closer to hand.

The men looked round the shop. The overcast day had made shadows of the furthest corners.

One said, "We want to talk to Calumiel Galdwin."

Cal eyed him levelly. "Why's that then?"

"Got a message for him."

Cal became sardonic. "Sure you can remember what it is? You look a bit old for a runner and you don't have a scroll, so a courier is out of the question."

The second man muttered, "You're 'im, ain't you?"

"Mind you the speech I'll give you. Certainly sound like people with a message. Go on; surprise me, what's the message?" From behind, the cold hilt of a sword was pressed into his right hand. He grasped it, praising the law that meant the lords were still permitted to carry weapons. The first man lunged forward and Cal parried the stroke with remarkable ease. The clash brought Master Galdwin out of the kitchen. He closed the kitchen door. The first man dropped his dagger holding his wrist. Cal's parry had been more forceful than expected. The second man drew a short sword from under his cloak. They squared up to each other, the well-worn, scarred face of Cal's opponent showed scorn, Cal's concentration.

Master Galdwin eyes darted around as Finian moved towards him. Cal's opponent lunged. Cal parried, stepped forward, placed two blows. Clatter. The short sword crashed to the floor. Cal sent it skimming over the floor to Finian, whose long sword was at the attacker's chest.

"You can tell whoever sent you that I'm not willing to accept messages from thugs who can't handle weapons," said Cal, "and if either of you show your face on this street again, you might not have any limbs left," he added. "Understand?" The man sneered as their eyes met, Cal applied slight pressure. The resistance of sword tip on bone restrained his hand.

The first man lunged. Cal kicked out, spinning him into the door. The second man edged away from Cal towards where his friend was extricating himself from the mass of splintered debris.

Two moments later, arms folded, Cal watched as they nonchalantly walked down the street without a backward glance, sheathing the knives they'd entered with. He picked up the remains of the door, propping it against the wall before re-entering the shop. Ignoring his father, he handed Finian back his sword.

"You'd have thought better assailants could have been found, wouldn't you, my lord? Thank you for the loan."

"I see you've not lost any of your skill," replied Finian sheathing the blade.

Cal grinned. It was now useless pretending to his father he couldn't fight. "Lord Rale, might I introduce my father to you?"

"Of course you can. I'm pleased to meet you at last, Master Galdwin."

Master Galdwin was looking between the two lads as though he was trying to work out if he was dreaming. "I you, my lord. Will you excuse me one moment?" Master Galdwin turned to Cal. "Since when have you been able to handle a sword?"

"Since I was nine, Pa," replied Cal, matter-of-factly.

"No-one mentioned it to me."

"It was part of the education at Ceardlann."

"You don't need to handle a sword as a cloth merchant!"

Finian weighed in, trying to help, "I think the events that just occurred rather prove that, cloth merchant or not, *Cal* will need to handle a sword. Like it or not Master Galdwin, Cal is a confidant of the King. He, more than most, will need to be able to protect not only himself but also his friend. Also, even cloth merchants, if they travel, should be able to protect themselves from bandits. Don't be angry with Cal, I expect King Adeone had a hand in the secrecy somewhere and, if there is one thing I am certain of, you *never* break faith with the King."

Master Galdwin turned to Cal. "He told you to lie, did he?"

Cal's blood began to boil. "No, father, he certainly did not! He always told me to lie was the worst thing I could do. You never asked. If you had asked, I'd have told you. It is too late to go back and change the fact that I can defend myself from people who want me dead."

Master Galdwin was stunned to silence by the tone his son had used.

About to take his leave, Finian saw Cal whiten slightly.

"What has the door ever done to you, Cal?" asked Tain entering.

"I think it was more the two men with weapons Cal objected to, Your Highness," remarked Finian, catching the Prince's eye.

By now well into the shop, Tain stilled. "What?"

Cal grimaced at Finian, who ignored him and explained. Tain's posture hardened with each sentence. When Finian finished the recital, the Prince called for the captain of his guards.

"Smithers, send one of the men to the Palace. Ask him to see the palace carpenter and request joiners and carpenters are despatched down here to replace a door. They'll need to bring everything with them. The wood included." When Smithers saluted and left, Tain turned to Master Galdwin. "I'm sorry that my acquaintance with Cal has resulted in this, Master Galdwin. Measures will be taken so it should never occur again. Lord Rale, my thanks are added to those you've no doubt received."

Finian smiled. "Thank you, sir. Cal did the hard work… How are you?"

"I was fine until this fiasco. Alcis preserve us; I'd have thought he'd have waited!"

Cal gently shook his head. "No, sir. He's so annoyed that he didn't get what he thought he would he has to make the point somehow. I was ready for something to happen. I just can't carry a sword in Oedran."

Tain looked at him. "We'll get that sorted! Master Galdwin, would you have writing materials? I left my administrator tidying my office. It keeps him busy."

As his father found what Tain had asked for, Cal said, sotto voce, "Yes, for years!"

Tain shot him a look. "At least a few days anyway. Thank you, Master Galdwin. Lord Rale, ask Smithers to join us please."

Smithers entered and Tain passed him a quickly scribbled note with the words, "Send this to the King, for his immediate attention. Ask the guard who goes to wait for a response."

Taking the note, Smithers said, "I'm afraid that would leave only myself and one other guard Your Highness. In the current circumstances, that is against the rules set down by Lord Landis as the King's Defender."

Tain nodded. "Messenger for a couple more. I promise I won't run off in Oedran without the required guards, Smithers."

"Thank you, sir. Though, I think I'm still fit enough to keep up."

"I'll race you another day." Tain turned to Finian. "I've sent a summary of the coronation proceedings to your secretary, my lord. You'll need to read them carefully; they had me confused, and I helped compile them."

Finian grinned. "I'm sure I'll cope, Your Highness. If you'll excuse me, I'll go and see if they've been received yet. Will you give my regards to the King?"

"Certainly." Once Finian had gone, Tain visibly relaxed. Much as he liked Finian, he didn't want to see any Lord of Oedran other than Landis. He turned to Master Galdwin. "I'm sorry; I've been infernally rude and taken over your shop. Is there somewhere Cal and I could talk which wouldn't be so intrusive?"

Master Galdwin said, "I don't know that there is. Not where you could be private. Only place is upstairs and I can't promise you won't be disturbed there."

Tain nodded. "Cal, how about we take a walk?"

"You did promise Smithers, sir..."

"Damn!" cursed Tain. Maybe it was better to get Cal to come to him.

"Look, sir, come up to my room. We'll be as private there as anywhere."

"If you're sure. I didn't want to encroach on your privacy that much."

Cal simply laughed. "I encroached on yours for years, sir. I'm sure I can cope if you can. Do you mind, Pa?"

Master Galdwin eyed his son. "I hope Cris has tidied up."

Cal smiled. "I'm sure he has." What could his friend have to say that his pa couldn't hear?

* * *

A few moments later, he opened the door to the room he shared with Crispin, who was sprawled on his back, tossing a rag ball up and catching it. The ten-year-old jumped up and bowed.

Tain said, "Hello, Cris. How's life?"

"Fine thank you, Your Highness."

"Good. Mind if I perch?"

"No, he doesn't, sir, and he should be downstairs cleaning the shoes," remarked Cal with brotherly affection.

Crispin muttered, "I've finished them."

Cal eyed him. "You'd better make sure. I put pa in a bad mood."

Crispin slouched out of the room. Cal grinned and waved to a bed.

"He didn't seem happy," observed Tain sitting down.

"He'll cope. He's not tidied up either, my apologies, sir."

"We made the same amount of mess when we were ten."

"True. How are things?"

Tain sighed. "They've been better. My closest friend and confidant was attacked—"

"One of the men was the one being disarmed at the King's Gate," revealed Cal.

"And you let him leave?"

"Oddly enough, sir, my first thought was my family."

Tain snorted. "Fair enough. Do you think they'll be back?"

"No. I think they'll report that I am not an easy target. After that, who knows but I'm safe for a time."

Tain sighed. "Do you want a guard?"

"As target practice?" asked Cal. "I won't have someone like Captain Marsh on my conscience."

"All right. Does this mean I can point out that you're not a safe person to be around as well?"

Cal watched him, the question hadn't got any spark of fun to lighten it. Tain was responding by rote still. It appeared light-hearted but wasn't truly his friend. "I need a bit more practice to match you, sir. Do you need to talk?"

Tain shrugged. "Not yet. I came to say that after some persuasion Arkyn agreed to us both swearing fealty. He wasn't particularly convinced by my reasons, at least I don't think he was but then I'd confused him, Lord Iris and Rayburn by explaining fealties."

Cal said, "I wouldn't have thought that they needed them explaining."

"It was their complicated background rather than the fact of them."

"Ah. What's the procedure at the Fealty Swear then?"

Tain settled down to explain.

* * *

Halfway through, Fafnir appeared. Tain accepted the link.

The King said, "Tell me that note was a joke."

"Unfortunately not."

"Two men?"

"Yes, sir, apparently. Lord Rale was here."

"Were you ever worried when you were training with Cal?"

"No, but I think I should have been."

"Yes, I think so should I. It's lucky he's our friend; I wouldn't want him as my enemy. Tell him the token for carrying weapons is under control."

"You're not sending it with the guard?"

"No. I'll let you finish your discussion. I need to prepare for the Military Audience."

Tain nodded, confused but not wanting to push the matter as Arkyn was being obviously official.

* * *

Once out of the link Tain finished the explanation as to the Fealty Swear. "I've got a copy of the coronation proceedings for you as you'll be there for most of it. Julius, Irvin and Emrys have all agreed as well, but I've not mentioned it to Arkyn; I'd like it to be a surprise. The tailor will be visiting. Your official wear will be a dark blue tunic, with silver stars. We want you sitting on the dais during the feast and I've also got a message from Arkyn saying that argument is fruitless and simply to accept it."

"No, sir. I'll be there quite happily but it would be wrong for me to be seated so high."

Tain eyed him. "Come on, Cal, you can't be seated on the lower tables, you mean much more to him than that."

"Yes, sir, you know that, the King knows that and I know that. What's

378

more, half the King's Hall will know that, but it would still be wrong for me to be seated on the dais. By being seated lower it shows to the world that I don't mean to be anything other than a friend. It might help diffuse any tension caused by the fact I was held in high enough trust to be in the room when the King ordered out six Lords of Oedran. Whatever we wish for, it will have been noted that I was there. Lady Phylicia's presence can be explained away by her father's standing in the empire and by the fact she is the heiress to that standing. Mine cannot. I witnessed the schemes of those lords disintegrate, whilst their authority and freedom was stripped from them. It is better I remain in the background, at least for the time being. I expect the attack today wouldn't have happened if my part in your lives wasn't so obvious."

Tain studied his friend's implacable face. "If that is your final decision, I shall tell Arkyn. I can't pretend he'll be anything other than disappointed but you might have a point about today."

Cal nodded. "I know he'll be disappointed, sir, and I'm sorry for it, but this way is best. I think there's trouble enough brewing for me anyway, however easily I might be able to escape major trouble."

Tain's eyes narrowed. "It would be better if you never had to resort to that skill. I think the time for revealing that isn't yet."

"So do I, sir. Mind you, I thought revealing I could wield a sword to my father wasn't a good idea. I had no choice as it turned out."

"How did he take it?" asked Tain picking up Crispin's abandoned ball, rolling it in his hands.

"Not well but he couldn't shout too much with Lord Rale there."

"No that was fortunate," said Tain glumly.

"Tain, don't overdo things… there's only so much can be done in a day and you've officials for a reason."

"Problem is we're all working hard."

"Yes, but the officials don't all have to look healthy and bright-eyed on the day of the coronation," pointed out Cal.

Tain swallowed. "Too true. It's an age since I've laughed properly."

Cal nodded. "I know what you mean. It seems wrong."

"You can say that again and yet I know father wouldn't want us to become sombre. Why did he have to let it happen?"

Cal hesitated. In all that had happened it was one question Tain had never asked. "To avoid civil war, to protect the empire and, I think, to prevent your uncle killing you or the King, sir. He knew Scanlon was determined to succeed soon with at least one of you."

"I know that, it was in his letter but '*why*'? Cal… I know what he said, and I believe it all but all I really want is for him to walk in through the door and give me a hug to tell me the world isn't collapsing around us."

"You're not the only one. There's one thing though, the world collapsing means you can rebuild it anew; if that writes out Lord Scanlon, all well and good. We've got to make sure the world is somewhere we want to live…"

"*We*…? *You* won't even sit on the dais."

Cal smiled conspiratorially. "I'm the secret weapon. Because if you think I'm going to watch my two closest friends fight for everything that is right and good, let alone their lives, without doing anything then, I'm afraid to say, Your Highness, you're wrong, a hundred times over!"

Tain blinked. "Thank you. I'll hold you to that."

Chapter 86
MILITARY AUDIENCE
Afternoon
King's Chambers – Audience Chamber

Arkyn GLARED AT the fresh scarlet tunic Kadeem had laid ready. It wasn't a military uniform, but it felt as restrictive. Banded with black is spoke of death, of loss. The gold buckle for his belt, the sword laid beside it ready to be sheathed in the ornate scabbard spoke of rank without a breastplate. He shrugged into the tunic trying to find a sense of calm in wearing it. He strapped the black leather belt on. The ornate scabbard's weight pulled him down. As his manservant passed him the sword, he sheathed it asking if everyone was gathered.

"Just arriving, Sire," replied Kadeem handing him a dagger hilt first.

Two minutes later, Arkyn squared his shoulders and entered the Audience Chamber. Nineteen officers of the army were present: eleven from the barracks, eight who were on leave in Oedran. The General and Major were standing by the dais. As Arkyn entered, Paturn shouted the men to attention. Every salute was exact. Every gaze fixed on Arkyn. There were no bows here, no servility, no wariness. There was discipline and concealed curiosity.

Arkyn crossed to the dais and sat on the throne. Eyeing the room, he avoided meeting anyone's gaze. As he took his place, the General moved forward to swear allegiance to his fourth King. Arkyn spoke the words numbly. The audience had to happen, had to happen before he was crowned. Having an army at one's back when lords were scheming was a good idea, as Rayburn had pointed out, but he didn't feel ready to call the army his yet, not within himself.

The Major stood forward next. Arkyn noted Wynfeld's unusually clammy

380

hands. His eyes narrowed. There was no time to think as he took the oath from a man whose support had been unwavering for years.

After Wynfeld, the commander stepped forward, then the captains from the barracks before those who were on leave. Not one of them put a foot wrong, not even to trip on the dais steps. All spoke the words with seeming sincerity, even Chander Teran. Captain Edmonds eyes were full of emotion he wouldn't let his fellow officers see. Arkyn tried to offer tacit support. Unbeknownst to many Edmonds had been a true friend of his father.

Arkyn's gaze swept over the room in the moments between each officer stepping forward. One Captain Foss, from outside Oedran, watched everyone rather than standing with gaze fixed forward. His eyes roved over every detail, the Audience Chamber's murals, the participant's faces, the guards and staff standing by. What was he seeing? Was he seeing a historical event, or one that no-one had expected a fortnight before? History never waited to be called upon. It made its own path in the world.

Arkyn drew the official proceedings to an end. Descending from the dais, he caught the eye of the General, Major and Captain Rathgar. The first two inclined their heads slightly in acknowledgement but Peaga's gaze was evaluating.

Arkyn motioned to Edward. "I'd like to see the doc, about Wynfeld."

Edward glanced at the Major and nodded. "Very good, sir. I'll ask him to attend on you."

* * *

Captain Rathgar had understood the message. He forged a path to wait by the door to the Outer Office. Part of him dreading the audience, part of him longing for it.

After a quick word with the General, Arkyn crossed to him. "Come and talk, Peaga."

The captain followed his second cousin into the Inner Office where he closed the door.

Arkyn stayed in front of the desk, letting out a long breath. "I'm sorry I couldn't include you in the family group at the funeral… It was one of the hardest decisions I've had to make."

"It was better, sir. If nothing else my inherited name is against me."

Arkyn hesitated. "That should never matter."

"Not to you, Sire, but it does to others. The link is so frail to the FitzAlcis that some aren't aware of its existence. They see me as a Rathgar, I suppose for years I've seen myself as one but not now, not within myself. I realise that I could never have done what my cousin did and therefore I can't be part of his family. I'll keep up the pretence though."

381

"Don't put yourself in danger, Peaga."

"Let me decide that, Sire. I do not mean to be rude, but King Adeone helped my mother when she most needed it; he'd a heart bigger than the empire and I want to repay that memory. I'm not the best captain in your army, not by a long way and I don't look for anything from you; I happen to agree with meritocracy as an ideal, but I'll do what I can and if that means being devious, then please don't order me not to be. My friends are my friends and I'll find it hard but, frankly, trust in our circle is not something that comes easily if at all. Cousin Rathgar and the others distrust each other; they may not seem to, but they're always watching for who is most in favour, and where their own fortunes lie. I'm not saying men in your camp don't, but it's a lot more circumspect and honest. Men know what to do to get your notice, or at least they knew what to do to get King Adeone's, but with Lord Scanlon it's not so easy – you can go from favour to fall quicker than an espien can disappear."

Arkyn considered him. There was a couple of years between them in age, with Peaga being the senior. They'd spent time together as young children. There was still something of that under the surface. Peaga had never been given access to Ceardlann, and Arkyn idly wondered whose decision that had been. His grandfather's? His father's? When had it been decided? When Neassa married Rufus Rathgar? She and Rhian had been to Ceardlann. Arkyn shook himself out of the preoccupation. Either Peaga was family or he wasn't. Whether he had access to the Rex Dallin or not didn't change the blood tie. He waved to the comfortable seats. He'd just taken Peaga's oath of loyalty. His second cousin could have excused himself from that obligation with the blood bond and he hadn't.

"You've been on your feet long enough."

"I'm used to it these days," said Peaga. "This room feels odd."

Arkyn sighed. "Yes. It's mourning father as well. Did you mean all you said?"

Peaga never hesitated. "Yes, sir. Father's always treated me like a disappointment. When mother suggested I joined the army, I didn't want to because I thought I'd show up Cousin Adeone. That I'd disappoint him. Father basically told me I would do just that. Mother persuaded me, with a helping hand from grandmother and Aunt Rhian. How do you manage grandmother?"

Arkyn chuckled. "Father taught me never to try."

Peaga laughed to himself. "I understand why. You know father and Cousin Rathgar never invited her to dine, don't you? It was all mother. They'd talk when they thought no-one would hear. You can't trust them, any of them."

"Given events, that won't be a problem."

"I don't even think they like Cousin Scanlon. They are scared of him. You know Kenelm Para had daughters that went missing, don't you?"

Arkyn's eyes narrowed. "I did not."

"He swears he doesn't know what we're talking about when we ask after them. He's furious about the exiles though. Absolutely livid. His sister's taken to hiding from him at our house. She's not stupid though. She just sits and reads. Doesn't get involved in the conversations. Well, not with the girls. She talks with young Simeon and with me on occasion. I think she misses Chandra."

"Well, she seems happy with Penrod Silvano." Arkyn sank onto a chair. "Please sit, Peaga." Once his second cousin had done so, Arkyn leaned forward. "I must ask you this. Did you have any inkling of what was planned?"

Peaga shook his head. "I don't think anyone but the exiles did, sir."

Arkyn maintained eye contact. "Will you swear it to me?"

"I swear I had no foreknowledge that the assassination would be attempted, my liege."

Arkyn let out a long breath. "Listen to me, Peaga. Don't ask questions and on your fealty don't mention it elsewhere. You are in danger. You're a male child from the line of kings. FitzAlcis women carry power in their blood as much as the men. You're acknowledged family. In desperate times that might be manipulated. You are higher in precedence than Tyler Galwood but you're mostly disregarded by those that play for power. One day they may realise—"

"I am also therefore a danger to you."

Arkyn looked at him levelly, "Are you planning to usurp me?"

Peaga smiled. "No, sir. I wouldn't know where to start. I meant simply that others may twist and manipulate me, or at least your perception of me. I'll swear any oath you want, even to a life-bind to prove where my loyalties lie – though that may make spying difficult. Say the word—"

"Thank you, but maybe not yet. Just be careful of your own safety, and if I distance myself, it's not because I do not want to acknowledge you as kin but, rather, I don't want you to be in danger as well."

"Thank you for saying it, Sire, and if I'm to be of any help, I can only suppose it is by listening to others around me. It may, therefore, be better if it seems you don't wish to acknowledge me."

Arkyn nodded as a knock at the door heralded Doctor Chapa.

The King said, "Well then, Captain Rathgar, remember that in the army you're a captain first and that's where I expect your allegiance to lie. You will acknowledge that the General is your commanding officer."

Peaga said simply, "Sire," saluted and left.

"Let's hope your secretaries were fooled, Sire," remarked Chapa, when the door closed.

"What does that mean, doc?"

"I know you as a person and you're rarely that officious. What can I do for you, sir?"

"Stop changing the subject *before* I berate your manner; however, now that you have, I think Wynfeld's unwell…"

Chapter 87
GUILT AND GRIEF
Mid-Afternoon
Audience Chamber

IN THE AUDIENCE CHAMBER, Edward had exited from the link with the doctor and realised the King had left. He relaxed and caught the Major's eye and Wynfeld walked over to join him.

"Don't go anywhere, Major. The King will want to see you shortly."

Wynfeld nodded. "Very good, Administrator. How is… are you?" amended Wynfeld, realising the room was full of departing officers.

"I feel so damned guilty, Major."

Wynfeld watched the veneer Edward maintained crack. Drawing the administrator to the end of the dais where they couldn't be overheard, he quietly asked, "What have you to feel guilty for, Edward?"

"I knew what was coming…"

Wynfeld froze, startled; a thousand thoughts ran through his head including the incredulous one that Edward was a traitor.

Edward saw the flicker. "King Adeone told me, but I couldn't break his faith to tell King Arkyn and yet I feel so damned awful."

"You might have warned us."

"I was under oath to tell no-one, Major, *no-one*. It was slightly more than my normal oath as well."

The Major studied him. "Speech-bound?"

"No, King Adeone didn't seem to think that level was necessary but… The King obviously feels, or felt, that I betrayed him and I did, didn't I? I know, logically, that I couldn't do anything else but my heart isn't made of logic. For the first time since I became his administrator, I can't see where I fit. Does that sound stupid? I'm sorry; I didn't mean to tell you any of this."

Wynfeld said, "It's my speciality, getting people talking, and no, Edward, it doesn't sound stupid."

"Thank you. How are things at the barracks?"

"Dispirited. I can't focus on anything. All I know is that we *did* fail the FitzAlcis, and we weren't under oaths preventing us doing anything. I can't find Jacobs, and Stuart obviously knows nothing about his whereabouts – even with Lord Wealsman's help that was clear. I can't get a lead on the actual assassin and I'm trying to organise the regiments for the coronation proceedings. Everything else has had to wait. Summer recruitment is postponed for the first time in centuries." He glanced around the room; they were now alone. "How is our King, Edward?"

Edward swallowed. "Not his normal self, Major. I don't just mean that because he's become King. He's obviously grieving and he will for months but because of it his temper is erratic… I think he wants solitude but it's not possible, is it?"

Wynfeld shook his head, "No, it's not, not for a long time. He was the same when Queen Ira died but I, perhaps, shouldn't have mentioned it."

"I'm glad you did. I didn't know him then."

Wynfeld said, "Neither did I; I blundered in."

"I doubt that, Major."

"I wouldn't."

Edward nodded. Noticing the doctor entering the Audience Chamber he said, "Excuse me for a moment, please, Major. Doctor Chapa, would you like announcing?"

Doctor Chapa looked between the administrator and Major, "Is everyone being announced, Edward?"

"No, doc, some aren't giving me a chance to."

Chapa smiled. "Then I shall follow in their footsteps."

Once he'd gone the Major asked, "Why is the doc here, Edward? The King's not ill is he?"

"No, Major, not to my knowledge."

A few moments later, Secretary Kenton entered the Audience Chamber. "Major, the King would like to see you."

The Major turned to Edward. "I'm not ill either."

Edward said, "I think the doc should be the one to say, don't you, Major? Please don't keep King Arkyn waiting."

Once he'd gone, Edward let out a long breath and entered the Outer Office.

* * *

In the Inner Office, the Major saluted and searched his King's face. Arkyn looked remarkably calm but the Major, used to reading him, realised that he wasn't truly calm and contentment was a long way away.

"Sire?"

"Doctor Chapa is just going to assure me that you're well."

"Sir, I'm—"

"Please come over here, Major," said Chapa, "and stop distressing the King with insubordination."

A few minutes later the doctor said, "Flu, sir."

Arkyn glanced over at them, "I thought it might be. Major, you're good at hiding what you feel but you can't hide sweat in a cool room. I'm speaking from experience. Now, you're to go to the barracks, you're to go to bed and you're to let others worry about this fiasco."

Wynfeld said, "Sire, in all conscience…"

Arkyn glanced in dismissal, with a nod of thanks, at Doctor Chapa. He waited for the door to close. "I gave you an instruction, Major Wynfeld."

"Sir, it's your coronation; I can't, I haven't time…"

"I don't want to order you, Wynfeld, but I will. I realise you have duties for the coronation but quite frankly you're not well enough and I'd rather have you around during my reign. Let the General delegate to the commander. If you are well enough on the day, I shall be very glad to see you but you're to rest and get better."

Major Wynfeld swallowed. "Sir…"

"Go to bed, Wynfeld, and if I discover you haven't, I'll send your aunt."

Wynfeld sighed. "Sire, that's surely slightly unfair."

Arkyn grinned. "I can't imagine what you mean. Maria is only ever caring."

Wynfeld rubbed the back of his head. "I experienced her care from a different perspective, Sire. Thank you. I will go and rest but before I do can I say something?"

"As you've accepted my bullying, I suppose it's only fair."

"Thank you, sir. It's about Edward…"

Arkyn frowned, that wasn't what he'd expected. "What about him?"

"He feels desperately guilty, and feels he betrayed you by not informing you of King Adeone's suspicions about approaching events, but he was under a binding oath. He's obviously distracted by these feelings."

Arkyn said quietly, "I've already done enough damage there. I don't want to make Edward feel any worse than he does. I know he's suffering but I don't know what to say. One reaction was that he betrayed me, but I know, like others before him, he had no choice. Sicla, if we follow that line of thought, Cal betrayed me also. Surely his betrayal would be the greater… Wynfeld, I can't grasp what's happened yet, not truly. There might be audiences and arrangements but they all mask the time in which to think, in which to absorb."

Wynfeld threw convention to the wind. "My King, I shouldn't have blundered into the matter but other than the fact I'm concerned about Edward's state of mind and the possibility of traitors taking advantage, you need to take a break from work, if only for a couple of hours. It is never easy to come to terms with loss, I'm willing to listen if you need to talk again but you need to take that time to absorb, to stop, in fact, flying on the wings of emotion to the eyrie in the cliffs for the fall will be all the harder."

Arkyn didn't even look at him. "Wynfeld, stop there. As for listening to me pour my heart out again, you're not well enough to and you really ought to stop talking to Kadeem…"

Wynfeld smiled softly. "He has a lot to answer for. Shall I go?"

"Yes, but that is no rebuke. You mentioned Edward was under a binding oath. How do you know?"

"He's just told me. I shouldn't have asked him anything, but he wanted to talk to someone and I thought I was the safest person."

"Thank you. Now, go and get better and ask Edward to join me."

Wynfeld left the office to find that Edward was still looking drawn. He simply squeezed his shoulder.

"He wants to see you. Don't blame me for my actions."

* * *

Hardly reassured, Edward entered the Inner Office. He let the door close softly behind him and faced Arkyn, whose face spoke a thousand words of loss and grief. For some reason Edward could never explain, he knelt; it seemed the right thing to do.

Arkyn got up, shaking. He watched his administrator for a moment, trying to imagine what his father would do. He couldn't, couldn't make that connection. In that instant the realisation hit him. Shock had rolled through him, grief had burned a path through his heart, but realisation had slept, it had been a dream, unreal, before. Mentally, he grasped at something faded, gone, beyond his reach. He sucked in air; the room was spinning. He stumbled trying to free himself from desk and chair. Caught by supportive arms he tried to right himself. He was lowered into the chair he'd been trying to escape. The presence was gone. The slosh of water into a glass. Nausea rose and he was retching. Arms encircled him, half helping, half carrying him to the couch. He stumbled onto it. Closing his eyes. Gradually the spinning stopped and he could hear his manservant telling Edward to get the doc. He lay down. He had a few minutes to pull himself together. It didn't work.

"You can lie and tell me you're fine, Sire, but there's plenty of evidence to the contrary."

The doc was kneeling by him, checking his pulse, his temperature, his pallor. Six minutes hadn't been enough to fool him.

"I *am* fine, doc. I was being foolish."

"You know I can't answer that one, Sire, but Lady Amara could."

Arkyn snorted. After threatening Wynfeld with an aunt he didn't know whether to appreciate the irony or sympathise.

"Doc, you know you wouldn't do that to yourself or me."

"Probably not, I like an easy life. Now, you're taking the afternoon off. You're to go and lie down, before that lethargy reasserts itself."

"Doc, I've got meetings lined up..."

"Edward can reorganise them; it'll keep him busy and everyone else assured of your authority."

Arkyn said, "I ought to talk to him first, alone."

Chapa and Kadeem left the room.

Arkyn motioned Edward over and then grasped him by his shoulder. He looked into his administrator's eyes and the force of the gaze meant Edward couldn't look away.

The King said, "You're not to blame, Edward, you did only what you could and what you should have done. The question of betrayal is nonsense, there would have been more questions had you informed me. I... I'm in support of what you did but don't you ever bloody try it again."

Edward searched Arkyn's eyes. "I will promise you that, Sire. Alcis, I'm sorry..."

Arkyn nodded. "What oath were you under, Edward? I had assumed it was your oath as my administrator. If it wasn't, then it might change perceptions and explain things better."

Edward knelt. "Fealty, Sire. I... Your father requested of me."

"Did you feel it was forced from you?"

"No, sir, but then I didn't know what he'd bind on it."

Arkyn saw a way out of their mutual guilt: Edward's for having accepted Adeone's orders and his for overreacting.

"Pass me your hands, Edward."

The administrator swallowed, but did as requested.

Placing his hands palm to palm with his administrator's, Arkyn said, "On your oaths and fealty forget that your actions annoyed me, forget my harsh words and accept that I do not blame you, for that is truth, and I shall also forget."

Edward's face cleared of preoccupation. He realised something had happened but not what. It was the strangest sensation he'd ever experienced but after a vague moment of uneasiness and grasping at a faded memory, he said, "Sire, you're shaking…" He hesitated. "My apologies, sir, I shouldn't have mentioned it."

Arkyn's grip tightened. Was it the binding magic of fealties draining him or was it the emotion of relief, of acceptance and of a clear conscience? He'd didn't know. "No. I'm sorry, Edward, for you'll have to reorganise my day."

"At least I am used to that, Sire," replied Edward with a smile.

"Anyone would think I made your life difficult. Get Kadeem and tell the doctor that I'm being good and going for a lie down. If my brother should show his face… think of something appropriate. I don't want to concern him or give him chance to fuss."

"I'll do my best, Sire. How is he?"

"Still flying on the wings of outrage…"

Chapter 88
OF OFFICERS AND LORDS
Mid to Late Afternoon
Barracks – Lyndon's Office

LYNDON RETURNED from the Military Audience with apprehension racing at his heels. He'd sworn to serve Arkyn as his Captain of Intelligence, to collect and collate information in pursuit of protection of the empire and the lives of the FitzAlcis. His new regiment wasn't a mystery to him. Far from it. He'd used their work when guarding the FitzAlcis, but being in charge was something else entirely. Beaver had left for Lufia that morning, taking his knowledge and support with him.

He'd told the sergeants to carry on as normal and that finding Jacobs and the assassin was their priority. They were having no luck with either. They'd obviously missed something. He entered the office, *his* office. He'd helped empty it when Wynfeld converted it from a storage room. Long and thin it seemed neither one thing nor the other to him. He flung his cloak onto a peg on the back of the door. Everything in its place except him. What had they missed? He sank onto the chair behind the desk – his chair, his desk. He gazed blankly at the surface in front of him. Ink stains dotted the plain wood. How long had he got before the King summoned him to explain the lack of arrests? If he was lucky, it would be after the coronation. It wouldn't make much difference if they couldn't make progress. He pulled his commission from his breastplate and placed it back in the drawer. Still new enough to hold its shape, he felt its burden. Why did men see a desk as a positive thing? It was just imprisonment by any other name. His commission landed on top of a file. He eyed the papyrus covering. It accused him of inaction. He pulled it out. He had to start somewhere. Beaver's file on Jacobs might just be the place.

Some time later he leant forward and spread the papers out, trying to construct a timeline, with associated statements. He glanced around the room and called for his corporal.

"Have you got some string and nails, oh and also some sort of clips?"

The corporal looked blank.

"A scroll parchment might be easier then, or even better everything… whilst we're at it, some sort of colour, that I can use to mark things with. Oh, and a hammer and nails…"

The corporal crooked an eyebrow. "I'll see what I can do, sir. How soon do you want it?"

Lyndon took a breath; he'd served under some abrupt captains in his time. "In the next six minutes but I won't shout for half an hour."

The corporal grinned, "At least you didn't say yesterday, Captain."

"I could if it would make you feel more comfortable."

Twelve minutes later he and the corporal were laying everything out and piecing it together along the long wall of the narrow room.

Lyndon eventually said, "Where's the statements from the gate guards the night he ran?"

"I've not seen them, sir. Are they still left in that pile?"

"No."

Lyndon opened the door halfway along his office and said to the startled clerks in the next room, "Do we have statements from the gate guards the night Jacobs ran?"

The clerks passed glances volunteering each other to speak.

"Aren't they in the file, Captain?" enquired one.

"Come and see if you can find them. I and the corporal can't."

"Well, if they're not there, Captain, no, we don't have them but I'll come and check."

The clerk entered Lyndon's office. "Do you know how long it takes us to get files in order, Captain?" he enquired, astounded and annoyed.

Lyndon shrugged. "Do you know how long we have before the King gets irate we've not found Jacobs?"

"No, sir."

"I don't want to find out."

They didn't find the statements.

Lyndon dismissed the clerk and gazed blankly ahead at the wall of paper. He cursed, frustrated. Had they discovered why they'd had no luck in finding their fugitive? At least, no luck in finding one of them.

"I'm going to have to go to the Major."

Factually, the corporal said, "He's confined to bed, Captain. Word came just before you called me in. Apparently, it's flu."

"Damn and blast. I don't want to disturb the General."

"What about the commander?"

Lyndon shook his head. "No. Orders are the Major, then General, then King. I don't answer to the commander, apparently. Unless he's in a bad temper and I'm being diplomatic – that was Beaver's way of putting it. I'll have to see the General. Sort this lot out, will you?"

The corporal said, jovially, "Of course, *Captain*."

Lyndon grinned. "Ask a clerk to help – that way it will be to their satisfaction."

* * *

Paturn nodded in acknowledgement as Lyndon saluted. "Well?"

"I've been reading the notes about Jacobs, sir. Given his belongings are missing, and that no-one saw him after he delayed the message to the Major, if he left, he left that night. Yet, I can't find any statement from the person who saw him leave the barracks. I wondered if I had the authority to talk to the duty captain and gate guards from that shift."

"Why wouldn't you? You're of equal rank to the captain."

Lyndon swallowed. "It's Captain Rathgar, sir, and, well, he is the King's cousin."

"Second cousin but here he's a captain first and foremost. Why do you think it's important to talk to him?"

"We're hunting for Jacobs in Oedran and its environs but, if no-one actually saw him leave, he could still be here."

"Someone would have seen him."

"Possibly but if he were careful and had a good place to hide, maybe not. Put a man in uniform and he disappears here. He is someone you've not seen before from a different regiment who is in your area of the barracks for one reason or another."

The General considered Lyndon for a few moments and called for his corporal. He said abruptly, "I want to see Captain Rathgar, now, with the men who were on the gates the night after the assassination."

The corporal, who'd barely managed a salute, left without a word.

Lyndon swallowed. "I didn't mean for you to interview them, sir."

"Good. I'm going to watch you do that."

Lyndon *wasn't* reassured.

391

* * *

When the men reported, the General said, "Captain Lyndon has taken over from Fysher and Beaver. He's got some questions for you."

"Thank you, sir. Does everyone know Jacobs?" asked Lyndon. When they all nodded, he momentarily wondered if it were true but then realised, they often had gate duties and civilians entering the barracks regularly were a minority. "Good. So, who saw him leave the barracks after the news came about the arrests?"

They gazed at each other blankly before Peaga said, satirically, "Seems none of us did, Lyndon."

The General gave a slight cough. The captain swallowed.

"Sorry, sir. It seems none of us did, Captain Lyndon."

"Thank you, my… Captain Rathgar. There's no-one missing? No-one took a break and asked someone to cover?"

A general shaking of the heads met this idea of breaking orders.

Without thinking, Lyndon said, "Blimey, first time ever to my knowledge."

Captain Rathgar looked at his squad. With a sigh, he said, "Own up!"

Three further men were called to the General's office but the result was the same, no-one recalled having seen Jacobs leave.

The General and Lyndon exchanged a significant look.

Paturn called once more for his corporal. "Close the barracks."

His corporal hesitated.

The General continued tolerantly, "Just tell the Maj… Commander and tell him I want to see him as soon as the barracks is secure."

* * *

An hour and a half later, a body was found, covered by rubbish, on the barracks' midden, which wasn't due to have been emptied until the end of the month. Paturn and Lyndon went to examine the discovery.

The General said, "Well done, Lyndon."

"Outsider's perspective, sir, that's all."

"Now you've just got to discover who stabbed him and where…"

"He's got to be identified, sir," advised Lyndon.

"That's Jacobs."

"By someone without a vested interest in seeing him caught, sir."

The General, aware of onlookers said, "Whom would you suggest?"

"Lord Faran?" suggested Lydon.

Paturn mused on that answer. "Why him?"

"He has no personal reason for wanting a body identified as Jacobs. Family might want to misidentify so he's safe, and people here need to find him quickly. Lord Faran doesn't need to cover his back, prove himself or is emotionally attached. He'll want *Jacobs* caught not someone

392

else named as him. It also needs to be someone the King can trust.”

The General frowned. “We’ll do it your way, but I’ll see you in my office as soon as the *formal* identification has been made.” He turned to the men around them. “Find where he was killed or you’ve all got bloody short careers.”

* * *

When Faran arrived, he glanced at the body now in the cool surrounds of the infirmary. “That’s definitely Jacobs. Congratulations, Lyndon.”

“Thank you, my lord, but I now have to find who killed him.”

As General Paturn entered, Faran knelt by the corpse. “It was either someone he knew or didn’t see coming for him. There are no defensive wounds.” He turned the remains over. “Ah, that could be why. He’s been slashed across the back. A word in private, please, Captain Lyndon. General, how are you?”

Lyndon led the way to his office, listening to the General and Lord of Lufian exchanging news, and hoping his corporal and the clerk had finished sorting out the mayhem. Entering the office, Lyndon glanced at the two men.

“Finish off later, please.”

The General said, “Sicla, death and damnation, Lyndon, what on Erinna have you been doing in here?”

“Trying to piece together what we missed, sir, and it worked.”

“Hmm. Your Lordship, please take a seat.”

Lyndon paused. “My apologies for the state of my office, Lord Faran.”

Faran said, “Not at all. I’m intrigued by your methods. I’ll come back another day for a talk about them but I am due at Lord Landis’. I simply wanted to say Jacobs’ wounds reminded me of King Adeone’s description of Captain Jones’ murder in Paras during the last Review of Anapara.”

The General said, “Sicla.” He pulled the door to the clerks’ office open. “Get me Captain Jones’ file, now.”

Two minutes later he was flicking through it. “The murderer was never caught and, you’re right, the wounds are identical. Butterworth and Marsh had the good sense to have sketches taken. Do the same with Jacobs.”

Lyndon nodded. “Very good, sir.”

Faran got to his feet. “Well, this was a pleasure, General, Lyndon, but I am due at Lord Landis’ and my conscience won’t let me be late. At least I shall have the topic for discussion at my fingertips.”

The General said, “Thank you for your help, Lord Faran. I’m sorry to have dragged you away from the Palace.”

“As I said, a pleasure. Please don’t feel you have to see me to the gates; I know my way.”

Once he'd gone the General's eyes narrowed at Lyndon. "My office."

* * *

The walk to the General's office was taken in silence. Paturn obviously had something to say about Lyndon's handling of the situation but the captain was determined to stick to his reasons for asking for Lord Faran. The General stood behind his desk and Lyndon realised why he was feared by officers of the militia. The General's gaze scorched over him and took in everything from his hair to his boots.

"You might have been autonomous of my command in the FitzAlcis' Guards but you damn well aren't now! You *do not* undermine a senior officer in public or private! I'll have you on every charge you can think of and more besides if you question my judgement in such a way again. You have a lot of licence as Captain of Intelligence but you don't abuse it or I'll advise the King to replace you and I'll then dismiss you if he doesn't. Is that understood?"

"Yes, sir."

"Bloody good job too." The General paused. "Apart from your choice of location to air your concerns you were right. It was inspired work that made you realise Jacobs could still be here and you've saved your men some valuable time, if not their reputations. You've also given them more to do. Why did you doubt you could do the job? No, don't answer that; I'm not in the mood for novice captain introspection. You've got a good brain, carry on using it. Your first day of true command – without your predecessor telling you what's what – you've closed the barracks, undermined me, and had the cheek to be proved right. Depending on your outlook that's either good or inauspicious. Dismiss."

* * *

Lyndon returned to his office, collapsed into his chair and considered what he needed was a drink.

He entered the officers' mess and obtained a tankard of beer. He sank onto a chair, hunched forward, clasping the tankard with both hands.

There were three other captains there who watched him, they glanced at each other and every glance volunteered a colleague to speak.

Finally, one of them said, "Who are you then?"

"Lyndon. I've taken over from Beaver and Fysher."

"Are they under arrest? I noticed they weren't at the audience."

"No."

"So what have you taken over for?"

Lyndon said, "The King didn't explain in detail."

"You're as bad as they were for answering obliquely."

"I suppose it's the job. I don't know any of you…"

394

"Quite right too. Never trust anyone who doesn't declare themselves. I'm surprised you lot have any friends…"

One of the others sniggered, "Quite right too, my lord."

Lyndon's hindbrain said, '*Just what I didn't need.*' Before he enquired, "Lord?"

The man smiled. "Lord Chander Teran. I tried to get your post but obviously it required men of lesser skill."

His companions sniggered.

"I'm sure that's not possible," replied Lyndon.

"Say that again and I'll see you don't keep your post," snapped Chander.

"We're all captains in here, I thought."

"You thought wrong."

"Has your father reached Tera yet, *my lord*?" asked Lyndon not knowing how he dared.

Suddenly the room was alive with the atmosphere of a fight. Three against one. The odds weren't good but Lyndon was willing to bet that he could take them all down; he'd been training hard to be able to guard the FitzAlcis. He itched for that fight, to rid himself of the angst and horror of the last few days. Would he survive even if he lived? Much as he wanted to wipe the superiority from Chander's face, he couldn't face the consequences today. Working for the FitzAlcis had shown him there were other ways to win. He got to his feet without menace.

"I'm off to see if a murder scene has been found and whether, therefore, the barracks can be reopened."

The shock of the revelation diffused the atmosphere.

The second captain said, "*You* had the audacity to close the barracks?"

"No, that was the General. I presume you won't argue with his authority? I merely gave him the evidence which led to his decision."

He left them looking significantly at each other. When he reached his office a smile played around his lips; it didn't feel so strange anymore.

Chapter 89

CISAN-AGE GIFT

Evening

Galdwins' House

THAT EVENING, Cal had a drink in hand and was talking to his parents about his decisions and what was happening, or at least those bits he could explain and would become general knowledge. Banging on the door disturbed them. Cal frowned, who would call so late? He looked at his father and saw his own thoughts mirrored there. Whatever it was couldn't be good.

Master Galdwin opened the spy hatch. "Yes?"

"Palace courier, sir, for Master Calumiel Galdwin."

"Alone?"

"No, sir, with two of the Prince's Guard."

Cal said, "Who, exactly?"

It was a well-known voice who replied, "Smithers, sir, and Halien."

Cal nodded to his father and when the door opened said, "Sorry, Smithers, but..."

"I'd have been more concerned if you hadn't checked, Master Calumiel."

The courier stepped forward bearing a medium-sized package. Cal looked at it, then at the courier. He crooked an eyebrow, slightly amused. Arkyn had obviously picked the courier as well as the guards.

"From the King, sir."

"Any other message, Cas?"

"There's a letter, Master Calumiel. We were told not to expect a reply."

Cal gave a slight nod of acknowledgement. He was intrigued.

Smithers said, "We'll leave you to unwrap it in peace, Master Calumiel."

Once they'd gone Cal hesitantly looked at his mother and father before taking a deep breath and unwrapping a beautifully inlaid box. He took the letter from the top of it hesitantly; it wasn't Arkyn's writing but King Adeone's. He stared at the letter, almost unwilling to open it. In the end he broke the seal and read it. It was only a page but not less poignant for that. No-one in his family would be reading it for a long time. Folding it into a square, he put it in his belt pouch, before picking up the box: a cisan-age gift from Adeone. With a shaking hand, he lifted the lid. There, in a tooled leather scabbard, lay a beautiful but not ornate dagger and also a small round, jewelled case: moonstones and amethysts. Cal lifted the dagger, and, with a practised motion, drew it from the scabbard, weighing it in his hand. He flipped and caught it; it felt perfect in his grip. Smiling, he re-sheathed the blade, but there was a lump in his throat: etched on the blade were his initials. Carefully, he placed the sheathed dagger in the box and picked up the small jewelled case. It seemed more appropriate for a woman's trinkets, but he opened it. There, in the centre, was an official token to allow him to carry weapons in Oedran and a small note in King Adeone's writing to say he thought it might come in useful. He snapped the jewelled box shut and replaced it before closing the box and fastening it with the key that had been inside. He ran his hand over the polished box.

"Well?"

His father's question startled him. Absorbed by the gift, its meaning and the box, he'd forgotten he wasn't alone. "A cisan-age gift from King Adeone, Pa."

Master Galdwin eyed his son. Where had the confidence come from? He had a different stance after he opened the box, as though the contents had made his situation bearable. "Oh. Well, I suppose it was kind of them to send it on."

"It must have been found with his things," replied Cal sadly. "They'll be clearing his chambers ready for King Arkyn to take them after the coronation. Ma, Pa, do you mind if I go to bed, I'm rather drained."

His father said, "Go to bed. We're not stopping you. Take the gift as well."

Cal simply nodded, kissed his mother goodnight and left.

Once he'd gone, Master Galdwin said, "He wasn't going to show us that letter, was he?"

"No but then I think I understand why. From what he's said King Adeone knew what was coming. That letter was no doubt his farewell. Cal lived with them for years."

Master Galdwin sighed. "Aye. I just hope it helps the lad."

Chapter 90
FAMILY AND FEALTY
Evening
Oedran – Iris Lordship – Iris House

WHILST CAL WAS UNWRAPPING his present, across the city, Aldwy and Galaloth entered Iris House curiously. Neither of them had visited before, even though their wives had grown up in its elegant surrounds. They took in the pleasant atrium with its central pool curiously. It wasn't a particularly common feature of houses north of Tradere, where the weather was cooler, but the atrium still felt inviting. They handed over their cloaks to the hovering footman with a nod of thanks as their wed-father walked to greet them and their wives.

"Welcome home, girls. It's certainly been too long."

Their wives smiled at their father and the hug they exchanged was honest.

"Well, if you hadn't been so good at getting our husbands significant posts we might have made it home sooner," said Farie with a grin. "Where's Idris and Lina?"

"Drawing room. Dinner will be serv— Oh, why do I bother. It's like they're sixteen again."

Galaloth chuckled. "Dana hasn't changed since I met her, Lord Iris."

Iris nodded. "Well, I feel younger with them here. Come on in. Did you manage to meet Irvin and Indria properly last night?"

"Not really," admitted Aldwy. "They seemed to be deep in conversation with their friends."

"Second cousins mainly. They were with the Landis siblings and Lord Rale, I believe."

"Yes, and a merchant's son?" replied Aldwy grasping at the memory.

"Calumiel Galdwin. The King and Prince Tain's confidant. Don't mistake him for a mere member of the Court," said Lord Iris gravely.

"No. ReJean apparently got short shrift for doing so," added Galaloth.

"Cal's all right," remarked Irvin with a grin. "You must be my uncles Aldwy and Galaloth. I'm sorry we didn't get a chance to meet last time I passed through Amphi, Uncle Galaloth."

Iris introduced them and turned to take a note from a footman. He broke the seal and turned on his heel, leaving his family together.

Galaloth's eyes followed him, confused. What was so urgent to disturb a family reunion?

Irvin smiled. "Grandfather has taken on many of Lord Landis' duties. He'll join us for dinner if he can."

* * *

Dinner was announced a few minutes later. They'd just sat down when Iris joined them saying,

"That's the last interruption tonight."

Idris hmphed. "It's rarely the last interruption."

"Rayburn understands," was all Iris said. He turned to his wed-sons. "How have you found Oedran?"

As talk turned, Iris watched everyone with his shrewd assessment. The ladies were talking amongst themselves for the most part. Indria joining in with her mother and aunts, exchanging stories and family gossip about the cousins. The men, accepting his lead, stayed away from topics to do with the FitzAlcis, until Galaloth said,

"Do we know how Lord Scanlon is? He must be devastated by the death of his brother."

Iris avoided Aldwy's eye. "The King has been very clear we are not to speculate on Lord Scanlon's state of mind." His gaze slipped to Irvin and, for the first time, he understood that his grandson had more than an inkling about Lord Scanlon's aims. Had the King told him? Or had he just put events together in that quick mind of his?

His son said, "Don't worry, Galaloth. You get used to this. We can't talk about anything to do with the FitzAlcis."

Galaloth hesitated. "I wasn't meaning to gossip."

"It is better the King's wishes are followed," said Aldwy carefully. "He will have made them known for a reason."

Galaloth frowned to himself. Why would concern for the Justiciar be a taboo topic of conversation? For the first time since arriving in Oedran, he felt his position acutely. His wed-father was the King's Counsellor. His wed-brother had been Tuchlin of the Low Plains until a week ago. He was just a Lord of Areal, definitely not in the King's confidence and barely in Governor ReJean's it seemed.

Irvin said, "Uncle Galaloth, does Amphi really have poles between the different levels of your markets that people use to descend quickly?"

"It does. You should come and visit properly if your grandfather can spare you. Indria as well. We'd love to have you to stay. You could explore the city. I'm sure you'd find much of it fascinating and we've some excellent bookbinders and sellers."

Lord Iris smiled. "If the King can spare Irvin's company for a time, I'm sure we can arrange something."

Aldwy nodded. "You're always welcome in Eyllyn too…"

Talk turned back and forth before Lord Aldwy said, "I've heard Lord Kenelm Para received a ban on attending Court last night. Do we know why?"

Iris pursed his lips and avoided Irvin's eye. "I believe he insulted King Arkyn and failed to follow his wishes when it came to the toast to Lord Landis for his actions at the Munewid Feast."

Galaloth frowned. "Why would anyone not observe that toast? Landis was selfless from everything I've heard."

"And his actions did save King Adeone's body being mutilated further," added Aldwy.

"Yes," said Iris. "My nephew was remarkably brave. I hope the wound heals without complications. Have you both received the information for the coronation?"

Galaloth caught Aldwy's eye. Was *everything* that might tangentially touch the FitzAlcis really off limits for discussion? Well, their wed-father might not talk about such things but they would need to so they could explain events to their governors.

* * *

When the dinner ended, Iris pushed himself to his feet and caught Aldwy's eye, then collected Galaloth in a glance. "Maybe we should discuss the coronation, as you're here. It will save time later. Come through to my study. I'm sure everyone will cope without us for a time."

Once in Iris' shelf-lined study, Aldwy let out a long breath. "How is the King? I was worried last night."

Iris shrugged. "Coping. I don't know where he gets his strength from.

It's remarkable how well they're both coping. Prince Tain will be crowning King Arkyn. Won't hear of anything else. Festus advised them not to do the homage, but other than that, they've taken the lead in everything."

Galaloth hesitated. "Do you want me to leave?"

Iris shook his head. "You're an ambassador. I've had precise instructions from King Arkyn that, when in private, I may explain matters to the ambassadors. The dinner table was not private."

Aldwy sank into a chair. "What on Erinna were your fellow lords thinking, Iris?"

"Only the King and Prince Tain have heard their explanation. I don't think my peers expected any consequences."

"Well, I'm exceptionally glad they got them. Sicla. Daioch and I had just shaken hands as he became Tuchlin when he grabbed his chest. I thought he was having a heart attack. He went so white I honestly thought he was about to die. So did everyone else. We got him sitting down and he grasped my wrist. I caught his eye and, somehow, I knew what must have happened. Of course, we couldn't get hold of anyone here and we didn't like to disturb King Arkyn or Prince Tain if we were wrong, but, Aluna preserve us, I never want to experience that again."

Iris nodded. "Nor me. King Adeone had survived so much. I shall never forgive the conspirators."

Galaloth sighed. "Nor will Lord Scanlon from what was said at—"

"Put it together!" snapped Aldwy. "You can't be so naïve, Galaloth. Six Lords of Oedran sign away King Adeone's life. Lord Scanlon isn't trusted enough to become Protector for his nephew? Doesn't attend the funeral? Won't be at the coronation? Leaving Oedran already? Honestly, do you need it spelling out to you?"

"That's enough, Aldwy!" ordered Iris.

Galaloth whitened. "The Justiciar— Sicla. Proof?"

Aldwy shrugged. "I don't know. There is enough circumstantial though. Sorry, Iris, but it's true. I didn't resign because I wanted to retire as Tuchlin. I resigned because Daioch has a much better chance of keeping the Low Plains loyal to King Adeone, King Arkyn now. You know it. King Adeone suspected it. Oh, I dressed it up as you suggested, but it was clear which way the sap ran. I've heard good things about King Arkyn. I hope he manages to survive. If I were you, Galaloth, I'd hope so as well. Areal will be in trouble if Lord Scanlon takes power."

"Why? ReJean's post is hereditary."

"Yes, and that stops an awful lot of the politics that exist elsewhere in the empire. Whilst he's in post, whilst his daughter is recognised as his heiress, lords will only vie for her hand, not her life or the lives of others who might take power. I was very pleased when King Adeone suggested Daioch as my deputy. He didn't have reason to work against me. He had the King's ear. His wed-brother is Lord Landis. His wife my wed-cousin. At the moment in Areal, you're the only one who has a strong link to Oedran other than the ReJeans. I'd watch your back."

Iris pursed his lips. "How did you survive so long as Tuchlin, Aldwy?"

Aldwy snorted. "I was noted for my straight talking in private, Iris. If nothing else, as a family, we need to watch out for each other and the truth helps with that. How much does Idris know?"

"Not as much as you both do," said Iris with a sigh. "Oh, he can see Lord Scanlon isn't in favour and he knows that the King will have reasons for it. King Arkyn has been as clear as King Adeone was. Lord Scanlon is still FitzAlcis. He is to be treated with respect."

"That's—" Galaloth paused. "Why? I mean, if he's at the root of these troubles, why?"

Iris held his gaze. "They will not risk civil war for what is a family disagreement. For which, they have my admiration."

Galaloth nodded slowly. "I agree. Can I ask how much do our fellow ambassadors know?"

"I haven't spoken with any others. I am unaware of how much Lady Phylicia has been told. I would assume nothing. King Adeone discussed some matters with his Representatives as events unfolded. Daioch's life-bind was one such moment; however, as you're here, and family, the King saw it would be awkward if you were ignorant. He has shown great faith in you by allowing me to discuss this."

Galaloth nodded. "I appreciate the mark of trust. I don't mean to worry you, Iris, but I'd be keeping an eye on Tradere. ReJean wants me to talk to their ambassador and get his side of a dispute that's running with Denshire about trade. We're seeing more traders coming through Areal for the Frander of Byfa. I'm not sure what's at the back of it, but it now feels like something more serious might be happening."

"Tradere? Lord Eleneth hasn't mentioned anything to either King to my knowledge. Are you certain?"

"No, but Denshirian traders are coming through Areal instead of entering Tradere on their border. Why would they do that if all was well?"

Aldwy shrugged. "It's a good question. We didn't have any issues like that on the Low Plains."

Iris sighed. "Let's get through the coronation. Is it going to cause trouble before the Ambassadors' Court starts?"

Galaloth considered. "I doubt it. I'll see what I can discover from Lords Buckler and Salman. Would that help?"

"Yes," admitted Iris. "If I speak to them about it first, they'll know you've spoken to me. I'll ask Wynfeld if there're any rumours the King needs to be aware of following the coronation."

Galaloth nodded. "Can I ask how the military audience went?"

Iris smiled. "That was a success. Everyone spoke the right words, including Chander Teran."

Aldwy crooked an eyebrow. "I expect he did in that company. I know the King doesn't want civil war, but if it comes to it, the Low Plains will be with him. Not just the army, but our villagers are still training with the plainstools since the decree of 1169 and our service defeating Bayan."

Iris grimaced. "Yes. I remember how well your villagers could fight. I shall tell the King he won't need his army."

Aldwy chuckled. "Don't you fancy fighting someone wielding a plainstaff?"

"No," said Iris. "Cracked heads were the least of the issues. Mind you, those staffs were useful when marching."

Chapter 91
SCANLON
Late Evening
Anapara – Black Hills House

LORD SCANLON looked at the man in front of him and considered if he'd trusted him a bit too much, if he was being undermined if not double-crossed. Events in Oedran were becoming twisted.

"Who attacked the boy?"

His companion shrugged. "Not my men. I thought they were yours."

"They were scarred! That's the mark of your best men!"

"I've lost the best men I ever had to your schemes already, Greatness."

"You've been recompensed."

"Money can't buy skill," said his companion silkily.

"Training can't produce it either, it seems. I warned you he was meant to be good. Or don't you believe Lord Landis' assessment?"

"Gave it to you himself, did he?"

"Never you mind."

"Oh, but I do mind, Greatness. Especially when I'm being accused of something that went wrong that I didn't have a hand in. I would have made sure the boy—"

"That wasn't the only thing that's gone wrong recently. What happened to the crossbow?"

"Why are you concerned? It's a crossbow. It can't be linked to you."

"I want it out of the way."

"It's out of the way. It's where no-one will ever find it – or rather it's where it's unlikely anyone will ever find it. Don't you trust me, Greatness?"

"No."

"At least that feeling is mutual."

Scanlon said, "I don't trust anyone at the moment…"

"What's so special about now? You don't trust anyone!"

Scanlon pushed himself to his feet so suddenly most men would have jumped but not his companion, icily cold and obviously schooled in every reaction he continued to sit, a slight smile on his face.

Scanlon crossed to him and stood directly in front of him, so close that his companion now couldn't get to his feet as he should have done.

"Who betrayed me?"

"I have no idea what you're on about, Greatness."

Scanlon's hand moved so quickly that reaction was almost impossible but his companion caught the Justiciar's wrist.

"I *have no idea*, Greatness."

Scanlon wrenched his hand free and made it clear by a simple look that, if his companion moved, it would be worse for him. Scanlon grabbed the man's chin and turned his head away, with his own knee in an indelicate place he leant down and whispered,

"Someone betrayed me, someone told Adeone what was planned, and if I ever find out it was you, then dispositions made or not, you will not escape. I've made myself clear." He withdrew his dagger and carefully held it to the man's throat. "Who betrayed me?"

The man never flinched but he had to be in a great deal of pain. "I *did not*, Greatness. I'll make enquiries."

"Will you now? Will I find out the results of them?"

The man, his face still turned away, a dagger against his throat and his private parts being crushed said normally, "If there's anything to tell."

"Swear it!"

"I swear, sir," replied the man silkily.

"I've had enough of your impertinence…"

"The feeling's mutual, Greatness."

Scanlon applied a bit more pressure and bent his head to whisper, "If, next time I rise, you don't get up, I'll have your legs removed."

"I won't be much use to you then." The pressure released.

Scanlon sheathed his dagger. "Oh, I expect you would be." He released the man's head before swiping him backhanded. "You will remember who you are and who I am."

The man said, "It's a little hard to forget, Greatness," and filed all the insults away for future use. As Scanlon resumed his seat, he continued, as though nothing had happened, "What were you trying to achieve with a protectorship. You'd not have managed much in a week and a half—"

"Do you think I'm so naïve as to tell you? You'd be surprised what can be achieved in a week."

"*I* wouldn't." He moved off the subject wanting to mull over the possibilities before he made any move or plans himself. "I hear Kenelm has been banned from Court. Is he defying your orders to be careful?"

Scanlon's eyes narrowed. "He was rash and foolish. He'll learn his lesson, and, if not, well, someone that unpredictable can only be a threat. His memory has been modified once. If I have to, I'll break him with more usual methods. We need to find a husband for Malandra soon as well. She can help secure us support elsewhere."

His companion snorted. "I can just see the eligible lords of the empire fighting over her hand. A daughter of a disgraced and exiled Lord of Oedran, why wouldn't the King give his permission?"

"He won't care what happens to the brats, not the girls. He doesn't see them as a threat. He's too blind."

"And you do care? Of course not, which of us does? Once wedded and bedded, however that happens, they play your game. Of course, Chandra didn't and I hear you've lost Bantling as well."

"He was only ever there as a chance and experiment to see what bindings could do. I altered his whole personality with relatively few simple words; it was interesting in the extreme and it's fortunate that the oath-breaker is lost. I admit that I expected him to be manhandled sooner. He was oath-bound to annoy Tain at every insolent point possible but that idiot boy is too dense to do anything about it. I expected Bantling to receive several whippings – any one of which would have resulted in the boy being attacked."

His companion smiled again. "Didn't you know that Prince Tain's household rules have changed from the traditional ones? Oh dear. Did no-one ever tell you that whippings have been forgone?"

"You little snake—"

"Not so much of the little, thank you. I had thought your admirable spy network would have told you, but maybe they didn't realise the significance, or they're just not bothering to tell you things. Are they keeping vital information from you? Are your methods reliant on flawed fundamentals? How unfortunate if they are. Adapt and survive."

Scanlon's eyes narrowed. "Get out!"

"Of course, Greatness. Have you had any scheme work in the way you wanted it to recently? Even your moment of triumph was tinged by unforeseen disaster, wasn't it? I admire your late brother's style – he certainly knew how to wind you up and I thought there was only one bastard in the family; obviously blood *is* thicker than water. Are you sure you want to dispose of such kin?"

"Say that again and you'll not leave this house alive."

"And your arrest would soon follow. I keep saying you don't want to antagonise me, I know too much and the skills I have, which you so recently put to good use, can be used in other ways." As he passed Scanlon, he said silkily, "Attack me again and you won't wake up. You'll not see me coming but I'll be there. Sweet dreams, *Greatness*?"

Chapter 92
ON DEFERENCE
Cisadai, Week 2 – 9th Cearal, 9th Cearcis 1215
Tain's Chambers

THE FOLLOWING DAY, with King Arkyn and Prince Tain ensconced in meetings, Kadeem did an inspection of the Prince's chambers. His quick, perceptive and perfectionist eye swept over everything. He nodded at several points but at the end tutted slightly.

"Robert, we need a word."

"Sir?" enquired Robert. What defect had been noticed? He was ticking everything off in his mind. True, he wasn't happy about some arrangements in the sitting room, but with the coronation so close all the palace specialists had informed him alterations would have to wait. Kadeem wouldn't blame him for that, would he? Then the antechamber, he knew the light wasn't the best and a couple of the tiles had cracks, but the same applied.

Kadeem said, "I'm concerned."

"Why, Master Kadeem?"

Kadeem eyed him. "Because I've rarely seen a room so well organised, let alone chambers. I'm willing to consider it as a one off, rather than rivalry."

"Rivalry, sir?" Robert relaxed.

"Yes. Your perfectionist endeavours won't escape King Arkyn's notice."

"I would hope that they do, sir."

"Hmm. Perfection comes at a price, Robert."

"But it is not, necessarily, one I am unwilling to pay, sir."

Kadeem regarded him levelly. "Then make sure debts don't run high. Now, this evening the King will be here for dinner and the evening will be private: the King, His Highness, Lady Elantha and Master Calumiel.

In this situation we announce and serve the meal and leave; we do not stay in the room; we allow them complete privacy. I say we but I mean you. King Arkyn has said I'm not required to be here, which means he's been comfortable with your presence, personally I might get worried. Unless you're rung for, you're not to disturb them, is that clear?"

"Yes, sir. Is there anything else I should be aware of?"

"There are more things known to the stars than to mortals," said Kadeem as he left.

"Yet the stars can't impart their wisdom to mortals," muttered Robert.

"I heard that," came the reply as the door to the antechamber closed.

* * *

That evening, Cal entered Tain's sitting room having handed Robert his cloak and received the news that Tain was still at the Courthouse but wouldn't be long by return.

His friend's sitting room was spacious but not expansive. A painted screen covered the fireplace. There was no need for a fire in the heat of summer. It depicted a summer evening. Cal tried to place the view. It had a valley feel to it. Was it one Lachlan had commissioned? Or did it reach further back? He was oddly relaxed. The room seemed to have acquired a lighter, happier feel in the last week. That was strange, he would have expected Tain's struggle to come to terms with his father's death, and his new position, would have had a more subduing effect on his rooms. Yet Tain was hardly ever in them, so it was probably down to Robert. The sun streamed through the windows and Cal wandered over to them. He gazed at the gardens and over the palace wall to the Administrative Quarter for some time. He barely heard the door behind him click shut.

"Observant as ever, Cal!"

Cal turned and gave a half bow.

Tain shook his head gently. "Won't you ever stop?"

"Unfortunately, sir, I don't think I can. Protocols are there to be observed."

"Unless requested otherwise, although, Alcis only knows why I'm having this discussion with you again." He walked over and rang the bell. When Robert entered, Tain said, "I'm afraid Jenkins will be coming with some documents for me to read. Collect them from him, for the King and Lady Elantha are also due to arrive at about the same time for dinner. Stow the papers in my bedchamber for now. I'll read them later."

"Very good, Your Highness. Can I get you anything now?"

"No, thank you, Robert." After Robert left, Tain asked, "What was he like when you got here, Cal?"

Cal smiled. "A lot more obliging and polite than Linnt ever was. Just one thing, sir... I thought you were meant to be having a night off.

Jenkins coming here with work for you is hardly that."

"Lost the deferential, I see," muttered Tain.

"Mostly, *Your Highness.*"

"Very funny. It shouldn't be much, but it's information on the legalities of the coronation. As Scanlon isn't going to be there, I need to know the laws."

"I'm sure your heart bleeds at the thought of him being miles away."

"Let's hope, because he's miles away, my heart doesn't bleed in the literal sense of the phrase. After all, he made sure he wasn't there when my father's did and when Tancred died."

Cal blushed. "I'm sorry, sir; it was a thoughtless phrase."

"I'll forgive you. How's living at home?"

"Noisy, sir. I'll cope though. There's been enough going on to make it eventful as well. It's odd to think we won't be going to Ceardlann soon."

"Yes, it is. Everything's changed."

"Yet most of the world will never notice."

Tain sighed. "I know. They will simply see a change of monarch, nothing more. I suppose that is a good thing. Better than open rebellion."

There was a knock at the door and Robert announced Arkyn.

Once the door had closed behind Robert, Arkyn said, "If either of you use any honorifics tonight, I will not be responsible for my actions. I mean that, Cal. My brother might be able to manage it but…"

"Experience has taught you I'm pretty useless. I know."

Arkyn nodded. "You can say that again. Alcis, I'm sick of sycophants."

Tain said, "It can only get…"

"Worse! If this is what they're like before I'm crowned what on Erinna will they be like afterwards?"

Cal smiled. "Probably far too annoying for words to describe."

"Makes you wonder why, when we have such a diverse language, there are any circumstances that those words can't describe," mused Tain.

"You mean like 'pedant' or 'facetious' or…"

Arkyn said, "How about 'highly annoying'?"

Tain sighed. "I get the message. You don't appreciate my unique outlook on situations at all. Come…"

The door opened and Robert announced Elantha before once again leaving. Tain thought he caught sight of Jenkins in the antechamber.

He said to Elantha, "Come and save me, cousin. Cal and Arkyn are ganging up on me."

Elantha smiled. "Why would I want to do that, Tain?" With that question she went and gave Arkyn a hug.

"You're fair minded and think that whatever the argument each side has a point," responded Tain dryly.

"I'm sure Elantha likes other people giving her opinions for her, Tain," pointed out Cal.

Tain threw a cushion at him. "Very funny. Don't I get a hug, Elantha?"

Elantha crossed to her cousin as Cal tossed the cushion back. She dodged it and Tain caught it neatly before giving her a hug.

"What's happened, Cal? You've dropped the honorifics..." asked Elantha suspiciously.

Cal grinned sheepishly. "I'd rather not see Arkyn pushed to the point where he isn't responsible for his actions. He has threatened dire retribution on anyone who dares address him formally tonight."

"Nice one, Arkyn. Can't you make it all the time?"

Arkyn sighed. "If I could, little flower, I would – especially if I have to talk business with anyone else today."

"So the man in the antechamber must have been bringing Tain work."

Tain cursed under his breath as Arkyn shot him a look before saying, "You were having the evening off!"

"I mentioned that as well," stated Cal smugly.

Tain explained again.

Arkyn caught Cal's eye. "Ring for Robert please." When the manservant entered, Arkyn said, "The information Jenkins brought for His Highness, return it to him. His Highness will deal with it tomorrow. That's all."

Rather perplexed, Robert bowed and left without saying a word.

"So, this is you avoiding responsibility for the evening?" muttered Tain sardonically. His brother was unbelievable at times.

"I'm never going to avoid being responsible for your welfare for another five years so don't expect me to stop looking out for it. You need a night off as much as me."

Tain sighed, defeated. "I see I'm cornered."

Elantha smiled at him. "Yes, you are. Arkyn, can I have wine tonight?"

Arkyn hesitated. She was still only eleven, his father would probably have said 'no' but the events of the last week, and the way Elantha had handled them, meant leeway was called for.

Trying to keep the agreement from his voice, he said, "I don't know, El."

She knelt, looking up into his face with bright eyes and a smile that was hard to resist.

"Sweet and innocent, Elantha, gets you nowhere..."

She changed her features slightly so they became mock sad.

Arkyn considered drawing out the teasing, but failed. "Maybe a goblet."

She jumped up and gave him another hug. Arkyn shook his head gently at her enthusiasm. She'd get two goblets of wine out of him without trying. He found it hard to see her as his cousin; he viewed her more as he would have done Ella, his sister, if she'd survived. Elantha used it to her advantage on occasion.

Seeing his brother wrestle with his conscience, Tain said, "Shouldn't you have asked your host that, Elantha?"

Arkyn shot him an amused glance as Elantha tried the same treatment on him, with exactly the same results – although Tain managed to pretend he wouldn't let her for a couple more moments than Arkyn had managed.

Cal sat grinning at the scene. He had sisters who had other methods of getting what they wanted but when it came down to it, wheedling always worked. Seeing Cal's grin, Elantha looked away in imitation of being demure. Cal laughed openly.

"I'm not fooled even if your cousins are, El."

"Are you saying Arkyn and I are easily hoodwinked?" retorted Tain.

"Evidence points that way."

"Fooled or not it worked," said El, bright-eyed.

"I wasn't fooled or manipulated!" exclaimed Tain.

Cal's eyes sparked with amusement. "My last comment is still true."

Elantha sat on the arm of Arkyn's chair, watching in amusement as the two friends wrangled.

"Do you think they'll ever stop, Arkyn?"

"It would be a shame to deprive us of the entertainment."

Tain and Cal both turned to them, then carried on wrangling for a couple more minutes to make a point. Arkyn and Elantha let them; they sat listening, forgetting the rest of the world. For those minutes, they could pretend nothing had happened or was happening. It ended when Robert entered to announce dinner. Tain playing the host waved everyone to the table. Robert served the meal with a deftness that Arkyn noticed and appreciated. His presence was never intrusive, simply competent. Once they were settled and contented, he removed himself from the room. When they'd finished, Robert served everyone's favourite drinks without having to ask what they were. Arkyn was impressed; the manservant had done his research well.

Chapter 93

GIFTS

Later Evening
Tain's Sitting Room

Once the meal was over Cal looked at his friends. "Was there a reason for tonight, other than the fact you need to relax?"

Arkyn smiled. "We thought we might exchange our gifts."

"You might have warned me, I'd have brought yours."

"But that cloth…"

"Was our family gift, not mine," replied Cal.

"Oh, right. Erm…"

"I'll nip and get them. It won't take me long, but I'll have to be careful."

Arkyn nodded and they sat talking until Cal returned a few minutes later with two small packages.

He handed one to Arkyn and one to Tain. They were heavier than they looked and the brothers frowned at each other in confusion as Cal simply grinned and winked at Elantha.

Arkyn opened his and laughed. There, in his hand, was a beautifully carved sleeping cat, made out of soapstone; it was tactile and had brought a smile. "Is this a reference to anything in particular, Cal?"

"I believe cats turn somnolent in the heat of day…"

Arkyn said softly, "So they do, Cal. Thank you."

Having watched Arkyn, Tain unwrapped his present with apprehension. Knowing Cal's sense of humour, the fact these were milestone birthdays would have meant nothing. The presents had obviously been conceived as a reminder of their life at Ceardlann that, even had Adeone not been killed, they were leaving behind.

Tain fought to keep a straight face as he unwrapped the small ornament: a monkey. The carver had caught an expression of mischief perfectly.

"I'm not sure whether this is appropriate, Cal."

"Everyone else is," muttered Elantha.

Cal grinned. "I couldn't resist."

Tain rolled his eyes. "I'm not sure I'm glad about that."

Arkyn chuckled and rang the bell for Robert. "There should be chests in the antechamber, Robert. Could you bring them in, please?" Once the manservant had done so and left, Arkyn said, "Tain, you go first, it was your birthday a week ago."

"I'll get Cal's." He handed Cal a present with the words, "It's not as apt as yours."

Cal unwrapped a tooled leather satchel. "Actually, sir, I think it is…

Sorry, Tain, I mean… Oh, Sicla, it's just *habit*."

"He said 'sir', Arkyn," pointed out Tain mischievously.

"Not to me he didn't and he better not. Now, Cal, I think you might find that these fit into that satchel…" He handed over a present and grinned as Cal opened it.

Inside were various weapons, all small and all beautifully made. Cal looked at Arkyn. "Are you sure it's safe to give me these?"

Arkyn grinned. "Yes, just not for anyone who annoys you."

Cal explored the selection: wrist knives, knuckle-dusters and a small weighted cosh on a length of thong. He opened the leather satchel to put them safely away and found that there were straps already there for them. He glanced at Tain.

"Not as apt?"

"It might have been *planned*, Cal, but that's different."

Cal said, "I should have known. Now I just need to get myself a proper sword, the one I was using at Ceardlann is fine but it hardly matches all my cisan-age gifts."

"Father left you the Skifta's Sword," stated Arkyn holding his gaze.

Cal gaped, speechless.

Seeing disbelief, Tain said, "Arkyn's right. It was part of the bequests."

Cal glanced between them. "I can't accept that. I… It belongs at Ceardlann and anyway it's a relic of the Cearcall, it's not right for me to have it, I mean—"

"Cal, you're a shifter. If you'd got the relevant star stone then you'd be the Skifta. How is it not right?"

"Because I haven't got the stone and anyway…"

"Cal, I'm tired of arguing with people over father's generosity, of making them see reason," stated Arkyn in a voice that matched his words. "Tell me you'll accept it, because quite frankly it was a last wish of a king and there's not much you can actually do about it, or that I or Tain can do about it."

Cal swallowed. "If I use any honorific you'll kill me, won't you?"

"Yes."

"Damn. All right, thank you, Arkyn. I still don't think…"

Elantha said, "Cal, you don't have to think."

"Fortunately," muttered Tain.

Cal subsided shaking his head.

Tain continued. "Anyway, you'd also need a dagger."

"Your father gave me this one."

Tain examined the dagger. Its practicality was oddly reassuring. "Oh. Right. You're all kitted out then, aren't you?" He passed the blade back.

Arkyn handed Tain an inlaid box. "This was from father."

Hesitatingly, Tain took it. He, as Cal had with his, ran his hands over it. Elantha put a hand on his arm and he looked at her sadly before opening the cantilevered lid. On the top level was a beautifully ornate and bejewelled dagger, set solely with emeralds in gold; it was certainly a statement. Tain looked at it, almost uncomprehendingly. He eventually put the box on the table and took out the dagger. It felt odd in his hand, it was too ornate to use but this wasn't designed as a practical tool. It was beautiful but impractical. He put it down and lifted the cover from the bottom of the box. It had covered two more practical daggers, each in a beautiful scabbard. Tain gazed at them and nodded to himself. A dagger was a traditional present for a cisan-age birthday and his father had melded that with practicality. As Tain closed the box, his practised fingers and quick mind detected hints of something else. He took the daggers from the box, turning it every which way.

Arkyn watched him. "What is it?"

"It's a puzzle box. I'm sure of it. Hang on…" Tain examined all the carvings, he found the carving of the moons and considering it was a cisan-age gift pressed in the representation of Cisluna.

"Go on, what now?" enquired Arkyn leaning forward.

Tain felt inside the box. Finding a catch, he pressed it. The inlaid front came away. At the bottom was a small drawer. He hesitated.

Arkyn said, "Just open it, this is father we're on about and I had this with me in Amphi."

Tain pulled out the drawer, there in his father's hand was a note to congratulate him on finding the compartment and also several discs and spinners. Tain took them out, putting the box on the floor. He started spinning all the discs and spinners and obviously relaxed.

Arkyn chuckled, crooking an eyebrow. "You didn't think father would have followed tradition, did you?"

Tain swallowed. "For a moment, I did. What did he give you?"

Arkyn lifted a box that had been found in his father's rooms. "I have no idea."

Tain put the spinners away. "Open it, Arkyn."

Elantha sat on Arkyn's chair arm and put her arm round his shoulders.

Arkyn looked at her. "Shall I, little flower?" When she nodded, he lifted the lid of the box and smiled to himself. Instead of weapons there were several jewelled and or precious metal buckles, all of different shapes. None of them were formal. Tain got up to see what Arkyn was looking at. He had some inkling but wanted to see for himself.

"Well, you will be twenty."

Arkyn nodded. "I know. I like them, I really do. I just wish I could wear one on my birthday."

Tain looked at them. "I'm sure you could manage it, if you tried."

"I'll try."

Elantha said, "Do you want my presents now?"

"Of course, if you want to give us them," replied Arkyn.

She grinned. "Cal was easy. Well, no-one else had thought of it..." She handed over a small box, "Uncle Adeone thought it was a good idea."

Cal opened the box and found a signet ring with his initials on. It was the same design as had been used on his dagger and, in fact, his initials overlaid a dagger.

"What is it?" asked Tain.

He handed it to his friend.

"Now you *are* grown up, you've got a seal."

"No. Now I'm scared."

Elantha said, "I didn't think of it like that, I just thought people might like to know the tome of a letter they've received is from you before they open it."

"Tome of a letter, little flower?" Cal watched her.

Elantha grinned. "I've seen you write them, remember."

"Will someone please give me an argument I can win tonight?"

"Probably not," replied Tain honestly.

Elantha said, "Tain, I didn't know whether to give you this or not... I think it might... well, erm..."

Tain took a small package with interest but also concern. "I'm sure it will be fine, El."

He unwrapped it, swallowed, got up and crossed to the windows, trying to collect himself. He looked at the miniature in his hand, and then turned back to the room. Everyone was watching him with concern, especially Elantha. He held out an arm to her, giving her a strong hug when she reached him.

"Thank you."

"You're not upset?"

"Yes, I am, but it will help, I promise."

"What is it?" asked Arkyn.

Elantha answered, "The portrait I did of the Judge at Ceardlann."

Tain placed the portrait on the bureau next to him. "So, little flower, dare I ask what you're giving Arkyn?"

Elantha grinned. "Well, I had to think a bit more and Uncle Adeone was obliging and Lord Irvin was really helpful..."

Arkyn said, "I'm worried. Is anyone else worried?"

They shook their heads, and Elantha continued, "Actually it's this."

She handed over what was obviously a book. Arkyn took it curiously, opening the silk wrapped package carefully. Inside was a beautifully bound and jewelled copy of the earliest account of the Cearcall known to exist – the original was carefully conserved in Denshire.

Arkyn gazed at it wide-eyed. "Little flower… You're unbelievable at times. Thank you. How did you persuade the Visir to let anyone handle the original?"

"I did say Uncle Adeone had helped and you are going to be twenty. It's an important date. Do you like it?"

Arkyn nodded. "Yes. Thank you."

Tain said, "Can I borrow it?"

"No, you can't, not until I've read it. Now, Tain, this is from me…"

Tain took the tiniest package yet and opened it, intrigued. Inside was a tiny key. "You did this to me last year as well, you know."

Arkyn grinned and handed over a much larger box. The key unlocked it and Tain looked at a selection of books, all were about either the Cearcall or the Bard. "You've got copies of most of these, haven't you?"

"Yes, but I thought it would be better if you had your own. I might know where mine are then."

For all the flippancy and seeming self-interest, Tain recognised how generous the gift was. Books weren't cheap, scroll copies weren't either because of the time needed to make them, but bound books were in a different league. These copies were in another league again: each of the fifteen volumes was embossed with gold and each spine held a solitary emerald at the top and the bottom.

"Thank you."

Arkyn grinned. "That's all right. This is from Lord Landis…"

Tain groaned as he recognised what it was. "Can't we remove his sense of humour?"

"See it as a challenge."

"What exactly? Removing his sense of humour or archery?"

"Well, both," replied Arkyn matter-of-factly.

Cal grinned. "I'd take it as a compliment."

"How is this a compliment?" demanded Tain. "I'm useless at archery."

"Not as bad as you have been," pointed out Cal. "Not since Lord Landis took your training in hand."

Tain ran his hands over the carvings on the bow. "Hmm. I'll try to find a way of thanking him."

Arkyn said, "Cal, this was his present for you."

Cal looked surprised. "Me? But…"

Arkyn held out a small box and Cal took it. Inside was a small pistol-bow and also a weapons belt.

"I'm going to be a walking armoury at this rate."

Arkyn chuckled. "Play to your strengths."

Tain ignored him. "Arkyn, this is from me."

Arkyn opened the proffered present with interest. There were two parts: a tooled leather belt and a small box. He took out the latter and opened the lid curiously; half wondering exactly what his brother's sense of humour had produced. He found a beautiful timepiece. He looked at Tain in thanks.

Tain gaze never changed. "Well, the Amser's Watch isn't much good for telling the time so this seemed to be called for. At least you'll know when I'm late. There's a stand for it as well."

"The belt with it is incongruous though."

"Try it with the buckles. Father mentioned in passing that he was commissioning them and I thought a decent belt might be needed."

Arkyn shook his head. "Your schemes, Tain, don't get any better."

They sat talking for an hour before Elantha began to droop. She excused herself and left the other three to talk for a couple more. By the time the sun had set and the palace gates had shut for the night they were ready for sleep. Arkyn and Cal left Tain to retire. Arkyn jokingly asking if Cal wanted a chitty to let him through the gates into the Lower City. Cal said he'd not trouble Arkyn to provide it and disappear instead, which when they reached a deserted corridor he did, in the blink of an eye.

Chapter 94
LEGALITIES

Tretaldai, Week 2 – 10th Cearal, 10th Cearcis 1215

Tain's Sitting Room

The Courthouse was officially closed on Tretaldai, so Tain talked to Jenkins in his chambers.

"Do you have the information on the legalities of the coronation?"

"Yes, sir. Once we'd worked our way down the documents in our offices, we found it well buried at the bottom of the pile."

"Wouldn't it have been easier to recompile it?" enquired Tain.

"I had a couple of lawyers doing that as well. Amazingly it was all the same and no-one seems to have thought to mislead Your Highness, just to bury the information so it takes us days to find it."

Tain said, "It keeps you in a job, Jenkins."

"So does everything else, Your Highness. Now, everything seems to be as we've discussed before. I've obviously had a copy taken for Your Highness to read and digest at your leisure. There are multiple ways to commit treason on the day of the coronation but the most likely is someone drawing steel in the King's presence. If they've already sworn fealty and don't have the King's permission it's an instant sentence of execution; however, it might be better, if the felon has not sworn fealty, that fealty is sworn and a reading taken. If it's to defend the King, the King can instruct for mercy but it is not automatic. There is only one exception to that: the King's Defenders – or, in King Arkyn's case, Defender. The post means that His Lordship can have unsheathed steel at all times in the King's presence; for example, he doesn't have to have scabbards for his weapons. With regards to the guards, they can defend but it is wiser for them to defend without drawing steel. They are there as a show of strength and support. The coronation day is a day of peace, Your Highness, without any conflict. It is a day to honour the King, and as such it is believed that none will wish him harm."

Tain said, "Believed?"

"Yes, sir. The empire is an unquenching optimist at heart."

"Are you saying that it is inevitable that someone would wish my brother harm?" enquired Tain in too calm a voice.

"Ah. I didn't consider that side of the statement, did I, sir?"

"Obviously not. Be careful, Jenkins, about what you say and how you say it. I'll not remind you again. What else should I know about the legalities?"

* * *

An hour later, Tain entered the Inner Office and Arkyn looked over wearily. Was it the night before or the day's demands?

"Are you all right, Sire?"

"I'm fine, *Your Highness*."

"Ah. Sorry, Arkyn."

"So am I. It's not your fault, is it?"

Tain swallowed. "Depends what you're referring to but no, for once, I don't think it is. You're looking tired. You've been working too hard."

"I'm not the only one."

"I don't have a lethargy to manage."

"Carry on the way you are doing and you may well."

Tain said, "I doubt it, I've always been too full of energy. Now…"

"That's your official voice, isn't it? I'm learning to recognise it."

"Sorry. I've got some notes on the legalities of the coronation for you but they can wait."

"No, they can't. It's tomorrow. I ought to have some idea of what you're there for."

"I'm there to crown you, Arkyn."

"You don't need to highlight the fact again."

Tain bit his lip, moving away. He sat in a chair, his head in his hands.

Arkyn watched him. "This isn't right. I'll tell the Moonshi—"

"No, you won't. I'll be fine. I'll live with the notoriety. It's just the…" he trailed off.

"The what?"

"I know that after your coronation we're both going to be isolated."

"Our relationship is not wholly dictated by tradition and other people's conceptions of it," retorted Arkyn. "It's our choice what we make it. Traditions can be changed and I'll bloody change that one." He sat opposite his brother. "Have you been worrying about it?"

Tain simply nodded.

"You bloody fool." He took Tain's hand. "I'm your brother first. You'll know when I have to be the King but I'm your brother, Tain: as you've said before now, your annoying older brother."

"I'm being stupid," stated Tain, but he grasped Arkyn's hand tightly.

"I would say there's a first time for everything but that's come and gone."

Tain frowned, releasing his grip. "Annoying, was it?"

Arkyn grinned in reply. "Seemingly. I thought you were comfortable with the concepts…"

"That you're annoying?"

"No, that our relationship has had to alter."

Tain said, "I was, I am, I'm just having a moment, it's nothing, I'm being stupid."

"Tain?"

"The more I'm doing, the more I'm realising that things can't stay the same," admitted Tain despondently.

"Then you're obviously doing too much. Leave the information for me to read and have a break instead of briefing me."

"No, I can't, I—"

"We've got to leave the city at four. Please, for my sake, have a break."

"Is that an order?" muttered Tain.

"No, it's not," said Arkyn, barely keeping his temper. "It was a suggestion but if you want to be stuck in here feeling isolated, please do."

Tain got up. "I'll leave you to it then. I'm obviously not wanted."

Arkyn caught Tain by the arm. "Tain, that's not fair."

Tain bit at his trembling lip. "I'm sorry."

Arkyn pulled him into a hug. "So am I. Go on; go for a ride or something. Get some fresh air."

PART 6

Chapter 95
CAMP
Evening
Rex Dallin Road – Coronation Camp

AT FOUR IN THE EVENING, Arkyn left his chambers dressed in his formal wear and made his way to the stables, with Tain at his side. He mounted Ponder and led a procession through Oedran to the Dallin Gate, as that was the gate by which he'd entered Oedran after receiving the news of his accession. He crossed the River Edra, which encircled Oedran, by the Dallin Bridge and continued riding about quarter of a mile to where the flags of a military-looking camp fluttered in the lazy breeze. Every twenty yards, stood a sergeant of the militia in sparkling armour.

Tain slightly behind Arkyn said, "The Major's done a good job, sir."

"Yes, for saying he has flu. I do hope he's been sensible and let the General take over the arrangements for this."

"I've only dealt with the General, sir. He said the Major was occupied enough with other matters."

"He was, I hope, referring to him being confined to bed!" Arkyn reined in and dismounted swiftly. They were in the centre of the camp and it was the General waiting to greet them. He saluted smartly and Arkyn nodded in acknowledgement.

"My liege, welcome. Your tent awaits."

Arkyn said simply, "Thank you, General."

Tain followed Arkyn and entered the King's tent. It was so richly furnished it made the King's chambers look drab and utilitarian. Scarlet velvet and silk vied for position with cloth of gold. Emerald piping edged luxurious cushions, campaign furniture, of rich and rare woods, was polished until it gleamed, reflecting the opulence of their surroundings; Denshirian glass decanters and drinking vessels stood ready to hand, the finest Terasian ceramics were laid with rich delicacies. It spoke of an extravagant age of decadence forgone, and of status assured by tradition and primogeniture.

Arkyn's face showed his astonishment.

The General smiled. "I hope you find yourself comfortable here, my liege."

"I should think I will, General, yes. Thank you."

The General saluted and left. Arkyn walked forward and then turned on the spot. He caught Tain's eye.

"This is rather flamboyant."

"But highly appropriate. It was grandfather's during the Bayan Rebellion."

Arkyn swallowed. "He had a thing for ostentation. Now that I've left Oedran, what are we doing this evening?"

"Dinner and entertainment. You hold Court here this evening, Sire."

"Oh dear."

Tain said simply, "It won't be that bad."

* * *

It wasn't. The weather was warm and the evening pleasant. Arkyn managed to forget about many of his cares. He retired early knowing he had to be up the following morning. As he entered the tent, he said to Tain,

"I wish I'd had more time to watch the stars tonight."

"Come with me, Sire." Tain crossed to the rear of the tent and lifted a flap. Arkyn walked out into a small enclosure, the canvas walls of which were over six feet high but also richly draped. Tain said softly,

"Watch the stars, sir."

Arkyn grabbed his arm. "Together."

They sat on the grass. Arkyn lay back tracing the constellations with his eyes. Soon Tain lay beside him. They didn't talk, the chatter and clatter of the camp were distant from them, for their minds were elsewhere.

After an hour Arkyn pushed himself to his feet. "I should sleep."

Tain got up. "Of course you should, Sire, but you don't have to."

"See I told you nothing would change."

Tain held the flap of the tent up. The tent was large, about twelve feet high and fifteen feet in diameter; it was spectacular and had plenty of room for a separate sleeping area. Arkyn made his way to it and was surprised when Tain followed.

The King said, "Tain?"

"Sire, the ceremony of your coronation started when we left Oedran."

"Oh dear."

Arkyn entered his sleeping area and found Lord Landis was waiting patiently, on seeing Arkyn he knelt.

Arkyn said, "Lord Landis, you must still be in pain."

"Sire."

"That's Uncle Festus' way of avoiding the issue, sir," remarked Tain.

"Yes. Now, I don't need you two to put me to bed."

"But tradition does."

"Landis, I believe you have an expression fit for this moment."

"*Traditions can be changed*, Prince Tain," said Lord Landis gravely.

"Very amusing," retorted Tain in a long-suffering tone.

Arkyn nodded. "I thought so. Lord Landis, we shall pretend you have fulfilled tradition's needs. Deliver Tain to his own bed and look after yourself."

"My King's wish is my command," replied Landis.

"Can't we change *that* tradition?" enquired Tain, conversationally as he and Landis left the King's tent.

Landis said to the assembled crowd, "The King has retired."

Silence fell as people made their way towards their tents or the city.

"Where are you again?" asked Tain.

"Here, sir. I sleep in the King's tent."

"Are you going to change that tradition?"

"No, Your Highness, but I will be careful to be awake early," admitted Landis. "Let me show you to your tent, sir."

Tain entered his tent, looking at the emerald green and gold. "I take it this used to be Great-uncle Lachlan's during the rebellion."

"Yes, sir. It's the first time that it has been used since. I hope Your Highness has a comfortable night."

Tain nodded, noticing how formal his nearfather was being and worrying about it as Landis left.

* * *

Morning came, as the morning must, and Tain was woken early as had been his wish. He rose and dressed carefully. His tunic was crisp plain white but with emerald green banding, two-inches wide, around the hem, collar and cuffs. His belt was ornate, with a gold and emerald buckle and the ceremonial dagger that had been his father's present. Robert draped his mantle and fixed it with a badge of office. As Tain put on his signet ring, the manservant said simply,

"Stand still for a moment, Your Highness, whilst I sort your circlet out."

Tain did as requested, still wishing that the delicate filigree circlet of gold and emeralds wasn't needed.

* * *

As the Prince crossed the camp, others were stirring. He was pleased; they had a couple of hours but no more. He caught Lord Faran's eye and waved a good morning.

Faran returned the greeting before crossing to him. "Good morning, Your Highness. Is there anything I can do?"

Tain said, "You've no orders already?"

"No, sir. I'm just to be in the procession."

Tain nodded. "Then I don't think there is. Everything should be covered. Did you sleep well?"

"Yes, Your Highness, very pleasantly. Did you, sir? A military camp is not the most comfortable."

"My grandfather and great-uncle had other ideas about what a military camp should be," remarked Tain dryly.

"Ah. Then I should not have worried. I shall let you continue, sir."

* * *

Tain entered Arkyn's tent and greeted his nearfather quietly. "Morning, Uncle Festus. Has the King risen yet?"

"No, sir."

Tain bit his lip. "I think he should, we don't want to be hurrying."

"It is Your Highness' decision."

Tain sighed. "True." He walked in to Arkyn's sleeping area and knelt by him. "Sire…"

"Mm…"

"Time to get up."

Arkyn rolled onto his back, blinking. "Morning, Tain. Are you sure it's time to get up?"

"Yes, sorry."

"Oh." He pushed himself to his feet. "Where's Kadeem?"

"Preparing your bath, sir."

Arkyn sighed. "There's even ceremony attached to that?"

"Yes, sir. Your robe, Sire."

"Tain, we're in private."

"It's your coronation day, Sire."

Arkyn glared at him.

In the main area of the tent, Kadeem had filled the bath and added drops of lemon essence to it to try to lift the King's mood. He looked pointedly at Tain and Lord Landis.

Addressing his elder nearson, Landis said, "I shall see no-one disturbs you, Sire." He bowed as much as he could and left the tent.

Arkyn crooked an eyebrow at his brother. "Tain?"

Tain eyed Kadeem. "I see you took Uncle Festus' maxim to heart. I shall wait outside."

Once he'd gone, Kadeem said, "Take as much time as you need, sir."

Arkyn stripped off and eased himself into the water. "That might not be wise, Kadeem."

"The day may not wait but men are able to, sir."

Twenty-four minutes later Arkyn dried himself off and donned his tunic. Kadeem informed Landis and Tain that the King was ready for them.

Tain knelt on re-entering the tent.

Arkyn swallowed. "Prince Tain?"

"Today and always, your servant, Sire."

Arkyn closed his eyes; it might be private but it was poignant. "Then aid in my dressing."

Tain got up and moved forward, he took the ready prepared belt from Kadeem and knelt to strap it on; he paused and looked up at Arkyn.

"An apt gift," murmured Arkyn.

Tain's hands shook as he tightened the belt he'd given Arkyn for his birthday. He'd even forgotten to wish him happy birthday, and the moment seemed past. Over his brother's tunic – which had been made from the silk Master Galdwin had given him – Tain strapped on a breastplate and military belt without a word, but these were far from utilitarian, gold and rubies glinted and shone from every angle. He knelt once more to strap on greaves. Arkyn would wear no headgear and so when Tain finished belting on the greaves, he took the King's hand and kissed the signet ring.

Tain rocked back on his heels and stood up; he bowed and moved out of the way. Landis knelt, wincing.

"I am your Defender, Sire."

Arkyn said simply, "As you see I have protection."

Lord Landis said, "Yet not your weapons."

"Then arm me."

One arm in a sling, Landis silently praised Tain's foresight for having included the belts and scabbards as part of his duties. Kadeem, holding a long tray knelt, presenting the King's weapons to Lord Landis. One-handed, Landis sheathed the King's ceremonial sword and two daggers before kneeling once more,

"Sire."

"Thank you, Defender. You may rise. Let us toast the day."

Kadeem offered a salver of drinks and they all took one each.

Prince Tain lifted his slightly. "Happy birthday, Sire."

Lord Landis smiled. "Happy birthday, Sire."

Arkyn said, "I thought the toast was to something else?"

"Traditions can be changed, sir," replied Landis, tongue-in-cheek. "And let us not tempt fate today."

They ate a light breakfast of apples, oat biscuits and cheese, in preparation for the afternoon and evening feasting.

At the end of the meal Arkyn stood up. "How long?"

"Half an hour, Sire."

"I could have stayed in bed then."

"Apparently so, sir," said Tain.

"Then I think I might take a walk."

Tain and Landis glanced at one another.

"Ah, I take it that the arrangements don't include that possibility."

Tain said, "No but as long as you're back to leave your tent in line with the established practice, it shouldn't matter. It rather depends if you can face the horde that's assembling."

"Horde? It's a very quiet one."

"You are not to be disturbed today, Sire."

"Obviously my coronation is not disturbing at all."

Tain shook his head. "Shall I ask a couple of lords to join you, Sire?"

"Any not running around trying to sort something out?"

"There's always a couple, sir." He made his way from the tent.

Arkyn turned to Landis, "Keep an eye on him, Uncle Festus."

Landis nodded. "Of course, sir, but today is not about anyone but you."

"If anything happens to him…"

Lord Landis said simply, "I know, Sire."

A couple of minutes later, Tain announced Lord Faran without any fuss.

The Lord of Lufian entered the King's tent and whistled. "I see what Your Highness meant." He bowed to Arkyn, "Good morning, Sire."

Arkyn looked between him and Tain. "Good morning, my lord. What did your comment to Prince Tain mean?"

Chapter 96
PROCESSION
Imperadai, Week 2 – 11th Cearal, 11th Cearcis 1215
Coronation Camp

AFTER ABOUT HALF AN HOUR, Tain left the tent and glanced at the assembling crowd. Spotting him, the General walked over,

"We're ready, Your Highness. The city gates have been closed."

"Good. Tell me, General, have you apprehended the assassin yet?"

"No, sir, and we still have no idea who he was."

"Then keep a bloody good look out. Await the King's appearance. Where are our horses?"

"They are being brought round now, sir."

Tain glanced to where the General indicated and nearly didn't recognise Ponder, he had so much finery draped over him that Tain was sure there wasn't a bit of actual horse to be seen. Bandit, his own horse, had also been dressed up but by nothing close to Ponder's glory.

Tain returned to the tent and on entering knelt. "Sire, your city and empire await you."

Arkyn got up feeling utterly lost and alone. He wanted to tell Tain to stop fooling around but this wasn't a joke, it wasn't a fool's errand, it was history in the making.

"Then let me not keep them waiting."

Tain held the tent flap and moved aside to allow Arkyn to leave. A hand covered his.

"Let me, sir. You should be with the King."

Tain looked at Faran. "Thank you, my lord."

Arkyn walked out the tent with Tain and Landis behind him. Tain on his right, Landis on his left. As he took in the sight, he was almost blown off his feet by the cheer. He inclined his head slightly in acknowledgement and glanced in concern at Ponder, who was fidgeting with the noise. He walked over to his horse slowly and took the reins. He spoke softly to the spooked horse and went to mount.

Faran stepped forward, knelt and cupped his hands to make a step.

Arkyn smiled and nodded at him before accepting the help. He settled himself in the saddle and waited for Tain and Lord Landis to mount. Lord Landis had trouble, not surprisingly with one hand out of order. Lord Faran simply crossed to him and did the same as he had for the King.

Lord Landis once in the saddle said, "Thank you, Faran."

"My pleasure. Be careful, Landis." He mounted his own horse, smiling to himself. He'd found something to do.

* * *

Arkyn glanced at Tain. They set out for Oedran. Where the night before there had been sergeants every twenty yards now each side of the road was lined with men of the army, with white cloaks over their polished armour, and flanking the King and Prince were the Prince's Guard. Immediately behind them were the ambassadors and lords.

As they reached the bridge Tain held up a hand and the rest of the entourage stopped.

The Prince said, "Sire, your city awaits. Will you claim her?"

Arkyn glanced at him, glanced at the city walls and rode forward, alone, over the bridge, Tain and the entourage waited until he made the other side then Tain alone rode forward, also scanning the city walls for an assassin. He halted in the middle of the bridge and watched as Arkyn reined in before the gates of Oedran.

It was the most dangerous part of the procession and Tain's eyes never stopped moving as he heard his brother say,

"Why are the city gates closed? Oedran should be open for all whilst the sun shines on her."

From the shadow of the gatehouse a man in black walked forward,

427

"She mourns the loss of her King, the gates be closed for he is gone."

Arkyn said simply, "Your King is here."

"Our King does not travel alone, for our King is loved."

"I am not alone."

Tain raised his hand and waved the entourage forward; he rode to his brother's side.

"Is there none here within who will recognise their King?"

The gates of Oedran opened and the Moonshi walked forward. He stood in the middle of the gatehouse, the shadows cloaking his face but not the silver of his robes.

He said, "I recognise my King and in his features are the ancestors. Sire, come now for your crowning and let this day be joyous."

"Let us ride to the Alcium, Sire, for this day is blessed," added Tain.

"I would know he who didn't recognise me," stated Arkyn.

Lord Iris lowered his cowl and knelt. "My King, the shadows of the mind clouded sight. Yet now light pierces all to show your magnificence."

"Then cast aside the darkness and let the light guide your steps. Today is not a day for retribution, be welcomed and known as my Counsellor."

"Your wish is my sole command, Sire."

Arkyn nodded and Iris rose and moved off to one side, discarding the black cloak to reveal a white one below.

The King said, "Let us see the city and let the city see us."

The Moonshi bowed and turned to the city. Slowly he walked forward until he was clear of the gatehouse. The King urged Ponder forward through the gate and waited on the further side of it. Four men flanked him, helping to support the canopy that had been Tain's solution to the problem of potential assassins in the buildings. Arkyn looked to see who had been chosen: Lord Julius Landis, Lord Emrys Daioch, Lord Irvin Iris and Cal. The sight of his friends was balm to his soul, and he made a mental note to thank Tain for the foresight and understanding such a choice displayed.

They rode slowly through the city, Arkyn followed by Tain, with Lord Landis and Lord Iris flanking him then the remaining Lords of Oedran, ambassadors and Lord Faran, behind them more minor lords and officials and, behind them, the majority of the militia who had been lining the route.

Overnight there had been many preparations, bunting had been strewn between buildings, flowers were everywhere from window boxes on the buildings to the ladies' hair. He smiled; it really was a beautiful sight: Oedran bedecked for glory. People were cheering as he approached and he smiled whilst reassuring Ponder. Behind them Landis' horse was jittery; he didn't like crowds.

Tain noticed. "Landis, is everything all right?"

"It will be, sir. I should really be leading Skit with this noise."

Tain said, "Please don't. Would it help if someone walked with him?"

"Probably, sir."

Tain nodded and looked around; with the guards rode a couple of grooms, suitably dressed up. He motioned to one.

The man rode over. "Your Highness?"

"Could you just walk with Lord Landis' horse; he's a bit jittery – the horse, not Lord Landis."

Simon nodded. "Of course, sir. I'll be back momentarily." He moved off, manoeuvred his horse back into line and passed his reins to a guard to tie to his stirrup leather, before dismounting and nimbly running back.

Simon carefully put a hand on Skit's neck. "Now then, old boy, it's nothing to worry about. Shall we just take a walk? Eh? Nice and slow does it, lad, no throwing your rider. His Lordship's a little fragile..."

Landis muttered, "I'll give you '*a little fragile*', Simon Ambler."

Tain looked at him. "At least Skit is calmer."

They crossed The Strait, and Tain once more stopped the procession as the Chief Merchant knelt in front of Arkyn.

The King said, "Who now holds up my progress?"

"I am the Chief Merchant of Oedran, Sire, elected by my peers."

"Do you speak for those peers?"

"I do, Sire. We offer our loyalty, to you and your heir."

Tain stilled. The traditional line, the one that Merchant Figgis had been *advised* to say, included the plural not the singular.

Arkyn never hesitated. "My heirs may be manifold before my reign ends."

"Sire, our loyalty will not change be there one heir, as now, your brother, or many of your blood."

"Then rise and witness the day's proceedings for your peers."

They continued the ride through the Lower City until they reached the Alcium Plaza. There were crowds but a path was clear to the Alcium gate. Arkyn rode slowly forward and through that gate. The riders with the canopy moved closer together and Tain watched as the canopy passed safely over the wall. The supports were on a ball joint where they met the actual canopy meaning that they could fold in. Tain nodded to himself; the carpenter had done a good job. He rode through the gates himself and dismounted swiftly. Walking resolutely forward, he held Ponder as Arkyn dismounted, before passing the horse's reins to Simon, who'd moved forward to lead Ponder off.

Chapter 97

CORONATION

Late Morning
Oedran – City Alcium

ARKYN STOOD IN RESOLUTE SILENCE, hardly catching Tain's eye as the nobles of his entourage flowed around the circular building and into it by different doors. The canopy was now held by four of the Prince's Guard and the Moonshi had entered the Alcium.

Tain marking time frowned to himself; they should have been welcomed in already, the Alcium courtyard was empty of all but horses and the militia.

Two moments later, a calm Moonshi stood in the doorway to the Alcium. "I welcome you to this Hall of Ancestors, ancient and strong."

"May my companions enter here also?"

"Any who come are welcome."

"Then it is my pleasure to enter."

Arkyn followed the Moonshi; Tain, Lord Landis and Lord Iris behind them. Guards lined their path, all saluted as Arkyn passed but it was a one-handed salute, as though he were a prince. He supposed it was for emphasis that he was uncrowned.

He walked to the centre of the chamber: facing the exit towards the Palace, his back to the city. An ease washed over him. He closed his eyes momentarily. The presence of his ancestors was here. They had stood on this very spot and been crowned after the loss of their fathers. The day had always been inevitable and, somewhere within him, the weight of grief was eased but the sorrow remained starkly carved into his heart.

When he opened his eyes, a line of people had formed: side on, zig-zagging towards him, one on one side, one on the other.

Tain spoke, "At the beginning of all the years there was a King, Anaparus, from whom this country proudly takes her name. He was strong of will, valiant in battle and his sword brought greatness and peace. When he died, his sword was laid by, never to be wielded in battle again, but such was the potency of the blade, the very majesty of kingship was linked to it. His son King Abraxas made the sword into a crown. Bring forth that crown for a new king of the line claims it."

In front of Arkyn, at the end of the corridor of people, a young white clad alcia, his robes edged with gold, appeared bearing the crown on a scarlet cushion trimmed with gold.

Tain continued, "Do the Lords of Anapara recognise the man who wears this crown as their King?"

The Ambassador for Anapara, Lord Parchi, stood forward, "We do, Justiciar of Oedran." He placed a gold token shaped like an arrow on the cushion, then turned to Arkyn and knelt.

Arkyn swallowed; he'd known Lord Parchi's nephew well before a bandit attack had robbed him of life.

"But a country cannot survive with just its lords, who speaks now for our merchants and recognise the man who wears this crown as King?"

The Chief Merchant stood forward. "I do, Justiciar, for myself and all merchants of this city and country." He took the token Lord Parchi had placed on the cushion and fixed it into the crown before replacing it on the cushion and turning to kneel.

"The capital city of this country moved here to Oedran many years ago," said Tain, "and when the peace of twelve countries was destroyed our kings helped restore it. They formed the empire we know and together we maintain peace, but we cannot do it without a king. Who speaks now for Areal? Who will recognise the crown of Anapara for that country?"

Lady Phylicia, her stomach doing somersaults stood forward. "I, Lady Phylicia ReJean, descendant of the Bard, do." She attached a golden token shaped like a key to the crown and then turned and curtsied to Arkyn. Lord Galaloth, watching her carefully, admitted she'd done a good job and within him an attitude, he hadn't consciously realised he had, began to reform itself.

"The empire though is more than Anapara and Areal. Who speaks for the Low Plains? Who now will recognise this crown?" enquired Tain.

"I, Lord Aldwy, do recognise the crown and do commit my country's loyalty to it. We have no metal, precious or otherwise, so I offer a token of our loyalty a carving of obsidian, but there be no polished surface lest traitors spy on our King." He attached a black gemstone eye to the crown.

Arkyn wondered if the mention of treason at the coronation was quite correct. Would he need to talk with Aldwy later?

Tain took a breath. "Is there any here from Tradere to acknowledge the crown of Anapara for their country?"

Lord Buckler stepped forward. "For all of Tradere I offer here our token of tribute." He attached a golden hourglass to the crown.

"As the kings reigned the empire grew. In Denshire a treaty was made and remains unbroken, who here speaks for that country?"

Lord Salman stood forward. "For Denshire, the man who wears this crown is our King and has the majesty of the stars." He placed a golden token etched with a mystic rose onto the crown.

"Lufian, the home of light and illusion is a wondrous country and enhances this empire, who now stands forward for them to declare their tribute?"

Lord Toral stepped forward, attached a golden rose and snowflake to the crown, turned to Arkyn and knelt. "For King Arkyn."

Tain frowned. It wasn't a direct enough declaration of loyalty. When Arkyn died, Lufian could leave the empire. "Lord Toral, do you declare, for your country, loyalty to the *crown* of Anapara?"

Lord Toral looked at the young Prince's face and considered maybe he wasn't as dim or mentally unstable as rumour had suggested. "I do, Justiciar. May the man who wears it ever be our king."

Arkyn watching him was reminded of when he'd first met Lord Toral, shortly after the bandit attack which had killed Kensal Parchi, and Toral had made a fool of himself. He also considered that the Sagamore must believe wholeheartedly in his, Arkyn's, impartiality to send someone who had been known to annoy him – that or the Sagamore was stupid. Arkyn wondered which it was as Tain continued speaking.

"The empire spread south to the mountains and the provinces there bring much to this joining of nations. Is any here willing to speak for Gerymor?"

Lord Ogilvie stepped forward, "For Gerymor, for my country, I say the man who wears this crown will be our King." He attached a moonstone overlain with golden scales to the crown. He knelt.

Arkyn tried hard not to think about when he'd first met Ogilvie for his father had been there.

Tain continued, "Gerymor's sister province is Terasia and its tribute when joining the empire was withheld, it caused an Age of Tyranny. Long ago that was forgiven by our kings and now is immaterial for the tribute was gifted to the man who claims the crown and great honour was there done unto him. Will any from Terasia stand forth and declare the country's allegiance to the crown he will wear?"

Lord Kre stood forward. "For Terasia and her peoples I declare the man who lawfully wears this crown will ever be our King." He attached a small golden bear's paw to the crown. He knelt to Arkyn with a smile.

That was even worse for Arkyn, Terasia was where he'd proved himself, but it held many memories of his father as well.

"This empire is not landlocked, it spreads across the Ranaegir Sea to the east and the known lands, as others journeyed so did our kings. Who here will speak for Serpent Isle?"

Lord Aked stood forward. "Many leagues have I sailed. Here is our token to state that the man who wears this crown is our King." He attached a coiled snake to the crown and knelt.

Tain said, "At the edge of the empire lies the Pale Lands, a perpetual light bathes them. Has anyone travelled here from that country?"

"I, Lord Hawkson, do declare that the man who wears this crown will be our King and heal our hurts." The token he attached was that of a vial.

Tain mentally ticking off the provinces said, "Returning across the seas we find islands. Which man now speaks for the Macian Isles?"

Lord Longland said, "For the Macian Isles, split by sea but never by dispute, I declare the wearer of this crown is our monarch." He attached the triskele spirals, emblem of his province, to the crown.

Arkyn also considered Lord Longland's appointment, again it was known he found the lord arrogant and rude. Was the Fencible trying to annoy him or engineer the end of Longland's career? Either was a dangerous game. The Ambassador's Court would be interesting with this mix of temperaments.

Tain nodded as Longland knelt. "As Terasia and Gerymor are considered sister provinces, Anapara is considered to have a relative province. For years without count there have been battles but now peace reigns. Who here declares for the proudest of all the provinces that we are blessed to consider friends?"

Lord Whelan of Bayan said, "I do declare that the man who lawfully wears this crown is King of Anapara and our monarch." He attached a token shaped like a bird to the crown and knelt.

Tain looked at the kneeling lords. "All provinces have declared their allegiance to the crown of Oedran; however, there are travellers in our lands, in this empire. They are the nomadic Wanda, trapped here, since the Fall of the Cearcall, they roam without a home. Never have they declared allegiance. Their wanderings cross the provinces and no King of Oedran has ever borne them ill will. Is any here from the Wanda? Is there any here to declare allegiance?"

The chamber was silent. It was part of the ceremony to wait for a few moments. No-one was in any doubt the silence wouldn't be broken.

The doors opposite the King opened. Chief Darshan walked through the path left by kneeling lords, holding Arkyn's gaze. He reached the Alcia, who still stood in front of Arkyn and tapped him on the shoulder.

"Excuse me, lad."

As the Alcia sidestepped, Chief Darshan knelt, and took from around his neck a golden wheel, between each spoke was set a different coloured gem.

Tain gaped, swallowed, blinked. What was he meant to do? This wasn't in the established script, or any alternative one either – it had never happened, no-one considered it ever would, no request for allegiance was ever sent to the Wanda, they were recognised merely as a people who inhabited the same lands, not as a people of the empire. The guests were silent: the silence of astoundment, of expectation and of history being made.

Seeing Tain was lost for words, Chief Darshan said, "I, Chief Darshan of the Wanda, do declare in this Hall of Ancestors that we recognise and pay honour to the lawful King in Oedran. Let him call upon us in need, let this jewel be our token but set it not in a crown, we Wanda travel with our hearts, wear this next to yours, Arkyn Adeone FitzAlcis, and may your heart be ever protected."

Tain tried to ignore the swell of astonishment in the Alcium. He found his voice. "All peoples of the empire," he hesitated before continuing, "and the lands which form it, have declared allegiance to the crown of Anapara or the lawful King who wears it."

The Moonshi stepped forward and lifted the adorned crown from its cushion. "May the blessings of the ancestors fall on the wearer of the crown and may he ever be their guardian." He placed it back on the cushion. Landis laid his hand on the crown.

"As Ealdorman of Oedran, I hereby recognise the man who lawfully wears this crown as our King. Let the city and empire cast out all who attempt to crown another whilst he lives." He released it for Tain to take.

The Prince lifted the adorned crown and found it lighter than he'd expected. "I, Prince Tain Lachlan FitzAlcis, am of the line of kings. My ancestors are the kings I have spoken of and they ruled this empire, but I do declare, and have you all bear witness to my vow, that whilst my brother or heirs of his body, yet to be born, live, I shall not wear the Crown of Anapara and the Empire, nor shall I ever seek to do so." He turned to Arkyn. "Our ancestors are the same men and I ask you now, on their memory, will you rule this empire from the heavens to the deepest oceans, from the northern shore to the southern mountains and all the lands between, from the western seas to beyond the eastern isles, over land and sea, from the time the sun rises to the moons set, from the birth of man unto his death?"

"I will, Prince Tain."

"In forgoing my rights, this I ask of you, for our ancestors and empire: when rebels rise up be mighty, when mercy is needed be kind, when a voice needs to be heard, listen but when action is needed, proceed. Keep peace in the lands and bring contentment to lives. May the prosperity you bring never wane. Will you now so vow, swear and bind yourself to this life and duty?"

"I will and do, Prince Tain."

"Then, from our ancestors to your descendants yet to come, I name thee our King, monarch of all lands and their peoples. May your life be long and your reign peaceful. May the ancestors guard you and the heavens celebrate this day.”

With that, Tain gently placed the crown on Arkyn’s head. He took the pendant Chief Darshan had offered, placing it around his brother’s neck, noticing with curiosity the thong of another. Taking a ring from the Moonshi, he knelt placing it on Arkyn’s hand, before kissing his brother’s hand with a smile.

“Your Majesty.”

Every man and women in the chamber made a deep obeisance, leaving Arkyn alone, crowned, the only man standing.

Chapter 98
SACRIFICE
Afternoon
Oedran Palace

Arkyn ACCEPTED the Keys of the Palace solemnly, accepted the acknowledgement of his Court with a smile and left the King’s Hall for the King’s Chambers. He walked through the Palace with Tain, Landis and Iris at his side, entered the Audience Chamber and paused, taking in the sight in front of him. Most of the arched panels that lined each wall had been changed from murals to mirrors. Of the four panels on the right, two remained as murals. A landscape considered Terasian, with its depiction of mountains and forests, and one that depicted a seascape. On the opposite wall, one panel was still a mural, a valley scene opening out to show wide plains, likely the Jecian Plains in Lufian.

‘*Subtle,*’ thought Tain. ‘*Provinces that Arkyn’s visited.*’ Who had decided to leave them in place? He’d been specific in his instructions. Though the gold and scarlet drapes were certainly ostentatious enough without more mirrors reflecting their splendour back at each other.

Arkyn hesitated before walking confidently to the King’s Triniculum. That room had also been transformed but, although ostentatious, it wasn’t so flamboyant. Arkyn sighed as he entered and reached up to remove the crown. Tain took it from him, placing it on a central table, for none but they could handle it that day. Arkyn sank onto the couch and nodded for his companions to do likewise.

Tain said, “We’re here to serve you, Your Majesty.”

Arkyn eyed him. “I’ve been crowned and we’re in private, I’ll happily alter that tradition. Anyway, Lord Landis only has one hand in action, he won’t be much use. Sit down.”

Tain eyed him in return. “Are you going to be this bad all day, Sire?”

"Probably."

"Thank you for the warning. I will leave you to lunch; I have matters to attend to."

"Prince Tain!"

Tain bowed. "Sire?"

They eyed each other again. Arkyn sighed. "All right. Can you tell Chief Darshan he's welcome to camp in the Palace grounds?"

"With pleasure, sir."

When Tain had gone, Iris said, "Your Majesty, with your permission we'll continue with the traditional honours and dues."

Arkyn saw something fundamental in Iris' eyes, a challenge of perception and a need for a confirmation of role. Landis was obviously deferring to the older lord. Arkyn nodded, accepting the inevitable; as he accepted it, he realised he'd accepted the fact he was King.

* * *

Tain returned to the Audience Chamber. Spotting Hillbeck, he motioned him over. "Final checks?"

"Underway, Your Highness."

"Good, thank you. Once you're satisfied, we can gather everyone for the Fealty Swear."

Tain left the Audience Chamber. He walked quickly to the Court and ignored everyone's surprise as he entered. He searched the room and walked over to Chief Darshan. The man bowed slightly. He couldn't be more than forty but he had a gravitas to match Lord Iris'.

"Chief Darshan, I wonder if I might have a word?"

"Of course, Prince Tain."

Once in private, Tain said simply, "His Majesty has said you're welcome to camp within the Palace grounds, Chief."

"Thank him for me. We will be happy to accept the invitation."

Tain nodded. "Can I ask—"

"Why I did it? It was time. We know what you fight, Prince Tain, and thought we could help. We wander the roads and have ears everywhere."

"Our fights have never been yours."

Chief Darshan put a hand on his shoulder. "Even the innocent can get caught in the battle. In other times we have helped, and even thieves once helped kings. This time, we do so openly."

"What do you request in return?"

Chief Darshan laughed. "We ask nothing of kings. What we have pledged is out of respect. We shall return to the roads shortly."

Tain collapsed onto a chair. "You've made history, my brother will never be forgotten because of what you've done and all you can say is that you'll return to the roads shortly."

Chief Darshan sat opposite him, completely relaxed and as an equal. "The stars tell the future, men record history."

"You and Laioril must be related that's the type of oblique answer he's fond of giving."

Chief Darshan chuckled. "Chief Laioril is a law unto himself as I have been discovering. You must have much to do today. There will be other times for us to discuss my actions." His eyes bored into Tain. "For there is much you need to understand for your future."

* * *

Three-quarters of an hour later, Tain entered the Audience Chamber behind his brother. The expansive room felt claustrophobic with the hum of anticipation. Along with the four Lords of Oedran, and three heirs of the exiled lords, there were the twelve ambassadors, Lord Faran, five lords who had travelled from lands in southern Anapara, two who had ridden from central Anapara, the chief merchant and Cal, all waiting to swear fealty – twenty-nine men in total. Added to which, guards were stationed around the room: four along the dais, two at the bottom of the dais steps and two on each door – a total of ten. Thirty-nine men filled the room.

As Arkyn entered from the Outer Office, they knelt, all facing him from across the room. Tain's eyes darted along the lines. Lord of Oedran and the heirs were at the front, then ambassadors, then provincial lords. Cal had been talking to Landis, so was with the Lords of Oedran. That made Tain smile. He'd have to carefully edge back soon. Tain glanced to see where Merchant Figgis was and found him hidden at the furthest corner. Cal would have to swear last, as he didn't hold an official post.

Tain waited patiently as Arkyn ascended to the throne. He tried to focus on the moment not the memories, and when his brother had settled himself, without any fanfare he stepped forward, ascended the steps and became the first Justiciar in several generations to swear fealty. He spoke the words with sincerity, feeling nothing but calm within him. As he kissed his brother's signet ring, sealing the binding, a lump rose in his throat. He swallowed it, rose, bowed formally and descended the steps backwards, kneeling once more at the bottom. A susurration stirred behind him. Ignoring it, he walked to the end of the dais and climbed the far steps, walking back to his brother and stationing himself at his right hand. By the time he relaxed, Lord Landis was waiting at the bottom of the steps. Fealty sworn, the King's Defender walked to the end of the dais, and ascended to stand at Arkyn's left hand.

The susurration had increased. Tain scanned the mirrors. He couldn't see what was happening. Landis put a hand on Arkyn's shoulder. The guards were moving. A shout and curse. A struggle erupted. Guards pulled people apart. A clatter. A bloodied dagger clanged on the floor. Ryson fell, clutching his side. A guard went to draw his sword.

"No!" yelled Tain.

The crowd parted.

Ryson had fainted. Cal was kneeling by him, bloodied dagger inches from his hand. He reached out for it.

"No!" Tain yelled again.

A voice from the crowd, "It's his dagger! Look at his belt."

"Landis!" snapped Arkyn.

His Defender wasn't quick enough. Cal's fingers closed around the hilt. His fate in his hand.

CHARACTERS

FAMILIES

FITZALCIS*	KING ADEONE ALTARIUS	King of the Oedranian Empire 1204-1214
	KING ARKYN ADEONE	King of the Oedranian Empire 1215-present
	PRINCE TAIN LACHLAN	Justiciar of Oedran, King Arkyn's brother
	LADY AMARA TALITHA	King Altarius' sister
	LADY NEASSA RATHGAR	Lady Amara's elder daughter
	LADY RHIAN FAIRSON	Lady Amara's younger daughter
	LORD PEAGA RATHGAR	Lady Amara's grandson, Military captain stationed at the Barracks of Oedran
	LORD SCANLON AMARUS	Justiciar of the Empire excluding Oedran
	LADY ELANTHA	Lord Scanlon's daughter
	PRINCESS LILITH	King Altarius' cousin. Lives in Bayan
	LORD GALWOOD	Princess Lilith's son
LANDIS	LORD FESTUS LANDIS	Lord of Oedran, Defender of the King's Life, Chief Advisor, nearfather to Arkyn and Tain
	LADY CORNELIA LANDIS	Long-suffering, hardworking Lady of Oedran
	LORD JULIUS AND LADY JULIA	Eldest children, twins
	LADY MARCELEA	Second daughter
	ANTONIA, LUCIUS, IRA	Younger children
RALE	LORD FINIAN RALE	Lord of Oedran for Areal, in his minority, living at Landis House
FAIRSON	LORD GERENS FAIRSON	Lord of Oedran for Tradere
RYSON	LORD ELIDIR RYSON	Lord of Oedran for Gerymor
LUX	LORD DYFRIG LUX	Lord of Oedran for Lufian

*For deceased characters please see the family tree

IRIS	LORD IGNATIUS IRIS	Lord of Oedran for the Low Plains, King's Counsellor
	LORD IDRIS	Lord Iris' heir
	LADY LINA	Lord Idris' wife
	LORD IRVIN	Lord Iris' grandson
	LADY INDRIA	Lord Iris' granddaughter
	LADY FARIE ALDWY	Lord Iris' eldest daughter
	LORD ALDWY	Lady Farie's husband
	LADY DANA GALALOTH	Lord Iris' second daughter
	LORD GALALOTH	Lady Dana's husband
TERAN	LORD TYRON TERAN	Lord of Oedran for Terasia
	LADY AMALIA TERAN	Lord Teran's wife
	LORD CHANDER	Eldest son (twin), Military captain stationed at the Barracks of Oedran
	LADY CHANDRA	Eldest daughter (twin), lives in Tera
	LORD PENROD SILVANO	Lady Chandra's husband
PARA	LORD JOREN PARA	Lord of Oedran for Anapara
	LORD KENELM	Lord Para's heir
	LADY MALANDRA	Lord Para's daughter
RATHGAR	LORD REMUS RATHGAR	Lord of Oedran for Bayan
	LORD RUFUS	Lord Rathgar's uncle, Lord Peaga's father, former husband of Lady Neassa.
CEARIS	LORD JINAN CEARIS	Lord of Oedran for Denshire
ANGUIS	LORD RASHAD ANGUIS	Lord of Oedran for Serpent Isle
REJEAN	LORD LEANDER REJEAN	Hereditary Governor of Areal
	LADY PHYLICIA	Daughter and heiress

FARAN	LORD FARAN	Lord of Lufian
	LADY KYLA FARAN	Lord Faran's wife
	LUCILLE, ELEANOR, CAITLIN, MELANIE	Daughters
	DAMSO	Son (deceased)
	SAMARA	Youngest daughter, Arkyn's neardaughter
	JUAN	Coachman
WEALSMAN	LORD PERCIVAL WEALSMAN	Margrave of Terasia, Overlord of Terasia
	LADY KRISTINA WEALSMAN	Lord Wealsman's wife
	ADEONA	Daughter, Arkyn's neardaughter
	VIAN	Son, Arkyn's nearson
GALDWIN	MASTER GALDWIN	Cloth merchant, Cal's father
	MADAM GALDWIN	Cal's mother
	CALUMIEL (CAL)	Eldest son, Arkyn and Tain's friend
	HALTERN, LOUISA, CRISPIN, TABITHA, ELSIE, AMIN, AMINA	Younger children

ADEONE'S RETINUE

RICHARDSON	King's Administrator
SIMKINS	King's manservant
DOCTOR CHAPA	King's Physician and cousin
CAPTAIN PIXNEY	Head of the Palace Guard
SERGEANT HILLBECK	Head of the King's Guard
SERGEANT KILBRIDE	Sergeant of the King's Guard
KENTON	King's Secretary
ADVISOR RAYBURN	King's Deputy Chief Advisor, King's Military Advisor
APPOSER NALLVIR	Apposer who was sent to look into Lord Faran's affairs
MARIA	FitzAlcis Nurse

ARKYN'S RETINUE

KADEEM	Manservant
EDWARD	Administrator
ADVISOR CAPLE	Chief Advisor
THOMAS	Kadeem's deputy
ALAN	Footman
GLEW	Masseur
SIMON	Groom
CAPTAIN SMITHERS	Captain of the Prince's Guard
SERGEANT LYNDON	Sergeant of the Prince's Guard
SERGEANT HALIEN	Sergeant of the Prince's Guard

TAIN'S RETINUE

GAB LINNT	Manservant
PETER SELTH	Administrator
ROBERT BURNE	Footman
LAWYER JENKINS	Chief Lawyer

SCANLON'S RETINUE

DYER	Administrator

CEARDLANN & REX DALLIN

COMPTROLLER	Gentleman in charge of Ceardlann
SUSAN	Housekeeper
JOE, DAVID	Footmen
SERGEANT BARIS	Sergeant of the Rex Dallin guards
CARLON SILVERSLEY	Rex Dallin Guard

LANDIS HOUSE

WILLIAM KADEEM	Lord Landis' manservant
BACKERY	Footman

IN THE EMPIRE

BAYAN	LORD TYLER GALWOOD	Exarch of Bayan, Princess Lilith's grandson
	LORD CAMLYN	Lord of Bayan
	MELLONIA CAMLYN	Lord Camlyn's daughter
	HUME	Camlyn's Steward
	LORD DENNISON	Lord of Bayan, Mellonia's nearfather
	LADY DENNISON	Lady of Bayan, Mellonia's nearmother
AREAL	LAIRD SKANER	Lord of the Empire (mentioned only)
	LORD ARRIDGE	ReJean's wed-brother (mentioned only)
	LORD TYNAN	Lord of Areal, ReJean's wed-brother
	LADY TYNAN	Lady of Areal, ReJean's wed-sister
	COMMANDER CHEGWIN	Commander of Areal
	CAPTAIN NOLAN	Captain in the army in Areal
	BENNETT	ReJean's Secretary
OTHER	LORD IFOR DAIOCH	Tuchlin of the Low Plains
	LORD ADRIAN EAMES	Sagamore of Lufian
	ERNST	Deputy Governor of Terasia
	LADY DAIA SANSKY	A King's ward in Terasia
	LORD TYNAN	Lord of Areal
	LADY TYNAN	Lady of Areal
WANDA	LAIORIL	Chief of the Wanda
	MIRANDA	Wise woman of the Wanda
	CHIEF DARSHAN	High Chief of the Wanda

IN OEDRAN

PALACE	STEWARD	In charge of day-to-day running of the Palace
	CHAMBERLAIN	In charge of the individual rooms in the Palace
	HERALD	Mail routes, runners and couriers
	CAPTAIN PIXNEY	Captain of the Palace Guard
	DENNY	Chief Server of Upper Hall
	CASWAL HILLBECK	A courier. Susan's son. Hillbeck's nephew.
CITY	MERCHANT FIGGIS	Chief Merchant of Oedran
	MERCHANT CHAPA	Merchant of Oedran and King Adeone's cousin
	ALDHOUSE	Chief Yeoman of Oedran, head of law enforcement
	MOONSHI	Chief Alcia
	ASTROLOGER TALDHEN	King's Astrologer
	RUSHTON	A yeoman
COURT-HOUSE	KEEPER OF THE JUSTICE HALL	Superintendent of the Courthouse of Oedran
	JUDGE YARNE	Judge of Oedran
	JUDGE TANCRED	Deceased Judge of Oedran and mentor to Prince Tain
ARMY	GENERAL PATURN	Head of the King's Army
	MAJOR WYNFELD	Major of Oedran
	COMMANDER AURIFABER	Commander of the Barracks of Oedran
	CAPTAIN BEAVER	Captain of Intelligence
	CAPTAIN FYSHER	Captain of Intelligence
	CAPTAIN EDMONDS	Training Captain
	CAPTAIN FOGG	Captain on leave in Oedran
	WOODROYD	Intelligence Scryer

DELVINGS

Lexicon

OF THE MOONS

ALUNA	The larger of the two Erinnan moons
ALUNA-MONTH	Four weeks
ALUNAN	The higher section of society
ALUNAN-AGE	Twenty years old. Alunan become adults in law
CISLUNA	The smaller of the two Erinnan moons
CISLUNA-MONTH	Three weeks
CISAN	The lower section of society
CISAN-AGE	Fifteen years old. Cisan become adults in law

FOR THE ANCESTORS

ALCIA	A guardian of the ancestor's memory
ALCIUM	A place to remember the ancestors, for blessing new life, for contemplation and for funerals.
MOONSHI	Chief Alcia in Oedran

ON RELATIONSHIPS

NEAR*	Named when a child is born, *nearparents* act as mentors for a child and would act as guardians should the child be left orphaned. Nearparents' children are *nearcousins*, unless the child lives in the same house, then they're *nearsiblings*
WED*	This prefix denotes relatives married into the family, rather like the suffix *in-law*

IN OEDRAN

KING'S ADVOCATES	A group consisting of the King's Defenders, heir and Representatives in the empire
TRINICULUM	A formal dining room at the Palace
ETANES	The law-making body, made up of the Lords of Oedran and twelve cisan members
EALDORMAN	The person keeping order in the Etanes debates
YEOMEN	Law enforcers

STREET SLANG

DAL	Money
RES	Crescent – smallest denomination of coin

HONORIFICS

SIRE, MAJESTY	The King
GRACE	The Queen
HIGHNESS	Princes
ELEGANCE	Princesses
EXCELLENCY	King's Representatives
BENEVOLENCE	Moonshi
GREATNESS	Scanlon
MY LORD	Lords
MY LADY	Nobel Ladies

FEALTIES

FEALTY	A declaration of loyalty from one person to another: a declaration to take up the fight for the liege by the vassal
TRUTH- BINDING	In addition to fealty, the vassal swears to speak to the truth to the liege when required.
SPEECH- BINDING	In addition to truth-binding, the vassal swears never to reveal anything confidential, never to say anything to annoy the liege, to speak only for them not against them.
HONOUR-BINDING	In addition to truth-binding, the vassal swears only to work for the honour of the liege, not against them.
LIFE-BINDING	Melding all aspects of truth, speech and honour bindings, the vassal ties their life force to the wishes of the liege. If they annoy their liege, they feel pain. If they commit treason, the vassal will die immediately.
VALLEY-BINDING	Specific to the Rex Dallin, this binding is said to be life-binding but may stop short of death.
OTHER BINDINGS	There are oaths which fall short of the recognised fealties, that are sworn when taking on specific duties or when an employer requires it.

The Cearcall and Ull's Legacy

At the beginning of the reckoning of years, the Majistar Ull brought magic to Erinna. Twelve star sapphires controlled the creation of the magic. Ull gifted the star stones to twelve individuals, each with a magical spirit. For six hundred years they, and their successors, controlled magic on Erinna, formed laws around it and maintained peace. In the year 600, they died, blown to the winds when magic, wielded by the Tribility who held three spirits, destroyed the Cearcall Tower in Denshire. Since 600 magic has been weaker, almost dormant. Some stones were lost, their location hidden by history, along with some items related to the members of the Cearcall.

Title	Spirit	Stone Colour	Item
AMSER	TIMER	TURQUOISE	AMSER'S WATCH
BERAN	BEARER	BLACK	BERAN'S PENDANT
ESPIER	ESPIEN	YELLOW	ESPIER'S GLASS
JECI	ILLUSIONIST	BLUE	JECI'S RING
MEITHRIN	HEALER	PINK	MEITHRIN'S VIAL
MEMINI	MEMOR	GREY	MEMINI'S MANUSCRIPT
RHEOL	BALANCER	WHITE	RHEOL'S NEEDLE
SENNACHIE	SEER	GREEN	SENNACHIE'S BOWL
SENTIRE	SENSOR	RED	SENTIRE'S KNIFE
SKIFTA	SHIFTER	PURPLE	SKIFTA'S SWORD
SUNDRIAN	SPLITTER	ORANGE	SUNDRIAN'S WHISTLE
WRIGHT	MANIPULATOR	BROWN	WRIGHT'S BOX

Each magical spirit manifests differently from healing hurts to splitting the mind, from creating illusions to manipulating objects.

More than one person at any one time can hold a spirit, but only one spirit wielder can possess the star stone and unlock its full power.

Each spirit has a collection of *hues*, lesser forms of the spirit, which may manifest in anyone.

People who wield magic are said to be affected by Ull's Legacy.

Provincial Information

Province	Capital City	Lord of Oedran
ANAPARA	OEDRAN	PARA
AREAL	AMPHI	RALE
BAYAN	GARTH	RATHGAR
DENSHIRE	CEARDEN	CEARIS
GERYMOR	RY	RYSON
LOW PLAINS	EYLLYN	IRIS
LUFIAN	LUFIA	LUX
MACIAN ISLES	MACIA	MACARIA
PALE LANDS	MEITH	LANDIS
SERPENT ISLE	ANGUIN	ANGUIS
TERASIA	TERA	TERAN
TRADERE	BYFA	FAIRSON

Province	King's Representative	Chief Judge
ANAPARA	DOMINI OF PARAS	CHIEF JUDGE (PARAS)
AREAL	GOVERNOR	KENNER
BAYAN	EXARCH	ESCHERVIN
DENSHIRE	VISIR	HAKIM
GERYMOR	DEY	BORSHOLDER
LOW PLAINS	TUCHLIN	DOMESMAN
LUFIAN	SAGAMORE	DEEMSTER
MACIAN ISLES	FENCIBLE	DOMARE
PALE LANDS	JARL	LAGHMAN
SERPENT ISLE	PASHA	TUOMARI
TERASIA	MARGRAVE	TERAZI
TRADERE	SATRAP	ARCHON

Province	Symbol	Colour
ANAPARA	THREE CROSSED ARROWS	PURPLE
AREAL	A KEY	SILVER
BAYAN	A BIRD IN FLIGHT	ORANGE
DENSHIRE	A TWELVE-POINT MYSTIC ROSE	BROWN
GERYMOR	A SET OF SCALES ON A GEM	WHITE
LOW PLAINS	AN EYE	GREEN
LUFIAN	A FLOWER AND SNOWFLAKE	BLUE
MACIAN ISLES	A TRISKELE OF THREE SPIRALS	RED
PALE LANDS	A VIAL	PINK
SERPENT ISLE	A CURLED SNAKE	YELLOW
TERASIA	A BEAR'S PAW PRINT	BLACK
TRADERE	AN HOURGLASS	TURQUOISE

Notes on Time

<table>
<tr><td rowspan="7">WEEKDAYS</td><td>ALUNADAI</td><td rowspan="7">FESTIVALS</td><td rowspan="2">MUNEWID</td><td>FIRST DAY OF SUMMER</td></tr>
<tr><td>CISADAI</td><td>FIRST DAY OF THE YEAR</td></tr>
<tr><td>TRETALDAI</td><td>MUNPYRAM</td><td>FIRST DAY OF AUTUMN</td></tr>
<tr><td>IMPERADAI</td><td>MUNDIMRI</td><td>FIRST DAY OF WINTER</td></tr>
<tr><td>PENTADAI</td><td>MUNLUMEN</td><td>FIRST DAY OF SPRING</td></tr>
<tr><td>HEXADAI</td><td colspan="2" rowspan="2">These festivals are known as Alcis Days and are marked by both moons being full</td></tr>
<tr><td>SEPTADAI</td></tr>
</table>

ON TIME

1 MINUTE	=	60 SECONDS
1 HOUR	=	72 MINUTES (12 X 6 MINUTES)
1 DAY	=	24 HOURS
1 WEEK	=	7 DAYS
COURT CYCLE	=	12 DAYS
1 FORTNIGHT	=	2 WEEKS

Season	Aluna-month	Week	Cisluna-month	Season	Aluna-month	Week	Cisluna-month
SUMMER	CEARAL	1	CEARCIS	WINTER	RALAL	25	RALIS
		2				26	
		3				27	
	TRADAL	4	MIDDIS		ANAPAL	28	NORIS
		5				29	
		6				30	
		7	TRADIS			31	ANAPCIS
		8				32	
	LOWAL	9			BAYAL	33	
		10	LOWIS			34	BAYIS
		11				35	
		12				36	
AUTUMN	MACIAL	13	MACIS	SPRING	TERAL	37	TERIS
		14				38	
		15				39	
	MEITHAL	16	EASIS		GERYAL	40	SOUIS
		17				41	
		18				42	
		19	MEITHIS			43	GERYIS
		20				44	
	SERAL	21			LUFIAL	45	
		22	SERIS			46	LUFIS
		23				47	
		24				48	

POSTSCRIPT

To you, my reader…

Thank you.

I hope you enjoyed *Thrown,* the fifth book in the *Treason and Truth* series.

Please consider leaving an honest review of this book wherever you feel most comfortable. Reviews really help readers find their next book and help authors find their next reader.

Acknowledgements

Authors rarely get to publication without help and support. They sit and write in snatched hours or minutes. Sometimes stories flow unceasingly from their fingers, clamouring to be heard amongst the din of everyday life. When the last scratch of the pen and click of the keyboard is done, then comes the editing, the interior design, the cover…

My journey has not been solo. From my friends and family who have read, re-read and given me honest feedback to you, the reader that got this far, I say thank you.

This book is dedicated to Caz, once a flatmate, forever a friend.

Explore Erinna

Please visit https://erinna.co.uk for more about the Erinnan Legacy or sign up to The Court Newsletter for freebies and news.